I Am Legend

Hell House

BY RICHARD MATHESON

I Am Legend

Hell House

❧

RICHARD MATHESON

❧

Quality Paperback Book Club
New York

I Am Legend

To

HENRY KUTTNER

with my grateful thanks
for his help and encouragement
on this book.

CONTENTS

I AM LEGEND

PART ONE: January 1976

CHAPTER ONE

On those cloudy days, Robert Neville was never sure when sunset came, and sometimes they were in the streets before he could get back.

If he had been more analytical, he might have calculated the approximate time of their arrival; but he still used the lifetime habit of judging nightfall by the sky, and on cloudy days that method didn't work. That was why he chose to stay near the house on those days.

He walked around the house in the dull gray of afternoon, a cigarette dangling from the corner of his mouth, trailing threadlike smoke over his shoulder. He checked each window to see if any of the boards had been loosened. After violent attacks, the planks were often split or partially pried off, and he had to replace them completely; a job he hated. Today only one plank was loose. Isn't that amazing? he thought.

In the back yard he checked the hothouse and the water tank. Sometimes the structure around the tank might be weakened or its rain catchers bent or broken off. Sometimes they would lob rocks over the high fence around the hothouse, and occasionally they would tear through the overhead net and he'd have to replace panes.

Both the tank and the hothouse were undamaged today.

He went to the house for a hammer and nails. As he pushed open the front door, he looked at the distorted reflection of himself in the cracked mirror he'd fastened to the door a month ago. In a few days, jagged pieces of the silver-backed glass would start to fall off. Let 'em fall, he thought. It was the last damned mirror he'd put there; it wasn't worth it. He'd put garlic there instead. Garlic always worked.

He passed slowly through the dim silence of the living room, turned left into the small hallway, and left again into his bedroom.

Once the room had been warmly decorated, but that was in another time. Now it was a room entirely functional, and since Neville's bed and bureau took up so little space, he had converted one side of the room into a shop.

A long bench covered almost an entire wall, on its hardwood top a heavy band saw, a wood lathe, an emery wheel, and a vise. Above it, on the wall, were haphazard racks of the tools that Robert Neville used.

He took a hammer from the bench and picked out a few nails from one of the disordered bins. Then he went back outside and nailed the plank fast to the shutter. The unused nails he threw into the rubble next door.

For a while he stood on the front lawn looking up and down the silent length of Cimarron Street. He was a tall man, thirty-six, born of English-German stock, his features undistinguished except for the long, determined mouth and the bright blue of his eyes, which moved now over the charred ruins of the houses on each side of his. He'd burned them down to prevent *them* from jumping on his roof from the adjacent ones.

After a few minutes he took a long, slow breath and went back into the house. He tossed the hammer on the living-room couch, then lit another cigarette and had his midmorning drink.

Later he forced himself into the kitchen to grind up the five-day accumulation of garbage in the sink. He knew he should burn up the paper plates and utensils too, and dust the furniture and wash out the sinks and the bathtub and toilet, and change the sheets and pillowcase on his bed; but he didn't feel like it.

For he was a man and he was alone and these things had no importance to him.

✦

It was almost noon. Robert Neville was in his hothouse collecting a basketful of garlic.

In the beginning it had made him sick to smell garlic in such quantity; his stomach had been in a state of constant turmoil. Now the smell was in his house and in his clothes, and sometimes he thought it was even in his flesh. He hardly noticed it at all.

When he had enough bulbs, he went back to the house and dumped them on the drainboard of the sink. As he flicked the wall switch, the light flickered, then flared into normal brilliance. A disgusted hiss passed his clenched teeth. The generator was at it again. He'd have to get out that damned manual again and check the wiring. And, if it were too much trouble to repair, he'd have to install a new generator.

Angrily he jerked a high-legged stool to the sink, got a knife, and sat down with an exhausted grunt.

First, he separated the bulbs into the small, sickle-shaped cloves. Then he cut each pink, leathery clove in half, exposing the fleshy center buds. The air thickened with the musky, pungent odor. When it got too oppressive, he snapped on the air-conditioning unit and suction drew away the worst of it.

Now he reached over and took an icepick from its wall rack. He punched holes in each clove half, then strung them all together with wire until he had about twenty-five necklaces.

In the beginning he had hung these necklaces over the windows. But from a distance they'd thrown rocks until he'd been forced to cover the broken panes with plywood scraps. Finally one day he'd torn off the plywood and nailed up even rows of planks instead. It had made the house a gloomy sepulcher, but it was better than having rocks come flying into his rooms in a shower of splintered glass.

And, once he had installed the three air-conditioning units, it wasn't too bad. A man could get used to anything if he had to.

When he was finished stringing the garlic cloves, he went outside and nailed them over the window boarding, taking down the old strings, which had lost most of their potent smell.

He had to go through this process twice a week. Until he found something better, it was his first line of defense.

Defense? he often thought. For what?

All afternoon he made stakes.

He lathed them out of thick doweling, band-sawed into nine-inch lengths. These he held against the whirling emery stone until they were as sharp as daggers.

It was tiresome, monotonous work, and it filled the air with hot-smelling wood dust that settled in his pores and got into his lungs and made him cough.

Yet he never seemed to get ahead. No matter how many stakes he made, they were gone in no time at all. Doweling was getting harder to find, too. Eventually he'd have to lathe down rectangular lengths of wood. Won't *that* be fun? he thought irritably.

It was all very depressing and it made him resolve to find a better method of disposal. But how could he find it when they never gave him a chance to slow down and think?

As he lathed, he listened to records over the loudspeaker he'd set up in the bedroom—Beethoven's Third, Seventh, and Ninth symphonies. He was glad he'd learned early in life, from his mother, to appreciate this kind of music. It helped to fill the terrible void of hours.

From four o'clock on, his gaze kept shifting to the clock on the wall. He worked in silence, lips pressed into a hard line, a cigarette in the corner of his mouth, his eyes staring at the bit as it gnawed away the wood and sent floury dust filtering down to the floor.

Four-fifteen. Four-thirty. It was a quarter to five.

In another hour they'd be at the house again, the filthy bastards. As soon as the light was gone.

⬦

He stood before the giant freezer, selecting his supper. His jaded eyes moved over the stacks of meats down to the frozen vegetables, down to the breads and pastries, the fruits and ice cream.

He picked out two lamb chops, string beans, and a small box of orange sherbet. He picked the boxes from the freezer and pushed shut the door with his elbow.

Next he moved over to the uneven stacks of cans piled to the ceiling. He took down a can of tomato juice, then left the room that had once belonged to Kathy and now belonged to his stomach.

He moved slowly across the living room, looking at the mural that covered the back wall. It showed a cliff edge, sheering off to green-blue ocean that surged and broke over black rocks. Far up in the clear blue sky, white sea gulls floated on the wind, and over on the right a gnarled tree hung over the precipice, its dark branches etched against the sky.

Neville walked into the kitchen and dumped the groceries on the table, his eyes moving to the clock. Twenty minutes to six. Soon now.

He poured a little water into a small pan and clanked it down on a stove burner. Next he thawed out the chops and put them under the broiler. By this time the water was boiling and he dropped in the frozen string beans and covered them, thinking that it was probably the electric stove that was milking the generator.

At the table he sliced himself two pieces of bread and poured himself a glass of tomato juice. He sat down and looked at the red second hand as it swept slowly around the clock face. The bastards ought to be here soon.

After he'd finished his tomato juice, he walked to the front door and went out onto the porch. He stepped off onto the lawn and walked down to the sidewalk.

The sky was darkening and it was getting chilly. He looked up and down Cimarron Street, the cool breeze ruffling his blond hair. That's what was wrong with these cloudy days; you never knew when they were coming.

Oh, well, at least they were better than those damned dust storms. With a shrug, he moved back across the lawn and into the house, locking and bolting the door behind him, sliding the thick bar into place. Then he went back into the kitchen, turned his chops, and switched off the heat under the string beans.

He was putting the food on his plate when he stopped and his eyes moved quickly to the clock. Six-twenty-five today. Ben Cortman was shouting.

"Come out, Neville!"

Robert Neville sat down with a sigh and began to eat.

✦

He sat in the living room, trying to read. He'd made himself a whisky and soda at his small bar and he held the cold glass as he read a physiology text. From the speaker over the hallway door, the music of Schönberg was playing loudly.

Not loudly enough, though. He still heard them outside, their murmuring and their walkings about and their cries, their snarling and fighting among themselves. Once in a while a rock or brick thudded off the house. Sometimes a dog barked.

And they were all there for the same thing.

Robert Neville closed his eyes a moment and held his lips in a tight line. Then he opened his eyes and lit another cigarette, letting the smoke go deep into his lungs.

He wished he'd had time to soundproof the house. It wouldn't be so bad if it weren't that he had to listen to them. Even after five months, it got on his nerves.

He never looked at them any more. In the beginning he'd made a peephole in the front window and watched them. But then the women had seen him and had started striking vile postures in order to entice him out of the house. He didn't want to look at that.

He put down his book and stared bleakly at the rug, hearing *Verklärte Nacht* play over the loud-speaker. He knew he could put plugs in his ears to shut off the sound of them, but that would shut off the music too, and he didn't want to feel that they were forcing him into a shell.

He closed his eyes again. It was the women who made it so difficult, he thought, the women posing like lewd puppets in the night on the possibility that he'd see them and decide to come out.

A shudder ran through him. Every night it was the same. He'd be reading and listening to music. Then he'd start to think about soundproofing the house, then he'd think about the women.

Deep in his body, the knotting heat began again, and he pressed his lips together until they were white. He knew the feeling well and it enraged him that he couldn't combat it. It grew and grew until he couldn't sit still any more. Then he'd get up and pace the floor, fists bloodless at his sides. Maybe he'd set up the movie projector or eat something or have too much to drink or turn the music up so loud it hurt his ears. He had to do something when it got really bad.

He felt the muscles of his abdomen closing in like tightening coils. He picked up the book and tried to read, his lips forming each word slowly and painfully.

But in a moment the book was on his lap again. He looked at the bookcase across from him. All the knowledge in those books couldn't put out the fires in him; all the words of centuries couldn't end the wordless, mindless craving of his flesh.

The realization made him sick. It was an insult to a man. All right, it was a natural drive, but there was no outlet for it any more. They'd forced celibacy on him; he'd have to live with it. You have a mind, don't you? he asked himself. Well, *use* it!

He reached over and turned the music still louder, then forced himself to read a whole page without pause. He read about blood cells being forced through membranes, about pale lymph carrying the wastes through tubes blocked by lymph nodes, about lymphocytes and phagocytic cells.

". . . to empty, in the left shoulder region, near the thorax, into a large vein of the blood circulating system."

The book shut with a thud.

Why didn't they leave him alone? Did they think they could *all* have him? Were they so stupid they thought that? Why did they keep coming every night? After five months, you'd think they'd give up and try elsewhere.

He went over to the bar and made himself another drink. As he turned back to his chair he heard stones rattling down across the roof and landing with thuds in the shrubbery beside the house. Above the noises, he heard Ben Cortman shout as he always shouted.

"Come out, Neville!"

Someday I'll get that bastard, he thought as he took a big swallow of the bitter drink. Someday I'll knock a stake right through his goddamn chest. I'll make one a foot long for him, a special one with ribbons on it, the bastard.

Tomorrow. Tomorrow he'd soundproof the house. His fingers drew into white-knuckled fists. He couldn't stand thinking about those women. If he didn't hear them, maybe he wouldn't think about them. Tomorrow. Tomorrow.

The music ended and he took a stack of records off the turntable and slid them back into their cardboard envelopes. Now he could hear them even more clearly outside. He reached for the first new record he could get and put it on the turntable and twisted the volume up to its highest point.

"The Year of the Plague," by Roger Leie, filled his ears. Violins scraped and whined, tympani thudded like the beats of a dying heart, flutes played weird, atonal melodies.

With a stiffening of rage, he wrenched up the record and snapped it over his right knee. He'd meant to break it long ago. He walked on rigid legs to the kitchen and flung the pieces into the trash box. Then he stood in the dark kitchen, eyes tightly shut, teeth clenched, hands clamped over his ears. Leave me alone, leave me alone, *leave me alone!*

No use, you couldn't beat them at night. No use trying; it was their special time. He was acting very stupidly, trying to beat them. Should he watch a movie? No, he didn't feel like setting up the projector. He'd go to bed and put the plugs in his ears. It was what he ended up doing every night, anyway.

Quickly, trying not to think at all, he went to the bedroom and undressed. He put on pajama bottoms and went into the bathroom. He never wore pajama tops; it was a habit he'd acquired in Panama during the war.

As he washed, he looked into the mirror at his broad chest, at the dark hair swirling around the nipples and down the center line of his chest. He looked at the ornate cross he'd had tattooed on his chest one night in Panama when he'd been drunk. What a fool I was in those days! he thought. Well, maybe that cross had saved his life.

He brushed his teeth carefully and used dental floss. He tried to take good care of his teeth because he was his own dentist now. Some things could go to pot, but not his health, he thought. Then why don't you stop pouring alcohol into yourself? he thought. Why don't you shut the hell up? he thought.

Now he went through the house, turning out lights. For a few minutes he looked at the mural and tried to believe it was really the ocean. But how could he believe it with all the bumpings and the scrapings, the howlings and snarlings and cries in the night?

He turned off the living-room lamp and went into the bedroom.

He made a sound of disgust when he saw that sawdust covered the bed. He brushed it off with snapping hand strokes, thinking that he'd better build a partition between the shop and the sleeping portion of the room. Better do this and better do that, he thought morosely. There were so many damned things to do, he'd never get to the real problem.

He jammed in his earplugs and a great silence engulfed him. He turned off the light and crawled in between the sheets. He looked at the radium-faced clock and saw that it was only a few minutes past ten. Just as well, he thought. This way I'll get an early start.

He lay there on the bed and took deep breaths of the darkness, hoping for sleep. But the silence didn't really help. He could still see them out there, the white-faced men prowling around his house, looking ceaselessly for a way to get in at him. Some of them, probably, crouching on their haunches like dogs, eyes glittering at the house, teeth slowly grating together; back and forth, back and forth.

And the women . . .

Did he have to start thinking about *them* again? He tossed over on his stomach with a curse and pressed his face into the hot pillow. He lay there, breathing heavily, body writhing slightly on the sheet. Let the morning come. His mind spoke the words it spoke every night. Dear God, let the morning come.

He dreamed about Virginia and he cried out in his sleep and his fingers gripped the sheets like frenzied talons.

CHAPTER TWO

The alarm went off at five-thirty and Robert Neville reached out a numbed arm in the morning gloom and pushed in the stop.

He reached for his cigarettes and lit one, then sat up. After a few moments he got up and walked into the dark living room and opened the peephole door.

Outside, on the lawn, the dark figures stood like silent soldiers on duty. As he watched, some of them started moving away, and he heard them muttering discontentedly among themselves. Another night was ended.

He went back to the bedroom, switched on the light, and dressed. As he was pulling on his shirt, he heard Ben Cortman cry out, "Come out, Neville!"

And that was all. After that, they all went away weaker, he knew, than when they had come. Unless they had attacked one of their own. They did that often. There was no union among them. Their need was their only motivation.

After dressing, Neville sat down on his bed with a grunt and penciled his list for the day:

Lathe at Sears
Water
Check generator
Doweling (?)
Usual

Breakfast was hasty: a glass of orange juice, a slice of toast, and two cups of coffee. He finished it quickly, wishing he had the patience to eat slowly.

After breakfast he threw the paper plate and cup into the trash box and brushed his teeth. At least I have one good habit, he consoled himself.

The first thing he did when he went outside was look at the sky. It was clear, virtually cloudless. He could go out today. Good.

As he crossed the porch, his shoe kicked some pieces of the mirror. Well, the damn thing broke just as I thought it would, he thought. He'd clean it up later.

One of the bodies was sprawled on the sidewalk; the other one was half concealed in the shrubbery. They were both women. They were almost always women.

He unlocked the garage door and backed his Willys station wagon into the early-morning crispness. Then he got out and pulled down the back gate. He put on heavy gloves and walked over to the woman on the sidewalk.

There was certainly nothing attractive about them in the daylight, he thought, as he dragged them across the lawn and threw them up on the canvas tarpaulin. There wasn't a drop left in them; both women were the color of fish out of water. He raised the gate and fastened it.

He went around the lawn then, picking up stones and bricks and putting them into a cloth sack. He put the sack in the station wagon and then took off his gloves. He went inside the house, washed his hands, and made lunch: two sandwiches, a few cookies, and a ther- mos of hot coffee.

When that was done, he went into the bedroom and got his bag of stakes. He slung this across his back and buckled on the holster that held his mallet. Then he went out of the house, locking the front door behind him.

He wouldn't bother searching for Ben Cortman that morning; there were too many other things to do. For a second, he thought about the soundproofing job he'd resolved to do on the house. Well, the hell with it, he thought. I'll do it tomorrow or some cloudy day.

He got into the station wagon and checked his list. "Lathe at Sears"; that was first. After he dumped the bodies, of course.

He started the car and backed quickly into the street and headed for Compton Boulevard. There he turned right and headed east. On both sides of him the houses stood silent, and against the curbs cars were parked, empty and dead.

Robert Neville's eyes shifted down for a moment to the fuel gauge. There was still a half tank, but he might as well stop on Western Av- enue and fill it. There was no point in using any of the gasoline stored in the garage until he had to.

He pulled into the silent station and braked. He got a barrel of gasoline and siphoned it into his tank until the pale amber fluid came gushing out of the tank opening and ran down onto the cement.

He checked the oil, water, battery water, and tires. Everything was in good condition. It usually was, because he took special care of the car. If it ever broke down so that he couldn't get back to the house by sunset . . .

Well, there was no point in even worrying about that. If it ever happened, that was the end.

Now he continued up Compton Boulevard past the tall oil derricks, through Compton, through all the silent streets. There was no one to be seen anywhere.

But Robert Neville knew where they were.

The fire was always burning. As the car drew closer, he pulled on his gloves and gas mask and watched through the eyepieces the sooty pall of smoke hovering above the earth. The entire field had been excavated into one gigantic pit; that was in June 1975.

Neville parked the car and jumped out, anxious to get the job over with quickly. Throwing the catch and jerking down the rear gate, he pulled out one of the bodies and dragged it to the edge of the pit. There he stood it on its feet and shoved.

The body bumped and rolled down the steep incline until it settled on the great pile of smoldering ashes at the bottom.

Robert Neville drew in harsh breaths as he hurried back to the station wagon. He always felt as though he were strangling when he was here, even though he had the gas mask on.

Now he dragged the second body to the brink of the pit and pushed it over. Then, after tossing the sack of rocks down, he hurried back to the car and sped away.

After he'd driven a half mile, he skinned off the mask and gloves and tossed them into the back. His mouth opened and he drew in deep lungfuls of fresh air. He took the flask from the glove compartment and took a long drink of burning whisky. Then he lit a cigarette and inhaled deeply. Sometimes he had to go to the burning pit every day for weeks at a time, and it always made him sick.

Somewhere down there was Kathy.

On the way to Inglewood he stopped at a market to get some bottled water.

As he entered the silent store, the smell of rotted food filled his nostrils. Quickly he pushed a metal wagon up and down the silent, dust-thick aisles, the heavy smell of decay setting his teeth on edge, making him breathe through his mouth.

He found the water bottles in back, and also found a door opening on a flight of stairs. After putting all the bottles into the wagon, he went up the stairs. The owner of the market might be up there; he might as well get started.

There were two of them. In the living room, lying on a couch, was a woman about thirty years old, wearing a red housecoat. Her chest rose and fell slowly as she lay there, eyes closed, her hands clasped over her stomach.

Robert Neville's hands fumbled on the stake and mallet. It was always hard when they were alive; especially with women. He could feel that senseless demand returning again, tightening his muscles. He forced it down. It was insane, there was no rational argument for it.

She made no sound except for a sudden, hoarse intake of breath. As he walked into the bedroom, he could hear a sound like the sound of water running. Well, what *else* can I do? he asked himself, for he still had to convince himself he was doing the right thing.

He stood in the bedroom doorway, staring at the small bed by the window, his throat moving, breath shuddering in his chest. Then, driven on, he walked to the side of the bed and looked down at her.

Why do they all look like Kathy to me? he thought, drawing out the second stake with shaking hands.

Driving slowly to Sears, he tried to forget by wondering why it was that only wooden stakes should work.

He frowned as he drove along the empty boulevard, the only sound the muted growling of the motor in his car. It seemed fantastic that it had taken him five months to start wondering about it.

Which brought another question to mind. How was it that he always managed to hit the heart? It had to be the heart; Dr. Busch had said so. Yet he, Neville, had no anatomical knowledge.

His brow furrowed. It irritated him that he should have gone through this hideous process so long without stopping once to question it.

He shook his head. No, I should think it over carefully, he thought, I should collect all the questions before I try to answer them. Things should be done the right way, the scientific way.

Yeah, yeah, yeah, he thought, shades of old Fritz. That had been his father's name. Neville had loathed his father and fought the acquisition of his father's logic and mechanical facility every inch of the way. His father had died denying the vampire violently to the last.

At Sears he got the lathe, loaded it into the station wagon, then searched the store.

There were five of them in the basement, hiding in various shadowed places. One of them Neville found inside a display freezer. When he saw the man lying there in this enamel coffin, he had to laugh; it seemed such a funny place to hide.

Later, he thought of what a humorless world it was when he could find amusement in such a thing.

About two o'clock he parked and ate his lunch. Everything seemed to taste of garlic.

And that set him wondering about the effect garlic had on them. It must have been the smell that chased them off, but why?

They were strange, the facts about them: their staying inside by day, their avoidance of garlic, their death by stake, their reputed fear of crosses, their supposed dread of mirrors.

Take that last, now. According to legend, they were invisible in mirrors, but he knew that was untrue. As untrue as the belief that they transformed themselves into bats. That was a superstition that logic plus observation had easily disposed of. It was equally foolish to believe that they could transform themselves into wolves. Without a doubt there were vampire dogs; he had seen and heard them outside his house at night. But they were only dogs.

Robert Neville compressed his lips suddenly. Forget it, he told himself; you're not ready yet. The time would come when he'd take a crack at it, detail for detail, but the time wasn't now. There were enough things to worry about now.

After lunch, he went from house to house and used up all his stakes. He had forty-seven stakes.

CHAPTER THREE

"The strength of the vampire is that no one will believe in him."

Thank *you*, Dr. Van Helsing, he thought, putting down his copy of *Dracula*. He sat staring moodily at the bookcase, listening to Brahms' second piano concerto, a whisky sour in his right hand, a cigarette between his lips.

It was true. The book was a hodgepodge of superstitions and soap-opera clichés, but that line was true; no one had believed in them, and how could they fight something they didn't even believe in?

That was what the situation had been. Something black and of the night had come crawling out of the Middle Ages. Something with no framework or credulity, something that had been consigned, fact and figure, to the pages of imaginative literature. Vampires were passé, Summers' idylls or Stoker's melodramatics or a brief inclusion in the Britannica or grist for the pulp writer's mill or raw material for the B-film factories. A tenuous legend passed from century to century.

Well, it was true.

He took a sip from his drink and closed his eyes as the cold liquid trickled down his throat and warmed his stomach. True, he thought, but no one ever got the chance to know it. Oh, they knew it was something, but it couldn't be that—not *that*. *That* was imagination, *that* was superstition, there was no such thing as *that*.

And, before science had caught up with the legend, the legend had swallowed science and everything.

He hadn't found any doweling that day. He hadn't checked the generator. He hadn't cleaned up the pieces of mirror. He hadn't eaten supper; he'd lost his appetite. That wasn't hard. He lost it most of the time. He couldn't do the things he'd done all afternoon and then come home to a hearty meal. Not even after five months.

He thought of the eleven—no, the twelve children that afternoon, and he finished his drink in two swallows.

He blinked and the room wavered a little before him. You're getting blotto, Father, he told himself. So what? he returned. Has anyone more right?

He tossed the book across the room. Begone, Van Helsing and Mina and Jonathan and blood-eyed Count and all! All figments, all driveling extrapolations on a somber theme.

A coughing chuckle emptied itself from his throat. Outside, Ben Cortman called for him to come out. Be right out, Benny, he thought. Soon as I get my tuxedo on.

He shuddered and gritted his teeth edges together. Be right out. Well, why not? Why *not* go out? It was a sure way to be free of them. Be one of them.

He chuckled at the simplicity of it, then shoved himself up and walked crookedly to the bar. Why not? His mind plodded on. Why go through all this complexity when a flung-open door and a few steps would end it all?

For the life of him, he didn't know. There was, of course, the faint possibility that others like him existed somewhere, trying to go on, hoping that someday they would be among their own kind again. But how could he ever find them if they weren't within a day's drive of his house?

He shrugged and poured more whisky in the glass; he'd given up the use of jiggers months ago. Garlic on the windows and nets over the hothouse and burn the bodies and cart the rocks away and, fraction of an inch by fraction of an inch, reduce their unholy numbers. Why kid himself? He'd never find anyone else.

His body dropped down heavily on the chair. Here we are, kiddies, sitting like a bug in a rug, snugly, surrounded by a battalion of bloodsuckers who wish no more than to sip freely of my bonded, 100-proof hemoglobin. Have a drink, men, this one's really on me.

His face twisted into an expression of raw, unqualified hatred. *Bastards!* I'll kill every mother's son of you before I'll give in! His right hand closed like a clamp and the glass shattered in his grip.

He looked down, dull-eyed, at the fragments on the floor, at the jagged piece of glass still in his hand, at the whisky-diluted blood dripping off his palm.

Wouldn't they like to get some of it, though? he thought. He started up with a furious lurch and almost opened the door so he could wave the hand in their faces and hear them howl.

Then he closed his eyes and a shudder ran through his body. Wise up, buddy, he thought. Go bandage your goddamn hand.

He stumbled into the bathroom and washed his hand carefully, gasping as he daubed iodine into the sliced-open flesh. Then he bandaged it clumsily, his broad chest rising and falling with jerky movements, sweat dripping from his forehead. I need a cigarette, he thought.

In the living room again, he changed Brahms for Bernstein and lit a cigarette. What will I do if I ever run out of coffin nails? he wondered, looking at the cigarette's blue trailing smoke. Well, there wasn't much chance of that. He had about a thousand cartons in the closet of Kathy's—

He clenched his teeth together. In the closet of the *larder*, the *larder*, the *larder*.

Kathy's room.

He sat staring with dead eyes at the mural while "The Age of Anxiety" pulsed in his ears. Age of anxiety, he mused. You thought you had anxiety, Lenny boy. Lenny and Benny; you two should meet. Composer, meet corpse. Mamma, when I grow up I wanna be a wampir like Dada. Why, bless you, hon, of course you shall.

The whisky gurgled into the glass. He grimaced a little at the pain in his hand and shifted the bottle to his left hand.

He sat down and sipped. Let the jagged edge of sobriety be now dulled, he thought. Let the crumby balance of clear vision be expunged, but post haste. I hate 'em.

Gradually the room shifted on its gyroscopic center and wove and undulated about his chair. A pleasant haze, fuzzy at the edges, took over sight. He looked at the glass, at the record player. He let his head flop from side to side. Outside, they prowled and muttered and waited.

Pore vampires, he thought, pore little cusses, pussyfootin' round my house, so thirsty, so all forlorn.

A thought. He raised a forefinger that wavered before his eyes.

Friends, I come before you to discuss the vampire; a minority element if there ever was one, and there was one.

But to concision: I will sketch out the basis for my thesis, which thesis is this: Vampires are prejudiced against.

The keynote of minority prejudice is this: They are loathed because they are feared. Thus . . .

He made himself a drink. A long one.

At one time, the Dark and Middle Ages, to be succinct, the vampire's power was great, the fear of him tremendous. He was anathema and still remains anathema. Society hates him without ration.

But are his needs any more shocking than the needs of other animals and men? Are his deeds more outrageous than the deeds of the parent who drained the spirit from his child? The vampire may foster quickened heartbeats and levitated hair. But is he worse than the parent who gave to society a neurotic child who became a politician? Is he worse than the manufacturer who set up belated foundations with the money he made by handing bombs and guns to suicidal nationalists? Is he worse than the distiller who gave bastardized grain juice to stultify further the brains of those who, sober, were incapable of a progressive thought? (Nay, I apologize for this calumny; I nip the brew that feeds me.) Is he worse, then, than the publisher who filled ubiquitous racks with lust and death wishes? Really, now, search your soul, lovie—is the vampire so bad?

All he does is drink blood.

Why, then, this unkind prejudice, this thoughtless bias? Why cannot the vampire live where he chooses? Why must he seek out hiding places where none can find him out? Why do you wish him destroyed? Ah, see, you have turned the poor guileless innocent into a haunted animal. He has no means of support, no measures for proper education, he has not the voting franchise. No wonder he is compelled to seek out a predatory nocturnal existence.

Robert Neville grunted a surly grunt. Sure, sure, he thought, but would you let your sister marry one?

He shrugged. You got me there, buddy, you got me there.

The music ended. The needle scratched back and forth in the black grooves. He sat there, feeling a chill creeping up his legs. That's what was wrong with drinking too much. You became immune to drunken delights. There was no solace in liquor. Before you got happy, you collapsed. Already the room was straightening out, the sounds outside were starting to nibble at his eardrums.

"Come out, Neville!"

His throat moved and a shaking breath passed his lips. Come out.

The women were out there, their dresses open or taken off, their flesh waiting for his touch, their lips waiting for—

My blood, my *blood*!

As if it were someone else's hand, he watched his whitened fist rise up slowly, shuddering, to drive down on his leg. The pain made him suck in a breath of the house's stale air. Garlic. Everywhere the smell of garlic. In his clothes and in the furniture and in his food and even in his drink. Have a garlic and soda; his mind rattled out the attempted joke.

He lurched up and started pacing. What am I going to do now? Go through the routine again? I'll save you the trouble. Reading-drinking-soundproof-the-house—the women. The women, the lustful, bloodthirsty, naked women flaunting their hot bodies at him. No, not hot.

A shuddering whine wrenched up through his chest and throat. Goddamn them, what were they waiting for? Did they think he was going to come out and hand himself over?

Maybe I am, maybe I am. He actually found himself jerking off the crossbar from the door. Coming, girls, I'm coming. Wet your lips, now.

Outside, they heard the bar being lifted, and a howl of anticipation sounded in the night.

Spinning, he drove his fists one after the other into the wall until he'd cracked the plaster and broken his skin. Then he stood there trembling helplessly, his teeth chattering.

After a while it passed. He put the bar back across the door and went into the bedroom. He sank down on the bed and fell back on the pillow with a groan. His left hand beat once, feebly, on the bedspread.

Oh, *God*, he thought, how long, how long?

CHAPTER FOUR

The alarm never went off because he'd forgotten to set it. He slept soundly and motionlessly, his body like cast iron. When he finally opened his eyes, it was ten o'clock.

With a disgusted muttering, he struggled up and dropped his legs over the side of the bed. Instantly his head began throbbing as if his brains were trying to force their way through his skull. Fine, he thought, a hangover. That's all I need.

He pushed himself up with a groan and stumbled into the bathroom, threw water in his face and splashed some over his head. No good, his mind complained, no good. I still feel like hell. In the mirror his face was gaunt, bearded, and very much like the face of a man in his forties. Love, your magic spell is everywhere; inanely, the words flapped across his brain like wet sheets in a wind.

He walked slowly into the living room and opened the front door. A curse fell thickly from his lips at the sight of the woman crumpled across the sidewalk. He started to tighten angrily, but it made his head throb too much and he had to let it go. I'm sick, he thought.

The sky was gray and dead. Great! he thought. Another day stuck in this boarded-up rat hole! He slammed the door viciously, then winced, groaning, at the brain-stabbing noise. Outside, he heard the rest of the mirror fall out and shatter on the porch cement. Oh, *great!* His lips contorted back into a white twist of flesh.

Two cups of burning black coffee only made his stomach feel worse. He put down the cup and went into the living room. To hell with it, he thought, I'll get drunk again.

But the liquor tasted like turpentine, and with a rasping snarl he flung the glass against the wall and stood watching the liquor run down onto the rug. Hell, I'm runnin' out of glasses. The thought irritated him while breath struggled in through his nostrils and out again in faltering bursts.

He sank down on the couch and sat there, shaking his head slowly. It was no use; they'd beaten him, the black bastards had beaten him.

That restless feeling again; the feeling as if he were expanding and the house were contracting and any second now he'd go bursting through its frame in an explosion of wood, plaster, and brick. He got up and moved quickly to the door, his hands shaking.

On the lawn, he stood sucking in great lungfuls of the wet morning air, his face turned away from the house he hated. But he hated the other houses around there too, and he hated the pavement and the sidewalks and the lawns and everything that was on Cimarron Street.

It kept building up. And suddenly he knew he had to get out of there. Cloudy day or not, he had to get out of there.

He locked the front door, unlocked the garage, and dragged up the thick door on its overhead hinges. He didn't bother putting down the door. I'll be back soon, he thought. I'll just go away for a while.

He backed the station wagon quickly down the driveway, jerked it around, and pressed down hard on the accelerator, heading for Compton Boulevard. He didn't know where he was going.

He went around the corner doing forty and jumped that to sixty-five before he'd gone another block. The car leaped forward under his foot and he kept the accelerator on the floor, forced down by a rigid leg. His hands were like carved ice on the wheel and his face was the face of a statue. At eighty-nine miles an hour, he shot down the lifeless, empty boulevard, one roaring sound in the great stillness.

Things rank and gross in nature possess it merely, he thought as he walked slowly across the cemetery lawn.

The grass was so high that the weight of it had bent it over and it crunched under his heavy shoes as he walked. There was no sound but that of his shoes and the now senseless singing of birds. Once I thought they sang because everything was right with the world, Robert Neville thought. I know now I was wrong. They sing because they're feeble-minded.

He had raced six miles, the gas pedal pressed to the floor, before he'd realized where he was going. It was strange the way his mind and body had kept it secret from his consciousness. Consciously, he'd known only that he was sick and depressed and had to get away from the house. He didn't know he was going to visit Virginia.

But he'd driven there directly and as fast as he could. He'd parked at the curb and entered through the rusted gate, and now his shoes were pressing and crackling through the thick grass.

How long had it been since he'd come here? It must have been at least a month. He wished he'd brought flowers, but then, he hadn't realized he was coming here until he was almost at the gate.

His lips pressed together as an old sorrow held him again. Why couldn't he have Kathy there too? Why had he followed so blindly, listening to those fools who set up their stupid regulations during the plague? If only she could be there, lying across from her mother.

Don't start that again, he ordered himself.

Drawing closer to the crypt, he stiffened as he noticed that the iron door was slightly ajar. Oh, *no*, he thought. He broke into a run across the wet grass. If they've been at her, I'll burn down the city, he vowed. I swear to God, I'll burn it to the ground if they've touched her.

He flung open the door and it clanged against the marble wall with a hollow, echoing sound. His eyes moved quickly to the marble base on which the sealed casket rested.

The tension sank; he drew in breath again. It was still there, untouched.

Then, as he started in, he saw the man lying in one corner of the crypt, body curled up on the cold floor.

With a grunt of rage, Robert Neville rushed at the body, and, grabbing the man's coat in taut fingers, he dragged him across the floor and flung him violently out onto the grass. The body rolled onto its back, the white face pointing at the sky.

Robert Neville went back into the crypt, chest rising and falling with harsh movements. Then he closed his eyes and stood with his palms resting on the cover of the casket.

I'm here, he thought. I'm back. Remember me.

He threw out the flowers he'd brought the time before and cleared away the few leaves that had blown in because the door had been opened.

Then he sat down beside the casket and rested his forehead against its cold metal side.

Silence held him in its cold and gentle hands.

If I could die now, he thought; peacefully, gently, without a tremor or a crying out. If I could be with her. If I could believe I would be with her.

His fingers tightened slowly and his head sank forward on his chest.

Virginia. Take me where you are.

A tear, crystal, fell across his motionless hand. . . .

He had no idea how long he'd been there. After a while, though, even the deepest sorrow faltered, even the most penetrating despair lost its scalpel edge. The flagellant's curse, he thought, to grow inured even to the whip.

He straightened up and stood. Still alive, he thought, heart beating senselessly, veins running without point, bones and muscles and tissue all alive and functioning with no purpose at all.

A moment longer he stood looking down at the casket, then he turned away with a sigh and left, closing the door behind him quietly so as not to disturb her sleep.

He'd forgotten about the man. He almost tripped over him now, stepping aside with a muttered curse and starting past the body.

Then, abruptly, he turned back.

What's this? He looked down incredulously at the man. The man was dead; really dead. But how could that be? The change had occurred so quickly, yet already the man looked and smelled as though he'd been dead for days.

His mind began churning with a sudden excitement. Something had killed the vampire; something brutally effective. The heart had not been touched, no garlic had been present, and yet . . .

It came, seemingly, without effort. Of course—the daylight!

A bolt of self-accusation struck him. To know for five months that they remained indoors by day and never *once* to make the connection! He closed his eyes, appalled by his own stupidity.

The rays of the sun; the infrared and ultraviolet. It had to be them. But why? Damn it, why didn't he know anything about the effects of sunlight on the human system?

Another thought: That man had been one of the true vampires; the living dead. Would sunlight have the same effect on those who were still alive?

The first excitement he'd felt in months made him break into a run for the station wagon.

As the door slammed shut beside him, he wondered if he should have taken away the dead man. Would the body attract others, would they invade the crypt? No, they wouldn't go near the casket, anyway; it was sealed with garlic. Besides, the man's blood was dead now, it—

Again his thoughts broke off as he leaped to another conclusion. The sun's rays must have done something to their blood!

Was it possible, then, that all things bore relations to the blood? The garlic, the cross, the mirror, the stake, daylight, the earth some of them slept in? He didn't see how, and yet . . .

He had to do a lot of reading, a lot of research. It might be just the thing he needed. He'd been planning for a long time to do it, but lately it seemed as if he'd forgotten it altogether. Now this new idea started the desire again.

He started the car and raced up the street, turning off into a residential section and pulling up before the first house he came to.

He ran up the pathway to the front door, but it was locked and he couldn't force it in. With an impatient growl, he ran to the next house. The door was open and he ran to the stairs through the darkened living room and jumped up the carpeted steps two at a time.

He found the woman in the bedroom. Without hesitation, he jerked back the covers and grabbed her by the wrists. She grunted as her body hit the floor, and he heard her making tiny sounds in her throat as he dragged her into the hall and started down the stairs.

As he pulled her across the living room, she started to move.

Her hands closed over his wrists and her body began to twist and flop on the rug. Her eyes were still closed, but she gasped and muttered and her body kept trying to writhe out of his grip. Her dark nails dug into his flesh. He tore out of her grasp with a snarl and dragged her the rest of the way by her hair. Usually he felt a twinge when he realized that, but for some affliction he didn't understand, these people were the same as he. But now an experimental fervor had seized him and he could think of nothing else.

Even so, he shuddered at the strangled sound of horror she made when he threw her on the sidewalk outside.

She lay twisting helplessly on the sidewalk, hands opening and closing, lips drawn back from red-spotted lips. Robert Neville watched her tensely.

His throat moved. It wouldn't last, the feeling of callous brutality. He bit his lips as he watched her. All right, she's suffering, he argued with himself, but she's one of them and she'd kill me gladly if she got the chance. You've got to look at it that way, it's the only way. Teeth clenched, he stood there and watched her die.

In a few minutes she stopped moving, stopped muttering, and her hands uncurled slowly like white blossoms on the cement. Robert Neville crouched down and felt for her heartbeat. There was none. Already her flesh was growing cold.

He straightened up with a thin smile. It was true, then. He didn't need the stakes. After all this time, he'd finally found a better method.

Then his breath caught. But how did he know the woman was really dead? How could he know until sunset?

The thought filled him with a new, more restless anger. Why did each question blight the answers before it?

He thought about it as he sat drinking a can of tomato juice taken from the supermarket behind which he was parked.

How was he going to know? He couldn't very well stay with the woman until sunset came.

Take her home with you, fool.

Again his eyes closed and he felt a shudder of irritation go through him. He was missing all the obvious answers today. Now he'd have to go all the way back and find her, and he wasn't even sure where the house was.

He started the motor and pulled away from the parking lot, glancing down at his watch. Three o'clock. Plenty of time to get back before they came. He eased the gas pedal down and the station wagon pulled ahead faster.

It took him about a half hour to relocate the house. The woman was still in the same position on the sidewalk. Putting on his gloves, Neville lowered the back gate of the station wagon and walked over to the woman. As he walked, he noticed her figure. No, don't start that again, for God's sake.

He dragged the woman back to the station wagon and tossed her in. Then he closed the gate and took off his gloves. He held up the watch and looked at it. Three o'clock. Plenty of time to—

He jerked up the watch and held it against his ear, his heart suddenly jumping.

The watch had stopped.

CHAPTER FIVE

His fingers shook as he turned the ignition key. His hands gripped the wheel rigidly as he made a tight U turn and started back toward Gardena.

What a fool he'd been! It must have taken at least an hour to reach the cemetery. He must have been in the crypt for hours. Then going to get that woman. Going to the market, drinking the tomato juice, going back to get the woman again.

What time *was* it?

Fool! Cold fear poured through his veins at the thought of them all waiting for him at his house. Oh, my God, and he'd left the garage door open! The gasoline, the equipment—*the generator*!

A groan cut itself off in his throat as he jammed the gas pedal to the floor and the small station wagon leaped ahead, the speedometer needle fluttering, then moving steadily past the sixty-five mark, the seventy, the seventy-five. What if they were already waiting for him? How could he possibly get in the house?

He forced himself to be calm. He mustn't go to pieces now; he had to keep himself in check. He'd get in. Don't worry, you'll get inside, he told himself. But he didn't see how.

One hand ran nervously through his hair. This is fine, fine, commented his mind. You go to all that trouble to preserve your existence, and then one day you just don't come back in time. Shut up! his mind snapped back at itself. But he could have killed himself for forgetting to wind his watch the night before. Don't bother killing yourself, his mind reflected, they'll be glad to do it for you. Suddenly he realized he was almost weak from hunger. The small amount of canned meat he'd eaten with the tomato juice had done nothing to alleviate hunger.

The silent streets flew past and he kept looking from side to side to see if any of them were appearing in the doorways. It seemed as if it were already getting dark, but that could have been imagination. It couldn't be that late, it couldn't be.

He'd just gone hurtling past the corner of Western and Compton when he saw the man come running out of a building and shout at him. His heart was contracted in an icy hand as the man's cry fluttered in the air behind the car.

He couldn't get any more speed out of the station wagon. And now his mind began torturing him with visions of one of the tires going, the station wagon veering, leaping the curb and crashing into a house. His lips started to shake and he jammed them together to stop them. His hands on the wheel felt numb.

He had to slow down at the corner of Cimarron. Out of the corner of an eye he saw a man come rushing out of a house and start chasing the car.

Then, as he turned the corner with a screech of clinging tires, he couldn't hold back the gasp.

They were all in front of his house, waiting.

A sound of helpless terror filled his throat. He didn't want to die. He might have thought about it, even contemplated it. But he didn't want to die. Not like *this*.

Now he saw them all turn their white faces at the sound of the motor. Some more of them came running out of the open garage and his teeth ground together in impotent fury. What a stupid, brainless way to die!

Now he saw them start running straight toward the station wagon, a line of them across the street. And, suddenly, he knew he couldn't stop. He pressed down on the accelerator, and in a moment the car went plowing through them, knocking three of them aside like tenpins. He felt the car frame jolt as it struck the bodies. Their screaming white faces went flashing by his window, their cries chilling his blood.

Now they were behind and he saw in the rear-view mirror that they were all pursuing him. A sudden plan caught hold in his mind, and impulsively he slowed down, even braking, until the speed of the car fell to thirty, then twenty miles an hour.

He looked back and saw them gaining, saw their grayish-white faces approaching, their dark eyes fastened to his car, to *him*.

Suddenly he twitched with shock as a snarl sounded nearby and, jerking his head around, he saw the crazed face of Ben Cortman beside the car.

Instinctively his foot jammed down on the gas pedal, but his other foot slipped off the clutch, and with a neck-snapping jolt the station wagon jumped forward and stalled.

Sweat broke out on his forehead as he lunged forward feverishly to press the button. Ben Cortman clawed in at him.

With a snarl he shoved the cold white hand aside.

"Neville, Neville!"

Ben Cortman reached in again, his hands like claws cut from ice. Again Neville pushed aside the hand and jabbed at the starter button, his body shaking helplessly. Behind, he could hear them all screaming excitedly as they came closer to the car.

The motor coughed into life again as he felt Ben Cortman's long nails rake across his cheek.

"Neville!"

The pain made his hand jerk into a rigid fist, which he drove into Cortman's face. Cortman went flailing back onto the pavement as the gears caught and the station wagon jolted forward, picking up speed. One of the others caught up and leaped at the rear of the car. For a minute he held on, and Robert Neville could see his ashen face glaring insanely through the back window. Then he jerked the car over toward the curb, swerved sharply, and shook the man off. The man went running across a lawn, arms ahead of him, and smashed violently into the side of a house.

Robert Neville's heart was pounding so heavily now it seemed as if it would drive through his chest walls. Breath shuddered in him and his flesh felt numb and cold. He could feel the trickle of blood on his cheek, but no pain. Hastily he wiped it off with one shaking hand.

Now he spun the station wagon around the corner, turning right. He kept looking at the rear-view mirror, then looking ahead. He went the short block to Haas Street and turned right again. What if they cut through the yards and blocked his way?

He slowed down a little until they came swarming around the corner like a pack of wolves. Then he pressed down on the accelerator. He'd have to take the chance that they were all following him. Would some of them guess what he was trying?

He shoved down the gas pedal all the way and the station wagon jumped forward, racing up the block. He wheeled it around the corner at fifty miles an hour, gunned up the short block to Cimarron, and turned right again.

His breath caught. There was no one in sight on his lawn. There was still a chance, then. He'd have to let the station wagon go, though; there was no time to put it in the garage.

He jerked the car to the curb and shoved the door open. As he raced around the edge of the car he heard the billowing cry of their approach around the corner.

He'd have to take a chance on locking the garage. If he didn't, they might destroy the generator; they couldn't have had time to do it already. His footsteps pounded up the driveway to the garage.

"Neville!"

His body jerked back as Cortman came lunging out of the dark shadows of the garage.

Cortman's body drove into his and almost knocked him down. He felt the cold, powerful hands clamp on his throat and smelled the fetid breath clouding over his face. The two of them went reeling back toward the sidewalk and the white-fanged mouth went darting down at Robert Neville's throat.

Abruptly he jerked up his right fist and felt it drive into Cortman's throat. He heard the choking sound in Cortman's throat. Up the block the first of them came rushing and screaming around the corner.

With a violent movement, Robert Neville grabbed Cortman by his long, greasy hair and sent him hurtling down the driveway until he rammed head on into the side of the station wagon.

Robert Neville's eyes flashed up the street. No time for the garage! He dashed around the corner of the house and up to the porch.

He skidded to a halt. Oh, God, the keys!

With a terrified intake of breath he spun and rushed back toward the car. Cortman started up with a throaty snarl and he drove his knee into the white face and knocked Cortman back on the sidewalk. Then he lunged into the car and jerked the key chain away from the ignition slot.

As he scuttled back out of the car the first one of them came leaping at him.

He shrank back onto the car seat and the man tripped over his legs and went sprawling heavily onto the sidewalk. Robert Neville pushed himself out, dashed across the lawn, and leaped onto the porch.

He had to stop to find the right key and another man came leaping up the porch steps. Neville was slammed against the house by the impact of his body. The hot blood-thick breath was on him again, the bared mouth lunging at his throat. He drove his knee into the man's groin and then, leaning his weight against the house, he raised his foot high and shoved the doubled-over man into the other one who was rushing across the lawn.

Neville dived for the door and unlocked it. He pushed it open, slipped inside, and turned. As he slammed it shut an arm shot through the opening. He forced the door against it with all his strength until he heard bones snap, then he opened the door a little, shoved the broken arm out, and slammed the door. With trembling hands he dropped the bar into place.

Slowly he sank down onto the floor and fell on his back. He lay there in the darkness, his chest rising and falling, his legs and arms like dead limbs on the floor. Outside they howled and pummeled the door, shouting his name in a paroxysm of demented fury. They grabbed up bricks and rocks and hurled them against the house and they screamed and cursed at him. He lay there listening to the thud of the rocks and bricks against the house, listening to their howling.

After a while he struggled up to the bar. Half the whisky he poured splashed onto the rug. He threw down the contents of the glass and stood there shivering, holding onto the bar to support his wobbling legs, his throat tight and convulsed; his lips shaking without control.

Slowly the heat of the liquor expanded in his stomach and reached his body. His breath slowed down, his chest stopped shuddering.

He started as he heard the great crash outside.

He ran to the peephole and looked out. His teeth grated together and a burst of rage filled him as he saw the station wagon lying on its side and saw them smashing in the windshield with bricks and stones, tearing open the hood and smashing at the engine with insane club strokes, denting the frame with their frenzied blows. As he watched, fury poured through him like a current of hot acid and half-formed curses sounded in his throat while his hands clamped into great white fists at his sides.

Turning suddenly, he moved to the lamp and tried to light it. It didn't work. With a snarl he turned and ran into the kitchen. The refrigerator was out. He ran from one dark room to another. The freezer was off; all the food would spoil. His house was a dead house.

Fury exploded in him. Enough!

His rage-palsied hands ripped out the clothes from the bureau drawer until they closed on the loaded pistols.

Racing through the dark living room, he knocked up the bar across the door and sent it clattering to the floor. Outside, they howled as they heard him opening the door. I'm coming out, you bastards! his mind screamed out.

He jerked open the door and shot the first one in the face. The man went spinning back off the porch and two women came at him in muddy, torn dresses, their white arms spread to enfold him. He watched their bodies jerk as the bullets struck them, then he shoved them both aside and began firing his guns into their midst, a wild yell ripping back his bloodless lips.

He kept firing the pistols until they were both empty. Then he stood on the porch clubbing them with insane blows, losing his mind almost completely when the same ones he'd shot came rushing at him again. And when they tore the guns out of his hands he used his fists and elbows and he butted with his head and kicked them with his big shoes.

It wasn't until the flaring pain of having his shoulder slashed open struck him that he realized what he was doing and how hopeless his attempt was. Knocking aside two women, he backed toward the door. A man's arm locked around his neck. He lurched forward, bending at the waist, and toppled the man over his head into the others. He jumped back into the doorway, gripped both sides of the frame and kicked out his legs like pistons, sending the men crashing back into the shrubbery.

Then, before they could get at him again, he slammed the door in their faces, locked it, bolted it, and dropped the heavy bar into its slots.

Robert Neville stood in the cold blackness of his house, listening to the vampires scream.

He stood against the wall clubbing slowly and weakly at the plaster, tears streaming down his bearded cheeks, his bleeding hand pulsing with pain. Everything was gone, everything.

"Virginia," he sobbed like a lost, frightened child. "Virginia. *Virginia.*"

PART TWO: March 1976

CHAPTER SIX

The house, at last, was livable again.

Even more so than before, in fact, for he had finally taken three days and soundproofed the walls. Now they could scream and howl all they wanted and he didn't have to listen to them. He especially liked not having to listen to Ben Cortman any more.

It had all taken time and work. First of all was the matter of a new car to replace the one they'd destroyed. This had been more difficult than he'd imagined.

He had to get over to Santa Monica to the only Willys store he knew about. The Willys station wagons were the only ones he had had any experience with, and this didn't seem quite the time to start experimenting. He couldn't walk to Santa Monica, so he had to try using one of the many cars parked around the neighborhood. But most of them were inoperative for one reason or another: a dead battery, a clogged fuel pump, no gasoline, flat tires.

Finally, in a garage about a mile from the house, he found a car he could get started, and he drove quickly to Santa Monica to pick up another station wagon. He put a new battery in it, filled its tank with gasoline, put gasoline drums in the back, and drove home. He got back to the house about an hour before sunset.

He made sure of that.

Luckily the generator had not been ruined. The vampires apparently had no idea of its importance to him, for, except for a torn wire and a few cudgel blows, they had left it alone. He'd managed to fix it quickly the morning after the attack and keep his frozen foods from spoiling. He was grateful for that, because he was sure there were no places left where he could get more frozen foods now that electricity was gone from the city.

For the rest of it, he had to straighten up the garage and clean out the debris of broken bulbs, fuses, wiring, plugs, solder, spare motor parts, and a box of seeds he'd put there once; he didn't remember just when.

The washing machine they had ruined beyond repair, forcing him to replace it. But that wasn't hard. The worst part was mopping up all the gasoline they'd spilled from the drums. They'd really outdone themselves spilling gasoline, he thought irritably while he mopped it up.

Inside the house, he had repaired the cracked plaster, and as an added fillip he had put up another wall mural to give a different appearance to the room.

He'd almost enjoyed all the work once it was started. It gave him something to lose himself in, something to pour all the energy of his still pulsing fury into. It broke the monotony of his daily tasks: the carrying away of bodies, the repairing of the house's exterior, the hanging of garlic.

He drank sparingly during those days, managing to pass almost the entire day without a drink, even allowing his evening drinks to assume the function of relaxing nightcaps rather than senseless escape. His appetite increased and he gained four pounds and lost a little belly. He even slept nights, a tired sleep without the dreams.

For a day or so he had played with the idea of moving to some lavish hotel suite. But the thought of all the work he'd have to do to make it habitable changed his mind. No, he was all set in the house.

Now he sat in the living room, listening to Mozart's Jupiter Symphony and wondering how he was to begin, *where* he was to begin his investigation.

He knew a few details, but these were only landmarks above the basic earth of cause. The answer lay in something else. Probably in some fact he was aware of but did not adequately appreciate, in some apparent knowledge he had not yet connected with the over-all picture.

But what?

He sat motionless in the chair, a sweat-beaded glass in his right hand, his eyes fastened on the mural.

It was a scene from Canada: deep northern woods, mysterious with green shadows, standing aloof and motionless, heavy with the silence of manless nature. He stared into its soundless green depths and wondered.

Maybe if he went back. Maybe the answer lay in the past, in some obscure crevice of memory. Go back, then, he told his mind, go back.

It tore his heart out to go back.

There had been another dust storm during the night. High, spinning winds had scoured the house with grit, driven it through the cracks, sifted it through plaster pores, and left a hair-thin layer of dust across all the furniture surfaces. Over their bed the dust filtered like fine powder, settling in their hair and on their eyelids and under their nails, clogging their pores.

Half the night he'd lain awake trying to single out the sound of Virginia's labored breathing. But he couldn't hear anything above the shrieking, grating sound of the storm. For a while, in the suspension between sleeping and waking, he had suffered the illusion that the house was being sandpapered by giant wheels that held its framework between monstrous abrasive surfaces and made it shudder.

He'd never got used to the dust storms. That hissing sound of whirlwind granulation always set his teeth on edge. The storms had never come regularly enough to allow him to adapt himself to them.

Whenever they came, he spent a restless, tossing night, and went to the plant the next day with jaded mind and body.

Now there was Virginia to worry about too.

About four o'clock he awoke from a thin depression of sleep and realized that the storm had ended. The contrast made silence a rushing noise in his ears.

As he raised his body irritably to adjust his twisted pajamas, he noticed that Virginia was awake. She was lying on her back and staring at the ceiling.

"What's the matter?" he mumbled drowsily.

She didn't answer.

"Honey?"

Her eyes moved slowly to him.

"Nothing," she said. "Go to sleep."

"How do you feel?"

"The same."

"Oh."

He lay there for a moment looking at her.

"Well," he said then and, turning on his side, closed his eyes.

The alarm went off at six-thirty. Usually Virginia pushed in the stop, but when she failed to do so, he reached over her inert body and did it himself. She was still on her back, still staring.

"What is it?" he asked worriedly.

She looked at him and shook her head on the pillow.

"I don't know," she said. "I just can't sleep."

"Why?"

She made an indecisive sound.

"Still feel weak?" he asked.

She tried to sit up but she couldn't.

"Stay there, hon," he said. "Don't move." He put his hand on her brow. "You haven't got any fever," he told her.

"I don't feel sick," she said. "Just . . . tired."

"You look pale."

"I know. I look like a ghost."

"Don't get up," he said.

She was up.

"I'm not going to pamper myself," she said. "Go ahead, get dressed. I'll be all right."

"Don't get up if you don't feel good, honey."

She patted his arm and smiled.

"I'll be all right," she said. "You get ready."

While he shaved he heard the shuffling of her slippers past the bathroom door. He opened the door and watched her crossing the living room very slowly, her wrappered body weaving a little. He went back in the bathroom shaking his head. She should have stayed in bed.

The whole top of the washbasin was grimy with dust. The damn stuff was everywhere. He'd finally been compelled to erect a tent over Kathy's bed to keep the dust from her face. He'd nailed one edge of a shelter half to the wall next to her bed and let it slope over the bed, the other edge held up by two poles lashed to the side of the bed.

He didn't get a good shave because there was grit in the shaving soap and he didn't have time for a second lathering. He washed off his face, got a clean towel from the hall closet, and dried himself.

Before going to the bedroom to get dressed he checked Kathy's room.

She was still asleep, her small blonde head motionless on the pillow, her cheeks pink with heavy sleep. He ran a finger across the top of the shelter half and drew it away gray with dust. With a disgusted shake of his head he left the room.

"I wish these damn storms would end," he said as he entered the kitchen ten minutes later. "I'm sure . . ."

He stopped talking. Usually she was at the stove turning eggs or French toast or pancakes, making coffee. Today she was sitting at the table. On the stove coffee was percolating, but nothing else was cooking.

"Sweetheart, if you don't feel well, go back to bed," he told her. "I can fix my own breakfast."

"It's all right," she said. "I was just resting. I'm sorry. I'll get up and fry you some eggs."

"Stay there," he said. "I'm not helpless."

He went to the refrigerator and opened the door.

"I'd like to know what this *is* going around," she said.."Half the people on the block have it, and you say that more than half the plant is absent."

"Maybe it's some kind of virus," he said.

She shook her head. "I don't know."

"Between the storms and the mosquitoes and everyone being sick, life is rapidly becoming a pain," he said, pouring orange juice out of the bottle. "And speak of the devil."

He drew a black speck out of the orange juice in the glass.

"How the hell they get in the refrigerator I'll never know," he said.

"None for me, Bob," she said.

"No orange juice?"

"No."

"Good for you."

"No, thank you, sweetheart," she said, trying to smile.

He put back the bottle and sat down across from her with his glass of juice.

"You don't feel any pain?" he said. "No headache, nothing?"

She shook her head slowly.

"I wish I *did* know what was wrong," she said.

"You call up Dr. Busch today."

"I will," she said, starting to get up. He put his hand over hers.

"No, no, sweetheart, stay there," he said.

"But there's no *reason* why I should be like this."

She sounded angry. That was the way she'd been as long as he'd known her. If she became ill, it irritated her. She was annoyed by sickness. She seemed to regard it as a personal affront.

"Come on," he said, starting to get up. "I'll help you back to bed."

"No, just let me sit here with you," she said. "I'll go back to bed after Kathy goes to school."

"All right. Don't you want something, though?"

"No."

"How about coffee?"

She shook her head.

"You're *really* going to get sick if you don't eat," he said.

"I'm just not hungry."

He finished his juice and got up to fry a couple of eggs. He cracked them on the side of the iron skillet and dropped the contents into the melted bacon fat. He got the bread from the drawer and went over to the table with it.

"Here, I'll put it in the toaster," Virginia said. "You watch your . . . Oh, God."

"What is it?"

She waved one hand weakly in front of her face.

"A mosquito," she said with a grimace.

He moved over and, after a moment, crushed it between his two palms.

"Mosquitoes," she said. "Flies, sand fleas."

"We are entering the age of the insect," he said.

"It's not good," she said. "They carry diseases. We ought to put a net around Kathy's bed too."

"I know, I know," he said, returning to the stove and tipping the skillet so the hot fat ran over the white egg surfaces. "I keep meaning to."

"I don't think that spray works, either," Virginia said.

"It doesn't?"

"No."

"My God, and it's supposed to be one of the best ones on the market."

He slid the eggs onto a dish.

"Sure you don't want some coffee?" he asked her.

"No, thank you."

He sat down and she handed him the buttered toast.

"I hope to hell we're not breeding a race of superbugs," he said. "You remember that strain of giant grasshoppers they found in Colorado?"

"Yes."

"Maybe the insects are . . . What's the word? Mutating."

"What's that?"

"Oh, it means they're . . . changing. Suddenly. Jumping over dozens of small evolutionary steps, maybe developing along lines they might not have followed at all if it weren't for . . ."

Silence.

"The bombings?" she said.

"Maybe," he said.

"Well, they're causing the dust storms. They're probably causing a lot of things."

She sighed wearily and shook her head.

"And they say we won the war," she said.

"Nobody won it."

"The mosquitoes won it."

He smiled a little.

"I guess they did," he said.

They sat there for a few moments without talking and the only sound in the kitchen was the clink of his fork on the plate and the cup on the saucer.

"You looked at Kathy last night?" she asked.

"I just looked at her now. She looks fine."

"Good."

She looked at him studiedly.

"I've been thinking, Bob," she said. "Maybe we should send her East to your mother's until I get better. It may be contagious."

"We could," he said dubiously, "but if it's contagious, my mother's place wouldn't be any safer than here."

"You don't think so?" she asked. She looked worried.

He shrugged. "I don't know, hon. I think probably she's just as safe here. If it starts to get bad on the block, we'll keep her out of school."

She started to say something, then stopped.

"All right," she said.

He looked at his watch.

"I'd better finish up," he said.

She nodded and he ate the rest of his breakfast quickly. While he was draining the coffee cup she asked him if he'd bought a paper the night before.

"It's in the living room," he told her.

"Anything new in it?"

"No. Same old stuff. It's all over the country, a little here, a little there. They haven't been able to find the germ yet."

She bit her lower lip.

"Nobody knows what it is?"

"I doubt it. If anybody did they'd have surely said so by now."

"But they must have *some* idea."

"Everybody's got an idea. But they aren't worth anything."

"What do they say?"

He shrugged. "Everything from germ warfare on down."

"Do you think it is?"

"Germ warfare?"

"Yes," she said.

"The war's over," he said.

"Bob," she said suddenly, "do you think you should go to work?"

He smiled helplessly.

"What else can I do?" he asked. "We have to eat."

"I know, but . . ."

He reached across the table and felt how cold her hand was.

"Honey, it'll be all right," he said.

"And you think I should send Kathy to school?"

"I think so," he said. "Unless the health authorities say schools have to shut down, I don't see why we should keep her home. She's not sick."

"But all the kids at school."

"I think we'd better, though," he said.

She made a tiny sound in her throat. Then she said, "All right. If you think so."

"Is there anything you want before I go?" he asked.

She shook her head.

"Now you stay in the house today," he told her, "and in bed."

"I will," she said. "As soon as I send Kathy off."

He patted her hand. Outside, the car horn sounded. He finished the coffee and went to the bathroom to rinse out his mouth. Then he got his jacket from the hall closet and pulled it on.

"Good-by, honey," he said, kissing her on the cheek. "Take it easy, now."

"Good-by," she said. "Be careful."

He moved across the lawn, gritting his teeth at the residue of dust in the air. He could smell it as he walked, a dry tickling sensation in his nasal passages.

"Morning," he said, getting in the car and pulling the door shut behind him.

"Good morning," said Ben Cortman.

CHAPTER SEVEN

"Distilled from *Allium sativum*, a genus of Liliaceae comprising garlic, leek, onion, shallot, and chive. Is of pale color and penetrating odor, containing several allyl sulphides. Composition: water, 64.6%; protein, 6.8%; fat, 0.1%; carbohydrates, 26.3%; fiber, 0.8%; ash, 1.4.%."

There it was. He jiggled one of the pink, leathery cloves in his right palm. For seven months now he'd strung them together into aromatic necklaces and hung them outside his house without the remotest idea of why they chased the vampires away. It was time he learned why.

He put the clove on the sink ledge. Leek, onion, shallot, and chive. Would they all work as well as garlic? He'd really feel like a fool if they did, after searching miles around for garlic when onions were everywhere.

He mashed the clove to a pulp and smelled the acrid fluid on the thick cleaver blade.

All right, what now? The past revealed nothing to help him; only talk of insect carriers and virus, and they weren't the causes. He was sure of it.

The past had brought something else, though; pain at remembering. Every recalled word had been like a knife blade twisting in him. Old wounds had been reopened with every thought of her. He'd finally had to stop, eyes closed, fists clenched, trying desperately to accept the present on its own terms and not yearn with his very flesh for the past. But only enough drinks to stultify all introspection had managed to drive away the enervating sorrow that remembering brought.

He focused his eyes. All right, damn it, he told himself, *do* something!

He looked at the text again, water—was it that? he asked himself. No, that was ridiculous; all things had water in them. Protein? No. Fat? No. Carbohydrates? No. Fiber? No. Ash? No. What then?

"The characteristic odor and flavor of garlic are due to an essential oil amounting to about 0.2% of the weight, which consists mainly of allyl sulphide and allyl isothicyanate."

Maybe the answer was there.

Again the book: "Allyl sulphide may be prepared by heating mustard oil and potassium sulphide at 100 degrees."

His body thudded down into the living-room chair and a disgusted breath shuddered his long frame. And where the hell do I get mustard oil and potassium sulphide? *And* the equipment to prepare them in?

That's great, he railed at himself. The first step, and already you've fallen flat on your face.

He pushed himself up disgustedly and headed for the bar. But halfway through pouring a drink he slammed down the bottle. No, by God, he had no intention of going on like a blind man, plodding down a path of brainless, fruitless existence until old age or accident took him. Either he found the answer or he ditched the whole mess, life included.

He checked his watch. Ten-twenty A.M.; still time. He moved to the hallway resolutely and checked through the telephone directories. There was a place in Inglewood.

Four hours later he straightened up from the workbench with a crick in his neck and the allyl sulphide inside a hypodermic syringe, and in himself the first sense of real accomplishment since his forced isolation began.

A little excited, he ran to his car and drove out past the area he'd cleared out and marked with chalked rods. He knew it was more than possible that some vampires might have wandered into the cleared area and were hiding there again. But he had no time for searching.

Parking his car, he went into a house and walked to the bedroom. A young woman lay there, a coating of blood on her mouth.

Flipping her over, Neville pulled up her skirt and injected the allyl sulphide into her soft, fleshy buttock, then turned her over again and stepped back. For a half hour he stood there watching her.

Nothing happened.

This doesn't make sense, his mind argued. I hang garlic around the house and the vampires stay away. And the characteristic of garlic is the oil I've injected in her. But nothing's happened.

Goddamn it, nothing's happened!

He flung down the syringe and, trembling with rage and frustration, went home again. Before darkness, he built a small wooden structure on the front lawn and hung strings of onions on it. He spent a listless night, only the knowledge that there was still much left to do keeping him from the liquor.

In the morning he went out and looked at the matchwood on his lawn.

The cross. He held one in his hand, gold and shiny in the morning sun. This, too, drove the vampires away.

Why? Was there a logical answer, something he could accept without slipping on banana skins of mysticism?

There was only one way to find out.

He took the woman from her bed, pretending not to notice the question posed in his mind: Why do you always experiment on women? He didn't care to admit that the inference had any validity. She just happened to be the first one he'd come across, that was all. What about the man in the living room, though? For God's sake! he flared back. I'm not going to rape the woman!

Crossing your fingers, Neville? Knocking on wood?

He ignored that, beginning to suspect his mind of harboring an alien. Once he might have termed it conscience. Now it was only an annoyance. Morality, after all, had fallen with society. He was his own ethic.

Makes a good excuse, doesn't it, Neville? Oh, shut up.

But he wouldn't let himself pass the afternoon near her. After binding her to a chair, he secluded himself in the garage and puttered around with the car. She was wearing a torn black dress and too much was visible as she breathed. Out of sight, out of mind. . . . It was a lie, he knew, but he wouldn't admit it.

At last, mercifully, night came. He locked the garage door, went back to the house, and locked the front door, putting the heavy bar across it. Then he made a drink and sat down on the couch across from the woman.

From the ceiling, right before her face, hung the cross.

At six-thirty her eyes opened. Suddenly, like the eyes of a sleeper who has a definite job to do upon awakening; who does not move into consciousness with a vague entry, but with a single, clearcut motion, knowing just what is to be done.

Then she saw the cross and she jerked her eyes from it with a sudden rattling gasp and her body twisted in the chair.

"Why are you afraid of it?" he asked, startled at the sound of his own voice after so long.

Her eyes, suddenly on him, made him shudder. The way they glowed, the way her tongue licked across her red lips as if it were a separate life in her mouth. The way she flexed her body as if trying to move it closer to him. A guttural rumbling filled her throat like the sound of a dog defending its bone.

"The cross," he said nervously. "Why are you afraid of it?"

She strained against her bonds, her hands raking across the sides of the chair. No words from her, only a harsh, gasping succession of breaths. Her body writhed on the chair, her eyes burned into him.

"The cross!" he snapped angrily.

He was on his feet, the glass falling and splashing across the rug. He grabbed the string with tense fingers and swung the cross before her eyes. She flung her head away with a frightened snarl and re-coiled into the chair.

"*Look* at it!" he yelled at her.

A sound of terror-stricken whining came from her. Her eyes moved wildly around the room, great white eyes with pupils like specks of soot.

He grabbed at her shoulder, then jerked his hand back. It was dribbling blood from raw teeth wounds.

His stomach muscles jerked in. The hand lashed out again, this time smashing her across the cheek and snapping her head to the side.

Ten minutes later he threw her body out the front door and slammed it again in their faces. Then he stood there against the door breathing heavily. Faintly he heard through the soundproofing the sound of them fighting like jackals for the spoils.

Later he went to the bathroom and poured alcohol into the teeth gouges, enjoying fiercely the burning pain in his flesh.

CHAPTER EIGHT

Neville bent over and picked up a little soil in his right hand. He ran it between his fingers, crumbling the dark lumps into grit. How many of them, he wondered, slept in the soil, as the story went?

He shook his head. Precious few.

Where did the legend fit in, then?

He closed his eyes and let the dirt filter down slowly from his hand. Was there any answer? If only he could remember whether those who slept in soil were the ones who had returned from death. He might have theorized then.

But he couldn't remember. Another unanswerable question, then. Add it to the question that had occurred to him the night before.

What would a Mohammedan vampire do if faced with a cross?

The barking sound of his laugh in the silent morning air startled him. Good God, he thought, it's been so long since I've laughed, I've forgotten how. It sounded like the cough of a sick hound. Well, that's what I am, after all, isn't it? he decided. A very sick dog.

There had been a light dust storm about four that morning. Strange how it brought back memories. Virginia, Kathy, all those horrible days . . .

He caught himself. No, *no*, there was danger there. It was thinking of the past that drove him to the bottle. He was just going to have to accept the present.

He found himself wondering again why he chose to go on living. Probably, he thought, there's no real reason. I'm just too dumb to end it all.

Well—he clapped his hands with false decision—what now? He looked around as if there were something to see along the stillness of Cimarron Street.

All right, he decided impulsively, let's see if the running-water bit makes sense.

He buried a hose under the ground and ran it into a small trough constructed of wood. The water ran through the trough and out another hole into more hosing, which conducted the water into the earth.

When he'd finished, he went in and took a shower, shaved, and took the bandage off his hand. The wound had healed cleanly. But then, he hadn't been overly concerned about that. Time had more than proved to him that he was immune to their infection.

At six-twenty he went into the living room and stood before the peephole. He stretched a little, grunting at the ache in his muscles. Then, when nothing happened, he made himself a drink.

When he got back to the peephole, he saw Ben Cortman come walking onto the lawn.

"Come out, Neville," Robert Neville muttered, and Cortman echoed the words in a loud cry.

Neville stood there motionless, looking at Ben Cortman.

Ben hadn't changed much. His hair was still black, his body inclined to corpulence, his face still white. But there was a beard on his face now; mostly under the nose, thinner around his chin and cheeks and under his throat. That was the only real difference, though. Ben had always been immaculately shaved in the old days, smelling of cologne each morning when he picked up Neville to drive to the plant.

It was strange to stand there looking out at Ben Cortman; a Ben completely alien to him now. Once he had spoken to that man, ridden to work with him, talked about cars and baseball and politics with him, later on about the disease, about how Virginia and Kathy were getting along, about how Freda Cortman was about . . .

Neville shook his head. There was no point going into that. The past was as dead as Cortman.

Again he shook his head. The world's gone mad, he thought. The dead walk about and I think nothing of it. The return of corpses has become trivial in import. How quickly one accepts the incredible if only one sees it enough! Neville stood there, sipping his whisky and wondering who it was that Ben reminded him of. He'd felt for some time that Cortman reminded him of somebody, but for the life of him he couldn't think who.

He shrugged. What was the difference?

He put down the glass on the window sill and went into the kitchen. He turned on the water there and went back in. When he reached the peephole, he saw another man and a woman on the lawn. None of the three was speaking to either of the others. They never did. They walked and walked about on restless feet, circling each other like wolves, never looking at each other once, having hungry eyes only for the house and their prey inside the house.

Then Cortman saw the water running through the trough and went over to look at it. After a moment he lifted his white face and Neville saw him grinning.

Neville stiffened.

Cortman was jumping over the trough, then back again. Neville felt his throat tightening. The bastard knew!

With rigid legs he pistoned himself into the bedroom and, with shaking hands, pulled one of his pistols out of the bureau drawer.

Cortman was just about finishing stamping in the sides of the trough when the bullet struck him in the left shoulder.

He staggered back with a grunt and flopped onto the sidewalk with a kicking of legs. Neville fired again and the bullet whined up off the cement, inches from Cortman's twisting body.

Cortman started up with a snarl and the third bullet struck him full in the chest.

Neville stood there watching, smelling the acrid fumes of the pistol smoke. Then the woman blocked his view of Cortman and started jerking up her dress.

Neville pulled back and slammed the tiny door over the peephole. He wasn't going to let himself look at that. In the first second of it, he had felt that terrible heat dredging up from his loins like something ravenous.

Later he looked out again and saw Ben Cortman pacing around, calling for him to come out.

And, in the moonlight, he suddenly realized who Cortman reminded him of. The idea made his chest shudder with repressed laughter and he turned away as the shaking reached his shoulders.

My God—*Oliver Hardy*! Those old two-reelers he'd looked at with his projector. Cortman was almost a dead ringer for the roly-poly comedian. A little less plump, that was all. Even the mustache was there now.

Oliver Hardy flopping on his back under the driving impact of bullets. Oliver Hardy always coming back for more, no matter what happened. Ripped by bullets, punctured by knives, flattened by cars, smashed under collapsing chimneys and boats, submerged in water, flung through pipes. And always returning, patient and bruised. That was who Ben Cortman was—a hideously malignant Oliver Hardy buffeted and long-suffering.

My God, it was hilarious!

He couldn't stop laughing because it was more than laughter; it was release. Tears flooded down his cheeks. The glass in his hand shook so badly, the liquor spilled all over him and made him laugh harder. Then the glass fell thumping on the rug as his body jerked with spasms of uncontrollable amusement and the room was filled with his gasping, nerve-shattered laughter.

Later, he cried.

He drove it into the stomach, into the shoulder. Into the neck with a single mallet blow. Into the legs and the arms, and always the same result: the blood pulsing out, slick and crimson, over the white flesh.

He thought he'd found the answer. It was a matter of losing the blood they lived by; it was hemorrhage.

But then he found the woman in the small green and white house, and when he drove in the stake, the dissolution was so sudden it made him lurch away and lose his breakfast.

When he had recovered enough to look again, he saw on the bedspread what looked like a row of salt and pepper mixed; just about as long as the woman had been. It was the first time he'd ever seen such a thing.

Shaken by the sight, he went out of the house on trembling legs and sat in the car for an hour, drinking the flask empty. But even liquor couldn't drive away the vision.

It had been so *quick*. With the sound of the mallet blow still in his ears, she had virtually dissolved before his eyes.

He recalled talking once to a Negro at the plant. The man had studied mortuary science and had told Robert Neville about the mausoleums where people were stored in vacuum drawers and never changed their appearance.

"But you just let some air in," the Negro had said, "and *whoom!*— they'll look like a row of salt and pepper. Jus' like *that!*" And he snapped his fingers.

The woman had been long dead, then. Maybe, the thought occurred, she was one of the vampires who had originally started the plague. God only knew how many years she'd been cheating death.

He was too unnerved to do any more that day or for days to come. He stayed home and drank to forget and let the bodies pile up on the lawn and let the outside of the house fall into disrepair.

For days he sat in the chair with his liquor and thought about the woman. And, no matter how hard he tried not to, no matter how much he drank, he kept thinking about Virginia. He kept seeing himself entering the crypt, lifting the coffin lid.

He thought he was coming down with something, so palsied and nerveless was his shivering, so cold and ill did he feel.

Is *that* what she looked like?

CHAPTER NINE

Morning. A sun-bright hush broken only by the chorus of birds in the trees. No breeze to stir the vivid blossoms around the houses, the bushes, the dark-leaved hedges. A cloud of silent heat was suspended over everything on Cimarron Street.

Virginia Neville's heart had stopped.

He sat beside her on the bed, looking down at her white face. He held her fingers in his hand, his fingertips stroking and stroking. His body was immobile, one rigid, insensible block of flesh and bone. His eyes did not blink, his mouth was a static line, and the movement of his breathing was so slight that it seemed to have stopped altogether.

Something had happened to his brain.

In the second he had felt no heartbeat beneath his trembling fingers, the core of his brain seemed to have petrified, sending out jagged lines of calcification until his head felt like stone. Slowly, on palsied legs, he had sunk down on the bed. And now, vaguely, deep in the struggling tissues of thought, he did not understand how he could sit there, did not understand why despair did not crush him to the earth. But prostration would not come. Time was caught on hooks and could not progress. Everything stood fixed. With Virginia, life and the world had shuddered to a halt.

Thirty minutes passed; forty.

Then, slowly, as though he were discovering some objective phenomenon, he found his body trembling. Not with a localized tremble, a nerve here, a muscle there. This was complete. His body shuddered without end, one mass entire of nerves without control, bereft of will. And what operative mind was left knew that this was his reaction.

For more than an hour he sat in this palsied state, his eyes fastened dumbly to her face.

Then, abruptly, it ended, and with a choked muttering in his throat he lurched up from the bed and left the room.

Half the whisky splashed on the sink top as he poured. The liquor that managed to reach the glass he bolted down in a swallow. The thin current flared its way down to his stomach, feeling twice as intense in the polar numbness of his flesh. He stood sagged against the sink. Hands shaking, he filled the glass again to its top and gulped the burning whisky down with great convulsive swallows.

It's a dream, he argued vainly. It was as if a voice spoke the words aloud in his head.

"Virginia . . ."

He kept turning from one side to another, his eyes searching around the room as if there were something to be found, as if he had mislaid the exit from this house of horror. Tiny sounds of disbelief pulsed in his throat. He pressed his hands together, forcing the shaking palms against each other, the twitching fingers intertwining confusedly.

His hands began to shake so he couldn't make out their forms. With a gagging intake of breath he jerked them apart and pressed them against his legs.

"Virginia."

He took a step and cried aloud as the room flung itself off balance. Pain exploded in his right knee, sending hot barbs up his leg. He whined as he pushed himself up and stumbled to the living room. He stood there like a statue in an earthquake, his marble eyes frozen on the bedroom door.

In his mind he saw a scene enacted once again.

The great fire crackling, roaring yellow, sending its dense and grease-thick clouds into the sky. Kathy's tiny body in his arms. The man coming up and snatching her away as if he were taking a bundle of rags. The man lunging into the dark mist carrying his baby. Him standing there while pile driver blows of horror drove him down with their impact.

Then suddenly he had darted forward with a berserk scream.

"Kathy!"

The arms caught him, the men in canvas and masks drawing him back. His shoes gouged frenziedly at the earth, digging two ragged trenches in the earth as they dragged him away. His brain exploded, the terrified screams flooding from him.

Then the sudden bolt of numbing pain in his jaw, the daylight swept over with clouds of night. The hot trickle of liquor down his throat, the coughing, a gasping, and then he had been sitting silent and rigid in Ben Cortman's car, staring as they drove away at the gigantic pall of smoke that rose above the earth like a black wraith of all earth's despair.

Remembering, he closed his eyes suddenly and his teeth pressed together until they ached.

"No."

He wouldn't put Virginia there. Not if they killed him for it.

With a slow, stiff motion he walked to the front door and went out on the porch. Stepping off onto the yellowing lawn, he started down the block for Ben Cortman's house. The glare of the sun made his pupils shrink to points of jet. His hands swung useless and numbed at his sides.

The chimes still played "How Dry I Am." The absurdity of it made him want to break something in his hands. He remembered when Ben had put them in, thinking how funny it would be.

He stood rigidly before the door, his mind still pulsing. I don't care if it's the law, I don't care if refusal means death, I won't put her there!

His fist thudded on the door.

"Ben!"

Silence in the house of Ben Cortman. White curtains hung motionless in the front windows. He could see the red couch, the floor lamp with the fringed shade, the upright Knabe Freda used to toy with on Sunday afternoons. He blinked. What day *was* it? He had forgotten, he had lost track of the days.

He twisted his shoulders as impatient fury hosed acids through his veins.

"Ben!"

Again the side of his hard fist pummeled the door, and the flesh along his whitening jawline twitched. Damn him, where *was* he? Neville jammed in the button with a brittle finger and the chimes started the tippler's song over and over and over. "How dry I am, how dry I am, how dry I am, how dry I . . ."

With a frenzied gasp he lurched against the door and it flew open against the inside wall. It had been unlocked.

He walked into the silent living room.

"Ben," he said loudly. "Ben, I need your car."

They were in the bedroom, silent and still in their daytime comas, lying apart on the twin beds, Ben in pajamas, Freda in silk nightgown; lying on the sheets, their thick chests faltering with labored breath.

He stood there for a moment looking down at them. There were some wounds on Freda's white neck that had crusted over with dried blood. His eyes moved to Ben. There was no wound on Ben's throat. And he heard a voice in his mind that said: If only I'd wake up.

He shook his head. No, there was no waking up from this.

He found the car keys on the bureau and picked them up. He turned away and left the silent house behind. It was the last time he ever saw either of them alive.

The motor coughed into life and he let it idle a few minutes, choke out, while he sat staring out through the dusty windshield. A fly buzzed its bloated form around his head in the hot, airless interior of the car. He watched the dull green glitter of it and felt the car pulsing under him.

After a moment he pushed in the choke and drove the car up the street. He parked it in the driveway before his garage and turned off the motor.

The house was cool and silent. His shoes scuffed quietly over the rug, then clicked on the floor boards in the hall.

He stood motionless in the doorway looking at her. She still lay on her back, arms at her sides, the white fingers slightly curled in. She looked as if she were sleeping.

He turned away and went back into the living room. What was he going to do? Choices seemed pointless now. What did it matter *what* he did? Life would be equally purposeless no matter what his decision was.

He stood before the window looking out at the quiet, sun-drenched street, his eyes lifeless.

Why did I get the car, then? he wondered. His throat moved as he swallowed. I can't burn her, he thought. I *won't*. But what else was there? Funeral parlors were closed. What few morticians were healthy enough to practice were prevented from doing so by law. Everyone without exception had to be transported to the fires immediately upon death. It was the only way they knew now to prevent communication. Only flames could destroy the bacteria that caused the plague.

He knew that. He knew it was the law. But how many people followed it? He wondered that too. How many husbands took the women who had shared their life and love and dropped them into flames? How many parents incinerated the children they adored, how many children tossed their beloved parents on a bonfire a hundred yards square, a hundred feet deep?

No, if there was anything left in the world, it was his vow that she would not be burned in the fire.

An hour passed before he finally reached a decision.

Then he went and got her needle and thread.

He kept sewing until only her face showed. Then, fingers trembling, a tight knot in his stomach, he sewed the blanket together over her mouth. Over her nose. Her eyes.

Finished, he went in the kitchen and drank another glass of whisky. It didn't seem to affect him at all.

At last he went back to the bedroom on faltering legs. For a long minute he stood there breathing hoarsely. Then he bent over and worked his arms under her inert form.

"Come on, baby," he whispered.

The words seemed to loosen everything. He felt himself shaking, felt the tears running slowly down his cheeks as he carried her through the living room and outside.

He put her in the back seat and got in the car. He took a deep breath and reached for the starter button.

He drew back. Getting out of the car again, he went into the garage and got the shovel.

He twitched as he came out, seeing the man across the street approaching slowly. He put the shovel in the back and got in the car.

"Wait!"

The man's shout was hoarse. The man tried to run, but he wasn't strong enough.

Robert Neville sat there silently as the man came shuffling up.

"Could you . . . let me bring my . . . my mother too?" the man said stiffly.

"I . . . I . . . I . . ."

Neville's brain wouldn't function. He thought he was going to cry again, but he caught himself and stiffened his back.

"I'm not going to the . . . *there*," he said.

The man looked at him blankly.

"But your . . ."

"I'm not going to the fire, I said!" Neville blurted out, and jabbed in the starter button.

"But your wife," said the man. "You have your . . ."

Robert Neville jerked the gear shift into reverse.

"Please," begged the man.

"I'm not *going* there!" Neville shouted without looking at the man.

"But it's the *law*!" the man shouted back, suddenly furious.

The car raced back quickly into the street and Neville jerked it around to face Compton Boulevard. As he sped away he saw the man standing at the curb watching him leave. Fool! his mind grated. Do you think I'm going to throw my wife into a fire?

The streets were deserted. He turned left at Compton and started west. As he drove he looked at the huge lot on the right side of the car. He couldn't use any of the cemeteries. They were locked and watched. Men had been shot trying to bury their loved ones.

He turned right at the next block and drove up one block, turned right again into a quiet street that ended in the lot. Halfway up the block he cut the motor. He rolled the rest of the way so no one would hear the car.

No one saw him carry her from the car or carry her deep into the high-weeded lot. No one saw him put her down on an open patch of ground and then disappear from view as he knelt.

Slowly he dug, pushing the shovel into the soft earth, the bright sun pouring heat into the little clearing like molten air into a dish. Sweat ran in many lines down his cheeks and forehead as he dug, and the earth swam dizzily before his eyes. Newly thrown dirt filled his nostrils with its hot, pungent smell.

At last the hole was finished. He put down the shovel and sagged down on his knees. His body shuddered and sweat trickled over his face. This was the part he dreaded.

But he knew he couldn't wait. If he was seen they would come out and get him. Being shot was nothing. But she would be burned then. His lips tightened. No.

Gently, as carefully as he could, he lowered her into the shallow grave, making sure that her head did not bump.

He straightened up and looked down at her still body sewn up in the blanket. For the last time, he thought. No more talking, no more loving. Eleven wonderful years ending in a filled-in trench. He began to tremble. No, he ordered himself, there's no time for that.

It was no use. The world shimmered through endless distorting tears while he pressed back the hot earth, patting it around her still body with nerveless fingers.

❖

He lay fully clothed on his bed, staring at the black ceiling. He was half drunk and the darkness spun with fireflies.

His right arm faltered out for the table. His hand brushed the bottle over and he jerked out clawing fingers too late. Then he relaxed and lay there in the still of night, listening to the whisky gurgle out of the bottle mouth and spread across the floor.

His unkempt hair rustled on the pillow as he looked toward the clock. Two in the morning. Two days since he'd buried her. Two eyes looking at the clock, two ears picking up the hum of its electric chronology, two lips pressed together, two hands lying on the bed.

He tried to rid himself of the concept, but everything in the world seemed suddenly to have dropped into a pit of duality, victim to a system of twos. Two people dead, two beds in the room, two windows, two bureaus, two rugs, two hearts that . . .

His chest filled with night air, held, then pushed it out and sank abruptly. Two days, two hands, two eyes, two legs, two feet . . .

He sat up and dropped his legs over the edge of the bed. His feet landed in the puddle of whisky and he felt it soaking through his socks. A cold breeze was rattling the window blinds.

He stared at the blackness. What's left? he asked himself. What's left, anyway?

Wearily he stood up and stumbled into the bathroom, leaving wet tracks behind him. He threw water into his face and fumbled for a towel.

What's left? What's . . .

He stood suddenly rigid in the cold blackness.

Someone was turning the knob on the front door.

He felt a chill move up the back of his neck and his scalp began prickling. It's Ben, he heard his mind offering. He's come for the car keys.

The towel slipped from his fingers and he heard it swish down onto the tiles. His body twitched.

A fist thudded against the door; strengthless, as if it had fallen against the wood.

He moved into the living room slowly, his heartbeat thudding heavily.

The door rattled as another fist thudded against it weakly. He felt himself twitch at the sound. What's the matter? he thought. The door is open. From the open window a cold breeze blew across his face. The darkness drew him to the door.

"Who . . ." he murmured, unable to go on.

His hand recoiled from the doorknob as it turned under his fingers. With one step, he backed into the wall and stood there breathing harshly, his widened eyes staring.

Nothing happened. He stood there holding himself rigidly.

Then his breath was snuffed. Someone was mumbling on the porch, muttering words he couldn't hear. He braced himself; then, with a lunge, he jerked open the door and let the moonlight in.

He couldn't even scream. He just stood rooted to the spot, staring dumbly at Virginia.

"Rob . . . ert," she said.

CHAPTER TEN

The Science Room was on the second floor. Robert Neville's footsteps thudded hollowly up the marble steps of the Los Angeles Public Library. It was April 7, 1976.

It had come to him, after a half week of drinking, disgust, and desultory investigation, that he was wasting his time. Isolated experiments were yielding nothing, that was clear. If there was a rational answer to the problem (and he had to believe that there was), he could only find it by careful research.

Tentatively, for want of better knowledge, he had set up a possible basis, and that was blood. It provided, at least, a starting point. Step number one, then, was reading about blood.

The silence of the library was complete save for the thudding of his shoes as he walked along the second-floor hallway. Outside, there were birds sometimes and, even lacking that, there seemed to be a sort of sound outside. Inexplicable, perhaps, but it never seemed as deathly still in the open as it did inside a building.

Especially here in this giant, gray-stoned building that housed the literature of a world's dead. Probably it was being surrounded by walls, he thought, something purely psychological. But knowing that didn't make it any easier. There were no psychiatrists left to murmur of groundless neuroses and auditory hallucinations. The last man in the world was irretrievably stuck with his delusions.

He entered the Science Room.

It was a high-ceilinged room with tall, large-paned windows. Across from the doorway was the desk where books had been checked out in days when books were still being checked out.

He stood there for a moment looking around the silent room, shaking his head slowly. All these books, he thought, the residue of a planet's intellect, the scrapings of futile minds, the leftovers, the potpourri of artifacts that had no power to save men from perishing.

His shoes clicked across the dark tiles as he walked to the beginning of the shelves on his left. His eyes moved to the cards between the shelf sections. "Astronomy," he read; books about the heavens. He moved by them. It was not the heavens he was concerned about. Man's lust for the stars had died with the others. "Physics," "Chemistry," "Engineering." He passed them by and entered the main reading section of the Science Room.

He stopped and looked up at the high ceiling. There were two banks of dead lights overhead and the ceiling was divided into great sunken squares, each square decorated with what looked like Indian mosaics. Morning sunlight filtered through the dusty windows and he saw motes floating gently on the current of its beams.

He looked down the row of long wooden tables with chairs lined up before them. Someone had put them in place very neatly. The day the library was shut down, he thought, some maiden librarian had moved down the room, pushing each chair against its table. Carefully, with a plodding precision that was the cachet of herself.

He thought about that visionary lady. To die, he thought, never knowing the fierce joy and attendant comfort of a loved one's embrace. To sink into that hideous coma, to sink then into death and, perhaps, return to sterile, awful wanderings. All without knowing what it was to love and be loved.

That was a tragedy more terrible than becoming a vampire.

He shook his head. All right, that's enough, he told himself, you haven't got the time for maudlin reveries.

He bypassed books until he came to "Medicine." That was what he wanted. He looked through the titles. Books on hygiene, on anatomy, on physiology (general and specialized), on curative practices. Farther down, on bacteriology.

He pulled out five books on general physiology and several works on blood. These he stacked on one of the dust-surfaced tables. Should he get any of the books on bacteriology? He stood a minute, looking indecisively at the buckram backs.

Finally he shrugged. Well, what's the difference? he thought. They can't do any harm. He pulled out several of them at random and added them to the pile. He now had nine books on the table. That was enough for a start. He expected he'd be coming back.

As he left the Science Room, he looked up at the clock over the door.

The red hands had stopped at four-twenty-seven. He wondered what day they had stopped. As he descended the stairs with his armful of books, he wondered at just what moment the clock had stopped. Had it been morning or night? Was it raining or shining? Was anyone there when it stopped?

He twisted his shoulders irritably. For God's sake, what's the difference? he asked himself. He was getting disgusted at this increasing nostalgic preoccupation with the past. It was a weakness, he knew, a weakness he could scarcely afford if he intended to go on. And yet he kept discovering himself drifting into extensive meditation on aspects of the past. It was almost more than he could control, and it was making him furious with himself.

He couldn't get the huge front doors open from the inside, either; they were too well locked. He had to go out through the broken window again, first dropping the books to the sidewalk one at a time, then himself. He took the books to his car and got in.

As he started the car, he saw that he was parked along a red-painted curb, facing in the wrong direction on a one-way street. He looked up and down the street.

"Policeman!" he found himself calling. "Oh, pol*ice*man!"

He laughed for a mile without stopping, wondering just what was so funny about it.

✠

He put down the book. He'd been reading again about the lymphatic system. He vaguely remembered reading about it months before, during the time he now called his "frenzied period." But what he'd read had made no impression on him then because he'd had nothing to apply it to.

There seemed to be something there now.

The thin walls of the blood capillaries permitted blood plasma to escape into the tissue spaces along with the red and colorless cells. These escaped materials eventually returned to the blood system through the lymphatic vessels, carried back by the thin fluid called lymph.

During this return flow, the lymph trickled through lymph nodes, which interrupted the flow and filtered out the solid particles of body waste, thus preventing them from entering the blood system.

Now.

There were two things that activated the lymphatic system: (1) breathing, which caused the diaphragm to compress the abdominal contents, thus forcing blood and lymph up against gravity; (2) physical movement, which caused skeletal muscles to compress lymph vessels, thus moving the lymph. An intricate valve system prevented any backing up of the flow.

But the vampires didn't breathe; not the dead ones, anyway. That meant, roughly, that *half* of their lymph flow was cut off. This meant, further, that a considerable amount of waste products would be left in the vampire's system.

Robert Neville was thinking particularly of the fetid odor of the vampire.

He read on.

"The bacteria passes into the blood stream, where . . .

". . . the white corpuscles playing a vital part in our defense against bacterial attack.

"Strong sunlight kills many germs rapidly and . . .

"Many bacterial diseases of man can be disseminated by the mechanical agency of flies, mosquitoes . . .

". . . where, under the stimulus of bacterial attack, the phagocytic factories rush extra cells into the blood stream."

He let the book drop forward into his lap and it slipped off his legs and thumped down on the rug.

It was getting harder and harder to fight, because no matter what he read, there was always the relationship between bacteria and blood affliction. Yet, all this time, he'd been letting contempt fall freely on all those in the past who had died proclaiming the truth of the germ theory and scoffing at vampires.

He got up and made himself a drink. But it sat untouched as he stood before the bar. Slowly, rhythmically, he thudded his right fist down on the top of the bar while his eyes stared bleakly at the wall.

Germs.

He grimaced. Well, for God's sake, he snapped jadedly at himself, the word hasn't got thorns, you know.

He took a deep breath. All right, he ordered himself, is there any reason why it couldn't be germs?

He turned away from the bar as if he could leave the question there. But questions had no location; they could follow him around.

He sat in the kitchen staring into a steaming cup of coffee. Germs.

Bacteria. Viruses. Vampires. Why am I so against it? he thought. Was it just reactionary stubbornness, or was it that the task would loom as too tremendous for him if it were germs?

He didn't know. He started out on a new course, the course of compromise. Why throw out either theory? One didn't necessarily negate the other. Dual acceptance and correlation, he thought.

Bacteria could be the answer to the vampire.

Everything seemed to flood over him then.

It was as though he'd been the little Dutch boy with his finger in the dike, refusing to let the sea of reason in. There he'd been, crouching and content with his iron-bound theory. Now he'd straightened up and taken his finger out. The sea of answers was already beginning to wash in.

The plague had spread so quickly. Could it have done that if only vampires had spread it? Could their nightly maraudings have propelled it on so quickly?

He felt himself jolted by the sudden answer. Only if you accepted bacteria could you explain the fantastic rapidity of the plague, the geometrical mounting of victims.

He shoved aside the coffee cup, his brain pulsing with a dozen different ideas.

The flies and mosquitoes had been a part of it. Spreading the disease, causing it to race through the world.

Yes, bacteria explained a lot of things; the staying in by day, the coma enforced by the germ to protect itself from sun radiation.

A new idea: What if the bacteria were the strength of the true vampire?

He felt a shudder run down his back. Was it possible that the same germ that killed the living provided the energy for the dead?

He had to know! He jumped up and almost ran out of the house. Then, at the last moment, he jerked back from the door with a nervous laugh. God's *sake*, he thought, am I going out of my mind? It was nighttime.

He grinned and walked restlessly around the living room.

Could it explain the other things? The stake? His mind fell over itself trying to fit that into the framework of bacterial causation. Come on! he shouted impatiently in his mind. But all he could think of was hemorrhage, and that didn't explain that woman. And it wasn't the heart. . . .

He skipped it, afraid that his new-found theory would start to collapse before he'd established it.

The cross, then. No, bacteria couldn't explain that. The soil; no, that was no help. Running water, the mirror, garlic . . .

He felt himself trembling without control and he wanted to cry out loudly to stop the runaway horse of his brain. He had to find *something*! Goddamn it! he raged in his mind. I won't let it go!

He made himself sit down. Trembling and rigid, he sat there and blanked his mind until calm took over. Good Lord, he thought finally, what's the matter with me? I get an idea, and when it doesn't explain everything in the first minute, I panic. I must be going crazy.

He took that drink now; he needed it. He held up his hand until it stopped shaking. All right, little boy, he tried kidding himself, calm down now. Santa Claus is coming to town with all the nice answers. No longer will you be a weird Robinson Crusoe, imprisoned on an island of night surrounded by oceans of death.

He snickered at that, and it relaxed him. Colorful, he thought, tasty. The last man in the world is Edgar Guest.

All right, then, he ordered himself, you're going to bed. You're not going to go flying off in twenty different directions. You can't take that any more; you're an emotional misfit.

The first step was to get a microscope. That is the first step, he kept repeating forcefully to himself as he undressed for bed, ignoring the tight ball of indecision in his stomach, the almost painful craving to plunge directly into investigation without any priming.

He almost felt ill, lying there in the darkness and planning just one step ahead. He knew it had to be that way, though. That is the first step, that is the first step. Goddamn your bones, that is the first step.

He grinned in the darkness, feeling good about the definite work ahead.

One thought on the problem he allowed himself before sleeping. The bitings, the insects, the transmission from person to person— were even these enough to explain the horrible speed with which the plague spread?

He went to sleep with the question in his mind. And, about three in the morning, he woke up to find the house buffeted by another dust storm. And suddenly, in the flash of a second, he made the connection.

CHAPTER ELEVEN

The first one he got was worthless.

The base was so poorly leveled that any vibration at all disturbed it. The action of its moving parts was loose to the point of wobbling. The mirror kept moving out of position because its pivots weren't tight enough. Moreover, the instrument had no substage to hold condenser or polarizer. It had only one nosepiece, so that he had to remove the object lens when he wanted any variation in magnification. The lenses were impossible.

But, of course, he knew nothing about microscopes, and he'd taken the first one he'd found. Three days later he hurled it against the wall with a strangled curse and stamped it into pieces with his heels.

Then, when he'd calmed down, he went to the library and got a book on microscopes.

The next time he went out, he didn't come back until he'd found a decent instrument; triple nose stage, substage for condenser and polarizer, good base, smooth movement, iris diaphragm, good lenses.

It's just one more example, he told himself, of the stupidity of starting off half-cocked. Yeah, yeah, yeah, he answered disgustedly.

He forced himself to spend a good amount of time familiarizing himself with the instrument.

He fiddled with the mirror until he could direct a beam of light on the object in a matter of seconds. He acquainted himself with the lenses, varying from a three-inch power to a one-twelfth-inch power. In the case of the latter, he learned to place a drop of cedar-wood oil on the slide, then rack down until the lens touched the oil. He broke thirteen slides doing it.

Within three days of steady attention, he could manipulate the milled adjustment heads rapidly, could control the iris diaphragm and condenser to get exactly the right amount of light on the slide, and was soon getting a sharply defined clarity with the ready-made slides he'd got.

He never knew a flea looked so godawful.

Next came mounting, a process much more difficult, he soon discovered.

No matter how he tried, he couldn't seem to keep dust particles out of the mount. When he looked at them in the microscope, it looked as if he were examining boulders.

It was especially difficult because of the dust storms, which still occurred on an average of once every four days. He was ultimately obliged to build a shelter over the bench.

He also learned to be systematic while experimenting with the mounts. He found that continually searching for things allowed that much more time for dust to accumulate on his slides. Grudgingly, almost amused, he soon had a place for everything. Glass slips, cover glasses, pipettes, cells, forceps, Petri dishes, needles, chemicals—all were placed in systematic locations.

He found, to his surprise, that he actually gleaned pleasure from practicing orderliness. I guess I got old Fritz's blood in me, after all, he thought once in amusement.

Then he got a specimen of blood from a woman.

It took him days to get a few drops properly mounted in a cell, the cell properly centered on the slide. For a while he thought he'd never get it right.

But then the morning came when, casually, as if it were only of minor import, he put his thirty-seventh slide of blood under the lens, turned on the spotlight, adjusted the draw tube and mirror, racked down and adjusted the diaphragm and condenser. Every second that passed seemed to increase the heaviness of his heartbeat, for somehow he knew this was the time.

The moment arrived; his breath caught.

It wasn't a virus, then. You couldn't see a virus. And there, fluttering delicately on the slide, was a germ.

I dub thee *vampiris*. The words crept across his mind as he stood looking down into the eyepiece.

By checking in one of the bacteriology texts, he'd found that the cylindrical bacterium he saw was a bacillus, a tiny rod of protoplasm that moved itself through the blood by means of tiny threads that projected from the cell envelope. These hairlike flagella lashed vigorously at the fluid medium and propelled the bacillus.

For a long time he stood looking into the microscope, unable to think or continue with the investigation.

All he could think was that here, on the slide, was the cause of the vampire. All the centuries of fearful superstition had been felled in the moment he had seen the germ.

The scientists had been right, then; there *were* bacteria involved. It had taken him, Robert Neville, thirty-six, survivor, to complete the inquest and announce the murderer—the germ *within* the vampire.

Suddenly a massive weight of despair fell over him. To have the answer now when it was too late was a crushing blow. He tried desperately to fight the depression, but it held on. He didn't know where to start, he felt utterly helpless before the problem. How could he ever hope to cure those still living? He didn't know anything about bacteria.

Well, I *will* know! he raged inside. And he forced himself to study.

Certain kinds of bacilli, when conditions became unfavorable for life, were capable of creating, from themselves, bodies called spores.

What they did was condense their cell contents into an oval body with a thick wall. This body, when completed, detached itself from the bacillus and became a free spore, highly resistant to physical and chemical change.

Later, when conditions were more favorable for survival, the spore germinated again, bringing into existence all the qualities of the original bacillus.

Robert Neville stood before the sink, eyes closed, hands clasped tightly at the edge. Something there, he told himself forcefully, something there. But *what?*

Suppose, he predicated, the vampire got no blood. Conditions then for the *vampiris* bacillus would be unfavorable.

Protecting itself, the germ sporulates; the vampire sinks into a coma. Finally, when conditions become favorable again, the vampire walks again, its body still the same.

But how would the germ know if blood were available? He slammed a fist on the sink in anger. He read again. There was still something there. He felt it.

Bacteria, when not properly fed, metabolized abnormally and produced bacteriophages (inanimate, self-reproducing proteins). These bacteriophages destroyed the bacteria.

When no blood came in, the bacilli would metabolize abnormally, absorb water, and swell up, ultimately to explode and destroy all cells.

Sporulation again; it had to fit in.

All right, suppose the vampire didn't go into a coma. Suppose its body decomposed without blood. The germ still might sporulate and—

Yes! The dust storms!

The freed spores would be blown about by the storms. They could lodge in minute skin abrasions caused by the scaling dust. Once in the skin, the spore could germinate and multiply by fission. As this multiplication progressed, the surrounding tissues would be destroyed, the channels plugged with bacilli. Destruction of tissue cells and bacilli would liberate poisonous, decomposed bodies into surrounding healthy tissues. Eventually the poisons would reach the blood stream.

Process complete.

And all without blood-eyed vampires hovering over heroines' beds. All without bats fluttering against estate windows, all without the supernatural.

The vampire was real. It was only that his true story had never been told.

Considering that, Neville recounted the historical plagues.

He thought about the fall of Athens. That had been very much like the plague of 1975. Before anything could be done, the city had fallen. Historians wrote of bubonic plague. Robert Neville was inclined to believe that the vampire had caused it.

No, not the vampire. For now, it appeared, that prowling, vulpine ghost was as much a tool of the germ as the living innocents who were originally afflicted. It was the germ that was the villain. The germ that hid behind obscuring veils of legend and superstition, spreading its scourge while people cringed before their own fears.

And what of the Black Plague, that horrible blight that swept across Europe, leaving in its wake a toll of three-fourths of the population?

Vampires?

❈

By ten that night, his head ached and his eyes felt like hot blobs of gelatin. He discovered that he was ravenous. He got a steak from the freezer, and while it was broiling he took a fast shower.

He jumped a little when a rock hit the side of the house. Then he grinned wryly. He'd been so absorbed all day that he'd forgotten about the pack of them that prowled around his house.

While he was drying himself, he suddenly realized that he didn't know what portion of the vampires who came nightly were physically alive and what portion were activated entirely by the germ. Odd, he thought, that he didn't know. There had to be both kinds, because some of them he shot without success, while others had been destroyed. He assumed that the dead ones could somehow withstand bullets.

Which brought up another point. Why did the living ones come to his house? Why just those few and not everyone in that area?

He had a glass of wine with his steak and was amazed how flavorsome everything was. Food usually tasted like wood to him. I must have worked up an appetite today, he thought.

Furthermore, he hadn't had a single drink. Even more fantastic, he hadn't wanted one. He shook his head. It was painfully obvious that liquor was an emotional solace to him.

The steak he finished to the bone, and he even chewed on that. Then he took the rest of the wine into the living room, turned on the record player, and sat down in his chair with a tired grunt.

He sat listening to Ravel's Daphnis and Chloe Suites One and Two, all the lights off except the spotlight on the woods. He managed to forget all about vampires for a while.

Later, though, he couldn't resist taking another look in the microscope.

You bastard, he thought, almost affectionately, watching the minuscule protoplasm fluttering on the slide. You dirty little bastard.

CHAPTER TWELVE

The next day stank.

The sun lamp killed the germs on the slide, but that didn't explain anything to him.

He mixed allyl sulphide with the germ-ridden blood and nothing happened. The allyl sulphide was absorbed, the germs still lived.

He paced nervously around the bedroom.

Garlic kept them away and blood was the fulcrum of their existence. Yet, mix the essence of garlic with the blood and nothing happened. His hands closed into angry fists.

Wait a minute; that blood was from one of the living ones.

An hour later he had a sample of the other kind. He mixed it with allyl sulphide and looked at it through the microscope. Nothing happened.

Lunch stuck in his throat.

What about the stake, then? All he could think of was hemorrhage, and he knew it wasn't that. That damned woman . . .

He tried half the afternoon to think of something concrete. Finally, with a snarl, he knocked the microscope over and stalked into the living room. He thudded down onto the chair and sat there, tapping impatient fingers on the arm.

Brilliant, Neville, he thought. You're uncanny. Go to the head of the class. He sat there, biting a knuckle. Let's face it, he thought miserably, I lost my mind a long time ago. I can't think two days in succession without having seams come loose. I'm useless, worthless, without value, a dud.

All right, he replied with a shrug, that settles it. Let's get back to the problem. So he did.

There are certain things established, he lectured himself. There *is* a germ, it's transmitted, sunlight kills it, garlic is effective. Some vampires sleep in soil, the stake destroys them. They don't turn into wolves or bats, but certain animals acquire the germ and become vampires.

All right.

He made a list. One column he headed "Bacilli," the other he headed with a question mark.

He began.

The cross. No, that couldn't have anything to do with the bacilli. If anything, it was psychological.

The soil. Could there be something in the soil that affected the germ? No. How would it get in the blood stream? Besides, very few of them slept in the soil.

His throat moved as he added the second item to the column headed by a question mark.

Running water. Could it be absorbed porously and . . . No, that was stupid. They came out in the rain, and they wouldn't if it harmed them. Another notation in the right-hand column. His hand shook a little as he entered it.

Sunlight. He tried vainly to glean satisfaction from putting down one item in the desired column.

The stake. No. His throat moved. Watch it, he warned.

The mirror. For God's sake, how could a mirror have anything to do with germs? His hasty scrawl in the right-hand column was hardly legible. His hand shook a little more.

Garlic. He sat there, teeth gritted. He had to add at least one more item to the bacilli column; it was almost a point of honor. He struggled over the last item. Garlic, garlic. It *must* affect the germ. But how?

He started to write in the right-hand column, but before he could finish, fury came from far down like lava shooting up to the crest of a volcano.

Damn!

He crumpled the paper into a ball in his fist and hurled it away.

He stood up, rigid and frenzied, looking around. He wanted to break things, anything. So you thought your frenzied period was over, did you! he yelled at himself, lurching forward to fling over the bar.

Then he caught himself and held back. No, no, don't get started, he begged. Two shaking hands ran through his lank blond hair. His throat moved convulsively and he shuddered with the repressed craving for violence.

The sound of the whisky gurgling into the glass angered him. He turned the bottle upside down and the whisky spurted out in great gushes, splashing up the sides of the glass and over onto the mahogany top of the bar.

He swallowed the whole glassful at once, head thrown back, whisky running out the edges of his mouth.

I'm an animal! he exulted. I'm a *dumb, stupid* animal and I'm going to drink!

He emptied the glass, then flung it across the room. It bounced off the bookcase and rolled across the rug. Oh, so you won't break, won't you! he rasped inside his head, leaping across the rug to grind the glass into splinters under his heavy shoes.

Then he spun and stumbled to the bar again. He filled another glass and poured the contents down his throat. I wish I had a pipe with whisky in it! he thought. I'd connect a goddamn hose to it and flush whisky down me until it came out my ears! Until I *floated* in it!

He flung away the glass. Too slow, too *slow*, damn it! He drank directly from the uptilted bottle, gulping furiously, hating himself, punishing himself with the whisky burning down his rapidly swallowing throat.

I'll choke myself! he stormed. I'll strangle myself, I'll *drown* myself in whisky! Like Clarence in his malmsey, I'll die, die, *die!*

He hurled the empty bottle across the room and it shattered on the wall mural. Whisky ran down the tree trunks and onto the ground. He lurched across the room and picked up a piece of the broken bottle. He slashed at the mural and the jagged edge sliced through the scene and peeled it away from the wall. There! he thought, his breath like steam escaping. That for you!

He flung the glass away, then looked down as he felt dull pain in his fingers. He'd sliced open the flesh.

Good! he exulted viciously, and pressed on each side of the slices until the blood ran out and fell in big drops on the rug. Bleed to death, you stupid, worthless bastard!

An hour later he was totally drunk, lying flat on the floor with a vacuous smile on his face.

World's gone to hell. No germs, no science. World's fallen to the supernatural, it's a supernatural world. Harper's Bizarre and Saturday Evening Ghost and Ghoul Housekeeping. "Young Dr. Jekyll" and "Dracula's Other Wife" and "Death Can Be Beautiful." "Don't be half-staked" and Smith Brothers' Coffin Drops.

He stayed drunk for two days and planned on staying drunk till the end of time or the world's whisky supply, whichever came first.

And he might have done it, too, if it hadn't been for a miracle.

It happened on the third morning, when he stumbled out onto the porch to see if the world was still there.

There was a dog roving about on the lawn.

The second it heard him open the front door, it stopped snuffling over the grass, its head jerked up in sudden fright, and it bounded off to the side with a twitch of scrawny limbs.

For a moment Robert Neville was so shocked he couldn't move. He stood petrified, staring at the dog, which was limping quickly across the street, its ropelike tail pulled between its legs.

It was *alive*! In the *daytime*! He lurched forward with a dull cry and almost pitched on his face on the lawn. His legs pistoned, his arms flailed for balance. Then he caught himself and started running after the dog.

"Hey!" he called, his hoarse voice breaking the silence of Cimarron Street. "Come back here!"

His shoes thudded across the sidewalk and off the curb, every step driving a battering ram into his head. His heart pulsed heavily.

"Hey!" he called again. "Come 'ere, boy."

Across the street, the dog scrambled unsteadily along the sidewalk, its right hind leg curled up, its dark claws clicking on the cement.

"Come 'ere, boy, I won't hurt you!" Robert Neville called out.

Already he had a stitch in his side and his head throbbed with pain as he ran. The dog stopped a moment and looked back. Then it darted in between two houses, and for a moment Neville saw it from the side. It was brown and white, breedless, its left ear hanging in shreds, its gaunt body wobbling as it ran.

"Don't run away!"

He didn't hear the shrill quiver of hysteria in his voice as he screamed out the words. His throat choked up as the dog disappeared between the houses. With a grunt of fear he hobbled on faster, ignoring the pain of hangover, everything lost in the need to catch that dog.

But when he got into the back yard the dog was gone.

He ran to the redwood fence and looked over. Nothing. He twisted back suddenly to see if the dog were going back out the way it had entered.

There was no dog.

For an hour he wandered around the neighborhood on trembling legs, searching vainly, calling out every few moments, "Come 'ere, boy, come 'ere."

At last he stumbled home, his face a mask of hopeless dejection. To come across a living being, after all this time to find a companion, and then to lose it. Even if it was only a dog. *Only* a dog? To Robert Neville that dog was the peak of a planet's evolution.

He couldn't eat or drink anything. He found himself so ill and trembling at the shock and the loss that he had to lie down. But he couldn't sleep. He lay there shaking feverishly, his head moving from side to side on the flat pillow.

"Come 'ere, boy," he kept muttering without realizing it. "Come 'ere, boy, I won't hurt you."

In the afternoon he searched again. For two blocks in each direction from his house he searched each yard, each street, each individual house. But he found nothing.

When he got home, about five, he put out a bowl of milk and a piece of hamburger. He put a ring of garlic bulbs around it, hoping the vampires wouldn't touch it.

But later it came to him that the dog must be afflicted too, and the garlic would keep it away also. He couldn't understand that. If the dog had the germ, how could it roam outdoors during the daylight hours? Unless it had such a small dosing of bacilli in its veins that it wasn't really affected yet. But, if that were true, how had it survived the nightly attacks?

Oh, my God, the thought came then, what if it comes back tonight for the meat and they kill it? What if he went out the next morning and found the dog's body on the lawn and knew that he was responsible for its death? I couldn't take that, he thought miserably. I'll blow out my brains if that happens, I swear I will.

The thought dredged up again the endless enigma of why he went on. All right, there were a few possibilities for experiment now, but life was still a barren, cheerless trial. Despite everything he had or might have (except, of course, another human being), life gave no promise of improvement or even of change. The way things shaped up, he would live out his life with no more than he already had. And how many years was that? Thirty, maybe forty if he didn't drink himself to death.

The thought of forty more years of living as he was made him shudder.

And yet he hadn't killed himself. True, he hardly treated his body welfare with reverence. He didn't eat properly, drink properly, sleep properly, or do anything properly. His health wasn't going to last indefinitely; he was already cheating the percentages, he suspected.

But using his body carelessly wasn't suicide. He'd never even approached suicide. Why?

There seemed no answer. He wasn't resigned to anything, he hadn't accepted or adjusted to the life he'd been forced into. Yet here he was, eight months after the plague's last victim, nine since he'd spoken to another human being, ten since Virginia had died. Here he was with no future and a virtually hopeless present. Still plodding on.

Instinct? Or was he just stupid? Too unimaginative to destroy himself? Why hadn't he done it in the beginning, when he was in the very depths? What had impelled him to enclose the house, install a freezer, a generator, an electric stove, a water tank, build a hothouse, a workbench, burn down the houses on each side of his, collect records and books and mountains of canned supplies, even—it was fantastic when you thought about it—even put a fancy mural on the wall?

Was the life force something more than words, a tangible, mind-controlling potency? Was nature somehow, in him, maintaining its spark against its own encroachments?

He closed his eyes. Why think, why reason? There was no answer. His continuance was an accident and an attendant bovinity. He was just too dumb to end it all, and that was about the size of it.

Later he glued up the sliced mural and put it back into place. The slits didn't show too badly unless he stood very close to the paper.

He tried briefly to get back to the problem of the bacilli, but he realized that he couldn't concentrate on anything except the dog. To his complete astonishment, he later found himself offering up a stumbling prayer that the dog would be protected. It was a moment in which he felt a desperate need to believe in a God that shepherded his own creations. But, even praying, he felt a twinge of self-reproach, and knew he might start mocking his own prayer at any second.

Somehow, though, he managed to ignore his iconoclastic self and went on praying anyway. Because he wanted the dog, because he needed the dog.

CHAPTER THIRTEEN

In the morning when he went outside he found that the milk and hamburger were gone.

His eyes rushed over the lawn. There were two women crumpled on the grass but the dog wasn't there. A breath of relief passed his lips. Thank God for that, he thought. Then he grinned to himself. If I were religious now, he thought, I'd find in this a vindication of my prayer.

Immediately afterward he began berating himself for not being awake when the dog had come. It must have been after dawn, when the streets were safe. The dog must have evolved a system to have lived so long. But he should have been awake to watch.

He consoled himself with the hope that he was winning the dog over, if only with food. He was briefly worried by the idea that the vampires had taken the food, and not the dog. But a quick check ended that fear. The hamburger had not been lifted over the garlic ring, but dragged through it along the cement of the porch. And all around the bowl were tiny milk splashes, still moist, that could have been made only by a dog's lapping tongue.

Before he had breakfast he put out more milk and more hamburger, placing them in the shade so the milk wouldn't get too warm. After a moment's deliberation he also put out a bowl of cold water.

Then, after eating, he took the two women to the fire and, returning, stopped at a market and picked up two dozen cans of the best dog food as well as boxes of dog biscuit, dog candy, dog soap, flea powder, and a wire brush.

Lord, you'd think I was having a baby or something, he thought as he struggled back to the car with his arms full. A grin faltered on his lips. Why pretend? he thought. I'm more excited than I've been in a year. The eagerness he'd felt upon seeing the germ in his microscope was nothing compared with what he felt about the dog.

He drove home at eighty miles an hour, and he couldn't help a groan of disappointment when he saw that the meat and drink were untouched. Well, what the hell do you expect? he asked himself sarcastically. The dog can't eat every hour on the hour.

Putting down the dog food and equipment on the kitchen table, he looked at his watch. Ten-fifteen. The dog would be back when it got hungry again. Patience, he told himself. Get yourself at least *one* virtue, anyway.

He put away the cans and boxes. Then he checked the outside of the house and the hothouse. There was a loose board to fasten and a pane to repair on the hothouse roof.

While he collected garlic bulbs, he wondered once again why the vampires had never set fire to his house. It seemed such an obvious tactic. Was it possible they were afraid of matches? Or was it that they were just too stupid? After all, their brains could not be so fully operative as they had been before. The change from life to mobile death must have involved some tissue deterioration.

No, that theory wasn't any good, because there were living ones around his house at night too. Nothing was wrong with their brains, was there?

He skipped it. He was in no mood for problems. He spent the rest of the morning preparing and hanging garlic strands. Once he wondered about the fact that garlic bulbs worked. In legend it was always the blossoms of the garlic plant. He shrugged. What was the difference? The proof of the garlic was in its chasing ability. He imagined that the blossoms would work too.

After lunch he sat at the peephole looking out at the bowls and the plate. There was no sound anywhere except for the almost inaudible humming of the air-conditioning units in the bedroom, bathroom, and kitchen.

The dog came at four. Neville had almost fallen into a doze as he sat there before the peephole. Then his eyes blinked and focused as the dog came hobbling slowly across the street, looking at the house with white-rimmed, cautious eyes. He wondered what was wrong with the dog's paw. He wanted very much to fix it and get the dog's affection. Shades of Androcles, he thought in the gloom of his house.

He forced himself to sit still and watch. It was incredible, the feeling of warmth and normality it gave him to see the dog slurping up the milk and eating the hamburger, its jaws snapping and popping with relish. He sat there with a gentle smile on his face, a smile he wasn't conscious of. It was such a nice dog.

His throat swallowed convulsively as the dog finished eating and started away from the porch. Jumping up from the stool, he moved quickly for the front door.

Then he held himself back. No, that wasn't the way, he decided reluctantly. You'll just scare him if you go out. Let him go now, let him go.

He went back to the peephole and watched the dog wobbling across the street and moving in between those two houses again. He felt a tightness in his throat as he watched it leave. It's all right, he soothed himself, he'll be back.

He turned away from the peephole and made himself a mild drink. Sitting in the chair and sipping slowly, he wondered where the dog went at night. At first he'd been worried about not having it in the house with him. But then he'd realized that the dog must be a master at hiding itself to have lasted so long.

It was probably, he thought, one of those freak accidents that followed no percentage law. Somehow, by luck, by coincidence, maybe by a little skill, that one dog had survived the plague and the grisly victims of the plague.

That started him thinking. If a dog, with its limited intelligence, could manage to subsist through it all, wouldn't a person with a reasoning brain have that much more chance for survival?

He made himself think about something else. It was dangerous to hope. That was a truism he had long accepted.

The next morning the dog came again. This time Robert Neville opened the front door and went out. The dog immediately bolted away from the dish and bowls, right ear flattened back, legs scrambling frantically across the street.

Neville twitched with the repressed instinct to pursue. As casually as he could manage, he sat down on the edge of the porch.

Across the street the dog ran between the houses again and disappeared. After fifteen minutes of sitting, Neville went in again.

After a small breakfast he put out more food.

The dog came at four and Neville went out again, this time making sure that the dog was finished eating.

Once more the dog fled. But this time, seeing that it was not pursued, it stopped across the street and looked back for a moment.

"It's all right, boy," Neville called out, but at the sound of his voice the dog ran away again.

Neville sat on the porch stiffly, teeth gritted with impatience. Goddamn it, what's the matter with him? he thought. The damn *mutt*!

He forced himself to think of what the dog must have gone through. The endless nights of groveling in the blackness, hidden God knew where, its gaunt chest laboring in the night while all around its shivering form the vampires walked. The foraging for food and water, the struggle for life in a world without masters, housed in a body that man had made dependent on himself.

Poor little fella, he thought, I'll be good to you when you come and live with me.

Maybe, the thought came then, a dog had *more* chance of survival than a human. Dogs were smaller, they could hide in places the vampires couldn't go. They could probably sense the alien nature of those about them, probably *smell* it.

That didn't make him any happier. For always, in spite of reason, he had clung to the hope that someday he would find someone like himself—a man, a woman, a child, it didn't matter. Sex was fast losing its meaning without the endless prodding of mass hypnosis. Loneliness he still felt.

Sometimes he had indulged in daydreams about finding someone. More often, though, he had tried to adjust to what he sincerely believed was the inevitable—that he was actually the only one left in the world. At least in as much of the world as he could ever hope to know.

Thinking about it, he almost forgot that nightfall was approaching.

With a start he looked up and saw Ben Cortman running at him from across the street.

"Neville!"

He jumped up from the porch and ran into the house, locking and bolting the door behind him with shaking hands.

For a certain period he went out on the porch just as the dog had finished eating. Every time he went out the dog ran away, but as the days passed it ran with decreasing speed, and soon it was stopping halfway across the street to look back and bark at him. Neville never followed, but sat down on the porch and watched. It was a game they played.

Then one day Neville sat on the porch *before* the dog came. And, when it appeared across the street, he remained seated.

For about fifteen minutes the dog hovered near the curb suspiciously, unwilling to approach the food. Neville edged as far away from the food as he could in order to encourage the dog. Unthinking, he crossed his legs, and the dog shrank away at the unexpected motion. Neville held himself quietly then and the dog kept moving around restlessly in the street, its eyes moving from Neville to the food and back again.

"Come on, boy," Neville said to it. "Eat your food, that's a good dog."

Another ten minutes passed. The dog was now on the lawn, moving in concentric arcs that became shorter and shorter.

The dog stopped. Then slowly, very slowly, one paw at a time, it began moving up on the dish and bowls, its eyes never leaving Neville for a second.

"That's the boy," Neville said quietly.

This time the dog didn't flinch or back away at the sound of his voice. Still Neville made sure he sat motionless so that no abrupt movement would startle the dog.

The dog moved yet closer, stalking the plate, its body tense and waiting for the least motion from Neville.

"That's right," Neville told the dog.

Suddenly the dog darted in and grabbed the meat. Neville's pleased laughter followed its frantically erratic wobble across the street.

"You little son of a gun," he said appreciatively.

Then he sat and watched the dog as it ate. It crouched down on a yellow lawn across the street, its eyes on Neville while it wolfed down the hamburger. Enjoy it, he thought, watching the dog. From now on you get dog food. I can't afford to let you have any more fresh meat.

When the dog had finished it straightened up and came across the street again, a little less hesitantly. Neville still sat there, feeling his heart thud nervously. The dog was beginning to trust him, and somehow it made him tremble. He sat there, his eyes fastened on the dog.

"That's right, boy," he heard himself saying aloud. "Get your water now, that's a good dog."

A sudden smile of delight raised his lips as he saw the dog's good ear stand up. He's *listening*! he thought excitedly. He hears what I say, the little son of a gun!

"Come on, boy." He went on talking eagerly. "Get your water and your milk now, that's a good boy. I won't hurt you. Atta boy."

The dog went to the water and drank gingerly, its head lifting with sudden jerks to watch him, then dipping down again.

"I'm not doing anything," Neville told the dog.

He couldn't get over how odd his voice sounded. When a man didn't hear the sound of his own voice for almost a year, it sounded very strange to him. A year was a long time to live in silence. When you come live with me, he thought, I'll talk your ear off.

The dog finished the water.

"Come 'ere, boy," Neville said invitingly, patting his leg. "*Come* on."

The dog looked at him curiously, its good ear twitching again. Those eyes, Neville thought. What a world of feeling in those eyes! Distrust, fear, hope, loneliness— all etched in those big brown eyes. Poor little guy.

"Come on, boy, I won't hurt you," he said gently.

Then he stood up and the dog ran away. Neville stood there looking at the fleeing dog shaking his head slowly.

More days passed. Each day Neville sat on the porch while the dog ate, and before long the dog approached the dish and bowls without hesitation, almost boldly, with the assurance of the dog that knows its human conquest.

And all the time Neville would talk to it.

"That's a good boy. Eat up the food. That's *good* food, isn't it? Sure it is. I'm your friend. I gave you that food. Eat it up, boy, that's right. That's a *good* dog," endlessly cajoling, praising, pouring soft words into the dog's frightened mind as it ate.

And every day he sat a little bit closer to it, until the day came when he could have reached out and touched the dog if he'd stretched a little. He didn't, though. I'm not taking any chances, he told himself. I don't want to scare him.

But it was hard to keep his hands still. He could almost feel them twitching empathically with his strong desire to reach out and stroke the dog's head. He had such a terrible yearning to love something again, and the dog was such a beautifully ugly dog.

He kept talking to the dog until it became quite used to the sound of his voice. It hardly looked up now when he spoke. It came and went without trepidation, eating and barking its curt acknowledgment from across the street. Soon now, Neville told himself, I'll be able to pat his head. The days passed into pleasant weeks, each hour bringing him closer to a companion.

Then one day the dog didn't come.

Neville was frantic. He'd got so used to the dog's coming and going that it had become the fulcrum of his daily schedule, everything fitting around the dog's mealtimes, investigation forgotten, everything pushed aside but his desire to have the dog in his house.

He spent a nerve-racked afternoon searching the neighborhood, calling out in a loud voice for the dog. But no amount of searching helped, and he went home to a tasteless dinner. The dog didn't come for dinner that night or for breakfast the next morning. Again Neville searched, but with less hope. They've got him, he kept hearing the words in his mind, the dirty bastards have got him. But he couldn't really believe it. He wouldn't let himself believe it.

On the afternoon of the third day he was in the garage when he heard the sound of the metal bowl clinking outside. With a gasp he ran out into the daylight.

"You're *back!*" he cried.

The dog jerked away from the plate nervously, water dripping from its jaws.

Neville's heart leaped. The dog's eyes were glazed and it was panting for breath, its dark tongue hanging out.

"No," he said, his voice breaking. "Oh, *no.*"

The dog still backed across the lawn on trembling stalks of legs.

Quickly Neville sat down on the porch steps and stayed there trembling. Oh, no, he thought in anguish, oh, God, *no.*

He sat there watching it tremble fitfully as it lapped up the water. No. No. It's not true.

"Not true," he murmured without realizing it.

Then, instinctively, he reached out his hand. The dog drew back a little, teeth bared in a throaty snarl.

"It's all right, boy," Neville said quietly. "I won't hurt you." He didn't even know what he was saying.

He couldn't stop the dog from leaving. He tried to follow it, but it was gone before he could discover where it hid. He'd decided it must be under a house somewhere, but that didn't do him any good.

He couldn't sleep that night. He paced restlessly, drinking pots of coffee and cursing the sluggishness of time. He had to get hold of the dog, he had to. And soon. He had to cure it.

But how? His throat moved. There had to be a way. Even with the little he knew there *must* be a way.

The next morning he sat right beside the bowl and he felt his lips shaking as the dog came limping slowly across the street. It didn't eat anything. Its eyes were more dull and listless than they'd been the day before. Neville wanted to jump at it and try to grab hold of it, take it in the house, nurse it.

But he knew that if he jumped and missed he might undo everything. The dog might never return.

All through the meal his hand kept twitching out to pat the dog's head. But every time it did, the dog cringed away with a snarl. He tried being forceful. "*Stop* that!" he said in a firm, angry tone, but that only frightened the dog more and it drew away farther from him. Neville had to talk to it for fifteen minutes, his voice a hoarse, trembling sound, before the dog would return to the water.

This time he managed to follow the slow-moving dog and saw which house it squirmed under. There was a little metal screen he could have put up over the opening, but he didn't. He didn't want to frighten the dog. And besides, there would be no way of getting the dog then except through the floor, and that would take too long. He had to get the dog fast.

When the dog didn't return that afternoon, he took a dish of milk and put it under the house where the dog was. The next morning the bowl was empty. He was going to put more milk in it when he realized that the dog might never leave his lair then. He put the bowl back in front of his house and prayed that the dog was strong enough to reach it. He was too worried even to criticize his inept prayer.

When the dog didn't come that afternoon he went back and looked in. He paced back and forth outside the opening and almost put milk there anyway. No, the dog would *never* leave then.

He went home and spent a sleepless night. The dog didn't come in the morning. Again he went to the house. He listened at the opening but couldn't hear any sound of breathing. Either it was too far back for him to hear or . . .

He went back to the house and sat on the porch. He didn't have breakfast or lunch. He just sat there.

That afternoon, late, the dog came limping out between the houses, moving slowly on its bony legs. Neville forced himself to sit there without moving until the dog had reached the food. Then, quickly, he reached down and picked up the dog.

Immediately it tried to snap at him, but he caught its jaws in his right hand and held them together. Its lean, almost hairless body squirmed feebly in his grasp and pitifully terrified whines pulsed in its throat.

"It's all right," he kept saying. "It's all right, boy."

Quickly he took it into his room and put it down on the little bed of blankets he'd arranged for the dog. As soon as he took his hand off its jaws the dog snapped at him and he jerked his hand back. The dog lunged over the linoleum with a violent scrabbling of paws, heading for the door. Neville jumped up and blocked its way. The dog's legs slipped on the smooth surface, then it got a little traction and disappeared under the bed.

Neville got on his knees and looked under the bed. In the gloom there he saw the two glowing coals of eyes and heard the fitful panting.

"*Come* on, boy," he pleaded unhappily. "I won't hurt you. You're *sick.* You need help."

The dog wouldn't budge. With a groan Neville got up finally and went out, closing the door behind him. He went and got the bowls and filled them with milk and water. He put them in the bedroom near the dog's bed.

He stood by his own bed a moment, listening to the panting dog, his face lined with pain.

"Oh," he muttered plaintively, "why don't you *trust* me?"

❧

He was eating dinner when he heard the horrible crying and whining.

Heart pounding, he jumped up from the table and raced across the living room. He threw open the bedroom door and flicked on the light.

Over in the corner by the bench the dog was trying to dig a hole in the floor.

Terrified whines shook its body as its front paws clawed frenziedly at the linoleum, slipping futilely on the smoothness of it.

"Boy, it's all right!" Neville said quickly.

The dog jerked around and backed into the corner, hackles rising, jaws drawn back all the way from its yellowish-white teeth, a half-mad sound quivering in its throat.

Suddenly Neville knew what was wrong. It was nighttime and the terrified dog was trying to dig itself a hole to bury itself in.

He stood there helplessly, his brain refusing to work properly as the dog edged away from the corner, then scuttled underneath the workbench.

An idea finally came. Neville moved to his bed quickly and pulled off the top blanket. Returning to the bench, he crouched down and looked under it.

The dog was almost flattened against the wall, its body shaking violently, guttural snarls bubbling in its throat.

"All right, boy," he said. "All right."

The dog shrank back as Neville stuck the blanket underneath the bench and then stood up. Neville went over to the door and remained there a minute looking back. If only I could *do* something, he thought helplessly. But I can't even get close to him.

Well, he decided grimly, if the dog didn't accept him soon, he'd have to try a little chloroform. Then he could at least work on the dog, fix its paw and try somehow to cure it.

He went back to the kitchen but he couldn't eat. Finally he dumped the contents of his plate into the garbage disposal and poured the coffee back into the pot. In the living room he made himself a drink and downed it. It tasted flat and unappetizing. He put down the glass and went back to the bedroom with a somber face.

The dog had dug itself under the folds of the blanket and there it was still shaking, whining ceaselessly. No use trying to work on it now, he thought; it's too frightened.

He walked back to the bed and sat down. He ran his hands through his hair and then put them over his face. Cure it, cure it, he thought, and one of his hands bunched into a fist to strike feebly at the mattress.

Reaching out abruptly, he turned off the light and lay down fully clothed. Still lying down, he worked off his sandals and listened to them thump on the floor.

Silence. He lay there staring at the ceiling. Why don't I get up? he wondered. Why don't I try to *do* something?

He turned on his side. Get some sleep. The words came automatically. He knew he wasn't going to sleep, though. He lay in the darkness listening to the dog's whimpering. Die, it's going to die, he kept thinking, there's nothing in the world I can do.

At last, unable to bear the sound, he reached over and switched on the bedside lamp. As he moved across the room in his stocking feet, he heard the dog trying suddenly to jerk loose from the blanketing. But it got all tangled up in the folds and began yelping, terror-stricken, while its body flailed wildly under the wool.

Neville knelt beside it and put his hands on its body. He heard the choking snarl and the muffled click of its teeth as it snapped at him through the blanket.

"All right," he said. "Stop it now."

The dog kept struggling against him, its high-pitched whining never stopping, its gaunt body shaking without control. Neville kept his hands firmly on its body, pinning it down, talking to it quietly, gently.

"It's all right now, fella, *all* right. Nobody's going to hurt you. Take it easy, now. Come on, relax, now. Come on, boy. Take it easy. Relax. That's right, relax. That's it. Calm down. Nobody's going to hurt you. We'll take care of you."

He went on talking intermittently for almost an hour, his voice a low, hypnotic murmuring in the silence of the room. And slowly, hesitantly, the dog's trembling eased off. A smile faltered on Neville's lips as he went on talking, talking.

"That's right. Take it easy, now. We'll take care of you."

Soon the dog lay still beneath his strong hands, the only movement its harsh breathing. Neville began patting its head, began running his right hand over its body, stroking and soothing.

"That's a good dog," he said softly. "*Good* dog. I'll take care of you now. Nobody will hurt you. You understand, don't you, fella? Sure you do. Sure. You're *my* dog, aren't you?"

Carefully he sat down on the cool linoleum, still patting the dog.

"You're a good dog, a *good* dog."

His voice was calm, it was quiet with resignation.

After about an hour he picked up the dog. For a moment it struggled and started whining, but Neville talked to it again and it soon calmed down.

He sat down on his bed and held the blanket-covered dog in his lap. He sat there for hours holding the dog, patting and stroking and talking. The dog lay immobile in his lap, breathing easier.

It was about eleven that night when Neville slowly undid the blanket folds and exposed the dog's head.

For a few minutes it cringed away from his hand, snapping a little. But he kept talking to it quietly, and after a while his hand rested on the warm neck and he was moving his fingers gently, scratching and caressing.

He smiled down at the dog, his throat moving.

"You'll be all better soon," he whispered. "Real soon."

The dog looked up at him with its dulled, sick eyes and then its tongue faltered out and licked roughly and moistly across the palm of Neville's hand.

Something broke in Neville's throat. He sat there silently while tears ran slowly down his cheeks.

In a week the dog was dead.

CHAPTER FOURTEEN

There was no debauch of drinking. Far from it. He found that he actually drank less. Something had changed. Trying to analyze it, he came to the conclusion that his last drunk had put him on the bottom, at the very nadir of frustrated despair. Now, unless he put himself under the ground, the only way he could go was up.

After the first few weeks of building up intense hope about the dog, it had slowly dawned on him that intense hope was not the answer and never had been. In a world of monotonous horror there could be no salvation in wild dreaming. Horror he had adjusted to. But monotony was the greater obstacle, and he realized it now, understood it at long last. And understanding it seemed to give him a sort of quiet peace, a sense of having spread all the cards on his mental table, examined them, and settled conclusively on the desired hand.

Burying the dog had not been the agony he had supposed it would be. In a way, it was almost like burying threadbare hopes and false excitements. From that day on he learned to accept the dungeon he existed in, neither seeking to escape with sudden derring-do nor beating his pate bloody on its walls.

And, thus resigned, he returned to work.

❧

It had happened almost a year before, several days after he had put Virginia to her second and final rest.

Hollow and bleak, a sense of absolute loss in him, he was walking the streets late one afternoon, hands listless at his sides, feet shuffling with the rhythm of despair. His face mirrored nothing of the helpless agony he felt. His face was a blank.

He had wandered through the streets for hours, neither knowing nor caring where he was going. All he knew was that he couldn't return to the empty rooms of the house, couldn't look at the things they had touched and held and known with him. He couldn't look at Kathy's empty bed, at her clothes hanging still and useless in the closet, couldn't look at the bed that he and Virginia had slept in, at Virginia's clothes, her jewelry, all her perfumes on the bureau. He couldn't go near the house.

And so he walked and wandered, and he didn't know where he was when the people started milling past him, when the man caught his arm and breathed garlic in his face.

"Come, brother, come," the man said, his voice a grating rasp. He saw the man's throat moving like clammy turkey skin, the red-splotched cheeks, the feverish eyes, the black suit, unpressed, unclean. "Come and be saved, brother, *saved.*"

Robert Neville stared at the man. He didn't understand. The man pulled him on, his fingers like skeleton fingers on Neville's arm.

"It's never too late, brother," said the man. "Salvation comes to him who . . ."

The last of his words were lost now in the rising murmur of sound from the great tent they were approaching. It sounded like the sea imprisoned under canvas, roaring to escape. Robert Neville tried to loose his arm.

"I don't want to—"

The man didn't hear. He pulled Neville on with him and they walked toward the waterfall of crying and stamping. The man did not let go. Robert Neville felt as if he were being dragged into a tidal wave.

"But I don't—"

The tent had swallowed him then, the ocean of shouting, stamping, hand-clapping sound engulfed him. He flinched instinctively and felt his heart begin pumping heavily. He was surrounded now by people, hundreds of them, swelling and gushing around him like waters closing in. And yelling and clapping and crying out words Robert Neville couldn't understand.

Then the cries died down and he heard the voice that stabbed through the half-light like knifing doom, that crackled and bit shrilly over the loud-speaker system.

"Do you want to fear the holy cross of God? Do you want to look into the mirror and not see the face that Almighty God has given you? Do you want to come crawling back from the grave like a monster out of hell?"

The voice enjoined hoarsely, pulsing, driving.

"Do you want to be changed into a black unholy animal? Do you want to stain the evening sky with hell-born bat wings? I ask you— do you want to be turned into godless, night-cursed husks, into creatures of eternal damnation?"

"No!" the people erupted, terror-stricken. "No, *save* us!"

Robert Neville backed away, bumping into flailing-handed, white-jawed true believers screaming out for succor from the lowering skies.

"Well, I'm *telling* you! I'm *telling* you, so listen to the word of God! Behold, evil shall go forth from nation to nation and the slain of the Lord shall be at that day from one end of the earth even unto the other end of the earth! Is that a lie, is that a *lie*?"

"No! *No!*"

"I tell you that unless we become as little children, stainless and pure in the eyes of Our Lord—unless we stand up and shout out the glory of Almighty God and of His only begotten son, Jesus Christ, our Saviour—unless we fall on our *knees* and beg forgiveness for our grievous offenses—we are damned! I'll say it again, so *listen*! We are damned, we are damned, *we are damned*!

"Amen!"

"Save us!"

The people twisted and moaned and smote their brows and shrieked in mortal terror and screamed out terrible hallelujahs.

Robert Neville was shoved about, stumbling and lost in a tread-mill of hopes, in a crossfire of frenzied worship.

"God has punished us for our great transgressions! God has unleashed the terrible force of His almighty wrath! God has set loose the second deluge upon us—a deluge, a flood, a world-consuming torrent of creatures from *hell*! He has opened the grave, He has un-sealed the crypt, He has turned the dead from their black tombs— *and set them upon us*! And death and hell delivered up the dead which were in them! That's the word of God! O God, You have punished us, O God, You have seen the terrible face of our transgressions, O God, You have struck us with the might of Your almighty wrath!"

Clapping hands like the spatter of irregular rifle fire, swaying bodies like stalks in a terrible wind, moans of the great potential dead, screams of the fighting living. Robert Neville strained through their violent ranks, face white, hands before him like those of a blind man seeking shelter.

He escaped, weak and trembling, stumbling away from them. Inside the tent the people screamed. But night had already fallen.

He thought about that now as he sat in the living room nursing a mild drink, a psychology text resting on his lap.

A quotation had started the train of thought, sending him back to that evening ten months before, when he'd been pulled into the wild revival meeting.

"This condition, known as hysterical blindness, may be partial or complete, including one, several, or all objects."

That was the quotation he'd read. It had started him working on the problem again.

A new approach now. Before, he had stubbornly persisted in attributing all vampire phenomena to the germ. If certain of these phenomena did not fit in with the bacilli, he felt inclined to judge their cause as superstition. True, he'd vaguely considered psychological explanations, but he'd never really given much credence to such a possibility. Now, released at last from unyielding preconceptions, he did.

There was no reason, he knew, why some of the phenomena could not be physically caused, the rest psychological. And, now that he accepted it, it seemed one of those patent answers that only a blind man would miss. Well, I always was the blind-man type, he thought in quiet amusement.

Consider, he thought then, the shock undergone by a victim of the plague.

Toward the end of the plague, yellow journalism had spread a cancerous dread of vampires to all corners of the nation. He could remember himself the rash of pseudo-scientific articles that veiled an out-and-out fright campaign designed to sell papers.

There was something grotesquely amusing in that; the frenetic attempt to sell papers while the world died. Not that all newspapers had done that. Those papers that had lived in honesty and integrity died the same way.

Yellow journalism, though, *had* been rampant in the final days. And, in addition, a great upsurge in revivalism had occurred. In a typical desperation for quick answers, easily understood, people had turned to primitive worship as the solution. With less than success. Not only had they died as quickly as the rest of the people, but they had died with terror in their hearts, with a mortal dread flowing in their very veins.

And then, Robert Neville thought, to have this hideous dread vindicated. To regain consciousness beneath hot, heavy soil and know that death had not brought rest. To find themselves clawing up through the earth, their bodies driven now by a strange, hideous need.

Such traumatic shocks could undo what mind was left. And such shocks could explain much.

The cross, first of all.

Once they were forced to accept vindication of the dread of being repelled by an object that had been a focal point of worship, their minds could have snapped. Dread of the cross sprang up. And, driven on despite already created dreads, the vampire could have acquired an intense mental loathing, and this self-hatred could have set up a block in their weakened minds causing them to be blind to their own abhorred image. It could make them lonely, soul-lost slaves of the night, afraid to approach anyone, living a solitary existence, often seeking solace in the soil of their native land, struggling to gain a sense of communion with something, with anything.

The water? That he *did* accept as superstition, a carryover of the traditional legend that witches were incapable of crossing running water, as written down in the story of Tam O'Shanter. Witches, vampires—in all these feared beings there was a sort of interwoven kinship. Legends and superstitions could overlap, and did.

And the living vampires? That was simple too now.

In life there were the deranged, the insane. What better hold than vampirism for these to catch on to? He was certain that all the living who came to his house at night were insane, thinking themselves true vampires although actually they were only demented sufferers. And that would explain the fact that they'd never taken the obvious step of burning his house. They simply could not think that logically.

He remembered the man who one night had climbed to the top of the light post in front of the house and, while Robert Neville had watched through the peephole, had leaped into space, waving his arms frantically. Neville hadn't been able to explain it at the time, but now the answer seemed obvious. The man had thought he was a bat.

Neville sat looking at the half-finished drink, a thin smile fastened to his lips.

So, he thought, slowly, surely, we find out about them. Find out that they are no invincible race. Far from it; they are a highly perishable race requiring the strictest of physical conditions for the furtherance of their Godforsaken existence.

He put the drink down on the table.

I don't need it, he thought. My emotions don't need feeding any more. I don't need liquor for forgetting or for escaping. I don't have to escape from anything. Not now.

For the first time since the dog had died he smiled and felt within himself a quiet, well-modulated satisfaction. There were still many things to learn, but not so many as before. Strangely, life was be-coming almost bearable. I don the robe of hermit without a cry, he thought.

On the phonograph, music played, quiet and unhurried.

Outside, the vampires waited.

PART THREE: June 1978

CHAPTER FIFTEEN

He was out hunting for Cortman. It had become a relaxing hobby, hunting for Cortman; one of the few diversions left to him. On those days when he didn't care to leave the neighborhood and there was no demanding work to be done on the house, he would search. Under cars, behind bushes, under houses, up fireplaces, in closets, under beds, in refrigerators; any place into which a moderately corpulent male body could conceivably be squeezed.

Ben Cortman could be in any one of those places at one time or another. He changed his hiding place constantly. Neville felt certain that Cortman knew he was singled out for capture. He felt, further, that Cortman relished the peril of it. If the phrase were not such an obvious anachronism, Neville would have said that Ben Cortman had a zest for life. Sometimes he thought Cortman was happier now than he ever had been before.

Neville ambled slowly up Compton Boulevard toward the next house he meant to search. An uneventful morning had passed. Cortman was not found, even though Neville knew he was somewhere in the neighborhood. He had to be, because he was always the first one at the house at night. The other ones were almost always strangers. Their turnover was great, because they invariably stayed in the neighborhood and Neville found them and destroyed them. Not Cortman.

As he strolled, Neville wondered again what he'd do if he found Cortman. True, his plan had always been the same: immediate disposal. But that was on the surface. He knew it wouldn't be that easy. Oh, it wasn't that he felt anything toward Cortman. It wasn't even that Cortman represented a part of the past. The past was dead and he knew it and accepted it.

No, it wasn't either of those things. What it probably was, Neville decided, was that he didn't want to cut off a recreational activity. The rest were such dull, robot-like creatures. Ben, at least, had some imagination. For some reason, his brain hadn't weakened like the others'. It could be, Neville often theorized, that Ben Cortman was born to be dead. Undead, that is, he thought, a wry smile playing on his full lips.

It no longer occurred to him that Cortman was out to kill him. That was a negligible menace.

Neville sank down on the next porch with a slow groan. Then, reaching lethargically into his pocket, he took out his pipe. With an idle thumb he tamped rough tobacco shreds down into the pipe bowl. In a few moments smoke swirls were floating lazily about his head in the warm, still air.

It was a bigger, more relaxed Neville that gazed out across the wide field on the other side of the boulevard. An evenly paced hermit life had increased his weight to 230 pounds. His face was full, his body broad and muscular underneath the loose-fitting denim he wore. He had long before given up shaving. Only rarely did he crop his thick blond beard, so that it remained two to three inches from his skin. His hair was thinning and was long and straggly. Set in the deep tan of his face, his blue eyes were calm and unexcitable.

He leaned back against the brick step, puffing out slow clouds of smoke. Far out across that field he knew there was still a depression in the ground where he had buried Virginia, where she had unburied herself. But knowing it brought no glimmer of reflective sorrow to his eyes. Rather than go on suffering, he had learned to stultify himself to introspection. Time had lost its multidimensional scope. There was only the present for Robert Neville; a present based on day-today survival marked by neither heights of joy nor depths of despair. I am predominantly vegetable, he often thought to himself. That was the way he wanted it.

Robert Neville sat gazing at the white spot out in the field for several minutes before he realized that it was moving.

His eyes blinked once and the skin tightened over his face. He made a slight sound in his throat, a sound of doubting question. Then, standing up, he raised his left hand to shade the sunlight from his eyes.

His teeth bit convulsively into the pipestem.

A woman.

He didn't even try to catch the pipe when it fell from his mouth as his jaw went slack. For a long, breathless moment, he stood there on the porch step, staring.

He closed his eyes, opened them. She was still there. Robert Neville felt the increasing thud in his chest as he watched the woman.

She didn't see him. Her head was down as she walked across the long field. He could see her reddish hair blowing in the breeze, her arms swinging loosely at her sides. His throat moved. It was such an incredible sight after three years that his mind could not assimilate it. He kept blinking and staring as he stood motionless in the shade of the house.

A woman. Alive. *In the daylight.*

He stood, mouth partly open, gaping at the woman. She was young, he could see now as she came closer; probably in her twenties. She wore a wrinkled and dirty white dress. She was very tan, her hair was red. In the dead silence of the afternoon Neville thought he heard the crunch of her shoes in the long grass.

I've gone mad. The words presented themselves abruptly. He felt less shock at that possibility than he did at the notion that she was real. He had, in fact, been vaguely preparing himself for just such a delusion. It seemed feasible. The man who died of thirst saw mirages of lakes. Why shouldn't a man who thirsted for companionship see a woman walking in the sun?

He started suddenly. No, it wasn't that. For, unless his delusion had sound as well as sight, he now heard her walking through the grass. He knew it was real. The movement of her hair, of her arms. She still looked at the ground. Who was she? Where was she going? Where had she been?

He didn't know what welled up in him. It was too quick to analyze, an instinct that broke through every barrier of time-erected reserve.

His left arm went up.

"Hi!" he cried. He jumped down to the sidewalk. "*Hi*, there!"

A moment of sudden, complete silence. Her head jerked up and they looked at each other. Alive, he thought. Alive!

He wanted to shout more, but he felt suddenly choked up. His tongue felt wooden, his brain refused to function. Alive. The word kept repeating itself in his mind, Alive, alive, alive. . . .

With a sudden twisting motion the young woman turned and began running wildly back across the field.

For a moment Neville stood there twitching, uncertain of what to do. Then his heart seemed to burst and he lunged across the sidewalk. His boots jolted down into the street and thudded across.

"Wait!" he heard himself cry.

The woman did not wait. He saw her bronze legs pumping as she fled across the uneven surface of the field. And suddenly he realized that words could not stop her. He thought of how shocked he had been at seeing her. How much more shocked she must have felt hearing a sudden shout end long silence and seeing a great, bearded man waving at her!

His legs drove him up over the other curb and into the field. His heart was pounding heavily now. She's alive! He couldn't stop thinking that. Alive. *A woman alive!*

She couldn't run as fast as he could. Almost immediately Neville began catching up with her. She glanced back over her shoulder with terrified eyes.

"I won't hurt you!" he cried, but she kept running.

Suddenly she tripped and went crashing down on one knee. Her face turned again and he saw the twisted fright on it.

"I won't *hurt* you!" he yelled again.

With a desperate lunge she regained her footing and ran on.

No sound now but the sound of her shoes and his boots thrashing through the heavy grass. He began jumping over the grass to avoid its impending height and gained more ground. The skirt of her dress whipped against the grass, holding her back.

"Stop!" he cried, again, but more from instinct than with any hope that she would stop.

She didn't. She ran still faster and, gritting his teeth, Neville put another burst of speed into his pursuit. He followed in a straight line as the girl weaved across the field, her light reddish hair billowing behind her.

Now he was so close he could hear her tortured breathing. He didn't like to frighten her, but he couldn't stop now. Everything else in the world seemed to have fallen from view but her. He had to catch her.

His long, powerful legs pistoned on, his boots thudded on the earth.

Another stretch of field. The two of them ran, panting. She glanced back at him again to see how close he was. He didn't realize how frightening he looked; six foot three in his boots, a gigantic bearded man with an intent look.

Now his hand lurched out and he caught her by the right shoulder.

With a gasping scream the young woman twisted away and stumbled to the side. Losing balance, she fell on one hip on the rocky ground. Neville jumped forward to help her up. She scuttled back over the ground and tried to get up, but she slipped and fell again, this time on her back. Her skirt jerked up over her knees. She shoved herself up with a breathless whimper, her dark eyes terrified.

"Here," he gasped, reaching out his hand.

She slapped it aside with a slight cry and struggled to her feet. He caught her by the arm and her free hand lashed out, raking jagged nails across his forehead and right temple. With a grunt he jerked back his arm and she whirled and began running again.

Neville jumped forward again and caught her by the shoulders.

"What are you afraid—"

He couldn't finish. Her hand drove stingingly across his mouth. Then there was only the sound of gasping and struggling, of their feet scrabbling and slipping on the earth, crackling down the thick grass.

"Will you *stop!*" he cried, but she kept battling.

She jerked back and his taut fingers ripped away part of her dress. He let go and the material fluttered down to her waist. He saw her tanned shoulder and the white brassiere cup over her left breast.

She clawed out at him and he caught her wrists in an iron grip. Her right foot drove a bone-numbing kick to his shin.

"Damn it!"

With a snarl of rage he drove his right palm across her face. She staggered back, then looked at him dizzily. Abruptly she started crying helplessly. She sank to her knees before him, holding her arms over her head as if to ward off further blows.

Neville stood there gasping, looking down at her cringing form. He blinked, then took a deep breath.

"Get up," he said. "I'm not going to *hurt* you."

She didn't raise her head. He looked down confusedly at her. He didn't know what to say.

"I said I'm not going to hurt you," he told her again.

She looked up. But his face seemed to frighten her again, for she shrank back. She crouched there looking up at him fearfully.

"What are you afraid of?" he asked.

He didn't realize that his voice was devoid of warmth, that it was the harsh, sterile voice of a man who had lost all touch with humanity.

He took a step toward her and she drew back again with a frightened gasp. He extended his hand.

"Here," he said. "Stand up."

She got up slowly but without his help. Noticing suddenly her exposed breast, she reached down and held up the torn material of her dress.

They stood there breathing harshly and looking at each other. And, now that the first shock had passed, Neville didn't know what to say. He'd been dreaming of this moment for years. His dreams had never been like this.

"What . . . what's your name?" he asked.

She didn't answer. Her eyes stayed on his face, her lips kept trembling.

"Well?" he asked loudly, and she flinched.

"R-Ruth." Her voice faltered.

A shudder ran through Robert Neville's body. The sound of her voice seemed to loosen everything in him. Questions disappeared. He felt his heart beating heavily. He almost felt as if he were going to cry.

His hand moved out, almost unconsciously. Her shoulder trembled under his palm.

"Ruth," he said in a flat, lifeless voice.

His throat moved as he stared at her.

"Ruth," he said again.

The two of them, the man and the woman, stood facing each other in the great, hot field.

CHAPTER SIXTEEN

The woman lay motionless on his bed, sleeping. It was past four in the afternoon. At least twenty times Neville had stolen into the bedroom to look at her and see if she were awake. Now he sat in the kitchen drinking coffee and worrying.

What if she *is* infected, though? he argued with himself.

The worry had started a few hours before, while Ruth was sleeping. Now, he couldn't rid himself of the fear. No matter how he reasoned, it didn't help. All right, she was tanned from the sun, she had been walking in the daylight. The dog had been in the daylight too.

Neville's fingers tapped restlessly on the table.

Simplicity had departed; the dream had faded into disturbing complexity. There had been no wondrous embrace, no magic words spoken. Beyond her name he had got nothing from her. Getting her to the house had been a battle. Getting her to enter had been even worse. She had cried and begged him not to kill her. No matter what he said to her, she kept crying and begging. He had visualized something on the order of a Hollywood production; stars in their eyes, entering the house, arms about each other, fade-out. Instead he had been forced to tug and cajole and argue and scold while she held back. The entrance had been less than romantic. He had to drag her in.

Once in the house, she had been no less frightened. He'd tried to act comfortingly, but all she did was cower in one corner the way the dog had done. She wouldn't eat or drink anything he gave her. Finally he'd been compelled to take her in the bedroom and lock her in. Now she was asleep.

He sighed wearily and fingered the handle of his cup.

All these years, he thought, dreaming about a companion. Now I meet one and the first thing I do is distrust her, treat her crudely and impatiently.

And yet there was really nothing else he could do. He had accepted too long the proposition that he was the only normal person left. It didn't matter that she looked normal. He'd seen too many of them lying in their coma that looked as healthy as she. They weren't, though, and he knew it. The simple fact that she had been walking in the sunlight wasn't enough to tip the scales on the side of trusting acceptance. He had doubted too long. His concept of the society had become ironbound. It was almost impossible for him to believe that there were others like him. And, after the first shock had diminished, all the dogma of his long years alone had asserted itself.

With a heavy breath he rose and went back to the bedroom. She was still in the same position. Maybe, he thought, she's gone back into coma again.

He stood over the bed, staring down at her. Ruth. There was so much about her he wanted to know. And yet he was almost afraid to find out. Because if she were like the others, there was only one course open. And it was better not to know anything about the people you killed.

His hands twitched at his sides, his blue eyes gazed flatly at her. What if it had been a freak occurrence? What if she had snapped out of coma for a little while and gone wandering? It seemed possible. And yet, as far as he knew, daylight was the one thing the germ could not endure. Why wasn't that enough to convince him she was normal?

Well, there was only one way to make sure.

He bent over and put his hand on her shoulder.

"Wake up," he said.

She didn't stir. His mouth tightened and his fingers drew in on her soft shoulder.

Then he noticed the thin golden chain around her throat. Reaching in with rough fingers, he drew it out of the bosom of her dress.

He was looking at the tiny gold cross when she woke up and recoiled into the pillow. She's not in coma; that was all he thought.

"What are you d-doing?" she asked faintly.

It was harder to distrust her when she spoke. The sound of the human voice was so strange to him that it had a power over him it had never had before.

"I'm . . . nothing," he said.

Awkwardly he stepped back and leaned against the wall. He looked at her a moment longer. Then he asked, "Where are you from?"

She lay there looking blankly at him.

"I asked you where you were from," he said.

Again she said nothing. He pushed himself away from the wall with a tight look on his face.

"Ing-Inglewood," she said hastily.

He looked at her coldly for a moment, then leaned back against the wall.

"I see," he said. "Did . . . did you live alone?"

"I was married."

"Where is your husband?"

Her throat moved. "He's dead."

"For how long?"

"Last week."

"And what did you do after he died?"

"Ran." She bit into her lower lip. "I ran away."

"You mean you've been wandering all this time?"

"Y-yes."

He looked at her without a word. Then abruptly he turned and his boots thumped loudly as he walked into the kitchen. Pulling open a cabinet door, he drew down a handful of garlic cloves. He put them on a dish, tore them into pieces, and mashed them to a pulp. The acrid fumes assailed his nostrils.

She was propped up on one elbow when he came back. Without hesitation he pushed the dish almost to her face.

She turned her head away with a faint cry.

"What are you doing?" she asked, and coughed once.

"Why do you turn away?"

"Please . . ."

"Why do you turn away?"

"It *smells!*" Her voice broke into a sob. "Don't! You're making me sick!"

He pushed the plate still closer to her face. With a gagging sound she backed away and pressed against the wall, her legs drawn up on the bed.

"Stop it! *Please!*" she begged.

He drew back the dish and watched her body twitching as her stomach convulsed.

"You're one of them," he said to her, quietly venomous.

She sat up suddenly and ran past him into the bathroom. The door slammed behind her and he could hear the sound of her terrible retching.

Thin-lipped, he put the dish down on the bedside table. His throat moved as he swallowed.

Infected. It had been a clear sign. He had learned over a year before that garlic was an allergen to any system infected with the *vampiris* bacillus. When the system was exposed to garlic, the stimulated tissues sensitized the cells, causing an abnormal reaction to any further contact with garlic. That was why putting it into their veins had accomplished little. They had to be exposed to the odor.

He sank down on the bed. And the woman had reacted in the wrong way.

After a moment Robert Neville frowned. If what she had said was true, she'd been wandering around for a week. She would naturally be exhausted and weak, and under those conditions the smell of so much garlic *could* have made her retch.

His fists thudded down onto the mattress. He still didn't know, then, not for certain. And, objectively, he knew he had no right to decide on inadequate evidence. It was something he'd learned the hard way, something he knew and believed absolutely.

He was still sitting there when she unlocked the bathroom door and came out. She stood in the hall a moment looking at him, then went into the living room. He rose and followed. When he came into the living room she was sitting on the couch.

"Are you satisfied?" she asked.

"Never mind that," he said. "You're on trial, not me."

She looked up angrily as if she meant to say something. Then her body slumped and she shook her head. He felt a twinge of sympathy for a moment. She looked so helpless, her thin hands resting on her lap. She didn't seem to care any more about her torn dress. He looked at the slight swelling of her breast. Her figure was very slim, almost curveless. Not at all like the woman he'd used to envision. Never mind that, he told himself, that doesn't matter any more.

He sat down in the chair and looked across at her. She didn't return his gaze.

"Listen to me," he said then. "I have every reason to suspect you of being infected. Especially now that you've reacted in such a way to garlic."

She said nothing.

"Haven't you anything to say?" he asked.

She raised her eyes.

"You think I'm one of them," she said.

"I think you *might* be."

"And what about this?" she asked, holding up her cross.

"That means nothing," he said.

"I'm awake," she said. "I'm not in a coma."

He said nothing. It was something he couldn't argue with, even though it didn't assuage doubt.

"I've been in Inglewood many times," he said finally. "Why didn't you hear my car?"

"Inglewood is a big place," she said.

He looked at her carefully, his fingers tapping on the arm of the chair.

"I'd . . . like to believe you," he said.

"Would you?" she asked. Another stomach contraction hit her and she bent over with a gasp, teeth clenched. Robert Neville sat there wondering why he didn't feel more compassion for her. Emotion was a difficult thing to summon from the dead, though. He had spent it all and felt hollow now, without feeling.

After a moment she looked up. Her eyes were hard.

"I've had a weak stomach all my life," she said. "I saw my husband killed last week. Torn to pieces. Right in front of my eyes I saw it. I lost two children to the plague. And for the past week I've been wandering all over. Hiding at night, not eating more than a few scraps of food. Sick with fear, unable to sleep more than a couple of hours at a time. Then I hear someone shout at me. You chase me over a field, hit me, drag me to your house. Then when I get sick because you shove a plate of reeking garlic in my face, you tell me I'm infected!"

Her hands twitched in her lap.

"What do you *expect* to happen?" she said angrily.

She slumped back against the couch back and closed her eyes. Her hands picked nervously at her skirt. For a moment she tried to tuck in the torn piece, but it fell down again and she sobbed angrily.

He leaned forward in the chair. He was beginning to feel guilty now, in spite of suspicions and doubts. He couldn't help it. He had forgotten about sobbing women. He raised a hand slowly to his beard and plucked confusedly as he watched her.

"Would . . ." he started. He swallowed. "Would you let me take a sample of your blood?" he asked. "I could—"

She stood up suddenly and stumbled toward the door.

He got up quickly.

"What are you doing?" he asked.

She didn't answer. Her hands fumbled awkwardly with the lock.

"You can't go out there," he said, surprised. "The street will be full of them in a little while."

"I'm not staying here," she sobbed. "What's the difference if they kill me?"

His hands closed over her arm. She tried to pull away.

"Leave me alone!" she cried. "I didn't ask to come here. You dragged me here. Why don't you leave me alone?"

He stood by her awkwardly, not knowing what to say.

"You can't go out," he said again.

He led her back to the couch. Then he went and got her a small tumbler of whisky at the bar. Never mind whether she's infected or not, he thought, never mind.

He handed her the tumbler. She shook her head.

"Drink it," he said. "It'll calm you down."

She looked up angrily. "So you can shove more garlic in my face?"

He shook his head.

"Drink it now," he said.

After a few moments she took the glass and took a sip of the whisky. It made her cough. She put the tumbler on the arm of the couch and a deep breath shook her body.

"Why do you want me to stay?" she asked unhappily.

He looked at her without a definite answer in his mind. Then he said, "Even if you *are* infected, I can't let you go out there. You don't know what they'd do to you."

Her eyes closed. "I don't care," she said.

CHAPTER SEVENTEEN

"I don't understand it," he told her over supper.

"Almost three years now, and still there are some of them alive. Food supplies are being used up. As far as I know, they still lie in a coma during the day." He shook his head. "But they're not dead. Three years and they're not dead. What keeps them going?"

She was wearing his bathrobe. About five she had relented, taken a bath, and changed. Her slender body was shapeless in the voluminous terry-cloth folds. She'd borrowed his comb and drawn her hair back into a pony tail fastened with a piece of twine.

Ruth fingered her coffee cup.

"We used to see them sometimes," she said. "We were afraid to go near them, though. We didn't think we should touch them."

"Didn't you know they'd come back after they died?"

She shook her head. "No."

"Didn't you wonder about the people who attacked your house at night?"

"It never entered our minds that they were . . ." She shook her head slowly. "It's hard to believe something like that."

"I suppose," he said.

He glanced at her as they sat eating silently. It was hard too to believe that here was a normal woman. Hard to believe that, after all these years, a companion had come. It was more than just doubting her. It was doubting that anything so remarkable could happen in such a lost world.

"Tell me more about them," Ruth said.

He got up and took the coffeepot off the stove. He poured more into her cup, into his, then replaced the pot and sat down.

"How do you feel now?" he asked her.

"I feel better, thank you."

He nodded and spooned sugar into his coffee. He felt her eyes on him as he stirred. What's she thinking? he wondered. He took a deep breath, wondering why the tightness in him didn't break. For a while he'd thought that he trusted her. Now he wasn't sure.

"You still don't trust me," she said, seeming to read his mind.

He looked up quickly, then shrugged.

"It's . . . not that," he said.

"Of course it is," she said quietly. She sighed. "Oh, very well. If you have to check my blood, check it."

He looked at her suspiciously, his mind questioning: Is it a trick? He hid the movement of his throat in swallowing coffee. It was stupid, he thought, to be so suspicious.

He put down the cup.

"Good," he said. "Very good."

He looked at her as she stared into the coffee.

"If you *are* infected," he told her, "I'll do everything I can to cure you."

Her eyes met his. "And if you can't?" she said.

Silence a moment.

"Let's wait and see," he said then.

They both drank coffee. Then he asked, "Shall we do it now?"

"Please," she said, "in the morning. I . . . still feel a little ill."

"All right," he said, nodding. "In the morning."

They finished their meal in silence. Neville felt only a small satisfaction that she was going to let him check her blood. He was afraid he might discover that she *was* infected. In the meantime he had to pass an evening and a night with her, perhaps get to know her and be attracted to her. When in the morning he might have to . . .

Later, in the living room, they sat looking at the mural, sipping port, and listening to Schubert's Fourth Symphony.

"I wouldn't have believed it," she said, seeming to cheer up. "I never thought I'd be listening to music again. Drinking wine."

She looked around the room.

"You've certainly done a wonderful job," she said.

"What about *your* house?" he asked.

"It was nothing like this," she said. "We didn't have a—"

"How did you protect your house?" he interrupted.

"Oh.—" She thought a moment. "We had it boarded up, of course. And we used crosses."

"They don't always work," he said quietly, after a moment of looking at her.

She looked blank. "They don't?"

"Why should a Jew fear the cross?" he said. "Why should a vampire who had been a Jew fear it? Most people were afraid of becoming vampires. Most of them suffer from hysterical blindness before mirrors. But as far as the cross goes—well, neither a Jew nor a Hindu nor a Mohammedan nor an atheist, for that matter, would fear the cross."

She sat holding her wineglass and looking at him with expressionless eyes.

"That's why the cross doesn't always work," he said.

"You didn't let me finish," she said. "We used garlic too."

"I thought it made you sick."

"I was already sick. I used to weigh a hundred and twenty. I weigh ninety-eight pounds now."

He nodded. But as he went into the kitchen to get another bottle of wine, he thought, She would have adjusted to it by now. After three years.

Then again, she might not have. What was the point in doubting her now? She was going to let him check her blood. What else could she do? It's me, he thought. I've been by myself too long. I won't believe anything unless I see it in a microscope. Heredity triumphs again. I'm my father's son, damn his moldering bones.

Standing in the dark kitchen, digging his blunt nail under the wrapping around the neck of the bottle, Robert Neville looked into the living room at Ruth.

His eyes ran over the robe, resting a moment on the slight promi-
nence of her breasts, dropping then to the bronzed calves and ankles,
up to the smooth kneecaps. She had a body like a young girl's. She
certainly didn't look like the mother of two.

The most unusual feature of the entire affair, he thought, was that
he felt no physical desire for her.

If she had come two years before, maybe even later, he might have
violated her. There had been some terrible moments in those days,
moments when the most terrible of solutions to his need were considered, were often dwelt upon until they drove him half mad.

But then the experiments had begun. Smoking had tapered off,
drinking lost its compulsive nature. Deliberately and with surprising
success, he had submerged himself in investigation.

His sex drive had diminished, had virtually disappeared. Salvation
of the monk, he thought. The drive had to go sooner or later, or no
normal man could dedicate himself to any life that excluded sex.

Now, happily, he felt almost nothing; perhaps a hardly discernible
stirring far beneath the rocky strata of abstinence. He was content to
leave it at that. Especially since there was no certainty that Ruth
was the companion he had waited for. Or even the certainty that he
could allow her to live beyond tomorrow. *Cure* her?

Curing was unlikely.

He went back into the living room with the opened bottle. She
smiled at him briefly as he poured more wine for her.

"I've been admiring your mural," she said. "It almost makes you
believe you're in the woods."

He grunted.

"It must have taken a lot of work to get your house like this," she
said.

"You should know," he said. "You went through the same thing."

"We had nothing like this," she said. "Our house was small. Our
food locker was half the size of yours."

"You must have run out of food," he said, looking at her carefully.

"Frozen food," she said. "We were living out of cans."

He nodded. Logical, his mind had to admit. But he still didn't like it. It was all intuition, he knew, but he didn't like it.

"What about water?" he asked then.

She looked at him silently for a moment.

"You don't believe a word I've said, do you?" she said.

"It's not that," he said. "I'm just curious how you lived."

"You can't hide it from your voice," she said. "You've been alone too long. You've lost the talent for deceit."

He grunted, getting the uncomfortable feeling that she was playing with him. That's ridiculous, he argued. She's just a woman. She was probably right. He probably *was* a gruff and graceless hermit. What did it matter?

"Tell me about your husband," he said abruptly.

Something flitted over her face, a shade of memory. She lifted the glass of dark wine to her lips.

"Not now," she said. "Please."

He slumped back on the couch, unable to analyze the formless dissatisfaction he felt. Everything she said and did could be a result of what she'd been through. It could also be a lie.

Why should she lie? he asked himself. In the morning he would check her blood. What could lying tonight profit her when, in a matter of hours, he'd know the truth?

"You know," he said, trying to ease the moment, "I've been thinking. If three people could survive the plague, why not more?"

"Do you think that's possible?" she asked.

"Why not? There must have been others who were immune for one reason or another."

"Tell me more about the germ," she said.

He hesitated a moment, then put down his wineglass. What if he told her everything? What if she escaped and came back after death with all the knowledge that *he* had?

"There's an awful lot of detail," he said.

"You were saying something about the cross before," she said. "How do you know it's true?"

"You remember what I said about Ben Cortman?" he said, glad to restate something she already knew rather than go into fresh material.

"You mean that man you—"

He nodded. "Yes. Come here," he said, standing. "I'll show him to you."

As he stood behind her looking out the peephole, he smelled the odor of her hair and skin. It made him draw back a little. Isn't that remarkable? he thought. I don't like the smell. Like Gulliver returning from the logical horses, I find the human smell offensive.

"He's the one by the lamppost," he said.

She made a slight sound of acknowledgment. Then she said, "There are so few. Where are they?"

"I've killed off most of them," he said, "but they manage to keep a few ahead of me."

"How come the lamp is on out there?" she said. "I thought they destroyed the electrical system."

"I connected it with my generator," he said, "so I could watch them."

"Don't they break the bulb?"

"I have a very strong globe over the bulb."

"Don't they climb up and try to break it?"

"I have garlic all over the post."

She shook her head. "You've thought of everything."

Stepping back, he looked at her a moment. How can she look at them so calmly, he wondered, ask me questions, make comments, when only a week ago she saw their kind tear her husband to pieces? Doubts again, he thought. Won't they ever stop?

He knew they wouldn't until he knew about her for sure.

She turned away from the window then.

"Will you excuse me a moment?" she said.

He watched her walk into the bathroom and heard her lock the door behind her. Then he went back to the couch after closing the peephole door. A wry smile played on his lips. He looked down into the tawny wine depths and tugged abstractedly at his beard.

"Will you excuse me a moment?"

For some reason the words seemed grotesquely amusing, the carry-over from a lost age. Emily Post mincing through the graveyard. Etiquette for Young Vampires.

The smile was gone.

And what now? What did the future hold for him? In a week would she still be here with him, or crumpled in the never cooling fire?

He knew that, if she were infected, he'd have to try to cure her whether it worked or not. But what if she were free of the bacillus? In a way, that was a more nerve-racking possibility. The other way he would merely go on as before, breaking neither schedule nor standards. But if she stayed, if they had to establish a relationship, perhaps become husband and wife, have children . . .

Yes, that was more terrifying.

He suddenly realized that he had become an ill-tempered and inveterate bachelor again. He no longer thought about his wife, his child, his past life. The present was enough. And he was afraid of the possible demand that he make sacrifices and accept responsibility again. He was afraid of giving out his heart, of removing the chains he had forged around it to keep emotion prisoner. He was afraid of loving again.

When she came out of the bathroom he was still sitting there, thinking. The record player, unnoticed by him, let out only a thin scratching sound.

Ruth lifted the record from the turntable and turned it. The third movement of the symphony began.

"Well, what about Cortman?" she asked, sitting down.

He looked at her blankly. "Cortman?"

"You were going to tell me something about him and the cross."

"Oh. Well, one night I got him in here and showed him the cross."

"What happened?"

Shall I kill her now? Shall I not even investigate, but kill her and burn her?

His throat moved. Such thoughts were a hideous testimony to the world he had accepted; a world in which murder was easier than hope.

Well, he wasn't that far gone yet, he thought. I'm a man, not a destroyer.

"What's wrong?" she said nervously.

"What?"

"You're staring at me."

"I'm sorry," he said coldly. "I . . . I'm just thinking."

She didn't say any more. She drank her wine and he saw her hand shake as she held the glass. He forced down all introspection. He didn't want her to know what he felt.

"When I showed him the cross," he said, "he laughed in my face."

She nodded once.

"But when I held a torah before his eyes, I got the reaction I wanted."

"A what?"

"A torah. Tablet of law, I believe it is."

"And that . . . got a reaction?"

"Yes. I had him tied up, but when he saw the torah he broke loose and attacked me."

"What happened?" She seemed to have lost her fright again.

"He struck me on the head with something. I don't remember what. I was almost knocked out. But, using the torah, I backed him to the door and got rid of him."

"Oh."

"So you see, the cross hasn't the power the legend says it has. My theory is that, since the legend came into its own in Europe, a continent predominantly Catholic, the cross would naturally become the symbol of defense against powers of darkness."

"Couldn't you use your gun on Cortman?" she asked.

"How do you know I had a gun?"

"I . . . assumed as much," she said. "*We* had guns."

"Then you must know bullets have no effect on vampires."

"We were . . . never sure," she said, then went on quickly: "Do you know why that's so? Why don't bullets affect them?"

He shook his head. "I don't know," he said.

They sat in silence listening to the music.

He did know, but, doubting again, he didn't want to tell her.

Through experiments on the dead vampires he had discovered that the bacilli effected the creation of a powerful body glue that sealed bullet openings as soon as they were made. Bullets were enclosed almost immediately, and since the system was activated by germs, a bullet couldn't hurt it. The system could, in fact, contain almost an indefinite amount of bullets, since the body glue prevented a penetration of more than a few fractions of an inch. Shooting vampires was like throwing pebbles into tar.

As he sat looking at her, she arranged the folds of the robe around her legs and he got a momentary glimpse of brown thigh. Far from being attracted, he felt irritated. It was a typical feminine gesture, he thought, an artificial movement.

As the moments passed he could almost sense himself drifting farther and farther from her. In a way he almost regretted having found her at all. Through the years he had achieved a certain degree of peace. He had accepted solitude, found it not half bad. Now this . . . ending it all.

In order to fill the emptiness of the moment, he reached for his pipe and pouch. He stuffed tobacco into the bowl and lit it. For a second he wondered if he should ask if she minded. He didn't ask.

The music ended. She got up and he watched her while she looked through his records. She seemed like a young girl, she was so slender. Who is she? he thought. Who is she really?

"May I play this?" she asked, holding up an album.

He didn't even look at it. "If you like," he said.

She sat down as Rachmaninoff's Second Piano Concerto began. Her taste isn't remarkably advanced, he thought, looking at her without expression.

"Tell me about yourself," she said.

Another typical feminine question, he thought. Then he berated himself for being so critical. What was the point in irritating himself by doubting her?

"Nothing to tell," he said.

She was smiling again. *Was* she laughing at him?

"You scared the life out of me this afternoon," she said. "You and your bristly beard. And those wild eyes."

He blew out smoke. Wild eyes? That was ridiculous. What was she trying to do? Break down his reserve with cuteness?

"What do you look like under all those whiskers?" she asked.

He tried to smile at her but he couldn't.

"Nothing," he said. "Just an ordinary face."

"How old are you, Robert?"

His throat moved. It was the first time she'd spoken his name. It gave him a strange, restless feeling to hear a woman speak his name after so long. Don't call me that, he almost said to her. He didn't want to lose the distance between them. If she were infected and he couldn't cure her, he wanted it to be a stranger that he put away.

She turned her head away.

"You don't have to talk to me if you don't want to," she said quietly. "I won't bother you. I'll go tomorrow."

His chest muscles tightened.

"But . . ." he said.

"I don't want to spoil your life," she said. "You don't have to feel any obligation to me just because . . . we're the only ones left."

His eyes were bleak as he looked at her, and he felt a brief stirring of guilt at her words. Why should I doubt her? he told himself. If she's infected, she'll never get away alive. What's there to fear?

"I'm sorry," he said. "I . . . I *have* been alone a long time."

She didn't look up.

"If you'd like to talk," he said, "I'll be glad to . . . tell you anything I can."

She hesitated a moment. Then she looked at him, her eyes not committing themselves at all.

"I *would* like to know about the disease," she said. "I lost my two girls because of it. And it caused my husband's death."

He looked at her and then spoke.

"It's a bacillus," he said, "a cylindrical bacterium. It creates an iso-tonic solution in the blood, circulates the blood slower than normal, activates all bodily functions, lives on fresh blood, and provides en-ergy. Deprived of blood, it makes self-killing bacteriophages or else sporulates."

She looked blank. He realized then that she couldn't have under-stood. Terms so common to him now were completely foreign to her.

"Well," he said, "most of those things aren't so important. To sporulate is to create an oval body that has all the basic ingredients of the vegetative bacterium. The germ does that when it gets no fresh blood. Then, when the vampire host decomposes, these spores go flying out and seek new hosts. They find one, germinate—and one more system is infected."

She shook her head incredulously.

"Bacteriophages are inanimate proteins that are also created when the system gets no blood. Unlike the spores, though, in this case ab-normal metabolism destroys the cells."

Quickly he told her about the imperfect waste disposal of the lymphatic system, the garlic as allergen causing anaphylaxis, the various vectors of the disease.

"Then why are we immune?" she asked.

For a long moment he looked at her, withholding any answer. Then, with a shrug, he said, "I don't know about you. As for me, while I was stationed in Panama during the war I was bitten by a vampire bat. And, though I can't prove it, my theory is that the bat had previously encountered a true vampire and acquired the *vampiris* germ. The germ caused the bat to seek human rather than animal blood. But, by the time the germ had passed into my system, it had been weakened in some way by the bat's system. It made me terribly ill, of course, but it didn't kill me, and as a result, my body built up an immunity to it. That's my theory, anyway. I can't find any better reason."

"But . . . didn't the same thing happen to others down there?"

"I don't know," he said quietly. "I killed the bat." He shrugged. "Maybe I was the first human it had attacked."

She looked at him without a word, her surveillance making Neville feel restive. He went on talking even though he didn't really want to.

Briefly he told her about the major obstacle in his study of the vampires.

"At first I thought the stake had to hit their hearts," he said. "I believed the legend. I found out that wasn't so. I put stakes in all parts of their bodies and they died. That made me think it was hemorrhage. But then one day . . ."

And he told her about the woman who had decomposed before his eyes.

"I knew then it couldn't be hemorrhage," he went on, feeling a sort of pleasure in reciting his discoveries. "I didn't know what to do. Then one day it came to me."

"What?" she asked.

"I took a dead vampire. I put his arm into an artificial vacuum. I punctured his arm inside that vacuum. Blood spurted out." He paused. "But that's all."

She stared at him.

"You don't see," he said.

"I. . . . No," she admitted.

"When I let air back into the tank, the arm decomposed," he said. She still stared.

"You see," he said, "the bacillus is a facultative saprophyte. It lives with or without oxygen; but with a difference. Inside the system, it is anaerobic and sets up a symbiosis with the system. The vampire feeds it fresh blood, the bacteria provides the energy so the vampire can get more fresh blood. The germ also causes, I might add, the growth of the canine teeth."

"Yes?" she said.

"When air enters," he said, "the situation changes instantaneously. The germ becomes aerobic and, instead of being symbiotic, it becomes virulently parasitic." He paused. "It eats the host," he said.

"Then the stake . . ." she started.

"Lets air in. Of course. Lets it in and keeps the flesh open so that the body glue can't function. So the heart has nothing to do with it. What I do now is cut the wrists deep enough so that the body glue can't work." He smiled a little. "When I think of all the time I used to spend making stakes!"

She nodded and, noticing the wineglass in her hand, put it down.

"That's why the woman I told you about broke down so rapidly," he said. "She'd been dead so long that as soon as air struck her system the germs caused spontaneous dissolution."

Her throat moved and a shudder ran down through her.

"It's horrible," she said.

He looked at her in surprise. Horrible? Wasn't that odd? He hadn't thought that for years. For him the word "horror" had become obsolete. A surfeiting of terror soon made terror a cliché. To Robert Neville the situation merely existed as natural fact. It had no adjectives.

"And what about the . . . the ones who are still alive?" she asked.

"Well," he said, "when you cut their wrists the germ naturally becomes parasitic. But mostly they die from simple hemorrhage."

"Simple—"

She turned away quickly and her lips were pressed into a tight, thin line.

"What's the matter?" he asked.

"N-nothing. Nothing," she said.

He smiled. "One gets used to these things," he said. "One has to."

Again she shuddered, the smooth column of her throat contracting.

"You can't abide by Robert's Rules of Order in the jungle," he said. "Believe me, it's the only thing I can do. Is it better to let them die of the disease and return—in a far more terrible way?"

She pressed her hands together.

"But you said a lot of them are—are still living," she said nervously. "How do you know they're not going to *stay* alive?"

"I know," he said. "I know the germ, know how it multiplies. No matter how long their systems fight it, in the end the germ will win. I've made antibiotics, injected dozens of them. But it doesn't work, it can't work. You can't make vaccines work when they're already deep in the disease. Their bodies can't fight germs and make antibodies at the same time. It can't be done, believe me. It's a trap. If I didn't kill them, sooner or later they'd die and come after me. I have no choice; no choice at all."

They were silent then and the only sound in the room was the rasping of the needle on the inner grooves of the record. She wouldn't look at him, but kept staring at the floor with bleak eyes. It was strange, he thought, to find himself vaguely on the defensive for what yesterday was accepted necessity. In the years that had passed he had never once considered the possibility that he was wrong. It took her presence to bring about such thoughts. And they were strange, alien thoughts.

"Do you actually think I'm wrong?" he asked in an incredulous voice.

She bit into her lower lip.

"Ruth," he said.

"It's not for me to say," she answered.

CHAPTER EIGHTEEN

"Virge!"

The dark form recoiled against the wall as Robert Neville's hoarse cry ripped open the silent blackness.

He jerked his body up from the couch and stared with sleep-clouded eyes across the room, his chest pulsing with heartbeats like maniac fists on a dungeon wall.

He lurched up to his feet, brain still foggy with sleep, unable to define time or place.

"Virge?" he said again, weakly, shakily. "Virge?"

"It—it's me," the faltering voice said in the darkness.

He took a trembling step toward the thin stream of light spearing through the open peephole. He blinked dully at the light.

She gasped as he put his hand out and clutched her shoulder.

"It's Ruth. *Ruth*," she said in a terrified whisper.

He stood there rocking slowly in the darkness, eyes gazing without comprehension at the dark form before him.

"It's Ruth," she said again, more loudly.

Waking came like a hose blast of numbing shock. Something twisted cold knots into his chest and stomach. It wasn't Virge. He shook his head suddenly, rubbed shaking fingers across his eyes.

Then he stood there staring, weighted beneath a sudden depression.

"Oh," he muttered faintly. "Oh, I . . ."

He remained there, feeling his body weaving slowly in the dark as the mists cleared from his brain.

He looked at the open peephole, then back at her.

"What are you doing?" he asked, voice still thick with sleep.

"Nothing," she said nervously. "I . . . couldn't sleep."

He blinked his eyes suddenly at the flaring lamplight. Then his hands dropped down from the lamp switch and he turned around. She was against the wall still, blinking at the light, her hands at her sides drawn into tight fists.

"Why are you dressed?" he asked in a surprised voice.

Her throat moved and she stared at him. He rubbed his eyes again and pushed back the long hair from his temples.

"I was . . . just looking out," she said.

"But why are you dressed?"

"I couldn't sleep."

He stood looking at her, still a little groggy, feeling his heartbeat slowly diminish. Through the open peephole he heard them yelling outside, and he heard Cortman shout, "Come out, Neville!" Moving to the peephole, he pushed the small wooden door shut and turned to her.

"I want to know why you're dressed," he said again.

"No reason," she said.

"Were you going to leave while I was asleep?"

"No, I . . ."

"*Were* you?"

She gasped as he grabbed her wrist.

"No, no," she said quickly. "How could I, with them out there?"

He stood breathing heavily, looking at her frightened face. His throat moved slowly as he remembered the shock of waking up and thinking that she was Virge.

Abruptly he dropped her arm and turned away. And he'd thought the past was dead. How long did it take for a past to die?

She said nothing as he poured a tumblerful of whisky and swallowed it convulsively. Virge, Virge, he thought miserably, still with me. He closed his eyes and jammed his teeth together.

"Was that her name?" he heard Ruth ask.

His muscles tightened, then went slack.

"It's all right," he said in a dead voice. "Go to bed."

She drew back a little. "I'm sorry," she said. "I didn't mean . . ."

Suddenly he knew he didn't want her to go to bed. He wanted her to stay with him. He didn't know why, he just didn't want to be alone.

"I thought you were my wife," he heard himself saying. "I woke up and I thought—"

He drank a mouthful of whisky, coughing as part of it went down the wrong way. Ruth stayed in the shadows, listening.

"She came back, you see," he said. "I buried her, but one night she came back. She looked like—like you did. An outline, a shadow. *Dead.* But she came back. I tried to keep her with me. I tried, but she wasn't the same any more . . . you see. All she wanted was—"

He forced down the sob in his throat.

"My own wife," he said in a trembling voice, "coming back to drink my blood!"

He jammed down the glass on the bar top. Turning away, he paced restlessly to the peephole, turned, and went back and stood again before the bar. Ruth said nothing; she just stood in the darkness, listening.

"I put her away again," he said. "I had to do the same thing to her I'd done to the others. My own wife." There was a clicking in his throat. "A stake," he said in a terrible voice. "I had to put a stake in her. It was the only thing I knew to do. I—"

He couldn't finish. He stood there a long time, shivering helplessly, his eyes tightly shut.

Then he spoke again.

"Almost three years ago I did that. And I still remember it, it's still with me. What can you do? What can you *do*?" He drove a fist down on the bar top as the anguish of memory swept over him again. "No matter how you try, you can't forget or—or adjust or—*ever* get away from it!"

He ran shaking fingers through his hair.

"I know what you feel, I know. I didn't at first, I didn't trust you. I was safe, secure in my little shell. Now . . ." He shook his head slowly, defeatedly. "In a second, it's all gone. Adjustment, security, peace—all gone."

"Robert."

Her voice was as broken and lost as his.

"Why were we punished like this?" she asked.

He drew in a shuddering breath.

"I don't know," he answered bitterly. "There's no answer, no reason. It just is."

She was close to him now. And suddenly, without hesitation or drawing back, he drew her against him, and they were two people holding each other tightly in the lost measure of night.

"Robert, *Robert*."

Her hands rubbed over his back, stroking and clutching, while his arms held her firmly and he pressed his eyes shut against her warm, soft hair.

Their mouths held together for a long time and her arms gripped with desperate tightness around his neck.

Then they were sitting in the darkness, pressing close together, as if all the heat in the world were in their bodies and they would share the warmth between them. He felt the shuddering rise and fall of her breasts as she held close to him, her arms tight around his body, her face against his neck. His big hands moved roughly through her hair, stroking and feeling the silky strands.

"I'm sorry, Ruth."

"Sorry?"

"For being so cruel to you, for not trusting you."

She was silent, holding tight.

"Oh, Robert," she said then, "it's so unfair. So *unfair*. Why are we still alive? Why aren't we all dead? It would be better if we were all dead."

"Shhh, shhh," he said, feeling emotion for her like a released current pouring from his heart and mind. "It'll be all right."

He felt her shaking her head slowly against him.

"It will, it will," he said.

"How can it?"

"It *will*," he said, even though he knew he really couldn't believe it, even though he knew it was only released tension forming words in his mind.

"No," she said. "No."

"Yes, it will. It will, Ruth."

He didn't know how long it was they sat there holding each other close. He forgot everything, time and place; it was just the two of them together, needing each other, survivors of a black terror embracing because they had found each other.

But then he wanted to do something for her, to help her.

"Come," he said. "We'll check you."

She stiffened in his arms.

"No, no," he said quickly. "Don't be afraid. I'm sure we won't find anything. But if we do, I'll cure you. I swear I'll cure you, Ruth."

She was looking at him in the darkness, not saying a word. He stood and pulled her up with him, trembling with an excitement he hadn't felt in endless years. He wanted to cure her, to help her.

"Let me," he said. "I won't hurt you. I promise I won't. Let's *know*. Let's find out for sure. Then we can plan and work. I'll save you, Ruth. I will. Or I'll die myself."

She was still tense, holding back.

"Come with me, Ruth."

Now that the strength of his reserve had gone, there was nothing left to brace himself on, and he was shaking like a palsied man.

He led her into the bedroom. And when he saw in the lamplight how frightened she was, he pulled her close and stroked her hair.

"It's all right," he said. "All right, Ruth. No matter what we find, it'll be all right. Don't you understand?"

He sat her down on the stool and her face was completely blank, her body shuddering as he heated the needle over a Bunsen flame.

He bent over and kissed her on the cheek.

"It's all right now," he said gently. "It's all right."

She closed her eyes as he jabbed in the needle. He could feel the pain in his own finger as he pressed out blood and rubbed it on the slide.

"There. There," he said anxiously, pressing a little cotton to the nick on her finger. He felt himself trembling helplessly. No matter how he tried to control it, he couldn't. His fingers were almost incapable of making the slide, and he kept looking at Ruth and smiling at her, trying to take the look of taut fright from her features.

"Don't be afraid," he said. "Please don't. I'll cure you if you're infected. I will, Ruth, I will."

She sat without a word, looking at him with listless eyes as he worked. Her hands kept stirring restlessly in her lap.

"What will you do if—if I *am*," she said then.

"I'm not sure," he said. "Not yet. But there are a lot of things we can do."

"What?"

"Vaccines, for one."

"You said vaccines didn't work," she said, her voice shaking a little.

"Yes, but . . ." He broke off as he slid the glass slide onto the microscope.

"Robert, what could you do?"

She slid off the stool as he bent over the microscope.

"Robert, don't look!" she begged suddenly, her voice pleading.

But he'd already seen.

He didn't realize that his breath had stopped. His blank eyes met hers.

"Ruth," he whispered in a shocked voice.

The wooden mallet crashed down on his forehead.

A burst of pain filled Robert Neville's head and he felt one leg give way. As he fell to one side he knocked over the microscope. His right knee hit the floor and he looked up in dazed bewilderment at her fright-twisted face. The mallet came down again and he cried out in pain. He fell to both knees and his palms struck the floor as he toppled forward. A hundred miles away he heard her gasping sob.

"Ruth," he mumbled.

"I *told* you not to!" she cried.

He clutched out at her legs and she drove the mallet down a third time, this time on the back of his skull.

"Ruth!"

Robert Neville's hands went limp and slid off her calves, rubbing away part of the tan. He fell on his face and his fingers drew in convulsively as night filled his brain.

CHAPTER NINETEEN

When he opened his eyes there was no sound in the house.

He lay there a moment looking confusedly at the floor. Then, with a startled grunt, he sat up. A package of needles exploded in his head and he slumped down on the cold floor, hands pressed to his throbbing skull. A clicking sound filled his throat as he lay there.

After a few minutes he pulled himself up slowly by gripping the edge of the bench. The floor undulated beneath him as he held on tightly, eyes closed, legs wavering.

A minute later he managed to stumble into the bathroom. There he threw cold water in his face and sat on the bathtub edge pressing a cold, wet cloth to his forehead.

What had happened? He kept blinking and staring at the white-tiled floor.

He stood up and walked slowly into the living room. It was empty. The front door stood half open in the gray of early morning. She was gone.

Then he remembered. He struggled back to the bedroom, using the walls to guide him.

The note was on the bench next to the overturned microscope. He picked up the paper with numbed fingers and carried it to the bed. Sinking down with a groan, he held the letter before his eyes. But the letters blurred and ran. He shook his head and pressed his eyes shut. After a little while he read:

Robert:

Now you know. Know that I was spying on you, know that almost everything I told you was a lie.

I'm writing this note, though, because I want to save you if I can.

When I was first given the job of spying on you, I had no feelings about your life. Because I *did* have a husband, Robert. You killed him.

But now it's different. I know now that you were just as much forced into your situation as we were forced into ours. We *are* infected. But you already know that. What you don't understand yet is that we're going to stay alive. We've found a way to do that and we're going to set up society again slowly but surely. We're going to do away with all those wretched creatures whom death has cheated. And, even though I pray otherwise, we may decide to kill you and those like you.

Those like me? he thought with a start. But he kept reading.

I'll try to save you. I'll tell them you're too well armed for us to attack now. Use the time I'm giving you, Robert! Get away from your house, go into the mountains and save yourself. There are only a handful of us now. But sooner or later we'll be too well organized, and nothing I say will stop the rest from destroying you. For God's sake, Robert, go now, while you can!

I know you may not believe this. You may not believe that we can live in the sun for short periods now. You may not believe that my tan was only make-up. You may not believe that we can live with the germ now.

That's why I'm leaving one of my pills.

I took them all the time I was here. I kept them in a belt around my waist. You'll discover that they're a combination of defebrinated blood and a drug. I don't know myself just what it is. The blood feeds the germs, the drug prevents its multiplication. It was the discovery of this pill that saved us from dying, that is helping to set up society again slowly.

Believe me, it's true. And escape!

Forgive me, too. I didn't mean to hit you, it nearly killed me to do it. But I was so terribly frightened of what you'd do when you found out.

Forgive me for having to lie to you about so many things. But please believe this: When we were together in the darkness, close to each other, I wasn't spying on you. I was loving you.

Ruth

He read the letter again. Then his hands fell forward and he sat there staring with empty eyes at the floor. He couldn't believe it. He shook his head slowly and tried to understand, but adjustment eluded him.

He walked unsteadily to the bench. He picked up the small amber pill and held it in his palm, smelled it, tasted it. He felt as if all the security of reason were ebbing away from him. The framework of his life was collapsing and it frightened him.

Yet how did he refute the evidence? The pill, the tan coming off her leg, her walking in the sun, her reaction to garlic.

He sank down on the stool and looked at the mallet lying on the floor. Slowly, ploddingly, his mind went over the evidence.

When he'd first seen her she'd run from him. Had it been a ruse? No, she'd been genuinely frightened. She must have been startled by his cry, then, even though she'd been expecting it, and forgotten all about her job. Then later, when she'd calmed down, she'd talked him into thinking that her reaction to garlic was the reaction of a sick stomach. And she had lied and smiled and feigned hopeless acceptance and carefully got all the information she'd been sent after. And, when she'd wanted to leave, she couldn't because of Cortman and the others. He had awakened then. They had embraced, they had . . .

His white-knuckled fist jolted down on the bench. "I was loving you." Lie. Lie! His fingers crumpled up the letter and flung it away bitterly.

Rage made the pain in his head flare hotly and he pressed both hands against it and closed his eyes with a groan.

Then he looked up. Slowly he slid off the stool and placed the microscope back on its base.

The rest of her letter wasn't a lie, he knew that. Without the pill, without any evidence of word or memory, he knew. He knew what even Ruth and her people didn't seem to know.

He looked into the eyepiece for a long time. Yes, he knew. And the admission of what he saw changed his entire world. How stupid and ineffective he felt for never having foreseen it! Especially after reading the phrase a hundred, a thousand times. But then he'd never really appreciated it. Such a short phrase it was, but meaning so much.

Bacteria can mutate.

PART FOUR: January 1979

CHAPTER TWENTY

They came by night. Came in their dark cars with their spotlights and their guns and their axes and pikes. Came from the blackness with a great sound of motors, the long white arms of their spotlights snapping around the boulevard corner and clutching out at Cimarron Street.

Robert Neville was sitting at the peephole when they came. He had put down a book and was sitting there watching idly when the beams splashed white across the bloodless vampire faces and they whirled with a gasp, their dark animal eyes staring at the blinding lights.

Neville jumped back from the peephole, his heart thudding with the abrupt shock. For a moment he stood there trembling in the dark room, unable to decide what to do. His throat contracted and he heard the roar of the car motors even through the soundproofing on his house. He thought of the pistols in his bureau, the submachine gun on his workbench, thought of defending his house against them.

Then he pressed his fingers in until the nails dug at his palms. No, he'd made his decision, he'd worked it out carefully through the past months. He would not fight.

With a heavy, sinking sensation in the pit of his stomach he stepped back to the peephole and looked out.

The street was a scene of rushing, violent action illuminated by the bald glare of the spotlights. Men rushed at men, the sound of running boots covered the pavement. Then a shot rang out, echoing hollowly; more shots.

Two male vampires went thrashing down onto their sides. Four men grabbed them by the arms and jerked them up while two other men drove the glittering lance points of their pikes into the vampires' chests. Neville's face twitched as screams filled the night. He felt his chest shuddering with labored breath as he watched from his house.

The dark-suited men knew exactly what they were doing. There were about seven vampires visible, six men and a woman. The men surrounded the seven, held their flailing arms, and drove razor-tipped pikes deep into their bodies. Blood spouted out on the dark pavement and the vampires perished one by one. Neville felt himself shivering more and more. Is this the new society? The words flashed across his mind. He tried to believe that the men were forced into what they were doing, but shock brought terrible doubt. Did they have to do it like this, with such a black and brutal slaughtering? Why did they slay with alarum by night, when by day the vampires could be dispatched in peace?

Robert Neville felt tight fists shaking at his sides. He didn't like the looks of them, he didn't like the methodical butchery. They were more like gangsters than men forced into a situation. There were looks of vicious triumph on their faces, white and stark in the spotlights. Their faces were cruel and emotionless.

Suddenly Neville felt himself shudder violently, remembering. Where was Ben Cortman?

His eyes fled over the street but he couldn't see Cortman. He pressed against the peephole and looked up and down the street. He didn't want them to get Cortman, he realized, didn't want them to destroy Cortman like that. With a sense of inward shock he could not analyze in the rush of the moment, he realized that he felt more deeply toward the vampires than he did toward their executioners.

Now the seven vampires lay crumpled and still in their pools of stolen blood. The spotlights were moving around the street, flaying open the night. Neville turned his head away as the brilliant glare blazed across the front of his house. Then the spotlight had turned about and he looked again.

A shout. Neville's eyes jumped toward the focus of the spotlights. He stiffened.

Cortman was on the roof of the house across the street. He was pulling himself up toward the chimney, body flattened on the shingles.

Abruptly it came to Neville that it was in that chimney that Ben Cortman had hidden most of the time, and he felt a wrench of despair at the knowledge. His lips pressed together tightly. Why hadn't he looked more carefully? He couldn't fight the sick apprehension he felt at the thought of Cortman's being killed by these brutal strangers. Objectively, it was pointless, but he could not repress the feeling. Cortman was not theirs to put to rest.

But there was nothing he could do.

With bleak, tortured eyes he watched the spotlights cluster on Cortman's wriggling body. He watched the white hands reaching out slowly for handholds on the roof. Slowly, slowly, as if Cortman had all the time in the world. Hurry up! Neville felt himself twitch with the unspoken words as he watched. He felt himself straining with Cortman's agonizingly slow movements.

The men did not shout, they did not command. They raised their rifles now and the night was torn open again with their exploding fire.

Neville almost felt the bullets in his own flesh. His body jerked with convulsive shudders as he watched Cortman's body jerk under the impact of the bullets.

Still Cortman kept crawling, and Neville saw his white face, his teeth gritted together. The end of Oliver Hardy, he thought, the death of all comedy and all laughter. He didn't hear the continuous fusillade of shots. He didn't even feel the tears running down his cheeks. His eyes were riveted on the ungainly form of his old friend inching up the brightly lit roof.

Now Cortman rose up on his knees and clutched at the chimney edge with spasmodic fingers. His body lurched as more bullets struck. His dark eyes glared into the blinding spotlights, his lips were drawn back in a soundless snarl.

Then he was standing up beside the chimney and Neville's face was white and taut as he watched Cortman start to raise his right leg.

And then the hammering machine gun splattered Cortman's flesh with lead. For a moment Cortman stood erect in the hot blast, palsied hands raised high over his head, a look of berserk defiance twisting his white features.

"Ben," Neville muttered in a croaking whisper.

Ben Cortman's body folded, slumped forward, fell. It slid and rolled slowly down the shingled incline, then dropped into space. In the sudden silence Neville heard the thump of it from across the street. Sick-eyed, he watched the men rush at the writhing body with their pikes.

Then Neville closed his eyes and his nails dug furrows in the flesh of his palms.

A clumping of boots. Neville jerked back into the darkness. He stood in the middle of the room, waiting for them to call to him and tell him to come out. He held himself rigidly. I'm not going to fight, he told himself strongly. Even though he wanted to fight, even though he already hated the dark men with their guns and their bloodstained pikes.

But he wasn't going to fight. He had worked out his decision very carefully. They were doing what they had to do, albeit with unnecessary violence and seeming relish. He had killed their people and they had to capture him and save themselves. He would not fight. He'd throw himself upon the justice of their new society. When they called to him he would go out and surrender; it was his decision.

But they didn't call. Neville lurched back with a gasp as the ax blade bit deeply into the front door. He stood trembling in the dark living room. What were they doing? Why didn't they call on him to surrender? He wasn't a vampire, he was a man like them. What were they doing?

He whirled and stared at the kitchen. They were chopping at the boarded-up back door too. He took a nervous step toward the hallway. His frightened eyes rushed from the back to the front door. He felt his heart pumping. He didn't understand, he didn't understand!

With a grunt of shocked surprise he jumped into the hall as the enclosed house rang with the gun explosion. The men were shooting away the lock on the front door. Another reverberating shot made his ears ring.

And, suddenly, he knew. They weren't going to take him to their courts, to their justice. They were going to exterminate him.

With a frightened murmur he ran into the bedroom. His hands fumbled in the bureau drawer.

He straightened up on trembling legs, the guns in his hands. But what if they *were* going to take him prisoner? He'd only judged by the fact that they hadn't called on him to come out. There were no lights in the house; maybe they thought he was already gone.

He stood shivering in the darkness of the bedroom, not knowing what to do, mutters of terror filling his throat. Why hadn't he left! Why hadn't he listened to her and left? Fool!

One of his guns fell from nerveless fingers as the front door was crushed in. Heavy feet thudded into the living room and Robert Neville shuffled back across the floor, his remaining pistol held out with rigid, blood-drained fingers. They weren't going to kill him without a fight!

He gasped as he collided with the bench. He stood there tautly. In the front room a man said something he couldn't understand, then flashlight beams shone into the hall. Neville caught his breath. He felt the room spinning around him. So this is the end. It was the only thing he could think. So this is the end.

Heavy shoes thumped in the hall. Neville's fingers tightened still more on the pistol and his eyes stared with wild fright at the doorway.

Two men came in.

Their white beams played around the room, struck his face. The two men recoiled abruptly.

"He's got a gun!" one of them cried, and fired his pistol.

Neville heard the bullet smash into the wall over his head. Then the pistol was jolting in his hand, splashing his face with bursts of light. He didn't fire at any one of them; he just kept pulling the trigger automatically. One of the men cried out in pain.

Then Neville felt a violent club blow across his chest. He staggered back, and jagged, burning pain exploded in his body. He fired once more, then crashed to his knees, the pistol slipping from his fingers.

"You got him!" he heard someone cry as he fell on his face. He tried to reach out for the pistol but a dark boot stamped on his hand and broke it. Neville drew in his hand with a rattling gasp and stared through pain-glazed eyes at the floor.

Rough hands slid under his armpits and pulled him up. He kept wondering when they would shoot him again. Virge, he thought, Virge, I'm coming with you now. The pain in his chest was like molten lead poured over him from a great height. He felt and heard his boot tips scraping over the floor and waited for death. I want to die in my own house, he thought. He struggled feebly but they didn't stop. Hot pain raked saw-toothed nails through his chest as they dragged him through the front room.

"No," he groaned. "No!"

Then pain surged up from his chest and drove a barbed club into his brain. Everything began spinning away into blackness.

"Virge," he muttered in a hoarse whisper.

And the dark men dragged his lifeless body from the house. Into the night. Into the world that was theirs and no longer his.

CHAPTER TWENTY-ONE

Sound; a murmured rustle in the air. Robert Neville coughed weakly, then grimaced as the pain filled his chest. A bubbling groan passed his lips and his head rolled slightly on the flat pillow. The sound grew stronger, it became a rumbling mixture of noises. His hands drew in slowly at his sides. Why didn't they take the fire off his chest? He could feel hot coals dropping through openings in his flesh. Another groan, agonized and breathless, twitched his graying lips. Then his eyes fluttered open.

He stared at the rough plaster ceiling for a full minute without blinking. Pain ebbed and swelled in his chest with an endless, nerve-clutching throb. His face remained a taut, lined mask of resistance to the pain. If he relaxed for a second, it enveloped him completely; he had to fight it. For the first few minutes he could only struggle with the pain, suffering beneath its hot stabbing. Then, after a while, his brain began to function; slowly, like a machine faltering, starting and stopping, turning and jamming gears.

Where am I? It was his first thought. The pain was awful. He looked down at his chest and saw that it was bound with a wide bandage, a great, moist spot of red rising and falling jerkily in the middle of it. He closed his eyes and swallowed. I'm hurt, he thought. I'm hurt badly. His mouth and throat felt powdery dry. Where am I, what am I . . .

Then he remembered; the dark men and the attack on his house. And he knew where he was even before he turned his head slowly, achingly, and saw the barred windows across the tiny cubicle. He looked at the windows for a long time, face tight, teeth clenched together. The sound was outside; the rushing, confused sound.

He let his head roll back on the pillow and lay staring at the ceiling. It was hard to understand the moment on its own terms. Hard to believe it wasn't all a nightmare. Over three years alone in his house. Now this.

But he couldn't doubt the sharp, shifting pain in his chest and he couldn't doubt the way the moist, red spot kept getting bigger and bigger. He closed his eyes. I'm going to die, he thought.

He tried to understand that. But that didn't work either. In spite of having lived with death all these years, in spite of having walked a tightrope of bare existence across an endless maw of death—in spite of that he couldn't understand it. Personal death still was a thing beyond comprehension.

He was still on his back when the door behind him opened.

He couldn't turn; it hurt too much. He lay there and listened to footsteps approach the bed, then stop. He looked up but the person hadn't come into view yet. My executioner, he thought, the justice of this new society. He closed his eyes and waited.

The shoes moved again until he knew the person was by the cot. He tried to swallow but his throat was too dry. He ran his tongue over his lips.

"Are you thirsty?"

He looked up with dulled eyes at her and suddenly his heart began throbbing. The increased blood flow made the pain billow up and swallow him for a moment. He couldn't cut off the groan of agony. He twisted his head on the pillow, biting his lips and clutching at the blanket feverishly. The red spot grew bigger.

She was on her knees now, patting perspiration from his brow, touching his lips with a cool, wet cloth. The pain began to subside slowly and her face came into gradual focus. Neville lay motionless, staring at her with pain-filled eyes.

"So," he finally said.

She didn't answer. She got up and sat on the edge of the bed. She patted his brow again. Then she reached over his head and he heard her pouring water into a glass.

The pain dug razors into him as she lifted his head a little so he could drink. This is what they must have felt when the pikes went into them, he thought. This cutting, biting agony, the escape of life's blood.

His head fell back on the pillow.

"Thank you," he murmured.

She sat looking down at him, a strange mixture of sympathy and detachment on her face. Her reddish hair was drawn back into a tight cluster behind her head and clipped there. She looked very clean-cut and self-possessed.

"You wouldn't believe me, would you?" she said.

A little cough puffed out his cheeks. His mouth opened and he sucked in some of the damp morning air.

"I . . . believed you," he said.

"Then why didn't you go?"

He tried to speak but the words jumbled together. His throat moved and he drew in another faltering breath.

"I . . . couldn't," he muttered. "I almost went several times. Once I even packed and . . . started out. But I couldn't, I couldn't . . . go. I was too used to the . . . the house. It was a habit, just . . . just like the habit of living. I got . . . used to it."

Her eyes ran over his sweat-greased face and she pressed her lips together as she patted his forehead again.

"It's too late now," she said then. "You know that, don't you?"

Something clicked in his throat as he swallowed.

"I know," he said.

He tried to smile but his lips only twitched.

"Why did you fight them?" she said. "They had orders to bring you in unharmed. If you hadn't fired at them they wouldn't have harmed you."

His throat contracted.

"What difference . . ." he gasped.

His eyes closed and he gritted his teeth tightly to force back the pain.

When he opened them again she was still there. The expression on her face had not changed.

His smile was weak and tortured.

"Your . . . your society is . . . certainly a fine one," he gasped. "Who are those . . . those gangsters who came to get me? The . . . the council of justice?"

Her look was dispassionate. She's changed, he thought suddenly.

"New societies are always primitive," she answered. "You should know that. In a way we're like a revolutionary group—repossessing society by violence. It's inevitable. Violence is no stranger to you. You've killed. Many times."

"Only to . . . to survive."

"That's exactly why we're killing," she said calmly. "To survive. We can't allow the dead to exist beside the living. Their brains are impaired, they exist for only one purpose. They *have* to be destroyed. As one who killed the dead *and* the living, you know that."

The deep breath he took made the pain wrench at his insides. His eyes were stark with pain as he shuddered. It's got to end soon, he thought. I can't stand much more of this. No, death did not frighten him. He didn't understand it, but he didn't fear it either.

The swelling pain sank down and the clouds passed from his eyes. He looked up at her calm face.

"I hope so," he said. "But . . . but did you see their faces when they . . . they killed?" His throat moved convulsively. "Joy," he mumbled. "Pure joy."

Her smile was thin and withdrawn. She *has* changed, he thought, entirely.

"Did you ever see *your* face," she asked, "when you killed?" She patted his brow with the cloth. "I saw it—remember? It was frightening. And you weren't even killing then, you were just chasing me."

He closed his eyes. Why am I listening to her? he thought. She's become a brainless convert to this new violence.

"Maybe you did see joy on their faces," she said. "It's not surprising. They're young. And they *are* killers—assigned killers, legal killers. They're respected for their killing, admired for it. What can you expect from them? They're only fallible men. And men can learn to enjoy killing. That's an old story, Neville. You know that."

He looked up at her. Her smile was the tight, forced smile of a woman who was trying to forgo being a woman in favor of her dedication.

"Robert Neville," she said, "the last of the old race."

His face tightened.

"Last?" he muttered, feeling the heavy sinking of utter loneliness in him.

"As far as we know," she said casually. "You're quite unique, you know. When you're gone, there won't be anyone else like you within our particular society."

He looked toward the window.

"Those are . . . people . . . outside," he said.

She nodded. "They're waiting."

"For my death?"

"For your execution," she said.

He felt himself tighten as he looked up at her.

"You'd better hurry," he said, without fear, with a sudden defiance in his hoarse voice.

They looked at each other for a long moment. Then something seemed to give in her. Her face grew blank.

"I knew it," she said softly. "I knew you wouldn't be afraid."

Impulsively she put her hand over his.

"When I first heard that they were ordered to your house, I was going to go there and warn you. But then I knew that if you were still there, nothing would make you go. Then I was going to try to help you escape after they brought you in. But they told me you'd been shot and I knew that escape was impossible too."

A smile flitted over her lips.

"I'm glad you're not afraid," she said. "You're very brave." Her voice grew soft. "Robert."

They were silent and he felt her hand tighten on his.

"How is it you can . . . come in here?" he asked then.

"I'm a ranking officer in the new society," she said.

His hand stirred under hers.

"Don't . . . let it get . . ." He coughed up blood. "Don't let it get . . . too brutal. Too heartless."

"What can I—" she started, then stopped. She smiled at him. "I'll try," she said.

He couldn't go on. The pain was getting worse. It twisted and turned like a clutching animal in his body.

Ruth leaned over him.

"Robert," she said, "listen to me. They mean to execute you. Even though you're wounded. They have to. The people have been out there all night, waiting. They're terrified of you, Robert, they hate you. And they want your life."

She reached up quickly and unbuttoned her blouse. Reaching under her brassiere, she took out a tiny packet and pressed it into his right palm.

"It's all I can do, Robert," she whispered, "to make it easier. I warned you, I *told* you to go." Her voice broke a little. "You just can't fight so many, Robert."

"I know." The words were gagging sounds in his throat.

For a moment she stood over his bed, a look of natural compassion on her face. It was all a pose, he thought, her coming in and being so official. She was afraid to be herself. I can understand that.

Ruth bent over him and her cool lips pressed on his.

"You'll be with her soon," she murmured hastily.

Then she straightened up, her lips pressed together tightly. She buttoned the two top buttons of her blouse. A moment longer she looked down at him. Then her eyes glanced at his right hand.

"Take them soon," she murmured, and turned away quickly.

He heard her footsteps moving across the floor. Then the door was shutting and he heard the sound of it being locked. He closed his eyes and felt warm tears pushing out from beneath the lids. Good-by, Ruth.

Good-by, everything.

Then, suddenly, he drew in a quick breath. Bracing himself, he pushed himself up to a sitting position. He refused to let himself collapse at the burning pain that exploded in his chest. Teeth grating together, he stood up on his feet. For a moment he almost fell, but, catching his balance, he stumbled across the floor on vibrating legs he could hardly feel.

He fell against the window and looked out.

The street was filled with people. They milled and stirred in the gray light of morning, the sound of their talking like the buzzing of a million insects.

He looked out over the people, his left hand gripping the bars with bloodless fingers, his eyes fever-lit.

Then someone saw him.

For a moment there was an increased babbling of voices, a few startled cries.

Then sudden silence, as though a heavy blanket had fallen over their heads. They all stood looking up at him with their white faces. He stared back. And suddenly he thought, I'm the abnormal one now. Normalcy was a majority concept, the standard of many and not the standard of just one man.

Abruptly that realization joined with what he saw on their faces—awe, fear, shrinking horror—and he knew that they *were* afraid of him. To them he was some terrible scourge they had never seen, a scourge even worse than the disease they had come to live with. He was an invisible specter who had left for evidence of his existence the bloodless bodies of their loved ones. And he understood what they felt and did not hate them. His right hand tightened on the tiny envelope of pills. So long as the end did not come with violence, so long as it did not have to be a butchery before their eyes . . .

Robert Neville looked out over the new people of the earth. He knew he did not belong to them; he knew that, like the vampires, he was anathema and black terror to be destroyed. And, abruptly, the concept came, amusing to him even in his pain.

A coughing chuckle filled his throat. He turned and leaned against the wall while he swallowed the pills. Full circle, he thought while the final lethargy crept into his limbs. Full circle. A new terror born in death, a new superstition entering the unassailable fortress of forever.

I am legend.

BURIED TALENTS

A man in a wrinkled, black suit entered the fairgrounds. He was tall and lean, his skin the color of drying leather. He wore a faded sport shirt underneath his suit coat, white with yellow stripes. His hair was black and greasy, parted in the middle and brushed back flat on each side. His eyes were pale blue. There was no expression on his face. It was a hundred and two degrees in the sun but he was not perspiring.

He walked to one of the booths and stood there watching people try to toss ping-pong balls into dozens of little fish bowls on a table. A fat man wearing a straw hat and waving a bamboo cane in his right hand kept telling everyone how easy it was. "Try your luck!" he told them. "Win a prize! There's nothing to it!" He had an unlit, half-smoked cigar between his lips which he shifted from side to side as he spoke.

For awhile, the tall man in the wrinkled, black suit stood watching. Not one person managed a ping-pong ball into a fish bowl. Some of them tried to throw the balls in. Others tried to bounce them off the table. None of them had any luck.

At the end of seven minutes, the man in the black suit pushed between the people until he was standing by the booth. He took a quarter from his right hand trouser pocket and laid it on the counter. "Yes, sir!" said the fat man. "Try your luck!" He tossed the quarter into a metal box beneath the counter. Reaching down, he picked three grimy ping-pong balls from a basket. He clapped them on the counter and the tall man picked them up.

"Toss a ball in the fish bowl!" said the fat man. "Win a prize! There's nothing to it!" Sweat was trickling down his florid face. He took a quarter from a teenage boy and set three ping-pong balls in front of him.

The man in the black suit looked at the three ping-pong balls on his left palm. He hefted them, his face immobile. The man in the straw hat turned away. He tapped at the fish bowls with his cane. He shifted the stump of cigar in his mouth. "Toss a ball in the fish bowl!" he said. "A prize for everybody! Nothing to it!"

Behind him, a ping-pong ball clinked into one of the bowls. He turned and looked at the bowl. He looked at the man in the black suit. "There you are!" he said. "See that? Nothing to it! Easiest game on the fairgrounds!"

The tall man threw another ping-pong ball. It arced across the booth and landed in the same bowl. All the other people trying missed.

"Yes, sir!" the fat man said. "A prize for everybody! Nothing to it!" He picked up two quarters and set six ping-pong balls before a man and wife.

He turned and saw the third ping-pong ball dropping into the fish bowl. It didn't touch the neck of the bowl. It didn't bounce. It landed on the other two balls and lay there.

"See?" the man in the straw hat said. "A prize on his very first turn! Easiest game on the fairgrounds!" Reaching over to a set of wooden shelves, he picked up an ashtray and set it on the counter. "Yes, sir! Nothing to it!" he said. He took a quarter from a man in overalls and set three ping-pong balls in front of him.

The man in the black suit pushed away the ashtray. He laid another quarter on the counter. "Three more ping-pong balls," he said.

The fat man grinned. "Three more ping-pong balls it is!" he said.

He reached below the counter, picked up three more balls and set them on the counter in front of the man. "Step right up!" he said. He caught a ping-pong ball which someone had bounced off the table. He kept an eye on the tall man while he stooped to retrieve some ping-pong balls on the ground.

The man in the black suit raised his right hand, holding one of the ping-pong balls. He threw it overhand, his face expressionless. The ball curved through the air and fell into the fish bowl with the other three balls. It didn't bounce.

The man in the straw hat stood with a grunt. He dumped a handful of ping-pong balls into the basket underneath the counter. "Try your luck and win a prize!" he said. "Easy as pie!" He set three ping-pong balls in front of a boy and took his quarter. His eyes grew narrow as he watched the tall man raise his hand to throw the second ball. "No leaning in," he told the man.

The man in the black suit glanced at him. "I'm not," he said.

The fat man nodded. "Go ahead," he said.

The tall man threw the second ping-pong ball. It seemed to float across the booth. It fell through the neck of the bowl and landed on top of the other four balls.

"Wait a second," said the fat man, holding up his hand.

The other people who were throwing stopped. The fat man leaned across the table. Sweat was running down beneath the collar of his long-sleeved shirt. He shifted the soggy cigar in his mouth as he scooped the five balls from the bowl. He straightened up and looked at them. He hooked the bamboo cane over his left forearm and rolled the balls between his palms.

"Okay, folks!" he said. He cleared his throat. "Keep throwing! Win a prize!" He dropped the balls into the basket underneath the counter. Taking another quarter from the man in overalls, he set three ping-pong balls in front of him.

The man in the black suit raised his hand and threw the sixth ball. The fat man watched it arc through the air. It fell into the bowl he'd emptied. It didn't roll around inside. It landed on the bottom, bounced once, straight up, then lay motionless.

The fat man grabbed the ashtray, stuck it on the shelf and picked up a fish bowl like the ones on the table. It was filled with pink colored water and had a goldfish fluttering around in it. "There you go!" he said. He turned away and tapped on the empty fish bowls with his cane. "Step right up!" he said. "Toss a ball in the fish bowl! Win a prize! There's nothing to it!"

Turning back, he saw the man in the wrinkled suit had pushed away the goldfish in the bowl and placed another quarter on the counter. "Three more ping-pong balls," he said.

The fat man looked at him. He shifted the damp cigar in his mouth.

"Three more ping-pong balls," the tall man said.

The man in the straw hat hesitated. Suddenly, he noticed people looking at him and, without a word, he took the quarter and set three ping-pong balls on the counter. He turned around and tapped the fish bowls with his cane. "Step right up and try your luck!" he said. "Easiest game on the fairgrounds!" He removed his straw hat and rubbed the left sleeve of his shirt across his forehead. He was almost bald. The small amount of hair on his head was plastered to his scalp by sweat. He put his straw hat back on and set three ping-pong balls in front of a boy. He put the quarter in the metal box underneath the counter.

A number of people were watching the tall man now. When he threw the first of the three ping-pong balls into the fish bowl some of them applauded and a small boy cheered. The fat man watched suspiciously. His small eyes shifted as the man in the black suit threw his second ping-pong ball into the fish bowl with the other two balls. He scowled and seemed about to speak. The scatter of applause appeared to irritate him.

The man in the wrinkled suit tossed the third ping-pong ball. It landed on top of the other three. Several people cheered and all of them clapped.

The fat man's cheeks were redder now. He put the fish bowl with the goldfish back on its shelf. He gestured toward a higher shelf. "What'll it be?" he asked.

The tall man put a quarter on the counter. "Three more ping-pong balls," he said in a brisk voice. He picked up three more ping-pong balls from the basket and rolled them between his palms.

"Don't give him the bad ones now," someone said in a mocking voice.

"No bad ones!" the fat man said. "They're all the same!" He set the balls on the counter and picked up the quarter. He tossed it into the metal box underneath the counter. The man in the black suit raised his hand.

"Wait a second," the fat man said. He turned and reached across the table. Picking up the fish bowl, he turned it over and dumped the four ping-pong balls into the basket. He seemed to hesitate before he put the empty fish bowl back in place.

Nobody else was throwing now. They watched the tall man curiously as he raised his hand and threw the first of his three ping-pong balls. It curved through the air and landed in the same fish bowl, dropping straight down through the neck. It bounced once, then was still. The people cheered and applauded. The fat man rubbed his left hand across his eyebrows and flicked the sweat from his fingertips with an angry gesture.

The man in the black suit threw his second ping-pong ball. It landed on the same fish bowl.

"*Hold* it," said the fat man.

The tall man looked at him.

"What are you doing?" the fat man asked.

"Throwing ping-pong balls," the tall man answered. Everybody laughed. The fat man's face got redder. "I know that!" he said.

"It's done with mirrors," someone said and everybody laughed again.

"Funny," said the fat man. He shifted the wet cigar in his mouth and gestured curtly. "Go on," he said.

The tall man in the black suit raised his hand and threw the third ping-pong ball. It arced across the booth as though it were being carried by an invisible hand. It landed in the fish bowl on top of the other two balls. Everybody cheered and clapped their hands.

The fat man in the straw hat grabbed a casserole dish and dumped it on the counter. The man in the black suit didn't look at it. He put another quarter down. "Three more ping-pong balls," he said.

The fat man turned away from him. "Step right up and win a prize!" he called. "Toss a ping-pong ball—!"

The noise of disapproval everybody made drowned him out. He turned back, bristling. "Four rounds to a customer!" he shouted.

"Where does it say that?" someone asked.

"That's the rule!" the fat man said. He turned his back on the man and tapped the fish bowls with his cane. "Step right up and win a prize!" he said.

"I came here yesterday and played *five* rounds!" a man said loudly.

"That's because you didn't win!" a teenage boy replied. Most of the people laughed and clapped but some of them booed. "Let him play!" a man's voice ordered. Everybody took it up immediately. "Let him play!" they demanded.

The man in the straw hat swallowed nervously. He looked around, a truculent expression on his face. Suddenly, he threw his hands up. "All right!" he said. "Don't get so excited!" He glared at the tall man as he picked up the quarter. Bending over, he grabbed three ping-pong balls and slammed them on the counter. He leaned in close to the man and muttered, "If you're pulling something fast, you'd better cut it out. This is an honest game."

The tall man stared at him. His face was blank. His eyes looked very pale in the leathery tan of his face. "What do you mean?" he asked.

"No one can throw that many balls in succession into those bowls," the fat man said.

The man in the black suit looked at him without expression. *"I* can," he said.

The fat man felt a coldness on his body. Stepping back, he watched the tall man throw the ping-pong balls. As each of them landed in the same fish bowl, the people cheered and clapped their hands.

The fat man took a set of steak knives from the top prize shelf and set it on the counter. He turned away quickly. "Step right up!" he said. "Toss a ball in the fish bowl! Win a prize!" His voice was trembling.

"He wants to play again," somebody said.

The man in the straw hat turned around. He saw the quarter on the counter in front of the tall man. "No more prizes," he said.

The man in the black suit pointed at the items on top of the wooden shelves—a four-slice electric toaster, a short wave radio, a drill set and a portable typewriter. "What about them?" he asked.

The fat man cleared his throat. "They're only for display," he said. He looked around for help.

"Where does it say *that?*" someone demanded.

"That's what they are, so just take my word for it!" the man in the straw hat said. His face was dripping with sweat.

"I'll play for them," the tall man said.

"Now *look!*" The fat man's face was very red. "They're only for display, I said! Now get the hell—!"

He broke off with a wheezing gasp and staggered back against the table, dropping his cane. The faces of the people swam before his eyes. He heard their angry voices as though from a distance. He saw the blurred figure of the man in the black suit turn away and push through the crowd. He straightened up and blinked his eyes. The steak knives were gone.

Almost everybody left the booth. A few of them remained. The fat man tried to ignore their threatening grumbles. He picked a quarter off the counter and set three ping-pong balls in front of a boy. "Try your luck," he said. His voice was faint. He tossed the quarter into the metal box underneath the counter. He leaned against a corner post and pressed both hands against his stomach. The cigar fell out of his mouth. "God," he said.

It felt as though he was bleeding inside.

THE NEAR DEPARTED

The small man opened the door and stepped in out of the glaring sunlight. He was in his early fifties, a spindly, plain looking man with receding gray hair. He closed the door without a sound, then stood in the shadowy foyer, waiting for his eyes to adjust to the change in light. He was wearing a black suit, white shirt, and black tie. His face was pale and dry-skinned despite the heat of the day.

When his eyes had refocused themselves, he removed his Panama hat and moved along the hallway to the office, his black shoes soundless on the carpeting.

The mortician looked up from his desk. "Good afternoon," he said.

"Good afternoon." The small man's voice was soft.

"Can I help you?"

"Yes, you can," the small man said.

The mortician gestured to the arm chair on the other side of his desk. "Please."

The small man perched on the edge of the chair and set the Panama hat on his lap. He watched the mortician open a drawer and remove a printed form.

"Now," the mortician said. He withdrew a black pen from its onyx holder. "Who is the deceased?" he asked gently.

"My wife," the small man said.

The mortician made a sympathetic noise. "I'm sorry," he said.

"Yes." The small man gazed at him blankly.

"What is her name?" the mortician asked.

"Marie," the small man answered quietly. "Arnold."

The mortician wrote the name. "Address?" he asked.

The small man told him.

"Is she there now?" the mortician asked.

"She's there," the small man said.

The mortician nodded.

"I want everything perfect," the small man said. "I want the best you have."

"Of course," the mortician said. "Of course."

"Cost is unimportant," said the small man. His throat moved as he swallowed dryly. "Everything is unimportant now. Except for this."

"I understand."

"She always had the best. I saw to it."

"Of course."

"There'll be many people," said the small man. "Everybody loved her. She's so beautiful. So young. She has to have the very best. You understand?"

"Absolutely," the mortician reassured him. "You'll be more than satisfied, I guarantee you."

"She's so beautiful," the small man said. "So young."

"I'm sure," the mortician said.

The small man sat without moving as the mortician asked him questions. His voice did not vary in tone as he spoke. His eyes blinked so infrequently the mortician never saw them doing it.

When the form was completed, the small man signed and stood. The mortician stood and walked around the desk. "I guarantee you you'll be satisfied," he said, his hand extended.

The small man took his hand and gripped it momentarily. His palm was dry and cool.

"We'll be over at your house within the hour," the mortician told him.

"Fine," the small man said.

The mortician walked beside him down the hallway.

"I want everything perfect for her," the small man said. "Nothing but the very best."

"Everything will be exactly as you wish."

"She deserves the best." The small man stared ahead. "She's so beautiful," he said. "Everybody loved her. Everybody. She's so young and beautiful."

"When did she die?" the mortician asked.

The small man didn't seem to hear. He opened the door and stepped into the sunlight, putting on his Panama hat. He was halfway to his car when he replied, a faint smile on his lips, "As soon as I get home."

PREY

Amelia arrived at her apartment at six-fourteen. Hanging her coat in the hall closet, she carried the small package into the living room and sat on the sofa. She nudged off her shoes while she unwrapped the package on her lap. The wooden box resembled a casket. Amelia raised its lid and smiled. It was the ugliest doll she'd ever seen. Seven inches long and carved from wood, it had a skeletal body and an oversized head. Its expression was maniacally fierce, its pointed teeth completely bared, its glaring eyes protuberant. It clutched an eight-inch spear in its right hand. A length of fine, gold chain was wrapped around its body from the shoulders to the knees. A tiny scroll was wedged between the doll and the inside wall of its box. Amelia picked it up and unrolled it. There was handwriting on it. *This is He Who Kills,* it began. *He is a deadly hunter.* Amelia smiled as she read the rest of the words. Arthur would be pleased.

The thought of Arthur made her turn to look at the telephone on the table beside her. After a while, she sighed and set the wooden box on the sofa. Lifting the telephone to her lap, she picked up the receiver and dialed a number.

Her mother answered.

"Hello, Mom," Amelia said.

"Haven't you left yet?" her mother asked.

Amelia steeled herself. "Mom, I know it's Friday night—" she started.

She couldn't finish. There was silence on the line. Amelia closed her eyes. Mom, please, she thought. She swallowed. "There's this man," she said. "His name is Arthur Breslow. He's a high-school teacher."

"You aren't coming," her mother said.

Amelia shivered. "It's his birthday," she said. She opened her eyes and looked at the doll. "I sort of promised him we'd . . . spend the evening together."

Her mother was silent. There aren't any good movies playing tonight, anyway, Amelia's mind continued. "We could go tomorrow night," she said.

Her mother was silent.

"Mom?"

"Now even Friday night's too much for you."

"Mom, I see you two, three nights a week."

"To *visit*," said her mother. "When you have your own room here."

"Mom, *let's not start on that again*," Amelia said. I'm not a child, she thought. Stop treating me as though I were a child!

"How long have you been seeing him?" her mother asked.

"A month or so."

"Without telling me," her mother said.

"I had every intention of telling you." Amelia's head was starting to throb. I will *not* get a headache, she told herself. She looked at the doll. It seemed to be glaring at her. "He's a nice man, Mom," she said.

Her mother didn't speak. Amelia felt her stomach muscles drawing taut. I won't be able to eat tonight, she thought.

She was conscious suddenly of huddling over the telephone. She forced herself to sit erect. *I'm thirty-three years old,* she thought. Reaching out, she lifted the doll from its box. "You should see what I'm giving him for his birthday," she said. "I found it in a curio shop on Third Avenue. It's a genuine Zuni fetish doll, extremely rare. Arthur is a buff on anthropology. That's why I got it for him."

There was silence on the line. All right, *don't talk*, Amelia thought.

"It's a hunting fetish," she continued, trying hard to sound untroubled. "It's supposed to have the spirit of a Zuni hunter trapped inside it. There's a golden chain around it to prevent the spirit from—" She couldn't think of the word; ran a shaking finger over the chain. "—escaping, I guess," she said. "His name is He Who Kills. You should see his face." She felt warm tears trickling down her cheeks.

"Have a good time," said her mother, hanging up.

Amelia stared at the receiver, listening to the dial tone. Why is it always like this? she thought. She dropped the receiver onto its cradle and set aside the telephone. The darkening room looked blurred to her. She stood the doll on the coffee-table edge and pushed to her feet. I'll take my bath now, she told herself. I'll meet him and we'll have a lovely time. She walked across the living room. A lovely time, her mind repeated emptily. She knew it wasn't possible. Oh, *Mom!* she thought. She clenched her fists in helpless fury as she went into the bedroom.

In the living room, the doll fell off the table edge. It landed head down and the spear point, sticking into the carpet, braced the doll's legs in the air.

The fine, gold chain began to slither downward.

It was almost dark when Amelia came back into the living room. She had taken off her clothes and was wearing her terrycloth robe. In the bathroom, water was running into the tub.

She sat on the sofa and placed the telephone on her lap. For several minutes, she stared at it. At last, with a heavy sigh, she lifted the receiver and dialed a number.

"Arthur?" she said when he answered.

"Yes?" Amelia knew the tone—pleasant but suspecting. She couldn't speak.

"Your mother," Arthur finally said.

That cold, heavy sinking in her stomach. "It's our night together," she explained. "Every Friday—" She stopped and waited. Arthur didn't speak. "I've mentioned it before," she said.

"I know you've mentioned it," he said.

Amelia rubbed at her temple.

"She's still running your life, isn't she?" he said.

Amelia tensed. "I just don't want to hurt her feelings anymore," she said. "My moving out was hard enough on her."

"I don't want to hurt her feelings either," Arthur said. "But how many birthdays a year do I have? We *planned* on this."

"I know." She felt her stomach muscles tightening again.

"Are you really going to let her do this to you?" Arthur asked. "One Friday night out of the whole year?"

Amelia closed her eyes. Her lips moved soundlessly. I just can't hurt her feelings anymore, she thought. She swallowed. "She's my mother," she said.

"Very well," he said. "I'm sorry. I was looking forward to it, but—" He paused. "I'm sorry," he said. He hung up quietly.

Amelia sat in silence for a long time, listening to the dial tone. She started when the recorded voice said loudly, "Please hang up." Putting the receiver down, she replaced the telephone on its table. So much for my birthday present, she thought. It would be pointless to give it to Arthur now. She reached out, switching on the table lamp. She'd take the doll back tomorrow.

The doll was not on the coffee table. Looking down, Amelia saw the gold chain lying on the carpet. She eased off the sofa edge onto her knees and picked it up, dropping it into the wooden box. The doll was not beneath the coffee table. Bending over, Amelia felt around underneath the sofa.

She cried out, jerking back her hand. Straightening up, she turned to the lamp and looked at her hand. There was something wedged beneath the index fingernail. She shivered as she plucked it out. It was the head of the doll's spear. She dropped it into the box and put the finger in her mouth. Bending over again, she felt around more cautiously beneath the sofa.

She couldn't find the doll. Standing with a weary groan, she started pulling one end of the sofa from the wall. It was terribly heavy. She recalled the night that she and her mother had shopped for the furniture. She'd wanted to furnish the apartment in Danish modern. Mother had insisted on this heavy, maple sofa; it had been on sale. Amelia grunted as she dragged it from the wall. She was conscious of the water running in the bathroom. She'd better turn it off soon.

She looked at the section of carpet she'd cleared, catching sight of the spear shaft. The doll was not beside it. Amelia picked it up and set it on the coffee table. The doll was caught beneath the sofa, she decided; when she'd moved the sofa, she had moved the doll as well.

She thought she heard a sound behind her—fragile, skittering. Amelia turned. The sound had stopped. She felt a chill move up the backs of her legs. "It's He Who Kills," she said with a smile. "He's taken off his chain and gone—"

She broke off suddenly. There had definitely been a noise inside the kitchen; a metallic, rasping sound. Amelia swallowed nervously. What's going on? she thought. She walked across the living room and reached into the kitchen, switching on the light. She peered inside. Everything looked normal. Her gaze moved falteringly across the stove, the pan of water on it, the table and chair, the drawers and cabinet doors all shut, the electric clock, the small refrigerator with the cookbook lying on top of it, the picture on the wall, the knife rack fastened to the cabinet side—

—its small knife missing.

Amelia stared at the knife rack. Don't be silly, she told herself. She'd put the knife in the drawer, that's all. Stepping into the kitchen, she pulled out the silverware drawer. The knife was not inside it.

Another sound made her look down quickly at the floor. She

gasped in shock. For several moments, she could not react; then, stepping to the doorway, she looked into the living room, her heartbeat thudding. Had it been imagination? She was sure she'd seen a movement.

"Oh, come on," she said. She made a disparaging sound. She hadn't seen a thing.

Across the room, the lamp went out.

Amelia jumped so startledly, she rammed her right elbow against the doorjamb. Crying out, she clutched the elbow with her left hand, eyes closed momentarily, her face a mask of pain.

She opened her eyes and looked into the darkened living room. "Come on," she told herself in aggravation. Three sounds plus a burned-out bulb did not add up to anything as idiotic as—

She willed away the thought. She had to turn the water off. Leaving the kitchen, she started for the hall. She rubbed her elbow, grimacing.

There was another sound. Amelia froze. Something was coming across the carpet toward her. She looked down dumbly. No, she thought.

She saw it then—a rapid movement near the floor. There was a glint of metal, instantly, a stabbing pain in her right calf. Amelia gasped. She kicked out blindly. Pain again. She felt warm blood running down her skin. She turned and lunged into the hall. The throw rug slipped beneath her and she fell against the wall, hot pain lancing through her right ankle. She clutched at the wall to keep from falling, then went sprawling on her side. She thrashed around with a sob of fear.

More movement, dark on dark. Pain in her left calf, then her right again. Amelia cried out. Something brushed along her thigh. She scrabbled back, then lurched up blindly, almost falling again. She fought for balance, reaching out convulsively. The heel of her left hand rammed against the wall, supporting her. She twisted around and rushed into the darkened bedroom. Slamming the door, she fell against it, panting. Something banged against it on the other side, something small and near the floor.

Amelia listened, trying not to breathe so loudly. She pulled carefully at the knob to make sure the latch had caught. When there were no further sounds outside the door, she backed toward the bed. She started as she bumped against the mattress edge. Slumping down, she grabbed at the extension phone and pulled it to her lap. Whom could she call? The police? They'd think her mad. Mother? She was too far off.

She was dialing Arthur's number by the light from the bathroom when the doorknob started turning. Suddenly, her fingers couldn't move. She stared across the darkened room. The door latch clicked. The telephone slipped off her lap. She heard it thudding onto the carpet as the door swung open. Something dropped from the outside knob.

Amelia jerked back, pulling up her legs. A shadowy form was scurrying across the carpet toward the bed. She gaped at it. It isn't true, she thought. She stiffened at the tugging on her bedspread. *It was climbing up to get her.* No, she thought; *it isn't true.* She couldn't move. She stared at the edge of the mattress.

Something that looked like a tiny head appeared. Amelia twisted around with a cry of shock, flung herself across the bed and jumped to the floor. Plunging into the bathroom, she sprung around and slammed the door, gasping at the pain in her ankle. She had barely thumbed in the button on the doorknob when something banged against the bottom of the door. Amelia heard a noise like the scratching of a rat. Then it was still.

She turned and leaned across the tub. The level of the water was almost to the overflow drain. As she twisted shut the faucets, she saw drops of blood falling into the water. Straightening up, she turned to the medicine-cabinet mirror above the sink.

She caught her breath in horror as she saw the gash across her neck. She pressed a shaking hand against it. Abruptly, she became aware of pain in her legs and looked down. She'd been slashed along the calves of both legs. Blood was running down her ankles, dripping off the edges of her feet. Amelia started crying. Blood ran between the fingers of the hand against her neck. It trickled down her wrist. She looked at her reflection through a glaze of tears.

Something in her aroused her, a wretchedness, a look of terrified surrender. *No,* she thought. She reached out for the medicine-cabinet door. Opening it, she pulled out iodine, gauze and tape. She dropped the cover of the toilet seat and sank down gingerly. It was a struggle to remove the stopper of the iodine bottle. She had to rap it hard against the sink three times before it opened.

The burning of the antiseptic on her calves made her gasp. Amelia clenched her teeth as she wrapped gauze around her right leg.

A sound made her twist toward the door. She saw the knife blade being jabbed beneath it. It's trying to stab my feet, she thought; it thinks I'm standing there. She felt unreal to be considering its thoughts. *This is He Who Kills*; the scroll flashed suddenly across her mind. *He is a deadly hunter.* Amelia stared at the poking knife blade. God, she thought.

Hastily, she bandaged both her legs, then stood and, looking into the mirror, cleaned the blood from her neck with a washrag. She swabbed some iodine along the edges of the gash, hissing at the fiery pain.

She whirled at the new sound, heartbeat leaping. Stepping to the door, she leaned down, listening hard. There was a faint metallic noise inside the knob.

The doll was trying to unlock it.

Amelia backed off slowly, staring at the knob. She tried to visualize the doll. Was it hanging from the knob by one arm, using the other to probe inside the knob lock with the knife? The vision was insane. She felt an icy prickling on the back of her neck. *I mustn't let it in,* she thought.

A hoarse cry pulled her lips back as the doorknob button popped out. Reaching out impulsively, she dragged a bath towel off its rack. The doorknob turned, the latch clicked free. The door began to open.

Suddenly the doll came darting in. It moved so quickly that its figure blurred before Amelia's eyes. She swung the towel down hard, as though it were a huge bug rushing at her. The doll was knocked against the wall. Amelia heaved the towel on top of it and lurched across the floor, gasping at the pain in her ankle. Flinging open the door, she lunged into the bedroom.

She was almost to the hall door when her ankle gave. She pitched across the carpet with a cry of shock. There was a noise behind her. Twisting around, she saw the doll come through the bathroom doorway like a jumping spider. She saw the knife blade glinting in the light. Then the doll was in the shadows, coming at her fast. Amelia scrabbled back. She glanced over her shoulder, saw the closet and backed into its darkness, clawing for the doorknob.

Pain again, an icy slashing at her foot. Amelia screamed and heaved back. Reaching up, she yanked a topcoat down. It fell across the doll. She jerked down everything in reach. The doll was buried underneath a mound of blouses, skirts and dresses. Amelia pitched across the moving pile of clothes. She forced herself to stand and limped into the hall as quickly as she could. The sound of thrashing underneath the clothes faded from her hearing. She hobbled to the door. Unlocking it, she pulled the knob.

The door was held. Amelia reached up quickly to the bolt. It had been shot. She tried to pull it free. It wouldn't budge. She clawed at it with sudden terror. It was twisted out of shape. "No," she muttered. *She was trapped.* "Oh, God." She started pounding on the door. "Please help me! *Help* me!"

Sound in the bedroom. Amelia whirled and lurched across the living room. She dropped to her knees beside the sofa, feeling for the telephone, but her fingers trembled so much that she couldn't dial the numbers. She began to sob, then twisted around with a strangled cry. The doll was rushing at her from the hallway.

Amelia grabbed an ashtray from the coffee table and hurled it at the doll. She threw a vase, a wooden box, a figurine. She couldn't hit the doll. It reached her, started jabbing at her legs. Amelia reared up blindly and fell across the coffee table. Rolling to her knees, she stood again. She staggered toward the hall, shoving over furniture to stop the doll. She toppled a chair, a table. Picking up a lamp, she hurled it at the floor. She backed into the hall and, spinning, rushed into the closet, slammed the door shut.

She held the knob with rigid fingers. Waves of hot breath pulsed against her face. She cried out as the knife was jabbed beneath the door, its sharp point sticking into one of her toes. She shuffled back, shifting her grip on the knob. Her robe hung open. She could feel a trickle of blood between her breasts. Her legs felt numb with pain. She closed her eyes. Please, someone help, she thought.

She stiffened as the doorknob started turning in her grasp. Her flesh went cold. It couldn't be stronger than she: it *couldn't* be. Amelia tightened her grip. *Please,* she thought. The side of her head bumped against the front edge of her suitcase on the shelf.

The thought exploded in her mind. Holding the knob with her right hand, she reached up, fumbling, with her left. The suitcase clasps were open. With a sudden wrench, she turned the doorknob, shoving at the door as hard as possible. It rushed away from her. She heard it bang against the wall. The doll thumped down.

Amelia reached up, hauling down her suitcase. Yanking open the lid, she fell to her knees in the closet doorway, holding the suitcase like an open book. She braced herself, eyes wide, teeth clenched together. She felt the doll's weight as it banged against the suitcase bottom. Instantly, she slammed the lid and threw the suitcase flat. Falling across it, she held it shut until her shaking hands could fasten the clasps. The sound of them clicking into place made her sob with relief. She shoved away the suitcase. It slid across the hall and bumped against the wall. Amelia struggled to her feet, trying not to listen to the frenzied kicking and scratching inside the suitcase.

She switched on the hall light and tried to open the bolt. It was hopelessly wedged. She turned and limped across the living room, glancing at her legs. The bandages were hanging loose. Both legs were streaked with caking blood, some of the gashes still bleeding. She felt at her throat. The cut was still wet. Amelia pressed her shaking lips together. She'd get to a doctor soon now.

Removing the ice pick from its kitchen drawer, she returned to the hall. A cutting sound made her look toward the suitcase. She caught her breath. The knife blade was protruding from the suitcase wall, moving up and down with a sawing motion. Amelia stared at it. She felt as though her body had been turned to stone.

She limped to the suitcase and knelt beside it, looking with revulsion at the sawing blade. It was smeared with blood. She tried to pinch it with the fingers of her left hand, pull it out. The blade was twisted, jerked down, and she cried out, snatching back her hand. There was a deep slice in her thumb. Blood ran down across her palm. Amelia pressed the finger to her robe. She felt as though her mind was going blank.

Pushing to her feet, she limped back to the door and started prying at the bolt. She couldn't get it loose. Her thumb began to ache. She pushed the ice pick underneath the bolt socket and tried to force it off the wall. The ice pick point broke off. Amelia slipped and almost fell. She pushed up, whimpering. There was no time, no time. She looked around in desperation.

The window! She could throw the suitcase out! She visualized it tumbling through the darkness. Hastily, she dropped the ice pick, turning toward the suitcase.

She froze. The doll had forced its head and shoulders through the rent in the suitcase wall. Amelia watched it struggling to get out. She felt paralyzed. The twisting doll was staring at her. No, she thought, it isn't true. The doll jerked free its legs and jumped to the floor.

Amelia jerked around and ran into the living room. Her right foot landed on a shard of broken crockery. She felt it cutting deep into her heel and lost her balance. Landing on her side, she thrashed around. The doll came leaping at her. She could see the knife blade glint. She kicked out wildly, knocking back the doll. Lunging to her feet, she reeled into the kitchen, whirled, and started pushing shut the door.

Something kept it from closing. Amelia thought she heard a screaming in her mind. Looking down, she saw the knife and a tiny wooden hand. The doll's arm was wedged between the door and the jamb! Amelia shoved against the door with all her might, aghast at the strength with which the door was pushed the other way. There was a cracking noise. A fierce smile pulled her lips back and she pushed berserkly at the door. The screaming in her mind grew louder, drowning out the sound of splintering wood.

The knife blade sagged. Amelia dropped to her knees and tugged at it. She pulled the knife into the kitchen, seeing the wooden hand and wrist fall from the handle of the knife. With a gagging noise, she struggled to her feet and dropped the knife into the sink. The door slammed hard against her side; the doll rushed in.

Amelia jerked away from it. Picking up the chair, she slung it toward the doll. It jumped aside, then ran around the fallen chair. Amelia snatched the pan of water off the stove and hurled it down. The pan clanged loudly off the floor, spraying water on the doll.

She stared at the doll. It wasn't coming after her. It was trying to climb the sink, leaping up and clutching at the counter side with one hand. It wants the knife, she thought. It has to have its weapon.

She knew abruptly what to do. Stepping over to the stove, she pulled down the broiler door and twisted the knob on all the way. She heard the puffing detonation of the gas as she turned to grab the doll.

She cried out as the doll began to kick and twist, its maddened thrashing flinging her from one side of the kitchen to the other. The screaming filled her mind again and suddenly she knew it was the spirit in the doll that screamed. She slid and crashed against the table, wrenched herself around and, dropping to her knees before the stove, flung the doll inside. She slammed the door and fell against it.

The door was almost driven out. Amelia pressed her shoulder, then her back against it, turning to brace her legs against the wall. She tried to ignore the pounding scrabble of the doll inside the broiler. She watched the red blood pulsing from her heel. The smell of burning wood began to reach her and she closed her eyes. The door was getting hot. She shifted carefully. The kicking and pounding filled her ears. The screaming flooded through her mind. She knew her back would get burned, but she didn't dare to move. The smell of burning wood grew worse. Her foot ached terribly.

Amelia looked up at the electric clock on the wall. It was four minutes to seven. She watched the red second hand revolving slowly. A minute passed. The screaming in her mind was fading now. She shifted uncomfortably, gritting her teeth against the burning heat on her back.

Another minute passed. The kicking and the pounding stopped. The screaming faded more and more. The smell of burning wood had filled the kitchen. There was a pall of gray smoke in the air. That they'll see, Amelia thought. Now that it's over, they'll come and help. That's the way it always is.

She started to ease herself away from the broiler door, ready to throw her weight back against it if she had to. She turned around and got on her knees. The reek of charred wood made her nauseated. She had to know, though. Reaching out, she pulled down the door.

Something dark and stifling rushed across her and she heard the screaming in her mind once more as hotness flooded over her and into her. It was a scream of victory now.

Amelia stood and turned off the broiler. She took a pair of ice tongs from its drawer and lifted out the blackened twist of wood. She dropped it into the sink and ran water over it until the smoke had stopped. Then she went into the bedroom, picked up the telephone and depressed its cradle. After a moment, she released the cradle and dialed her mother's number.

"This is Amelia, Mom," she said. "I'm sorry I acted the way I did. I want us to spend the evening together. It's a little late, though. Can you come by my place and we'll go from here?" She listened. "Good," she said. "I'll wait for you."

Hanging up, she walked into the kitchen, where she slid the longest carving knife from its place in the rack. She went to the front door and pushed back its bolt, which now moved freely. She carried the knife into the living room, took off her bathrobe and danced a dance of hunting, of the joy of hunting, of the joy of the impending kill.

Then she sat down, cross-legged, in the corner. He Who Kills sat, cross-legged, in the corner, in the darkness, waiting for the prey to come.

WITCH WAR

Seven pretty little girls sitting in a row. Outside, night, pouring rain—war weather. Inside, toasty warm. Seven overalled little girls chatting. Plaque on the wall saying: P.G. CENTER.

Sky clearing its throat with thunder, picking and dropping lint lightning from immeasurable shoulders. Rain hushing the world, bowing the trees, pocking earth. Square building, low, with one wall plastic.

Inside, the buzzing talk of seven pretty little girls.

"So I say to him—'Don't give me *that*, Mr. High and Mighty.' So he says, 'Oh yeah?' And I say, 'Yeah!' "

"Honest, will I ever be glad when this thing's over. I saw the cutest hat on my last furlough. Oh, *what* I wouldn't give to wear it!"

"You too? Don't I *know* it! You just can't get your hair right. Not in *this* weather. Why don't they let us get rid of it?"

"*Men!* They make me sick."

Seven gestures, seven postures, seven laughters ringing thin beneath thunder. Teeth showing in girl giggles. Hands tireless, painting pictures in the air.

P.G. Center. Girls. Seven of them. Pretty. Not one over sixteen. Curls. Pigtails. Bangs. Pouting little lips—smiling, frowning, shaping emotion on emotion. Sparkling young eyes—glittering, twinkling, narrowing, cold or warm.

Seven healthy young bodies restive on wooden chairs. Smooth adolescent limbs. Girls—pretty girls—seven of them.

✦

An army of ugly shapeless men, stumbling in mud, struggling along the pitchblack muddy road.

Rain a torrent. Buckets of it thrown on each exhausted man. Sucking sound of great boots sinking into oozy yellow-brown mud, pulling loose. Mud dripping from heels and soles.

Plodding men—hundreds of them—soaked, miserable, depleted. Young men bent over like old men. Jaws hanging loosely, mouth gasping at black wet air, tongues lolling, sunken eyes looking at nothing, betraying nothing.

Rest.

Men sink down in the mud, fall on their packs. Heads thrown back, mouths open, rain splashing on yellow teeth. Hands immobile—scrawny heaps of flesh and bone. Legs without motion—khaki lengths of worm-eaten wood. Hundreds of useless limbs fixed to hundreds of useless trunks.

In back, ahead, beside, rumble trucks and tanks and tiny cars. Thick tires splattering mud. Fat treads sinking, tearing at mucky slime. Rain drumming wet fingers on metal and canvas.

Lightning flashbulbs without pictures. Momentary burst of light. The face of war seen for a second—made of rusty guns and turning wheels and faces staring.

Blackness. A night hand blotting out the brief storm glow. Windblown rain flitting over fields and roads, drenching trees and trucks. Rivulets of bubbly rain tearing scars from the earth. Thunder, lightning.

A whistle. Dead men resurrected. Boots in sucking mud again—deeper, closer, nearer. Approach to a city that bars the way to a city that bars the way to a . . .

An officer sat in the communication room of the P.G. Center. He peered at the operator, who sat hunched over the control board, phones over his ears, writing down a message.

The officer watched the operator. They are coming, he thought. Cold, wet and afraid they are marching at us. He shivered and shut his eyes.

He opened them quickly. Visions fill his darkened pupils—of curling smoke, flaming men, unimaginable horrors that shape themselves without words or pictures.

"Sir," said the operator, "from advance observation post. Enemy forces sighted."

The officer got up, walked over to the operator and took the message. He read it, face blank, mouth parenthesized. "Yes," he said.

He turned on his heel and went to the door. He opened it and went into the next room. The seven girls stopped talking. Silence breathed on the walls.

The officer stood with his back to the plastic window. "Enemies," he said, "two miles away. Right in front of you."

He turned and pointed out the window. "Right out there. Two miles away. Any questions?"

A girl giggled.

"Any vehicles?" another asked.

"Yes. Five trucks, five small command cars, two tanks."

"That's too easy," laughed the girl, slender fingers fussing with her hair.

"That's all," said the officer. He started from the room. "Go to it," he added and, under his breath, "Monsters!"

He left.

"Oh, me," sighed one of the girls, "here we go again."

"What a bore," said another. She opened her delicate mouth and plucked out chewing gum. She put it under her chair seat.

"At least it stopped raining," said a redhead, tying her shoelaces.

The seven girls looked around at each other. *Are you ready?* said their eyes. *I'm ready, I suppose.* They adjusted themselves on the chairs with girlish grunts and sighs. They hooked their feet around the legs of their chairs. All gum was placed in storage. Mouths were tightened into prudish fixity. The pretty little girls made ready for the game.

Finally they were silent on their chairs. One of them took a deep breath. So did another. They all tensed their milky flesh and clasped fragile fingers together. One quickly scratched her head to get it over with. Another sneezed prettily.

"Now," said a girl on the right end of the row.

Seven pairs of beady eyes shut. Seven innocent little minds began to picture, to visualize, to transport.

Lips rolled into thin gashes, faces drained of color, bodies shivered passionately. Their fingers twitching with concentration, seven pretty little girls fought a war.

❖

The men were coming over the rise of a hill when the attack came. The leading men, feet poised for the next step, burst into flame.

There was no time to scream. Their rifles slapped down into the muck, their eyes were lost in fire. They stumbled a few steps and fell, hissing and charred, into the soft mud.

Men yelled. The ranks broke. They began to throw up their weapons and fire at the night. More troops puffed incandescently, flared up, were dead.

"Spread out!" screamed an officer as his gesturing fingers sprouted flame and his face went up in licking yellow heat.

The men looked everywhere. Their dumb terrified eyes searched for an enemy. They fired into the fields and woods. They shot each other. They broke into flopping runs over the mud.

A truck was enveloped in fire. Its driver leaped out, a two-legged torch. The truck went bumping over the road, turned, wove crazily over the field, crashed into a tree, exploded and was eaten up in blazing light. Black shadows flitted in and out of the aura of light around the flames. Screams rent the night.

Man after man burst into flame, fell crashing on his face in the mud. Spots of searing light lashed the wet darkness—screams—running coals, sputtering, glowing, dying—incendiary ranks—trucks cremated—tanks blowing up.

A little blonde, her body tense with repressed excitement. Her lips twitch, a giggle hovers in her throat. Her nostrils dilate. She shudders in giddy fright. She imagines, imagines. . . .

A soldier runs headlong across a field, screaming, his eyes insane with horror. A gigantic boulder rushes at him from the black sky.

His body is driven into the earth, mangled. From the rock edge, fingertips protrude.

The boulder lifts from the ground, crashes down again, a shapeless trip hammer. A flaming truck is flattened. The boulder flies again to the black sky.

A pretty brunette, her face a feverish mask. Wild thoughts tumble through her virginal brain. Her scalp grows taut with ecstatic fear. Her lips draw back from clenching teeth. A gasp of terror hisses from her lips. She imagines, imagines. . . .

A soldier falls to his knees. His head jerks back. In the light of burning comrades, he stares dumbly at the white-foamed wave that towers over him.

It crashes down, sweeps his body over the muddy earth, fills his lungs with salt water. The tidal wave roars over the field, drowns a hundred flaming men, tosses their corpses in the air with thundering whitecaps.

Suddenly the water stops, flies into a million pieces and disintegrates.

A lovely little redhead, hands drawn under her chin in tight bloodless fists. Her lips tremble, a throb of delight expands her chest. Her white throat contracts, she gulps in a breath of air. Her nose wrinkles with dreadful joy. She imagines, imagines. . . .

A running soldier collides with a lion. He cannot see in the darkness. His hands strike wildly at the shaggy mane. He clubs with his rifle butt.

A scream. His face is torn off with one blow of thick claws. A jungle roar billows in the night.

A red-eyed elephant tramples wildly through the mud, picking up men in its thick trunk, hurling them through the air, mashing them under driving black columns.

Wolves bound from the darkness, spring, tear at throats. Gorillas scream and bounce in the mud, leap at falling soldiers.

A rhinoceros, leather skin glowing in the light of living torches, crashes into a burning tank, wheels, thunders into blackness, is gone.

Fangs—claws—ripping teeth—shrieks—trumpeting—roars. The sky rains snakes.

Silence. Vast brooding silence. Not a breeze, not a drop of rain, not a grumble of distant thunder. The battle is ended.

Gray morning mist rolls over the burned, the torn, the drowned, the crushed, the poisoned, the sprawling dead.

Motionless trucks—silent tanks, wisps of oily smoke still rising from their shattered hulks. Great death covering the field. Another battle in another war.

Victory—everyone is dead.

The girls stretched languidly. They extended their arms and rotated their round shoulders. Pink lips grew wide in pretty little yawns. They looked at each other and tittered in embarrassment. Some of them blushed. A few looked guilty.

Then they all laughed out loud. They opened more gumpacks,

drew compacts from pockets, spoke intimately with schoolgirl whispers, with late-night dormitory whispers.

Muted giggles rose up fluttering in the warm room.

"Aren't we awful?" one of them said, powdering her pert nose.

Later they all went downstairs and had breakfast.

DANCE OF THE DEAD

I wanna RIDE!
with my Rota-Mota honey
by my SIDE!
As we whiz along the highway
We will HUG and SNUGGLE
And we'll have a
little STRUGGLE!

STRUGGLE (strug′ ′l), n., act of promiscuous loveplay; usage evolved during WW III.

Double beams spread buttery lamplight on the highway. Rotor-Motors Convertible, Model C, 1997, rushed after it. Light spurted ahead, yellow glowing. The car pursued with a twelve-cylindered snarling pursuit. Night blotted in behind, jet and still. The car sped on. ST. LOUIS—10.

"I wanna FLY!" they sang, "with the Rota-Mota apple of my EYE!" they sang. "It's the only way of living. . . ."

The quartet singing:

Len, 23.

Bud, 24.

Barbara, 20.

Peggy, 18.

Len with Barbara, Bud with Peggy.

Bud at the wheel, snapping around tilted curves, roaring up black-shouldered hills, shooting the car across silent flatlands. At the top of three lungs (the fourth gentler), competing with wind that buffeted their heads, that whipped their hair to lashing threads—singing:

"You can have your walkin' under MOONLIGHT BEAMS! At a hundred miles an hour let me DREAM my DREAMS!"

Needle quivering at 130, two 5-mph notches from gauge's end. *A sudden dip!* Their young frames jolted and the thrown-up laughter of three was windswept into night. Around a curve, darting up and down a hill, flashing across a leveled plain—an ebony bullet skimming earth.

"In my *ROTORY, MOTORY, FLOATERY*, drivin' machi-i-i-ine!"

"YOU'LL BE A FLOATER IN YOUR ROTOR-MOTOR."

In the back seat:
"Have a jab, Bab."
"Thanks, I had one after supper" (pushing away needle fixed to eye-dropper).
In the front seat:
"You meana tell me this is the first time you ever been t'Saint Loo!"
"But I just started school in September."
"Hey, you're a *frosh*!"
Back seat joining front seat:
"Hey, *frosh*, have a mussle-tussle."
(Needle passed forward, eye bulb quivering amber juice.)
"*Live* it, girl!"

MUSSLE-TUSSLE (mus´ 'l-tus´ 'l), n., slang for the result of inject-ing a drug into a muscle; usage evolved during WW III.

Peggy's lips failed at smiling. Her fingers twitched.

"No, thanks, I'm not . . ."

"Come *on*, frosh!" Len leaning hard over the seat, white-browed under black blowing hair. Pushing the needle at her face. "Live it, girl! Grab a li'l mussle-tussle!"

"I'd rather not," said Peggy. "If you don't—"

"What's '*at*, frosh?" yelled Len and pressed his leg against the pressing leg of Barbara.

Peggy shook her head and golden hair flew across her cheeks and eyes. Underneath her yellow dress, underneath her white brassiere, underneath her young breast—a heart throbbed heavily. *Watch your step, darling, that's all we ask. Remember, you're all we have in the world now.* Mother words drumming at her; the needle making her draw back into the seat.

"*Come* on, frosh!"

The car groaned its shifting weight around a curve and centrifu-gal force pressed Peggy into Bud's lean hip. His hand dropped down and fingered at her leg. Underneath her yellow dress, underneath her sheer stocking—flesh crawled. Lips failed again; the smile was a twitch of red.

"Frosh, live it up!"

"Lay off, Len, jab your own dates."

"But we gotta teach frosh how to mussle-tussle!"

"Lay off, I said! She's my date!"

The black car roaring, chasing its own light. Peggy anchored down the feeling hand with hers. The wind whistled over them and grabbed down chilly fingers at their hair. She didn't want his hand there but she felt grateful to him.

Her vaguely frightened eyes watched the road lurch beneath the wheels. In back, a silent struggle began, taut hands rubbing, parted mouths clinging. Search for the sweet elusive at 120 miles-per-hour.

"*Rota-Mota honey,*" Len moaned the moan between salivary kisses. In the front seat a young girl's heart beat unsteadily. ST. LOUIS—6.

"No kiddin', you never been to Saint Loo?"

"No, I . . ."

"Then you never saw the loopy's dance?"

Throat contracting suddenly. "No, I . . . is that what . . . we're going to—"

"Hey, frosh never saw the loopy's dance!" Bud yelled back.

Lips parted, slurping; skirt was adjusted with blasé aplomb. "No kiddin'!" Len fired up the words. "Girl, you haven't *lived*!"

"Oh, she's *got* to see *that*," said Barbara, buttoning a button.

"Let's go there then!" yelled Len. "Let's give frosh a thrill!"

"Good enough," said Bud and squeezed her leg. "Good enough up here, right, Peg?"

Peggy's throat moved in the dark and the wind clutched harshly at her hair. She'd heard of it, she'd read of it but never had she thought she'd—

Choose your school friends carefully, darling. Be very careful.

But when no one spoke to you for two whole months? When you were lonely and wanted to talk and laugh and be alive? And some-one spoke to you finally and asked you to go out with them?

"I yam Popeye, the sailor man!" Bud sang.

In back, they crowed artificial delight. Bud was taking a course in Pre-War Comics and Cartoons—2. This week the class was studying Popeye. Bud had fallen in love with the one-eyed seaman and told Len and Barbara all about him; taught them dialogue and song.

"I yam Popeye, the sailor man! I like to go swimmin' with bow-legged women! I yam Popeye, the sailor man!"

Laughter. Peggy smiled falteringly. The hand left her leg as the car screeched around a curve and she was thrown against the door. Wind

dashed blunt coldness in her eyes and forced her back, blinking.
110—115—120 miles-per-hour. ST. LOUIS—3. *Be very careful, dear.*

Popeye cocked wicked eye.

"O, Olive Oyl, you is my sweet patootie."

Elbow nudging Peggy. "You be Olive Oyl—*you.*"

Peggy smiled nervously. "I can't."

"*Sure!*"

In the back seat, Wimpy came up for air to announce, "I will gladly pay you Tuesday for a hamburger today."

Three fierce voices and a faint fourth raged against the howl of wind. "I fights to the *fin*-ish 'cause I eats my *spin*-ach! I yam Popeye, the sailor man! *Toot! Toot!*"

"I yam what I yam," reiterated Popeye gravelly and put his hand on the yellow-skirted leg of Olive Oyl. In the back, two members of the quartet returned to feeling struggle.

ST. LOUIS—1. The black car roared through the darkened suburbs. "On with the noises!" Bud sang out. They all took out their plasticate nose-and-mouth pieces and adjusted them.

ANCE IN YOUR PANTS WOULD BE A PITY!
WEAR YOUR NOSIES IN THE CITY!!

ANCE (anse), n., slang for anticivilian germs; usage evolved during WW III.

"You'll like the loopy's dance!" Bud shouted to her over the shriek of wind. "It's sen-*saysh!*"

Peggy felt a cold that wasn't of the night or of the wind. *Remember, darling, there are terrible things in the world today. Things you must avoid.*

"Couldn't we go somewhere else?" Peggy said but her voice was inaudible. She heard Bud singing, "I like to go swimmin' with bow-legged women!" She felt his hand on her leg again while, in the back, was the silence of grinding passion without kisses.

Dance of the dead. The words trickled ice across Peggy's brain.

ST. LOUIS.

The black car sped into the ruins.

It was a place of smoke and blatant joys. Air resounded with the bleating of revelers and there was a noise of sounding brass spinning out a cloud of music—1997 music, a frenzy of twisted dissonances. Dancers, shoe-horned into the tiny square of open floor, ground pulsing bodies together. A network of bursting sounds lanced through the mass of them; dancers singing:

"Hurt me! Bruise me! Squeeze me TIGHT!
Scorch my blood with hot DELIGHT!
Please abuse me every NIGHT!
LOVER, LOVER, LOVER, be a beast-to-me!"

Elements of explosion restrained within the dancing bounds— instead of fragmenting, quivering. "Oh, be a beast, beast, beast, *Beast*, BEAST to me!"

"How is *this*, Olive old goil?" Popeye inquired of the light of his eye as they struggled after the waiter. "Nothin' like this in Sykesville, eh?"

Peggy smiled but her hand in Bud's felt numb. As they passed by a murky lighted table, a hand she didn't see felt at her leg. She twitched and bumped against a hard knee across the narrow aisle. As she stumbled and lurched through the hot and smoky, thick-aired room, she felt a dozen eyes disrobing her, abusing her. Bud jerked her along and she felt her lips trembling.

"Hey, how about that!" Bud exulted as they sat. "Right by the stage!"

From cigarette mists, the waiter plunged and hovered, pencil poised, beside their table.

"What'll it be!" His questioning shout cut through cacophony.

"Whiskey-water!" Bud and Len paralleled orders, then turned to their dates. "What'll it be!" the waiter's request echoed from their lips.

"Green Swamp!" Barbara said and, *"Green Swamp* here!" Len passed it along. Gin, Invasion Blood (1997 Rum), lime juice, sugar, mint spray, splintered ice—a popular college girl drink.

"What about you, honey?" Bud asked his date.

Peggy smiled. "Just some ginger ale," she said, her voice a fluttering frailty in the massive clash and fog of smoke.

"What?" asked Bud and, "What's that, didn't hear!" the waiter shouted.

"Ginger ale."

"What?"

"Ginger ale!"

"GINGER ALE!" Len screamed it out and the drummer, behind the raging curtain of noise that was the band's music, almost heard it. Len banged down his fist. *One—Two—Three!*

CHORUS: *Ginger Ale was only twelve years old!*
Went to church and was as good as gold.
Till that day when—

"Come *on*, come *on!*" the waiter squalled. "Let's have that order, kids! I'm busy!"

"Two whiskey-waters and two Green Swamps!" Len sang out and the waiter was gone into the swirling maniac mist.

Peggy felt her young heart flutter helplessly. *Above all, don't drink when you're out on a date. Promise us that, darling, you must promise us that.* She tried to push away instructions etched in brain.

"How you like this place, honey? *Loopy*, ain't it?" Bud fired the question at her; a red-faced, happy-faced Bud.

LOOPY (lōō´ pī), adj., common alter. of L.U.P.

She smiled at Bud, a smile of nervous politeness. Her eyes moved around, her face inclined and she was looking up at the stage. *Loopy.* The word scalpeled at her mind. *Loopy, loopy.*

The stage was five yards deep at the radius of its wooden semicircle. A waist-high rail girdled the circumference, two pale purple spotlights, unlit, hung at each rail end. Purple on white— the thought came. *Darling, isn't Sykesville Business College good enough? No! I don't want to take a business course, I want to major in art at the University!*

The drinks were brought and Peggy watched the disembodied waiter's arm thud down a high, green-looking glass before her. *Presto!*—the arm was gone. She looked into the murky green swamp depths and saw chipped ice bobbing.

"A toast! Pick up your glass, Peg!" Bud clarioned.

They all clinked glasses:

"To lust primordial!" Bud toasted.

"To beds intemperate!" Len added.

"To flesh insensate!" Barbara added a third link.

Their eyes zeroed in on Peggy's face, demanding. She didn't understand.

"Finish it!" Bud told her, plagued by freshman sluggishness.

"To . . . u-*us*," she faltered.

"How o-*ri*-ginal," stabbed Barbara and Peggy felt heat licking up her smooth cheeks. It passed unnoticed as three Youths of America with Whom the Future Rested gurgled down their liquor thirstily. Peggy fingered at her glass, a smile printed to lips that would not smile unaided.

"Come on, *drink*, girl!" Bud shouted to her across the vast distance of one foot. "Chuggalug!"

"Live it, girl," Len suggested abstractedly, fingers searching once more for soft leg. And finding, under the table, soft leg waiting.

Peggy didn't want to drink, she was afraid to drink. Mother words kept pounding—*never on a date, honey, never*. She raised the glass a little.

"Uncle Buddy will help, will help!"

Uncle Buddy leaning close, vapor of whiskey haloing his head. Uncle Buddy pushing cold glass to shaking young lips. "Come on, Olive Oyl, old goil! Down the hatch!"

Choking sprayed the bosom of her dress with green swamp droplets. Flaming liquid trickled into her stomach, sending offshoots of fire into her veins.

Bangity boom crash smash POW!! The drummer applied the *coup de grâce* to what had been, in ancient times, a lover's waltz. Lights dropped and Peggy sat coughing and tear-eyed in the smoky cellar club.

She felt Bud's hand clamp strongly on her shoulder and, in the murk, she felt herself pulled off balance and felt Bud's hot wet mouth pressing at her lips. She jerked away and then the purple spots went on and a mottle-faced Bud drew back, gurgling, "I fights to the finish," and reaching for his drink.

"Hey, the loopy now, the loopy!" Len said eagerly, releasing exploratory hands.

Peggy's heart jolted and she thought she was going to cry out and run thrashing through the dark, smoke-filled room. But a sophomore hand anchored her to the chair and she looked up in white-faced dread at the man who came out on the stage and faced the microphone which, like a metal spider, had swung down to meet him.

"May I have your attention, ladies and gentlemen," he said, a grim-faced, sepulchral-voiced man whose eyes moved out over them like flicks of doom. Peggy's breath was labored, she felt thin lines of green swamp water filtering hotly through her chest and stomach. It made her blink dizzily. *Mother.* The word escaped cells of the mind and trembled into conscious freedom. *Mother, take me home.*

"As you know, the act you are about to see is not for the faint of heart, the weak of will." The man plodded through the words like a cow enmired. "Let me caution those of you whose nerves are not what they ought to be—*leave now.* We make no guarantees of responsibility. We can't even afford to maintain a house doctor."

No laughter appreciative. "Cut the crap and get off stage," Len grumbled to himself. Peggy felt her fingers twitching.

"As you know," the man went on, his voice gilded with learned sonority, "this is not an offering of mere sensation but an honest scientific demonstration."

"Loophole for Loopy's!" Bud and Len heaved up the words with the thoughtless reaction of hungry dogs salivating at a bell.

It was, in 1997, a comeback so rigidly standard it had assumed the status of a catechism answer. A crenel in the postwar law allowed the LUP performance if it was orally prefaced as an exposition of science. Through this legal chink had poured so much abusing of the law that few cared any longer. A feeble government was grateful to contain infractions of the law at all.

When hoots and shoutings had evaporated in the smoke-clogged air, the man, his arms upraised in patient benediction, spoke again.

Peggy watched the studied movement of his lips, her heart swelling, then contracting in slow, spasmodic beats. An iciness was creeping up her legs. She felt it rising toward the threadlike fires in her body and her fingers twitched around the chilly moisture of the glass. *I want to go, please take me home—* Will-spent words were in her mind again.

"Ladies and gentlemen," the man concluded, "brace yourselves."

A gong sounded its hollow, shivering resonance, the man's voice thickened and slowed.

"The L.U. Phenomenon!"

The man was gone; the microphone had risen and was gone. Music began; a moaning brassiness, all muted. A jazzman's conception of *the palpable obscure*—mounted on a pulse of thumping drum. A dolor of saxophone, a menace of trombone, a harnessed bleating of trumpet—they raped the air with stridor.

Peggy felt a shudder plaiting down her back and her gaze dropped quickly to the murky whiteness of the table. Smoke and darkness, dissonance and heat surrounded her.

Without meaning to, but driven by an impulse of nervous fear, she raised the glass and drank. The glacial trickle in her throat sent another shudder rippling through her. Then further shoots of liquored heat budded in her veins and a numbness settled in her temples. Through parted lips, she forced out a shaking breath.

Now a restless, murmuring movement started through the room, the sound of it like willows in a soughing wind. Peggy dared not lift her gaze to the purpled silence of the stage. She stared down at the shifting glimmer of her drink, feeling muscle strands draw tightly in her stomach, feeling the hollow thumping of her heart. *I'd like to leave, please let's leave.*

The music labored toward a rasping dissonant climax, its brass components struggling, in vain, for unity.

A hand stroked once at Peggy's leg and it was the hand of Popeye, the sailor man, who muttered roupily, "Olive Oyl, you is my goil." She barely felt or heard. Automatonlike, she raised the cold and sweating glass again and felt the chilling in her throat and then the flaring network of warmth inside her.

SWISH!

The curtain swept open with such a rush, she almost dropped her glass. It thumped down heavily on the table, swamp water cascading up its sides and raining on her hand. The music exploded shrapnel of ear-cutting cacophony and her body jerked. On the tablecloth, her hands twitched white on white while claws of uncontrollable demand pulled up her frightened eyes.

The music fled, frothing behind a wake of swelling drum rolls. The nightclub was a wordless crypt, all breathing checked. Cobwebs of smoke drifted in the purple light across the stage. No sound except the muffled, rolling drum.

Peggy's body was a petrifaction in its chair, smitten to rock around her leaping heart, while, through the wavering haze of smoke and liquored dizziness, she looked up in horror to where it stood.

It had been a woman.

Her hair was black, a framing of snarled ebony for the tallow mask that was her face. Her shadow-rimmed eyes were closed behind lids as smooth and white as ivory. Her mouth, a lipless and unmoving line, stood like a clotted sword wound beneath her nose. Her throat, her shoulders and her arms were white, were motionless. At her sides, protruding from the sleeve ends of the green transparency she wore, hung alabaster hands.

Across this marble statue, the spotlights coated purple shimmer.

Still paralyzed, Peggy stared up at its motionless features, her fingers knitted in a bloodless tangle on her lap. The pulse of drumbeats in the air seemed to fill her body, its rhythm altering her heartbeat.

In the black emptiness behind her, she heard Len muttering, "I love my wife but, oh, you corpse," and heard the wheeze of helpless snickers that escaped from Bud and Barbara. The cold still rose in her, a silent tidal dread.

Somewhere in the smoke-fogged darkness, a man cleared viscid nervousness from his throat and a murmur of appreciative relief strained through the audience.

Still no motion on the stage, no sound but the sluggish cadence of the drum, thumping at the silence like someone seeking entrance at a far-off door. The thing that was a nameless victim of the plague stood palely rigid while the distillation sluiced through its blood-clogged veins.

Now the drum throbs hastened like the pulsebeat of a rising panic.

Peggy felt the chill begin to swallow her. Her throat started tightening, her breathing was a string of lip-parted gasps.

The loopy's eyelid twitched.

Abrupt, black, straining silence webbed the room. Even the breath choked off in Peggy's throat when she saw the pale eyes flutter open. Something creaked in the stillness; her body pressed back unconsciously against the chair. Her eyes were wide, unblinking circles that sucked into her brain the sight of the thing that had been a woman.

Music again; a brass-throated moaning from the dark, like some animal made of welded horns mewling its derangement in a midnight alley.

Suddenly, the right arm of the loopy jerked at its side, the tendons contracted. The left arm twitched alike, snapped out, then fell back and thudded in purple-white limpness against the thigh. The right arm out, the left arm out, the right, the left-right-left-right—like marionette arms twitching from an amateur's dangling strings.

The music caught the time, drum brushes scratching out a rhythm for the convulsions of the loopy's muscles. Peggy pressed back further, her body numbed and cold, her face a livid, staring mask in the fringes of the stage light.

The loopy's right foot moved now, jerking up inflexibly as the distillation constricted muscles in its leg. A second and a third contraction caused the leg to twitch, the left leg flung out in a violent spasm and then the woman's body lurched stiffly forward, filming the transparent silk to its light and shadow.

Peggy heard the sudden hiss of breath that passed the clenching teeth of Bud and Len and a wave of nausea sprayed foaming sickness up her stomach walls. Before her eyes, the stage abruptly undulated with a watery glitter and it seemed as if the flailing loopy was headed straight for her.

Gasping dizzily, she pressed back in horror, unable to take her eyes from its now agitated face.

She watched the mouth jerk to a gaping cavity, then a twisted scar that split into a wound again. She saw the dark nostrils twitching, saw writhing flesh beneath the ivory cheeks, saw furrows dug and undug in the purple whiteness of the forehead. She saw one lifeless eye wink monstrously and heard the gasp of startled laughter in the room.

While music blared into a fit of grating noise, the woman's arms and legs kept jerking with convulsive cramps that threw her body around the purpled stage like a full-sized rag doll given spastic life.

It was a nightmare in an endless sleep. Peggy shivered in helpless terror as she watched the loopy's twisting, leaping dance. The blood in her had turned to ice; there was no life in her but the endless, pounding stagger of her heart. Her eyes were frozen spheres staring at the woman's body writhing white and flaccid underneath the clinging silk.

Then, something went wrong.

Up till then, its muscular seizures had bound the loopy to an area of several yards before the amber flat which was the background for its paroxysmal dance. Now its erratic surging drove the loopy toward the stage-encircling rail.

Peggy heard the thump and creaking strain of wood as the loopy's hip collided with the rail. She cringed into a shuddering knot, her eyes still raised fixedly to the purple-splashed face whose every feature was deformed by throes of warping convulsion.

The loopy staggered back and Peggy saw and heard its leprous hands slapping with a fitful rhythm at its silk-scaled thighs.

Again it sprang forward like a maniac marionette and the woman's stomach thudded sickeningly into the railing wood. The dark mouth gaped, clamped shut and then the loopy twisted through a jerking revolution and crashed back against the rail again, almost above the table where Peggy sat.

Peggy couldn't breathe. She sat rooted to the chair, her lips a trembling circle of stricken dread, a pounding of blood at her temples as she watched the loopy spin again, its arms a blur of flailing white.

The lurid bleaching of its face dropped toward Peggy as the loopy crashed into the waist-high rail again and bent across its top. The mask of lavender-rained whiteness hung above her, dark eyes twitching open into a hideous stare.

Peggy felt the floor begin to move and the livid face was blurred with darkness, then reappeared in a burst of luminosity. Sound fled on brass-shoed feet, then plunged into her brain again—a smearing discord.

The loopy kept on jerking forward, driving itself against the rail as though it meant to scale it. With every spastic lurch, the diaphanous silk fluttered like a film about its body and every savage collision with the railing tautened the green transparency across its swollen flesh. Peggy looked up in rigid muteness at the loopy's fierce attack on the railing, her eyes unable to escape the wild distortion of the woman's face with its black frame of tangled, snapping hair.

What happened then happened in a blurring passage of seconds.

The grim-faced man came rushing across the purple-lighted stage; the thing that had been a woman went crashing, twitching, flailing at the rail, doubling over it, the spasmodic hitching flinging up its muscle-knotted legs.

A clawing fall.

Peggy lurched back in her chair and the scream that started in her throat was forced back into a strangled gag as the loopy came crashing down onto the table, its limbs a thrash of naked whiteness.

Barbara screamed, the audience gasped and Peggy saw, on the fringe of vision, Bud jumping up, his face a twist of stunned surprise.

The loopy flopped and twisted on the table like a new-caught fish. The music stopped, grinding into silence; a rush of agitated murmur filled the room and blackness swept in brain-submerging waves across Peggy's mind.

Then the cold white hand slapped across her mouth, the dark eyes stared at her in purple light and Peggy felt the darkness flooding.

The horror-smoked room went turning on its side.

❊

Consciousness. It flickered in her brain like gauze-veiled candle-light. A murmuring of sound, a blur of shadow before her eyes.

Breath dripped like syrup from her mouth.

"Here, Peg."

She heard Bud's voice and felt the chilly metal of a flask neck pressed against lips. She swallowed, twisting slightly at the trickle of fire in her throat and stomach, then coughed and pushed away the flask with deadened fingers.

Behind her, a rustling movement. "Hey, she's *back*," Len said. "Ol' Olive Oyl is back."

"You feel all right?" asked Barbara.

She felt all right. Her heart was like a drum hanging from piano wire in her chest, slowly, slowly beaten. Her hands and feet were numb, not with cold but with a sultry torpor. Thoughts moved with a tranquil lethargy, her brain a leisurely machine imbedded in swaths of woolly packing.

She felt all right.

Peggy looked across the night with sleepy eyes. They were on a hilltop, the braked convertible crouching on a jutting edge. Far below, the country slept, a carpet of light and shadow beneath the chalky moon.

An arm snake moved around her waist. "Where are we?" she asked him in a languid voice.

"Few miles outside school," Bud said. "How d'ya feel, honey?"

She stretched, her body a delicious strain of muscles. She sagged back, limp, against his arm.

"*Wonderful,*" she murmured with a dizzy smile and scratched the tiny itching bump on her left shoulder. Warmth radiated through her flesh; the night was a sabled glow. There seemed—*somewhere*—to be a memory, but it crouched in secret behind folds of thick content.

"Woman, you were *out*," laughed Bud; and Barbara added and Len added, "*Were* you!" and "Olive Oyl went *plunko!*"

"Out?" Her casual murmur went unheard.

The flask went around and Peggy drank again, relaxing further as the liquor needled fire through her veins.

"Man, I never saw a loopy dance like that!" Len said.

A momentary chill across her back, then warmth again. "Oh," said Peggy, "that's right. I forgot."

She smiled.

"That was what I calls a grand finale!" Len said, dragging back his willing date, who murmured, "*Lenny* boy."

"LUP," Bud muttered, nuzzling at Peggy's hair. "Son of a gun." He reached out idly for the radio knob.

LUP (Lifeless Undead Phenomenon)—This freak of physiological abnormality was discovered during the war when, following certain germ-gas attacks, many of the dead troops were found erect and performing the spasmodic gyrations which, later, became known as the "loopy's" (LUP's) dance. The particular germ spray responsible was later distilled and is now used in carefully controlled experiments which are conducted only under the strictest of legal license and supervision.

Music surrounded them, its melancholy fingers touching at their hearts. Peggy leaned against her date and felt no need to curb exploring hands. Somewhere, deep within the jellied layers of her mind, there was something trying to escape. It fluttered like a frantic moth imprisoned in congealing wax, struggling wildly but only growing weaker in attempt as the chrysalis hardened.

Four voices sang softly in the night.

"If the world is here tomorrow
I'll be waiting, dear, for you
If the stars are there tomorrow
I'll be wishing on them too."

Four young voices singing, a murmur in immensity. Four bodies, two by two, slackly warm and drugged. A singing, an embracing— a wordless accepting.

"Star light, star bright
Let there be another night."

The singing ended but the song went on.
A young girl sighed.
"Isn't it romantic?" said Olive Oyl.

DRESS OF WHITE SILK

Quiet is here and all in me.

Granma locked me in my room and wont let me out. Because its happened she says. I guess I was bad. Only it was the dress. Mommas dress I mean. She is gone away forever. Granma says your momma is in heaven. I dont know how. Can she go in heaven if shes dead?

Now I hear granma. She is in mommas room. She is putting mommas dress down the box. Why does she always? And locks it too. I wish she didnt. Its a pretty dress and smells sweet so. And warm. I love to touch it against my cheek. But I cant never again. I guess that is why granma is mad at me.

But I amnt sure. All day it was only like everyday. Mary Jane came over to my house. She lives across the street. Everyday she comes to my house and play. Today she was.

I have seven dolls and a fire truck. Today granma said play with your dolls and it. Dont you go inside your mommas room now she said. She always says it. She just means not mess up I think. Because she says it all the time. Dont go in your mommas room. Like that.

But its nice in mommas room. When it rains I go there. Or when granma is doing her nap I do. I dont make noise. I just sit on the bed and touch the white cover. Like when I was only small. The room smells like sweet.

I make believe momma is dressing and I am allowed in. I smell her white silk dress. Her going out for night dress. She called it that I dont remember when.

I hear it moving if I listen hard. I make believe to see her sitting at the dressing table. Like touching on perfume or something I mean. And see her dark eyes. I can remember.

Its so nice if it rains and I see eyes on the window. The rain sounds like a big giant outside. He says shushshush so every one will be quiet. I like to make believe that in mommas room.

What I like almost best is to sit at mommas dressing table. It is like pink and big and smells sweet too. The seat in front has a pillow sewed in it. There are bottles and bottles with bumps and have colored perfume in them. And you can see almost your whole self in the mirror.

When I sit there I make believe to be momma. I say be quiet mother I am going out and you can not stop me. It is something I say I dont know why like I hear it in me. And oh stop your sobbing mother they will not catch me I have my magic dress.

When I pretend I brush my hair long. But I only use my own brush from my room. I didnt never use mommas brush. I dont think granma is mad at me for that because I never use mommas brush. I wouldnt never.

Sometimes I did open the box up. Because I know where granma puts the key. I saw her once when she wouldnt know I saw her. She puts the key on the hook in mommas closet. Behind the door I mean.

I could open the box lots of times. Thats because I like to look at mommas dress. I like best to look at it. It is so pretty and feels soft and like silky. I could touch it for a million years.

I kneel on the rug with roses on it. I hold the dress in my arms and like breathe from it. I touch it against my cheek. I wish I could take it to sleep with me and hold it. I like to. Now I cant. Because granma says. And she says I should burn it up but I loved her so. And she cries about the dress.

I wasnt never bad with it. I put it back neat like it was never

touched. Granma never knew. I laughed that she never knew before.
But she knows now I did it I guess. And shell punish me. What did
it hurt her? Wasnt it my mommas dress?

What I like real best in mommas room is look at the picture of
momma. It has a gold thing around it. Frame is what granma says.
It is on the wall on top the bureau.

Momma is pretty. Your momma was pretty granma says. Why
does she? I see momma there smiling on me and she *is* pretty. For always.

Her hair is black. Like mine. Her eyes are even pretty like black.
Her mouth is red so red. I like the dress and its the white one. It is
all down on her shoulders. Her skin is white almost white like the
dress. And so are her hands. She is so pretty. I love her even if she is
gone away forever. I love her so much.

I guess I think thats what made me bad. I mean to Mary Jane.

Mary Jane came from lunch like she does. Granma went to do her
nap. She said dont forget now no going to your mommas room. I
told her no granma. And I was saying the truth but then Mary Jane
and I was playing fire truck. Mary Jane said I bet you havent no
mother I bet you made up it all she said.

I got mad at her. I have a momma I know. She made me mad at
her to say I made up it all. She said Im a liar. I mean about the bed
and the dressing table and the picture and the dress even and every
thing.

I said well Ill show you smarty.

I looked into granmas room. She was doing her nap still. I went
down and said Mary Jane to come on because granma wont know.

She wasnt so smart after then. She giggled like she does. Even she
made a scaredy noise when she hit into the table in the hall upstairs.
I said youre a scaredy cat to her. She said back well *my* house isnt so
dark like this. Like that was so much.

We went in mommas room. It was more dark than you could see.
I said this is my mommas room I suppose I made up it all.

She was by the door and she wasnt smart then either. She didnt say any word. She looked around the room. She jumped when I got her arm. Well come on I said.

I sat on the bed and said this is my mommas bed see how soft it is. She didnt say nothing. Scaredy cat I said. Am not she said like she does.

I said to sit down how can you tell if its soft if you dont sit down. She sat down by me. I said feel how soft it is. Smell how sweet it is.

I closed my eyes but funny it wasnt like always. Because Mary Jane was there. I told her to stop feeling the cover. You said to she said. Well stop it I said.

See I said and I pulled her up. Thats the dressing table. I took her and brought her there. She said let go. It was so quiet and like always. I started to feel bad. Because Mary Jane was there. Because it was in my mommas room and momma wouldnt like Mary Jane there.

But I had to show her the things because. I showed her the mirror. We looked at each other in it. She looked white. Mary Jane is a scaredy cat I said. Am not am not she said anyway nobodys house is so quiet and dark inside. Anyway she said it smells.

I got mad at her. No it doesnt smell I said. Does so she said you said it did. I got madder too. It smells like sugar she said. It smells like sick people in your mommas room.

Dont say my mommas room is like sick people I said to her.

Well you didnt show me no dress and youre lying she said there isnt no dress. I felt all warm inside so I pulled her hair. Ill show you I said youre going to see my mommas dress and youll better not call me a liar.

I made her stand still and I got the key off the hook. I kneeled down. I opened the box with the key.

Mary Jane said pew that smells like garbage.

I put my nails in her and she pulled away and got mad. Dont you pinch me she said and she was all red. Im telling my mother on you she said. And anyway its not a white dress its dirty and ugly she said.

Its not dirty I said. I said it so loud I wonder why granma didnt hear. I pulled out the dress from the box. I held it up to show her how its white. It fell open like the rain whispering and the bottom touched on the rug.

It is too white I said all white and clean and silky.

No she said she was so mad and red it has a hole in it. I got more madder. If my momma was here shed show you I said. You got no momma she said all ugly. I hate her.

I have. I said it way loud. I pointed my finger to mommas picture. Well who can see in this stupid dark room she said. I pushed her hard and she hit against the bureau. See then I said mean look at the picture. Thats my momma and shes the most beautiful lady in the world.

Shes ugly she has funny hands Mary Jane said. She hasnt I said shes the most beautiful lady in the world!

Not not she said *she has buck teeth.*

I dont remember then. I think the dress moved in my arms. Mary Jane screamed. I dont remember what. It got dark and the curtains were closed I think. I couldnt see anyway. I couldnt hear nothing except buck teeth funny hands buck teeth funny hands even when no one was saying it.

There was something else because I think I heard some one call *dont let her say that!* I couldnt hold to the dress. And I had it on me I cant remember. Because I was grown up strong. But I was a little girl still I think. I mean outside.

I think I was terrible bad then.

Granma took me away from there I guess. I dont know. She was screaming god help us its happened its happened. Over and over. I dont know why. She pulled me all the way here to my room and locked me in. She wont let me out. Well Im not so scared. Who cares if she locks me in a million billion years? She doesn't have to even give me supper. Im not hungry anyway.

Im full.

MAD HOUSE

He sits down at his desk. He picks up a long, yellow pencil and starts to write on a pad. The lead point breaks.

The ends of his lips turn down. The eye pupils grow small in the hard mask of his face. Quietly, mouth pressed into an ugly, lipless gash, he picks up the pencil sharpener.

He grinds off the shavings and tosses the sharpener back in the drawer. Once more he starts to write. As he does so, the point snaps again and the lead rolls across the paper.

Suddenly his face becomes livid. Wild rage clamps the muscles of his body. He yells at the pencil, curses it with a stream of outrage. He glares at it with actual hate. He breaks it in two with a brutal snap and flings it into the wastebasket with a triumphant, "There! See how you like it in *there!*"

He sits tensely on the chair, his eyes wide, his lips trembling. He shakes with a frenzied wrath; it sprays his insides with acid.

The pencil lies in the wastebasket, broken and still. It is wood, lead, metal, rubber; all dead, without appreciation of the burning fury it has caused.

And yet . . .

He is quietly standing by the window, peering out at the street. He is letting the tightness sough away. He does not hear the rustle in the wastebasket which ceases immediately.

Soon his body is normal again. He sits down. He uses a foun-tain pen.

✦

He sits down before his typewriter.

He inserts a sheet of paper and begins tapping on the keys.

His fingers are large. He hits two keys at once. The two strikers are jammed together. They stand in the air, hovering impotently over the black ribbon.

He reaches over in disgust and slaps them back. They separate, flap back into their separate berths. He starts typing again.

He hits a wrong key. The start of a curse falls from his lips, un-finished. He snatches up the round eraser and rubs the unwanted let-ter from the sheet of paper.

He drops the eraser and starts to type again. The paper has shifted on the roller. The next sentences are on a level slightly above the orig-inal. He clenches a fist, ignores the mistake.

The machine sticks. His shoulders twitch, he slams a fist on the space bar with a loud curse. The carriage jumps, the bell tinkles. He shoves the carriage over and it crashes to a halt.

He types faster. Three keys stick together. He clenches his teeth and whines in helpless fury. He smacks the type arms. They will not come apart. He forces them to separate with bent, shaking fingers. They fall away. He sees that his fingers are smudged with ink. He curses out loud, trying to outrage the very air for revenge on the stu-pid machine.

Now he hits the keys brutally, fingers falling like the stiff claws of a derrick. Another mistake, he erases savagely. He types still faster. Four keys stick together.

He screams.

He slams his fist on the machine. He clutches at the paper and rips it from the machine in jagged pieces. He welds the fragments in his fist and hurls the crumpled ball across the room. He beats the carriage over and slams the cover down on the machine.

He jumps up and glares down.

"You fool!" he shouts with a bitter, revolted voice. "You stupid, idiotic, asinine *fool*!"

Scorn drips from his voice. He keeps talking, he drives himself into a craze.

"You're no damn good. You're no damn good at all. I'm going to break you in pieces. I'm going to crack you into splinters, melt you, *kill* you! You stupid, moronic, lousy goddamn machine!"

He quivers as he yells. And he wonders, deep in the self-isolated recesses of his mind whether he is killing himself with anger, whether he is destroying his system with fury.

He turns and stalks away. He is too outraged to notice the cover of the machine slip down and hear the slight whirring of metal such as he might hear if the keys trembled in their slots.

He is shaving. The razor will not cut. Or the razor is too sharp and cuts too much.

Both times a muffled curse billows through his lips. He hurls the razor on the floor and kicks it against the wall.

He is cleaning his teeth. He draws the fine silk floss between his teeth. It shreds off. A fuzzy bit remains in the gap. He tries to press another piece down to get that bit out. He cannot force the white thread down. It snaps in his fingers.

He screams. He screams at the man in the mirror and draws back his hand, throws the floss away violently. It hits the wall. It hangs there and waves in the rush of angry breeze from the man.

He has torn another piece of floss from the container. He is giving the dental floss another chance. He is holding back his fury. If the floss knows what is good for it, it will plunge down between the teeth and draw out the shredded bit immediately.

It does. The man is mollified. The systematic juices leave off bubbling, the fires sink, the coals are scattered.

But the anger is still there, apart. Energy is never lost; a primal law.

He is eating.

His wife places a steak before him. He picks up the knife and fork and slices. The meat is tough, the blade is dull.

A spot of red puffs up in the flesh of his cheeks. His eyes narrow. He draws the knife through the meat. The blade will not sever the browned flesh.

His eyes widen. Withheld tempest tightens and shakes him. He saws at the meat as though to give it one last opportunity to yield.

The meat will not yield.

He howls. *"God damn it!"* White teeth jam together. The knife is hurled across the room.

The woman appears, alarm etching transient scars on her forehead. Her husband is beyond himself. Her husband is shooting poison through his arteries. Her husband is releasing another cloud of animal temper. It is mist that clings. It hangs over the furniture, drips from the walls.

It is alive.

So through the days and nights. His anger falling like frenzied axe blows in his house, on everything he owns. Sprays of teeth-grinding hysteria clouding his windows and falling to his floors. Oceans of wild, uncontrolled hate flooding through every room of his house; filling each iota of space with a shifting, throbbing life.

He lay on his back and stared at the sun-mottled ceiling.

The last day, he told himself. The phrase had been creeping in and out of his brain since he'd awakened.

In the bathroom he could hear the water running. He could hear the medicine cabinet being opened and then closed again. He could hear the sound of her slippers shuffling on the tile floor.

Sally, he thought, don't leave me.

"I'll take it easy if you stay," he promised the air in a whisper.

But he knew he couldn't take it easy. That was too hard. It was easier to fly off the handle, easier to scream and rant and attack.

He turned on his side and stared out into the hall at the bathroom door. He could see the line of light under the door. Sally is in there, he thought. Sally, my wife, whom I married many years ago when I was young and full of hope.

He closed his eyes suddenly and clenched his fists. It came on him again. The sickness that prevailed with more violence every time he contracted it. The sickness of despair, of lost ambition. It ruined everything. It cast a vapor of bitterness over all his comings and goings. It jaded appetite, ruined sleep, destroyed affection.

"Perhaps if we'd had children," he muttered and knew before he said it that it wasn't the answer.

Children. How happy they would be watching their wretched father sinking deeper into his pit of introspective fever each day.

All right, tortured his mind, let's have the facts. He gritted his teeth and tried to make his mind a blank. But, like a dull-eyed idiot, his mind repeated the words that he muttered often in his sleep through restless, tossing nights.

I'm forty years old. I teach English at Fort College. Once I had hoped to be a writer. I thought this would be a fine place to write. I would teach class part of the day and write with the rest of my time. I met Sally at school and married her. I thought everything would be just fine. I thought success was inevitable. Eighteen years ago.

Eighteen years.

How, he thought, did you mark the passing of almost two decades? The time seemed a shapeless lump of failing efforts, of nights spent in anguish; of the secret, the answer, the revelation always being withheld from him. Dangled overhead like cheese swinging in a maddening arc over the head of a berserk rat.

And resentment creeping. Days spent watching Sally buy food and clothing and pay rent with his meager salary. Watching her buy new curtains or new chair covers and feeling a stab of pain every time because he was that much farther removed from the point where he could devote his time to writing. Every penny she spent he felt like a blow at his aspirations.

He forced himself to think that way. He forced himself to believe that it was only the time he needed to do good writing.

But once a furious student had yelled at him, "You're just a third-rate talent hiding behind a desk!"

He remembered that. Oh, God, how he remembered that moment. Remembered the cold sickness that had convulsed him when those words hit his brain. Recalled the trembling and the shaky unreason of his voice.

He had failed the student for the semester despite good marks. There had been a great to-do about it. The student's father had come to the school. They had all gone before Dr. Ramsay, the head of the English Department.

He remembered that too; the scene could crowd out all other memories. Him, sitting on one side of the conference table, facing the irate father and son. Dr. Ramsay stroking his beard until he thought he'd hurl something at him. Dr. Ramsay had said—well let's see if we can't straighten out this matter.

They had consulted the record book and found the student was right. Dr. Ramsay had looked up at him in great surprise. Well, I can't see what . . . he had said and let his syrupy voice break off and looked probingly at him, waiting for an explanation.

And the explanation had been hopeless, a jumbled and pointless affair. Irresponsible attitude, he had said, flaunting of unpardonable behavior; morally a failure. And Dr. Ramsay, his thick neck getting red, telling him in no uncertain terms that morals were not subject to the grading system at Fort College.

There was more but he'd forgotten it. He'd made an effort to forget it. But he couldn't forget that it would be years before he made a professorship. Ramsay would hold it back. And his salary would go on being insufficient and bills would mount and he would never get his writing done.

He regained the present to find himself clutching the sheets with taut fingers. He found himself glaring in hate at the bathroom door. Go on!—his mind snapped vindictively—Go home to your precious mother. See if I care. Why just a trial separation? Make it permanent. Give me some peace. Maybe I can do some writing then.

Maybe I can do some writing then.

The phrase made him sick. It had no meaning anymore. Like a word that is repeated until it becomes gibberish that sentence, for him, had been used to extinction. It sounded silly; like some bit of cliché from a soap opera. Hero saying in dramatic tones—Now, by God, maybe I can do some writing. Senseless.

For a moment, though, he wondered if it was true. Now that she was leaving could he forget about her and really get some work done? Quit his job? Go somewhere and hole up in a cheap furnished room and write?

You have $123.89 in the bank, his mind informed him. He pretended it was the only thing that kept him from it. But, far back in his mind, he wondered if he could write anywhere. Often the question threw itself at him when he was least expecting it. You have four hours every morning, the statement would rise like a menacing wraith. You have time to write many thousands of words. Why don't you?

And the answer was always lost in a tangle of becauses and wells and endless reasons that he clung to like a drowning man at straws.

The bathroom door opened and she came out, dressed in her good red suit.

For no reason at all, it seemed, he suddenly realized that she'd been wearing that same outfit for more than three years and never a new one. The realization angered him even more. He closed his eyes and hoped she wasn't looking at him. I hate her, he thought. I hate her because she has destroyed my life.

He heard the rustle of her skirt as she sat at the dressing table and pulled out a drawer. He kept his eyes shut and listened to the venetian blinds tap lightly against the window frame as morning breeze touched them. He could smell her perfume floating lightly on the air.

And he tried to think of the house empty all the time. He tried to think of coming home from class and not finding Sally there waiting for him. The idea seemed, somehow, impossible. And that angered him. Yes, he thought, she's gotten to me. She's worked on me until I am so dependent of her for really unessential things that I suffer under the delusion that I cannot do without her.

He turned suddenly on the mattress and looked at her.

"So, you're really going," he said in a cold voice.

She turned briefly and looked at him. There was no anger on her face. She looked tired.

"Yes," she said. "I'm going."

Good riddance. The words tried to pass his lips. He cut them off.

"I suppose you have your reasons," he said.

Her shoulders twitched a moment in what he took for a shrug of weary amusement.

"I have no intention of arguing with you," he said. "Your life is your own."

"Thank you," she murmured.

She's waiting for apologies, he thought. Waiting to be told that he didn't hate her as he'd said. That he hadn't struck *her* but all his twisted and shattered hopes; the mocking spectacle of his own lost faith.

"And just how long is this *trial* separation going to last?" he said, his voice acidulous.

She shook her head.

"I don't know, Chris," she said quietly. "It's up to you."

"Up to me," he said. "It's always up to me, isn't it?"

"Oh, please darl—Chris. I don't want to argue anymore. I'm too tired to argue."

"It's easier to just pack and run away."

She turned and looked at him. Her eyes were very dark and unhappy.

"Run away?" she said. "After eighteen years you accuse me of that? Eighteen years of watching you destroy yourself. And me along with you. Oh, don't look surprised. I'm sure you know you've driven me half insane too."

She turned away and he saw her shoulders twitch. She brushed some tears from her eyes.

"It's n-not just because you hit me," she said. "You kept saying that last night when I said I was leaving. Do you think it would matter if . . ." She took a deep breath. "If it meant you were angry with *me*? If it was that I could be hit every day. But you didn't hit me. I'm nothing to you. I'm not wanted."

"Oh, stop being so . . ."

"No," she broke in. "That's why I'm going. Because I can't bear to watch you hate me more every day for something that . . . that isn't my fault."

"I suppose you . . ."

"Oh, don't say anymore," she said, getting up. She hurried out of the room and he heard her walk into the living room. He stared at the dressing table.

Don't say anymore?—his mind asked as though she were still there. Well, there's more to say; lots more. You don't seem to realize what I've lost. You don't seem to understand. I had hopes, oh God, what hopes I had. I was going to write prose to make the people sit up and gasp. I was going to tell them things they needed badly to know. I was going to tell them in so entertaining a way that they would never realize that the truth was getting to them. I was going to create immortal works.

Now when I die, I shall only be dead. I am trapped in this depressing village, entombed in a college of science where men gape at dust and do not even know that there are stars above their heads. And what can I do, what can . . . ?

The thoughts broke off. He looked miserably at her perfume bottles, at the powder box that tinkled "Always" when the cover was lifted off.

I'll remember you. Always.

With a heart that's true. Always.

The words are childish and comical, he thought. But his throat contracted and he felt himself shudder.

"Sally," he said. So quietly that he could hardly hear it himself.

After a while he got up and dressed.

While he was putting on his trousers a rug slid from under him and he had to grab the dresser for support. He glared down, heart pounding in the total fury he had learned to summon in the space of seconds.

"Damn you," he muttered.

He forgot Sally. He forgot everything. He just wanted to get even with the rug. He kicked it violently under the bed. The anger plunged down and disappeared. He shook his head. I'm sick, he thought. He thought of going in to her and telling her he was sick.

His mouth tightened as he went into the bathroom. I'm not sick, he thought. Not in body anyway. It's my mind that's ill and she only makes it worse.

The bathroom was still damply warm from her use of it. He opened the window a trifle and got a splinter in his finger. He cursed the window in a muffled voice. He looked up. Why so quiet? he asked. So *she* won't hear me?

"Damn you!" he snarled loudly at the window. And he picked at his finger until he had pulled out the sliver of wood.

He jerked at the cabinet door. It stuck. His face reddened. He pulled harder and the door flew open and cracked him on the wrist. He spun about and grabbed his wrist, threw back his head with a whining gasp.

He stood there, eyes clouded with pain, staring at the ceiling. He looked at the crack that ran in a crazy meandering line across the ceiling. Then he closed his eyes.

And began to sense something. Intangible. A sense of menace. He wondered about it. Why it's myself, of course, he answered then. It is the moral decrepitude of my own subconscious. It is bawling out to me, saying: You are to be punished for driving your poor wife away to her mother's arms. You are not a man. You are a—

"Oh, shut up," he said.

He washed his hands and face. He ran an inspecting finger over his chin. He needed a shave. He opened the cabinet door gingerly and took out his straight razor. He held it up and looked at it.

The handle has expanded. He told himself that quickly as the blade appeared to fall out of the handle willfully. It made him shiver to see it flop out like that and glitter in the light from the cabinet light fixture.

He stared in repelled fascination at the bright steel. He touched the blade edge. So sharp, he thought. The slightest touch would sever flesh. What a hideous thing it was.

"It's my hand."

He said it involuntarily and shut the razor suddenly. It *was* his hand, it had to be. It couldn't have been the razor moving by itself. That was sick imagination.

But he didn't shave. He put the razor back in the cabinet with a vague sense of forestalling doom.

Don't care if we *are* expected to shave every day, he muttered. I'm not taking a chance on my hand slipping. I'd better get a safety razor anyway. This kind isn't for me, I'm too nervous.

Suddenly, impelled by those words, the picture of him eighteen years before flew into his brain.

He remembered a date he'd had with Sally. He remembered telling her he was so calm it was akin to being dead. Nothing bothers me, he'd said. And it was true, at the time. He remembered too telling her he didn't like coffee, that one cup kept him awake at night. That he didn't smoke, didn't like the taste or smell. I like to stay healthy, he'd said. He remembered the exact words.

"And now," he muttered at his lean and worn reflection.

Now he drank gallons of coffee a day. Until it sloshed like a black pool in his stomach and he couldn't sleep any more than he could fly. Now he smoked endless strings of finger-yellowing cigarettes until his throat felt raw and clogged, until he couldn't write in pencil because his hand shook so much.

But all that stimulation didn't help his writing any. Paper still remained blank in the typewriter. Words never came, plots died on him. Characters eluded him, mocking him with laughter from behind the veil of their non-creation.

And time passed. It flew by faster and faster, seeming to single him out for highest punishment. He—a man who had begun to value time so neurotically that it overbalanced his life and made him sick to think of its passing.

As he brushed his teeth he tried to recall when this irrational temper had first begun to control him. But there was no way of tracing its course. Somewhere in mists that could not be pierced, it had started. With a word of petulance, an angry contraction of muscles. With a glare of unrecallable animosity.

And from there, like a swelling amoeba, it had gone its own perverted and downward course of evolution, reaching its present nadir in him; a taut embittered man who found his only solace in hating.

He spit out white froth and rinsed his mouth. As he put down the glass, it cracked and a barb of glass drove into his hand.

"Damn!" he yelled.

He spun on his heel and clenched his fist. It sprang open instantly as the sliver sank into his palm. He stood with tears on his cheeks, breathing heavily. He thought of Sally listening to him, hearing once more the audible evidence of his snapping nerves.

Stop it!—he ordered himself. You can never do anything until you rid yourself of this enervating temper.

He closed his eyes. For a moment he wondered why it seemed that everything was happening to him lately. As if some revenging power had taken roost in the house, pouring a savage life into inanimate things. Threatening him. But the thought was just a faceless, passing figure in the crushing horde of thoughts that mobbed past his mind's eye; seen but not appreciated.

He drew the glass sliver from his palm. He put on his dark tie.

Then he went into the dining room, consulting his watch. It was ten thirty already. More than half the morning was gone. More than half the time for sitting and trying to write the prose that would make people sit up and gasp.

It happened that way more often now than he would even admit to himself. Sleeping late, making up errands, doing anything to forestall the terrible moment when he must sit down before his typewriter and try to wrench some harvest from the growing desert of his mind.

It was harder every time. And he grew more angry every time; and hated more. And never noticed until now, when it was too late, that Sally had grown desperate and could no longer stand his temper or his hate.

She was sitting at the kitchen table drinking dark coffee. She too drank more than she once had. Like him, she drank it black, without sugar. It jangled her nerves too. And she smoked now although she'd never smoked until a year before. She got no pleasure from it.

She drew the fumes deep down into her lungs and then blew them out quickly. And her hands shook almost as badly as his did.

He poured himself a cup of coffee and sat down across from her. She started to get up.

"What's the matter? Can't you stand the sight of me?"

She sat back and took a deep pull on the cigarette in her hand. Then she stamped it out on the saucer.

He felt sick. He wanted to get out of the house suddenly. It felt alien and strange to him. He had the feeling that she had renounced all claim to it, that she had retreated from it. The touch of her fingers and the loving indulgences she had bestowed on every room; all these things were taken back. They had lost tangibility because she was leaving. She was deserting it and it was not their home anymore. He felt it strongly.

Sinking back against the chair he pushed away his cup and stared at the yellow oilcloth on the table. He felt as if he and Sally were frozen in time; that seconds were drawn out like some fantastic taffy until each one seemed an eternity. The clock ticked slower. And the house was a different house.

"What train are you getting?" he asked, knowing before he spoke that there was only one morning train.

"Eleven forty-seven," she said.

When she said it, he felt as if his stomach were pulled back hard against his backbone. He gasped, so actual was the physical pain. She glanced up at him.

"Burned myself," he said hastily, and she got up and put her cup and saucer in the sink.

Why did I say that?—he thought. Why couldn't I say that I gasped because I was filled with terror at the thought of her leaving me? Why do I always say the things I don't mean to say? I'm not bad. But every time I speak I build higher the walls of hatred and bitterness around me until I cannot escape from them.

With words I have knit my shroud and will bury myself therein.

He looked at her back and a sad smile raised his lips. I can think of words when my wife is leaving me. It is very sad.

Sally had walked out of the kitchen. His mind reverted to its sullen attitude. This is a game we're playing. Follow the leader. You walk in one room, head high, the justified spouse, the injured party. I am supposed to follow, slope shouldered and contrite, pouring out apologetic hecatombs.

Once more conscious of himself, he sat tensely at the table, rage making his body tremble. Consciously he relaxed and pressed his left hand over his eyes. He sat there trying to lose his misery in silence and blackness.

It wouldn't work.

And then his cigarette really burned him and he sat erect. The cigarette hit the floor scattering ashes. He bent over and picked it up. He threw it at the wastecan and missed. To hell with it, he thought. He got up and dumped his cup and saucer in the sink. The saucer broke in half and nicked his right thumb. He let it bleed. He didn't care.

She was in the extra room finishing her packing.

The extra room. The words tortured him now. When had they stopped calling it "the nursery"? When had it begun to eat her insides out because she was so full of love and wanted children badly? When had he begun to replace this loss with nothing better than volcanic temper and days and nights of sheath-scraped nerves?

He stood in the doorway and watched her. He wanted to get out the typewriter and sit down and write reams of words. He wanted to glory in his coming freedom. Think of all the money he could save. Think of how soon he could go away and write all the things he'd always meant to write.

He stood in the doorway, sick.

Is all this possible?—his mind asked, incredulous. Possible that she was leaving? But she and he were man and wife. They had lived and loved in this house for more than eighteen years. Now she was leaving. Putting articles of clothing in her old black suitcase and leaving. He couldn't reconcile himself to that. He couldn't understand it or ally it with the functions of the day. Where did it fit into the pattern?—the pattern that was Sally right there cleaning and cooking and trying to make their home happy and warm.

He shivered and, turning abruptly, went back into the bedroom.

He slumped on the bed and stared at the delicately whirring electric clock on their bedside table.

Past eleven, he saw. In less than an hour I have to hold class for a group of idiot freshmen. And, on the desk in the living room, is a mountain of mid-term examinations with essays that I must suffer through, feeling my stomach turn at their paucity of intelligence, their adolescent phraseology.

And all that tripe, all those miles of hideous prose, had been wound into an eternal skein in his head. And there it sat unraveling into his own writing until he wondered if he could stand the thought of living anymore. I have digested the worst, he thought. Is it any wonder that I exude it piecemeal?

Temper began again, a low banking fire in him, gradually fanned by further thinking. I've done no writing this morning. Like every morning after every other morning as time passes. I do less and less. I write nothing. Or I write worthless material. I could write better when I was twenty than I can now.

I'll *never* write anything good!

He jolted to his feet and his head snapped around as he looked for something to strike at, something to break, something to hate with such hate that it would wither in the blast.

It seemed as though the room clouded. He felt a throbbing. His left leg banged against a corner of the bed.

He gasped in fury. He wept. Tears of hate and repentance and self commiseration. I'm lost, he thought. Lost. There is nothing.

He became very calm, icy calm. Drained of pity, of emotion. He put on his suit coat. He put on his hat and got his briefcase off the dresser.

He stopped before the door to the room where she still fussed with her bag. So she will have something to occupy herself with now, he thought, so she won't have to look at me. He felt his heart thudding like a heavy drum beat.

"Have a nice time at your mother's," he said dispassionately.

She looked up and saw the expression on his face. She turned away and put a hand to her eyes. He felt a sudden need to run to her and beg her forgiveness. Make everything right again.

Then he thought again of papers and years of writing undone. He turned away and walked across the living room. The small rug slipped a little and it helped to focus the strength of anger he needed. He kicked it aside and it fluttered against the wall in a rumpled heap.

He slammed the door behind him.

His mind gibbered. Now, soap opera like, she has thrown herself on the coverlet and is weeping tears of martyr-tinged sorrow. Now she is digging nails into the pillow and moaning my name and wishing she were dead.

His shoes clicked rapidly on the sidewalk. God help me, he thought. God help all us poor wretches who would create and find that we must lose our hearts for it because we cannot afford to spend our time at it.

It was a beautiful day. His eyes saw that but his mind would not attest to it. The trees were thick with green and the air warm and fresh. Spring breezes flooded down the streets. He felt them brush over him as he walked down the block, crossed Main Street to the bus stop.

He stood there on the corner looking back at the house.

She is in there, his mind persisted in analysis. In there, the house in which we've lived for more than eight years. She is packing or crying or doing something. And soon she will call the Campus Cab Company. A cab will come driving out. The driver will honk the horn, Sally will put on her light spring coat and take her suitcase out on the porch. She will lock the door behind her for the last time.

"No—"

He couldn't keep the word from strangling in his throat. He kept staring at the house. His head ached. He saw everything weaving. I'm sick, he thought.

"I'm *sick!*"

He shouted it. There was no one around to hear. He stood gazing at the house. She is going away forever, said his mind.

Very well then! I'll write, write, write. He let the words soak into his mind and displace all else.

A man had a choice, after all. He devoted his life to his work or to his wife and children and home. It could not be combined; not in this day and age. In this insane world where God was second to income and goodness to wealth.

He glanced aside as the green-striped bus topped the distant hill and approached. He put the briefcase under his arm and reached into his coat pocket for a token. There was a hole in the pocket. Sally had been meaning to sew it. Well, she would never sew it now. What did it matter anyway?

I would rather have my soul intact than the suit of clothes I wear.

Words, words, he thought, as the bus stopped before him. They flood through me now that she is leaving. Is that evidence that it is her presence that clogs the channels of thought?

He dropped the token in the coin box and weaved down the length of the bus. He passed a professor he knew and nodded to him distractedly. He slumped down on the back seat and stared at the grimy, rubberized floor boards.

This is a great life, his mind ranted. I am so pleased with this, my life and these, my great and noble accomplishments.

He opened the briefcase a moment and looked in at the thick prospectus he had outlined with the aid of Dr. Ramsay.

First week—1. *Everyman*. Discussion of. Reading of selections from *Classic Readings For College Freshmen*. 2. *Beowulf*. Reading of. Class discussion. Twenty minute quotation quiz.

He shoved the sheaf of papers back into the briefcase. It sickens me, he thought. I hate these things. The classics have become anathema to me. I begin to loathe the very mention of them. Chaucer, the Elizabethan poets, Dryden, Pope, Shakespeare. What higher insult to a man than to grow to hate these names because he must share them by part with unappreciative clods? Because he must strain them thin and make them palatable for the dullards who should better be digging ditches.

He got off the bus downtown and started down the long slope of Ninth Street.

Walking, he felt as though he were a ship with its hawser cut, prey to a twisted network of currents. He felt apart from the city, the country, the world. If someone told me I were a ghost, he thought, I would be inclined to believe.

What is she doing now?

He wondered about it as the buildings floated past him. What is she thinking as I stand here and the town of Fort drifts by me like vaporous stage flats? What are her hands holding? What expression has she on her lovely face?

She is alone in the house, our house. What might have been our *home*. Now it is only a shell, a hollow box with sticks of wood and metal for furnishings. Nothing but inanimate dead matter.

No matter what John Morton said.

Him with his gold leaves parting and his test tubes and his God of the microscope. For all his erudite talk and his papers of slide-ruled figures; despite all that—it was simple witchcraft he professed. It was idiocy. The idiocy that prompted that ass Charles Fort to burden the world with his nebulous fancies. The idiocy that made that fool of a millionaire endow this place and from the arid soil erect these huge stone structures and house within a zoo of wild-eyed scientists always searching for some fashion of elixir while the rest of the clowns blew the world out from under them.

No, there is nothing right with the world, he thought as he plodded under the arch and onto the wide, green campus.

He looked across at the huge Physical Sciences Center, its granite face beaming in the late morning sun.

Now she is calling the cab. He consulted his watch. No. She is in the cab already. Riding through the silent streets. Past the houses and down into the shopping district. Past the red brick buildings spewing out yokels and students. Through the town that was a potpourri of the sophisticated and the rustic.

Now the cab was turning left on Tenth Street. Now it was pulling up the hill, topping it. Gliding down toward the railroad station. Now . . .

"Chris!"

His head snapped around and his body twitched in surprise. He looked toward the wide-doored entrance to the Mental Sciences Building. Dr. Morton was coming out.

We attended school together eighteen years ago, he thought. But I took only a small interest in science. I preferred wasting my time on the culture of the centuries. That's why I'm an associate and he's a doctor and the head of his department.

All this fled like racing winds through his mind as Dr. Morton approached, smiling. He clapped Chris on the shoulder.

"Hello there," he said. "How are things?"

"How are they ever?"

Dr. Morton's smile faded.

"What is it, Chris?" he asked.

I won't tell you about Sally, Chris thought. Not if I die first. You'll never know it from me.

"The usual," he said.

"Still on the outs with Ramsay?"

Chris shrugged. Morton looked over at the large clock on the face of the Mental Sciences Building.

"Say, look," he said. "Why are we standing here? Your class isn't for a half hour yet, is it?"

Chris didn't answer. He's going to invite me for coffee, he thought. He's going to regale me with more of his inane theories. He's going to use me as whipping boy for his mental merry-go-round.

"Let's get some coffee," Morton said, taking Chris's arm. They walked along in silence for a few steps.

"How's Sally?" Morton asked then.

"She's fine," he answered in an even voice.

"Good. Oh, incidentally. I'll probably drop by tomorrow or the next day for that book I left there last Thursday night."

"All right."

"What were you saying about Ramsay now?"

"I wasn't."

Morton skipped that. "Been thinking anymore about what I told you?" he asked.

"If you're referring to your fairy tale about my house—no. I haven't been giving it any more thought than it deserves—which is none."

They turned the corner of the building and walked toward Ninth Street.

"Chris, that's an indefensible attitude," Morton said. "You have no right to doubt when you don't know."

Chris felt like pulling his arm away, turning and leaving Morton standing there. He was sick of words and words and words. He wanted to be alone. He almost felt as if he could put a pistol to his head now, get it over with. Yes, I could—he thought. If someone handed it to me now it would be done in a moment.

They went up the stone steps to the sidewalk and crossed over to the Campus Cafe. Morton opened the door and ushered Chris in. Chris went in back and slid into a wooden booth.

Morton brought two coffees and sat across from him.

"Now listen," he said, stirring in sugar, "I'm your best friend. At least I regard myself as such. And I'm damned if I'll sit by like a mute and watch you kill yourself."

Chris felt his heart jump. He swallowed. He got rid of the thoughts as though they were visible to Morton.

"Forget it," he said. "I don't care what proofs you have. I don't believe any of it."

"What'll it take to convince you, damn it?" Morton said. "Do you have to lose your life first?"

"Look," Chris said pettishly. "I don't believe it. That's *it*. Forget it now, let it go."

"Listen, Chris, I can show you . . ."

"You can show me nothing!" Chris cut in.

Morton was patient. "It's a recognized phenomenon," he said.

Chris looked at him in disgust and shook his head.

"What dreams you white-frocked kiddies have in the sanctified cloister of your laboratories. You can make yourself believe anything after a while. As long as you can make up a measurement for it."

"Will you listen to me, Chris? How many times have you complained to me about splinters, about closet doors flying open, about rugs slipping? How many times?"

"Oh, for God's sake, don't start *that* again. I'll get up and walk out of here. I'm in no mood for your lectures. Save them for those poor idiots who pay tuition to hear them."

Morton looked at him with a shake of his head.

"I wish I could get to you," he said.

"Forget it."

"Forget it?" Morton squirmed. "Can't you see that you're in danger because of your temper?"

"I'm telling you, John . . ."

"Where do you think that temper of yours goes? Do you think it disappears? No. It doesn't. It goes into your rooms and into your furniture and into the air. It goes into Sally. It makes everything sick; including you. It crowds you out. It welds a link between animate and inanimate. *Psychobolie.* Oh, don't look so petulant; like a child who can't stand to hear the word *spinach*. Sit down, for God's sake. You're an adult; listen like one."

Chris lit a cigarette. He let Morton's voice drift into a non-intelligent hum. He glanced at the wall clock. Quarter to twelve. In two minutes, if the schedule was adhered to, she would be going. The train would move and the town of Fort would pass away from her.

"I've told you any number of times," Morton was saying. "No one knows what matter is made of. Atoms, electrons, pure energy—all words. Who knows where it will end? We guess, we theorize, we make up means of measurement. But we don't know.

"And that's for matter. Think of the human brain and its still unknown capacities. It's an uncharted continent, Chris. It may stay that way for a long time. And all that time the suspected powers will still be affecting us and, maybe, affecting matter; even if we *can't* measure it on a gauge.

"And I say you're poisoning your house. I say your temper has become ingrained in the structure, in every article you touch. All of them influenced by you and your ungovernable rages. And I think too that if it weren't for Sally's presence acting as an abortive factor, well . . . you might actually be attacked by . . ."

Chris heard the last few sentences.

"Oh, stop this gibberish!" he snapped angrily. "You're talking like a juvenile after his first Tom Swift novel."

Morton sighed. He ran his fingers over the cup edge and shook his head sadly.

"Well," he said, "all I can do is hope that nothing breaks down. It's obvious to me that you're not going to listen."

"Congratulations on one statement I can agree with," said Chris. He looked at his watch. "And now if you'll excuse me I'll go and listen to saddle-shoed cretins stumble over passages they haven't the slightest ability to assimilate."

They got up.

"I'll take it," said Morton but Chris slapped a coin on the counter and walked out. Morton followed, putting his change into his pocket slowly.

In the street he patted Chris on the shoulder.

"Try to take it easy," he said. "Look, why don't you and Sally come out to the house tonight? We could have a few rounds of bridge."

"That's impossible," Chris said.

The students were reading a selection from *King Lear*. Their heads were bent over the books. He stared at them without seeing them.

I've got to resign myself to it, he told himself. I've got to forget her, that's all. She's gone. I'm not going to bewail the fact. I'm not going to hope against hope that she'll return. I don't *want* her back. I'm better off without her. Free and unfettered now.

His thoughts drained off. He felt empty and helpless. He felt as though he could never write another word for the rest of his life. Maybe, he thought, sullenly displeased with the idea, maybe it was only the upset of her leaving that enabled my brain to find words. For, after all, the words I thought of, the ideas that flourished, though briefly, were all to do with her—her going and my wretchedness because of it.

He caught himself short. No!—he cried in silent battle. I will not let it be that way. I'm strong. This feeling is only temporary, I'll very soon have learned to do without her. And then I'll do work. Such work as I have only dreamed of doing. After all, haven't I lived eighteen years more? Haven't those years filled me to overflowing with sights and sounds, ideals, impressions, interpretations?

He trembled with excitement.

Someone was waving a hand in his face. He focused his eyes and looked coldly at the girl.

"Well?" he said.

"Could you tell us when you're going to give back our mid-term papers, Professor Neal?" she asked.

He stared at her, his right cheek twitching. He felt about to hurl every invective at his command into her face. His fists closed.

"You'll get them back when they're marked," he said tensely.

"Yes, but . . ."

"You heard me," he said.

His voice rose at the end of the sentence. The girl sat down. As he lowered his head he noticed that she looked at the boy next to her and shrugged her shoulders, a look of disgust on her face.

"Miss . . ."

He fumbled with his record book and found her name.

"Miss Forbes!"

She looked up, her features drained of color, her red lips standing out sharply against her white skin. Painted alabaster idiot. The words clawed at him.

"You may get out of this room," he ordered sharply.

Confusion filled her face.

"Why?" she asked in a thin, plaintive voice.

"Perhaps you didn't hear me," he said, the fury rising. "I said get out of this room!"

"But . . ."

"Do you hear me!" he shouted.

Hurriedly she collected her books, her hands shaking, her face burning with embarrassment. She kept her eyes on the floor and her throat moved convulsively as she edged along the aisle and went out the doorway.

The door closed behind her. He sank back. He felt a terrible sickness in himself. Now, he thought, they will all turn against me in defense of an addle-witted little girl. Dr. Ramsay would have more fuel for his simple little fire.

And they were right.

He couldn't keep his mind from it. They *were* right. He knew it. In that far recess of mind which he could not cow with thoughtless passion, he knew he was a stupid fool. I have no right to teach others. I cannot even teach myself to be a human being. He wanted to cry out the words and weep confessions and throw himself from one of the open windows.

"The whispering will stop!" he demanded fiercely.

The room was quiet. He sat tensely, waiting for any signs of militance. I am your teacher, he told himself, I am to be obeyed, I am . . .

The concept died. He drifted away again. What were students or a girl asking about mid-term papers? What was anything?

He glanced at his watch. In a few minutes the train would pull into Centralia. She would change to the main line express to Indianapolis. Then up to Detroit and her mother. Gone.

Gone. He tried to visualize the word, put it into living terms. But the thought of the house without her was almost beyond his means. Because it wasn't the house without her; it was something else.

He began to think of what John had said.

Was it possible? He was in a mood to accept the incredible. It was incredible that she had left him. Why not extend the impossibilities that were happening to him?

All right then, he thought angrily. The house is alive. I've given it this life with deadly outpourings of wrath. I hope to God that when I get back there and enter the door, the roof collapses. I hope the walls buckle and I'm crushed to pulp by the crushing weight of plaster and wood and brick. That's what I want. Some agency to do away with me. I cannot drive myself to it. If only a gun would commit my suicide for me. Or gas blow its deadly fumes at me for the asking or a razor slice my flesh upon request.

The door opened. He glanced up. Dr. Ramsay stood there, face drawn into a mask of indignation. Behind him in the hall Chris could see the girl, her face streaked with tears.

"A moment, Neal," Ramsay said sharply and stepped back into the hall again.

Chris sat at the desk staring at the door. He felt suddenly very tired, exhausted. He felt as if getting up and moving into the hall was more than he could possibly manage. He glanced at the class. A few of them were trying to repress smiles.

"For tomorrow you will finish the reading of *King Lear*," he said. Some of them groaned.

Ramsay appeared in the doorway again, his cheeks pink.

"Are you coming, Neal?" he asked loudly.

Chris felt himself tighten with anger as he walked across the room and out into the hall. The girl lowered her eyes. She stood beside Dr. Ramsay's portly frame.

"What's this I hear, Neal?" Ramsay asked.

That's right, Chris thought. Don't ever call me professor. I'll never be one, will I? You'll see to that, you bastard.

"I don't understand," he said, as coolly as possible.

"Miss Forbes here claims you ejected her from class for no reason at all."

"Then Miss Forbes is lying quite stupidly," he said. Let me hold this anger, he thought. Don't let it flood loose. He shook with holding it back.

The girl gasped and took out her handkerchief again. Ramsay turned and patted her shoulder.

"Go in my office, child. Wait for me."

She turned away slowly. Politician!—cried Neal's mind. How easy it is for you to be popular with them. You don't have to deal with their bungling minds.

Miss Forbes turned the corner and Ramsay looked back.

"Your explanation had better be good," he said. "I'm getting a little weary, Neal, of your behavior."

Chris didn't speak. Why am I standing here?—he suddenly wondered. Why, in all the world, am I standing in this dimlit hall and, voluntarily, listening to this pompous boor berate me?

"I'm waiting, Neal."

Chris tightened. "I told you she was lying," he said quietly.

"I choose to believe otherwise," said Dr. Ramsay, his voice trembling.

A shudder ran through Chris. His head moved forward and he spoke slowly, teeth clenched.

"You can believe anything you damn well please."

Ramsay's mouth twitched.

"I think it's time you appeared before the board," he muttered.

"Fine!" said Chris loudly. Ramsay made a move to close the classroom door. Chris gave it a kick and it banged against the wall. A girl gasped.

"What's the matter?" Chris yelled. "Don't you want your students to hear me tell you off? Don't you even want them to suspect that you're a dolt, a windbag, an ass!"

Ramsay raised shaking fists before his chest. His lips trembled violently.

"This will do, Neal!" he cried.

Chris reached out and shoved the heavy man aside, snarling, "Oh, *get* out of my way!"

He started away. The hall fled past him. He heard the bell ring. It sounded as though it rang in another existence. The building throbbed with life; students poured from classrooms.

"Neal!" called Dr. Ramsay.

He kept walking. Oh, God, let me out of here, I'm suffocating, he thought. My hat, my briefcase. Leave them. Get out of here. Dizzily he descended the stairs surrounded by milling students. They swirled about him like an unidentifiable tide. His brain was far from them.

Staring ahead dully he walked along the first floor hall. He turned and went out the door and down the porch steps to the campus sidewalk. He paid no attention to the students who stared at his ruffled blond hair, his mussed clothes. He kept walking. I've done it, he thought belligerently. I've made the break. I'm *free*!

I'm sick.

All the way down to Main Street and out on the bus he kept renewing his stores of anger. He went over those few moments in the hallway again and again. He summoned up the vision of Ramsay's stolid face, repeated his words. He kept himself taut and furious. I'm glad, he told himself forcibly. Everything is solved. Sally has left me. Good. My job is done. Good. Now I'm free to do as I like. A strained and angry joy pounded through him. He felt alone, a stranger in the world and glad of it.

At his stop, he got off the bus and walked determinedly toward the house pretending to ignore the pain he felt at approaching it. It's just an empty house, he thought. Nothing more. Despite all puerile theories, it is nothing but a house.

Then, when he went in, he found her sitting on the couch.

He almost staggered as if someone had struck him. He stood dumbly, staring at her. She had her hands tightly clasped. She was looking at him.

He swallowed.

"Well," he managed to say.

"I . . ." Her throat contracted. "Well . . ."

"Well *what*!" he said quickly and loudly to hide the shaking in his voice.

She stood up. "Chris, please. Won't you . . . ask me to stay?" She looked at him like a little girl, pleading.

The look enraged him. All his day dreams shattered; he saw the growing thing of new ideas ground under foot.

"Ask you to stay!" he yelled at her. "By God, I'll ask you nothing!"

"Chris! Don't!"

She's buckling, cried his mind. She's cracking. Get her now. Get her out of here. Drive her from these walls!

"Chris," she sobbed, "be kind. Please be kind."

"Kind!"

He almost choked on the word. He felt a wild heat coursing his body.

"Have *you* been kind? Driving me crazy, into a pit of despair. I can't get out. Do you understand? Never. Never! Do you understand that! I'll never write. I *can't* write! You drained it out of me! You killed it! Understand *that*? *Killed* it!"

She backed away toward the dining room. He followed her, hands shaking at his sides, feeling that she had driven him to this confession and hating her the more for it.

"Chris," she murmured in fright.

It seemed as if his rage grew cell-like, swelling him with fury until he was nothing of bone and blood but a hating accusation made flesh.

"I don't want you!" he yelled. "You're right, I don't want you! Get out of here!"

Her eyes were wide, her mouth an open wound. Suddenly she ran past him, eyes glistening with tears. She fled through the front doorway.

He went to the window and watched her running down the block, her dark brown hair streaming behind her.

Dizzy suddenly, he sank down on the couch and closed his eyes. He dug his nails into his palms. Oh God, I *am* sick, his mind churned.

He twitched and looked around stupidly. What was it? This feeling that he was sinking into the couch, into the floorboards, dissolving in the air, joining the molecules of the house. He whimpered softly, looking around. His head ached; he pressed a palm against his forehead.

"What?" he muttered. "What?"

He stood up. As though there were fumes he tried to smell them. As though it were a sound he tried to hear it. He turned around to see it. As though there were something with depth and length and width; something menacing.

He wavered, fell back on the couch. He stared around. There was nothing; all intangible. It might only be in the mind. The furniture lay as it did before. The sunlight filtered through the windows, piercing the gauzelike curtains, making gold patterns on the inlaid wooden floor. The walls were still creamy, the ceiling was as it was before. Yet there was this darkening, darkening . . .

What?

He pushed up and walked dizzily around the room. He forgot about Sally. He was in the dining room. He touched the table, he stared at the dark oak. He went into the kitchen. He stood by the sink and looked out the window.

Far up the block, he saw her walking, stumbling. She must have been waiting for the bus. Now she couldn't wait any longer and she was walking away from the house, away from him.

"I'll go after her," he muttered.

No, he thought. No, I won't go after her like a . . .

He forgot like what. He stared down at the sink. He felt drunk. Everything was fuzzy on the edges.

She's washed the cups. The broken saucer was thrown away. He looked at the nick on his thumb. It was dried. He'd forgotten about it.

He looked around suddenly as if someone had sneaked behind him. He stared at the wall. Something was rising. He felt it. It's not me. But it had to be; it had to be imagination.

Imagination!

He slammed a fist on the sink. I'll write. Write, *write*. Sit down and drain it all away in words; this feeling of anguish and terror and loneliness. Write it out of my system.

He cried, "Yes!"

He ran from the kitchen. He refused to accept the instinctive fear in himself. He ignored the menace that seemed to thicken the very air.

A rug slipped. He kicked it aside. He sat down. The air hummed. He tore off the cover on the typewriter. He sat nervously, staring at the keyboard. The moment before attack. It was in the air. But it's *my* attack!—he thought triumphantly, my attack on stupidity and fear.

He rolled a sheet into the typewriter. He tried to collect his throbbing thoughts. Write, the word called in his mind. Write—*now*.

"Now!" he cried.

He felt the desk lurch against his shins.

The flaring pain knifed open his senses. He kicked the desk in automatic frenzy. More pain. He kicked again. The desk flung back at him. He screamed.

He'd seen it move.

He tried to back off, the anger torn from him. The typewriter keys moved under his hands. His eyes swept down. He couldn't tell whether he was moving the keys or whether they moved by themselves. He pulled hysterically, trying to dislodge his fingers but he couldn't. The keys were moving faster than his eye could see. They were a blur of motion. He felt them shredding his skin, peeling his fingers. They were raw. Blood started to ooze out.

He cried out and pulled. He managed to jerk away his fingers and jump back in the chair.

His belt buckle caught, the desk drawer came flying out. It

slammed into his stomach. He yelled again. The pain was a black cloud pouring over his head.

He threw down a hand to shove in the drawer. He saw the yellow pencils lying there. They glared. His hand slipped, it banged into the drawer.

One of the pencils jabbed at him.

He always kept the points sharp. It was like the bite of a snake. He snapped back his hand with a gasp of pain. The point was jammed under a nail. It was imbedded in raw, tender flesh. He cried out in fury and pain. He pulled at the pencil with his other hand. The point flew out and jabbed into his palm. He couldn't get rid of the pencil, it kept dragging over his hand. He pulled at it and it made black, jagged lines on his skin. It tore the skin open.

He heaved the pencil across the room. It bounced on the wall. It seemed to jump as it fell on the eraser. It rolled over and was still.

He lost his balance. The chair fell back with a rush. His head banged sharply against the floorboards. His outclutched hand grabbed at the window sill. Tiny splinters flashed into his skin like invisible needles. He howled in deathly fear. He kicked his legs. The mid-term papers showered down over him like the beating wings of insane bird flocks.

The chair snapped up again on its springs. The heavy wheels rolled over his raw, bloody hands. He drew them back with a shriek. He reared a leg and kicked the chair over violently. It crashed on the side against the mantelpiece. The wheels spun and chattered like a swarm of furious insects.

He jumped up. He lost his balance and fell again, crashing against the window sill. The curtains fell on him like a python. The rods snapped. They flew down and struck him across the scalp. He felt warm blood trickle across his forehead. He thrashed about on the floor. The curtains seemed to writhe around him like serpents. He screamed again. He tore at them wildly. His eyes were terror-stricken.

He threw them off and lurched up suddenly, staggering around for balance. The pain in his hands assailed him. He looked at them. They were like raw butcher meat, skin hanging down in shreds. He had to bandage them. He turned toward the bathroom.

At his first step the rug slid from under him, the rug he had kicked aside. He felt himself rush through the air. He reached down his hands instinctively to block the fall.

The white pain made his body leap. One finger snapped. Splinters shot into his raw fingers, he felt a burning pain in one ankle.

He tried to scramble up but the floor was like ice under him. He was deadly silent. His heart thudded in his chest. He tried to rise again. He fell, hissing with pain.

The bookshelf loomed over him. He cried out and flung up an arm. The case came crashing down on him. The top shelf drove into his skull. Black waves dashed over him, a sharp blade of pain drove into his head. Books showered over him. He rolled on his side with a groan. He tried to crawl out from underneath. He shoved the books aside weakly and they fell open. He felt the page edges slicing into his fingers like razor blades.

The pain cleared his head. He sat up and hurled the books aside. He kicked the bookcase back against the wall. The back fell off it and it crashed down.

He rose up, the room spinning before his eyes. He staggered into the wall, tried to hold on. The wall shifted under his hands it seemed. He couldn't hold on. He slipped to his knees, pushed up again.

"Bandage myself," he muttered hoarsely.

The words filled his brain. He staggered up through the quivering dining room, into the bathroom.

He stopped. No! Get out of the house! He knew it was not his will that brought him in there.

He tried to turn but he slipped on the tiles and cracked his elbow against the edge of the bathtub. A shooting pain barbed into his upper arm. The arm went numb. He sprawled on the floor, writhing in pain. The walls clouded; they welled around him like a blank shroud.

He sat up, breath tearing at his throat. He pushed himself up with a gasp. His arm shot out, he pulled open the cabinet door. It flew open against his cheek, tearing a jagged rip in the soft flesh.

His head snapped back. The crack in the ceiling looked like a wide idiot smile on a blank, white face. He lowered his head, whimpering in fright. He tried to back away.

His hand reached out. For iodine, for gauze!—his mind cried.

His hand came out with the razor.

It flopped in his hand like a new caught fish. His other hand reached in. For iodine, for gauze!—shrieked his mind.

His hand came out with dental floss. It flooded out of the tube like an endless white worm. It coiled around his throat and shoulders. It choked him.

The long shiny blade slipped from its sheath.

He could not stop his hand. It drew the razor heavily across his chest. It slit open the shirt. It sliced a valley through his chest. Blood spurted out.

He tried to hurl away the razor. It stuck to his hand. It slashed at him, at his arms and hands and legs and body.

At his throat.

A scream of utter horror flooded from his lips. He ran from the bathroom, staggering wildly into the living room.

"Sally!" he screamed, "Sally, Sally, Sally . . ."

The razor touched his throat. The room went black. Pain. Life ebbing away into the night. Silence over all the world.

The next day Dr. Morton came. He called the police. And later the coroner wrote in his report:

Died of self-inflicted wounds.

THE FUNERAL

Morton Silkline was in his office musing over floral arrangements for the Fenton obsequies when the chiming strains of "I am Crossing o'er the Bar to Join the Choir Invisible" announced an entrant into Clooney's Cut-Rate Catafalque.

Blinking meditation from his liver-colored eyes, Silkline knit his fingers to a placid clasp, then settled back against the sable leather of his chair, a smile of funereal welcome on his lips. Out in the stillness of the hallway, footsteps sounded on the muffling carpet, moving with a leisured pace and, just before the tall man entered, the desk clock buzzed a curt acknowledgment to 7:30.

Rising as if caught in the midst of a *tête-à-tête* with death's bright angel, Morton Silkline circled the glossy desk on whispering feet and extended one flaccid-fingered hand.

"Ah, good evening, sir," he dulceted, his smile a precise compendium of sympathy and welcome, his voice a calculated drip of obeisance.

The man's handshake was cool and bone-cracking but Silkline managed to repress reaction to a momentary flicker of agony in his cinnamon eyes.

"Won't you be seated?" he murmured, fluttering his bruised hand toward The Grieved One's chair.

"Thank you," said the man, his voice a baritoned politeness as he seated himself, unbuttoning the front of his velvet-collared overcoat and placing his dark homburg on the glass top of the desk.

"My name is Morton Silkline," Silkline offered as he recircled to his chair, settling on the cushion like a diffident butterfly.

"Asper," said the man.

"May I say that I am proud to meet you, Mister Asper?" Silkline purred.

"Thank you," said the man.

"Well, now," Silkline said, getting down to the business of bereavement, "what can Clooney's do to ease your sorrow?"

The man crossed his dark-trousered legs. "I should like," he said, "to make arrangements for a funeral service."

Silkline nodded once with an I-am-here-to-succor smile.

"Of course," he said, "you've come to the right place, sir." His gaze elevated a few inches beyond the pale. *"When loved ones lie upon that lonely couch of everlasting sleep,"* he recited, *"let Clooney draw the coverlet."*

His gaze returned and he smiled with a modest subservience. "Mrs. Clooney," he said, "made that up. We like to pass it along to those who come to us for comfort."

"Very nice," the man said. "Extremely poetic. But to details: I'd like to engage your largest parlor."

"I see," Silkline answered, restraining himself, only with effort, from the rubbing together of hands. "That would be our Eternal Rest Room."

The man nodded affably. "Fine. And I would also like to buy your most expensive casket."

Silkline could barely restrain a boyish grin. His cardiac muscle flexing vigorously, he forced back folds of sorrowful solicitude across his face.

"I'm sure," he said, "that can be effected."

"With gold trimmings?" the man said.

"Why . . . yes," said Director Silkline, clicking audibly as he swallowed. "I'm certain that Clooney's can satisfy your every need in this time of grievous loss. Naturally—" His voice slipped a jot from the condoling to the fiduciary "—it will entail a bit more expenditure than might, otherwise, be—"

"The cost is of no importance," said the man, waving it away. "I want only the best of everything."

"It will be so, sir, it *will* be so," declared a fervent Morton Silkline.

"Capital," said the man.

"Now," Silkline went on, briskly, "will you be wishing our Mr. Mossmound to deliver his sermon *On Crossing The Great Divide* or have you a denominational ceremony in mind?"

"I think not," said the man, shaking his head, thoughtfully. "A friend of mine will speak at the services."

"Ah," said Silkline, nodding, "I see."

Reaching forward, he plucked the gold pen from its onyx holder, then with two fingers of his left hand, drew out an application form from the ivory box on his desk top. He looked up with the accredited expression for the Asking of Painful Questions.

"And," he said, "what is the name of the deceased, may I ask?"

"Asper," said the man.

Silkline glanced up, smiling politely. "A relative?" he inquired.

"Me," said the man.

Silkline's laugh was a faint coughing.

"I beg your pardon?" he said. "I thought you said—"

"*Me,*" the man repeated.

"But, I don't—"

"You see," the man explained, "I never had a proper going off. It was catch-as-catch-can, you might say; all improvised. Nothing— how shall I put it?—*tasty.*" The man shrugged his wide shoulders. "I always regretted that," he said. "I always intended to make up for it."

Morton Silkline had returned the pen to its holder with a decisive jabbing of the hand and was on his feet, pulsing with a harsh distemper.

"Indeed, sir," he commented. "In*deed*."

The man looked surprised at the vexation of Morton Silkline.

"I—" he began.

"I am as fully prepared as the next fellow for a trifling badinage," Silkline interrupted, "but *not* during work hours. I think you fail to realize, sir, just where you are. This is Clooney's, a much respected ossuary; not a place for trivial joking or—"

He shrank back and stared, open-mouthed, at the black-garbed man who was suddenly on his feet, eyes glittering with a light most unseemly.

"This," the man said, balefully, "is not a joke."

"Is not—" Silkline could manage no more.

"I came here," said the man, "with a most serious purpose in mind." His eyes glowed now like cherry-bright coals. "And I expect this purpose to be gratified," he said. "Do you understand?"

"I—"

"On Tuesday next," the man continued, "at 8:30 p.m., my friends and I will arrive here for the service. You will have everything prepared by then. Full payments will be made directly following the exequies. Are there any questions?"

"I—"

"I need hardly remind you," said the man, picking up his homburg, "that this affair is of the utmost importance to me." He paused potently before allowing his voice to sink to a forbidding basso profundo. "I expect all to go well."

Bowing a modicum from the waist, the man turned and moved in two regal strides across the office, pausing a moment at the door.

"Uh . . . one additional item," he said. "That mirror in the foyer . . . *remove it*. And, I might add, any others that my friends and I might chance upon during our stay in your parlors."

The man raised one gray-gloved hand. "And now good night."

When Morton Silkline reached the hall, his customer was just flapping out a small window. Quite suddenly, Morton Silkline found the floor.

⊐⊏

They arrived at 8:30, conversing as they entered the foyer of Clooney's to be met by a tremble-legged Morton Silkline about whose eyes hung the raccoon circles of sleepless nights.

"Good evening," greeted the tall man, noting, with a pleased nod, the absence of the wall mirror.

"Good—" was the total of Silkline's wordage.

His vocal cords went slack and his eyes, embossed with daze, moved from figure to figure in the tall man's coterie—the gnarl-faced hunchback whom Silkline heard addressed as Ygor; the peak-hatted crone upon whose ceremented shoulder a black cat crouched; the hulking hairy-handed man who clicked yellow teeth together and regarded Silkline with markedly more than casual eyes; the waxen-featured little man who licked his lips and smiled at Silkline as though he possessed some inner satisfaction; the half-dozen men and women in evening dress, all cherry-eyed and -lipped and—Silkline cringed—superbly toothed.

Silkline hung against the wall, mouth a circular entrance way, hands twitching feebly at his sides as the chatting assemblage passed him by, headed for the Eternal Rest Room.

"Join us," the tall man said.

Silkline stirred fitfully from the wall and stumble-wove an erratic path down the hallway, eyes still saucer-round with stupor.

"I trust," the man said pleasantly, "everything is well prepared."

"Oh," Silkline squeaked. "Oh—oh, yes."

"Sterling," said the man.

When the two of them entered the room, the others were grouped in an admiring semicircle about the casket.

"Is good," the hunchback was muttering to himself. "Is good box."

"Aye, be that a casket or be that a casket, Delphinia?" cackled the ancient crone and Delphinia replied, "Mrrrr*ow.*"

While the others nodded, smiling felicitous smiles and murmuring, "Ah. Ah."

Then one of the evening-dressed women said, "Let Ludwig see," and the semicircle split open so the tall man could pass.

He ran his long fingers over the gold work on the sides and top of the casket, nodding appreciatively. "Splendid," he murmured, voice husky with emotion. "Quite splendid. Just what I always wanted."

"You picked a beauty, lad," said a tall white-haired gentleman.

"Well, try it on fer size!" the chuckling crone declared.

Smiling boyishly, Ludwig climbed into the casket and wriggled into place. "A perfect fit," he said, contentedly.

"Master look good," mumbled Ygor, nodding crookedly. "Look good in box."

Then the hairy-handed man demanded they begin because he had an appointment at 9:15, and everyone hurried to their chairs.

"Come, duck," said the crone, waving a scrawny hand at the ossified Silkline. "Sit by my side. I likes the pretty boys, I do, eh, Delphinia?" Delphinia said, "Mrrrrrow."

"Please, Jenny," Ludwig Asper asked her, opening his eyes a moment. "I'm serious. You know what this means to me."

The crone shrugged. "Aye. Aye," she muttered, then pulled off her peaky hat and fluffed at dank curls as the zombie-stiff Silkline quivered into place beside her, aided by the guiding hand of the little waxen-faced man.

"Hello, pretty boy," the crone whispered, leaning over and jabbing a spear-point elbow into Silkline's ribs.

Then the tall white-haired gentleman from the Carpathian zone rose and the service began.

"Good friends," said the gentleman, "we have gathered ourselves within these bud-wreathed walls to pay homage to our comrade, Ludwig Asper, whom the pious and unyielding fates have chosen to pluck from existence and place within that bleak sarcophagus of all eternity."

"Ci-git," someone murmured; *"Chant du cygne,"* another. Ygor wept and the waxen-featured little man, sitting on the other side of Morton Silkline, leaned over to murmur, *"Tasty,"* but Silkline wasn't sure it was in reference to the funeral address.

"And thus," the gentleman from Carpathia went on, "we collect our bitter selves about this, our comrade's bier; about this litter of sorrow, this cairn, this cromlech, this unhappy tumulus—"

"Clearer, clearer," demanded Jenny, stamping one pointy-toed and petulant shoe. "Mrrrrow," said Delphinia and the crone winked one blood-laced eye at Silkline who shrank away only to brush against the little man who gazed at him with berry eyes and murmured once again, *"Tasty."*

The white-haired gentleman paused long enough to gaze down his royal nose at the crone. Then he continued, "—this mastaba, this sorrowing tope, this ghat, this dread dokhma—"

"What did he say?" asked Ygor, pausing in mid-sob. "What, what?"

"This ain't no declamation tourney, lad," the crone declared. "Keep it crisp, I say."

Ludwig raised his head again, a look of pained embarrassment on his face. "Jenny," he said. *"Please."*

"Aaaah . . . *toad's teeth!"* snapped the crone jadedly, and Delphinia moaned.

"Requiescas in pace, dear brother," the Count went on, testily. "The memory of you shall not perish with your untimely sepulture. You are, dear friend, not so much out of the game as playing on another field."

At which the hairy-handed man rose and hulked from the room with the guttural announcement, *"Go,"* and Silkline felt himself rendered an icicle as he heard a sudden padding of clawed feet on the hallway rug and a baying which echoed back along the walls.

"Ullgate says he has a dinner appointment," the little man asided with a bright-eyed smile. Silkline's chair creaked with shuddering.

The white-haired gentleman stood tall and silent, his red eyes shut, his mouth tight-lipped with aristocratic pique.

"*Count,*" pleaded Ludwig. "Please."

"Am I to endure these vulgar calumnies?" asked the Count. "These—"

"Well, *la-de-da,*" crooned Jenny to her cat.

"Silence, woman!" roared the Count, his head disappearing momentarily in a white, trailing vapor, then reappearing as he gained control.

Ludwig sat up, face a twist of aggravation. "Jenny," he declared, "I think you'd better leave."

"You think to throw old Jenny of Boston out?" the crone challenged. "Well, you got a think that's coming then!"

And, as a shriveling Silkline watched, the crone slapped on her pointed hat and sprouted minor lightning at the fingertips. A snail-backed Delphinia bristled ebony hairs as the Count stepped forward, hand outstretched, to clamp onto the crone's shoulder, then stiffened in mid-stride as sizzling fire ringed him.

"Haa!" crowed Jenny while a horror-stricken Silkline gagged, "My *rug!*"

"Jen-*ny!*" Ludwig cried, clambering out. The crone gestured and all the flowers in the room began exploding like popcorn.

"*No-o,*" moaned Silkline as the curtains flared and split. Chairs were overthrown. The Count bicarbonated to a hissing stream of white which flew at Jenny—who flung up her arms and vanished, cat and all, in an orange spume as the air grew thick with squeaks and rib-winged flapping.

Just before the bulbous-eyed Morton Silkline toppled forward, the waxen-faced man leaned over, smiling toothfully, squeezed the Director's numbed arm and murmured, "*Tasty.*"

Then Silkline was at one with the rug.

Morton Silkline slumped in his sable-leathered chair, still twitching slightly even though a week had passed since the nerve-splitting event. On his desk lay the note that Ludwig Asper had left pinned to his unconscious chest.

Sir, it read. *Accept, in addition to this bag of gold (which I trust will cover all costs) my regrets that full decorum was not effected by the guests at my funeral. For, save for that, the entire preparation was most satisfactory to me.*

Silkline put down the note and grazed a loving touch across the hill of glinting coins on his desk. Through judicious inquiry, he had gleaned the information that a connection in Mexico (namely, a cosmetician nephew in Carillo's Cut-Rate Catacomb) could safely dispose of the gold at mutual profit. All things considered, the affair had not been really as bad as all—

Morton Silkline looked up as something entered his office.

He would have chosen to leap back screaming and vanish in the flowered pattern of the wallpaper but he was too petrified. Once more gape-mouthed he stared at the huge, tentacled, ocher-dripping shapelessness that weaved and swayed before him.

"A friend," it said politely, "recommended you to me."

Silkline sat bug-eyed for a lengthy moment but then his twitching hand accidentally touched the gold again. And he found strength.

"You've come," he said, breathing through his mouth, "to the right place—uh . . . *sir. Pomps*—" He swallowed mightily and braced himself "*—for all circumstances.*"

He reached for his pen, blowing away the yellow-green smoke which was beginning to obscure the office.

"Name of the deceased?" he asked, businesslike.

FROM SHADOWED PLACES

Dr. Jennings hooked in toward the curb, the tires of his Jaguar spewing out a froth of slush. Braking hard, he jerked the key loose with his left hand while his right clutched for the satchel at his side. In a moment, he was on the street, waiting for a breach in traffic.

His gaze leaped upward to the windows of Peter Lang's apartment. Was Patricia all right? She'd sounded awful on the phone—tremulous, near to panic. Jennings lowered his eyes and frowned uneasily at the line of passing cars. Then, as an opening appeared in the procession, he lunged forward.

The glass door swung pneumatically shut behind him as he strode across the lobby. *Father, hurry! Please! I don't know what to do with him!* Patricia's stricken voice re-echoed in his mind. He stepped into the elevator and pressed the tenth-floor button. *I can't tell you on the phone! You've got to come!* Jennings stared ahead with sightless eyes, unconscious of the whispering closure of the doors.

Patricia's three-month engagement to Lang had certainly been a troubled one. Even so, he wouldn't feel justified in telling her to break it off. Lang could hardly be classified as one of the idle rich. True, he'd never had to face a job of work in his entire twenty-seven years. Still, he wasn't indolent or helpless. One of the world's ranking hunter-sportsmen, he handled himself and his chosen world with graceful authority. There was a readily mined vein of humor in him and a sense of basic justice despite his air of swagger. Most of all, he seemed to love Patricia very much.

Still, all this trouble—

Jennings twitched, blinking his eyes into focus. The elevator doors were open. Realizing that the tenth floor had been reached, he lurched into the corridor, shoe heels squeaking on the polished tile. Without thinking, he thrust the satchel underneath his arm and began pulling off his gloves. Before he'd reached the apartment, they were in his pocket and his coat had been unbuttoned.

A pencilled note was tacked unevenly to the door. *Come in.* Jennings felt a tremor at the sight of Pat's misshapen scrawl. Bracing himself, he turned the knob and went inside.

He froze in unexpected shock. The living room was a shambles, chairs and tables overturned, lamps broken, a clutter of books hurled across the floor, and, scattered everywhere, a debris of splintered glasses, matches, cigarette butts. Dozens of liquor stains islanded the white carpeting. On the bar, an upset bottle trickled Scotch across the counter edge while, from the giant wall speakers, a steady rasping flooded the room. Jennings stared, aghast. *Peter must have gone insane.*

Thrusting his bag onto the hall table, he shed his hat and coat, then grabbed his bag again, and hastened down the steps into the living room. Crossing to the built-in sound system, he switched it off.

"Father?"

"Yes." Jennings heard his daughter sob with relief and hurried towards the bedroom.

They were on the floor beneath the picture window. Pat was on her knees embracing Peter who had drawn his naked body into a heap, arms pressed across his face. As Jennings knelt beside them, Patricia looked at him with terror-haunted eyes.

"He tried to jump," she said. "He tried to kill himself." Her voice was fitful, hoarse.

"All right." Jennings drew away the rigid quiver of her arms and tried to raise Lang's head. Peter gasped, recoiling from his touch, and bound himself again into a ball of limbs and torso. Jennings stared at his constricted form. Almost in horror, he watched the crawl of muscles in Peter's back and shoulders. Snakes seemed to writhe beneath the sun-darkened skin.

"How long has he been like this?" he asked.

"I don't know." Her face was a mask of anguish. "I don't know."

"Go in the living room and pour yourself a drink," her father ordered, "I'll take care of him."

"He tried to jump right through the window."

"Patricia."

She began to cry and Jennings turned away; tears were what she needed. Once again, he tried to uncurl the inflexible knot of Peter's body. Once again, the young man gasped and shrank away from him.

"Try to relax," said Jennings, "I want to get you on your bed."

"No!" said Peter, his voice a pain-thickened whisper.

"I can't help you, boy, unless—"

Jennings stopped, his face gone blank. In an instant, Lang's body had lost its rigidity. His legs were straightening out, his arms were slipping from their tense position at his face. A stridulous breath swelled out his lungs.

Peter raised his head.

The sight made Jennings gasp. If ever a face could be described as tortured, it was Lang's. Darkly bearded, bloodless, stark-eyed, it was the face of a man enduring inexplicable torment.

"What *is* it?" Jennings asked, appalled.

Peter grinned; it was the final, hideous touch that made the doctor shudder. "Hasn't Patty told you?" Peter answered.

"Told me what?"

Peter hissed, apparently amused. "I'm being hexed," he said. "Some scrawny—"

"Darling, *don't,*" begged Pat.

"What are you talking about?" demanded Jennings.

"Drink?" asked Peter. "Darling?"

Patricia pushed unsteadily to her feet and started for the living room. Jennings helped Lang to his bed.

"What's this all about?" he asked.

Lang fell back heavily on his pillow. "What I said," he answered. "Hexed. Cursed. Witch doctor." He snickered feebly. "Bastard's killing me. Been three months now—almost since Patty and I met."

"Are you—?" Jennings started.

"Codeine ineffectual," said Lang. "Even morphine—got some. Nothing." He sucked in at the air. "No fever, no chills. No symptoms for the AMA. Just—someone killing me." He peered up through slitted eyes. "Funny?"

"Are you serious?"

Peter snorted. "Who the hell knows?" he said. "Maybe it's delirium tremens. God knows I've drunk enough today to—" The tangle of his dark hair rustled on the pillow as he looked towards the window. "Hell, it's night," he said. He turned back quickly. "Time?" he asked.

"After ten," said Jennings. "What about—?"

"Thursday, isn't it?" asked Lang.

Jennings stared at him.

"No, I see it isn't." Lang started coughing dryly. "Drink!" he called. As his gaze jumped towards the doorway, Jennings glanced across his shoulder. Patricia was back.

"It's all spilled," she said, her voice like that of a frightened child.

"All right, don't worry," muttered Lang. "Don't need it. I'll be dead soon anyway."

"Don't talk like that!"

"Honey, I'd be glad to die right now," said Peter, staring at the ceiling. His broad chest hitched unevenly as he breathed. "Sorry, darling, I don't mean it. Uh-oh, here we go again." He spoke so mildly that his seizure caught them by surprise.

Abruptly, he was floundering on the bed, his muscle-knotted legs kicking like pistons, his arms clamped down across the drumhide tautness of his face. A noise like the shrilling of a violin wavered in his throat, and Jennings saw saliva running from the corners of his mouth. Turning suddenly, the doctor lurched across the room for his bag.

Before he'd reached it, Peter's thrashing body had fallen from the bed. The young man reared up, screaming, on his face the wide-mouthed, slavering frenzy of an animal. Patricia tried to hold him back but, with a snarl, he shoved her brutally aside and staggered for the window.

Jennings met him with the hypodermic. For several moments, they were locked in reeling struggle, Peter's distended, teeth-bared face inches from the doctor's, his vein-corded hands scrabbling for Jennings's throat. He cried out hoarsely as the needle pierced his skin and, springing backwards, lost his balance, fell. He tried to stand, his crazed eyes looking towards the window. Then the drug was in his blood and he was sitting with the flaccid posture of a rag doll. Torpor glazed his eyes. "Bastard's killing me," he muttered.

They laid him on the bed and covered up the sluggish twitching of his body.

"Killing me," said Lang. "Black bastard."

"Does he really *believe* this?" Jennings asked.

"Father, *look* at him," she answered.

"You believe it too?"

"*I* don't know." She shook her head impotently. "All I know is that I've seen him change from what he was to—*this*. He isn't sick, father. There's nothing wrong with him." She shuddered. "Yet he's dying."

"Why didn't you call me sooner?"

"I couldn't," she said. "I was afraid to leave him for a second."

Jennings drew his fingers from the young man's fluttering pulse. "Has he been examined at all?"

She nodded tiredly. "Yes," she answered, "when it started getting

worse, he went to see a specialist. He thought, perhaps his brain—"
She shook her head. "There's nothing wrong with him."

"But why does he say he's being—?" Jennings found himself unable to speak the word.

"I don't know," she said. "Sometimes, he seems to believe it. Mostly he jokes about it."

"But on what grounds—?"

"Some incident on his last safari," said Patricia. "I don't really know what happened. Some—Zulu native threatened him; said he was a witch doctor and was going to—" Her voice broke into a wracking sob. "Oh, God, how can such a thing be true? How can it *happen?*"

"The point, I think, is whether Peter, actually, believes it's happening," said Jennings. He turned to Lang. "And, from the look of him—"

"Father, I've been wondering if—" Patricia swallowed. "If maybe Dr. Howell could help him."

Jennings stared at her for a moment. Then he said, "You *do* believe it, don't you?"

"Father, *try to understand.*" There was a trembling undertone of panic in her voice, "You've only seen Peter now and then. I've watched it happening to him almost day by day. Something is destroying him! I don't know what it is, but I'll try anything to stop it. *Anything.*"

"All right." He pressed a reassuring hand against her back. "Go phone while I examine him."

After she'd gone into the living room—the telephone connected in the bedroom had been ripped from the wall—Jennings drew the covers down and looked at Peter's bronzed and muscular body. It was trembling with minute vibrations—as if, within the chemical imprisoning of the drug, each separate nerve still pulsed and throbbed.

Jennings clenched his teeth in vague distress. Somewhere, at the core of his perception, where the rationale of science had yet to fil-ter, he sensed that medical inquiry would be pointless. Still, he felt distaste for what Patricia might be setting up. It went against the grain of learned acceptance. It offended mentality.

It, also, frightened him.

❖

The drug's effect was almost gone now, Jennings saw. Ordinarily, it would have rendered Lang unconscious for six to eight hours. Now—in *forty minutes*—he was in the living room with them, lying on the sofa in his bathrobe, saying, "Patty, it's ridiculous. What good's another doctor going to do?"

"All right then, it's ridiculous!" she said. "What would you *like* for us to do—just stand around and watch you—?" She couldn't finish.

"Shhh." Lang stroked her hair with trembling fingers. "Patty, Patty. Hang on, darling. Maybe I can beat it."

"You're *going* to beat it." Patricia kissed his hand. "It's both of us, Peter. I won't go on without you."

"Don't *you* talk like that." Lang twisted on the sofa. "Oh, Christ, it's starting up again." He forced a smile. "No, I'm all right," he told her, "just—crawly, sort of." His smile flared into a sudden grimace of pain. "So this Dr. Howell is going to solve my problem, is he? How?"

Jennings saw Patricia bite her lip. "It's a—*her*, darling," she told Lang.

"Great," he said. He twitched convulsively. "That's what we need. What is she, a chiropractor?"

"She's an anthropologist."

"*Dandy*. What's she going to do, explain the ethnic origins of su-perstition to me?" Lang spoke rapidly as if trying to outdistance pain with words.

"She's been to Africa," said Pat. "She—"

"So have I," said Peter. "Great place to visit. Just don't screw around with witch doctors." His laughter withered to a gasping cry. "Oh, God, you scrawny, black bastard, if I had you here!" His hands clawed out as if to throttle some invisible assailant.

"I beg your pardon—"

They turned in surprise. A young black woman was looking down at them from the entrance hall.

"There was a card on the door," she said.

"Of course; we'd forgotten." Jennings was on his feet now. He heard Patricia whispering to Lang, "I *meant* to tell you. Please don't be biased." Peter looked at her sharply, his expression even more surprised now. *"Biased?"* he said.

Jennings and his daughter moved across the room.

"Thank you for coming." Patricia pressed her cheek to Dr. Howell's.

"It's nice to see you, Pat," said Dr. Howell. She smiled across Patricia's shoulder at the doctor.

"Had you any trouble getting here?" he asked.

"No, no, the subway never fails me." Lurice Howell unbuttoned her coat and turned as Jennings reached to help her. Pat looked at the overnight bag that Lurice had set on the floor, then glanced at Peter.

Lang did not take his eyes from Lurice Howell as she approached him, flanked by Pat and Jennings.

"Peter, this is Dr. Howell," said Pat. "She and I went to Columbia together. She teaches anthropology at City College."

Lurice smiled. "Good evening," she said.

"Not so very," Peter answered. From the corners of his eyes Jennings saw the way Patricia stiffened.

Dr. Howell's expression did not alter. Her voice remained the same. "And who's the scrawny, black bastard you wish you had here?" she asked.

Peter's face went momentarily blank. Then, his teeth clenched against the pain, he answered, "What's that supposed to mean?"

"A question," said Lurice.

"If you're planning to conduct a seminar on race relations, skip it," muttered Lang, "I'm not in the mood."

"*Peter.*"

He looked at Pat through pain-filmed eyes. "What do you want?" he demanded. "You're already convinced I'm prejudiced, so—" He dropped his head back on the sofa arm and jammed his eyes shut. "Jesus, stick a *knife* in me," he rasped.

The straining smile had gone from Dr. Howell's lips. She glanced at Jennings gravely as he spoke. "I've examined him," he told her. "There's not a sign of physical impairment, not a hint of brain injury."

"How should there be?" she answered, quietly. "It's not disease. It's juju."

Jennings stared at her. "You—"

"*There* we go," said Peter, hoarsely. "Now we've got it." He was sitting up again, whitened fingers digging at the cushions. "That's the answer. *Juju.*"

"Do you doubt it?" asked Lurice.

"I *doubt* it."

"The way you doubt your prejudice?"

"Oh, Jesus. *God.*" Lang filled his lungs with a guttural, sucking noise. "I was hurting and I wanted something to hate so I picked on that lousy savage to—" He fell back heavily. "The hell with it. Think what you like." He clamped a palsied hand across his eyes. "Just let me die. Oh, Jesus, Jesus God, sweet Jesus, *let me die.*" Suddenly, he looked at Jennings. "Another shot?" he begged.

"Peter, your heart can't—"

"*Damn* my heart!" Peter's head was rocking back and forth now. "*Half* strength then! You can't refuse a dying man!"

Pat jammed the edge of a shaking fist against her lips, trying not to cry.

"*Please!*" said Peter.

After the injection had taken effect, Lang slumped back, his face and neck soaked with perspiration. "Thanks," he gasped. His pale lips twitched into a smile as Patricia knelt beside him and began to dry his face with a towel. "Greetings, love," he muttered. She couldn't speak.

Peter's hooded eyes turned to Dr. Howell. "All right, I'm sorry, I apologize," he told her curtly. "I thank you for coming, but I don't believe it."

"Then why is it working?" asked Lurice.

"I don't even know what's happening!" snapped Lang.

"I think you do," said Dr. Howell, an urgency rising in her voice, "and *I* know, Mr. Lang. Juju is the most fearsome pagan sorcery in the world. Centuries of mass belief alone would be enough to give it terrifying power. It *has* that power, Mr. Lang. You know it does."

"And how do *you* know, Dr. Howell?" he countered.

"When I was twenty-two," she said, "I spent a year in a Zulu village doing field work for my Ph.D. While I was there, the *ngombo* took a fancy to me and taught me almost everything she knew."

"*Ngombo?*" asked Patricia.

"*Witch doctor,*" said Peter, in disgust.

"I thought witch doctors were men," said Jennings.

"No, most of them are women," said Lurice. "Shrewd, observant women who work very hard at their profession."

"*Frauds,*" said Peter.

Lurice smiled at him. "Yes," she said, "they are. Frauds. Parasites. Loafers. Scaremongers. Still—" Her smile grew hard. "—what do you suppose is making you feel as though a thousand spiders were crawling all over you?"

For the first time since he'd entered the apartment, Jennings saw a look of fear on Peter's face. "*You know that?*" Peter asked her.

"I know everything you're going through," said Dr. Howell. "I've been through it myself."

"*When?*" demanded Lang. There was no derogation in his voice now.

"During that year," said Dr. Howell, "a witch doctor from a nearby village put a death curse on me. Kuringa saved me from it."

"Tell me," said Peter, breaking in on her. Jennings noticed that the young man's breath was quickening. It appalled him to realize that the second injection was already beginning to lose its effect.

"Tell you what?" said Lurice. "About the long-nailed fingers scraping at your insides? About the feeling that you have to pull yourself into a ball in order to crush the snake uncoiling in your belly?"

Peter gaped at her.

"The feeling that your blood has turned to acid?" said Lurice. "That, if you move, you'll crumble because your bones have all been sucked hollow?"

Peter's lips began to shake.

"The feeling that your brain is being eaten by a pack of furry rats? That your eyes are just about to melt and dribble down your cheeks like jelly? That—?"

"That's enough." Lang's body seemed to jolt, he shuddered so spasmodically.

"I only said these things to convince you that I know," said Lurice. "I remember my own pain as if I'd suffered it this morning instead of seven years ago. I can help you if you'll let me, Mr. Lang. Put aside your skepticism. You *do* believe it or it couldn't hurt you, don't you see that?"

"Darling, *please*," said Patricia.

Peter looked at her. Then his gaze moved back to Dr. Howell.

"We mustn't wait much longer, Mr. Lang," she warned.

"All *right*!" He closed his eyes. "All right then, *try*. I sure as hell can't get any worse."

"*Quickly*," begged Patricia.

"Yes." Lurice Howell turned and walked across the room to get her overnight bag.

It was as she picked it up that Jennings saw the look cross her face—as if some formidable complication had just occurred to her. She glanced at them. "Pat," she said.

"*Yes.*"

"Come here a moment."

Patricia pushed up hurriedly and moved to her side. Jennings watched them for a moment before his eyes shifted to Lang. The young man was starting to twitch again. It's *coming*, Jennings thought. *Juju is the most fearsome pagan sorcery in the world—*

"What?"

Jennings glanced at the women. Pat was staring at Dr. Howell in shock.

"I'm sorry," said Lurice, "I should have told you from the start, but there wasn't any opportunity."

Pat hesitated. "It has to be that way?" she asked.

"Yes. It does."

Patricia looked at Peter with a questioning apprehension in her eyes. Abruptly, then, she nodded. "All right," she said, "but *hurry.*"

Without another word, Lurice Howell went into the bedroom. Jennings watched his daughter as she looked intently at the door behind which the black woman had closeted herself. He could not fathom the meaning of her look. For now the fear in Pat's expression was of a different sort.

⟐

The bedroom door opened and Dr. Howell came out. Jennings, turning from the sofa, caught his breath. Lurice was naked to the waist and garbed below with a skirt composed of several colored handkerchiefs knotted together. Her legs and feet were bare. Jennings gaped at her. The blouse and skirt she'd worn had revealed nothing of her voluptuous breasts, the sinuous abundance of her hips. Suddenly conscious of his blatant observation, Jennings turned his eyes towards Pat. Her expression, as she stared at Dr. Howell, was unmistakable now.

Jennings looked back at Peter. Due to its masking of pain, the young man's face was more difficult to read.

"Please understand, I've never done this before," said Lurice, embarrassed by their staring silence.

"We understand," said Jennings, once more unable to take his eyes from her.

A bright red spot was painted on each of her tawny cheeks and, over her twisted, twine-held hair, she wore a helmet-like plume of feathers, each of a chestnut hue with a vivid white eye at the tip. Her breasts thrust out from a tangle of necklaces made of animals teeth, skeins of brightly colored yarn, beads, and strips of snake skin. On her left arm—banded at the biceps with a strip of angora fleece—was slung a small shield of dappled oxhide.

The contrast between the bag and her outfit was marked enough. The effect of her appearance in the Manhattan duplex created a ripple of indefinable dread in Jennings as she moved towards them with a shy, almost childlike defiance—as if her shame were balanced by a knowledge of her physical wealth. Jennings was startled to see that her stomach was tattooed, hundreds of tiny welts forming a design of concentric circles around her navel.

"Kuringa insisted on it," said Lurice as if he'd asked. "It was her price for teaching me her secrets." She smiled fleetingly. "I managed to dissuade her from filing my teeth to a point."

Jennings sensed that she was talking to hide her embarrassment and he felt a surge of empathy for her as she set her bag down, opened it and started to remove its contents.

"The welts are raised by making small incisions in the flesh," she said, "and pressing into each incision a dab of paste." She put, on the coffee table, a vial of grumous liquid, a handful of small, polished bones. "The paste I had to make myself. I had to catch a land crab with my bare hands and tear off one of its claws. I had to tear the skin from a living frog and the jaw from a monkey." She put on the table a bundle of what looked like tiny lances. "The claws, the skin, and the jaw, together with some plant ingredients, I pounded into the paste."

Jennings looked surprised as she withdrew an LP from the bag and set it on the turntable.

"When I say *'Now,'* Doctor," she asked, "will you put on the turntable arm?"

Jennings nodded mutely, watching her with what was close to fascination. She seemed to know exactly what she was doing. Ignoring the slit-eyed stare of Lang, the uncertain surveillance of Patricia, Lurice set the various objects on the floor. As she squatted, Pat could not restrain a gasp. Underneath the skirt of handkerchiefs, Lurice's loins were uncovered.

"Well, I may not live," said Peter—his face was almost white now—"but it looks as if I'm going to have a fascinating death."

Lurice interrupted him. "If the three of you will sit in a circle," she said. The prim refinement of her voice coming from the lips of what seemed a pagan goddess struck Jennings forcibly as he moved to assist Lang.

The seizure came as Peter tried to stand. In an instant, he was in the throes of it, groveling on the floor, his body doubled, his knees and elbows thumping at the rug. Abruptly, he flopped over, forcing back his head, the muscles of his spine tensed so acutely that his back arched upward from the floor. Pale foam ribboned from the slash of his mouth, his staring eyes seemed frozen in their sockets.

"Lurice!" screamed Pat.

"There's nothing we can do until it passes," said Lurice. She stared at Lang with sickened eyes. Then, as his bathrobe came undone and he was thrashing naked on the rug, she turned away, her face tightening with a look that Jennings, glancing at her, saw, to his added disquietude, was a look of fear. Then he and Pat were bent across Lang's afflicted body, trying to hold him in check.

"Let him go," said Lurice. "There's nothing you can do."

Patricia glared at her in frightened animosity. As Peter's body finally shuddered into immobility, she drew the edges of his robe together and refastened the sash.

"*Now.* Into the circle, quickly," said Lurice, clearly forcing herself against some inner dread. "No, he has to sit alone," she said, as Patricia braced herself beside him, supporting his back.

"He'll *fall*," said Pat, an undercurrent of resentment in her voice.

"Patricia, if you want my help—!"

Uncertainly, her eyes drifting from Peter's pain-wasted features to the harried expression on Lurice's face, Patricia edged away and settled herself.

"Cross-legged, please," said Lurice. "Mr. Lang?"

Peter grunted, eyes half-closed.

"During the ceremony, I'll ask you for a token of payment. Some unimportant personal item will suffice."

Peter nodded. "All right; let's *go*," he said, "I can't take much more."

Lurice's breasts rose, quivering, as she drew in breath. "No talking now," she murmured. Nervously, she sat across from Peter and bowed her head. Except for Lang's stentorian breathing, the room grew deathly still. Jennings could hear, faintly, in the distance, the sounds of traffic. It seemed impossible to adjust his mind to what was about to happen; an attempted ritual of jungle sorcery—in a New York City apartment.

He tried, in vain, to clear his mind of misgivings. He didn't believe in this. Yet here he sat, his crossed legs already beginning to cramp. Here sat Peter Lang, obviously close to death with not a symptom to explain it. Here sat his daughter, terrified, struggling mentally against that which she herself had initiated. And there most bizarre of all, sat—not Dr. Howell, an intelligent professor of anthropology, a cultured, civilized woman—but a near-naked African witch doctor with her implements of barbarous magic.

There was a rattling noise. Jennings blinked his eyes and looked at Lurice. In her left hand, she was clutching the sheaf of what looked like miniature lances. With her right, she was picking up the cluster of tiny, polished bones. She shook them in her palm like dice and tossed them onto the rug, her gaze intent on their fall.

She stared at their pattern on the carpeting, then picked them up again. Across from her, Peter's breath was growing tortured. What if he suffered another attack? Jennings wondered. Would the ceremony have to be restarted?

He twitched as Lurice broke the silence.

"Why do you come here?" she asked. She looked at Peter coldly, almost glaring at him. "Why do you consult me? Is it because you have no success with women?"

"What?" Peter stared at her bewilderedly.

"Is someone in your house sick? Is that why you come to me?" asked Lurice, her voice imperious. Jennings realized abruptly that she was—completely now—a witch doctor questioning her male client, arrogantly contemptuous of his inferior status.

"Are *you* sick?" She almost spat the words, her shoulders jerking back so that her breasts hitched upwards. Jennings glanced involuntarily at his daughter. Pat was sitting like a statue, cheeks pale, lips a narrow, bloodless line.

"Speak up, man!" ordered Lurice—ordered the scowling *ngombo.*

"Yes! I'm sick!" Peter's chest lurched with breath. "I'm *sick.*"

"Then speak of it," said Lurice. "Tell me how this sickness came upon you."

Either Peter was in such pain now that any notion of resistance was destroyed—or else he had been captured by the fascination of Lurice's presence. Probably it was a combination of the two, thought Jennings as he watched Lang begin to speak, his voice compelled, his eyes held by Lurice's burning stare.

"One night, this man came sneaking into camp," he said. "He tried to steal some food. When I chased him, he got furious and threatened me. He said he'd kill me." Jennings wondered if Lurice had hypnotized Peter, the young man's voice was so mechanical.

"And he carried, in a sack at his side—" Lurice's voice seemed to prompt like a hypnotist's.

"He carried a doll," said Peter. His throat contracted as he swallowed. "It spoke to me," he said.

"The fetish spoke to you," said Lurice. "What did the fetish say?"

"It said that I would die. It said that, when the moon was like a bow, I would die."

Abruptly, Peter shivered and closed his eyes. Lurice threw down the bones again and stared at them. Abruptly, she flung down the tiny lances.

"It is not Mbwiri nor Hebiezo," she said. "It is not Atando nor Fuofuo nor Sovi. It is not Kundi or Sogbla. It is not a demon of the forest that devours you. It is an evil spirit that belongs to a *ngombo* who has been offended. The *ngombo* has brought evil to your house. The evil spirit of the *ngombo* has fastened itself upon you in revenge for your offense against its master. Do you understand?"

Peter was barely able to speak. He nodded jerkily. "Yes."

"Say—*Yes, I understand.*"

"Yes." He shuddered. "Yes. I understand."

"You will pay me now," she told him.

Peter stared at her for several moments before lowering his eyes. His twitching fingers reached into the pockets of his robe and came out empty. Suddenly, he gasped, his shoulders hitching forward as a spasm of pain rushed through him. He reached into his pockets a second time as if he weren't sure that they were empty. Then, frantically, he wrenched the ring from the third finger of his left hand and held it out. Jennings's gaze darted to his daughter. Her face was like stone as she watched Peter handing over the ring she'd given him.

"Now," said Lurice.

Jennings pushed to his feet and, stumbling because of the numbness in his legs, he moved to the turntable and lowered the stylus in place. Before he'd settled back into the circle, the record started playing.

In a moment, the room was filled with drumbeats, with a chanting of voices and a slow, uneven clapping of hands. His gaze intent on Lurice, Jennings had the impression that everything was fading at the edges of his vision, that Lurice, alone, was visible, standing in a dimly nebulous light.

She had left her oxhide shield on the floor and was holding the bottle in her hand. As Jennings watched, she pulled the stopper loose and drank the contents with a single swallow. Vaguely, through the daze of fascination that gripped his mind, Jennings wondered what it was she'd drunk.

The bottle thudded on the floor.

Lurice began to dance.

She started languidly. Only her arms and shoulders moved at first, their restless sinuating timed to the cadence of the drumbeats. Jennings stared at her, imagining that his heart had altered its rhythm to that of the drums. He watched the writhing of her shoulders, the serpentine gestures she was making with her arms and hands. He heard the rustling of her necklaces. Time and place were gone for him. He might have been sitting in a jungle glade, watching the somnolent twisting of her dance.

"Clap hands," said the *ngombo*.

Without hesitation, Jennings started clapping in time with the drums. He glanced at Patricia. She was doing the same, her eyes still fixed on Lurice. Only Peter sat motionless, looking straight ahead, the muscles of his jaw quivering as he ground his teeth together. For a fleeting moment, Jennings was a doctor once again, looking at his patient in concern. Then turning back, he was redrawn into the mindless captivation of Lurice's dance.

The drumbeats were accelerating now, becoming louder. Lurice began to move within the circle, turning slowly, arms and shoulders still in undulant motion. No matter where she moved, her eyes remained on Peter, and Jennings realized that her gesturing was exclusively for Lang—drawing, gathering gestures as if she sought to lure him to her side.

Suddenly, she bent over, her breasts dropping heavily, then jerking upward as their muscles caught. She shook herself with feverish abandon, swinging her breasts from side to side and rattling her necklaces, her wild face hovering inches over Peter's. Jennings felt his stomach muscles pulling in as Lurice drew her talon-shaped fingers over Peter's cheeks, then straightened up and pivoted, her shoulders thrust back carelessly, her teeth bared in a grimace of savage zeal. In a moment, she had spun around to face her client again.

A second time she bent herself, this time stalking back and forth in front of Peter with a catlike gait, a rabid crooning in her throat. From the corners of his eyes, Jennings saw his daughter straining forward and he glanced at her. The expression on her face was terrible.

Suddenly, Patricia's lips flared back as in a soundless cry and Jennings looked back quickly at Lurice. His breath choked off. Leaning over, she had clutched her breasts with digging fingers and was thrusting them at Peter's face. Peter stared at her, his body trembling. Crooning again, Lurice drew back. She lowered her hands and Jennings tightened as he saw that she was pulling at the skirt of handkerchiefs. In a moment, it had fluttered to the carpeting and she was back at Peter. It was then that Jennings knew exactly what she'd drunk.

"No." Patricia's vemon-thickened voice made him twist around, his heartbeat lurching. She was starting to her feet.

"Pat!" he whispered.

She looked at him and, for a moment, they were staring at each other. Then, with a violent shudder, she sank to the floor again and Jennings turned away from her.

Lurice was on her knees in front of Peter now, rocking back and forth and rubbing at her thighs with flattened hands. She couldn't seem to breathe. Her open mouth kept sucking at the air with wheezing noises. Jennings saw perspiration trickling down her cheeks; he saw it glistening on her back and shoulders. No, he thought. The word came automatically, the voicing of some alien dread that seemed to rise up, choking, in him. No. He watched Lurice's hand clutch upwards at her breasts again, proferring them to Peter. No. The word was lurking terror in his mind. He kept on staring at Lurice, fearing what was going to happen, fascinated at its possibility. Drumbeats throbbed and billowed in his ears. His heartbeat pounded.

No!

Lurice's hands had clawed out suddenly and torn apart the edges of Lang's robe. Patricia's gasp was hoarse, astounded. Jennings only caught a glimpse of her distorted face before his gaze was drawn back to Lurice. Swallowed by the frenzied thundering of the drums, the howl of chanting voices, the explosive clapping, he felt as if his head were going numb, as if the room were tilting. In a dreamlike haze, he saw Lurice's hands begin to rub at Peter's flesh. He saw a look of nightmare on the young man's face as torment closed a vise around him—torment that was just as much carnality as agony. Lurice moved closer to him. Closer. Now her writhing, sweat-laved body pendulated inches from his own, her hands caressing wantonly.

"Come into me." Her voice was bestial, gluttonous. "Come into me."

"Get away from him." Patricia's guttural warning tore Jennings from entrancement. Jerking around, he saw her reaching for Lurice— who, in that instant, clamped herself on Peter's body.

Jennings lunged at Pat, not understanding why he should restrain her, only sensing that he must. She twisted wildly in his grip, her hot breath spilling on his cheeks, her body violent in rage.

"Get away from him!" she screamed at Lurice. *"Get your hands away from him!"*

"Patricia!"

"Let me *go!*"

Lurice's scream of anguish paralyzed them. Stunned, they watched her flinging back from Peter and collapsing on her back, her legs jerked in, arms flung across her face. Jennings felt a burst of horror in himself. His gaze leaped up to Peter's face. The look of pain had vanished from it. Only stunned bewilderment remained.

"What *is* it?" gasped Patricia.

Jennings's voice was hollow, awed. *"She's taken it away from him,"* he said.

"Oh, my God—" Aghast, Patricia watched her friend.

The feeling that you have to pull yourself into a ball in order to crush the snake uncoiling in your belly. The words assaulted Jennings's mind. He watched the rippling crawl of muscles underneath Lurice's flesh, the spastic twitching of her legs. Across the room, the record stopped and, in the sudden stillness, he could hear a shrill whine quavering in Lurice's throat. *The feeling that your blood has turned to acid, that, if you move, you'll crumble because your bones have all been sucked hollow.* Eyes haunted, Jennings watched her suffering Peter's agony. *The feeling that your brain is being eaten by a pack of furry rats, that your eyes are just about to melt and dribble down your cheeks like jelly.* Lurice's legs kicked out. She twisted onto her back and started rolling on her shoulders. Her legs jerked in until her feet were resting on the carpet. Convulsively, she reared her hips. Her stomach heaved with tortured breath, her swollen breasts lolled from side to side.

"Peter!"

Patricia's horrified whisper made Jennings's head snap up. Peter's eyes were glittering as he watched Lurice's thrashing body. He had started pushing to his knees, a look not human drawn across his features. Now his hands were reaching for Lurice. Jennings caught him by the shoulders, but Peter didn't seem to notice. He kept reaching for Lurice.

"Peter."

Lang tried to shove him aside but Jennings tightened his grip. *"For God's sake—*Peter!"

The noise Lang uttered made Jennings's skin crawl. He clamped his fingers brutally in Peter's hair and jerked him around so that they faced each other.

"Use your mind, man!" Jennings ordered. "Your *mind!*"

Peter blinked. He stared at Jennings with the eyes of a newly awakened man. Jennings pulled his hands away and turned back quickly.

Lurice was lying motionless on her back, her dark eyes staring at the ceiling. With a gasp, Jennings leaned over and pressed a finger underneath her left breast. Her heartbeat was nearly imperceptible. He looked at her eyes again. They had the glassy stare of a corpse. He gaped at them in disbelief. Suddenly, they closed and a protracted, body-wracking shudder passed through Lurice. Jennings watched her, open-mouthed, unable to move. No, he thought. It was impossible. She couldn't be—

"*Lurice!*" he cried.

She opened her eyes and looked at him. After several moments, her lips stirred feebly as she tried to smile.

"It's over now," she whispered.

The car moved along Seventh Avenue, its tires hissing on the slush. Across the seat from Jennings, Dr. Howell slumped, motionless, in her exhaustion. A shamed, remorseful Pat had bathed and dressed her, after which Jennings had helped her to his car. Just before they'd left the apartment, Peter had attempted to thank her, then, unable to find the words, had kissed her hand and turned away in silence.

Jennings glanced at her. "You know," he said, "if I hadn't actually seen what happened tonight, I wouldn't believe it for a moment. I'm still not sure that I do."

"It isn't easy to accept," she said.

Jennings drove in silence for a while before he spoke again. "Dr. Howell?"

"Yes?"

He hesitated. Then he asked, "Why did you do it?"

"If I hadn't," said Lurice, "your future son-in-law would have died before the night was over. You have no idea how close he came."

"Granting that," said Jennings, "what I mean is—why did you deliberately subject yourself to such—abasement?"

"There was no alternative," she answered. "Mr. Lang couldn't possibly have coped with what was happening to him. I could. It was as simple as that. Everything else was—unfortunate necessity."

"And something of a Pandora's box as well," he said.

"I know," she said, "I was afraid of it but there was nothing I could do."

"You told Patricia what was going to happen?"

"No," said Lurice, "I couldn't tell her everything. I tried to brace her for the shock of what was coming but, of course, I had to withhold some of it. Otherwise she might have refused my help—and her fiancé would have died."

"It was an aphrodisiac in that bottle, wasn't it?"

"Yes," she answered, "I had to lose myself. If I hadn't, personal inhibitions would have kept me from doing what was necessary."

"What happened just before the end of it—" Jennings began.

"Mr. Lang's apparent lust for me?" said Lurice. "It was only a derangement of the moment. The sudden extraction of the pain left him, for a period of seconds, without conscious volition. Without, if you will, civilized restraint. It was an animal who wanted me, not a man. You saw that, when you ordered him to use his mind, the lust was controlled."

"But the animal was there," said Jennings, grimly.

"It's always there," she answered. "The trouble is that people forget it."

Minutes later, Jennings parked in front of Dr. Howell's apartment house and turned to her.

"I think we both know how much sickness you exposed—and cured tonight," he said.

"I hope so," said Lurice. "Not for myself but—" She smiled a little. *"Not for myself I make this prayer,"* she recited. "Are you familiar with that?"

"I'm afraid I'm not."

He listened quietly as Dr. Howell recited again. Then, as he started to get out of the car, she held him back. "Please don't," she said, "I'm fine now." Pushing open the door, she stood on the sidewalk. For several moments, they looked at each other. Then Jennings reached over and squeezed her hand.

"Good night, my dear," he said.

Lurice Howell returned his smile. "Good night, Doctor." She closed the door and turned away.

Jennings watched her walk across the sidewalk and enter her apartment house. Then, drawing his car into the street again, he made a U-turn and started back towards Seventh Avenue. As he drove, he began remembering the Countee Cullen poem that Lurice had spoken for him.

Not for myself I make this prayer
But for this race of mine
That stretches forth from shadowed places
Dark hands for bread and wine.

Jennings's fingers tightened on the wheel.

"Use your mind, man," he said. "Your *mind.*"

PERSON TO PERSON

The ringing telephone stirred Millman from his sleep. His eyelids fluttered as he drifted up toward consciousness. The telephone kept ringing and he groaned. "All right, all right."

Sliding his left arm from beneath the covers, he reached to the bedside table, feeling for the handset. His fingers closed around it and he carried the receiver to his ear. "Yes?" he mumbled.

He listened to the dial tone for a few seconds before grimacing irritably and reaching out to thump the handset back on its cradle.

His eyes opened wide as he looked toward the bedside table.

The telephone was still ringing.

He stretched out his arm and fumbled for the lamp switch. Twisting it, he averted his face from the glare, then picked up the handset again and pressed the receiver to his ear.

There was only the dial tone.

Millman stared, bewildered, at the handset. He could still hear the sound of a telephone ringing.

Several moments passed before it came to him that the ringing was inside his head.

"I have the test results," Dr. Vance told him.

Millman waited anxiously. "My immediate assumption was that it was *tinnitus*," Dr. Vance continued. "There's no sign of middle-ear infection, though, no symptoms such as earache, fever, a sensation of pressure in your ears."

"What *is* it then?" Millman asked.

"You know for a fact it doesn't ring all the time."

"Only at night," Millman answered. "It wakes me up."

"That wouldn't be the case if it was *tinnitus*," Dr. Vance said. "The ringing would be constant."

Millman looked at him in worried silence.

"Don't tell anyone I said this," Dr. Vance went on, "but you might try getting a chiropractic adjustment on your neck. I had a friend who suffered from what appeared to be *tinnitus*. After he got a neck adjustment, it went away."

"And if that doesn't work?" Millman asked.

"Try it first," the doctor said.

✦

Millman twisted on the bed with an angry groan.

The telephone was ringing again.

He reached out quickly with his left hand and grabbed the handset, carrying the earpiece to his head.

Then he slammed the handset down on its cradle. "Damn!" he cried.

He lay on his back, a look of apprehension on his face as he listened to the sound of the ringing telephone inside his head.

✦

"Everything's been tried?" Dr. Palmer asked.

"*Yes,*" Millman said despairingly. "There's no sign of a fracture or a concussion. Nothing wrong with my spine. No sign of any foreign body. No growths, no tumors, *nothing.* I even had a neck adjustment. It made no difference."

"The ringing happens every night?" Dr. Palmer asked.

"Yes."

"At the same time?"

"Three in morning," Millman answered. "I can't sleep any more. I just lie in bed waiting for it to start."

"And you're positive it sounds like a telephone ringing."

"It *is* a telephone ringing," Millman said impatiently.

"Try answering it then," suggested Dr. Palmer.

❈

Millman lay on his back in the darkness, listening to the ringing sound inside his head. He wanted desperately to make it stop. But Dr. Palmer's suggestion disturbed him. It seemed a bizarre thing for a therapist to say.

Still. . . .

The telephone kept ringing. Millman's left hand twitched as though about to reach for the telephone on the bedside table. But he knew that wasn't where the ringing was coming from.

Impulsively, he visualized a telephone inside his head. He visualized his left hand picking up the handset. "Hel-*lo*," he said aloud.

"Well, finally," said the voice.

❈

Millman felt himself recoil into the mattress, heartbeat pounding suddenly. *"My God,"* he said.

"Take it easy now," the voice responded, that of a man. "Don't get yourself in an uproar. There's a simple explanation."

Millman couldn't seem to breathe.

"Still there?" the man's voice asked.

Millman swallowed. He sucked in a wheezing breath and muttered, "Yes."

The voice said, "Good."

Millman had to ask, although he knew it was insane.

"Who *is* this?" he said.

"The name's not important," the man's voice replied. "I'm not allowed to tell you anyway."

"What are you talking about?" Millman's voice strained.

"Take it *easy*," the man's voice said. "You're getting yourself upset for nothing. I told you there's a simple explanation."

"*What?*" demanded Millman.

"Okay," the man's voice answered. "Here's what's going on. It's a government project; a *secret* project, it goes without saying. You'll have to keep it quiet. It's a matter of national security."

Millman's mouth slipped open. *National security?*

"I won't go into background," the man's voice continued. "You know the situation in the world. Our government maintains a constant policy of espionage. We have to know what's happening on the other side."

"But—" Millman started.

"Just listen," the man's voice interrupted. "We have agents all around the globe, sending us information. The transmission of their messages has always been a risk. Any device they use can be detected sooner or later. Which is why we're experimenting with inner-brain communication."

"*Inner-brain—?*"

"Yes." The man's voice cut Millman off. "A method by which agents can transmit information with no risk whatever of being intercepted. I don't mean telepathy or anything like that. I'm talking about a microscopic insert."

Millman tightened. "*What?*"

"*Relax,*" the man's voice told him. "If it's so minute it never even showed up on your medical tests, it's certainly too small to bother you."

Millman tried to speak but couldn't.

"You're probably wondering why you were chosen for this experiment," the man's voice continued. "Actually, you're not the only one.

I can't tell you how many there are, but the number is considerable. As to *how* you were chosen, it was mathematical; a random generator."

"I don't understand," Millman said.

"To be perfectly candid," the man's voice went on, "only a few of you have reached the stage of answering our call. The rest are still fixated at the point of thinking it's a physical affliction, making endless rounds of doctor visits. Congratulations on being imaginative enough to answer the ringing—it *is* that of an actual telephone, by the way."

Millman braced himself. "But—" he began.

"—we never asked," the man's voice finished Millman's thought. "True. And we're sorry it disturbed you. Still—under the circumstances, we couldn't very well have asked for your permission.

"At any rate," he added, "we won't be bothering you as much now. The connection's been made."

"For how long?" Millman asked.

"I'm sorry," the man's voice responded. "That's not my decision to make."

Inside his head, Millman heard the distinct sound of a telephone handset being placed on its cradle.

He fell back on the pillow; he'd been unaware that he was leaning on his right elbow throughout his conversation with the man. In spite of his distress, he felt relieved that the ringing noise had stopped.

In seconds, he was heavily asleep.

❈

The ringing of the telephone inside his head jarred Millman awake. His eyes sprang open and he twitched on the mattress. *"No,"* he said. It had been five days since he'd spoken with the man. He'd begun to hope it was over; that either the calls would not continue or that he'd imagined everything.

Grimacing, he snatched up the unseen handset. *"Yes,"* he said.

The ringing continued.

Millman looked confused. He visualized the telephone as clearly as he could, lifted the handset and brought it to his ear. "Hel-*lo*," he said.

The telephone kept ringing. Was it because he hadn't heard it for the past five nights that it sounded so painfully shrill to him?

In his mind, he visualized his hand grabbing at the handset. "Hello!" he said.

The ringing didn't stop. Millman made a pained noise. The sound seemed to pulse in stabbing waves against the tissues of his brain. He clenched his teeth, face contorted.

The telephone kept ringing. Millman kept snatching up the handset in his imagination, crying out, "Hel-*lo*!"

Abruptly, then, the man's voice answered. "You don't have to *shout*."

"For God's sake!" Millman cried.

"Take it *easy*," the man's voice told him.

"*Easy?*" Millman said. "The phone's been ringing in my head for ten minutes straight!"

"Five," the man corrected.

"Well, *why?*" demanded Millman.

"I've been *busy*." The man's voice had an edge to it. "You're not the only line I have to deal with, you know."

"I'm *sorry*," Millman said in a shaking voice. "But you—" He broke off, frowning. "Why did you keep *ringing* me then?"

"Oh, was I ringing you? I didn't realize," the man's voice said.

Millman looked astonished as he heard a handset click down in his head, breaking the connection.

Seconds later, the telephone began to ring again.

No matter how often he answered it, there was no response.

The ringing continued almost until dawn, Millman lying wide-eyed on his bed, teeth clenched, hands like talons clutching at the sheets.

-◼◻◼-

"I was wondering what happened to you," Dr. Palmer said.

Millman drew in labored breath. "I thought I knew what it was," he said. "I thought I had to keep it quiet."

"Keep what quiet?" Dr. Palmer asked.

When Millman had finished telling him what happened, Dr. Palmer gazed at him without acknowledgment.

Millman swallowed nervously. "I'm still not sure I'm not making a mistake in telling you," he said, unable to endure the silence. "But he's driving me crazy, ringing me every night from three a.m. to six and never answering."

Dr. Palmer began to speak, hesitated, then finally said, "You believe this?"

Millman regarded him blankly.

"You believe it's a secret government project?" the therapist asked.

"Well—" Millman broke off in confusion. "That's what he *said*. He—"

The expression on Dr. Palmer's face stopped him.

"David," the therapist said. "Does it really make sense to you?"

Millman struggled for an answer. "I—" He stopped; braced himself. "I *hear* the telephone ringing," he said. "I *answer* it. The man's voice *speaks* to me. I'm not imagining it."

Dr. Palmer sighed. "David, think about it," he said. "A secret government project? Citizens picked at random? Microscopic telephones implanted in their brains without them knowing it? Espionage agents of the United States government transmitting information this way?" He looked at Millman challengingly.

Millman stared back, feeling a heavy weight on his back. Dear God, he thought.

He fought against the feeling. "But I *hear* the ringing," he insisted. "I *hear* the man's voice."

"David, not to alarm you," Dr. Palmer replied, "but hearing voices in one's head has been in the symptomatology tradition for a long time."

Millman drank black coffee with supper that evening. He wanted to remain alert.

Lying on his bed in the dark, propped on pillows leaned against the headboard, he waited for the ringing of the telephone to start.

And thought about what Dr. Palmer had said.

He'd gotten angry at the therapist's remark about hearing voices in one's head. Was Dr. Palmer implying that he'd gone insane?

"Not at all," the therapist had reassured him. "What I'm saying is that you're undergoing some kind of mental constraint. That your mind is seeking out a method of redressing it."

"By dreaming up a phone call from some secret government project?" Millman had responded tensely.

"The means by which the human mind attempts to deal with hidden problems can be infinite," Dr. Palmer had told him.

The room was still. Millman heard the whirring of the electric alarm clock on the bedside table.

Was Palmer right? he wondered.

True, it did seem awfully farfetched that the national government would go to such lengths to conduct a project so outlandish.

Still, the alternative. . . .

Millman bared his teeth in anger. It was all irrelevant anyway. If the man's voice didn't answer any more— and it hadn't in a week— what difference did it make? Palmer might be convinced that presently the voice would speak to him again because it needed to, but he was certainly not—

Millman caught his breath, jerking back against the headboard as the telephone began to ring. His gaze jumped to the clock. It was three.

He let the ringing go on for thirty seconds before mentally picking up the handset and saying, "Yes?"

"We're very displeased with you," the man's voice said; Millman tensed at the tone of it. "You were asked not to say anything about the project, weren't you?"

Millman swallowed nervously.

"Weren't you?" the man's voice snapped.

"Yes, but—"

"You were told it was a matter of national security," the man's voice cut him off. "Yet still you told your therapist."

Millman couldn't seem to fill his lungs with air. He made a wheezing sound. "How do you know?" he asked, his voice frail and breathless.

"Figure it out," the man's voice said. "If we can hear your voice when you speak to *us. . . .*"

He didn't finish. Millman shuddered. *Every word?* he thought in dismay. *Every single word I say?*

He struggled to resist. "You know what he told me then," he said. "You know what he thinks you are."

"Sure," the man's voice answered scornfully. "I'm not Agent 25409-J. I'm not William J. Lonsdale. I'm not married with three children. I don't work for the C.I.A. I'm your goddamn subconscious mind. Jesus, Millman. What the hell's the matter with you?"

Millman had no answer. He lay immobile, staring up into the darkness. He thought he heard the breathing of the man on the other end of the line.

"All right, listen to me," the man's voice said then. "We're going to try to cut you off the circuit. We *have* been trying for a week now; that's why we haven't spoken to you. I'll put it on priority now that you've blabbed to your therapist about us. Jesus, Millman!"

Millman heard the sound of a handset being set down.

Hard.

✠

"But don't you *see*?" Palmer said with a smile. "Your subconscious mind was reacting angrily to having its ruse exposed. A step forward, David."

"He said he was going to cut me off the circuit."

Dr. Palmer shook his head, still smiling. "He won't cut you off," he said. "He has things to say."

"What if I don't want to listen to him anymore?" Millman said.

"David," Dr. Palmer said. "*David. Consider.* You're being given an invaluable opportunity: to engage in dialogue with your own subconscious mind."

"What if the voice keeps picking on me?" Millman asked.

The therapist's gesture was casual.

"Hang up on him," he said.

✠

When the telephone began to ring in his head, Millman was loathe to answer it. The resonating jangle of the bell set his teeth on edge. Even so, it was preferable to the man's potentially abusive voice.

He remained immobile on the bed, a flinching expression on his face.

Could he hang up on the man?

Further, could he snatch up the invisible handset after the connection had been broken, making it impossible for the man to call him anymore? He imagined hearing a dial tone in his head, then an operator's voice, breaking in to tell him he should hang up if he wanted to make a call.

Millman scowled. Now he really *was* beginning to think like a man who was losing his mind.

Abruptly, he picked up the imaginary handset and said, "Hello."

"Thank you for answering," the man's voice said.

Millman tightened. *Now what?*" he thought.

"I apologize for speaking out of turn during our last conversation," the man's voice said. "It was uncalled for."

"*Yes, it was,*" Millman said impulsively.

"I'm sorry," the man replied. Before Millman could respond, he continued. "Listen," he said, "I'm going to level with you."

Millman's eyes narrowed. *Now* what? he wondered.

"This government project thing," the voice went on. "It's all a lie."

Without thinking, Millman drew his left hand near his face to stare at it as though he actually held a handset in his grip.

"There's no such thing," the man confessed. "Your Dr. Palmer was correct. It *doesn't* make sense. Microscopic telephones implanted secretly in people's brains? I can't believe you bought it."

Millman made a sound of spluttering exasperation.

"I'll tell you what it is," the man's voice said. "I won't give you my name because I'm afraid you might report me to the police. They'd lock me up and throw the key away if they found out what I'm doing."

"What are you talking about *now?*" Millman demanded furiously.

"I'm an inventor," the man's voice said. "I've developed an apparatus which radiates short-wave energy that penetrates the mind of anyone the beamer is directed at, enabling two-way conversation with them. You're the first."

Millman couldn't tell if he felt horrified or enraged. The clashing emotions kept him speechless.

"I know this is as hard to believe as the government project idea," the man's voice continued. "The government would love to get their hands on this, I guarantee you. I'd destroy it first though. It gives me the creeps thinking what our government would do with this device. I'd never—"

Millman broke in fiercely. "*Why are you doing this to me?*" he demanded.

"As I said," the man's voice answered patiently, "I chose you as my first subject. I didn't have the nerve to tell you what was really going on so I made up the story about a government project when all the time—"

It all burst out explosively from Millman. *"Bullshit!"* he snarled. "I don't believe this story any more than I believe the other! You're no inventor! My therapist's been right all the time! You're my own—"

"You *fool!*" the man's voice cut him off. "You goddamned fool!"

Millman tried to answer but the words choked in his throat.

"You just can't leave well enough alone, can you?" the man's voice criticized him. "Just can't let me do this my own way. No! Not you! You're too goddamned smart for that!"

The animal-like sound the man made drowned out Millman's faint reply. "Well, you're *not* smart! Not at all!" the man's voice cried. "You're *dumb!* You always *have* been dumb! A dumb boy and a stupid man! Davie, you're an *idiot!*"

Millman lurched in shock as the handset crashed down in his head.

He lay in silence, struggling for breath.

He knew the voice.

✦

Dr. Palmer gazed at him without a word.

Millman drew in a laboring breath. "I have to tell you something about my family," he said. "Something I never told you before."

"Yes?" asked Dr. Palmer.

"My mother suffered from dissociated consciousness," Millman said. "I mean, she was psychic. I won't go into details but she proved it many times."

"Yes?" Dr. Palmer's tone was still noncommittal.

"I think I inherited her ability," Millman told him.

The therapist had difficulty repressing a look of aggravation. "You're suggesting—" he began.

"I'm *telling*," Millman broke in irritably. "You were *right*. It's not a secret government project and it's certainly not what the man's voice told me last night."

"Instead—" Dr. Palmer prodded.

"It's my father," Millman answered.

The therapist didn't reply. He rubbed his lowered eyelids with the thumb and forefinger of his left hand. Millman felt a tightening of resentment in his body.

Dr. Palmer opened his eyes. "You believe that he's communicating with you from 'the other side' as it were?" he asked.

Millman nodded, features hardening. "I *do*."

The therapist sighed.

"Very well," he said. "Let's talk about it."

❖

The instant the telephone rang in his head, Millman snatched up the imagined handset. "I'm here," he said.

"That was prompt," the man's voice replied.

"I know who you are," Millman told him.

"You do." Millman had a fleeting impression of his father's face, a smile of faint amusement on it.

"Yes, I do," Millman answered. "Father."

The man chuckled. "So you've caught me," he said.

Millman was unable to control a throat-catching sob. *"Why are you doing this?"* he asked.

"Why?" the voice responded incredulously. "Why do I want to speak to my only begotten son? You ask such a question, *Davie*? Is it so difficult to comprehend?"

Millman was crying now. Tears ran off the sides of his face, soaking into the pillow case. *"Pop,"* he murmured.

"I want you to listen to me now," his father's voice continued.

Millman's chest hitched as he sobbed.

"Are you listening?" his father's voice inquired.

"Yes." Millman rubbed the trembling fingertips of his right hand over his eyes.

"The reason I'm calling you," his father's voice went on, "is that I feel you should be cognizant of certain things."

"What things?" Millman asked.

"You don't know?" his father's voice responded.

"No," Millman sniffled, rubbing a finger underneath his dripping nostrils.

His father's sigh was deep. "I'll have to tell you then," he said.

Millman waited.

"You're a loser," his father's voice told him.

"What?" asked Millman.

"I have to *explain?*" said his father's voice. "You leave me *nothing?* All right; I'll lay it on the line then. You married a bitch. You let her bleed you dry in every way. You let her poison the minds of your two sons against you. You let her divorce proceeding take you to the cleaners. You let her rip away your *manhood.*

"On top of that, you're a loser at your job. You let that moron boss of yours kick you around like a ball. You scrape to him and let him treat you like a piece of dog shit. *Dog shit*, Davie! Don't bother to deny! You know it's true! You're a loser in every department of life and you *know* it!"

Millman felt as though paralysis had gripped him, body and mind.

"Can you deny a single word I've spoken?" his father's voice challenged.

Millman sobbed. "Pop," he murmured pleadingly.

"Don't Pop me, you goddamn loser!" his father's voice lashed back. "I'm ashamed to call you my son! Thank God I'm dead and don't have to see you getting kicked around day after day!"

Millman cried out, agonized. "Pop, *don't!*"

❖

Dr. Palmer rose from his chair and walked to the window. He had never done that before and Millman watched him uneasily, dabbing at his reddened eyes with a tear-clotted handkerchief. The therapist stood with his back to Millman, looking out at the street.

After a while, he returned to his chair and sat down with a tired grunt. He gazed at Millman silently. What kind of gaze was it? Millman wondered. Compassionate?

Or fed up?

"I don't do this ordinarily," Dr. Palmer began. "You know my method: to let you find the answers yourself. However—"

He exhaled heavily and clasped his hands beneath his chin. "I feel as though I simply can't allow this to proceed the way it's going," he continued. "I have to say something to you. I have to say—" he winced "—*enough*, David."

Millman stared at the therapist.

"I do not believe—any more than I believe it was a secret government project or an isolated inventor—that your father is communicating with you from beyond the grave. I believe, as I have from the start, that your subconscious mind has, somehow, found a way to speak to you *audibly*. Trying to establish some kind of resolution to your mental problems."

"But it's *his voice*," Millman insisted.

"David," Dr. Palmer's voice was firm now. "You believed it was the voice of Secret Agent 25409-J. You then believed, albeit briefly, that it was the voice of some inventor. Can't you see that this subconscious voice of yours *can make itself sound like anyone it chooses?*"

David felt helpless. He knew he couldn't bear any more of the abuse his father's voice had heaped on him. At the same time, he felt sick about the possibility of losing touch with his father.

"What should I do?" he asked in a feeble voice.

"*Confront it,*" Dr. Palmer urged. "Stop just listening and suffering and *talk back*. Start *retaliating*. Demand answers; explanations. Speak *up* for yourself. It's *your* subconscious, David. Hear it out but don't permit it to harass you mercilessly. *Take control*."

Millman felt exhausted. "If only I could sleep," he murmured.

"That I can give you something for," the therapist said.

He couldn't confront the voice that night. He did as Dr. Palmer prescribed and took two capsules, sleeping deeply and without remembrance. If the telephone rang in his head, he didn't hear it.

It relaxed him enough to enjoy a good night's rest. At work the following day, he even found Mr. Fitch endurable. Once, he almost spoke back to him but managed to repress the impulse. There was no point in losing his job on top of everything else.

During the evening, Millman thought about Elaine and the boys. Had the voice—whoever it belonged to—spoken the truth? *Was* Elaine a bitch who'd poisoned the minds of his sons against him? Was that why their behavior, when they saw him, was so remote? He'd told himself it was because they got together so infrequently; that he was virtually a stranger to them.

What if it was more than that?

It *was* true that the divorce settlement had left him very little. Still, it had been *his* choice. He didn't have to give her so much.

Thinking of it all made Millman tense and edgy, ready to confront the voice.

At three a.m., when the ringing in his head began, he grabbed the unseen handset and yanked it to his head. "I'm here," he said.

"*Are* you, Davie?" his father's voice responded scornfully.

"You can cut it out now," Millman answered.

"Cut what out, little boy?" his father's voice inquired mockingly.

Millman braced himself. It took all the will he had to resist that voice which had intimidated him throughout his childhood and adolescence.

"You're not my father," he said.

Silence.

Then his father's voice said, "I'm not?"

"No, you're not," Millman said, trying to keep his voice strong.

"Who *am* I then?" his father's voice asked. "The King of Siam?"

Millman shuddered with uncertain anger. *"I don't know,"* he admitted. "I only know you're not my father."

"You're a stupid boy," his father's voice responded. "You've always been a stupid boy."

"I defy you!" Millman cut him off. *"You're not my father!"*

"Who *am* I then?" the voice demanded.

"Me!" cried Millman. "My subconscious mind!"

"Your *subconscious mind?"* The voice broke into sudden laughter; totally insane, the laughter of a maniac.

"Stop it," Millman said.

The laughing continued, uncontrolled, deranged. Millman visualized a face behind it—white and twisted, staring, wild-eyed.

"Stop it," he ordered.

The laughter rose in pitch and volume. It began to echo in his head.

He had to mentally slam down the handset three times before the laughter cut off.

His hands almost vibrating they shook so badly, he washed down a pair of capsules.

When the telephone began to ring inside his head again, he tried to ignore it, waiting tensely for the drug to lower him into a heavy, deafened sleep.

❂

The tiny, black-haired woman opened the door to her apartment and looked at Millman questioningly. She didn't look as old as he knew her to be.

"I spoke to you on the telephone this afternoon," he said. "I'm Myra Millman's son."

"Ah, yes." Mrs. Danning's false teeth showed in a smile as she stepped back to admit him.

There was a smell of burning incense in the dimly lit living room. Millman noticed crosses and religious paintings on the walls while he moved to the chair the tiny woman pointed at. He sat down, hoping that he wasn't making a mistake. Momentarily, he imagined Dr. Palmer's reaction to this. The idea made his throat feel dry.

Mrs. Danning perched on a chair across from him and asked him to repeat his story.

Millman told her everything from its beginning to the manic laughter. Mrs. Danning nodded when he spoke about the laughter. "That may well provide the clue," she declared. He wondered what she meant by that.

He watched in anxious silence as she closed her eyes and began to draw in deep, laboring breaths, both hands on her lap, palms facing upward.

Several minutes later, her features hardened with a look of disdain. "So," she said. "Now you see a psychic." Mrs. Danning bared her teeth so much that Millman saw her pale gums. "You just won't listen, will you?" she said. "You have to keep investigating. *Asshole!*"

Millman twitched on his chair, eyes fixed on the psychic. She had begun to rock back and forth, a humming in her throat. "Oh, yes," she said after a while. "Oh, yes." She repeated the words so many times that Millman lost count of them.

After ten minutes, she opened her eyes and looked at Millman. He began to speak but she raised her right hand to prevent it. He waited as she picked up a glass of water from the table beside her chair and gulped down every drop of it. She sighed.

"I think we have it now," she said.

—✺—

"For God's sake, David!" Dr. Palmer cried. Millman had never heard such disapproval in the therapist's voice.

"I wasn't going to come back," he said defensively. "Wasn't going to tell you. But I thought you might be sympathetic."

"To what this woman told you?" Dr. Palmer asked, appalled. "That you're being possessed by some— some—?" He gestured angrily.

"*Earthbound spirit,*" Millman said, willfully. "A disincarnate soul held prisoner by the magnetism of the living, doing everything he can to—"

"David, David." Dr. Palmer looked exasperated and despairing at the same time. "We're losing ground. Every time we get together, we seem to fall back a little more."

"*The spirit is not at peace.*" Millman's voice was stubbornly insistent. "It wants to experience life again. So it invades my mind—"

"David—!" the therapist cut him off. "*Please!*"

Millman pushed up from his chair. "Oh, what's the use?" he muttered.

"Sit down," Dr. Palmer told him. Millman stood before the chair, unable to decide.

"Please sit down," the therapist requested quietly.

Millman didn't move at first. Then he sat back down, a look of sullen accusation on his face. "I don't think you appreciate—" he began.

"I appreciate that you are going through one hell of an ordeal," Dr. Palmer broke in.

"But you don't believe a word I've said."

"David, use your head," the therapist replied. "*Did you really think I would?*"

Millman blew out tired breath.

"I suppose not," he conceded.

He had never in his life felt so divided in his mind—so torn between desire and dread.

On the one hand, he wanted the telephone to ring in his head so he could resolve this madness.

On the other hand, he was terror-stricken by what might happen if he answered it.

Easy enough for Palmer to repeat his conviction that it was his subconscious mind.

What if he was wrong?

Millman was thinking that for what might well have been the hundredth time when the telephone began to ring in his head.

He drew in a long, slow, chest-expanding breath of air, then let it out until his lungs felt empty. All right, he told himself.

The time had come.

He saw the handset in his mind. Saw his left hand pick it up. Almost felt the earpiece press against his head. *"Yes,"* he said aloud.

"This is your father," the voice replied.

Millman answered, "No."

"What did you say?" The image of his father's face appeared in Millman's mind: thin-lipped, critical.

"You're not my father," he said.

"Who am I then?"

"I don't know," Millman answered desolately. "I just know you're not my father." Amazingly, he *did* know it now.

"You're right," the man's voice told him.

Millman started. *Was this the beginning of some new ploy?* he wondered. "Who *are* you then?" he demanded.

"This is a secret government project and I'm Agent 25409-J—" the man's voice started.

"Stop it," Millman said through clenched teeth. "Don't start that again. I won't have it."

"I'm an inventor," said the voice. "I've created a device that—"

"*Stop* it," Millman cut him off.

"Right," the man's voice said. "This is your father."

"*Stop* it, damn it!" Millman cried.

"Correct," the man's voice said. "I'm an earthbound spirit possessing you."

"God damn it, that's enough!" Millman shouted. He felt his heartbeat pound.

"*Right,*" the man's voice said. "This is Krol. I'm speaking to you from the planet Mars."

"I'm hanging up," Millman said.

He imagined doing it.

"You can't hang up," the voice informed him. "It's too late for that."

Millman stiffened. "Yes, I can," he said. He tried again to put the handset down.

"I'm *telling* you," the voice said coldly. "You can't *do* it anymore."

Millman made a frightened sound and tried again.

"You *should* be frightened," said the voice. "I'm going to kill you now."

Millman's body spasmed with a shudder. He slammed the handset down on its invisible cradle.

"I'm going to kill you now," the voice repeated.

"Get away from me," said Millman.

"Not so." The man's voice was one of cruel amusement. "You're mine now, little porker. Don't you know who this really is?"

"*Get away from me.*" Millman's voice was trembling now.

"All right, I'll tell you who I am," the man's voice said. "I have many names. One of them is Prince of Liars. Isn't that a gas?"

Millman shook his head, teeth gritted hard. Again and again, he slammed down the unseen handset.

"You're wasting time, little porker," said the man's voice. "I'm in charge now. Want to hear some other names? Lord of Vermin. Prince of Sinners. Serpent. Goat. Old Nick. Old *Davy*! Isn't *that* a gas?!"

"Get away from me!" cried Millman. "I won't listen to you anymore!"

"Yes you will!" the voice cried back. "You're mine now and I'm going to kill you!" The maniacal laughter began again.

Millman reached for the vial of capsules.

"That won't do you any good," the man's voice told him gleefully. "You can't escape me now."

Millman didn't try to answer. Shaking uncontrollably, he picked the cap off, shaking two capsules onto his palm.

"*Two?*" the man's voice asked. "Not half enough, old man. You'll never get away from me. You're mine, I'm going to kill you dead."

The laughter started in again, booming in some cavern in his mind.

Millman washed a pair of capsules down his throat, water spilling across his chin.

"Not half enough!" the man's voice cried, exultantly. He continued laughing with demented joy.

Millman pressed another capsule in his mouth, another, washed them down.

"*Not half enough!*" the man's voice yelled at him. "*You've let me in too long!*"

Millman's palsied hand shoved capsules in his mouth. He washed them down. The glass was empty now. He gulped down capsules dry, his face a mask of terror.

"Secret government project!" howled the voice. "Inventor! Father! Earthbound spirit! Krol from Mars! The Devil! Take another capsule, David!"

Millman lay on his right side on the bed, legs drawn up, twitching. *God, please take me out of here!* he kept begging, sobbing helplessly.

"*Your wish is my command,*" the voice said finally.

Inside his head, the telephone began to ring.

He lay in his bed, hands clasped behind his head, grinning at the sound.

Then he chuckled, picking up the handset in his mind. *"Ye-es,"* he said musically.

"Please," the man's voice said.

"Please?" he said as though he didn't understand. "Please what?"

"Please let me back."

"Oh, no," he chided. "After all the trouble I went to? Keeping you so occupied you never dreamed what was coming? After all that work, you want me to let you *back*?"

His face became a mask of feral animosity.

"Never, asshole," he said. "You are out of here for good."

"No!" the man's voice cried.

He snickered. "Gotta go now, babe," he said.

He put the handset down, giggling as he visualized the look of shock on Davie's face. The little shit would try again of course, he knew.

While he waited for the ringing to begin, he made his plans for to-morrow.

First, a call to Elaine. Not another fucking nickel, bitch. And tell that pair of cretins you dropped not to bother me again.

As for Fitch—his eyes lit up—what sheer delight it was going to be to smash that ugly bastard in the mouth and stalk out on that nowhere job.

Then off to enjoy himself. Travel. Women. Fun. Women.

He'd worry about money when he ran out of it.

As for Palmer—he laughed aloud—the clever son of a bitch had it right all the time.

Now let him try to collect his bill!

He was cackling at the idea when the telephone began to ring in his head.

With a hissing smirk, he reached into his mind and yanked out all the wires. The ringing stopped abruptly. There, he thought.

He wouldn't need that line any more.

Hell House

With love, for my daughters
Bettina and Alison,
who have haunted my life so sweetly

DECEMBER 18, 1970

3:17 P.M.

It had been raining hard since five o'clock that morning. Brontean weather, Dr. Barrett thought. He repressed a smile. He felt rather like a character in some latter-day Gothic romance. The driving rain, the cold, the two-hour ride from Manhattan in one of Deutsch's long black leather-upholstered limousines. The interminable wait in this corridor while disconcerted-looking men and women hurried in and out of Deutsch's bedroom, glancing at him occasionally.

He drew his watch from its vest pocket and raised the lid. He'd been here more than an hour now. What did Deutsch want of him? Something to do with parapsychology, most likely. The old man's chain of newspapers and magazines were forever printing articles on the subject. "Return from the Grave"; "The Girl Who Wouldn't Die"—always sensational, rarely factual.

Wincing at the effort, Dr. Barrett lifted his right leg over his left. He was a tall, slightly overweight man in his middle fifties, his thinning blond hair unchanged in color, though his trimmed beard showed traces of white. He sat erect on the straight-back chair, staring at the door to Deutsch's bedroom.

Edith must be getting restless downstairs. He was sorry she'd
come. Still, he'd had no way of knowing it would take this
long.

The door to Deutsch's bedroom opened, and his male secretary, Hanley, came out. "Doctor," he said.

Barrett reached for his cane and, standing, limped across
the hallway, stopping in front of the shorter man. He waited
while the secretary leaned in through the doorway and announced, "Doctor Barrett, sir." Then he stepped past Hanley,
entering the room. The secretary closed the door behind him.

The darkly paneled bedroom was immense. Sanctum of
the monarch, Barrett thought as he moved across the rug.
Stopping by the massive bed, he looked at the old man sitting
in it. Rolf Rudolph Deutsch was eighty-seven, bald, and skeletal, his dark eyes peering out from bony cavities. Barrett
smiled. "Good afternoon." Intriguing that this wasted creature ruled an empire, he was thinking.

"You're crippled." Deutsch's voice was rasping. "No one
told me that."

"I beg your pardon?" Barrett had stiffened.

"Never mind." Deutsch cut him off. "It's not that vital,
I suppose. My people have recommended you. They say
you're one of the five best in your field." He drew in laboring
breath. "Your fee will be one hundred thousand dollars."

Barrett started.

"Your assignment is to establish the facts."

"Regarding what?" asked Barrett.

Deutsch seemed hesitant about replying, as though he felt
it was beneath him. Finally he said, "Survival."

"You want me—?"

"—to tell me if it's factual or not."

Barrett's heart sank. That amount of money would make

all the difference in the world to him. Still, how could he in conscience accept it on such grounds?

"It isn't lies I want," Deutsch told him. "I'll buy the answer, either way. So long as it's definitive."

Barrett felt a roil of despair. "How can I convince you, either way?" He was compelled to say it.

"By giving me *facts*," Deutsch answered irritably.

"Where am I to find them? I'm a physicist. In the twenty years I've studied parapsychology, I've yet to—"

"If they exist," Deutsch interrupted, "you'll find them in the only place on earth I know of where survival has yet to be refuted. The Belasco house in Maine."

"Hell House?"

Something glittered in the old man's eyes.

"Hell House," he said.

Barrett felt a tingling of excitement. "I thought Belasco's heirs had it sealed off after what happened—"

"That was thirty years ago." Deutsch cut him off again. "They need the money now; I've bought the place. Can you be there by Monday?"

Barrett hesitated, then, seeing Deutsch begin to frown, nodded once. "Yes." He couldn't let this chance go by.

"There'll be two others with you," Deutsch said.

"May I ask who—?"

"Florence Tanner and Benjamin Franklin Fischer."

Barrett tried not to show the disappointment he felt. An over-emotive Spiritualist medium, and the lone survivor of the 1940 debacle? He wondered if he dared object. He had his own group of sensitives and didn't see how Florence Tanner or Fischer could be of any help to him. Fischer had shown incredible abilities as a boy, but after his breakdown had obviously lost his gift, been caught in fraud a number of

times, finally disappearing from the field entirely. He listened, half-attentive, as Deutsch told him that Florence Tanner would fly north with him, while Fischer would meet
them in Maine.

The old man noted his expression. "Don't worry, you'll
be in charge," he said; "Tanner's only going because my people tell me she's a first-class medium—"

"But a mental medium," said Barrett.

"—and I want that line of approach employed, as well as
yours," Deutsch went on, as though Barrett hadn't spoken.
"Fischer's presence is obvious."

Barrett nodded. There was no way out of it, he saw. He'd
have to bring up one of his own people after the project was
under way. "As to costs—" he started.

The old man waved him off. "Take that up with Hanley.
You have unlimited funds."

"And time?"

"That you don't have," Deutsch replied. "I want the answer in a week."

Barrett looked appalled.

"Take it or leave it!" the old man snapped, sudden, naked
rage in his expression. Barrett knew he had to accede or lose
the opportunity—and there *was* a chance if he could get his
machine constructed in time.

He nodded once. "A week," he said.

3:50 P.M.

nything else?" asked Hanley.

Barrett reviewed the items in his mind again. A list of all
phenomena observed in the Belasco house. Restoration of its
electrical system. Installation of telephone service. The swim-

ming pool and steam room made available to him. Barrett had ignored the small man's frown at the fourth item. A daily swim and steam bath were mandatory for him.

"One more item," he said. He tried to sound casual but felt that his excitement showed. "I need a machine. I have the blueprints for it at my apartment."

"How soon will you need it?" Hanley asked.

"As soon as possible."

"Is it large?"

Twelve years, Barrett thought. "Quite large," he said.

"That's it?"

"All I can think of at the moment. I haven't mentioned living facilities, of course."

"Enough rooms have been renovated for your use. A couple from Caribou Falls will prepare and deliver your meals." Hanley seemed about to smile. "They've refused to sleep in the house."

Barrett stood. "It's just as well. They'd only be in the way."

Hanley walked him toward the library door. Before they reached it, it was opened sharply by a stout man, who glared at Barrett. Although he was forty years younger and a hundred pounds heavier, William Reinhardt Deutsch bore an unmistakable resemblance to his father.

He shut the door. "I'm warning you right now," he said, "I'm going to block this thing."

Barrett stared at him.

"The truth," Deutsch said. "This is a waste of time, isn't it? Put it in writing, and I'll make you out a check for a thousand dollars right now."

Barrett tightened. "I'm afraid—"

"There's no such thing as the supernatural, is there?" Deutsch's neck was reddening.

"Correct," said Barrett. Deutsch began to smile in triumph. "The word is *'supernormal.'* Nature cannot be transcen—"

"What the hell's the difference?" interrupted Deutsch. "It's superstition, all of it!"

"I'm sorry, but it isn't." Barrett started past him. "Now, if you'll excuse me."

Deutsch caught his arm. "Now, *look*, you better drop this thing. I'll see you never get that money—"

Barrett pulled his arm free. "Do what you will," he said. "I'll proceed until I hear otherwise from your father."

He closed the door and started down the corridor. In light of present knowledge, his mind addressed Deutsch, anyone who chooses to refer to psychic phenomena as superstition simply isn't aware of what's going on in the world. The documentation is immense—

Barrett stopped and leaned against the wall. His leg was starting to ache again. For the first time, he allowed himself to recognize what a strain on his condition it might be to spend a week in the Belasco house.

What if it was really as bad as the two accounts claimed it was?

4:37 P.M.

The Rolls-Royce sped along the highway toward Manhattan.

"That's an awful lot of money." Edith still sounded incredulous.

"Not to him," said Barrett. "Especially when you consider that what he's paying for is an assurance of immortality."

"But he must know that you don't believe—"

"I'm sure he does," Barrett interrupted. He didn't want to consider the possibility that Deutsch hadn't been told.

"He's not the sort of man who goes into anything without being totally informed."

"But a hundred thousand dollars."

Barrett smiled. "I can scarcely believe it myself," he said. "If I were like my mother, I'd undoubtedly consider this a miracle from God. The two things I've failed to accomplish both supplied at once—an opportunity to prove my theory, and provision for our later years. Really, I could ask no more."

Edith returned his smile. "I'm happy for you, Lionel," she said.

"Thank you, my dear." He patted her hand.

"Monday afternoon, though." Edith looked concerned. "That doesn't give us too much time."

Barrett said, "I'm wondering if I shouldn't go alone on this one."

She stared at him.

"Well, not alone, of course," he said. "There are the two others."

"What about your meals?"

"They'll be provided. All I'll have to do is work."

"I've always helped you, though," she said.

"I know. It's just that—"

"What?"

He hesitated. "I'd rather you weren't along this time, that's all."

"*Why*, Lionel?" She looked uneasy when he didn't answer. "Is it me?"

"Of course not." Barrett's smile was quick, distracted. "It's the house."

"Isn't it just another so-called haunted house?" she asked, using his phrase.

"I'm afraid it isn't," he admitted. "It's the Mount Everest of haunted houses, you might say. There were two attempts to investigate it, one in 1931, the other in 1940. Both were disasters. Eight people involved in those attempts were killed, committed suicide, or went insane. Only one survived, and I have no idea how sound he is—Benjamin Fischer, one of the two who'll be with me.

"It's not that I fear the ultimate effect of the house," he continued, trying to ameliorate his words. "I have confidence in what I know. It's simply that the details of the investigation may be"—he shrugged—"a little nasty."

"And yet you want me to let you go there alone?"

"My dear—"

"What if something happens to you?"

"Nothing will."

"What if it does? With me in New York, and you in Maine?"

"Edith, nothing's going to happen."

"Then there's no reason I can't go." She tried to smile. "I'm not afraid, Lionel."

"I know you're not."

"I won't get in your way."

Barrett sighed.

"I know I don't understand much of what you're doing, but there are always things I can do to help. Pack and unload your equipment, for instance. Help you set up your experiments. Type the rest of your manuscript; you said you wanted to have it ready by the first of the year. And I want to be with you when you prove your theory."

Barrett nodded. "Let me think about it."

"I won't be in your way," she promised. "And I know there are any number of things I can do to help."

He nodded again, trying to think. It was obvious she didn't want to stay behind. He could appreciate that. Except for his three weeks in London in 1962, they'd never been separated since their marriage. Would it really hurt that much to take her? Certainly, she'd experienced enough psychic phenomena by now to be accustomed to it.

Still, that house was such an unknown factor. It hadn't been called Hell House without reason. There was a power there strong enough to physically and/or mentally demolish eight people, three of whom had been scientists like himself.

Even believing that he knew exactly what that power was, dare he expose Edith to it?

DECEMBER 20, 1970

10:39 P.M.

Florence Tanner crossed the yard which separated her small house from the church and walked along the alley to the street. She stood on the sidewalk and gazed at her church. It was only a converted store, but it had been everything to her these past six years. She looked at the sign in the painted window: TEMPLE OF SPIRITUAL HARMONY. She smiled. It was indeed. Those six years had been the most spiritually harmonious of her life.

She walked to the door, unlocked it, and went inside. The warmth felt good. Shivering, she turned on the wall lamp in the vestibule. Her eye was caught by the bulletin board:

Sunday Services—11:00 a.m., 8:00 p.m.

Healing and Prophecy—Tuesdays, 7:45 p.m.

Lectures and Spirit Greetings—Wednesdays, 7:45 p.m.

Messages and Revelations—Thursdays, 7:45 p.m.

Holy Communion—1st Sunday of Month

She turned and gazed at her photograph tacked to the wall, the printed words above it: *The Reverend Florence Tanner.*

For several moments she was pleased to be reminded of her beauty. Forty-three, she still retained it unimpaired, her long red hair untouched by grayness, her tall, Junoesque figure almost as trim as it had been in her twenties. She smiled in self-depreciation then. Vanity of vanities, she thought.

She went into the church, walked along the carpeted aisle, and stepped onto the platform, taking a familiar pose behind the lectern. She looked at the rows of chairs, the hymnals set on every third one. She visualized her congregation sitting before her. "My dears," she murmured.

She had told them at the morning and evening services. Told them of the need for her to be away from them for the next week. Told them of the answer to their prayers—the means to build a true church on their own property. Asked them to pray for her while she was gone.

Florence clasped her hands on the lectern and closed her eyes. Her lips moved slightly as she prayed for the strength to cleanse the Belasco house. It had such a dreadful history of death and suicide and madness. It was a house most horribly defiled. She prayed to end its curse.

The prayer completed, Florence lifted her head and gazed at her church. She loved it deeply. Still, to be able to build a real church for her congregation was truly a gift from heaven. And at Christmastime . . . She smiled, eyes glistening with tears.

God was good.

11:17 P.M.

Edith finished brushing her teeth and gazed at her reflection in the mirror—at her short-cut auburn hair, her strong, almost masculine features. Her expression was a worried one. Disturbed by the sight of it, she switched off the bathroom light and returned to the bedroom.

Lionel was asleep. She sat on her bed and looked at him, listening to the sound of his heavy breathing. Poor dear, she thought. There had been so much to do. By ten o'clock he'd been exhausted, and she'd made him go to bed.

Edith lay on her side and continued looking at him. She'd never seen him so concerned before. He'd made her promise that she'd never leave his side once they'd entered the Belasco house. Could it be that bad? She'd been to haunted houses with Lionel and never been frightened. He was always so calm, so confident; it was impossible to be afraid when he was near.

Yet, he was disturbed enough about the Belasco house to make an issue of her staying by his side at all times. Edith shivered. Would her presence harm him? Would looking after her use up so much of his limited energy that his work would suffer? She didn't want that. She knew how much his work meant to him.

Still, she had to go. She'd face anything rather than be alone. She'd never told Lionel how close she'd come to a mental breakdown during those three weeks he'd been gone in 1962. It would only have distressed him, and he'd needed all his concentration for the work he was doing. So she'd lied and sounded cheerful on the telephone the three times he'd called—and, alone, she'd wept and shaken, taken tranquilizers, hadn't slept or eaten, lost thirteen pounds, fought off compulsions to end it all. Met him at the airport finally, pale and smiling, told him that she'd had the flu.

Edith closed her eyes and drew her legs up. She couldn't face that again. The worst haunted house in the world threatened her less than being alone.

11:41 P.M.

He couldn't sleep. Fischer opened his eyes and looked around the cabin of Deutsch's private plane. Strange to be sitting in an armchair in an airplane, he thought. Strange to be sitting in an airplane at all. He'd never flown in his life.

Fischer reached for the coffeepot and poured himself another cupful. He rubbed a hand across his eyes and picked up one of the magazines lying on the coffee table in front of him. It was one of Deutsch's. What else? he thought.

After a while his eyes went out of focus, and the words on the page began to blur together. Going back, he thought. The only one of nine people still walking around, and he was going back for more.

They'd found him lying on the front porch of the house that morning in September 1940, naked, curled up like a fetus, shivering and staring into space. When they'd put him on a stretcher, he'd begun to scream and vomit blood, his muscles knotting, rocklike. He'd lain in a coma three months in the Caribou Falls Hospital. When he'd opened his eyes, he'd looked like a haggard man of thirty, a month short of his sixteenth birthday. Now he was forty-five, a lean, gray-haired man with dark eyes, his expression one of hard, suspicious readiness.

Fischer straightened in the chair. Never mind; it's time, he thought. He wasn't fifteen anymore, wasn't naïve or gullible, wasn't the credulous prey he'd been in 1940. Things would be different this time.

He'd never dreamed in his wildest fancies that he'd be given a second chance at the house. After his mother had died, he'd traveled to the West Coast. Probably, he later realized, to get as far away as possible from Maine. He'd committed clumsy fraud in Los Angeles and San Francisco, deliberately alienating Spiritualists and scientists alike in order to be free of them. He'd existed barely for thirty years, washing dishes, doing farmwork, selling door to door, janitoring, anything to earn money without using his mind.

Yet, somehow, he'd protected his ability and nurtured it. It was still there, maybe not as spectacular as it had been when he was fifteen, but very much intact—and backed now by the thoughtful caution of a man rather than the suicidal arrogance of a teenager. He was ready to shake loose the dormant psychic muscles, exercise and strengthen them, use them once more. Against that pesthole up in Maine.

Against Hell House.

DECEMBER 21, 1970

11:19 A.M.

The two black Cadillacs moved along the road, which twisted through dense forest. In the lead car was Deutsch's representative. Dr. Barrett, Edith, Florence Tanner, and Fischer rode in the second, chauffeur-driven limousine, Fischer sitting on the pull-down seat, facing the other three.

Florence put her hand on Edith's. "I hope you didn't think me unfriendly before," she said. "It was only that I felt concern for you, going into that house."

"I understand," said Edith. She drew her hand away.

"I'd appreciate it, Miss Tanner," Barrett told her, "if you wouldn't alarm my wife prematurely."

"I had no intention of doing that, Doctor. Still—" Florence hesitated, then went on. "You *have* prepared Mrs. Barrett, I trust."

"My wife has been advised that there will be occurrences."

Fischer grunted. "One way of putting it," he said. It was the first time he'd spoken in an hour.

Barrett turned to him. "She has also been advised," he

said, "that these occurrences will not, in any way, signify the presence of the dead."

Fischer nodded, taking out a pack of cigarettes. "All right if I smoke?" he asked. His gaze flicked across their faces. Seeing no objection, he lit one.

Florence was about to say something more to Barrett, then changed her mind. "Odd that a project such as this should be financed by a man like Deutsch," she said. "I would never have thought him genuinely interested in these matters."

"He's an old man," Barrett said. "He's thinking about dying, and wants to believe it isn't the end."

"It isn't, of course."

Barrett smiled.

"You look familiar," Edith said to Florence. "Why is that?"

"I used to be an actress years ago. Television mostly, an occasional film. My acting name was Florence Michaels."

Edith nodded.

Florence looked at Barrett, then at Fischer. "Well, this *is* exciting," she said. "To work with two such giants. How can that house not fall before us?"

"Why is it called Hell House?" Edith asked.

"Because its owner, Emeric Belasco, created a private hell there," Barrett told her.

"Is he supposed to be the one who haunts the house?"

"Among many," Florence said. "The phenomena are too complex to be the work of one surviving spirit. It's obviously a case of multiple haunting."

"Let's just say there's something there," said Barrett.

Florence smiled. "Agreed."

"Will you get rid of it with your machine?" asked Edith.

Florence and Fischer looked at Barrett. "I'll explain it presently," he said.

They all looked toward the windows as the car angled

downward. "We're almost there," Barrett said. He looked at Edith. "The house is in the Matawaskie Valley."

All of them gazed at the hill-ringed valley lying ahead, its floor obscured by fog. Fischer stubbed his cigarette in the ashtray, blowing out smoke. Looking forward again, he winced. "We're going in."

The car was suddenly immersed in greenish mist. Its speed was decreased by the driver, and they saw him leaning forward, peering through the windshield. After several moments he switched on the fog lights and wipers.

"How could anyone want to build a house in such a place?" asked Florence.

"This was sunshine to Belasco," Fischer said.

They all stared through the windows at the curling fog. It was as though they rode inside a submarine, slowly navigating downward through a sea of curdled milk. At various moments, trees or bushes or boulder formations would appear beside the car, then disappear. The only sound was the hum of the engine.

At last the car was braked. They all looked forward to see the other Cadillac in front of them. There was a faint sound as its door was closed. Then the figure of Deutsch's representative loomed from the mist. Barrett depressed a button, and the window by his side slid down. He grimaced at the fetid odor of the mist.

The man leaned over. "We're at the turnoff," he said. "Your chauffeur is going into Caribou Falls with us, so one of you will have to drive to the house—it's just a little way. The telephone has been connected, the electricity is on, and your rooms are ready." He glanced at the floor. "The food in that basket should see you through the afternoon. Supper will be delivered at six. Any questions?"

"Will we need a key for the front door?" Barrett asked.

"No, it's unlocked."

"Get one anyway," Fischer said.

Barrett looked at him, then back at the man. "Perhaps we'd better."

The man withdrew a ring of keys from his overcoat pocket and disconnected one of them, handing it to Barrett. "Anything else?"

"We'll phone if there is."

The man smiled briefly. "Good-bye, then," he said. He turned away.

"I trust he meant *au revoir*," said Edith.

Barrett smiled as he raised the window.

"I'll drive," Fischer said. He clambered over the seat and got in front. Starting the motor, he turned left onto the rutted blacktop road.

Edith drew in sudden breath. "I wish I knew what to expect."

Fischer answered without looking back. "Expect anything," he said.

11:47 A.M.

For the past five minutes Fischer had been inching the Cadillac along the narrow, fog-bound road. Now he braked and stopped the engine. "We're here." he said. He wrenched up the door handle and ducked outside, buttoning his Navy pea coat.

Edith turned as Lionel opened the door beside him. She waited as he struggled out, then edged across the seat after him. She shivered as she got out. "Cold," she said, "and that *smell*."

"Probably a swamp around here somewhere."

Florence joined them, and the four stood silent for a few moments, looking around.

.   "That way," Fischer said then. He was gazing across the hood of the car.

"Let's take a look," said Barrett. "We can get our luggage afterward." He turned to Fischer. "Would you lead?"

Fischer moved off.

They had gone only a few yards when they reached a narrow concrete bridge. As they walked across it, Edith looked over the edge. If there was water below, the mist obscured it from sight. She glanced back. Already the limousine was swallowed by fog.

"Don't fall in the tarn." Fischer's voice drifted back. Edith turned and saw a body of water ahead, a gravel path curving to its left. The surface of the water looked like clouded gelatin sprinkled with a thin debris of leaves and grass. A miasma of decay hovered above it, and the stones which lined its shore were green with slime.

"Now we know where the odor comes from," Barrett said. He shook his head. "Belasco *would* have a tarn."

"Bastard Bog," said Fischer.

"Why do you call it that?"

Fischer didn't answer. Finally he said, "I'll tell you later."

They walked in silence now, the only sound the crunching of gravel underneath their shoes. The cold was numbing, a clammy chill that seemed to dew itself around their bones. Edith drew up the collar of her coat and stayed close to Lionel, holding on to his arm and looking at the ground. Just behind them walked Florence Tanner.

When Lionel stopped at last, Edith looked up quickly.

It stood before them in the fog, a massive, looming specter of a house.

"*Hideous*," said Florence, sounding almost angry. Edith looked at her. "We haven't even gone inside, Miss Tanner," Barrett said.

"I don't have to go inside." Florence turned to Fischer,

who was staring at the house. As she looked at him, he shuddered. Reaching out, she put her hand in his. He gripped it so hard it made her wince.

Barrett and Edith gazed up at the shrouded edifice. In the mist, it resembled some ghostly escarpment blocking their path. Edith leaned forward suddenly. *"It has no windows,"* she said.

"He had them bricked up," Barrett said.

"Why?"

"I don't know. Perhaps—"

"We're wasting time," Fischer cut him off. He let go of Florence's hand and lurched forward.

They walked the final yards along the gravel path, then started up the wide porch steps. Edith saw that all the steps were cracked, fungus and frosted yellow grass sprouting from the fissures.

They stopped before the massive double doors.

"If they open by themselves, I'm going home," Edith said, trying to sound amused. Barrett gripped the handle on the door and depressed its thumb plate. The door held fast. He glanced at Fischer. "This happen to you?"

"More than once."

"Good we have the key, then." Barrett removed it from his overcoat pocket and slid it into the lock. It wouldn't turn. He wiggled the key back and forth, attempting to loosen the bolt.

Abruptly the key turned over, and the heavy door began to swing in. Edith twitched as Florence caught her breath. "What is it?" she asked. Florence shook her head. "No cause for alarm," Barrett said. Edith glanced at him in surprise.

"It's just reaction, Mrs. Barrett," Florence explained. "Your husband is quite right. It's nothing to be alarmed about."

Fischer had been reaching in to locate the light switch.

Now he found it, and they heard him flick it up and down without result. "So much for restored electrical service," he said.

"Obviously the generator is too old," Barrett said.

"Generator?" Edith looked surprised again. "There's no electrical service here?"

"There aren't enough houses in the valley to make it worth the effort," Barrett answered.

"How could they put in a telephone, then?"

"It's a field telephone," Barrett said. He looked into the house. "Well, Mr. Deutsch will have to provide us with a new generator, that's all."

"You think that's the answer, do you?" Fischer sounded dubious.

"Of course," said Barrett. "The breakdown of an antique generator can scarcely be classified as a psychic phenomenon."

"What are we going to do?" asked Edith. "Stay in Caribou Falls until the new generator is installed?"

"That might take days," said Barrett. "We'll use candles until it arrives."

"Candles," Edith said.

Barrett smiled at her expression. "Just for a day or so."

She nodded, her returned smile wan. Barrett looked inside the house. "The question now," he said, "is how do we find some candles? I assume there must be some inside—" He broke off, looking at the flashlight Fischer had taken out of his coat pocket. "*Ah*," he said.

Fischer switched on the flashlight, pointed the beam inside, then, bracing himself, stepped across the threshold.

Barrett went in next. He stepped through the doorway, seemed to listen briefly. Turning then, he extended his hand to Edith. She entered the house, clutching at his hand. "That *smell*," she said. "It's even worse than outside."

"It's a very old house with no aeration," Barrett said. "It

could also be the furnace, which hasn't been used in more than twenty-nine years." He turned to Florence. "Coming, Miss Tanner?" he asked.

She nodded, smiling faintly. "Yes." She took a deep breath, held herself erect, and stepped inside. She looked around. "The *atmosphere* in here—" She sounded queasy.

"An atmosphere of this world, not the next," said Barrett dryly.

Fischer played the flashlight beam around the dark immensity of the entry hall. The narrow cone of light jumped fitfully from place to place, freezing momentarily on hulking groups of furniture; huge, leaden-colored paintings; giant tapestries filmed with dust; a staircase, broad and curving, leading upward into blackness; a second-story corridor overlooking the entry hall; and far above, engulfed by shadows, a vast expanse of paneled ceiling.

"Be it ever so humble," Barrett said.

"It isn't humble at all," said Florence. "It reeks of arrogance."

Barrett sighed. "It reeks, at any rate." He looked to his right. "According to the floor plan, the kitchen should be that way."

Edith walked beside him as they started across the entry hall, the sound of their footsteps loud on the hardwood floor.

Florence looked around. "It knows we're here," she said.

"Miss Tanner—" Barrett frowned. "Please don't think I'm trying to restrict you—"

"Sorry." Florence said. "I'll try to keep my observations to myself."

They reached a corridor and walked along it, Fischer in the lead, Barrett and Edith behind him, Florence last. At the end of the corridor stood a pair of metal-faced swinging doors. Fischer pushed one of them open and stepped into the kitchen, holding the door ajar for the others. When all of them had gone inside, he let the door swing back and turned.

"Good Lord." Edith's eyes moved with the flashlight beam as Fischer shifted it around the room.

The kitchen was twenty-five by fifty feet, its perimeter rimmed by steel counters and dark-paneled cupboards, a long, double-basin sink, a gigantic stove with three ovens, and a massive walk-in refrigerator. In the center of the room, like a giant's steel-topped casket, stood a huge steam table.

"He must have entertained a good deal," Edith said.

Fischer pointed the flashlight at the large electric wall clock above the stove. Its hands were stopped at 7:31. A.M. or P.M., and on what day? Barrett wondered as he limped along the wall to his right, pulling open drawers. Edith and Florence stood together, watching him. Barrett pulled open one of the cupboard doors and grunted as Fischer shone the light over. "Genuine spirits," he said, looking at the shelves of dust-filmed bottles. "Perhaps we'll raise some after supper."

Fischer pulled a sheet of yellow-edged cardboard from one of the drawers and pointed the flashlight at it.

"What's that?" Barrett asked.

"One of their menus, dated March 27, 1928. Shrimp bisque. Sweetbreads in gravy. Stewed capon. Bread sauce in gravy. Creamed cauliflower. For dessert, *amandes en crème:* crushed almonds in whipped egg whites and heavy cream."

Barrett chuckled. "His guests must have all had heartburn."

"The food wasn't aimed at their hearts," said Fischer, taking a box of candles from the drawer.

12:19 P.M.

They started back across the entry hall, each carrying a candle in a holder. As they moved, the flickering illumination made their shadows billow on the walls and ceiling.

"This must be the great hall over here," said Barrett.

They moved beneath an archway six feet deep and stopped, Edith and Florence gasping almost simultaneously. Barrett whistled softly as he raised his candle for a maximum of light.

The great hall measured ninety-five by forty-seven feet, its walls two stories high, paneled in walnut to a height of eight feet, rough-hewn blocks of stone above. Across from where they stood was a mammoth fireplace, its mantel constructed of antique carved stone.

The furnishings were all antique except for scattered chairs and sofas upholstered in the fashion of the twenties. Marble statues stood on pedestals in various locations. In the northwest corner was an ebony concert grand piano, and in the center of the hall stood a circular table, more than twenty feet across, with sixteen high-backed chairs around it and a large chandelier suspended over it. Good place to set up my equipment, Barrett thought; the hall had obviously been cleaned. He lowered his candle. "Let's push on," he said.

They left the great hall, moved across the entry hall, beneath the overhanging staircase, and turned right into another corridor. Several yards along its length, they reached a pair of swinging walnut doors set to their left. Barrett pushed one in and peered inside. "The theater," he said.

They went inside, reacting to the musty smell. The theater was designed to seat a hundred people, its walls covered with an antique red brocade, its sloping, three-aisled floor with thick red carpeting. On the stage, gilded Renaissance columns flanked the screen, and spaced along the walls were silver candelabra wired for electricity. The seats were custom-made, upholstered with wine-red velvet.

"Just how wealthy *was* Belasco?" Edith asked.

"I believe he left in excess of seven million dollars when he died," Barrett answered.

"Died?" said Fischer. He held open one of the doors.

"If there's anything you care to tell us . . ." Barrett said as he stepped into the corridor.

"What's to tell? The house tried to kill me; it almost succeeded."

Barrett looked as though he meant to speak. Then he changed his mind and peered down the corridor. "I think that staircase leads down to the pool and steam room," he said. "No point in going there until the electricity's on." He limped across the corridor and opened a heavy wooden door.

"What is it?" Edith asked.

"Looks like a chapel."

"A *chapel?*" Florence looked appalled. As she neared the door, she started making sounds of apprehension in her throat. Edith glanced at her uneasily.

"Miss Tanner?" Barrett said.

She didn't answer. Almost to the door, she held back.

"Better not," said Fischer.

Florence shook her head. "I must." She began to enter.

With a faint, involuntary cry, she shrank back. Edith started. "What *is* it?" Florence was unable to reply. She sucked in breath and shook her head with tiny movements. Barrett put his hand on Edith's arm. She looked at him and saw his lips frame the words, "It's all right."

"I can't go in," Florence said, as though apologizing. "Not now, anyway." She swallowed. "The atmosphere is more than I can bear."

"We'll only be a moment," Barrett told her.

Florence nodded, turning away.

As she went inside the chapel, Edith braced herself, expecting a shock of some kind. Feeling nothing, she turned to Lionel in confusion, started to speak, then waited until they were apart from Fischer. "Why couldn't she come in?" she whispered then.

"Her system is attuned to psychic energy," Barrett explained. "Obviously it's very strong in here."

"Why here?"

"Contrast, perhaps. A church in hell; that sort of thing."

Edith nodded, glancing back at Fischer. "Why doesn't it bother him?" she asked.

"Perhaps he knows how to protect himself better than she does."

Edith nodded again, stopping as Lionel did to look around the low-ceilinged chapel. There were wooden pews for fifty people. In front was an altar; above it, glinting in the candle-light, a life-size, flesh-colored figure of Jesus on the cross.

"It *looks* like a chapel," she started to say, breaking off in shock as she saw that the figure of Jesus was naked, an enormous phallus jutting upward from between the legs. She made a sound of revulsion, staring at the obscene crucifix. The air seemed suddenly thick, coagulating in her throat.

Now she noticed that the walls were covered with pornographic murals. Her eye was caught by one on her right, depicting a mass orgy involving half-clothed nuns and priests. The faces on the figures were demented—leering, slavering, darkly flushed, distorted by maniacal lust.

"Profanation of the sacred," Barrett said. "A venerable sickness."

"He *was* sick," Edith murmured.

"Yes, he was." Barrett took her arm. As he escorted her along the aisle, Edith saw that Fischer had already left.

They found him in the corridor.

"She's gone," he said.

Edith stared at him. "How can she—?" She broke off, looking
around.

"I'm sure it's nothing," Barrett said.

"Are you?" Fischer sounded angry.

"I'm sure she's all right," said Barrett firmly. "Miss Tanner!" he called. "Come along, my dear." He started down the
corridor. "Miss Tanner!" Fischer followed him without making a sound.

"Lionel, why would she—?"

"Let's not jump to conclusions," Barrett said. He called
again. "Miss Tanner! Can you hear me?"

As they reached the entry hall, Edith pointed. There was
candlelight inside the great hall.

"Miss Tanner!" Barrett called.

"Yes!"

Barrett smiled at Edith, then glanced over at Fischer. Fischer's expression had not relaxed.

She was standing on the far side of the hall. Their footsteps clicked in broken rhythm on the floor as they crossed to
her. "You shouldn't have done that, Miss Tanner," Barrett
said. "You caused us undue alarm."

"I'm sorry," Florence said, but it was only a token apology. "I heard a voice in here."

Edith shuddered.

Florence gestured toward the piece of furniture she was
standing beside, a phonograph installed inside a walnut Spanish cabinet. Reaching down to its turntable, she lifted off a
record and showed it to them. "It was this."

Edith didn't understand. "How could it play without electricity?"

"You forget they used to wind up phonographs." Barrett set his candle holder on top of the cabinet and took the record from Florence. "Homemade," he said.

"Belasco."

Barrett looked at her, intrigued. "His voice?" She nodded, and he turned to put it back on the turntable. Florence looked at Fischer, who was standing several yards away, staring at the phonograph.

Barrett wound the crank tight, ran a fingertip across the end of the steel needle, and set it on the record edge. There was a crackling noise through the speaker, then a voice.

"Welcome to my house," said Emeric Belasco. "I'm delighted you could come."

Edith crossed her arms and shivered.

"I am certain you will find your stay here most illuminating." Belasco's voice was soft and mellow, yet terrifying—the voice of a carefully disciplined madman. "It is regrettable I cannot be with you," it said, "but I had to leave before your arrival."

Bastard, Fischer thought.

"Do not let my physical absence disturb you, however. Think of me as your unseen host and believe that, during your stay here, I shall be with you in spirit."

Edith's teeth were set on edge. *That voice.*

"All your needs have been provided for," Belasco's voice continued. "Nothing has been overlooked. Go where you will, and do what you will—these are the cardinal precepts of my home. Feel free to function as you choose. There are no responsibilities, no rules. 'Each to his own device' shall be the only standard here. May you find the answer that you seek. It is here, I promise you." There was a pause. "And now . . . *auf Wiedersehen.*"

The needle made a scratching noise on the record. Barrett

raised the needle arm and switched off the phonograph. The great hall was immensely still.

"Auf Wiedersehen" said Florence. *"Until we meet again."*

"Lionel—?"

"The record wasn't meant for us," he said.

"But—"

"It was cut a good half-century ago," said Barrett. "Look at it." He held it up. "It's merely a coincidence that what he said seems applicable to us."

"What made the phonograph go on by itself, then?" Florence asked.

"That is a separate problem," Barrett said. "I'm only discussing the record now." He looked at Fischer. "Did it play by itself in 1940? The accounts say nothing of it."

Fischer shook his head.

"Do you know anything about the record?"

It appeared that Fischer wasn't going to answer. Then he said, "Guests would arrive, to find him gone. That record would be played for them." He paused. "It was a game he played. While the guests were here, Belasco spied on them from hiding."

Barrett nodded.

"Then, again, maybe he was invisible," Fischer continued. "He claimed the power. Said that he could will the attention of a group of people to some particular object, and move among them unobserved."

"I doubt that," Barrett said.

"Do you?" Fischer's smile was strange as he looked at the phonograph. "We all had our attention on that a few moments ago," he said. "How do you know he didn't walk right by us while we were listening?"

12:46 P.M.

They were moving up the staircase when an icy breeze passed over them, causing their candle flames to flicker. Edith's flame went out. "What was that?" she whispered.

"A breeze," said Barrett instantly. He declined his candle to relight hers. "We'll discuss it later."

Edith swallowed, glancing at Florence. Barrett took her by the arm, and they started up the stairs again. "There'll be many things like that during the week," he said. "You'll get used to them."

Edith said no more. As she and Lionel ascended the stairs, Florence and Fischer exchanged a look.

They reached the second floor and, turning to the right, started along the balcony corridor. On their right, the heavy balustrade continued. To their left, set periodically along a paneled wall, were bedroom doors. Barrett approached the first of these and opened it. He looked inside, then turned to Florence. "Would you like this one?" he asked.

She stepped into the doorway. After several moments, she turned back to them. "Not too bad," she said. She smiled at Edith. "You'll rest more comfortably here."

Barrett was about to comment, then relented. "Fine," he said. He gestured toward the room.

He followed Edith inside and shut the door. Edith watched as he limped around the bedroom. To her left were a pair of carved walnut Renaissance beds, between them a small table with a lamp and a French-style telephone on it. A fireplace was centered on the opposite wall, in front of it a heavy walnut rocking chair. The teakwood floor was almost covered by a twenty-by-thirty-foot blue Persian rug, in the middle of which stood an octagonal-topped table with a matching chair upholstered in red leather.

Barrett glanced into the bathroom, then returned to her. "About that breeze," he said. "I didn't want to get involved in a discussion with Miss Tanner. That's why I glossed over it."

"It really happened, didn't it?"

"Of course," he answered, smiling. "A manifestation of simple kinetics: unguided, unintelligent. No matter what Miss Tanner thinks. I should have mentioned that before we left."

"Mentioned what?"

"That you'll need to inure yourself to what she'll be saying in the next week. She's a Spiritualist, as you know. Survival of and communication with the so-called disincarnate is the foundation of her belief; an erroneous foundation, as I intend to prove. In the meantime, though"—he smiled—"be prepared to hear her views expressed. I can't very well ask that she remain mute."

To her right, their heads against the wall, were a pair of beds with elaborately carved headboards, between them a huge chest of drawers. Above the chest, suspended from the ceiling, was a large Italian silver lamp.

Directly across from her, by the paneled window shutters, was a Spanish table with a matching chair. On top of the table was a Chinese lamp and a French-style telephone. Florence crossed the room and picked up the receiver. It was dead. Did I expect it to be working? she thought, amused. At any rate, it had doubtless been used only for calls made within the house.

She turned and looked around the room. There was something in it. What, though? A personality? A residue of emotion? Florence closed her eyes and waited. Something in the air; no doubt of it. She felt it shift and throb, advancing on her, then retreating like some unseen, timorous beast.

After several minutes she opened her eyes. *It will come,* she thought. She crossed to the bathroom, squinting slightly as its white tile walls glittered with reflected candlelight. Setting the holder on the sink, she turned the hot-water faucet. For a moment, nothing happened. Then, with a gurgling rattle, a gout of darkly rusted water splattered into the basin. Florence waited until the water cleared before she held her hand beneath it. She hissed at its coldness. *I hope the water heater isn't broken too,* she thought. Bending over, she started patting water onto her face.

I should have gone into the chapel, she thought. *I shouldn't have backed off from the very first challenge.* She winced, remembering the violent nausea she'd felt as she was about to enter. *An awful place,* she thought. She'd have to work her way up to it, that was all. If she forced it now, she might lose consciousness. *I'll get in there soon enough,* she promised herself. *God will grant the power when it's time.*

His room was smaller than the other two. There was only one bed with a canopy top. Fischer sat at the foot of it, staring at the intricate pattern on the rug. He could feel the house around him like some vast, invisible being. *It knows I'm here,* he thought; *Belasco knows, they all know that I'm here: their single failure.* They were watching him, waiting to see what he'd do.

He wasn't going to do anything prematurely, that was certain. He wasn't going to do a thing until he got the feel of the place.

2:21 P.M.

Fischer came into the great hall carrying his flashlight. He had changed into a black turtleneck sweater, black corduroy trousers, and a pair of scuffed white tennis shoes. His steps were soundless as he moved toward the huge round table where Barrett, seated, and Edith, standing, were opening wooden boxes and unloading equipment. In the fireplace, a fire was burning.

Edith started as Fischer emerged from the shadows. "Need help?" he asked.

"No, it's going fine," said Barrett, smiling. "Thank you for the offer, though."

Fischer sat in one of the chairs. His eyes remained on Barrett as the tall, bearded man removed an instrument from protective excelsior, wiped it carefully with a cloth, and set it on the table. Fussy about his equipment, Fischer thought. He pulled a pack of cigarettes from his pocket and lit one, watching the gamboling deformity of Edith's shadow on the wall as she picked up another wooden box and carried it to the table.

"Still teach physics?" he asked.

"Limitedly, because of health." Barrett hesitated, then continued. "I had polio when I was twelve; my right leg is partially paralyzed."

Fischer gazed at him in silence. Barrett took another instrument from its box and wiped it off. He set the instrument on the table and looked at Fischer. "It won't affect our project in any way," he said.

Fischer nodded.

"You referred to the tarn before as Bastard Bog," Barrett said, returning to his work. "Why was that?"

"Some of Belasco's female guests got pregnant while they were here."

"And they actually—?" Barrett broke off, glancing up.

"Thirteen times."

"That's hideous," said Edith.

Fischer blew out smoke. "A lot of hideous things happened here," he said.

Barrett ran his eyes across the instruments already on the table: astatic galvanometer, mirror galvanometer, quadrant electrometer, Crookes balance, camera, gauze cage, smoke absorber, manometer, weighing platform, tape recorder. Still to be unpacked were the contact clock, electroscope, lights (standard and infrared), maximum and minimum thermometer, hygroscope, sthenometer, phosphorescent sulfide screen, electric stove, the box of vessels and tubes, the molding materials, and the cabinet equipment. And the most important instrument of all, Barrett thought with satisfaction.

He was unpacking the rack of red, yellow, and white lights when Fischer asked, "How are you going to use those when there's no electricity?"

"There will be by tomorrow," Barrett said. "I telephoned Caribou Falls; the phone is near the front door, incidentally. They'll install a new generator in the morning."

"And you think it will work?"

Barrett repressed a smile. "It will work."

Fischer said no more. Across the hall, a burning log popped, making Edith twitch as she walked to one of the larger wooden boxes.

"Not that one, it's too heavy," Barrett told her.

"I'll do it." Rising from his chair, Fischer walked to Edith and, stooping, lifted the box. "What is it, an anvil?" he asked as he set it on the table.

Barrett was aware of Fischer's curious gaze as he pried up the boards on top of the box. "Would you—?" he asked. Fischer lifted out the bulky metal instrument and set it on the table. It was cube-shaped, painted dark blue, an uncomplicated dial in front of it numbered 0-900, the thin red needle

pointed at zero. Across the top of the instrument was sten-
ciled, in black letters: BARRETT—EMR.

"EMR?" asked Fischer.

"I'll explain it later," said Barrett.

"This your machine?"

Barrett shook his head. "That's being constructed."

They all turned toward the archway at the sound of heels.
Florence was approaching, carrying a candle in its holder. She
had changed to a heavy green, long-sleeved sweater, thick
tweed skirt, and low-heeled shoes. "Hello," she said cheer-
fully.

As she came up to them, her gaze ran across the array of
devices on the table, and she smiled. She turned to Fischer.
"Like to take a walk with me?" she asked.

"Why not?"

After they were gone, Edith saw a typed list on the table
and picked it up. It was headed, "Observed Psychic Phenomena at the Belasco House":

Apparitions; Apports; Asports; Automatic drawing; Automatic
painting; Automatic speaking ; Automatic writing; Autoscopy;
Bilocation; Biological phenomena; Book tests; Breezes; Catalepsy;
Chemical phenomena; Chemicographs; Clairaudience; Clairsenti-
ence; Clairvoyance; Communication; Control; Crystal gazing; De-
materialization; Direct drawing; Direct painting; Direct voice;
Direct writing; Divination; Dreams; Dream communications;
Dream prophecies; Ectoplasm; Eidolons; Electrical phenomena;
Elongation; Emanations; Exteriorization of motricity; Exteriori-
zation of sensation; Extras; Extratemporal perception; Eyeless
sight; Facsimile writing; Flower clairsentience; Ghosts;
Glossolalia; Hyperamnesia; Hyperesthesia; Ideomorphs;
Ideoplasm; Impersonation; Imprints; Independent voice;
Interpenetration of matter; Knot tying; Levitation; Luminous
phenomena; Magnetic phenomena; Materialization; Matter

through matter; Metagraphology; Monition; Motor automatism;
Newspaper tests; Obsession; Paraffin molds; Parakinesis; Param-
nesia; Paresthesia; Percussion; Phantasmata; Poltergeist phe-
nomena; Possession; Precognition; Presentiment; Prevision;
Pseudopods; Psychic photography; Psychic rods; Psychic sounds;
Psychic touches; Psychic winds; Psychokinesis; Psychometry;
Radiesthesia; Radiographs; Raps; Retrocognition; Scriptograph;
Sensory automatism; Skin writing; Skotography; Slate writing;
Smells; Somnambulism; Stigmata; Telekinesis; Teleplasm; Tele-
scopic vision; Telesthesia; Transcendental music; Transfiguration;
Transportation; Typtology; Voices; Water sprinkling; Xenoglossy.

Edith put the list down numbly. My God, she thought.
What kind of week was it going to be?

2:53 P.M.

The garage had been built to accommodate seven
automobiles. Now it was empty. As they entered, Fischer
thumbed off his flashlight, enough daylight filtering through
the grimy door windows for them to see. He looked at the
greenish mist which pressed against the panes of glass.
"Maybe we should keep the car in here," he said.

Florence didn't answer. She was walking across the oil-
spotted floor, turning her head from side to side. She paused
by a shelf and touched a dirty, rust-flecked hammer.

"What did you say?" she asked.

"Maybe we should keep the car in here."

Florence shook her head. "If a generator can be tampered
with, so can a car."

Fischer watched the medium move around the garage. As

she passed close by, he caught a scent of the cologne she wore. "Why did you give up acting?" he asked.

Florence glanced at him with a fleeting smile. "It's a long story, Ben. When we've settled down a bit, I'll tell it to you. Right now, I'd better get the feeling of the place." She stopped in a patch of light and closed her eyes.

Fischer stared at her. In the dim illumination, the medium's ivory skin and lustrous red hair gave her the appearance of a Dresden doll.

After a while she returned to Fischer. "Nothing here," she said. "You agree?"

"Whatever you say."

Fischer switched on his flashlight as they ascended the steps to the corridor. "Which way now?" she asked.

"I don't know the place that well. I was here only three days."

"We'll just explore, then," Florence said. "No need—" She broke off suddenly and stopped, head twisted to the right, as though she heard a noise behind them. "Yes," she murmured. "*Yes*. Sorrow. Pain." She frowned and shook her head. "No, no." At length she sighed and looked at Fischer. "You felt it," she said.

Fischer didn't answer. Florence smiled and looked away. "Well, let's see what else we can find," she said.

"Have you read Doctor Barrett's article in which he compares sensitives to Geiger counters?" she asked as they walked along the corridor.

"No."

"It's not a bad comparison. We *are* like Geiger counters in a way. Expose us to psychic emanations, and we tick. Of course, the difference is that we are judge as well as instrument, not only picking up impressions, but evaluating them as well."

"Uh-huh," said Fischer. Florence glanced at him.

They started down the flight of stairs across from the chapel, Fischer pointing the flashlight beam at their feet. "I wonder if we're going to need the full week," Florence said.

"A full year wouldn't be too long."

Florence tried to make her sound of disagreement mild. "I've seen the most abstruse of psychic problems solved overnight. We mustn't—" She stopped, hand clamping on the banister rail. *"This goddamn sewer,"* she muttered in a savage voice. She jolted in dismay and shook her head. "Oh, dear. Such fury. Such destructive venom." She drew in trembling breath. "A very hostile man," she said. "No wonder. Who can blame him, imprisoned in this house?" She glanced at Fischer.

Reaching the lower corridor, they moved to a pair of swinging metal doors with porthole windows in them. Fischer pushed at one of the doors and held it open for Florence. As they went inside, their footsteps sounded sharply on a tile floor and reverberated off the ceiling.

The pool was Olympic size. Fischer shone his flashlight into the murky green depths of it. He walked to the end of the pool and knelt at its corner. Pulling up the sleeve of his sweater, he put his hand in the water. "Not too cold," he said, surprised. He felt around. "And water's coming in. The pool must work on a separate generator."

Florence gazed across the glinting pool. The ripples made by Fischer were gliding across its surface. "Something in here," she said. She did not look to Fischer for verification.

"Steam room's down the other end." Fischer returned to her side.

"Let's look at it."

The ringing echoes of their footsteps as they walked along the edge of the pool made it sound as though someone were following them. Florence glanced across her shoulder. "Yes," she murmured, unaware that she had spoken.

Fischer pulled open the heavy metal door and held it ajar, playing the flashlight beam inside. The steam room was twelve feet square, its walls, floor, and ceiling tiled in white. Built-in wooden benches lined the walls, and spiraling across the floor like some petrified serpent was a length of faded green hose connected to a water outlet.

Florence grimaced. "Perverted," she said. "In there—" She swallowed as though to rid her throat of sour bile. "In *there*," she said. "But what?"

Fischer let the door swing shut, the thumping closure of it echoing loudly. Florence glanced at him; then, as he turned away, she fell into step beside him. "Doctor Barrett is certainly well equipped, isn't he?" she said, trying to lighten his mood. "It's strange to think he really believes that science alone can end the power of this house."

"What will?"

"Love," she answered. She squeezed his arm. "We know that, don't we?"

Fischer held open the swinging door for her, and they went back into the corridor. "What's over there?" Florence crossed the hallway and opened a wooden door. Fischer pointed the flashlight beam inside. It was a wine cellar, all its shelves and racks empty. Florence winced. "I see this room completely filled with bottles." She turned away. "Let's not go in."

They went back up the staircase and started along the first-floor corridor. As they passed the chapel door, Florence shuddered. "That place is the worst of all," she said. "Even though I haven't seen the entire house, somehow I have the feeling . . ." Her voice faded as she spoke. She cleared her throat. "I'll get in there," she said.

They turned into an adjoining corridor. Twenty yards along its right wall was an archway. "What have we here?"

Florence walked beneath the archway and caught her breath. *"This house,"* she said.

The ballroom was immense, its lofty, brocaded walls adorned with red velvet draperies. Three enormous chandeliers hung, spaced, along the paneled ceiling. The floor was oak, elaborately parqueted. At the far end of the room was an alcove for musicians.

"A theater, yes, but this?" said Florence. "Can a ballroom be an evil place?"

"The evil came later," Fischer said.

Florence shook her head. "Contradictions." She looked at Fischer. "You're right, it's going to take a while. I feel as if I'm standing in the center of a labyrinth of such immeasurable intricacy that the prospect of emerging is—" She caught herself. "We *will* emerge, however."

Overhead, there was a tinkling noise. Fischer jerked up his arm, pointing the flashlight at the parabola of heavy hanging crystal above them. Its pendants refracted the light, splaying colors of the spectrum across the ceiling. The chandelier was motionless.

"The challenge is met," whispered Florence.

"Don't be too quick to accept it," Fischer warned.

Florence looked at him abruptly. "You're blocking it off," she said.

"What?"

"You're blocking it off. That's why you didn't feel those things."

Fischer's smile was cold. "I didn't feel them because they weren't there. I was a Spiritualist too, remember. I know how you people find things in every corner when you want to."

"Ben, that isn't true." Florence looked hurt. "Those things *were* there. You would have felt them just as I did if you weren't obstructing—"

"I'm not obstructing anything," he cut her off. "I'm just

not sticking my head on the block a second time. When I came here in 1940, I was just like you—no, worse, much worse. I really thought I was something. God's gift to psychical research."

"You were the most powerful physical medium this country has ever known, Ben."

"Still am, Florence. Just a little bit more careful now, that's all. I suggest the same approach for you. You're walking around this house like an open nerve. When you really *do* hit something, it'll tear your insides out. This place isn't called Hell House for nothing, you know. It intends to kill every one of us, so you'd damn well better learn to protect yourself until you're ready. Or you'll just be one more victim on the list."

They looked at each other in silence for a long time. Finally she touched his hand. " 'But he who buried his talent—' " she began

"Oh, shit." Turning on his heel, he stalked away from her.

6:42 P.M.

The dining hall was sixty feet in length, and as high as it was wide—twenty-seven feet in both directions. There were two entrances to it—one an archway from the great hall, the other a swinging door leading to the kitchen.

Its ceiling was divided into a series of elaborately carved panels, its floor polished travertine. Its walls were paneled to a height of twelve feet, stone-blocked above. In the center of the west wall was a giant fireplace, its Gothic mantel reaching to the ceiling. Spaced at intervals above the length of the forty-foot table in the center of the hall hung four immense sanctuary lamps, wired for electricity. Thirty chairs stood around the table, all of them constructed of antique walnut with wine-red velvet upholstery.

The four were sitting at one end of the table, Barrett at its head. The unseen couple from Caribou Falls had left the supper at six-fifteen.

"If no one objects, I'd like to try a sitting tonight," Florence said.

Barrett's hand froze momentarily before continuing to spoon himself a second portion of broccoli. "I have no objection," he said.

Florence glanced at Edith, who shook her head. She looked at Fischer. "Fine," he said, reaching for the coffeepot.

Florence nodded. "After supper, then." Her plate was empty; she'd been drinking only water since they'd sat down.

"Would *you* care to sit in the morning, Mr. Fischer?" Barrett asked.

Fischer shook his head. "Not yet."

Barrett nodded. There; it's done, he thought. He'd asked and been refused. Since his part in the project required the services of a physical medium, Deutsch couldn't object to his sending for one of his own people. *Excellent*, he thought. He'd get it settled in the morning.

"Well," he said, "I must say that the house has scarcely lived up to its reputation so far."

Fischer looked up from the scraps of food on his plate. "It hasn't taken our measure yet," he said. His lips flexed briefly in a humorless smile.

"I think we'd be mistaken to consider the house as the haunting force," Florence said. "Quite evidently, the trouble is created by surviving personalities—whoever they may be. The only one we can be sure of is Belasco."

"You contacted him today, did you?" Barrett asked. His tone was mild, but Florence sensed the goading in it. "No," she said. "But Mr. Fischer did when he was here in 1940. And Belasco's presence *has* been documented."

"Reported," Barrett said.

Florence hesitated. Finally she said, "I think it might be well for us to lay our cards on the table, Doctor Barrett. I take it you are still convinced that no such things as ghosts exist."

"If, by that, you mean surviving personalities," said Barrett, "you are quite correct."

"Despite the fact that they've been observed throughout the ages?" Florence asked. "Have been seen by more than one person at a time? Been seen by animals? Been photographed? Have imparted information that was later verified? Have touched people? Moved objects? Been weighed?"

"These are facts in evidence of a phenomenon, Miss Tanner, not proof of ghosts."

Florence smiled wearily. "I don't know how to answer that," she said.

Barrett returned her smile, gesturing with his hands as though to say: We don't agree, so why not let it go at that?

"You don't accept survival, then," Florence persisted.

"It's a charming notion," Barrett said. "I have no objection to it, so long as I am not expected to give credence to the concept of communicating with the so-called survivors."

Florence regarded him sadly. "You can say that, having heard the sobs of joy at séances?"

"I've heard similar sobs in mental institutions."

"Mental institutions?"

Barrett sighed. "No offense intended. But the evidence is clear that belief in communication with the dead has led more people to madness than to peace of mind."

"That isn't true," said Florence. "If it were, all attempts at spirit communication would have ended long ago. They haven't, though; they've lasted through the centuries." She looked intently at Barrett, as though trying to understand his point of view. "You call it a charming notion, Doctor. Surely

it's more than that. What about the religions that accept the idea of life after death? Didn't Saint Paul say: 'If the dead rise not from the grave, then is our religion vain'?"

Barrett didn't respond.

"But you don't agree," she said.

"I don't agree."

"Have you any alternative to offer, though?"

"*Yes.*" Barrett returned her gaze with challenge. "An alternative far more interesting, albeit far more complex and demanding; namely, *the subliminal self*, that vast, concealed expanse of the human personality which, iceberglike, inheres beneath the so-called threshold of consciousness. That is where the fascination lies, Miss Tanner. Not in the speculative realms of afterlife, but *here, today; the challenge of ourselves.* The undiscovered mysteries of the human spectrum, the infrared capacities of our bodies, the ultraviolet capacities of our minds. This is the alternative I offer: *the extended faculties of the human system not as yet established.* The faculties by which, I am convinced, all psychic phenomena are produced."

Florence remained silent for a few moments before she smiled. "We'll see," she said.

Barrett nodded once. "Indeed we shall."

Edith looked around the dining hall. "When was this house built?" she asked.

Barrett looked at Fischer. "Do you know?"

"Nineteen-nineteen," Fischer answered.

"From several things you said today, I have the impression that you know quite a bit about Belasco," Barrett said. "Would you care to tell us what you know? It might not be amiss to"—he repressed a smile—"know our adversary."

Amused? thought Fischer. You won't be when Belasco

and the others get to work. "What do you want to know?" he asked.

"Whatever you can tell us," Barrett said. "A general account of his life might be helpful."

Fischer poured himself another cupful of coffee, then set the pot back on the table, wrapped his hands around the cup, and began to speak.

"He was born in 1879, the illegitimate son of Myron Sandler, an American munitions maker, and Noelle Belasco, an English actress."

"Why did he take his mother's name?" Barrett asked.

"Sandler was married," Fischer said. He paused, went on. "His childhood is a blank except for isolated incidents. At five he hanged a cat to see if it would revive for the second of its nine lives. When it didn't, he became infuriated and chopped the cat to pieces, flinging the parts from his bedroom window. After that, his mother called him Evil Emeric."

"He was raised in England, I presume," Barrett interjected.

Fischer nodded. "The next verified incident was a sexual assault on his younger sister," he said.

Barrett frowned. "Is it all to be like this?"

"He didn't live an exemplary life, Doctor," Fischer said, a caustic edge to his voice.

Barrett hesitated. "Very well." he said. He looked at Edith. "You object, my dear?" Edith shook her head. He glanced at Florence. "Miss Tanner?"

"Not if it will help us understand," she said. Barrett gestured toward Fischer, bidding him continue.

"The assault put his sister in the hospital for two months," Fischer said. "I won't go into details. Belasco was sent to a private school—he was ten and a half at the time. There, he was abused for a number of years, mostly by one of the homosexual teachers. Belasco later invited the man to visit his house for a week; at the end of that time, the retired teacher went home and hanged himself."

"What did Belasco look like?" Barrett asked, attempting to guide the course of Fischer's account.

Fischer stared into his memory. After a while, he began to quote: " 'His teeth are those of a carnivore. When he bares them in a smile, it gives one the impression of an animal snarling. His face is white, for he despises the sun, eschews the out-of-doors. He has astonishingly green eyes, which seem to possess an inner light of their own. His forehead is broad, his hair and short-trimmed beard jet black. Despite his handsomeness, his is a frightening visage, the face of some demon who has taken on a human aspect' "

"Whose description is that?" asked Barrett.

"His second wife's. She committed suicide here in 1927."

"You know that description word for word," said Florence. "You must have read it many times."

Fischer's smile was somber. "As the Doctor said," he answered, "know thine adversary."

"Was he tall or short?" asked Barrett.

"Tall, six-foot-five. 'The Roaring Giant,' he was called."

Barrett nodded. "Education?"

"New York. London. Berlin. Paris. Vienna. No specific course of study. Logic, ethics, religion, philosophy."

"Just enough with which to rationalize his actions, I imagine," Barrett said. "He inherited his money from his father, did he?"

"Mostly. His mother left him several thousand pounds, but his father left him ten and a half million dollars—his share of the proceeds from the sales of rifles and machine guns."

"That could have given him a sense of guilt," said Florence.

"Belasco never felt a twinge of guilt in his life."

"Which only serves to verify his mental aberration," Barrett said.

"His mind may have been aberrant, but it was brilliant, too," Fischer went on. "He could master any subject he chose to study. He spoke and read a dozen languages. He was versed in natural and metaphysical philosophy. He'd studied all the religions, cabalist and Rosicrucian doctrines, ancient mysteries. His mind was a storehouse of information, a powerhouse of energy." He paused. *"A charnelhouse of fancies."*

"Did he ever love a single person in his life?" asked Florence.

"He didn't believe in love," Fischer answered. "He believed in will. 'That rare *vis viva* of the self, that magnetism, that most secret and prevailing delectation of the mind: influence.' Unquote. Emeric Belasco, 1913."

"What did he mean by 'influence'?" asked Barrett.

"The power of the mind to dominate," Fischer said. "The control of one human being by another. He obviously had the kind of hypnotic personality men like Cagliostro and Rasputin had. Quote: 'No one ever went too close to him, lest his terrible presence overpower and engulf them.' His second wife, again." .

"Did Belasco have any children?" Florence asked.

"A son, they say. No one's really sure, though."

"You said the house was built in 1919," Barrett said. "Did the corruption start immediately?"

"No, it was innocent at first. *Haut monde* dinner parties. Lavish dances in the ballroom. Soirées. People traveling from all over the country and world to spend a weekend here. Belasco was a perfect host—sophisticated, charming.

"Then—" He raised his right hand, thumb and index finger almost touching. "In 1920: *'un peu,'* as he referred to it. A *soupçon* of debasement. The introduction, bit by bit, of open sensuality—first in talk, then in action. Gossip. Court intrigues. Aristocratic machinations. Flowing wine and bedroom-hopping. All of it induced by Belasco and his *influences.*

"What he did, in this phase, was create a parallel to eighteenth-century European high society. It would take too long to describe in detail how he did it. It was subtle, though, engineered with great finesse."

"I presume that the result of this was primarily sexual license," Barrett said.

Fischer nodded. "Belasco formed a club he called Les Aphrodites. Every night—later, two and three times a day—they'd hold a meeting; what Belasco called his Sinposium. Having all partaken of drugs and aphrodisiacs, they'd sit around that table in the great hall talking about sex until everyone was what Belasco referred to as 'lubricous.' Then an orgy would commence.

"Still, it wasn't exclusively sex. The principle of excess was applied to every phase of life here. Dining became gluttony, drinking turned to drunkenness. Drug addiction mounted. And, as the physical spectrum of his guests was perverted, so, too, was their mental."

"How?" asked Barrett.

"Visualize twenty to thirty people set loose upon each other mentally—encouraged to do whatever they wanted to one another; no limits set but those of imagination. As their minds began to open up—or close in, if you like—so did every aspect of their lives together. People stayed here months, then years. The house became their way of life. A way of life that grew a little more insane each day. Isolated from the contrast of normal society, the society in this house became the norm. Total self-indulgence became the norm. Debauchery became the norm. Brutality and carnage soon became the norm."

"How could all this . . . bacchanalia take place without re-
percussions?" Barrett asked. "Surely someone must have—
what's the expression?—blown the whistle on Belasco?"

"The house is isolated; really isolated. There were no outside telephones. But, just as important, no one dared to im-
plicate Belasco; they were too afraid of him. Once in a while,
private detectives might do a little probing. They never found
a thing. Everyone was on their best behavior while the investigation was taking place. There was never any evidence. Or,
if there was, Belasco bought it."

"And, during all this time, people kept coming to the
house?" Barrett asked, incredulous.

"In droves," said Fischer. "After a while, Belasco got so
tired of having only eager sinners in his house, he started to
travel around the world enlisting young, creative people for a
visit to his 'artistic retreat'—to write or compose, paint or
meditate. Once he got them here, of course—" He gestured.
"Influences."

"The most vile of evils," Florence said, "corruption of the
innocent." She looked at Fischer almost pleadingly. "Had the
man no trace of decency at all?"

"None," said Fischer. "One of his favorite hobbies was
destroying women. Being so tall and imposing, so magnetic,
he could make them fall in love with him at will. Then, when
they were in the deepest throes of adoration, he'd dump
them. He did it to his own sister—the same one he'd assaulted. She was his mistress for a year. After he rejected her,
she became a drug addict and the leading lady of his Little
Theater Company. She died here of an overdose of heroin in
1923."

"Did Belasco take drugs?" asked Barrett.

"In the beginning. Later on, he started to withdraw from
all involvement with his guests. He had it in mind to make a

study of evil, and he decided that he couldn't do that if he was an active participant. So he began to remove himself, concentrating his energies on the mass corruption of his people.

"About 1926, he started his final thrust. He increased his efforts at encouraging guests to conceive of every cruelty, perversion, and horror they could. He conducted contests to see who could come up with the ghastliest ideas. He started what he termed 'Days of Defilement,' twenty-four-hour periods of frenzied, nonstop depravities. He attempted a literal enactment of de Sade's *120 Days of Sodom*. He began to import monstrosities from all over the world to mingle with his guests—hunchbacks, dwarfs, hermaphrodites, grotesques of every sort."

Florence closed her eyes and bowed her head, pressing tightly clasped hands against her forehead.

"About that time," continued Fischer, "everything began to go. There were no servants to maintain the house; they were indistinguishable from the guests by then. Laundry service failed, and everyone was forced to wash their own clothes—which they refused to do, of course. There being no cooks, everyone had to prepare their own meals with whatever was at hand—which was less and less, because the pickups of food and liquor had dwindled so much, with no acting servants.

"An influenza epidemic hit the house in 1927. Believing the reports of several of his doctor guests that the Matawaskie Valley fog was injurious to health, Belasco had the windows sealed. About that time, the main generator, no longer being maintained, started functioning erratically, and everyone was forced to use candles most of the time. The furnace went out in the winter of 1928, and no one bothered to relight it. The house became as cold as a refrigerator. Pneumonia killed off thirteen guests.

"None of the others cared. By then they were so far gone

that all they were concerned with was their 'daily diet of de-baucheries,' as Belasco put it. They were at the bottom by 1928, delving into mutilation, murder, necrophilia, cannibal-ism."

The three sat motionless and silent, Florence with her head inclined, Barrett and Edith staring at Fischer as he kept on speaking, quietly, virtually without expression, as though he were recounting something very ordinary.

"In June of 1929, Belasco held a version of the Roman circus in his theater," he said. "The highlight was the eating of a virgin by a starving leopard. In July of the same year, a group of drug-addicted doctors started to experiment on ani-mals and humans, testing pain thresholds, exchanging organs, creating monstrosities.

"By then everyone but Belasco was at an animal level, rarely bathing, wearing torn, soiled clothes, eating and drink-ing anything they could get their hands on, killing each other for food or water, liquor, drugs, sex, blood, even for the taste of human flesh, which many of them had acquired by then.

"And, every day, Belasco walked among them, cold, with-drawn, unmoved. Belasco, a latter-day Satan observing his rab-ble. Always dressed in black. A giant, terrifying figure, looking at the hell incarnate he'd created."

"How did it end?" asked Barrett.

"If it had ended, would we be here?"

"*It will end now,*" Florence said.

Barrett persisted. "What happened to Belasco?"

"No one knows," said Fischer. "When relatives of some of his guests had the house broken into in November of 1929, everyone inside was dead—twenty-seven of them.

"Belasco was not among them."

8:46 P.M.

Florence came walking back across the great hall. For the past ten minutes, she'd been sitting in a corner, "preparing herself," she'd told them. Now she was ready. "As ready as one can be in this kind of climate. Excessive dampness is always a handicap." She smiled. "Shall we take our places?"

The four sat at the huge round table, Fischer across from Florence, Barrett several chairs away from her, Edith next to him.

"It's occurred to me," Florence said as she settled herself, "that the evil in this house is so intensely concentrated that it might be a constant lure to earthbound spirits everywhere. In other words, the house might be acting like a giant magnet for degraded souls. This could explain its complicated texture."

What is one supposed to say to that? Barrett thought. He glanced at Edith, forced to repress a smile at her expression as she gazed at Florence. "You're certain this equipment isn't going to bother you?" he said.

"Not at all. As a matter of fact, it might not be amiss for you to switch on your tape recorder when Red Cloud starts to speak. He might say something valuable."

Barrett nodded noncommittally.

"It works on battery as well, doesn't it?"

Barrett nodded again.

"Good." Florence smiled. "The rest of the instruments, of course, are of no use to me." She looked at Edith. "Your husband has explained to you, I'm sure, that I'm not a physical medium. Mine is solely a mental contact with those in spirit. I admit them only in the form of thought." She glanced around. "Will you put out your candles now?"

Edith tensed as Lionel wet two fingers and crimped out

the wick of his candle, Fischer blew his out. Only hers remained, a tiny, pulsing aura of light in the vastness of the hall;
the fire had gone out an hour earlier. Edith was unable to
make herself extinguish it. Barrett reached out and did it for
her.

Blackness seemed to crash across her like a tidal wave,
taking her breath. She groped for Lionel's hand, the moment
reminding her of a visit she had made once to the Carlsbad
Caverns. In one of the caverns, the guide had turned out the
lights, and the darkness had been so intense that she had felt
it pressing at her eyes.

"O Spirit of Love and Tenderness," Florence began. "We
gather here tonight to discover a more perfect understanding
of the laws which govern our being."

Barrett felt how cold Edith's hand was and smiled in sympathy. He knew what she was going through; he'd been
through the same thing dozens of times in the early days of
his work. True, she'd been to séances with him before, but
never in a place with such an awesome size and history.

"Give us, O Divine Teacher, avenues of communication
with those beyond, particularly those who walk this house in
restless torment."

Fischer pulled in a long, erratic breath. He recalled his first
sitting here in 1940—in this hall, at this very table. Objects
had been hurled about; Dr. Graham had been knocked unconscious by one of them. A greenish, glowing mist had filled
the air. Fischer's throat felt parched. I shouldn't be sitting in
on this, he thought.

"May the work of bridging the chasm of death be, by us,
so faithfully accomplished that pain may be transformed into
joy, sorrow into peace. All this we ask in the name of our
infinite Father. Amen."

It was silent for a while. Then Edith's legs retracted as
Florence began to sing in a soft, melodious voice: " 'The world

hath felt a quickening breath from heaven's eternal shore. And souls, triumphant over death, return to earth once more.' " Something about the sound of her muted singing in the darkness made Edith's flesh crawl.

When the hymn had ended. Florence started to breathe in deeply, making passes in front of her face. After several minutes, she began to rub both hands over her arms and shoulders, down across her breasts, and over her stomach and thighs. The strokings were almost sensual as she massaged herself, lips parted, eyes half-closed, an expression of torpid abandonment on her face. Her breathing became slower and louder. Soon it was a hoarsely sibilant, wheezing sound. By then, her hands lay flaccid in her lap, her arms and legs twitching slightly. Bit by bit, her head leaned back until it touched the chair. She drew in an extended, quavering breath, then was still.

The great hall was without a sound. Barrett stared at the place where Florence sat, though nothing was visible to him. Edith had closed her eyes, preferring an individual darkness to that of the room. Fischer sat tensely in his chair, waiting.

Florence's chair made a creaking noise. "Me Red Cloud," she said in a sonorous voice. Her face, in the darkness, was stonelike, her expression imperious. "Me Red Cloud," she repeated.

Barrett sighed. "Good evening."

Florence grunted, nodding. "Me come from afar. Bring greeting to you from realm of Eternal Peace. Red Cloud happy see you. Always happy see earthlings gather in circle of belief. We with you always, watch and ward. Death not end of road. Death but door to world without end. This we know."

"Could you—?" Barrett started.

"Earthling souls in prison," Florence interrupted. "Bound in dungeons of flesh."

"Yes," said Barrett. "Could you—?"

"Death the pardon, the release. Leave behind what poet call 'muddy vesture of decay.' Find freedom—light—eternal joy."

"Yes, but do you think—?"

Edith bit her lower lip to keep from laughing as Florence interrupted again. "Tanner woman say put on machine, get voice on ribbon. Not know what she mean. You do that?"

Barrett grunted. "Very well." Reaching across the table, he felt around for the tape recorder, switched it on, and pushed the microphone toward Florence. "Now, if you'd—"

"Red Cloud Tanner woman guide. Guide second medium on this side. Talk with Tanner woman. Bring other spirits to her."

Florence looked around abruptly, teeth bared, eyebrows pressing down, a growl of disapproval rumbling in her throat "Bad house. Place of sickness. Evil here. Bad medicine." She shook her head and growled again. "*Bad* medicine."

She twisted around the other way, grunting in surprise, as though someone had come up behind her and attracted her attention. "Man here. Ugly man. Like caveman. Long hair. Dirt on face. Scratches, sores. Yellow teeth. Man bent over, twisted. No clothes. Like animal. Breathing hard. In pain. Very sick. Say: 'Give me peace. Let free.' "

Edith clutched at Lionel's hand, afraid to open her eyes lest she see the figure Florence had described.

Florence shook her head, then slowly raised her arm and pointed toward the entry hall. "Go. Leave house." She stared into the darkness, turned back with a grunt. "No good. Here too long. Not listen. Not understand." She tapped her head with an index finger. "Too much sick inside."

She made a sound as though something interesting had been imparted to her. "Limits," she said. "Nations. Terms. Not know what that mean. Extremes and limits. Terminations and extremities." She shook her head. "Not know."

She jerked around as though someone had grabbed her rudely by the shoulder. "No. Go away." She grunted. "Young man here. Say must talk—must talk." She made a grumbling noise and then was still.

All three twitched as Florence cried out, "I don't know you people!" She looked around the table, her expression one of rabid agitation. "Why are you here? It does no good. Nothing ever changes. *Nothing!* Get out of here, or I'll hurt you! I can't help myself! God damn you filthy sons of bitches!"

Edith pressed back hard against her chair. The voice was totally unlike Florence's—hysterical, unbalanced, threatening. "Can't you see I'm helpless! I don't want to hurt you, but I *must!*" Florence's head shifted forward, eyes hooding, lips drawn back from clenching teeth. "I warn you," she told them in a guttural voice. "*Get out of this house before I kill you all.*"

Edith cried out as a series of loud, staccato rappings sounded on the table. "What's that?" she asked. Her voice was lost beneath the chain of savage blows. It sounded as though a berserk man were pounding a hammer on the table-top as hard and fast as he could. Barrett started to reach for his instruments, then remembered that there was no electricity. Damn! he thought.

Abruptly, the rappings ceased. Edith looked toward Florence as the medium started making groaning noises. She could still hear the blows ringing in her ears. Her body felt numb, as though the vibrations had deadened her flesh.

She started as Lionel pulled his hand free. She heard a rustling of his clothes, then started again as a small red light appeared where he was sitting. He had taken the pencil flashlight from his pocket and was pointing it at Florence. In the dim illumination, Edith could see the medium's head lolling back against the chair, eyes shut, mouth hanging open.

She stiffened, suddenly aware of a mounting coldness underneath the table. Shuddering, she crossed her arms. Fischer clenched his teeth together, willing himself not to jump from his chair.

Barrett tugged at the microphone wire, the scraping of the microphone across the table making Edith shudder. Picking it up, he noted quickly, "Temperature decline. Strictly tactile. Instrument reading impossible. Physical phenomena commenced with series of severe percussions." He pointed the flashlight at Florence again. "Miss Tanner reacting erratically. Trance state retained, but variable. Possible confusion at onset of unexpected physical phenomena. Absence of cabinet a probable factor. Handing subject tube of uranium-salt solution."

Edith watched the red light flicking around the tabletop. She saw Lionel's dark hand pick up the tube. The coldness beneath the table was making her legs and ankles ache. Still, she felt a little better, the unruffled tone of Lionel's voice having had a quieting effect on her. She watched as he pressed the tube into Florence's hands.

Florence sat up quickly, opening her eyes.

Barrett frowned in disappointment. "Subject out of trance." He switched off the tape recorder and struck a match. Florence averted her face while he relit the candles.

Fischer stood and moved around the table to a pitcher of water. As he poured some into a glass, the lip of the pitcher rattled on the glass edge. Barrett glanced at him. Fischer handed the glass to Florence, who drank its contents in a single swallow. "There." She smiled at Fischer. "Thank you." She set the glass down, shivering. "What happened?"

When Barrett told her, she stared at him in confusion. "I don't understand. I'm not a physical medium."

"You were just now. The embryo of one, at any rate."

Florence looked disturbed. "That doesn't make sense. Why should I suddenly become a physical medium after all these years?"

"I have no idea."

Florence gazed at him. Finally she nodded with reluctance. "Yes; this house." She looked around. At last she sighed. "God's will, not mine," she said. "If my part in the cleansing is to alter my mediumship, so be it. All that matters is the end." She didn't look at Fischer as she spoke. The weight's been lifted from his shoulders to be put on mine, she thought.

"We can work together now if you're amenable," said Barrett.

"Yes, of course."

"I'll telephone Deutsch's man and have him see to the construction of a cabinet tomorrow morning." Barrett wasn't convinced that what had happened indicated a physical mediumship in Florence extensive enough for his needs. There was certainly no immediate harm in seeing if she had the capability, however. If she did it would be more expeditious to work with her than be forced to wait for Deutsch's permission to bring up one of his own people.

Seeing her expression still reflect uneasy doubt, he asked, "You really want this?"

"*Yes, yes.*" Her smile was disconcerted. "It's just that . . . well, it's difficult for me to understand. All these years, a mental medium." She shook her head. "Now this." She made a sound of wry amusement. "The Lord moves in mysterious ways indeed."

"So does this house," said Fischer.

Florence looked at him in surprise. "You think the house had something to do with me—?"

"Just watch your step," he cut her off. "The Lord may not have too much influence in Hell House."

9:49 P.M.

Science is more than a body of facts. It is, first and foremost, a method of investigation, and there is no acceptable reason why parapsychological phenomena should not be investigated by this method, for, as much as physics and chemistry, parapsychology is a science of the natural.

This, then, is the intellectual barrier through which man must inevitably break. No longer can parapsychology be classified as a philosophical concept. It is a biological reality, and science cannot permanently avoid this fact. Already it has wasted too much time skirting the borders of this irrefutable realm. Now it must enter, to study and learn. Morselli expressed it thus: "The time has come to break with this exaggerated, negative attitude, this constant casting of the shadow of doubt with its smile of sarcasm."

It is a sorry condemnation of our times that these words were published sixty years ago—because the negative attitude of which Morselli wrote still persists. Indeed—

"Lionel?"

Barrett looked up from his manuscript.

"Can I help?"

"No, I'll be finished in a few moments." He looked at her propped against a bank of pillows. She was wearing blue ski pajamas, and with her short hair and slight figure she looked, somehow, like a child. Barrett smiled at her. "Oh, it can wait," he said, deciding with the words.

He put the manuscript back in its box, looking briefly at the title page: "Borders of the Human Faculty, by Lionel Barrett, B.S., M.A., Ph.D.'' The sight of it gratified him. Really, everything was going wonderfully. The chance to prove his theory, ample funds for retirement, and the book almost completed. Perhaps he'd add an epilogue about the week here; maybe even do a thin, appending volume. Smiling, he extinguished the candle on the octagonal table, stood, and crossed the room. He had a momentary vision of himself as some baronial lord crossing a palace chamber to converse with his lady. The vision amused him, and he chuckled.

"What?" she asked.

He told her, and she smiled. "It is a fantastic house, isn't it? A museum of treasures. If it weren't haunted—" Lionel's expression made her stop.

Barrett sat down on her bed and put aside his cane. "Were you frightened before?" he asked. "You were very quiet after the sitting."

"It was a bit unnerving. Especially the coldness; I can never get used to that."

"You know what it is," he said. "The medium's system drawing heat from the air to convert it into energy."

"What about those things she said?"

Barrett shrugged. "Impossible to analyze. It might take years to trace down each remark and determine its source. We only have a week. The physical effects are where the answer lies."

He broke off as she looked across his shoulder with a gasp. Twisting around, he saw that the rocking chair had begun to move.

"What is it?" Edith whispered.

Barrett stood and limped across the room. He stood beside the chair and watched it rocking back and forth. "It's likely the breeze," he told her.

"It moves as though someone were sitting in it." Edith had unconsciously pressed back against the pillows.

"No one's sitting in it, that I guarantee you," Barrett said. "Rocking chairs are easy to set in motion. That's why the phenomenon is so frequent in haunted houses. The least application of pressure suffices."

"But—"

"—what applies the pressure?" Barrett finished for her. "Residual energy." Edith tensed as he reached out and stopped the chair. "See?" His hand had withdrawn, and the chair remained motionless. "It's dissipated now." He pushed the chair. It rocked a few times, then was still again. "All gone," he said.

He returned to her bed and sat beside her. "I'm not very good parapsychologist material, I'm afraid," she said.

Barrett smiled and patted her hand.

"Why does this residual energy suddenly make a chair rock?" she asked.

"No specific reason I've been able to discover. Although our presence in the room undoubtedly has something to do with it. It's a kind of random mechanics which follows the line of least resistance—sounds and movements which occurred most often in the past, establishing a pattern of dynamics: breezes, door slams, rappings, footsteps, rocking chairs."

She nodded, then touched the tip of his nose. "You have to sleep," she said.

Barrett kissed her on the cheek, then stood and moved to the other bed. "Shall I leave the candle on?" he asked.

"Would you mind?"

"No. We'll use a night light while we're here. No harm in it."

They settled down, and Edith looked up at the shell design carved in the walnut ceiling panels. "Lionel?" she asked.

"Yes?"

"Are you sure there are no such things as ghosts?"

Barrett chuckled. "Nary a one."

10:21 P.M.

The hot stream of water sprayed off Florence's upper chest and rivuleted down between her breasts. She stood in the shower stall, head back, eyes shut, feeling the ribbons of water lace across her stomach and down her thighs and legs.

She was thinking about the tape recording of her sitting. Only one thing in it seemed of import: that crazed and trembling voice which had told them to get out of the house or be killed. There was something there. It was amorphous, just beginning, but most compelling. *Can't you see I'm helpless?* she heard the pitiful voice in her mind. *I don't want to hurt you, but I must!*

It could be part of the answer.

She twisted off the faucets and, pushing open the shower door, stepped out onto the bathmat. Hissing at the cold, she grabbed a bath towel from its rack and rubbed herself briskly. Dry, she pulled the heavy flannel gown across her head and thrust her arms into its full-length sleeves. She brushed her teeth, then moved across the bedroom with the candle, set it down, and got into the bed closest to the bathroom door. She thrashed her legs to warm the sheets, then stretched out, pulling the bedclothes to her chin. After a while, her shivering stopped. She wet two fingers and, reaching out, crimped the candle flame between them.

The house was massively silent. I wonder what Ben is doing, she thought. She clucked in distress. Poor, deluded man. She brushed aside the thought. That was for tomorrow. Now she had to think about her part in the project. That voice. Whose had it been? Beneath its threatening had been such despair, such harrowed anguish.

Florence turned her head. The door to the corridor had just been opened. She looked across the darkness of the room. The door closed quietly.

Footsteps started toward her.

"Yes?" she said.

The footsteps kept approaching, muffled on the rug. Florence started reaching for the candle, then withdrew her hand, knowing it was not one of the other three. "All right," she murmured.

The footsteps halted. Florence listened carefully. There was a sound of breathing at the foot of the bed. "Who's there?" she asked.

Only the sound of breathing. Florence peered into the darkness, but it was impenetrable. She closed her eyes. Her tone was even, undismayed. "Who is it, please?"

The breathing continued.

"You wish to speak to me?"

Breathing.

"Are you the one who warned us to get out?"

The sound of breathing quickened. "*Yes,*" she said. "It *is* you, isn't it?"

The breathing grew more labored. It was that of a young man. She could almost visualize him standing at the foot of the bed, his posture tense, his face tormented.

"You must speak or give me some sign," she said. She waited. There was no reply. "I wait for you with God's love. Let me help you find the peace I know you hunger for."

Was that a sob? She tightened. "Yes, I hear, I understand. Tell me who you are, and I can help you."

Suddenly the room was still. Florence cupped her hands behind her ears and listened intently.

The sound of breathing had stopped.

With a sigh of disappointment, she reached to the left until her fingers found the matchbook on the chest of drawers. Striking one, she lit her candle and looked around. There was still something in the room.

"Shall I put out the candle?" she asked.

Silence.

"Very well." She smiled. "You know where I am. Any-time you want—"

She broke off, gasping, as the bedspread leaped into the air and sailed across the foot of the bed, then stopped and settled downward flutteringly.

A figure stood beneath it.

Florence regained her breath. "Yes, I can see you now," she said. She estimated height. "How tall you are." She shivered as Fischer's words flashed across her mind. *"The Roaring Giant," he was called.* She stared at the figure. She could see its broad chest rise and fall, as though with breath.

"No," she said abruptly. It was not Belasco. She began to rise, easing the bedclothes from her body, gazing at the figure. She let her legs slide off the mattress, stood. The head of the figure turned, as though to watch her while she drifted toward it. "You're not Belasco, are you? Such pain would not be in Belasco. And I feel your anguish. Tell me who—"

The bedspread suddenly collapsed. Florence stared at it awhile, then leaned over to pick it up.

She reared with a gasp as a hand caressed her buttocks. Angrily, she looked around the room. There was a chuckling— low-pitched, sly. Florence drew in a shaking breath. "You've proved your sex to me, at any rate," she said. The chuckling deepened. Florence shook her head in pity. "If you're all that clever, why are you a prisoner in this house?"

The chuckling stopped, and all three blankets flew from the bed as though someone were pulling them away in rage. The sheets went next, the pillows, then the mattress cover. In seven seconds, all the bedclothes lay in scattered heaps across the rug, the mattress shifted to the side.

Florence waited. When nothing more occurred, she spoke. "Feel better now?"

Smiling to herself, she started gathering up the bedclothes.

Something tried to pull a blanket from her hands. She jerked it back. "That's enough! I'm not amused!" She turned to the bed. "Go away, and don't come back until you're ready to behave."

As she started to remake the bed, the corridor door was opened. She didn't even look around to watch it shut.

DECEMBER 22, 1970

7:01 A.M.

I'm afraid not." Barrett drew his foot from the water. "Maybe it'll be warm enough by tomorrow morning." He dried the foot and pulled his slipper on again. Pushing to his feet, he looked at Edith with a rueful smile. "I could have let you sleep."

"That's all right."

Barrett looked around. "I wonder if the steam room works."

Edith pulled the heavy metal door and held it open for him. Barrett limped inside and turned to watch her follow. The door thumped shut. Barrett raised his candle and peered around, then leaned forward, squinting.

"Ah." Setting down his cane and candle, he eased himself into a kneeling position. He reached underneath and tried to turn the tap wheel of the steam outlet.

Edith sat across from him and leaned against the tile wall, straightening as the chill of it pierced her robe. She stared at Lionel sleepily. The flickering of their candles and his bobbing shadow on the walls and ceiling seemed to pulse against her eyes. She closed them momentarily, then opened them again.

She found herself beginning to appraise the shadow hovering on the ceiling over Lionel. It seemed, somehow, to be expanding. How could that be? There was no movement of air in the room; the candle flames burned straight up now. Only Barrett's shifting as he labored with the tap wheel was reflected on the walls and ceiling.

She blinked and shook her head. She could swear the edges of the shadow were extending like a spreading inkblot. She shifted on the bench. The room was still except for Lionel's breathing. Let's go, she thought. She tried to speak the words aloud, but something kept her from it.

She stared at the shadow. It hadn't gone across that corner before, had it? Let's get out of here, she thought. It's probably nothing, but let's go.

She felt her body going rigid. She was sure she'd seen a patch of lighted wall go black. "Lionel?" The sound she made was barely audible, a feeble stirring in her throat. She swallowed hard. "Lionel?"

Her voice came so abruptly that Barrett jerked around with a gasp. "What *is* it?"

Edith blinked. The shadow on the ceiling looked normal now.

"Edith?"

She filled her lungs with air. "Let's go?"

"Nervous?"

"Yes, I'm . . . seeing things." Her smile was wan. She didn't want to tell him. Still, she had to. If it did mean something, he would want to know. "I thought I saw your shadow start to grow." He stood and picked up his cane and candle holder, turning back to join her. "It's possible," he said, "but following your sleepless night in this particular house, I'm more inclined to think it was imagination."

They left the steam room and started back along the pool

edge. It *was* imagination, Edith thought. She repressed a smile
Who ever heard of a ghost in a steam room?

7:33 A.M.

Florence knocked softly on the door to Fischer's
room. When there was no answer, she knocked again. "Ben?"
she called.

He was sitting up in bed, eyes closed, head leaning back
against the wall. On the table to his right, his candle was
almost guttered. Florence drifted across the room, protecting
the flame of her candle with an upraised hand. Poor man, she
thought, stopping by the bed. His face was drawn and pale.
She wondered when he'd gotten to sleep. Benjamin Franklin
Fischer: the greatest American physical medium of the century. His sittings in Professor Galbreath's house at Marks College had been the most incredible display of power since the
heyday of Home and Palladino. She shook her head with pity.
Now he was emotionally crippled, a latter-day Samson, self-
shorn of might.

She returned to the corridor and shut the door as quietly
as possible. She looked toward the door to Belasco's room.
She and Fischer had gone there yesterday afternoon, but its
atmosphere had been curiously flat, not at all what she'd expected.

She crossed the corridor and entered it again. It was the
only duplex apartment in the house, its sitting room and bath
located on the lower level, its bedroom on a balcony reached
by a curved stairway. Florence moved to it and ascended the
steps.

The bed had been constructed in seventeenth-century
French style, its intricately carved columns as thick as tele-

phone poles, the initials "E. B." carved in the center of the headboard. Sitting down on it, Florence closed her eyes and opened herself to impressions, wanting to verify that it had not been Belasco in her room the night before. She released her mind as much as possible without going into a trance.

A tumble of images began to cross her consciousness. The room at night, lamps burning. Someone lying on the bed. A figure chuckling. Lucid, staring eyes. A calendar for 1921. A man in black. A smell of pungent incense in her nostrils. A man and woman on the bed. A painting. A cursing voice. A wine bottle hurled against the wall. A sobbing woman flung across the balcony rail. Blood oozing on the teakwood floor. A photograph. A crib. New York. A calendar for 1903. A pregnant woman.

The birth of a child; a boy.

Florence opened her eyes. "Yes." She nodded. *"Yes."*

She went down the stairs and left the room. A minute later, she was entering the dining hall, where Barrett and his wife were breakfasting.

"Ah, good, you're up," Barrett said. "Breakfast just arrived."

Florence sat at the table and served herself a small portion of scrambled eggs, a piece of toast; she wouldn't be sitting until later in the day, since they had to wait for a cabinet to be built. She exchanged a few remarks with Mrs. Barrett, answered Barrett's questions by saying that she felt it would be better to let Fischer sleep than wake him up, then, finally, said, "I think I have a partial answer to the haunting of the house."

"Oh?" Barrett looked at her with interest that was clearly more polite than genuine.

"That voice warning us. That pounding on the table. The personality that approached me in my room last night. A young man."

"Who?" asked Barrett.

"Belasco's son."

They looked at her in silence.

"You recall that Mr. Fischer mentioned him."

"But didn't he say that no one was sure whether Belasco had a son or not?" Barrett said.

Florence nodded. "But he did. He's here now, suffering, tormented. He must have gone into spirit at an early age— just past twenty, I feel. He's very young and very frightened— and, because he's frightened, very angry, very hostile. I believe if we can convince him to go on, a portion of the haunting force will be eliminated."

Barrett nodded. Don't believe a word of it, he thought. "That's very interesting."

Florence thought, I know he doesn't believe me, but it's better that I tell him what I think.

She was about to change the subject when there was a loud knocking on the front door. Edith, who was drinking coffee, spilled some as her hand jerked. Barrett smiled at her. "Our generator, I imagine, And a carpenter, I hope."

Standing, he picked up his candle holder and cane and started toward the great hall. He stopped to look back at Edith. "Well, I guess it's safe to leave you long enough to answer the door," he said after a few moments.

He crossed the great hall and moved into the entry hall. Opening the front door, he saw Deutsch's representative standing on the porch, coat collar raised, an umbrella in his hand. To Barrett's surprise, he saw that it was raining.

"I've got your generator and your carpenter," the man said.

Barrett nodded. "What about the cat?"

"That too."

Barrett smiled with satisfaction. Now he could move.

1:17 P.M.

The lights went on, and, in unison, all four uttered sounds of pleasure. "I'll be damned," said Fischer. They exchanged spontaneous smiles. "I never thought electric lights could look so good," Edith said.

Bathed with light, the great hall was another place entirely. Now its size seemed regal rather than ominous. No longer black with looming shadows, it was a massive chamber in some art museum, and not a haunted cavern. Edith looked at Fischer. He was obviously pleased, his posture different, apprehension cleansed from his eyes. She looked at Florence, who was sitting with the cat on her lap. The lights on, she thought. That cat resting peacefully. She smiled. It didn't seem like a haunted house at all now.

She gasped as the lights flickered, went out, then on again. Immediately, they began to dim. "Oh, no," she murmured.

"Easy," Barrett said. "They'll get it."

A minute later, the lights were bright and steady. When another minute passed without a change, Barrett smiled. "There, you see?"

Edith nodded. Her relief had ended, though. From relaxed assurance, she had fallen back to a nagging dread that, any second, they might once more be in darkness.

Florence looked at Fischer, caught his eye, and smiled at him. He did not return it. Idiots, he thought. Some bulbs go on, and they all think the danger's over.

1:58 P.M.

The cabinet had been constructed in the northeast corner of the great hall by the installation of an eight-foot-long round wooden bar between the walls. A pair of heavy green draperies was hanging from the bar on rings, forming a triangular enclosure seven feet high. Inside the enclosure was a straight-backed wooden armchair.

Barrett edged aside the draperies on each side until there was an opening in the middle large enough to accommodate a small wooden table he had asked Fischer to carry in. Pushing the table in front of the opening, he placed on top of it a tambourine, a small guitar, a tea bell, and a length of rope. He looked at the cabinet appraisingly for several moments, then turned to the others.

They watched as he rummaged through the contents of the wooden chest from which he'd gotten the rope, tea bell, guitar, and tambourine. He lifted out a pair of black tights and a black long-sleeved smock and held them out to Florence. "I believe they'll fit," he said.

Florence stared at him.

"You don't object, do you?"

"Well—"

"You know it's standard procedure."

"Yes, but"—Florence hesitated, then went on—"as a precaution against fraud."

"Primarily."

Florence's smile was awkward. "Surely you don't think I'm capable of perpetrating fraud with a form of mediumship I didn't even know I had before last night."

"I'm not implying that, Miss Tanner. It's simply that I must maintain a standard. If I don't, the results of the sitting are scientifically unacceptable."

Finally she sighed. "Very well." She took the tights and smock, looked around, then went inside the cabinet to change, pulling the draperies together. Barrett turned to Edith. "Would you examine her, my dear?" he asked. Bending over the box, he lifted out a spool of black thread with a needle pushed through the thread, and handed it to her.

Edith moved toward the cabinet, a discomfited look on her face. She'd always hated doing this, although she'd never indicated it to Lionel. Stopping by the cabinet, she cleared her throat. "May I come in?"

There was a momentary silence before Florence answered. "Yes." Edith pushed between the drapery edges, stepping into the cabinet.

Florence had removed her skirt and sweater and was leaning over, stepping from her half-slip. Straightening, she draped the slip across the chair back. As she reached back to unhook her white brassiere, Edith stepped aside. "I'm sorry," she murmured; "I know it's—"

"Don't be embarrassed," Florence said. "Your husband is quite right. It's standard procedure."

Edith nodded, keeping her eyes on Florence's face as the medium hung her brassiere across the chair back. Her gaze dropped as Florence bent forward to remove her underpants. She was startled by the fullness of the medium's breasts, and looked up quickly. Florence stood erect. "All right," she said. Edith saw a stippling of gooseflesh on the medium's arms.

"We'll make it quick so you can dress," she said. "Your mouth?"

Florence opened her mouth, and Edith looked inside. She felt ridiculous. "Well, unless you have a hollow tooth or something—"

Florence closed her mouth and smiled. "It's just a technicality. Your husband knows I'm not concealing anything."

Edith nodded. "Your hair?"

Florence reached up both hands to unpin her hair. The movement made her breasts hitch, so their hardened nipples brushed against Edith's sweater. Edith twitched back, watching the tresses of thick red hair as they rippled downward, spilling over Florence's creamy shoulders. She'd never examined a woman so beautiful before.

"All right," Florence said.

Edith started fingering through the medium's hair. It was warm and silky to the touch. The fragrance of Florence's perfume drifted over her. Balenciaga, she thought. She drew in a labored breath. She could feel the pressing weight of Florence's breasts against her own. She wanted to step back but couldn't do it. She looked into the medium's green eyes, looked down quickly. Turning Florence's head, she looked into her ears. I will not look up her nose, she thought. She drew her hands back awkwardly. "Armpits?" she said.

Florence raised her arms and caused her breasts to jut again. Edith edged away from her and glanced down at her shaved armpits. She nodded once, and Florence lowered her arms. Edith felt her heartbeat thudding. The inside of the cabinet seemed very close. She looked at Florence unhappily. It seemed as if the two of them were stopped in time. Then she noted Florence glancing down, and lowered her gaze. She started at the sight of Florence's hands cupped beneath her breasts, holding them up. This is ridiculous, she thought. She nodded once, and Florence took her hands away. That's enough, Edith decided. I'll just say I did the rest. Obviously she has no intention of committing fraud.

She watched as the medium sat in the chair, hissing at its coldness. She looked up at Edith. I'll just say I did the rest, Edith thought.

Leaning back, Florence spread her legs apart.

Edith stared down at the medium's body: the heavy, ovate loll of her breasts, the swell of her stomach, the milk-white fullness of her thighs, the parted tuft of glossy copper hair between her legs. She couldn't take her eyes away. She felt a drawing hotness in her stomach.

She jerked her head around so quickly, looking up, that it sent a shooting pain through her neck.

"What *is* it?" Florence asked.

Edith swallowed, staring up across the wooden rod. There was only ceiling visible. She looked at Florence. *"What?"* the medium asked.

Edith shook her head. "I think we can assume—" She broke off, gesturing with a trembling hand, then turned and pushed from the cabinet.

She nodded to Lionel and crossed to the fireplace. She was sure she looked completely disconcerted, but hoped he wouldn't ask her why.

She stared into the fire. There was something in her hand. She looked at it; the spool of thread. Now she'd have to bring it back. She closed her eyes. Her neck still hurt from the wrenching she'd given it. Had she really seen a movement? There'd been nothing there. Still, she could have sworn that someone had been looking down into the cabinet.

At her.

2:19 P.M.

Too tight?" asked Barrett.

"No, it's fine," Florence answered quietly.

Barrett finished tying the gloves at her wrists. As he did, Florence looked across his shoulder at Edith, who was sitting by the equipment table, the cat resting on her lap.

"Put your palms on the chair plates," Barrett instructed. The gloves he'd fastened to Florence had metal plates attached to their palms. As Florence rested them on the plates nailed to the chair arms, a pair of tiny bulbs on the equipment table lighted.

"So long as your hands remain in place, the bulbs will burn," Barrett told her. "Break contact—" He lifted her hands, and the bulbs went out.

Florence watched as Barrett unrolled the wire for the shoe plates. It disturbed her that Edith had looked up the way she had, when she'd been conscious of nothing.

"Will the foot plates activate the same two bulbs?" she asked.

"Two others."

"Isn't that a lot of light?"

"The combined wattage of all four bulbs is less than ten," he answered as he connected the shoe plates.

"I'd assumed we'd be in darkness."

"I can't accept darkness as a test condition." Barrett glanced up. "Would you try the foot plates?"

Florence set the plates attached to the soles of her shoes on the pair of plates Barrett had placed on the floor. On the equipment table, two more small bulbs went on. Barrett pushed up, wincing. "Don't be concerned," he said. "There'll be just enough illumination to observe by."

Florence nodded. Barrett's words failed to reassure her, though. Why do I feel so upset? she thought.

Fischer sat looking at the medium, her luxuriant figure outlined by the skin-tight costume. The sight did not arouse him. Those damned black outfits, he was thinking. How many of them had he worn? The memory of his early teen years was of endless sittings like this, his mother and himself riding from city to city on buses, from one test to another.

He lit another cigarette and watched as Barrett connected wire leads to Florence's arms and thighs, roped her to the chair, then picked up a folded piece of mosquito netting to which tiny bells had been sewn. Shaking it open, Barrett fastened it to the wooden rod so that the netting hung down in the space uncovered by the draperies. He pulled the small table several inches toward himself. Now the netting filled the space between the table and Florence, weights on its bottom holding it taut.

Barrett arranged the infrared lights so they'd shine across the surface of the table in front of the cabinet. Switching on the invisible lights, he moved his hand across the cabinet table. There was a clicking noise as the synchronized shutters of the two cameras were activated. Satisfied, Barrett checked the dynamometer and the globe of the telekinetoscope. He set out modeling clay and briefly stirred the melted paraffin wax in its pot on the small electric stove.

"We're ready now," he said.

As if it understood his words, the cat jumped suddenly from Edith's lap and loped across the room, heading for the entry hall. "Isn't that encouraging?" she said.

"Doesn't mean a thing," Barrett told her. Adjusting the red and yellow lights to minimum illumination, he moved to the wall switch and depressed it. The great hall darkened. Barrett took his place at the table, switching on the tape recorder. "December 22, 1970," he said into the microphone. "Sitters: Doctor and Mrs. Lionel Barrett, Mr. Benjamin Franklin Fischer. Medium: Miss Florence Tanner." Quickly he recited the details of arrangements and precautions, then sat back. "Proceed," he said.

The three sat quietly as Florence spoke an invocation and sang a hymn. After she was finished, she began to take in deep breaths. Soon, her hands and legs began to twitch as though she were being subjected to a series of galvanic shocks. Her head began to loll from side to side, her face becoming flushed. Low-pitched groans quavered in her throat. "No," she muttered. "No, not now." Gradually her noises faded, until, following a wheezing inhalation, she relapsed into silence.

"Two-thirty-eight p.m.; Miss Tanner in apparent trance," Barrett said into the microphone. "Pulse rate: eighty-five. Respiration: fifteen. Four electric contacts maintained." He checked the self-recording thermometer. "No change in temperature. Steady at seventy-three-point-two degrees. Dyna-mometer reading: eighteen hundred and seventy."

Twenty seconds later, he spoke again. "Dynamometer reading decreased to eighteen hundred and twenty-three. Temperature lowering; now at sixty-six-point-six degrees. Pulse rate: ninety-four-point-five and rising."

Edith drew in her legs, pressing them together as she felt coldness underneath the table. Fischer sat immobile. Even sheltered, he could feel the power gathering around him.

Barrett checked the thermometer again. "Temperature drop now twelve-point-three degrees. Dynamometer tension reduced to seventeen hundred and seventy-nine. Pressurome-ter negative. Electric contacts still maintained. Rate of breath increasing. Fifty . . . fifty-seven . . . sixty; rising steadily."

Edith stared at Florence. In the feeble light, all she could make out was the medium's face and hands. She seemed to be lying back against the chair, eyes shut. Edith swallowed. There was a cold knot in her stomach, which even Lionel's assured tones could not dispel.

She started as the camera shutters clicked. "Infrared rays broken, cameras activated," Barrett said. He looked at the dark blue instrument and tightened with excitement. "Evi-dence of EMR commencing."

Fischer looked at him. What was EMR? Clearly it was something vital to Barrett.

"Medium's respiration now two hundred and ten," Bar-rett was saying. "Dynamometer fourteen hundred and sixty. Temperature—"

He broke off at the sound of Edith's gasp. "Ozone present in the air," he said. Remarkable, he thought.

A minute passed, then two, the smell and coldness steadily increasing. Abruptly Edith closed her eyes. She waited, opened them again, and stared at Florence's hands. It had not been her imagination.

Threads of pale white, viscous matter were oozing from the medium's fingertips.

"Teleplasm forming," Barrett said. "Separate filaments uniting into single filmy strand. Will attempt matter penetration." He waited until the teleplasm strand was longer, then said to Florence, "Lift the bell." He paused before repeating the instruction.

The viscous tentacle began to rear up slowly like a serpent. Edith drew back in her chair, staring at it as it glided forward through the air, penetrated the net, and headed for the table.

"Teleplasmic stalk through net and moving toward the table." Barrett said. "Dynamometer reading: thirteen hundred and forty, dropping steadily. Electric contacts still maintained."

His voice became a blur of meaningless sounds to Fischer as he watched the moist, glistening tentacle inch its way across the table like a giant worm. A photograph flared briefly in his mind: him, fourteen, deep in trance, a similar extrusion from his mouth. He shivered as the filmy member twined itself around the handle of the tea bell. The tentacle began to tighten slowly. Suddenly it raised the bell, and Fischer's legs twitched spastically as the bell was shaken.

"Thank you. Put it down, please," Barrett said. Edith looked at him, astounded by his casual tone. Her gaze returned to the table as the gray extremity put down the bell, uncurling itself from the handle.

"Will try for specimen retrieval," Barrett said. Standing, he set a porcelain bowl on the cabinet table; at his approach, the tentacle jerked back as though in startled retreat. "Leave a section in the bowl, please," Barrett said, returning to his chair.

The gray appendage started swaying back and forth like the stalk of some undersea plant undulating in the current. "Leave a section in the bowl, please," Barrett repeated. He looked at the EMR recorder. The needle had passed the 300 mark. He felt a glow of satisfaction. Turning back to the cabinet, he repeated his instruction once more.

He was forced to speak the words seven times more before the glistening filament began to move. Slowly it started toward the bowl. Edith stared at it, repelled yet fascinated. It looked like an eyeless, gray-scaled serpent. As it reached the bowl, it slithered up across the rim. She flinched as it recoiled. Again it advanced on the bowl, with perceptible caution in its movement. Once again it snapped back soundlessly.

On the fifth advance, the tentacle remained in place, coiling with a languid, spiraling movement, until it filled the bowl. Thirty seconds later it withdrew. Edith started as it disappeared from sight.

Barrett rose and transferred the bowl to the equipment table. Edith glanced at the transparent liquid inside it. "Specimen retained in bowl," Barrett said, looking at it. "No odor. Colorless and slightly turbid."

"Lionel." Edith's urgent whisper made him look up.

Across the bottom half of Florence's face, a cloudy mass was starting to form.

"Teleplasmic matter being generated across lower part of medium's face," Barrett said. "Issuance from mouth and nostrils."

As he continued speaking into the microphone, describing the materialization and noting the flux of instrument readings, Edith stared at the formation in front of Florence's face. Now it resembled a torn, grimy handkerchief, the lower part of which hung down in shreds. The upper part was starting to rise. It spread with a swaying movement, first obscuring Florence's nose, then her eyes, finally her brow, so that her face was cloaked entirely, the formation like a ragged veil through which her pale features could be seen.

"Teleplasmic veil beginning to condense," said Barrett.

This really was remarkable, he thought. For a mental medium to produce such striking teleplasm at her first physical sitting was almost unprecedented. He watched with mounting interest.

The texture of the mistlike veil looked curdled now; in less than half a minute, Florence's face had vanished behind it. Soon, her head, then upper shoulders, were concealed beneath folds of what appeared to be a soggy, grayish shroud. The bottom of this dingy fabric was descending toward her lap, lengthening into a solid strip several inches wide. As it descended, it began to take on coloration.

"Separate filament extending downward," Barrett said. "Reddish hue impinging on the grayness. Stretching tissue seems to be inflamed. Getting brighter . . . brighter. The color of open flesh now."

Fischer felt numb. His chair seemed to be tilting backward as he watched the altering vesture on Florence's head and body. Sudden panic struck him. He was going under! He dug his nails into his palms until pain overshadowed all else.

The shroud on Florence was becoming more albescent every moment, starting to resemble linen dipped in white paint, transparent in some places, solid in others. Veillike strips and patches were beginning to appear at other spots on her body—her right arm and leg, her right breast, the center of her lap. It looked as though a solid bedsheet had been dipped into some iridescent liquid, then torn apart, the fragments thrown across her indiscriminately, the largest piece settling on her head and shoulders.

Edith pressed back hard against her chair, unaware that she was doing so. She had witnessed physical phenomena before, but never anything like this. Her face was masklike as she watched the teleplasmic sections start to coalesce. Bit by bit, they started to assume a shape. The filament, now pale again, looked vaguely like an arm and wrist.

"Something taking form," said Barrett.

Twenty-seven seconds later, a white figure stood before the cabinet, garbed in a shapeless robe, sexless, incomplete, its hands like rudimentary claws. There was a mouth, and two dark spots for nostrils, and it had two eyes which seemed to gaze at them. Edith drew in a rasping breath. "Easy," Barrett said. "Teleplasmic figure formed. Imperfectly—"

He broke off as the figure chuckled.

Edith made a stricken noise. *"Easy,"* Barrett told her.

The figure laughed: a rolling laugh, deep and resonant, which seemed to gorge the air. Edith felt her scalp begin to crawl. *The figure was turning to look at her.* It seemed to be coming closer. A frightened whimper filled her throat. *"Hold still,"* Barrett whispered.

Suddenly the figure reached for her, and Edith screamed, throwing her arms across her face. With a noise that sounded like the snapping of a giant rubber band, the figure vanished. Florence cried out hoarsely, making Edith jump again. Fischer struggled to his feet. "Hold it!" Barrett ordered.

Fischer stood beside the table rigidly as Barrett drew up the netting and shone the red beam of his pencil flashlight into Florence's face. Immediately he turned it off and checked his instruments. "Miss Tanner coming out of trance," he said. "Premature retraction, causing brief systemic shock." He looked at Fischer.

"Help her now," he said.

4:23 P.M.

Edith woke with a start. She checked her watch and saw that she'd been sleeping more than an hour.

Lionel was sitting at the octagonal table, looking into his microscope and making notes. Edith dropped her feet across the mattress edge and worked them into her shoes. Standing, she walked across the rug. Barrett looked up, smiling. "Feeling better?"

She nodded. "I apologize for what I did before."

"No problem."

Edith made a pained face. "I caused a 'premature retraction,' didn't I?"

"Don't worry, she'll get over it; I'm sure it's not the worst thing that's ever happened to her during a sitting." Barrett looked at her a moment, then asked, "What was it that upset you before the sitting? The examination?"

Edith was aware of restraining her reply. "It was a little awkward, yes."

"You've done it before."

"I know." She felt herself tensing. "I just felt awkward this time."

"You should have told me. I could have done it."

"I'm glad you didn't." Edith managed a smile. "Compared to her, I look like a boy."

Barrett made a scoffing noise. "As if that would matter."

"Anyway, I'm sorry I ruined the sitting." Edith was conscious of changing the subject.

"You didn't ruin anything. I couldn't be more satisfied."

"What are you doing?"

Barrett gestured toward the microscope. "Take a look."

Edith peered into the eyepiece. On the slide, she saw groups of shapeless forms and groups of oval and polygonal bodies. "What am I looking at?" she asked.

"A specimen of that teleplasm prepared in water. What you see are conglomerates of etiolated, lamellar, cohesive bodies, as well as single laminae of varied forms resembling epithelium without nuclei."

Edith looked up chidingly. "Now, do you really think I understood what you just said?"

Barrett smiled. "Just showing off. What I'm trying to say is that the specimen consists of cell detritus, epithelium cells, veils, lamellae, filmy aggregates, isolated fat grains, mucus, and so on."

"Which means—?"

"Which means that what the Spiritualists refer to as ectoplasm is derived almost entirely from the medium's body, the remainder being admixtures from the air and the medium's costume—fibrous vegetable remains, bacterial spores, starch grains, food and dust particles, et cetera. The bulk of it, however, is organic, living matter. Think of it, my dear. *An organic externalization of thought.* Mind reduced to matter, subject to scientific observation, measurement, and analysis." He shook his head in wonderment. "The concept of ghosts seems dreadfully prosaic compared to that."

"You mean Miss Tanner made that figure from her own body."

"Essentially."

"*Why?*"

"To prove a point. That figure was undoubtedly supposed to be Belasco's son—a son who, I'm convinced, never existed."

4:46 P.M.

The cat lay warmly indolent beside her. Its body throbbed with purrs as Florence stroked its neck.

When she'd come upstairs, she'd found it cowering outside her door and, despite her wretchedness, had picked it up and carried it inside. She'd held it in her lap until its trembling had stopped, then had put it on the bed and taken a hot shower. Now she was lying in her robe, the bedspread pulled across her.

"Poor puss," she murmured. "What a place to bring you."
She ran the edge of a finger along the front of its neck, and
the cat raised its head with a languid movement, eyes still
closed. Barrett had said that he needed it as an additional verification of "presence" in the house. It seemed a harsh measure, though, merely to acquire a slight scientific validation.
Maybe she could get it taken away by the couple who brought
their meals. She'd ask Barrett to let her know the moment
the cat had served its purpose.

Florence closed her eyes again. She wished she could
sleep, but things kept nagging at her mind. Mrs. Barrett's
strained embarrassment—the way she'd jerked around, as
though someone were looking at her; Barrett's overzealous
safeguards against fraud; the onset of physical mediumship in
herself; her inability to go inside the chapel; her concern for
Fischer; her feeling of dissatisfaction with herself; her fear that
she was giving more importance to Belasco's son than he war-
ranted. After all—

She jolted, gasping, as the cat leaped from the bed. Sitting
up, she saw it rushing to the door and crouching there, back
arched, fur on end, its pupils expanded so completely that its
eyes looked black. Hastily she stood and crossed to it. The
instant she opened the door, it darted out into the corridor
and disappeared.

Something flapped behind her, and she whirled, to see the
spread and blankets landing on the rug.

There was something underneath the sheet.

Florence stared at it. It was the figure of a man. She started
toward the bed, tightening as she saw that the figure was
nude. She could make out every body contour, from the swelling broadness of the chest to the bulge of genitals. She felt a
stir of sensual awareness in her body. No, she told herself;
that's what he wants. "If you're here only to impress me with
your cleverness again, I'm not interested," she said.

The figure made no sound. It lay immobile underneath the sheet, chest expanding and contracting in a perfect simulation of breath. Florence peered at its face. "Are you Emeric Belasco's son?" she asked. She edged along the side of the bed. "If you are, you said that nothing changes. Yet, with love, all things are possible. This is true of life, and true of life beyond life." She leaned across him, trying to make out his features. "Tell me who you are," she said.

"Boo!" the figure shouted. Florence jumped back with a cry. Instantly the sheet collapsed, and there was nothing on the bed. The air began to ring with mocking laughter. Florence tightened with resentment. "Very funny," she said. The laughter rose in pitch, taking on a frenzied quality. Florence clenched her hands. "If practical jokes are all you're interested in, stay away from me!" she ordered.

For almost twenty seconds, it was deathly still inside the room. Florence felt her stomach muscles slowly tightening. Suddenly the Chinese lamp was pitched to the floor, shattering its bulb; only the light from the bathroom kept the room from total darkness. Florence twitched as footsteps thudded across the rug. The door to the corridor was flung open so hard that it crashed against the wall.

She waited for a while before she crossed the room to shut the door. Switching on the overhead light, she moved to the fallen lamp and picked it up. Such anger, she thought. Yet it wasn't only anger; that was clear.

It was a plea as well.

6:21 P.M.

Florence walked into the dining hall. "Good evening," she said.

Fischer's smile was cursory. Florence sat down. "Have you

seen this couple yet?" she asked, gesturing toward the table, which was set for supper.

"No."

She smiled. "Funny if there wasn't any couple."

Fischer showed no sign of amusement. Florence glanced toward the great hall. "I wonder where the Barretts are," she said. She looked back at him. "Well, what have you been doing?"

"Scouting." Fischer lifted the cover from one of the serving dishes and eyed the heap of lamb chops. He replaced the cover.

"You should eat," she said.

He pushed the dish toward her. "Maybe we should wait," she said.

"Go ahead."

Florence waited a few more seconds. Then she said, "I'll have some salad." She served her plate and looked at him. He shook his head. "A little?" Fischer shook his head again.

Florence ate some salad before she spoke again. "Were you in contact with Belasco's son when you were here before?"

"All I was in contact with was a live wire."

The sound of footsteps made them look around. "Good evening," Florence said.

"Good evening." Barrett smiled politely; Edith nodded. "Are you feeling better?" Barrett asked.

Florence nodded. "Yes, I'm fine."

"Good," Barrett and his wife sat down, served themselves, and started eating.

"We were talking about Belasco's son," Florence said.

"Ah, yes; Belasco's son."

Something in Barrett's tone made Florence bristle. Suddenly the thought of having been subjected by him to the indignity of a physical examination galled her. The costume, those ridiculous precautions: ropes and nets and infrared lamps, hand and foot plates turning lights on, cameras. She tried to repress a mounting anger but couldn't. How dare Barrett treat her this way? Her position in this project was just as vital as his.

"Will it never end?" she said.

The others looked at her. "Were you addressing me?" inquired Barrett.

"I was." Again she tried to quell her anger, but again the vision of the physical examination flashed across her mind, the costume, the absurd safeguards against fraud.

"Will what never end?" asked Barrett.

"This attitude of doubt. Distrust."

"Distrust?"

"Why should mediums be expected to produce phenomena only under conditions which science dictates?" she demanded. "We're not machines. We're human beings. These rigid, unyielding demands by science have done more harm than good to parapsychology."

"Miss Tanner—" Barrett looked confused. "What brought this on? Have I—"

"I'm not a medium for the fun of it, you know." Florence cut him off. The more she spoke, the more infuriated she became. "It's often painful, often unrewarding."

"Don't you think—?"

"It just so happens I believe that mediumship is God's manifestation in man." She couldn't stop herself. " 'When I speak with thee,' " she quoted angrily. " 'I will open thy mouth, and thou shalt say to them: Thus saith the Lord.' "

"Miss Tanner—"

"There is nothing in the Bible—not a single recorded phenomenon—which does not occur today, whether it be sights or sounds, shaking of the house, or coming through closed doors: rushing winds, levitations, automatic writing, or the speaking in tongues."

There was a heavy silence. Florence glared at Barrett, conscious of Fischer and Edith staring at her. Somewhere, deep inside her mind, she heard a warning cry, but fury stilled it. She watched Barrett pour himself some coffee, watched him pick up his cup. He looked at her. "Miss Tanner," he said, "I don't know what's bothering you, but—"

He broke off as the cup exploded in his hand. Edith jerked back, gasping. Barrett, frozen, gaped at the shard of handle still in his fingers. Blood was starting to drip from the cut in his thumb. Florence felt a pounding at her temples. Fischer looked around in startlement. "What in God's name—?" Barrett started.

He was drowned out as the glass beside his plate burst apart, its fragments scattering across the table. Edith jerked her hands back as her plate leaped from the table, flipping over rapidly and dumping food across the floor before it landed, shattering. She recoiled as the top part of her glass broke off with a cracking noise and jumped across the table toward her husband. Barrett, pulling out a handkerchief, twisted to the side. The glass top thudded off his arm and tumbled to the floor. Fischer's glass exploded, and he lurched back, flinging an arm in front of his face.

Florence's plate somersaulted, scattering salad over the table. She reached out to grab it, then jolted back as the plate went flying across the table. Barrett jerked his head aside. The plate scaled past his ear and landed on its edge, rolling rapidly across the floor, to break against the wall. Edith cried out as a heavy serving dish began to slide across the table toward him. Barrett jumped up, toppling his chair. He almost fell, then leaned against the table. The serving dish slid off the table edge and crashed to the floor. Mashed potatoes splattered over his shoes and trouser cuffs.

Fischer was on his feet now. He tried to turn from the table, but was slammed against it as his chair lurched hard against his legs. He saw his cup go leaping from the table, gouting coffee over Barrett's shirt front as it struck him in the middle of the chest. Edith's scream choked off as Fischer's plate was catapulted from the tabletop, flying closely over her head. The chair slid back from Fischer, and he crumpled to his knees, his face a mask of shock.

Barrett tried to twist the handkerchief around his bleeding thumb. The silver pot fell over and began to spin across the table at him, spouting coffee. Barrett lurched aside to avoid it, slipped on the potatoes, flailed for balance, then went crashing onto his right side. The coffeepot fell off the table, bouncing off his left calf. He cried out at the burning impact. Edith tried to stand to help him, but her chair rocked backward, throwing her off balance. A knife and spoon went flying past her cheek.

Florence shrank into her chair as another serving dish began to skid across the table, headed for Barrett. Barrett scrabbled aside with a gasp. The serving dish crashed down beside him, the edge of its cover striking his shin. Edith struggled to her feet. "Under the table!" Fischer cried. Florence slid from the chair, falling to her knees. Fischer flung himself beneath the table. Overhead, the hanging lamp began to pendulum, the length of its swings increasing rapidly.

They were barely in the shelter of the table when the objects on the monastery table against the east wall came to life. A heavy silver chafing dish arced across the room and hit their table with a deafening impact. Edith cried out. Barrett started reaching for her automatically, then went back to wrapping his thumb. A silver bowl came hurtling at them, struck a table leg, and spun around in a blur of movement. Florence glanced at Fischer. He was on his knees, eyes staring, face a frozen mask of dread. She wanted to help him but felt too dazed. There was a churning coldness in her stomach.

All of them looked up in shock as the dining table started rocking back and forth. The silver creamer landed nearby, contents splattering across the floor like a gout of ivory paint. The silver sugar bowl fell beside it as the table rocked with mounting violence, legs crashing down like pounding horse hooves. The table shifted suddenly, and Barrett had to jerk his hand away to keep from getting it crushed. The chairs began to overturn, banging one by one against the floor, the noise like rifle shots.

Suddenly the table surged away from them, sliding fast across the polished floor. It smashed against the fire screen and bent it out of shape. Above them, all the sanctuary lamps were swinging violently. One of them tore loose and hurtled sideways, creating a shower of sparks as it collided violently with the stone mantel, then crashed to the tabletop. A silver candelabrum flew across the room and landed on the floor by Barrett, thudding against his side. He fell with a gasp of pain. Florence cried out. *"No!"*

All movement ceased abruptly, except for the decreasing arcs of the remaining sanctuary lamps. Edith bent over Barrett anxiously. "Lionel?" She touched his shoulder. He managed to nod.

"Ben, you've got to leave this house."

Fischer turned to Florence, startled by her words.

"You aren't up to it," she told him.

"What the hell are you talking about?"

Florence turned to Barrett for support. "Doctor—" she began, then stopped, seeing how he looked at her as Edith helped him to his feet. "Are you all right?" she asked.

He didn't answer, leaning against the table with a groan. Edith looked at him in fright. "Lionel?"

"I'll be all right." He tightened the handkerchief around his thumb. The cut was deep; it stung. There were islands of pain all over his body—his arm, his chest, his shin, his ankle, mostly his side. His leg ached horribly.

Florence stared at him. Why had he looked at her that way? Suddenly she thought she knew. "I'm sorry I spoke so angrily," he said. "But please support me in this. I think it's important that Ben—that Mr. Fischer leave the house."

Barrett clenched his teeth against the pain. "Trying to get us both out now?" he muttered. Florence looked at him in surprise. "Help me to our room, please?" Barrett asked his wife. Edith nodded faintly, handed him his cane, and took his arm.

Florence didn't understand. "What do you mean, Doctor Barrett?"

He threw a glance around the wreckage of the hall. "I should think that was obvious," he said.

Stunned into silence, Florence watched the Barretts leave. After they were gone, she looked at Fischer. "What is he saying?" she asked. "That I—?"

Fischer turned away from her.

"Ben, it isn't true!"

He lurched away. Still moving, he glanced back at her. "You're the one who'd better leave," he said. "You're the one who's being used, not me."

6:48 P.M.

Barrett sat down gingerly. "My bag," he murmured. Edith let go of his arm and hurried to the Spanish

table, lifting off the small black bag in which he kept his codeine and first-aid kit. Returning quickly to the bed, she set
the bag beside him. Lionel was removing the handkerchief
from his thumb with slow, careful movements, his teeth
clenched at the pain.

The sight of the deep, blood-oozing cut made Edith hiss.
"It's all right," Barrett told her. Reaching into the bag, he took
out the first-aid kit and opened it. Removing a packet of sulfa
powder, he tore it open. "Would you get me a glass of water,
please?"

Edith turned to the bathroom. Barrett drew a box of gauze
from the first-aid kit and started to break the seal on its cover.
When Edith returned, he handed her the box. "Would you
bandage it?" he asked. She nodded, giving him the glass of
water. Taking his container of pills from the black bag, he got
one out and washed it down.

Edith winced as she started bandaging. "This needs
stitches."

"I don't think so." Barrett gritted his teeth, eyes narrowing, as she wrapped the gauze around the thumb. "Make it
tight."

When the thumb was bandaged and taped, he eased up
his left trouser leg. There was a dark-red burn on the calf.
Edith looked at it in dismay. "You have to see a doctor."

"Put some Butesin picrate on it."

She looked at him for several moments indecisively. Then,
kneeling beside him, she spread the yellow cream across the
burn. Barrett hissed and closed his eyes. "It's all right," he
muttered, knowing she was looking at him.

Edith wrapped some gauze around his leg, then helped
him lie down. Barrett groaned and shifted onto his left side.
"I am one gigantic mass of bruises," he said, trying to make
it sound like a joke.

"Lionel, let's go home."

Barrett took another sip of water and handed her the glass. He slumped back on the pillows she had propped behind him. "I'm all right," he said.

"What if it happens again?"

He shook his head. "It won't." He looked at her a moment. "You could go, though."

"*Leave* you here?"

Barrett raised his right hand as though making a pledge. "Believe me, it won't happen again."

"Then why should I leave?"

"I just don't want you hurt."

"You're the one who's hurt."

Barrett chuckled. "That I am. It had to be that way, of course. I'm the one who angered her."

"You're saying"—Edith hesitated—"*she* did all that?"

"Making use of the power in the room," he said. "Converting it to poltergeist-type phenomena directed at me."

Edith thought about the violence of what had happened. The gigantic table rocking back and forth, then hurled across the floor like an express train. The whipping movement of those massive hanging lamps. "My God," she said.

"I made a mistake," Barrett told her. "I accepted her genial attitude toward me at face value. You can never do that with a medium. You never know what's underneath. It might be absolute hostility, and if it is"—he blew out breath—"by making unconscious use of their power, they can inflict tremendous damage. Especially when that power can be amplified a hundredfold by the kind of energy that fills this house." His smile was grim. "I'll not make that mistake again."

"Is it so important that we stay?" she asked.

Lionel answered quietly. "You know it means everything to me."

Edith nodded, trying to suppress the rise of panic in herself. *Five more days of this*, she thought.

8:09 P.M.

As she paced restlessly, her mind kept going over it again and again. Was Barrett right? She couldn't make herself believe it. Yet the evidence was there. She *had* been furious with him. The poltergeist phenomena *had* been directed primarily at him. Her body *did* feel enervated, as it always did after psychic use.

She turned and crossed her room again. I was angry with him, yes, she thought, but I wouldn't try to hurt him just because our views are different.

No. She wouldn't accept it. She respected Dr. Barrett; loved him as a fellow human being, as a fellow soul. She'd die before she'd harm him. Truly. Truly!

With a faint sob, Florence knelt beside the bed and bowed her head to rest it on tightly clasping hands. Dear God, please help me. Show me the path to follow. I am yours to lead. I consecrate my heart and soul to your exalted works. Dear Lord, I beg you for an answer. Reach down your hand and lift my spirit, help me to walk in your light, along your blessed way.

She looked up suddenly, eyes opened. For several moments she was frozen to the spot, her expression one of indecision. Then a radiant smile pulled back her lips, and standing eagerly, she crossed the room and went into the corridor. She glanced at her wristwatch; they would still be awake. Walking to the door of the Barretts' room, she knocked four times in quick succession.

Edith opened the door. Across her shoulder, Florence could see Dr. Barrett sitting up in bed, his legs beneath the covers.

"May I speak to you?" she asked.

Barrett hesitated, his face drawn with pain.

"I'll only be a moment," she said.

"Very well."

Edith stepped aside, and Florence crossed the room to Barrett's bed. "I know what happened now," she said. "It wasn't me. It was Belasco's son."

Barrett looked at her without response.

"Don't you see? He wants to separate us. Disunited, we are far less of a challenge to him."

Barrett didn't speak.

"Please believe me," Florence said. "I know I'm right. He's trying to turn us against each other." She looked at him with anxious eyes. "If you don't believe me, he'll have succeeded; can't you see that?"

Barrett sighed. "Miss Tanner—"

"I'll sit for you first thing in the morning," she broke in. "You'll see."

"There'll be no further sittings."

Florence stared at him, incredulous. "No further sittings?"

"It isn't necessary."

"But we've barely begun. We can't stop now. We've so much to learn."

"I've learned everything I wish to learn." Barrett was trying to control his temper, but the pain was making it difficult.

"You're cutting me off because of what happened before," Florence objected. "It wasn't my fault. I've told you that."

"Telling me is not convincing me," Barrett answered in a tightly restrained voice. "Now, if you don't mind—"

"Doctor, we can't stop the sittings!"

"I am doing so, Miss Tanner."

"You think it was me who—"

"Not only think it, Miss Tanner, but know it," he interrupted. "Now, *please*, I'm in considerable pain."

"Doctor, I was not responsible! It was Belasco's son!"

"Miss Tanner, *there is no such person!*"

The sharpness of his voice made Florence shrink away from him. "I know you're in pain—" she started faintly.

"Miss Tanner, will you *go?*" he asked through gritted teeth.

"Miss Tanner—" Edith began.

Florence looked around at her. She wanted desperately to convince Barrett, but the look of concern on his wife's face stopped her. She looked back at him. "You're wrong," she said. Turning away, she started for the door. "I'm sorry," she murmured to Edith. "Please forgive me."

She held herself in check until she'd returned to her room. There she sat down on the edge of her bed and started to cry. "You're wrong," she whispered. "Don't you see? You're wrong. You're *wrong.*"

10:18 P.M.

Edith lay on her back, staring at the ceiling. She'd closed her eyes a dozen times, only to open them again in seconds. She couldn't conceive of falling asleep. It seemed an impossibility to her.

She turned her head on the pillow and looked at Lionel. He was heavily asleep. It was no wonder, after what he'd been through. She'd been appalled when she'd helped him undress and put on his pajamas. His entire body was discolored by bruises.

She closed her eyes again, a terrible uneasiness inside her—nervousness with no apparent source. It was probably the house that made her feel it. What in God's name was this power Lionel kept talking about? That it was present was undeniable. What had happened in the dining hall had been terrifying proof of its existence. The thought that Miss Tanner could utilize that power against them was unnerving.

Edith sat up, turning back the bedclothes. Frowning, she slid her feet into her slippers and stood. She wandered across the rug and stopped by the octagonal table, looking at the box in which Lionel kept his manuscript. Abruptly she turned and walked across the room. Stopping in front of the fireplace, she looked inside. There was a low-burning fire, mostly glowing wood coals. She thought of putting on another log, sitting in the rocking chair, and staring at the fire until sleep came. She glanced uneasily at the rocking chair. What would she do if it started moving by itself again?

She rubbed a hand across her face. There was a tingling underneath the skin. She drew in a shaking breath and looked around. She should have brought a book to read. Something light and undemanding. A mystery novel would be good. Better still, some humor; that would be perfect. Some H. Allen Smith or Perelman.

She moved to the cabinet to the right of the fireplace and opened one of its doors. "Oh, good," she murmured. There were shelves of leatherbound volumes inside. None of them were titled. She pulled one out and opened it. It was a treatise on *Conation and Volition*. She frowned and slid it back onto its shelf, drew out another. It was printed in German. "Wonderful." She replaced it on the shelf, pulled out a third book. It dealt with eighteenth-century military tactics. Edith's smile was pained. Water, water everywhere, she thought. Sighing, she pushed the book back onto its shelf and pulled out a larger volume bound in blue leather with gold-edged pages.

The book was false, its center hollowed out. As she opened the cover, a pack of photographs fell out and spilled across the rug. Edith started, almost dropping the book. Her heartbeat quickened as she stared down at the fading photographs.

Swallowing, she stooped and picked one up. A shudder rippled through her flesh. The photograph was of two women

in a sexual embrace. All the photographs were pornographic—
men and women in a variety of poses. Some of them made it
evident that the men and women were performing on the
huge round table in the great hall while other men and women
sat around the table, watching avidly.

Edith pressed her lips together as she picked up all the
photographs and pressed them into a bundle. What an ugly
house this is, she thought. She put the photographs into the
hollow book and thrust it back onto its shelf. As she closed
the cabinet door, she saw, on one of the upper shelves, a decanter of brandy on a silver tray with two small silver cups
beside it.

She walked across the room and sat on her bed again. She
felt uncomfortable and restless. Why did she have to look in
that cabinet? Why, of all the books inside it, did she have to
pick out that one?

She lay down on her side and drew her legs up, crossing
her arms. She shivered. *Cold,* she thought. She stared at Lionel. If only she could lie beside him; not for sex, just to feel
his warmth.

Not for sex. She closed her eyes, a look of self-reproach on
her face. Had she ever wanted sex with him? She made a
pained sound. Would she have even married him if he hadn't
been twenty years her senior and left virtually impotent by
the polio?

Edith twisted on her back and glared up at the ceiling.
What's the matter with me, anyway? she thought. Just because my mother told me sex is evil and degrading, do I have
to fear it all my life? My mother was a bitter woman, married
to an alcoholic woman-chaser. I'm married to another kind of
man entirely. I have no reason to feel like this; no reason at
all.

She sat up suddenly and looked around in terror. *Someone's watching me again,* she thought. She felt the skin on the

back of her neck begin to crawl. Her scalp was covered with
an icy tingling. Someone's looking at me, knowing what I feel.

Pushing up, she walked to Lionel's bed and looked at him.
She mustn't wake him up; he needed rest. Turning hurriedly,
she moved to the octagonal table and dragged its chair beside
Lionel's bed. She sat on the chair, and carefully, so as not to
wake him, put her hand on his arm. There couldn't be anyone
looking at her. There were no such things as ghosts. Lionel
had said so; Lionel knew. She closed her eyes. There are no
such things as ghosts, she told herself. No one is looking at
me. There are no such things as ghosts. *Dear God in heaven,
there are no such things as ghosts.*

11:23 P.M.

Fischer broke the seal on the bottle and unscrewed
its cap. He poured two inches of bourbon into a glass and set
down the bottle. Picking up the glass, he swirled the liquor
around. He hadn't had a drink in years. He wondered if it was
a mistake to start again. There had been a time when he
couldn't stop once he'd started. He didn't want to sink to that
again. Especially here.

He took a sip, grimacing as he swallowed. He coughed,
and his eyes watered; he rubbed a finger over them. Then he
leaned against the cupboard and began to take tiny sips of the
bourbon. It felt comfortingly warm as it trickled down his
throat and settled in his stomach.

Better thin it down, he thought. He walked around the
steam table and over to the sink, where he turned on the cold
water. After it had cleared, he held the glass of bourbon underneath the faucet and added an inch of water. That was
better. Now the relaxation could come without the danger of
his getting drunk.

Fischer lifted himself onto the sink counter and took judicious sips of his drink as he thought about the house. What was it doing this time? he wondered. There *was* a plan; of that he had no doubt. That was the horror of the place. It was not amorphously haunted. Hell House had a method. It worked against invaders systematically. How it did this, no one had ever found out. Until December 1970, he thought, when B. F. Fischer, moving just as systematically—

His right hand twitched so violently as the corridor door was opened that he spilled half his drink across the floor. Florence came into the kitchen, looking harried and exhausted.

"Why aren't you in bed?" she asked.

"Why aren't you?"

"I'm looking for Belasco's son."

He didn't speak.

"You don't think he exists either, do you?"

Fischer didn't know what to say.

"I'll find him," she said, turning away.

Fischer watched her go. He wondered if he should offer to accompany her. He shook his head. Things always happened around her, because she was too open. He didn't want to experience anything more today. He watched her push through the swinging door and disappear into the dining hall. Her footsteps faded. It was still again.

All right, the house, he thought; his plan. Two days had passed. He had the feel of the place now. It was time to start figuring what his approach was going to be. Obviously, it could not consist of working in tandem with Barrett or Florence. He'd have to function on his own. But how?

Fischer sat immobile, staring at the floor. After a while, he took a sip of his drink. It had to be something clever, he thought, something different, something that would circumvent the house's method.

He tapped the fingers of his left hand on the drainboard.

Clever. Different. Florence was right about the multiple-haunting idea; that much he could agree on. Belasco and a host of others were in this house. How to best them, though?

After several minutes Fischer put the drink down, jumped abruptly to the floor, and started toward the entry hall. A walk around the house, he thought. All by himself this time, without Florence Tanner to distract his train of thought. Those things she'd "felt." Jesus Christ. He shook his head, a mirthless smile on his lips. Those Spiritualists were too damn much.

He was crossing the entry hall when he froze in his tracks, his heartbeat leaping. A figure was drifting down the staircase. Fischer blinked his eyes and squinted, trying to see who or what it was; there were no lights on the stairs.

He started as the figure reached the foot of the steps and started toward the front door. It was Edith in a pair of light blue ski pajamas, her eyes staring straight ahead. Fischer stood motionless as she glided like a wraith across the entry hall and pulled open the front door.

She went outside, and Fischer, starting, ran across the entry hall. He dashed through the open doorway, gasping in shock as he saw that she had disappeared into the mist. He ran across the porch and down the steps, hearing a crackling of frost beneath his tennis shoes as he ran along the path. He saw a blur of movement ahead. *Is it really her?* he thought in sudden horror. Or was he being tricked? He started slowing down, then caught his breath. The figure was headed toward—

"No!" He bolted forward, grabbing. Two emotions flared in him at once—relief that it was flesh and skin he clutched, and fierce elation that he'd thwarted the will of the house. He pulled Edith away from the edge of the tarn. She looked at him without a sign of recognition, eyes like glass.

"Come back inside," he said.

Edith held back stiffly, face expressionless.

"Come on. It's cold out here." He turned her toward the house. "Come on."

Edith began to shiver as he led her. For several frightening moments he thought he'd lost his sense of direction; that they were going to walk into the freezing night to die of exposure. Then he saw, through the swirling mist, the nebulous rectangle of the front doorway, and hurried toward it, one arm around Edith, drawing her along beside him. He led her up the porch steps and into the house, pushing the door shut as they went inside. As quickly as he could, he guided her across the entry hall and into the great hall. Standing Edith before the hearth, he bent over and picked up a log, tossing it onto the coals. He grabbed a poker and jabbed at the log until it caught fire. Tongues of flame leaped upward cracklingly. "There we go," he said. He turned to look at Edith. She was staring at the mantel, her expression taut, unreadable. Fischer turned and looked. There were pornographic carvings on the mantel he hadn't noticed before.

Edith's groan was one of such revulsion that Fischer looked back sharply. She was shivering. He pulled off his sweater and held it out to her. She didn't take it. Her eyes were fixed on his face. "I'm not," she said.

Fischer stiffened as she reached up and began to remove her pajama top. "What are you doing?" he asked. His heartbeat quickened as she pulled the pajama top over her head and dropped it on the floor. Her skin was covered with gooseflesh, but she didn't seem aware of being cold. She started to work the pajama bottoms over her hips. Her blank expression was unnerving. "Stop it," Fischer told her.

She didn't seem to hear. She pushed down hard, and the pajama bottoms slipped down her legs. She stepped out of them and moved toward Fischer. "No," he muttered, as she stepped up close to him. She pressed against him with a moan and slid her arms around his back. She pushed her loins against him. Fischer started as she kissed his neck. She started reaching down to touch him. Fischer pulled back. Edith's eyes were blank. He braced himself and slapped her as hard as he could.

Edith spun around with a gasp and almost fell. Fischer grabbed her arm and pulled her back to her feet. She stared at him in shock. Suddenly she looked down at herself, gasping in horror. She yanked free of his grip so violently that it made her stagger backward. She almost fell again. Regaining her balance, she snatched her pajamas off the floor and held them in front of herself.

"You were walking in your sleep," he told her. "I found you outside, starting to go into the tarn."

She didn't respond. Her eyes were wide with fear. She backed away from him, heading toward the archway.

"Mrs. Barrett, it was the house—"

He broke off as she whirled and ran across the room. He started after her, then stopped and listened. After almost a minute, he heard a door being closed upstairs. His shoulders slumped. Turning, he stared into the fire.

Now the house was getting to her as well.

11:56 P.M.

Something kept drawing her to the cellar. Florence descended the stairs and pushed through the swinging metal door that opened on the swimming pool. She remembered the feeling she'd had when she and Fischer had looked into the steam room yesterday: a sense of something perverted, something unwholesome. She could not resign that feeling to what she felt about Belasco's son. Still, she had to be sure.

Her footsteps echoed and re-echoed as she walked along the edge of the pool. She blinked. Her eyes were tired. She felt badly in need of sleep. But she couldn't go to bed the way things were. Before she slept, she had to prove—to herself, at least—that Belasco's son was not imagination.

She pulled open the door to the steam room, looked inside. The pipe valve had been fixed, she saw. The room was filled with steam. She stared into the curling depths of it. There was something in there, without a doubt, something terribly malignant. But Belasco's son was not that way. His fury was defensive. He was desperately in need of help, and desperately desired that help, yet, at the same time, had such scarified malaise of soul that he fought against help in almost suicidal fashion.

She turned from the steam room and walked back along the length of the pool. She'd better warn Dr. Barrett not to use the steam room. She looked around. If Belasco's son was not here, why had she felt a compulsion to come to the cellar? There was only the pool and steam room. No, that wasn't true; she remembered now. There was a wine cellar across the corridor.

The moment she remembered it, it seemed as though a burst of cognizance exploded through her. An excited smile beginning on her lips, she hurried to the swinging door and pushed it open. Running across the corridor, she opened the wine-cellar door and felt around for a light switch. After a moment she found it, pushed it up. The light was dim, the overhead bulb filmed with dust and grime.

Florence walked into the room and looked around. The feeling was intense. Her gaze jumped from wall to wall, across the empty wine racks. Suddenly it froze on the wall across from the door. She stared at it. *Yes*, she thought. She started toward it.

She cried out as unseen hands clutched her by the throat. She reached up and began to grapple with the hands. They were cold and moist. She yanked them away and staggered to the side. Regaining direction, she lunged for the wall. The hands grabbed her arm and slung her sideways. She reeled across the floor and crashed against a wine rack. "Don't!" she cried. She turned and looked around the room. "I'm here to help!"

She pushed away from the wine rack, started for the wall again. Again the hands were on her, clutching at her shoulders. She was turned and hurled away. She almost hit the door before she caught her balance, whirling. *"You will not deter me."* She started forward slowly, praying in a soft, determined voice. The hands grabbed hold of her again. They jerked free as she spoke out loudly: "In the name of the Father, the Son, and the Holy Ghost!" Florence rushed to the wall and pressed herself against it. She was flooded with awareness. "Yes!" she cried. A vision leaped across her mind: a lion's den—a young man looking at her pleadingly. She sobbed with joy. "Daniel!" She had found him! *"Daniel!"*

DECEMBER 23, 1970

6:47 A.M.

The distant scream cut like a knife into Edith's sleep. She twitched awake, staring upward in confusion. A sound of rustling made her jerk around. Lionel was propped on his left elbow, looking at her.

"What *was* it?" she asked.

Barrett shook his head.

"I mean, was it real?"

Barrett didn't answer.

The second scream made her gasp. Barrett caught his breath. "Miss Tanner." He dropped his legs across the mattress edge and felt for his slippers. Edith started sitting up. She gasped again as Lionel's legs gave way. He fell against his bed, hissing at the pain in his thumb.

"Are you all right?" she asked.

He nodded once and pushed erect again, grabbing for his cane. Edith stood up, pulling on her quilted robe. She followed Lionel quickly to the door. He pulled it open, and they moved into the corridor, Lionel hobbling badly. Edith walked beside him, buttoning her robe. She glanced toward Fischer's room. Surely he had heard.

Barrett stopped at Florence Tanner's door and knocked three times in quick succession. When she failed to answer, he opened the door and went inside. The room was dark. Edith felt herself stiffen with anticipation as Lionel flicked up the wall switch.

Florence Tanner was on her back, arms clutched across her chest. Barrett limped to her bed, Edith close behind him. "What is it?" he asked.

Florence stared at him with narrowed, pain-glazed eyes. He leaned down, wincing at the pull of stiffened muscles. "Miss Tanner?"

She shuddered, digging teeth into her lower lip to keep from crying. Slowly she withdrew her arms, and Edith started as she saw him begin to unbutton the medium's gown. There were two damp patches on it, one above each breast. Florence closed her eyes as Barrett drew aside the edges of the gown. Edith shrank back.

There were deep teeth marks ringing the nipples on Florence's breasts.

Abruptly Florence pulled the blankets to her chin. Despite her will, a sob convulsed her throat; she tried in vain to check it. "Don't fight it," Barrett told her. Florence sobbed again, tears spilling down her cheeks.

Edith stared at Florence as she cried. For the first time since they'd met, the medium seemed vulnerable, and Edith felt a rush of sympathy. "Is there anything I can do?" she asked.

Florence shook her head. "I'll be all right."

Edith glanced aside as Fischer entered the room and joined them by the bed. "What happened?" he asked.

Florence hesitated before drawing down the covers briefly. Edith tried not to look, but couldn't help herself. Her breath shook as she saw the bites on Florence Tanner's breasts again.

"He's punishing me," Florence said.

Edith's face went blank. She glanced at Lionel, who was looking at the medium without expression.

"I found him last night," Florence told him. "Daniel Belasco."

There was heavy silence. Barrett looked embarrassed. Florence managed a smile. "No, I'm not imagining it." She laid a hand on her breasts. "Did I imagine these?"

Barrett gestured inconclusively.

"His body is in the wine cellar."

Edith could see how awkward Lionel felt. She knew that he wanted to be sympathetic but didn't know what to say that wouldn't hurt her further.

"Will you help exhume the body?" Florence asked.

"I would, but after last night, I'm afraid I'm in no condition for heavy labor."

Florence stared at him in disbelief. "But, Doctor, he's *there*. Doesn't that mean anything to you?"

"Miss Tanner—"

Florence turned to Fischer. "Will you help me, then?"

Fischer looked at her in silence. He *had* heard her scream, Edith realized abruptly; heard but been afraid to come until Lionel had arrived. Now he was afraid to offer help. It was not surprising. Whenever something violent occurred, Miss Tanner was always there.

When he didn't answer, Florence clenched her teeth, forcing back a sob. "All right, I'll do it myself." The pain of the bites seemed to overwhelm her, and she closed her eyes.

"I'll help you," Fischer said.

Florence opened her eyes and tried to smile. "Thank you."

Barrett put his hand on Edith's arm and started turning.

"Are you so afraid I might be right, Doctor?" Florence asked him.

Barrett looked at her appraisingly. At last he nodded. "Very well. We'll go downstairs with you. I can't dig, however, if that's what you intend to do."

"Ben and I will do that," Florence told him.

Edith glanced at Fischer. He was standing at the foot of the bed, looking at Florence without expression. Suddenly she felt a shiver plaiting up her back.

Was there really something down there?

7:29 A.M.

Fischer drove the crowbar edge into the cleft, and, straining, levered out another chunk of brick and mortar. It had taken him more than twenty minutes to gouge away an opening no larger than his fist. His pants and tennis shoes were streaked with mortar stains; there was a film of powder on his hands. He sneezed as mortar dust got up his nostrils. Turning, he withdrew his handkerchief and blew his nose. He looked at Florence, who was watching him with anxious eyes. She forced a smile. "I know it's hard."

Fischer nodded, drawing in a ragged breath. He almost sneezed again, controlled it, then, raising the crowbar, jammed its edge into the breach. It slipped as he began to pry away another clump of brick, and, losing balance, he pitched against the wall. "Damn!" he muttered. He straightened up, teeth set on edge, and once more drove the crowbar edge into the wall gap.

He jimmied out another piece of brick, which bounced across the floor, then looked at Florence. "This could take all day," he said.

"I know it's hard," she said again. Fischer stretched his back. "Let me do it for a while," she offered. Fischer shook his head and raised the crowbar.

"Before you continue—" Barrett said.

Fischer turned.

"Since this is clearly going to take a long time," Barrett said to Florence. "you won't mind if I go upstairs and get off this leg. It's rather painful."

"Yes, of course," she said. "We'll call you when we've found him."

"Quite." Barrett took hold of Edith's arm and turned for the door. Florence exchanged a look with Fischer as he turned back to the gap in the wall.

He was about to thrust the crowbar when he saw it. *"Wait."* Barrett and Edith looked around as he picked up his flashlight and shone the beam of light into the opening.

"What is it?" Florence was unable to contain her eagerness.

Fischer squinted through the haze of dust. He blew into the gap, then pointed the flashlight beam again. "Looks like a rope," he answered.

Florence came over, and Fischer handed her the flashlight. "Keep pointing it in there." She nodded quickly. Fischer reached into the opening and clamped his fingers on the dusty rope. He pulled down, but there was no give. He pulled up, felt the rope grow slack, then tauten as he let go. "I think there's a weight on the end of it," he said.

Florence caught her breath. "A *counterbalance.*"

Fischer grabbed the crowbar and started jabbing its beveled edge at the sides of the hole, widening it as quickly as he could. After a minute of forceful digging he dropped the crowbar, and before the clanging resonance had faded, had both hands through the opening. Clutching at the rope, he started pulling upward. The resistance was too strong. He braced himself and pulled with all his might, forehead pressed against the wall, eyes closed, teeth gritted. Move, you bastard, *move*, he thought.

Suddenly the rope lurched upward, slamming the edge of
his right wrist against the jagged brick edge. Fischer jerked his
hands back. He was examining his wrist when a rumbling
noise began inside the wall. He looked up, startled.

A section of wall was hitching slowly to the right. Fischer
braced himself for what they'd see—or wouldn't see. He was
conscious of Florence standing beside him tensely as the wall
section creaked and shuddered to the side.

Edith made a gagging noise and turned away. Fischer's lips
pulled back in a grimace. Florence's sigh of relief fell strangely
on his ears.

Shackled to the wall inside the narrow passage were the
mummified remains of a man.

Barrett murmured, "Shades of Poe."

"I told you he was here," Florence said.

Fischer stared at the grayish, parchmentlike features of the
corpse. Its eyes were like dark, hardened berries, its lips drawn
back and frozen in a soundless scream. Obviously, he'd been
tied behind the wall while still alive.

"Well, Doctor?" Florence asked.

Barrett drew in a faltering breath. "Well, what?" he asked.
"I see the mummy of a man. How do you know it's Daniel
Belasco?"

"I *know*," she said.

"Beyond a doubt? Beyond the slightest doubt?"

"*Yes.*" She looked incredulous.

Barrett smiled. "I think more proof than that is called
for."

Florence stared at him. "You're right," she said abruptly.

Turning to the opening, she reached out for the left hand
of the shackled figure. Fischer watched her remove a ring.
"Here." She held it out to Barrett.

Barrett hesitated before taking it. Fischer glanced at Edith.

She was staring at her husband with a look of apprehension. He looked at Barrett. The physicist was handing back the ring, a forced smile on his lips. "Very good," he said.

"Do you believe me now?"

"I'll think it over."

"*Think it over?*" Florence gaped at him. "Are you telling me—?"

"I'm telling you nothing," Barrett cut her off. "I'm saying that I need more time to digest this information and work out my interpretation of it. I must advise you, however, not to presume that one cadaver with a ring can reverse the scientific convictions of a lifetime."

"Doctor, I'm not *trying* to reverse your convictions. All I'm asking is that we work together. Can't you see that both of us can be right?"

Barrett shook his head. "I'm sorry, no. That I cannot see; and never will." He turned abruptly, limping toward the corridor. "My dear?" he said.

Edith looked at Florence for a moment, then turned to follow her husband across the room. Fischer took the ring from Florence. It was made of gold, with an oval crest.

Across the crest, in scroll-like letters, were the initials "D. B."

8:16 A.M.

They had eaten in silence for almost twenty minutes now. Barrett pushed aside his plate and drew his cup of coffee in front of himself. He stared across the table at the EMR indicator. Awkward that they had to take their meals at the same table on which his equipment was placed. Still, there was no help for it, since the dining hall was wrecked.

He glanced at Edith. She was sitting motionless, both hands wrapped around her coffee cup, as if for warmth. She looked like a frightened child.

He thrust aside his thinking on the problem. "Edith?" She looked at him, and Barrett smiled. "Disturbed?"

"Aren't you?"

He shook his head. "No, not at all. Is that why you think I've been quiet?"

Edith seemed to hesitate, as if afraid to bring up points he might not be able to refute. "There *was* a figure," she finally said.

"Quite a dreadful one."

Edith gazed at him uneasily.

"Not necessarily *the* figure, however," he said.

"But the ring."

"D. B. doesn't *have* to stand for Daniel Belasco."

She did not look reassured.

"It could stand for David Bart," he said. "Donald Bascomb." He smiled. "Doctor Barrett."

"But—"

"On the other hand, it might actually *be* Daniel Belasco— assuming such a person existed at all."

"Doesn't that prove her story, then?"

"It would appear to."

"I don't understand, then."

"The point is not the evidence or what it seems to prove, but *who found* that evidence."

Edith still looked bewildered. Barrett smiled. "My dear," he said, "Miss Tanner is a sensitive of considerable development. Add to that the vast power residuum in this house to which she, as a medium, has access. The result is a loaded psychic situation in which she is enabled to create any number of effects to validate her views. She was responsible for that 'poltergeist' attack on me last night, later claiming its source as Daniel Belasco. Next she became 'aware' of his body and 'discovered' it this morning, thus verifying her story even further. The fact that those may actually be the remains of Daniel Belasco is irrelevant. The point is simply that Miss Tanner is manipulating her power and the power in the house to build a case for herself."

Edith looked at him anxiously. Barrett knew she wanted to believe him but was still thrown off by what had happened. "What about the teeth marks, though?" he said.

She started.

"That *is* what you're thinking, isn't it?"

Her smile was faint. "You must be psychic, too."

Barrett chuckled. "Not a bit. It has to be the only point remaining on which you're still uncertain."

"Isn't it proof?"

"To her it is."

"They *were* teeth marks."

"They appeared to be."

"Lionel—" Edith looked more confused than ever. "Are you telling me they *weren't* teeth marks?"

"They may have been," he said. "All I'm saying is that they most certainly were not inflicted by Daniel Belasco."

Edith grimaced. "She did it to herself?"

"Perhaps not directly, although I can't discount the possibility," he said. "More likely, though, it falls under the category of stigmata."

Edith looked a little ill.

"Stranger things have happened." Barrett hesitated, then went on. "I never did tell you what happened to Martin Wrather that time; if you recall, I merely said he'd suffered injury while sitting. What happened was that his genitals were nearly severed. He did it to himself in a moment of hysteria. To this day, however, he remains convinced that 'forces from the other side' attempted to emasculate him." He smiled somberly. "Which is a far cry from a few small bites on female breasts—although I'm sure the pain she's suffering is considerable.

"You see how she's rounding out her case, though," he continued. "She comes upon the body last night—and this morning, in a rage at having his secret discovered, Daniel Belasco punishes her, tries to frighten her away."

"But you"—she gestured weakly—"don't believe any of it."

"None."

She sighed, as if surrendering. "What's going to happen, then?"

"What's going to happen is that my machine will arrive this morning, and by tomorrow I'll end the so-called curse of Hell House by purely scientific means."

They looked around as Fischer entered the great hall and walked over to the table, wearing his pea jacket, his clothes and hands streaked with earth stains. He said nothing as he sat and poured himself a cup of coffee, lit a cigarette.

"Are the services completed?" Barrett asked, the faintest edge of gibing in his voice.

Fischer glanced at him, then lifted the silver cover from the platter of bacon and eggs and looked at them before he dumped the cover back in place.

"Isn't Miss Tanner having breakfast?" Barrett asked.

Fischer shook his head, then drank some coffee. Barrett studied him. The man was obviously under pressure. He'd never given it much thought, but for Fischer to have come back to this house after what had happened must have required a tremendous act of will.

"Mr. Fischer," he said.

Fischer raised his eyes.

"I didn't respond to Miss Tanner last night because I was in pain and . . . well, to be quite frank, angry with her, too.

But I do think she was right when she suggested that you leave."

Fischer eyed him coldly.

"Please don't take this as criticism. I simply think that, for your own good, it might be wise for you to go."

Fischer's smile was bitter. "Thanks."

Barrett laid his napkin on the table. "Well, I've given you my feelings on the matter. The decision is yours to make, of course." He took out his pocket watch and raised the lid. As he put the watch back into its pocket, he noticed Edith glancing away from Fischer. "Perhaps we should bring some food to Miss Tanner," he suggested.

"She wants to be alone right now," Fischer said.

Barrett nodded, then pushed to his feet, flinching as he set his weight down on his burned leg. "My dear?" he said. She nodded with a faint smile, standing.

"He seems particularly tense today," he said as they started across the entry hall.

"Mmm."

He looked at her. "So do you."

"It's the house."

"Of course." He smiled. "Wait until tomorrow. You'll notice quite a change."

He looked around with an elated smile as someone knocked on the front door. "My machine," he said.

8:31 A.M.

So this broken body has released the spirit which shall never return to it again. This body has served its purpose, it can serve that purpose no more. Earth to earth, ashes to ashes, dust to dust. Amen."

She had spoken the words of the funeral service three

times now, the first time when she and Fischer had laid Daniel Belasco's body to rest, twice more upon returning to her room. Now his soul could rest.

It had been bitterly cold outside, the ground as hard as iron. Fischer's attempt to dig a pit finally had to be abandoned. They had searched the area around the house until they'd found a hollow in the earth, placed the body in that, and covered it with leaves and stones. Then she had recited the words of the funeral service, both of them standing beside the makeshift grave, heads bowed, eyes closed.

Florence smiled. She'd see to it that Daniel had a proper burial as soon as possible. What mattered now was that he was released from this house.

Reaching into the pocket of her sweater, she drew out Daniel's ring and held it in her palm, closing her fingers over it.

The images began immediately. She saw him: dark-haired, handsome, imperious in attitude, yet, underneath the superficial arrogance, as defenseless as a child. She saw him laughing at the table in the dining hall, saw him in the ballroom, waltzing with a beautiful young woman. There was only youth and tenderness in his smile.

The visions darkened. Daniel in the theater, looking at a play, face taut, eyes glittering. Florence tightened. This was not what he desired; but he was young, impressionable. Everything degrading was available. She saw him reeling down a corridor, a drunken woman on his arm. She saw him in this very bedroom, trying, in spite of everything, to find a sense of beauty in the sex act.

The corruption deepened. Drunkenness. Despair. A brief escape, then, helplessly, retreat to Hell House, never to escape again. Florence winced. She saw him in the great hall, naked, sitting at the huge round table, watching avidly. She saw him sliding a hypodermic needle into his arm, saw him venting sexual desires that made her tremble in the darkness. Yet, always, behind the mask—the face that Hell House had created—cowered the boy; wanting to flee, but incapable of doing so; wanting love, but finding only license.

She caught her breath, seeing him approach his father. She could not make out the face of Emeric Belasco; the figure stood in shadows, giant, menacing. She moved her lips in prayer, the ring gripped tightly in her hand. The shadows started to contract. In a moment she would see him. Something cold began to fill her chest; the vision faltered. Florence groaned. She mustn't lose it! She descended deeper with a surge of will. If only she could see the father, get inside the father, understand the father. Sweat broke out across her brow. She felt a snake uncoiling in her stomach, cold and wet. "No," she murmured. She must not surrender. There was meaning here, an answer.

She cried out as a violent shock coursed through her body. Instantly her hand unclasped, the ring slipped off. She heard it thumping on the rug, a vast distance below. She felt as though she lay in some great cavern, wounded. She could not perceive the walls or ceiling; in every direction lay only darkness and distance. She tried to open her eyes but couldn't. Blackness trickled sluggishly across her mind, blotting out awareness. Power, she thought. Dear God, the *power.*

She started slipping down the wall of a gigantic pit, moving downward toward a darkness which was blacker than any she had ever known. She tried to stop herself but couldn't. The sensation was physical—her body sliding down and down, the walls of the pit adhesive enough to keep her from pitching into space, not enough to stop her inexorable descent toward the darkness below. The darkness that waited had a character, a personality. It's him, she thought. He waits for me.

Oh, God, he waits for me!

She fought against it, praying to her guides, her spirit doctors, all those who had helped her in the past. Keep me from falling deeper, she entreated them. Take my hand and bear me up. I ask this in the name of our eternal God. Help me, help me!

Abruptly she was back inside the room, the pit and cavern gone. She was asleep, yet not asleep. She knew that she was on the bed, unconscious; knew she was aware, as well. She heard the opening and closing of a door. Was it the door of her room, or some imagined door within her mind? All she knew was that her eyes were fastened shut; that she slept, yet was awake. She heard footsteps drawing near.

She saw a figure. With her eyes closed, she could see it coming toward her like a silhouette cut from black paper. Did she imagine it? Was the figure in the room, or in her mind?

It reached the bed and sat beside her; she could feel the mattress yielding as it sat. Suddenly she knew that it was Daniel, and a groaning noise enveloped her. Was it a real groan, issuing from her lips, or a thought sound which expressed the shock she felt? *It could not be him.* He was at rest. She and Fischer had placed his body in a consecrated grave. He could not be back again; it was impossible. Asleep, awake, she saw him sitting on the bed beside her, a figure in black. Was he looking at her? Were there eyes in that dark head?

"Is it you?" she asked. She heard her voice but couldn't tell if it was thought or real.

"It is."

"*Why?*" she asked, she thought. "You should have gone on."

"I cannot."

She tried to wake herself, unable to endure this limbo of fragmentary awareness. "You have to go," she told him. "You were given your release."

"It's not the release I seek."

"What *is*, then?" She became more conscious of the battle to awaken. She had to separate herself before it was too late.

"You know what it is," he said.

She did know, suddenly. The knowledge was a chilling wind across her heart. *"You must go on,"* she said.

"You know what you must do," he answered.

"No."

"I need it, or I cannot leave."

"No!" she answered. *Wake!* she thought.

Daniel said, "Then I must kill you, Florence."

Icy hands were clamped around her neck. Florence cried out in her sleep. She reached up, clawing at them. Suddenly she woke. The hands were gone. She started pushing up, then froze in shock, her heartbeat staggering.

There was a hideous sound beside her on the bed; an eerie sound, half-animal, half-human, liquid, and deranged. She couldn't move. What was it? Very slowly Florence turned her eyes. The bathroom door was open slightly, faint illumination clouding through the room.

It was the cat.

She watched it staring at her. Its eyes were glittering, insane. It kept making the wavering, unnatural sound in its throat. She began to lift her hand. "In the name of God," she whispered.

With a savage yowl, the cat leaped at her face. Florence jerked back, both arms flung before her. The cat thrashed into her, its sharp claws hooking deep into her arms. She cried out as she felt its teeth dig brutally into her head. She tried to push it loose but couldn't; it was sprawled across her face, its hot fur in her eyes and mouth. Its teeth dug deeper, front claws buried in her arms, the harsh, demented sound still bubbling in its throat. Florence jerked her left arm free and dug her fingers into fur and skin, trying to pull its head back. The teeth pulled loose. Instantly the cat's head lunged berserkly at her throat. Florence blocked its way with her right arm, and the cat's teeth sank into her flesh again. She sobbed in pain and tried to jerk its head away. The cat began to kick its rear legs. Florence grabbed its throat and started squeezing. It began to make a gurgling noise, its rear legs thrashing, clawing at her chest and stomach through the sweater. Suddenly the teeth pulled free. Florence hurled the cat to the floor.

She sat up quickly, gasping for breath. In the faint light from the bathroom she could see the cat roll over and regain its feet. She jumped from the bed and lunged toward the bathroom. The cat hurled itself against her legs, digging teeth and claws into her calves. She cried out, almost falling. Struggling to regain balance, she toppled against the Spanish table, right arm crashing on the telephone. Instantly she snatched up the receiver, swung down at the cat with it. The first blow smashed against her knee. She sobbed and swung again, hitting the cat's head. She began to hit it again and again, battering at its skull until, abruptly, the teeth jerked out. Kicking the cat away, she spun around and dashed for the bathroom. The cat raked to a halt, then darted after her. Lurching through the doorway, Florence slammed the door and fell against it as the cat crashed against the other side and started clawing frenziedly at the wood.

Florence stumbled to the sink and looked at her reflection in the mirror. She gasped in shock, seeing the deep holes in her forehead, blood oozing from the cavities. Tugging up her sweater, she pulled it over her head, groaning at the sight of her chest and stomach crisscrossed with a network of bleeding lacerations, her torn bra spotted with bloodstains.

She looked at her arms, wincing at the perforations the cat's teeth had dug into her flesh. She whimpered, turning on the cold water. Dragging a washcloth off its rack, she held it underneath the faucet until it was soaked, then began to pat it on the bites and scratches. She started crying at the pain, digging teeth into her lower lip. Hot tears blurred her sight.

As she washed the wounds, she heard the cat outside the door, raking its claws through the wood and making the horrible noise in its throat.

9.14 A.M.

It's big," Edith said.

Barrett grunted as he jimmied the end of a plank from the side of a plank from the side of the crate stamped FRONT. His movements were excited, overquick. The crowbar slipped.

"Don't overdo it, now."

He nodded, prying at the other end of the plank. She hadn't seen him so worked up in years. "Can I help you?"

Barrett shook his head.

Edith watched uneasily as he leaned forward in his chair and pried the boards loose, cracking several of them, pulling off jagged pieces with his left hand, and tossing them onto the floor. "They packed it well enough," he muttered. She couldn't tell if he was pleased or annoyed by the fact.

The crate was eight by ten feet in width and length, and taller than Barrett by a foot. What was in it? Edith wondered. His machine, yes; but what was his machine, and how was it supposed to end the haunting of a house?

"Damn!"

She twitched as Barrett cursed and dropped the crowbar with a hiss of pain to clutch at his bandaged thumb.

"Lionel, please don't overdo it."

"All *right*," he said impatiently. He picked up the crowbar and returned to the crate.

"Why don't you ask Fischer to help you?"

"Do it myself," he muttered.

Edith flinched as he drove the crowbar in between two planks and started jimmying out one of them. "Lionel, *take it easy*," she said. "You look as though you mean to tear that crate apart with your teeth."

Barrett stopped and looked at her, his chest rising and falling heavily, a dew of perspiration on his forehead. He made a sound which might have been amusement. "It's just that this is—well, the culmination of all my years in parapsychology," he said. "You can understand why I'm excited."

"And you can understand why I'm concerned."

He nodded. "I'll restrain myself," he promised. "I guess I can spare a few more minutes after twenty years."

Edith leaned back in her chair, relieved. Maybe if she kept him talking while he worked, he wouldn't get too overwrought.

"Lionel?"

"Yes?"

"Should we report that body to the police?"

"We will," he said, "when the week is up."

Edith nodded, wondering what to talk about next.

"Was Fischer really a powerful psychic?" she asked, wondering why the question came to mind.

"At one time, it was generally conceded that he ranked with Home and Palladino."

"What did he do?"

"Oh"—Barrett pried away another plank end from the front of the crate and set the board aside, revealing a line of glass-fronted dials—"the usual: levitation, direct voice, biological phenomena, imprints, percussion, materialization—that sort of thing. At one sitting, a table that weighed almost five hundred pounds was raised to the ceiling in full light, him with it, and the combined strength of six men couldn't pull it down.

"Later, when the lights were out in the testing room—

full controls in operation—a group of seven perfectly formed faces floated around the room. One of the testers—Doctor Wells, the famous Harvard chemist—had his face blown into by one of them, and another tried to kiss him. I believe he was rather a cynic about the entire subject until that night."

"What else?" Edith prompted as he fell silent again.

"Oh, a . . . dark shadow in the shape of a man walked around the testing room with a tread that shook the walls. Green phosphorescent lights, like outsize butterflies, fluttered around the table and nested in the sitters' hair. A mandolin floated near the ceiling, playing 'My Bonny Lies Over the Ocean.' Professor Mulvaney of the Pittsburgh Parapsychological Association held a perfectly formed materialized hand for more than ten minutes, describing it as possessing bones, skin, hair, nails, and warmth. It dissolved in his grip in less than a second.

"Finally, a mass of teleplasm flooded from Fischer's mouth and formed the figure of a Chinese mandarin, seven feet tall, complete to the finest detail. It spoke to the group for twenty minutes before being retracted into Fischer's body." Barrett set aside another plank. "Fischer was all of thirteen at the time."

"He was genuine, then."

"Oh, yes, completely." Barrett started working on the final plank. "Unfortunately, that was long ago. It's like a muscle, you see. Fail to use it, and it atrophies." He set aside the final plank and stood with his cane. *"Now,"* he said.

Edith rose and walked over to him. He was peeling off a large envelope that was taped to the front of the machine. As he opened it and slid out his blueprints, Edith looked at the control panel with its array of switches, dials, and knobs. "What did this cost to build?" she asked.

"I'd say in excess of seventy thousand dollars."

"My God." Edith ran her gaze over the dials. "EMR," she

murmured, reading the metal plate fastened below the largest dial. The numbers on it ranged from zero to 120,000.

"What *is* EMR, Lionel?"

"I'll explain it later, dear," he said distractedly. "I'll tell all of you exactly what the Reversor is designed to do."

"The Reversor," she said.

He nodded, looking at the top blueprint. Pulling the pencil flashlight from his pocket, he shone its thin beam through a grille-like opening on the side of the machine. He frowned and, limping to the table, set down the blueprints, and picked up a screwdriver. Returning to the machine, he began to unfasten a plate.

Edith moved to the fireplace and held her hands toward the flames. She'd stood right here, she thought after a moment. She could remember nothing before being slapped from sleep, to find herself naked in front of Fischer. She shuddered, trying not to think about it.

She was moving back toward Lionel when Fischer suddenly came dashing in. Edith started as he called out, "Doctor!"

Barrett whirled.

"It's Miss Tanner!"

Edith froze. My God, what's happened now? she thought.

"She's been hurt again."

Barrett nodded once and, limping to the table, grabbed his black bag. "Where?" he asked.

"In her room."

The three moved hurriedly across the great hall, Barrett setting the pace as best he could. "How bad is it?" he asked.

"She's scratched—torn—bitten."

"How did it happen?"

"I don't know; the cat, I think."

"The *cat?*"

"I was bringing her some food. When she didn't answer

my knock, I opened the door. The second I did, the cat shot
out and disappeared."

"And Miss Tanner?"

"She was in the bathroom," Fischer said. "At first she
wouldn't come out. When she did—" He stopped, grimacing.

She was lying on her bed when they came in; she opened
her eyes and turned her head as they crossed the room. Edith
made a sound of shock. The medium's skin was as pale as
wax, deep, blood-encrusted indentations on her head, puffy
scratches on her face and neck.

Barrett put his bag by her bed and sat down beside her.
"Have you disinfected these?" he asked, looking at the bites
on her head.

She shook her head. Barrett opened his bag and removed
a small brown bottle and a box of Q-Tips. He glanced at the
rips in Florence's sweater. "Your body, too?"

She nodded, tears welling in her eyes.

"You'd better take the sweater off."

"I've washed myself."

"That's not enough. There could be infection."

Florence glanced at Fischer. Without a word, he turned
and walked to the other bed, sitting down on it, his back to
them. Florence started to remove her sweater. "Would you
help her, Edith?" Barrett asked.

Edith moved to the side of the bed, wincing as she saw
the pattern of the jagged slashes across Florence's chest and
stomach, the bites and lacerations on her arms. She reached
behind the medium to unhook her bra, stepping back as Florence slipped it off. The medium's breasts were covered with
scratches as well.

Barrett unscrewed the cap of the bottle. "This is going to
hurt," he said. "Would you like a codeine?"

Florence shook her head. Barrett dipped a Q-Tip into the
bottle and began to swab out one of the puncture wounds in

her forehead. Florence hissed and closed her eyes, tears pressing out beneath the lids. Edith couldn't watch. She turned away and looked at Fischer. He was staring at the wall.

Several minutes passed, the only sound Florence's hissing and an occasional murmur of apology from Barrett. When he was done, he drew a blanket across her chest. "Thank you," she said. Edith turned back.

"The cat attacked me," Florence said. "It was possessed by Daniel Belasco."

Edith looked at her husband. His expression was unreadable.

The medium tried to smile. "I know, you think—"

"It doesn't really matter what I think, Miss Tanner," Barrett cut her off. "What matters is your being mauled."

"I'll be all right."

"I wonder if that's so, Miss Tanner. I wonder if it might not be advisable for *you* to leave rather than Mr. Fischer."

Edith was aware of Fischer twisting around to look at them.

"No, Doctor." Florence shook her head. "I don't think it would be advisable at all."

Barrett looked at the medium for several moments before he spoke again. "Mr. Deutsch needn't know," he said.

Florence looked confused.

"I mean"—he hesitated—"you've more than contributed your share to the project."

"And you'll see to it that I get paid off, is that it?"

"I'm only trying to help. Miss Tanner."

Florence started to reply, then held back. She averted her eyes before she looked at Barrett again. "All right," she said, "I'll accept that. But I'm not going to leave."

Barrett nodded. "Very well. It's up to you, of course." He paused, then added, "But I would feel derelict in my responsibility toward you if I didn't urge, no, *warn* you to leave this house while you can." He paused again. "Furthermore, if I think your life is in danger, I may *see* to it that you go."

Florence looked appalled.

"I don't intend to stand by knowingly and allow you to become yet one more victim of Hell House," Barrett told her. He snapped his bag shut, picked it up. "My dear?" he said. Struggling to his feet, he turned for the door.

10:43 A.M.

Edith turned onto her right side and looked at the other bed. Lionel was asleep. She should never have let him work on that crate. They should have asked Fischer to open it.

She thought about what Lionel had said before he'd gone to sleep: that Florence Tanner was becoming so anxious to prove her case that she was sacrificing her bodily well-being to do it.

"Dissociation of mind resulting in a modification of self is the basic cause of mediumistic phenomena," he had said. "I don't know if there really was a Daniel Belasco or not, but the personality Miss Tanner claims to be in touch with is nothing more than a division of her own personality."

Edith blew out a harried breath and turned onto her back. If only she could understand as Lionel did. All she could think of were those horrible teeth marks around Florence Tanner's nipples; the scratches and bites which Florence claimed the cat had inflicted. How could she have done those things to herself, even unconsciously?

Edith slipped her legs across the mattress edge and sat up. She stared at her shoes for several minutes before pushing her feet into them. Standing, she moved to the octagonal table and looked at the manuscript. She ran a finger over the title page. Would it really hurt? she thought. It was ridiculous to have this almost mindless dread of alcohol. Just because her father's drinking had made her childhood miserable was no reason to condemn liquor per se. All she was contemplating was one small drink in order to relax.

She moved to the cabinet and opened the door. Lifting out the decanter and one of the small silver cups, she carried them to the table. She pulled a tissue from her purse and cleaned out the silver cup before she poured it full of brandy. It was very dark. She wondered suddenly if it could be poisoned. That would be a grisly way to end things.

She dipped a finger into the brandy, touched it to her tongue. Would she know if it was poisoned? Her tongue began to burn, and she swallowed nervously. The warmth spread delicately to the tissues of her throat. Edith raised the silver cup and held it underneath her nostrils. The aroma was pleasing. How could it be poisoned? Surely someone had tasted it before this.

She took a tiny sip, closing her eyes as it trickled down her throat. The inside of her mouth grew warm. She made a sound of pleasure as the brandy reached her stomach and a tiny core of heat began expanding there. She took another sip. It's what I need, she thought. I'm not a potential drunk just because I sip a little brandy. She moved to the rocking chair, hesitated, then sat down. Leaning back, she closed her eyes and drank the brandy with deliberate sips.

When the cup was empty, she opened her eyes and looked toward the table. No, she thought. One was enough. She felt relaxed now; that was all she wanted. She held the cup before her eyes, examining the intricacies of its silverwork. Maybe she'd take it home as a souvenir when the week was over. She smiled. There; that was better. She was planning ahead.

She thought about Fischer. She really should apologize to

him for avoiding him so rudely this morning. She should thank
him for saving her life. She shivered, thinking of the stagnant
water in the tarn, and stood up, wavering slightly as she
crossed the room. She opened the door and stepped into the
corridor, closing the door behind herself as quietly as possible.

A wave of dread swept over her for an instant as she realized that she was alone for the first time since they'd entered
the house. She scoffed away the dread. She was being foolish.
Lionel was just inside the room. Florence was probably in her
room, Fischer in his. She moved along the hallway to his door.
Was she making a mistake? No, she thought; I owe him an
apology, I owe him thanks.

She knocked on Fischer's door and waited. There was no
sound inside the room. After several moments she knocked
again, but there was no response. Edith turned the knob and
pushed at the door. What am I doing? she thought. She
couldn't stop herself. Opening the door, she looked inside.

The room was considerably smaller than the one she and
Lionel were in. There was only one massive bed with a high,
square-cut canopy. To its right was a table with a French telephone and an ashtray on it. Edith looked at the ashtray filled
with mashed cigarette butts. He smokes too much, she
thought.

She drifted to the armchair beside the table. Fischer's tote
bag was on it, its zipper undone. Edith looked inside and saw
some T-shirts and an open carton of cigarettes. She swallowed,
reaching down to touch the bag.

She whirled with a gasp.

Fischer was standing in the doorway, looking at her.

For a terribly extended time, it seemed to her, they stared
at each other. Edith's heartbeat raced; she felt a licking heat
across her face.

"What is it, Mrs. Barrett?"

She tried to get control of herself. What must he be thinking to find her here like this? "I came to thank you," she managed.

"Thank me?"

"For saving my life last night."

She drew back unconsciously as Fischer walked over to her. "You shouldn't have left your husband."

She didn't know what to say.

"Are you all right?"

"Of course."

Fischer looked at her closely. "I think you should go back to your room now," he said.

He moved beside her as she crossed the rug. "Try tying your wrist to the bed at night," he told her.

Edith nodded as he followed her into the corridor and to her room. She turned to face him. "Thank you."

"Don't leave your husband again," he said. "You should never—"

He broke off, leaning forward suddenly as though to kiss her. Edith twitched and drew back. "Have you been drinking?" he asked.

She tightened. "Why?"

"Because it isn't safe to drink here. It isn't safe to lose control."

"*I am not losing control,*" she told him stiffly. She turned and went inside her room.

11:16 A.M.

Florence started as someone knocked on the door. "Come in."

Fischer entered.

"Ben." She tried to rise.

"Don't get up," he told her. He started across the room. "I'd like to talk to you."

"Of course." She patted the bed. "Sit here beside me."

Fischer settled on the mattress edge. "I'm sorry you're in pain."

"It will pass."

He nodded, unconvinced, then looked at her in silence, until Florence smiled. "Yes?" she asked.

He braced himself for her reaction. "I agree with Doctor Barrett. I think you should leave."

"*Ben.*"

"You're being torn to pieces, Florence. Can't you see that?"

"You don't think I'm doing these things to *myself*, do you?"

"No, I don't," he answered. "But I don't know who *is* doing them, either. You say it's Daniel Belasco. What if you're wrong? What if you're being fooled?"

"Fooled?"

"There was a woman medium here with us in 1940. Grace Lauter. She became convinced that a pair of sisters haunted the house. She built a very convincing case for it. The only trouble was, she was wrong. She cut her throat the third day we were here."

"But Daniel Belasco *does* exist. We found his body, found his ring with his initials on it."

"We also put him to rest. *Why isn't he at rest, then?*"

Florence shook her head. "I don't know." Her voice was faltering. "I just don't know."

"I'm sorry." He patted her hand. "I'm not trying to pick at you. I'm just concerned, that's all."

"Thank you, Ben." After several moments she smiled at him. "Benjamin Franklin Fischer," she said. "Whoever gave you such a name?"

"My father. He was nuts for Benjamin Franklin."

"Tell me about him."

"There's nothing to tell. He left my mother when I was two. I don't blame him. She must have driven him mad."

Florence's smile faded.

"She was a fanatic," Fischer said. "When I started showing signs of mediumship at nine, she devoted her existence to it." His smile was humorless. "My existence, too."

"Do you regret it?"

"I regret it."

"Truly, Ben?" She looked at him with deep concern.

Fischer smiled abruptly. "You said you were going to tell me about Hollywood when we settled down." His smile went wry. "Not that things have settled down much."

"It's a long story, Ben."

"We have time."

She gazed at him in silence. "All right," she finally said. "I'll tell you briefly."

Fischer waited, looking at her.

"Perhaps you read about it," Florence said. "The gossip columns made a lot of it at the time. *Confidential* even did a story on the Spiritualist meetings I held in my home. They made it sound like something else, of course.

"It wasn't, Ben. It was exactly what I claimed. As for the stories about me never marrying because I wanted to 'play the field,' as they called it, they weren't true either. I never married because I never met a man I wanted to marry."

"How did you become an actress?"

"I loved to act. When I was a child, I put on little shows for my parents and relatives. Later on, I joined the high-school drama club, a local theater group, majored in dramatics at college. The progression was remarkably smooth; it happens that way sometimes. A God-given appearance, a combination of fortunate events." She smiled a little ruefully. "I was never

a great success at it. I didn't apply myself enough. But there
was never anything questionable, either. No dark past, no
scars covering childhood wounds. I had a wonderful childhood. My parents loved me, and I loved them. They were
Spiritualists; I became a Spiritualist."

"Were you an only child?"

"I had a brother. David. He died when he was seventeen—spinal meningitis." She looked into the past. "It was
the only real sorrow of my life."

She smiled again. "It was the 'waning' of my career, they
said, that made me 'flee' from Hollywood, 'turning to religion'
for comfort. They always neglected to mention that I'd been
a Spiritualist all my life. Actually, I blessed my fading career.
It gave me the opportunity to do what I always knew I should
do—devote myself exclusively to mediumship.

"I didn't fear Hollywood—or flee from it. There's nothing
fearful about it. It's a location and an enterprise, nothing
more. What those involved in it make of their lives is their
own choice. The so-called 'corrupting' influences are no
greater than similar influences that exist in any line of work.
It isn't the business that matters, but the corruptibility of
those who enter it.

"Not that I was unaware of the moral vacuum which usually surrounded me. On crowded sets, at parties, I was often
overwhelmed by the atmosphere of unwholesome tension in
the air." She smiled, remembering. "One night, when I went
to bed, I said the Lord's Prayer as I always do. Suddenly I
realized that what I'd said was 'Our Father which art in
heaven, Hollywood be thy name.' " She shook her head in
amusement. "I left within the month and came East to stay."

Fischer began to speak, then broke off as somewhere,
faintly, in the distance, the cat yowled. *End of pleasant inter-
lude*, he thought. Florence looked pained. "The wretched
thing." She started to rise.

Fischer pressed her back against the pillows. "I'll look."

"But—"

"Rest." he told her, standing.

"Before you go, would you get my purse?"

Fischer walked across the room and got it for her. Florence opened it and removed a medallion, holding it out to him. Fischer took it. There was a single word engraved on it: BE-LIEVE.

"It's all within you if you do," she said.

He started to hand it back to her. "No, keep it," she said. "From me to you, with love."

Fischer forced a smile. "Thank you." He slipped the medallion into his pocket. "I'm really all right, though. Worry about yourself, not me."

"Will you sit with me after I rest?" she asked. "I've got to contact Daniel Belasco, and trance is the quickest way. But I don't want to sit alone."

"You won't consider leaving, then?"

"I can't, Ben, you know that." She paused. "Will you sit with me?"

Fischer looked at her uneasily. Finally he nodded. "Right."

He left the room without another word.

12:16 P.M.

The cool water rippling against his face felt good. The skin of his burned calf had contracted, making it painful to kick, but he didn't want to stop. Every time he lifted his right hand from the water, the pain in his thumb intensified. I need this, though, he thought. He hadn't been swimming for almost a week.

He reached the shallow end of the pool and stopped, holding on to the coping with his left hand. Edith was sitting on

a wooden bench near the steam-room door. "Don't overdo,"
she said.

"I won't. I'll just do two more laps."

Twisting around, Barrett began to swim again. He closed
his eyes and listened to the splashing sounds his arms and feet
made.

He wondered how badly the atmosphere of the house was
affecting Edith. When he'd waked up, he'd tried to rise without disturbing her, but the moment he'd stirred, her eyes had
opened. There'd been a smell of brandy on her breath, and
when he'd gotten up he'd seen a decanter of it on the table,
a small silver cup beside it. She'd told him that she'd found
them in the cabinet and taken one cupful to relax. He'd put
the decanter back in the cabinet, telling her she'd taken a
serious risk drinking anything in this house. She'd promised
not to touch any more.

Barrett's hand touched the far end of the pool and, turning, he started swimming back. We should be out of here by
tomorrow night, he thought. If he could get the Reversor
functioning without delay, he was certain they could leave by
then. He smiled to himself, wondering if Edith had any concept at all how the Reversor was going to change the atmosphere of the house.

He reached the shallow end and stood up, hissing at the
coldness of the air on his body. Edith helped him up the steps
and wrapped a towel around his shoulders. "Can you stand a
few minutes in the steam room?" he asked.

She nodded, handing him his cane.

"I think it would do me good."

"Yes. Go in." She pulled open the heavy door.

"You'd better remove your outer clothes," he told her.

"All right."

Barrett tossed the towel onto the wooden bench and
limped inside the steam room as Edith let the door thud shut.

He groaned in pleasure at the feeling of the wet heat on his body. Breathing through his teeth, he felt around until he found a bench. The top of it was burning hot. He eased around the room, feeling with his cane, until it touched the hose. Moving his left hand along its length until he reached the wall, he turned the spigot once. Cold water gushed from the end of the hose. Barrett washed it over the bench top and sat down, putting aside his cane. Reaching down, he worked the bathing suit across his hips. It slithered down his legs, and he shook it off.

He looked toward the door. Edith was taking rather a long time. He frowned. He didn't want to stand again. Still, he mustn't leave her alone for more than seconds.

He was on the verge of getting to his feet when the door opened and he saw the outline of her figure. He was surprised to see that she had taken all her clothes off. As the door jarred shut, he said, "Over here." He'd have to remember to put in a brighter bulb. The one overhead was either deficient in wattage or covered with grime; probably both.

Edith moved cautiously across the steam-obscured room. She made a faint sound as she walked through the gush of cold water. Barrett pulled the hose until the end was in his hand, then washed off the bench beside himself, wincing as some of the water sprayed against his leg. He tossed down the hose, and Edith sat beside him. Barrett heard her drawing in erratic breaths, trying not to let the hot air down her throat. "All right?" he asked.

She coughed. "I never could get used to breathing in steam rooms."

"Try putting water on your face and taking a breath as you do."

"I'm all right."

Barrett closed his eyes and felt the damp heat seeping into

his flesh. He twitched as Edith's hand settled on his leg. He covered it with his. After several moments she leaned over and kissed his cheek. "I love you," she said.

Barrett put his arm across her shoulders. "I love you, too," he said. She kissed him on the cheek again, then on the corner of his lips. He felt a stirring in his body as she pressed her lips to his, moving her head as she kissed him. Barrett opened his eyes as one of her hands ran down his stomach. Edith? he thought.

After several moments she swung around and straddled him, her lips never leaving his. He felt her hot, slick stomach thrust against his. Reaching down, she took hold of his sex and began to rub it against herself. Barrett's breath began to labor. The hot air seared his throat and chest. He made a startled sound as she dug her teeth into his lower lip. He could smell the brandy on her breath.

Her lips ran across his cheek, her tongue trailing over the skin. "Make it hard," she whispered in his ear. Her voice was almost fierce. Barrett caught his breath as she grabbed his injured hand and pulled it up against her breast. He jerked it back as fiery pain ran up his wrist. *"Don't!"* she ordered, clutching it again.

"My thumb!" he cried. The pain was so severe, his vision started blurring. He could hardly breathe, his lungs struggling with the scalding air. Edith didn't seem to hear. She clutched at his organ, groaning so loudly it made Barrett's heartbeat leap. "For Christ's sake, make it hard!" she cried. She jammed her lips on his again.

Barrett couldn't breathe. Gagging, he jerked his head back, slamming it against the tile wall. He cried out in new pain, his face contorted. Edith fell against him, sobbing. Barrett tried to catch his breath. "Edith," he gasped.

She wrenched to her feet and turned away. "Don't," he

muttered, reaching for her dazedly. He felt a rush of cold air as she opened the door, saw her outline vaguely. Then the door thumped shut again.

Wincing, he bent over, feeling for the hose. He rubbed cold water on his face, drawing in a breath through clenched teeth. My God, what's come over her? he thought. He knew that the curtailment of their sex life must have had a damaging effect on her, but she'd never shown desire like this. The house *must* be affecting her. Standing groggily with his cane, he inched his way across the steam-filled room, grimacing at the increase of heat on his face. The ceiling bulb had all but disappeared from view now, no more than a spot of pale light overhead. Barrett reached the door and felt for the handle. Finding it, he closed his fingers over it and pushed. The door held fast. He pushed it harder. The door wouldn't move. His features tightened. Clutching the handle as hard as he could, he pushed again.

The door refused to budge.

A flicker of uneasiness oppressed him. Barrett willed it off. "Edith?" he called. He hit the door with the palm of his left hand. "Edith, the door is stuck!"

There was no reply. *My God, she didn't go upstairs*, he thought with sudden dread. He pushed at the handle again. The door was wedged in its frame. The heat and dampness, he told himself; the door had warped, expanded. "Edith!" he called. He pounded on the door with his fist.

"What *is* it?" he heard her answer faintly.

"The door is stuck! Try to open it from your side!"

He waited. There was a thump on the door, and he felt it stir. He grabbed the handle again and pulled with all his strength as she thrust her weight against the door on the other side.

The door held.

"What are we going to do?" he heard her ask. She sounded frightened.

Could she possibly use the bench to batter open the door? No, it was too heavy. Barrett scowled. The heat seemed to be getting worse. He'd better turn it off.

"Lionel?"

"I'm all right!" He lowered himself gingerly to his left knee to get below the worst of the heat. He made a worried sound. Well, there was no other way. He couldn't stay in here. "You'd better get Fischer!" he called.

"What?" He couldn't tell if she hadn't heard or was appalled by what he'd said.

"You'd-better-get-Fischer!"

Silence. Barrett knew the thought of going alone through the house was terrifying to her. "It's the only way!" he shouted.

Edith didn't answer for a long time. Then he heard her call. "All right! I'll be right back!"

Barrett remained motionless for a while. He hoped to God she didn't run into anything. In her mental state, it could be catastrophic. He scowled. I can't just stay like this, he thought. I'd better turn off that steam.

He looked abruptly to his right; he thought he'd heard a sound. There was nothing but swirling steam. He stared at it with slitted eyes. It was thick and white and coiling, and made shapes. A person with an uncontrolled imagination might see all sorts of things in it.

Barrett hissed. "Ridiculous." He stood and edged his way across the floor until his shins bumped against the edge of the wooden bench. Kneeling again, he reached beneath the bench for the tap wheel. He couldn't find it and began to crawl along the bench, feeling for it.

He froze. He was certain that he'd heard something this

time, a kind of—*slithering* noise? Barrett shivered despite the
heat. "Ri*dic*ulous," he muttered. He continued crawling. No
wonder this house had claimed so many victims. Its atmosphere was incredibly conducive to delusions. The sound he'd
heard was probably coming from the tap wheel he was searching for—an escape of steam, probably too much pressure. It
was getting awfully hot in here.

His hand came in contact with the tap wheel, and he felt
a burst of relief. He tried to turn the wheel, but it stuck. He
fought off premonition, gritting his teeth against the pain in
his leg as he wrapped both hands around the wheel. "Stuck,"
he said aloud, as though to convince somebody in the room
that the problem was a normal one. He strained the muscles
of his arms and back, trying to revolve the wheel.

It wouldn't move.

"Oh, no." He swallowed, flinching at the scorch of air in
his throat and chest. This is not good, definitely not good, he
thought. Still, it was a physical problem: a door stuck in its
frame, a steam valve stuck—things to be expected in an old
house. Edith would be back with Fischer in a few moments.
If worse came to worst, he could lie on the floor and wash his
face off with the water while—

He jerked around. The noise again, too definite to be
imagination. It *was* a slithering noise, no doubt of it, like the
stirring of some torpid serpent on the floor. Barrett's face
hardened. Come *on*, he told himself; don't go childish on me
now. He turned around slowly, leaning his back against the
bench and trying to see through the steam. If it *was* some
phenomenon, he had only to keep his wits about him. There
was nothing in the house that could harm him so long as he
didn't panic.

He listened carefully, wincing at the throb of pain in his
thumb. After what seemed to be a minute or more, he heard
the sound again, a liquid, sliding noise. He imagined lava pour-

ing slowly down a coal chute, splattering like smoky gruel into a bin. He shuddered. "*Stop* it," he ordered himself. He was reacting as credulously as Miss Tanner now.

The hose! he thought abruptly. If wet heat could cause the door to warp out of shape, wet coldness might reverse the process. He began to feel around for the hose.

He heard the sound again, ignored it this time. *Psi phenomena abound in realms of credulity.* The sentence flashed across his mind. Precisely, he thought. He gulped in breath without thinking, groaning at the fire of it in his throat and chest. Where the hell was that damned hose, anyway? The tile floor was beginning to hurt both legs now.

He felt the gush of water then and made a sound of gruff satisfaction. He reached for the hose, edging his hand across the floor.

He cried out, jerking back his hand. It had touched what felt like hot slime. Barrett held his hand to his face and looked at it. The light was very dim; he had to squint. He felt his heartbeat catch. There seemed to be a kind of darkish ooze clinging to his palm and fingers. With a gagging sound, he reached down quickly, rubbing his palm on the floor. What in God's name? Melted grout from between the tiles? Some sort of—?

He jerked around so fast it made his neck hurt. He stared into the roiling steam, heartbeat jolting. The sound had started up again, louder now, moving toward him. Barrett drew back unconsciously, trying to see. He rubbed his hand across his eyes without thinking, smearing some of the slime on his face. He made an angry, sickened noise and rubbed it off with his left hand. It had a vaguely familiar smell. Where the hell *is* she? he suddenly thought. For an instant he felt a rush of panic as he imagined her not telling anyone, leaving him imprisoned here because of what had happened between them.

"No," he muttered. That was ludicrous. She'd be back

any moment. He'd better get to the door and wait. He wavered to his feet and moved haltingly away from the sound, visualizing a gigantic jellyfish heaving its transparent, quivering bulk across the floor at him. "That's enough," he muttered, furious at himself. He had to get to the door. He stared into the steam but couldn't see which way the door was. The noise continued—a dragging, soggy noise. Barrett felt a chill of dread lace up his back. He'd best prepare himself. He mustn't panic.

He cried out in shock as his feet sank into hot, thick slime. He started jumping back and slipped, landing on his left elbow and crying out again as jagged pain shot up his arm. He writhed in agony on the floor.

Suddenly he felt the slime push up against his side like heated gelatin. He thrashed away from it, the odor welling over him. It was the smell of rot—*the odor of the tarn!* It's come inside! his mind cried, terrified. He flung himself to his knees. The door; where was the door? He guessed and, shoving to his feet, hobbled clumsily in that direction.

Something blocked his way—something near the floor that had size and bulk and was alive. With a cry of horror, Barrett fell across it. It reared up, shoving him onto his back, hot and jellylike, reeking of stagnation. Barrett screamed as it flopped across his legs. He struck out wildly with his left foot, feeling it sink into muculent slime, then strike what felt like skin the texture of cooked mushroom.

Suddenly it was before his eyes, bulbous, glistening darkly. "No!" he screamed. He kicked at it again, thrashing back across the floor, until his back slammed violently against the door. He felt the ropy form start oozing up his legs adhesively. Shrieks of terror flooded from his lips. The room began to swirl and darken. He could not dislodge the glutinous weight. He felt the hotness of it sucking at his flesh.

Suddenly the door was shoving in behind him, pushing

him directly into the gelatinous form. It struck his face; his screaming mouth was filled with turgid jelly. Coldness washed across his side. He felt hands slip beneath his arms. He thought he heard Edith screaming. Someone started dragging him across the floor. Looking up, he made out Fischer's face above him, pale and indistinct. Just before he lost consciousness, Barrett saw his body. There was nothing on it.

12:47 P.M.

Fischer gulped down coffee, holding the cup with both hands. Once again the couple from Caribou Falls had come and gone, unseen.

He'd been in the theater, searching for the cat, when he'd heard Mrs. Barrett's shouting. Rushing to the entry hall, he'd met her, and she'd told him, frightenedly, that her husband was locked in the steam room.

In there; he'd suddenly remembered Florence's words. Without a word, he'd dashed downstairs, shoved through the swinging doors, and raced along the side of the pool, the rapid padding of his tennis shoes echoing off the walls and ceiling.

He'd heard Barrett's screams before he reached the steam-room door. He'd jarred to a halt and almost turned around when Mrs. Barrett had come running in. He'd been unable to retreat before her look of panic. Turning back, he'd sprinted to the steam-room door and thrown his weight against it, to no avail. Mrs. Barrett had come rushing up behind him, begging him to save her husband, her voice unnatural, shrill.

Grabbing one end of the wooden bench against the wall, he'd dragged it to the steam-room door and rammed it hard against it. Immediately the door had given, and dropping the bench, he'd shoved the door in. Inside, Barrett's screams had cut off suddenly, and Fischer had felt his weight against the door and reached around to grab him in the burning steam and pull him out, forced to strain every muscle because of Barrett's weight. By then Barrett's wife was shaking uncontrollably, her face almost gray. Somehow the two of them had managed to get Barrett upstairs and put him on his bed. Fischer had offered to help put Barrett's pajamas on, but Mrs. Barrett, in a tight, almost inaudible voice, had told him she could do it. He'd left immediately and come downstairs.

He set down the empty cup and covered his eyes with his left hand, mind a jumble of confusions. The unlocked door that had been locked by the time they'd reached the house. The restored electrical system that had failed to work. Florence's inability to enter the chapel. The record playing by itself. The cold breeze on the stairs. The tinkling chandelier. The pounding noises during the séance; Florence suddenly, inexplicably, becoming a physical medium. The figure at the séance; its hysterical warning to them. The poltergeist attack. Mrs. Barrett being led to the tarn in her sleep; removing her pajamas; acting so peculiarly this morning. The bites on Florence's breasts. The body in the wall; the ring. The attack on Florence by the cat. Now the attack on Barrett in the steam room.

He slumped back in the chair. Nothing fitted, he thought. Nothing added up. They were exactly nowhere in their quest. But Florence was being torn apart emotionally and physically. Mrs. Barrett was losing control. Barrett had been violently assaulted twice. And, as for himself—

His mind leaped back, remembering. Faces sprang before him: Grace Lauter's, Dr. Graham's, Professor Rand's, and Fenley's. Grace Lauter working by herself, convinced that she, alone, would solve the mystery of Hell House; not even talking to the rest of them. Him working with Dr. Graham and

Professor Rand, who, in turn, refused to work with Professor
Fenley because he was a Spiritualist and not a "man of science."

Three demoralizing days before it ended. Grace Lauter
with her throat cut by her own hand; Dr. Graham, dead
drunk, wandering outdoors to perish in the woods; Professor
Rand dying of a cerebral hemorrhage after an experience in
the ballroom he'd been unable to describe before he died;
Professor Fenley still in Medview Sanatorium, hopelessly insane. Himself found naked on the front porch, horror-ridden,
old before his time.

"And now I'm back," he muttered in a trembling voice.
"I'm *back.*" He closed his eyes and couldn't stop from shaking.
How? he thought. I'm not afraid to try, but how do I begin?
A rage of bewilderment clamped his muscles suddenly. Jerk-
ing open his eyes, he grabbed his cup and hurled it far across
the room. *It's too damn complicated!* screamed his mind.

1:57 P.M.

She blinked her eyes. Lionel was awake. She put
her hand in his. "Are you all right?"

He nodded, didn't smile. Edith forced control into her
voice. "I'll pack our bags," she said. She waited. Lionel returned her look without expression.

"We'll go today," she said.

"I want you to go."

Edith stared at him. "We'll both go, Lionel."

"Not until I'm finished."

She couldn't believe it, even though she'd anticipated his
response. Her lips twitched, words unspoken stammering in
her mind.

"You go into Caribou Falls," he told her. "I'll join you tomorrow."

"Lionel, I want both of us to go."

"Edith—"

"No. I don't want to hear a word. You can't convince me, anymore, you know what's happening. You would have died down there if Fischer hadn't come. You would have been killed by . . . *what*? By *what*? We have to go before this house destroys us all. *Now*, Lionel. *Now*."

"Listen to me," he said. "I know it's gone beyond the point of endurance for you. It hasn't for me, however. I'm not going to let what happened frighten me away. I've waited twenty years for this. Twenty long years of work and research, and I'm not about to lose it all because of—something in a steam room."

Edith stared at him, a pulsing at her temple.

"It was a shock," he said. "I admit it. It was a terrible shock. I've never experienced anything remotely like it in my life. But it was not the dead. You hear me, Edith? *It was not the dead*."

He closed his eyes. "Please," he said. "Go into Caribou Falls. Fischer will drive you there. I'll join you tomorrow."

He opened his eyes after a while and looked at her. "Tomorrow, Edith. After twenty years, there's only one more day before I prove my theory. *One more day*. I can't retreat when I'm so close. What happened was ghastly, yes, but I can't, I *won't* let it chase me away." His hand closed tightly over hers. "*I'd rather die than leave*."

The room was still. Edith felt her heartbeat like a slow, erratic drumbeat in her chest.

"Tomorrow," she said.

"I swear to you I'll end the reign of terror in this house by then."

She stared at him, feeling lost and helpless. She had no

faith of her own remaining. She could only cling to his. God help us if you're wrong, she thought.

2:21 P.M.

"O Spirit of Immortal Truth," Florence began, "help us, this day, to rise above the doubts and fears of this life. Open our natures to mighty revelations. Give us eyes to see, and ears to hear. Bless us in our efforts to lift the darkness from the world."

The bathroom light cast dim illumination on the place where they sat. Florence sat in the chair beside the table, eyes closed, hands on her lap, knees and feet pressed tightly together. Fischer had pulled the other chair across the floor and sat facing her at a distance of four feet.

"The sweetest expression of spiritual life is service," Florence was saying. "We offer ourselves for the service of the spirits. May they find us ready, and may they, so that naught may impede our free expression, commune with us this day and reveal their light to us. Most of all, may they impart to us the power to communicate with that tortured soul who still hovers in this place, unsanctified, imprisoned: Daniel Belasco." She raised her face. "Attend us, ministering angels. Help us in our effort to lift the burden from this soul. All this we ask in the name of the Eternal and Most Everlasting Spirit. Amen."

There was momentary silence. Fischer heard the crackling noise his throat made as he swallowed. Then Florence began to sing: " 'Sweet souls around us, watch us still. Press nearer to our side. Into our thoughts, into our prayers, with gentle helpings glide.' "

When the song was ended, Florence began to take in deep breaths, drawing air into her lungs convulsively through clenched teeth as she rubbed both hands over her body. Soon her month fell open, and her head began to loll back. The heavy breathing continued. Florence slouched down in the chair, head rolling from side to side. At last she was still.

Minutes passed. Fischer began to shiver. Coldness was starting to gather between them, rising slowly like ice water, until he felt as though he were submerged to the waist in it.

He twitched as faint spots of light began to appear in front of Florence. *Focuses of condensation*; the phrase drifted across his mind. He stared at the spots as they grew in size and number, hovering in the air in front of Florence like a galaxy of pale, miniature suns. His legs felt almost numb now. Soon, he thought.

His fingers dug into the chair arms as teleplasm started oozing from the medium's nostrils. The viscous filaments resembled twin gray serpents gliding downward from her nose. As Fischer watched in dry-mouthed silence, they joined to form a heavier coil, which started to unravel, then began to rise and cover Florence's face. Fischer lowered his eyes. He heard a sound like rustling paper, closed his eyes.

The smell of ozone penetrated his nostrils like the odor of a badly chlorinated swimming pool. Compelled, he opened his eyes and looked up, wincing. The teleplasm had covered Florence's head, hanging over it like a wet, filmy sack. As he stared at it, he saw it being shaped as though by some invisible sculptor, the eye pits pressed in, a ridge of nose appearing, nostrils, ears, a line of mouth. In less than a minute, it was complete; the face of a young man, dark-haired, handsome, grave in its expression.

Fischer cleared his throat. His heartbeat felt unreal. "Have you a voice?" he asked.

There was a labored, gurgling noise like the sound of a death rattle. Fischer felt his skin crawl. After half a minute, the sound stopped, and there was silence again.

"Can you speak now?" Fischer asked.

"I can." The voice was undeniably masculine.

Fischer hesitated, then drew in a quick breath. "Who are you?"

"Daniel Belasco." The lips of the face did not move, but the voice was coming from the pallid features of the young man.

"Was it your body we found behind the wall of the wine cellar this morning?"

"It was."

"We gave you proper services outside. Why are you still here?"

"I cannot leave."

"Why?"

There was no answer.

"Why?"

No answer. Fischer clutched his hands together on his lap. "Did you have anything to do with the attack on Doctor Barrett in the steam room?"

"No."

"Who did it, then?"

There was no answer.

"Did you attack Doctor Barrett in the dining hall last night?" Fischer asked.

"I did not."

"Who did?"

Silence.

"Did you bite Miss Tanner this morning?"

"I did not."

"Who did?"

Silence.

"Did you possess the cat to attack her?"

"I did not."

"Who did, then?"

Silence.

"Who did, then?" Fischer persisted. "Who attacked Doctor Barrett? Who bit Miss Tanner? Who possessed the cat?"

Silence.

"Who?" demanded Fischer.

"Cannot say."

"Why not?"

"Cannot."

"Why?"

Silence.

"You have to tell me. Who attacked Doctor Barrett in the dining hall and steam room? Who bit Miss Tanner? Who possessed the cat?"

He heard a quickening of breath.

"Who?" he demanded.

"Cannot—"

"You have to tell me."

The voice began to plead. "Cannot—"

"Who?" asked Fischer.

"Cannot say—"

"Who?"

"Please—"

"Who?"

He heard something like a sob.

"Him," said the voice.

"Who?"

"Him."

"*Who?*"

"Him. Him!"

"*Who?*"

"*Him!*" cried the voice. "The Giant! Him! Father, Father!"

Fischer sat in rigid silence as the face lost form, the tele-

plasm rippling. Suddenly it began to steam back into Florence's nostrils. As it vanished, Fischer heard her moan with
pain. In less than seven seconds it was gone.

He sat immobile for almost a minute before standing. He
felt numb as he walked into the bathroom, ran some water
into a glass, and carried it back into the bedroom, standing
motionless beside the chair until she opened her eyes.

After she had drunk the water in one long swallow, he
moved to the wall switch and turned on the hanging lamp
beside her bed.

He sank down heavily on the chair across from hers.

"Did he come through?" she asked.

As he told her what had happened, her expression tensed
to one of deep excitement.

"*Belasco,*" she said. "Of course. Of *course*. We should
have realized it."

Fischer did not respond.

"Daniel would never have hurt me. He would never have
hurt Doctor Barrett. I *knew* it couldn't have been him, despite
the evidence; it simply didn't *feel* right. He's as much a victim
of the house as anyone." She looked at Fischer's unconvinced
expression. "Don't you see?" she said. "*He's being kept here
by his father.*"

Fischer regarded her in silence, wanting to believe what
she was saying but afraid to commit his mind.

"Don't you *see?*" she asked him eagerly. "They're warring
together, Daniel trying to escape from Hell House, his father
doing everything he can to prevent it by trying to turn me
against Daniel, trying to make me believe that Daniel means
me harm, when he doesn't. When all he wants is—"

She stopped so quickly that Fischer's eyes narrowed.
"Wants *what?*" he asked.

"My help."

"That's not what you were going to say."

"Yes, it was. I'm the only one who *can* help. I'm the only one he trusts. Don't you see?"

Fischer eyed her guardedly. "I hope I do," he said.

3:47 P.M.

Edith sat up and slid her legs across the mattress edge. Reaching out, she picked up Lionel's watch from the table and raised its lid. Nearly four o'clock. How could he possibly get his machine ready by tomorrow?

She stared at him as he slept, wondering if he still believed everything he said. Somehow, she had the uncomfortable feeling that he was no longer as confident as he claimed. Not that he would ever show it, not even to her. When it came to his work, he was a man of unrelenting pride, always had been.

Standing abruptly, Edith moved to the cabinet and opened the door. All right, both of them had warned her. Nothing had happened, had it? The brandy had relaxed her, nothing more. If she was going to stay in this house until tomorrow, she was damned well going to take a few steps to make that stay endurable.

She carried the decanter and one of the silver cups to the table. Setting down the cup, she pulled out the decanter top and poured the cup full of brandy. Picking up the cup, she drank its contents with a swallow. She threw her head back, eyes closed, mouth open wide, sucking at the air as brandy scalded down her throat. It was like pouring hot syrup into her chest and stomach. Heat pulsed outward, radiating through her veins.

She poured herself another cupful, took a sip of it, and eased herself onto the table, pushing aside the box with Lionel's manuscript in it. She took another sip of brandy, then swallowed the entire cupful, head laid back again, eyes closed, a look of sensual enjoyment on her face.

She thought about being in the steam room with Lionel, trying not to face the nagging qualm that, beyond a certain point, she'd been infuriated at his impotence, as if, somehow, it were his fault and not that of the polio. She tightened, thinking that the real reason he wanted her to go to Caribou Falls was that he didn't want to be annoyed by her needs; that he wanted to concentrate on his machine.

She blinked. That was a terrible thing to think of Lionel. If he'd been able to, he would have made love to her.

Would he? her mind demanded. Or did he really care at all whether they ever had sex?

With an impulsive movement, she reached around for the decanter, knocking the box off the table, spilling pages of the manuscript across the rug. She started to get up, then, with a frown, ignored it. Let it lie, she thought. I'll get it later. She closed her eyes, emptying another cupful of brandy into her mouth and swallowing it.

She slipped off the table, almost fell. I'm *drunk*, she thought. A momentary pang of guilt assailed her. Mom was right, I am like him, she thought. She fought it off. I'm *not!* she told her unseen mother; I'm a good girl. "*Hell*—" She scowled. I'm not a girl at all, I'm a woman. With desires. He should know that. He's not *that* old. Or that impotent. It was his damned religious mother, not the polio. It was—

She frowned away the thought, weaving across the bedroom toward the cabinet. Her limbs felt warm and silky, and there was a lovely numbness in her head. They were wrong; getting drunk was the only answer. She thought about the cabinet of liquor in the kitchen. Maybe she'd get a bottle of bourbon from it—maybe two bottles. Maybe she'd just drink herself insensible until tomorrow came.

She removed the hollowed book so quickly that it slipped

from her fingers and thudded on the rug, the photographs scattering. She sank to her knees and started looking at them one by one. She licked her upper lip unconsciously. She stared at a photograph of the two women lying on the great hall table, performing mutual cunnilingus. The room seemed to get hotter and hotter.

Abruptly she flung away the photograph as though it was burning her fingers. *"No,"* she muttered frightenedly. She started, looking back toward Lionel as he stirred, then pushed clumsily to her feet and looked around the bedroom like a cornered animal.

She walked across the room quickly. Opening the door, she moved into the hall and closed the door, flinching at the noise; she'd meant to be more quiet. Shaking her head to clear it, she walked to Fischer's room.

He wasn't there. Edith stared into his room and wondered what to do. Closing the door, she turned and started back along the hallway, drifting to her left until she reached the banister rail. She held on to it for balance as she headed for the staircase. For some strange reason, the house did not seem frightening to her. Further proof that alcohol was just the thing, she thought.

She had the sensation of floating down the staircase. Vaguely she recalled some film about the South she'd seen at a revival. All she could remember clearly was some woman in hoop skirts gliding down the stairs as though she were descending on a track. She felt the same way. She wondered why she felt so confident.

A glimmer, faint, too fleeting to be captured. Edith blinked and hesitated. Nothing. She continued down the stairs. He's in the great hall, she decided. He was always where the coffee was. She couldn't recall ever seeing him eat. No wonder he was so thin.

As she crossed the entry hall, she heard a sound of splintering wood. Again she stopped. She hesitated, then moved forward once again. Of course, she thought. She smiled. She'd never felt so fuzzy in her life. She closed her eyes. I'm floating, said her mind. Father and daughter, drunks forever.

She stopped in the archway and leaned against it dizzily. She blinked her eyes, refocusing with effort. Fischer had his back to her. He was using the crowbar to pry apart the crate. That's sweet, she thought.

She started as Fischer spun around, the crowbar raised as though to strike at some attacker. He whirled so quickly that the cigarette between his lips arced to the floor.

"*Kamerad,*" she said. She raised her arms as though surrendering.

Fischer stared at her without a sound. She saw his chest rise and fall with agitated breath. "Are you angry?" she began to say.

He cut her off. "What the hell are you doing here?"

"Nothing." She pushed off from the archway and started toward him weavingly.

"Are you *drunk?*" He sounded stunned.

"I've had a few drinks, if that's any of your business."

Fischer dumped the crowbar on the table, moving toward her. "Lionel will be pleased that you—" She gestured airily toward the machine.

Fischer reached her, took her arm. "Come on."

She pulled away from him. "Come on, yourself." She staggered slightly, then regained her balance, turning toward the machine.

"Mrs. Barrett—"

"Edith."

Fischer took her arm again. "Come *on.* You shouldn't leave your husband."

"He's all right. He's sleeping."

Fischer tried to turn her, but she wouldn't do it. Snickering, she pulled away from him again. "For Christ's sake!" he snapped.

A teasing smile drew back her lips. "No, not for his sake." Fischer looked at her confusedly.

As she started toward the table, the room was nebulous around her, and she had the vague impression it was filled with people standing just beyond the limits of her vision. That's imagination, said her mind. All there is in here is mindless energy.

She reached the table and rubbed a finger on its surface. Fischer rejoined her. "You've got to go upstairs."

"No, I don't." She took hold of his right hand. Fischer pulled it away. Edith smiled and rubbed her finger on the table again. "This is where they met," she said.

"Who?"

"Les Aphrodites. Here. Around this table."

Fischer took her arm again. Edith jerked it in against herself so that his hand was pinned against her breast. "Here. Around this table," she repeated.

"You don't know what you're saying." Fischer pulled his hand away.

"I know exactly what I'm saying. Mr. Fischer." Edith snickered. "Mr. B. F. Fischer."

"Edith—"

He tightened as she pushed against him, sliding her arms around him. "Don't you like me at all?" she asked. "I know I'm not as beautiful as Florence, but I—"

"Edith, it's the house. It's making you—"

"*The house is doing nothing,*" she broke in. "*I'm* doing it."

He tried to pull away her arms. She pressed against him harder. "Are you impotent too?" she teased.

Fischer wrenched her arms loose, pushing her away. "Wake up!" he shouted.

Fury burst inside her. "Don't tell *me* to wake up! *You*

wake up!—you sexless bastard." Edith stumbled back against the table, wriggled up on top of it, and yanked her skirt with clawing fingers. "What's the matter, little man?" she jeered. "Never had a woman?" Grabbing at her sweater front, she jerked it open, popping buttons. Dragging aside the edges, she undid the front hook of her bra and, clutching at her breasts with palsied fingers, held them up, a look of furious derision on her face. "What's the *matter*, little man?" she ranted. "Never had a tit before? *Try* it! It's delicious!"

Sliding off the table, she advanced on Fischer, fingers gouging at her breasts. "Suck them," she said, her voice trembling with hatred. Her face convulsed with sudden fury. "Suck them, you fairy bastard, or I'll get myself a woman who will!"

His head jerked sideways. Edith scanned the movement, and a sudden weight crashed down on her.

Lionel was standing in the archway.

A wave of darkness billowed up at her. Her legs gave way; she started falling. Fischer leaped to catch her. "No!" she screamed. She twisted to the left and fell against a marble statue on a pedestal. She caught at it; the cold stone pressed against her breasts. It seemed as though the face was leering at her Edith cried out as the weight of it fell backward from her grasp and shattered on the floor. She landed on her knees and toppled forward.

Darkness swallowed her.

4:27 P.M.

Somewhere there was music playing, slowly, tenderly; a waltz. She was dancing to the music, gliding through a kind of mist. Was she in the ballroom? She could not be sure. Her partner's face was indistinct, yet she felt certain it was Daniel's. She could feel his arm around her and his left hand holding out her right. It was warm. There was a scent of flowers in the air; roses, she decided. A summer dance. A small string orchestra performing. Florence danced in languorous circles with her partner.

"Are you happy?" he asked.

"Yes," she murmured. "Very."

Was she on a set? Was that it? Was she making a film? She tried to recall but couldn't. Still, how could it be a film? It was all too real; no camera, no banks of lights, no fourth wall missing and the crew in sight, the sound man at his board. No, it was a real ballroom. Florence tried again to see her partner's face, but couldn't focus her eyes. "Daniel?" she murmured.

"My dear?"

"It *is* you," Florence said.

She saw him then, his grave face very handsome, very gentle. His arm drew tight around her. "I love you," he said.

"And I love you."

"You'll never leave me? Always be beside me?"

"Yes, my darling, always; always."

Florence closed her eyes. The music quickened, and she felt herself being swept around the ballroom floor. She heard the rustling of a hundred skirts, the ballroom filled with dancers, lovers. Florence smiled. And she loved, too; loved Daniel. Daniel held her safely as they danced. She scarcely felt her feet; she seemed to float.

She felt a scented breeze across her face and smiled again. He'd danced her out onto the wide veranda. Overhead, the sky was filled with stars, like diamond fragments sprinkled on black velvet; she didn't have to look to know that they were there. The moon was full, pale silver, glowing. It shed soft radiance on the garden just beyond. She didn't have to look; she knew. Had she been drinking wine? She felt intoxicated. No; it was intoxication of the spirit. It was joy and love, sweet

music playing in the distance as she waltzed with her beloved
Daniel, around, around, dancing slowly toward—

He shouted. "No!"

Florence gasped in shock, all senses flooded. Daniel stood
before her in the mist, white-faced, frightened, gesturing for
her to stop. Icy water numbed her feet and ankles, cold wind
scored her face, the smell of rot assailed her nostrils; crying
out, she staggered back and fell. Something seemed to rush
away behind her. Florence thrashed around and caught a momentary view of someone very tall and dressed in black vanishing into the mist.

She shuddered as the freezing air sliced deep into her
flesh. She lay beside the tarn.

She had been walking into it.

With a sound of sickened dread, she pushed up, started
running for the house. Her shoes were wet, the bottoms of
her stockings. Shivering, she dashed along the gravel path. The
blind face of the house loomed darkly from the mist. She ran
across the gravel, up the steps. The doorway yawned. She ran
inside and slammed the door, falling back against it.

She was shaking from the cold, from fright. She couldn't
stop herself. *She'd almost walked into the tarn.* The knowledge
horrified her.

She started as a figure hurried down the hallway from the
kitchen. It was Fischer, with a glass in his hand. Seeing her,
he stopped a moment, then advanced again. "What happened?" he asked.

"Is that whiskey?"

Fischer nodded.

"Let me have some."

He handed her the glass, and Florence drank, choking as
the liquor scalded down her throat. She handed back the glass.

"What happened?" Fischer asked.

"He tried to kill me."

"Who?"

"*Belasco*," she said. She clutched at his arm. "I *saw* him, Ben. I actually caught a glimpse of him as he left me by the tarn."

She told him what had happened, how Belasco had made her think she was dancing in the ballroom with Daniel, while he'd led her to the tarn to drown her. How Daniel had warned her at the moment she was going in.

"How did Belasco get control of you?" he asked.

"I must have dozed off. I was tired after sitting, after everything that's happened today."

Fischer looked ill. "If he can get you in your sleep now—"

"*No.*" She shook her head. "He won't again. I'm warned now. I'll retain my strength." She shivered. "Can we go in by the fire?"

When they were sitting in front of the fire, her shoes and stockings off, her feet propped on a stool, a new log crackling on the fire, Florence said, "I think I know the secret of Hell House, Ben."

Fischer didn't speak for almost half a minute. "Do you?" he asked then.

"It's Belasco."

"How?"

"He safeguards the haunting of his house by reinforcing it," she said. "By acting as a hidden aide for every other haunting force."

Fischer did not respond, but she could tell from the sudden flare of interest in his eyes that she had gotten through to him. He sat up slowly, as though uncoiling, his eyes fixed on hers.

"Think of it, Ben," she said. "*Controlled multiple haunting.* Something absolutely unique in haunted houses: a surviving will so powerful that he can use that power to dominate every other surviving personality in the house."

"You think the others are aware of it?" he asked.

"I don't know about the others. All I know is that his son is. If he weren't, he couldn't have saved my life.

"It all fits, Ben," she said. "It's been Belasco from the start. He's the one who's kept me from the chapel. He's the one who tried to keep me from discovering Daniel's body last night. He's the one who made it seem that Daniel had bitten me, the one who possessed the cat. He's the one who caused the poltergeist attack on Doctor Barrett, trying to turn us against each other. He's the one who's keeping Daniel's soul imprisoned here.

"Think of what fantastic power he possesses, Ben. To actually be capable of keeping another's spirit from progression, *despite* a consecrated burial. Maybe it's because Daniel is his son, but, even so, it's incredible."

She leaned back in her chair, looking at the flames. "He's like a general with his army. Never entering the battle, but always controlling it."

"How can he be hurt, then? Generals don't get killed in war."

"We'll hurt him by decreasing the size of his army until he has no one left, until he has to fight his war alone." She looked at him with challenge in her eyes. "A general without an army is nothing."

"But we have only till Sunday."

Florence shook her head. "I'm staying here until the job is done," she said.

She closed the door and moved immediately to her bed. Kneeling beside it, she offered up a prayer of gratitude for the enlightenment which had been given her, a prayer of request for strength to deal with what she had discovered.

When the prayers were ended, she rose and moved into

the bathroom to cleanse her ankles and feet; there was still a
residue of odor from the tarn on them. As she washed and
dried them, she thought about the massive project which lay
ahead: to release the earthbound spirits from this house,
against the will of Emeric Belasco. It almost seemed too much
to accomplish.

"But I will," she said aloud, as though Belasco listened.
She'd have to be alert, though. What Ben had said was true.
"You've been fooled before," he'd said. "Make sure you aren't
fooled again."

"I'll be careful," she'd replied.

She would. She recognized the sense in what he'd said.
How thoroughly she had been fooled last night into believing
that, perhaps, she'd been responsible for the poltergeist attack
on Dr. Barrett. How thoroughly she had been fooled this
morning into thinking that Daniel was responsible for the bites
and for the cat's attack on her. She must not allow herself to
be fooled again. Daniel had not been responsible for any of
those things. He was tormented, not tormentor.

Florence closed her eyes, hands clasped in front of her.
Daniel, listen now, she whispered in her mind. I thank you,
with all my heart, for saving my life. But don't you see what
it means? If you can thwart your father's will in that way, you
can also thwart it by departing from this house. You don't
have to stay here any longer. You're free to go if only you
believe. Your father has no power to hold you prisoner. Ask
for the help of those beyond, and it will come to you. You
can leave this house. You *can!*

Florence opened her eyes abruptly. Moving to the Spanish
table, she opened her purse. She took out a pad and pencil,
laid the pad on the table, picked up the pencil, and held its
point against the paper. Instantly it started moving. She closed
her eyes and felt it writing by itself, tugging her hand this way

and that. In seconds it stopped, and the feeling of control drained from her hand. She looked at the pad.

"No!" She tore the top sheet off and crumpled it into a ball, flinging it to the floor, "No, Daniel! No!"

She stood beside the table, trembling, staring at the paper, the words engraved on her mind.

One way only.

6:11 P.M.

Fischer stood at the edge of the tarn, shining his flashlight at the turbid surface of the water. Twice now, he was thinking. Edith first, then Florence. He moved the cone of light across the water, grimacing at the stench which hovered over it. Once when he'd been working in a hospital, an old man had died of gangrenous wounds on his back. The smell of his room had been like this.

He looked around. Footsteps were approaching through the mist. Abruptly he switched off his flashlight and turned. Who was it? Florence? Surely she would not be coming back after what had happened. Barrett or his wife? He couldn't believe that they'd come out here either. Who, then? Fischer tensed as the footsteps drew closer. He could not determine their origin in the mist. He waited, rigid, heartbeat thudding.

They were on him suddenly. Seeing the glow of a lantern, he flicked on his flashlight. There was a strangled gasp. Fischer stared with blank confusion at the two gaunt faces in his light.

"Who's that?" the old man asked. His voice was trembling.

Fischer caught his breath and lowered the beam of light. "I'm sorry," he said. "I'm one of the four."

The old woman released a breath which sounded like a groan. "Lord," she muttered.

"I'm sorry, I was startled, too," Fischer apologized, "I didn't realize what time it was."

"You scared the livin' breath from us," the old man said resentfully.

"Sorry." Fischer turned away.

The couple mumbled indistinctly as they trailed him to the house. Fischer held the door for them, then followed as they hurried across the entry hall, looking around uneasily. They were wearing heavy overcoats, the woman a woolen scarf on her head, the man a battered gray fedora.

"How are things in the world?" asked Fischer.

"Mmm," the man responded. The old woman made a sound of disapproval.

"No matter," Fischer said. "We have our own world here."

He moved behind them into the great hall, observing as they set the covered dishes on the table. He saw them looking at Barrett's machine, exchanging glances. Quickly they gathered up the lunch things and started toward the entry hall. Fischer watched their departure, fighting an urge to yell "Boo!" and see what would happen. If they thought a flashlight beam in the face was frightening, what would they think of what had happened in the house since Monday?

"Thank you!" he called as they moved beneath the archway. The old man grunted sourly, and he saw them exchange another look.

When the front door had shut, Fischer moved to the table and lifted the covers of the trays. Lamb chops, peas and carrots, potatoes, biscuits, pie, and coffee. *A Meal Fit for a King*, he thought. His smile was dour. Or was it *The Last Supper*?

Removing his pea coat, he tossed it onto a chair, setting the flashlight on top of it. He forked a lamb chop onto a plate, added a spoonful of carrots and peas, poured himself a cup of coffee. Community meals seem to have gone by the board since last night, he thought. He sat at the table and drank some coffee, then began to eat. He'd bring some food to Florence in a while.

He began to think of what she'd said. He'd been thinking of it constantly, trying to find loopholes in it. So far he'd been unable to; it made sense, there was no escaping it.

This time Florence was on the right track.

It was a strange, not altogether satisfying certainty he felt. They'd always known that Belasco was here—he and Florence had, at any rate—but the knowledge had been an unexplored one, at least on his part. That they would come to terms with Belasco himself had never really occurred to him. True, he had contacted him in 1940, but the juncture had been evanescent, a nonconnective tissue in the body of Hell House.

This was more than that. This was integral. He'd tried to pick it apart a dozen different ways without success. It was too logical. By using these anomalous means, Belasco could act in any area without his presence ever being known. He could create an all but incomprehensible tapestry of effects by manipulating every entity within the house, shifting from one to the other, always in the background—as Florence had said, a general with his army.

He thought about the record suddenly. It had been no coincidence. It had been Belasco greeting them upon their entrance into his home—his battlefield. He heard the eerie, mocking voice inside his mind again. *Welcome to my house. I'm delighted you could come.*

Fischer turned to see Barrett limping across the room, looking pale and solemn. He wondered if the older man were going to speak to him. He'd said nothing earlier, obviously suffering humiliation on humiliation by the fact that he'd been unable to carry Edith upstairs himself.

He waited. Barrett stopped and looked at his machine with a confused expression. He looked at Fischer then. "Did you do that?" he asked, his voice subdued.

Fischer nodded.

The faintest tremor raised the ends of Barrett's mouth. "Thank you," he murmured.

"You're welcome."

Barrett limped to the table and began to put food on two plates, using his left hand. Fischer glanced at his right and saw how awkwardly the thumb was held.

"I haven't thanked you for what you did this afternoon," Barrett said. "In the steam room," he added quickly.

"Doctor?"

Barrett looked up.

"What happened in here before—"

"I'd rather not discuss it, if you don't mind."

Fischer felt obliged to speak. "I'm only trying to help."

"I appreciate that, but—"

"Doctor," Fischer interrupted, "something in this house is working on your wife. What happened before—"

"Mr. Fischer—"

"—was not her doing."

"If you don't mind, Mr. Fischer—"

"Doctor Barrett, this is life and death I'm talking about. Did you know she almost walked into the tarn last night?"

Barrett started, looking shocked. "When?" he demanded.

"Near midnight. You were asleep." Fischer paused for emphasis. "So was she."

"*She walked in her sleep?*" Barrett looked appalled.

"If I hadn't seen her go outside—"

"You should have told me sooner."

"*She* should have told you," Fischer said. "The fact that she didn't is—" He broke off at the look of offense on Barrett's face. "Doctor, I don't know what you think is going on in this house, but—"

"What I think is going on is irrelevant to this conversation, Mr. Fischer," Barrett said stiffly.

"*Irrelevant?*" Fischer looked amazed. "What the hell do you mean, irrelevant? Whatever's going on is getting to your wife. It's gotten to Florence, and it's gotten to you. Or maybe you haven't noticed."

Barrett regarded him in silence, his expression hard. "I've noticed a number of things, Mr. Fischer," he finally said. "One of which is that Mr. Deutsch is wasting approximately a third of his money."

Picking up the plates of food and two forks, he turned away.

For a long time after he'd gone, Fischer sat without moving, staring across the great hall.

"Like hell," he muttered then. What in the name of God did Barrett expect him to do?—commit progressive suicide like Florence? If he wasn't handling things the way they should be handled, how come he was the only one unharmed so far?

The truth crashed over him so violently it made him catch his breath. "*No,*" he muttered angrily. It wasn't true. He knew what he was doing. Of the three of them, he was the only one who—

The defensive thought broke off in fragments. Fischer felt a wave of nausea rush through him. Barrett was right. Florence was right.

Those thirty years of waiting had been nothing but delusion.

Standing with a muffled curse, he strode to the fireplace. No, it was impossible. He couldn't deceive himself so completely. He struggled to remember what he'd done since Monday. He'd known the door would be locked, hadn't he? His

mind rejected that. All right, he'd rescued Edith. Only because you couldn't sleep and happened to be downstairs, came
the answer. What about saving Barrett, then? *Nothing*, said his
mind. He'd been available, that was all—and even then he
might have fled if it hadn't been for Mrs. Barrett's presence.
What was left? He'd pulled the planking off the crate. Wonderful, he thought, in sudden rage. Deutsch hired himself a
hundred-thousand-dollar handyman!

"Christ," he muttered. He shouted, "*Christ!*" He'd been
the most powerful physical medium in the United States in
1940—and at fifteen. *Fifteen!* Now, at forty-five, he was a goddamned, self-deluding parasite, malingering his way through
the week in order to collect a hundred thousand dollars. Him!
The one who should be doing the most!

He paced back and forth in front of the fireplace. The
feeling he had was almost unendurable, compounded of
shame and guilt and fury. He'd never felt so meaningless. To
walk around in Hell House like a turtle with its head pulled
in, a blind shell seeing nothing, knowing nothing, doing nothing, waiting for the others to accomplish the work he should
be accomplishing. He'd wanted to come back here, hadn't he?
Well, he was back! Something—God only knew what—had
seen fit to give him a second chance.

Was he going to let it pass him by, untouched?

Fischer stopped and looked around the great hall with a
furious expression. Who the hell is Belasco? he thought. Who
the hell are any of the goddamned dead who glut this house
like maggots on a corpse? Was he going to let them terrify
him to his dying day? They hadn't been able to kill him in
1940, had they? He'd been a child, a thoughtless, over-
confident fool—and even so, they'd been unable to destroy
him. Grace Lauter they'd destroyed—one of the most respected mental mediums of the day. Dr. Graham they'd destroyed—a hardheaded, dauntless physician. Professor Rand

they'd destroyed—one of the nation's most noted chemistry teachers, head of his department at Hale University. Professor Fenley they'd destroyed—a shrewd, experienced Spiritualist who had survived a hundred psychic pitfalls.

Only he had lived and kept his sanity—a credulous boy of fifteen. Despite the fact that he had virtually begged to be annihilated, the house had been able to do no more than eject him, leaving him on its porch to die of exposure. It had not been able to kill him. Why had he never thought of it in just that way before? Despite the perfect opportunity, *it had not been able to kill him.*

Fischer moved to one of the armchairs and sat down hurriedly. Closing his eyes, he began to draw in deep breaths, starting to unlock the gates of consciousness before he had a chance to change his mind. Confidence suffused his mind and body. He was not a boy now, but a thinking man; not so blindly confident that he would make himself a vulnerable prey. He would open up with care, stage by stage, not allowing himself to be overwhelmed by impressions, as Florence did. Slowly, carefully, monitoring each step of the way with his adult intelligence, trusting only to himself, not allowing others to control his perception in any way.

He stopped his heavy breathing, waited, tense, alert. Nothing yet. A flatness and a vacancy about him. He waited longer, antennae feeling at the atmosphere. There was nothing. He drew in further breath, opening the gates a little wider, stopped again, and waited.

Nothing. Fischer felt a flicker of involuntary dread cross his mind. *Had he waited too long?* Had his power atrophied? His lips pressed hard together, whitening. *No.* He still possessed it. He breathed in deeply, inspiring further cognizance into his mind. He felt a tingling in his fingertips, the sensation of a spider web collecting on his face, his solar plexus drawing inward. He had not done this in years; too long. He had forgotten how it felt, that surging growth of awareness, all his senses widening in spectrum. Every sound was heard exaggeratedly: the crackling of the fire, the infinitesimal creaking of his chair, the sound of his breath soughing in and out. The smell of the house became intense. The texture of his clothes felt rough against his skin. He could feel the delicate waft of heat from the fire.

He frowned. But nothing else. What was happening? It made no sense to him. This house had to be gorged with impressions. The moment he'd walked in on Monday he'd sensed their presence like some cloud of influences, always ready to attack, take advantage of the slightest flaw, the least misstep in judgment.

It struck him suddenly. *Misstep in judgment!*

Instantly he started pulling back. But, already; something dark and vast was hurtling at him, something with discernment, something violent that meant to pounce on him and crush him. Fischer gasped and pressed back hard against the chair, recoiling his awareness desperately.

He was not in time. Before he could protect himself, the force swept over him, entering his system through the chink still open in his armor. He cried out loudly as it wrenched into his vitals, twisting, clawing, threatening to disembowel him, slice his brain to shreds. His eyes leaped open, staring, horror-stricken. Doubling over, he clapped both hands across his stomach. Something slammed against his back, his head, hurling him out of the chair. He crashed against a table edge, was flung back with a strangling gasp. The room began to spin around, its atmosphere a whirlpool of barbaric force. Fischer crumpled to his knees, arms crossed, trying to shut out the savage power. It tried to rip his arms apart. He fought it, teeth clenched, face a stonelike mask of agonized resistance, gurgling noises in his throat. You won't! he thought. You won't! You *won't!*

The power vanished suddenly, sucked back into the air. Fischer tottered on his knees, across his face the dazed expression of a man who'd just been bayoneted in the stomach. He tried to hold himself erect but couldn't. With a choking noise, he fell, landing on his side and drawing up his legs, bending forward at the neck until he had contracted to a fetal pose, eyes closed, body shivering uncontrollably. He felt the rug against his cheek. Nearby, he heard the pop and crackle of the fire. And it seemed as though someone were standing over him, someone who regarded him with cold, sadistic pleasure, gloating at the sight of his ravaged form, the helpless dissolution of his will.

And wondering, idly, casually, just how and when to finish him off.

6:27 P.M.

Barrett stood beside the bed, looking at Edith, wondering whether to wake her or not. The food was getting cold; but was it food she needed, or rest?

He moved to his own bed and sat with a groan. Crossing his left leg over his right, he touched the burn gingerly. He couldn't use his injured thumb. The cut should have been sutured. God knew how infected it was getting. He was afraid to remove the bandage and look.

He didn't see how he was going to work on the machine tonight. The least exertion brought on pain in his leg and lower back; just walking downstairs and up had been a strain. Grimacing, he eased off his left shoe. His feet were swelling too. He had to end it by tomorrow. He wasn't sure he could last beyond then.

The realization drained his waning confidence even further.

• • •

Noises had awakened him—the sound of something thumping on the rug. Slowly he had surfaced from a leaden sleep, thinking that he heard a door shut somewhere.

When he'd opened his eyes, Edith was gone.

For several groggy moments he had thought she was in the bathroom. Then, on the periphery of vision, he'd caught sight of something on the floor, and sat up, staring at the manuscript pages scattered across the rug. His gaze had shifted to the area beside the cabinet. Photographs were lying strewn about; a book had fallen.

Alarm had started rising in him then. Grabbing his cane, he'd stood, his attention caught by the brandy decanter on the table, the silver cup. Crossing to the cabinet, he'd looked down at the photographs, tensing as he saw what they were.

"Edith?" He'd turned toward the bathroom. "Edith, are you in there?" He'd limped to the bathroom door and knocked. "Edith?"

There'd been no reply. He'd waited several moments before turning the knob; the door was unlocked.

She was gone.

He'd turned in dismay, hobbling to the door as quickly as he could, trying not to panic; but everything about the situation was ominous: his manuscript thrown to the floor, those photographs, the brandy decanter back on the table, and on top of all that, Edith's absence.

He'd hurried into the corridor and moved to Florence Tanner's room. Knocking, he'd waited for several seconds, then knocked again. When there'd been no reply, he'd opened the door, to see Miss Tanner heavily asleep on her bed. He'd backed out, shut the door, and moved to Fischer's room.

There'd been no one there, and he'd begun to panic then. He'd moved across the corridor and looked into the entry hall below, thinking he heard voices. Frowning, he'd limped to the stairs and started to descend as quickly as he could, teeth set against the pain in his leg. He'd *told* her not to do this! What was the matter with her?

He'd heard her voice as he crossed the entry hall, her tone unnatural as she said, "It's delicious!" With renewed alarm, he'd hastened his steps.

Then he'd reached the archway and was frozen there, staring into the great hall with a stunned expression, watching Edith, sweater open, bra unhooked, advancing on Fischer, breasts in her hands, ordering him to—

Barrett closed his eyes and pressed a hand across them. He'd never heard such language from her in their married life, never seen a hint of such behavior, not even to himself, much less to any other man. That she was probably repressed, he'd always known; their sex life had been necessarily constrained. But this—

He dropped his hand and looked at her again. The pain was returning, the distrust, the anger, the desire for retaliation of some kind. He struggled against it. He wanted to believe that the house had done it all to her, but he could not expunge the nagging doubt that somewhere deep within her lay the real cause of what had happened. Which, of course, explained his sudden animosity toward Fischer's words, he recognized.

He stood and crossed to her. They had to talk; he couldn't stand this doubting any longer. Reaching down, he touched her shoulder.

She awakened with a gasp, eyes flung open, legs retracting suddenly. Barrett tried to smile but couldn't. "I've brought your supper," he said.

"Supper." She spoke the word as though she'd never heard it in her life.

He nodded once. "Why don't you wash up?"

Edith looked around the room. Was she wondering where

he'd put the photographs? he thought. He withdrew as she sat up, looking down at herself. He'd refastened her bra and closed her sweater with what buttons remained. Her right hand fluttered up the front of her sweater; then she stood and crossed to the bathroom.

Barrett limped to the octagonal table, picked up the boxed manuscript, and placed it on the library table against the wall. With great effort he pulled the chair beside her bed over to the octagonal table and sat down. He eyed the lamb chops and vegetables on his plate and sighed. He should never have brought her to this house. It had been a dreadful mistake.

He turned as the bathroom door opened. Edith, her face washed and hair combed, walked over to the table and sat. She did not pick up her fork, but sat hunched over, gaze deflected, looking like a chastened girl. Barrett cleared his throat. "The food is cold," he said, "but . . . well, you need something."

He saw her dig her teeth into her lower lip as it began to tremble. After several moments she replied, "You don't have to be polite to me."

Barrett felt a sudden need to shout at her, fought it off. "You shouldn't have had any more of that brandy," he said. "I examined it before, and unless I'm mistaken, it contains more than fifty percent absinthe."

She looked up questioningly.

"An aphrodisiac."

She gazed at him in silence.

"As for the rest," he heard himself say, "there *is* a powerful influence in this house. I think it's begun to affect you." Why am I saying this? he wondered. Why am I absolving her?

Still, the look. Barrett felt a tremor in his stomach.

"Is that all?" she finally asked.

"All?"

"You've . . . solved the problem?" There was an undertone of resentful mortification in her voice.

Barrett tensed. "I'm trying to be rational."

"I see," she whispered.

"Would you rather I ranted? Called you names?" He
pulled himself erect. "I'm trying, for the moment, to blame
it on outside forces."

Edith said nothing.

"I know I haven't provided sufficient . . . physical love,"
he said with difficulty. "There *is* the polio damage, but I suppose that's not a full excuse. Maybe it's my mother's influence, maybe my total absorption in my work, my inability
to—"

"*Don't.*"

"*I'm blaming it on that,*" he said determinedly. "On myself
and on the house." There was a sheen of perspiration on his
brow. He took out his handkerchief and wiped it off. "Kindly
permit me to do so," he said. "If there are other factors involved . . . we'll work them out later. After we've left this
house."

He waited. Edith managed a nod.

"You should have told me what happened last night."

She looked up quickly.

"About your almost walking into the tarn."

She looked as though she were about to speak; but as he
said no more, she changed her mind. "I didn't want to worry
you," she said.

"I understand." He stood with a groan. "I think I'll rest
my leg a bit before I go downstairs."

"You have to work tonight?"

"I have to finish by tomorrow."

She walked beside him to the bed and watched as he lay
down, lifting his right leg with effort. He saw her trying not

to show reaction to the swollen state of his ankles. "I'll be all right," he told her.

She stood beside the bed, looking at him worriedly. Finally she said, "Do you want me to leave, Lionel?"

He was quiet for a while before he answered. "Not if you'll stay with me all the time from now on."

"All right." She seemed to hold back, then, on impulse, sat beside him. "I know you can't forgive me now," she said. "I don't expect it—no, please don't speak. I know what I've done. I'd give twenty years of my life to undo it."

Her head dropped forward. "I don't know why I drank like that, except that I was nervous—frightened. I don't know why I went downstairs. I was conscious of what I was doing, yet, at the same time—"

She looked up, tears brimming in her eyes. "I'm not asking for forgiveness. Just try not to hate me too much. I need you, Lionel. I love you. And I don't know what's happening to me." She could hardly speak now. "I just don't know what's happening to me."

"My *dear*." Despite the pain, Barrett sat up and put his arms around her, pressing his cheek to hers. "It's all right, all right. It will all pass after we've left this house." He turned his face to kiss her hair. "I love you, too. But then, you've always known that, haven't you?"

Edith clung to him, sobbing. It's going to be all right, he told himself. It *had* been the house. Everything would be re-solved after they left.

7:31 P.M.

Florence straightened with a groan. Leaning her elbow on the mattress edge, she levered to her feet. What time is it? she wondered. Declining her head, she raised her watch. *That late*, she thought, dismayed.

And still he was here.

Sighing wearily, she trudged into the bathroom and rinsed her face with cold water. As she dried her skin, she gazed at her reflection in the mirror. She looked haggard.

For more than two hours she'd been praying for Daniel's release. Kneeling beside the bed, hands clasped tightly, she had called upon all those in the spirit world who had helped her in the past, asking them to aid Daniel in breaking the bonds which kept him a prisoner of Hell House.

It hadn't worked. When the hours of prayer were ended and she'd sent out feelers of awareness, Daniel had been nearby.

Waiting.

Florence hung up the towel and left the bathroom. Crossing the bedroom, she went into the corridor and started for the stairs. More and more, her deepening involvement with Daniel was disturbing her. I should be doing more, she thought. There were so many other souls to be reprieved as well. Could she really manage to remain in Hell House for as long as it would take to do that? Without light or heat or food, how could she subsist? It was obvious that, after Sunday, Deutsch would want the house closed up.

What about the other entities she'd contacted since Monday?—and that only a small percentage of the actual number, she was convinced. Recollections tided through her mind as she descended the staircase. The "something" in her room; it might not have been Daniel. That sense of pain and sorrow she'd experienced while leaving the garage on Monday afternoon. The furious entity on the staircase to the basement who had called this house a "goddamn sewer." The perverted evil in the steam room. She still felt a terrible guilt for failing to

warn Dr. Barrett. The spirit Red Cloud had described as like
a caveman covered with sores. Whatever it was in the chapel
which prevented her from entering; it might not be Belasco.
The figure at the sitting which had reached for Mrs. Barrett.
Florence shook her head. There were so many, she thought.
Unhappy presences filled this house wherever she moved.
Even now she felt that, if she opened herself, she would come
upon many more of them. They were everywhere. In the theater and the ballroom, in the dining hall, the great hall—everywhere. Would a *year* be long enough in which to contact
all of them?

She thought, with anguish, about the list which Dr. Barrett
had. *Apparitions; Apports . . . Bilocation . . . Chemical phenomena . . . Clairsentience . . . Direct voice . . . Elongation . . . Ideoplasm . . . Imprints . . .* There must be more than a hundred
items on the list. They had barely scratched the surface of
Hell House. A massive sense of hopelessness assailed her. She
tried to fight it off but found it impossible. It was one thing
to speak of solving the enigma, step by step, if one had unlimited time. But a week. No, less. Only a little more than four
days now.

Willfully, she thrust her shoulders back and walked erect.
I'm doing all I can, she told herself. I can do no more. If all
she did in the entire week was give Daniel peace, it would be
enough. She walked determinedly into the great hall. She
needed food. She wasn't going to sit anymore. She'd make
sure she ate well for the rest of the week. Moving to the table,
she began to serve herself some dinner.

She was about to sit at the table when she saw him. He
was sitting before the fireplace, staring at the lowering flames.
He hadn't even turned to look at her.

"I didn't see you," she said. She carried her plate of food
over to him. "May I sit with you?"

He glanced at her as though she were a stranger. Florence sat down on another armchair and began to eat.

"What's wrong, Ben?" she asked when he gave no indication of accepting her company.

"Nothing."

She hesitated, then went on. "Has something happened?"

Fischer didn't answer.

"You seemed so hopeful before, when we were talking."

He said nothing.

"What's happened, Ben?"

"Nothing."

Florence started at the anger in his voice. "Have I done something wrong?"

He drew in breath, said nothing.

"I thought we trusted each other, Ben."

"*I don't trust anyone or anything,*" he said. "And anyone who does, in this house, is a fool."

"Something *has* happened."

"A lot of things have happened," Fischer snapped.

"Nothing we can't handle."

"*Wrong.*" He turned on her, his dark eyes filled with venom—and with fear, she saw. "There's nothing in this house we *can* handle. Nothing anyone is *ever* going to handle."

"That isn't true, Ben. We've made wonderful progress."

"Toward what? *Our mutual graves?*"

"No." She shook her head. "We've discovered much. Daniel, for instance; and the way Belasco works."

"*Daniel,*" he said contemptuously. "How do you know there *is* a Daniel? Barrett thinks you made him up in your mind. How do you know he isn't right?"

"Ben, the body, the ring—"

"*A* body, *a* ring," he broke in. "Is that your proof? Your logic for putting your head on the block?"

Florence was shocked at the malevolence in his voice. What had *happened* to him?

"How do you know you haven't been deluding yourself from the first moment you entered this house?" he demanded. "How do you know Daniel Belasco isn't a figment of your imagination? How do you know his personality isn't exactly what you've made it, his problem exactly what you've made it? *How do you know?*"

He jarred to his feet, glaring at her. "You're *right*," he said. "I'm obstructed, shut off. And I'm going to *stay* shut off until the week is over. At which time I'll collect my hundred thousand clams and never come within a thousand miles of this goddamned house again. I suggest you do the same."

Turning on his heel, he moved across the floor with angry strides. "Ben—!" she called. He ignored her. Florence tried to stand to follow, but she didn't have the strength. She sat slumped on the chair, gazing toward the entry hall. After a while she set her plate aside. His words had had a terrible impact on her. She tried to repress them, but they would not be repressed. All the uncertainties were returning. She'd always been a mental medium. Why should she have, suddenly, become a physical one? It made no sense, it was unprecedented.

It threatened her faith.

"No." She shook her head. It wasn't true. Daniel *did* exist. She had to believe that. He'd saved her life. He'd spoken to her, pleaded with her.

Pleaded. Spoken. Saved her life.

How do you know Daniel Belasco isn't a figment of your imagination?

She tried to repel the notion, but it wouldn't leave. All she could think was that if he *were* a product of her imagination, she would have had him save her life exactly as he did. In trance, she would have taken herself down to the tarn to prove

Belasco's murderous intent, then awakened herself at the moment of entering the tarn in order to prove that Daniel existed and wanted to save her life; even given herself the vision of him standing before her, blocking the way; the vision of Belasco fleeing.

"*No.*" She shook her head again. It wasn't true. Daniel did exist; he *did.*

Are you happy? she thought, the words rising unexpectedly to the surface of consciousness. *Yes. Very.* The words she'd exchanged with Daniel as she'd danced with him—or thought that she was dancing with him. *Are you happy? Yes. Very. Are you happy? Yes. Very.*

"Oh, my God," she murmured.

She'd spoken those words in a television play once.

Her mind strained desperately to resist the onrush of doubt—but now the dam of her resistance had fallen, and the dark waters were flooding in. *I love you. And I love you.* "No," she whispered, tears welling in her eyes. *You'll never leave me, will you? You'll always be beside me? Yes, my darling, always; always.*

She saw him as he'd looked that evening in the hospital, pale, drawn, eyes bright with the glitter of impending death; her beloved David. The remembrance chilled her. He had whispered to her earlier of Laura, the girl he loved. He'd never shared her physical love, and now he was dying, and it was too late.

He'd held her hand so tightly it had hurt, his face a lined, gray mask, his lips bloodless as he'd spoken those words to her: *I love you.* She had whispered back: *I love you, too.* Had he known, by then, that it was her in the room with him? Dying, had he thought that she was Laura? *You'll never leave me, will you?* he'd murmured. *You'll always be beside me?* And she had answered: *Yes, my darling, always; always.*

A sob of terror broke inside her. No, it wasn't true! She

started crying. But it *was* true. *She had made up Daniel Belasco in her mind.* There *was* no Daniel Belasco. There was only the memory of her brother, and the way he'd died, the loss he'd felt, the need he'd carried to his grave.

"No, no, no, no, no." Her hands were clutching at the arms of the chair, her head slumped forward, shaking, hot tears spilling from her eyes. She couldn't seem to breathe, kept gulping at the air, as if her lungs were bursting. No, it wasn't true! She could not have done this thing, this blinded, terrible, deluded thing! There had to be some way of proving that! There had to be!

She jerked her head up with a gasp, staring at the fire through gelatinous tears. It seemed as though someone had whispered in her ear: two words.

The chapel.

A trembling smile drew back her lips. She wavered to her feet and started toward the entry hall, rubbing at her eyes. There was an answer in the chapel; she had always known that. Now, in an instant, she knew it was the answer she needed; it was proof and vindication.

This time she would get in.

She tried not to run but couldn't help herself. She rushed across the entry hall and past the staircase, skirts rustling, shoes thudding on the floor. Turning the corner, she started down the side corridor, running as fast as she could.

She reached the chapel door and placed her hands against it. Instantly the rush of cold resistance filled her vitals, the grinding churn of nausea. She pressed both palms against the door and started praying. Nothing in this world or in the next was going to stop her now.

The force within the chapel seemed to waver. Florence pressed her weight against the door. "In the name of the Father, the Son, and the Holy Ghost!" she said in a loud, clear voice. The force began retreating, drawing backward and inward, as though it were shrinking. Her lips moved quickly as she prayed. "You cannot keep me from this place, for God is with me! We will enter now, together! Open! You cannot repel me any longer! *Open!*"

Suddenly the force was gone. Florence pushed the door and went inside, switching on the lights. Leaning back against the door, she closed her eyes and spoke. "I thank thee, Lord, for giving me strength."

After several moments, she opened her eyes and looked around. The dim illumination of the wall lights barely held the darkness at bay. She was standing in a shadow, only her face in light as she searched the room with her eyes. The silence was intense; she seemed to feel its pressure on her eardrums.

Moving forward abruptly, she drifted down the center aisle, averting her shocked gaze from the crucifix above the altar. This was the way; she felt it unmistakably. Unseen filaments were drawing at her.

She reached the foot of the altar and looked at it. A massive Bible with metal clasps was set on top of it. A Bible in this hideous place, she thought, shuddering. Her gaze shifted around the wall. The drawing power was so intense it seemed as though invisible threads were tied to her, pulling her toward . . . what? The wall? The altar? Surely not the crucifix. Florence felt herself drawn forward, forward.

She gasped, all movement frozen, as the cover of the Bible was flung back violently. As she stared at it, the pages began to turn so rapidly that they became a blur of movement. Florence felt a throbbing at her temples. Suddenly the pages stopped, and bending down, she looked at the page which had been uncovered.

"Yes!" she whispered joyously. "Oh, *yes!*"

The top of the page was titled BIRTHS. Below it was a single faded entry: "Daniel Myron Belasco was born at 2:00 A.M. on November 4, 1903."

9:07 P.M.

There must be *something* I can do," she said. Barrett turned from the machine, where he was working on an uncovered circuit assembly, comparing its maze of wires and transistors with one of his blueprints. She had been watching him in restive silence for the past twenty minutes, noticing how tired he looked. Finally she'd had to speak.

"I'm afraid there isn't," he told her. "It's just too complicated. It would take ten times as long to explain what I wanted done as it does for me to do it myself."

"I know, but—" Edith broke off worriedly. "How much longer will it be?"

"Hard to say. I have to make certain everything's been done as specified. Otherwise there could be a malfunction, and all my work would be for nothing. I can't afford that." He tried to smile, but it was more like a grimace of pain. "I'll finish as soon as possible."

Edith nodded without assurance. She glanced at Lionel's watch on the table. He'd been at it for more than an hour now and had barely finished checking one circuit assembly. The Reversor was gigantic. At this rate it could take all night, and his energy simply wasn't up to it. She'd phone Dr. Wagman if she thought it would do any good, but she knew that Lionel would drop in his tracks before stopping now.

The cold weight in her stomach seemed to press down as she watched him work. He was not as confident as he had been. He'd been trying to conceal it from her but she knew his conviction had been badly shaken by the occurrence in the steam room. She knew how vulnerable she'd felt after what she'd done.

Despite his façade of certainty, Lionel must be feeling the same way.

She had to know. "What is your machine supposed to do?"

He looked across his shoulder. "I'd rather not explain it now, my dear. It's quite involved."

"Can't you tell me anything?"

"Well, in essence, I'm going to pull the plug on all the power in the house." He swallowed dryly, turned to get a drink of water. "I'll explain it in detail tomorrow," he continued, pouring water into a glass. "Suffice to say that any form of energy can be dissipated—which is what I plan to do."

She watched him take out a codeine pill and wash it down. He drew in a shaking breath and smiled. "I know it doesn't sound too satisfying at the moment, but you'll see." He set the glass down. "By this time tomorrow, Hell House will be drained, de-energized."

They looked around abruptly at the sound of measured clapping. Fischer stood in the archway, looking at them, a bottle underneath his right arm. "Bravo," he said.

Edith turned away, a dark flush on her face.

"Have you been drinking, Mr. Fischer?" Barrett asked.

"Have been, will continue to," said Fischer. "Not enough to lose control," he cut off Barrett's words. "Just enough to blunt the senses. Nothing in this goddamn house is going to get another crack at me. I've had it. I have *had* it."

"I'm sorry," Barrett said after a few moments. He felt, somehow, responsible for Fischer's black mood.

"Don't be sorry for me. Be sorry for yourself." Fischer pointed at the Reversor. "That goddamn pile of junk isn't

going to do a goddamn thing but make a lot of noise . . . assuming that it works at all. You think this house is going to
shape up 'cause you play your goddamn music box? The *hell*
it is. Belasco's going to laugh in your face. They're all going
to laugh in your face—the way they've been laughing all these
years at any idiot who tries to come in here and . . . de-
energize the place." He made a hissing sound. "De-energize,
my ass." He glared at Barrett, gesturing toward Edith. "Get
her out of here," he said. "Get yourself out. You don't have
a chance."

"What about yourself?" asked Barrett.

"I'm all right. I know the score. You don't fight this place,
it can't get at you. You don't let it get inside your skin, you're
fine. Hell House doesn't mind a guest or two. Anyone can
stay here if they don't mind fun and games. What it doesn't
like is people who attack it. Belasco doesn't like it. All his
people, *they* don't like it, and they fight back, and they kill
you. He's a general, did you know that? A general with an
army. He directs them!" Fischer gestured floridly. "Directs
them like a—*mess of goddamn troops!* No one makes a move
without him, not his son, not anybody."

Fischer pointed at Barrett, his expression suddenly rabid.

"I'm telling you," he said. "I'm *telling* you! Cut out this
bullshit! Leave that damn machine alone, forget it! Spend
your week here eating, resting, doing nothing. Then, when
Sunday comes, tell old man Deutsch anything he wants to
hear, and bank your money. Hear me, Barrett? Try anything
more than that, and you're a dead man, *a-dead-man.*" He
looked at Edith. "With a dead wife by your side."

He jerked himself around. "Oh, hell, why bother anyway?
No one listens. Florence doesn't listen. You don't listen. No
one listens. Die, then. Die!" He stumbled off. "I was the only
one who made it out alive in 1940, and I'll be the only one
to make it out alive in 1970." He weaved across the entry

hall. "You hear me, Belasco, you son of a bitch! I'm closed off! Try to get me! You never will! You *hear* me?"

Edith sat staring at her husband. He was watching Fischer's departure with a troubled look.

He looked at her. "Poor man. This house has really beaten him."

He's right; she heard the words in her mind. She hadn't the courage to voice them.

Barrett limped over, pulled a chair beside hers, and sat with a groan. He was silent for a while, then drew in a heavy breath and said, "He's wrong."

"Is he?" Edith's voice was faint.

He nodded. "What he calls a pile of junk"—he smiled at the words—"is nothing more or less than the key to Hell House." He raised a hand. "All right, grant you, things have happened which I don't quite comprehend—although I would if I had time." He rubbed his eyes. "That's not the point, however. Man controls electricity without understanding its true nature. What the details are of the energy inside this house is not as vital as the fact that I"—he pointed—"that *machine* . . . has the power of life and death over it."

He stood. "And *that* is *that*. I told you from the start that Miss Tanner is wrong in what she believes. I tell you now that Fischer is equally in error. And tomorrow I'll prove my case beyond a solitary doubt."

He turned away and hobbled back to the Reversor. Edith watched him go. She wished she could believe him, but Fischer's words had driven fear so deep inside her she could feel it in her blood, chill and acidic, eating at her.

10:19 P.M.

. . . Daniel, please. You have to understand. What you ask is inconceivable. You know that. It isn't that I have no sympathy. I do. I've opened up my heart completely to you. I believe in you and trust you. You saved my life. Now let me save your soul.

You don't have to stay in this house any longer. Help is present, if only you will ask for it. Believe me, Daniel. There are those who love you and will help you if you ask. Your father doesn't have the power to stop you. Not if you seek out those beyond, and take the hand they offer you. Let them help you. Take their hand. If you only knew the beauty which awaits you, Daniel. If you only knew how lovely are the realms which lie beyond this house. Would you keep yourself locked in a barren cell when all the beauties of the universe await you on the outside? Think! Accept! Don't close yourself to those who would so gladly help you. Try; only try. They wait for you with open arms. They will help you, give you comfort. Don't remain within these cheerless walls. You can be free. Believe that, Daniel. Believe it, and it will be so. I pledge you this. Trust me. Let go. Let go.

She could barely stand. Shuffling to the bathroom, she washed and changed into her nightgown with infirm movements. Her limbs were like iron. She had never felt such helpless enervation in her life.

Daniel wouldn't listen. He simply would not listen.

She returned to the other room and got into bed. Tomorrow, then, she told herself. He had to listen sooner or later. In the morning, she would start again. She slumped back heavily or the pillow, wincing at the flare of pain in her breasts. She lay on her back, staring at the ceiling with heavy-lidded eyes. Tomorrow, she thought.

She turned her head.

There was a figure standing by the door. She gazed at it without alarm. There was no menace in it.

"Daniel?"

The figure advanced. In the feeble light from the bathroom she saw its features clearly: youthful, handsome, the expression grave, the eyes filled with despair.

"Can you speak?" she asked.

"Yes." His voice was gentle, pained.

"Why won't you go?"

"I cannot."

"But you must."

"Not without—"

"Daniel, no," she said.

He turned his face away.

"Daniel—"

"I love you," he said. "You're the only woman I've ever said that to. I never met another like you. You're so good . . . so good . . . the kindest person I have ever known."

His face turned back to her, dark eyes searching her face. "I need—" He broke off, twisting toward the door. "I *will* speak to her!" he said frightenedly. "You can't stop me!" He looked back at her. "I can't remain much longer; he won't let me," he said. "I beg of you. Please give me what I ask. If I am driven from this house without fulfillment . . ."

"Driven?" Florence tensed.

"Your Doctor Barrett has the means."

She gazed at him, stunned.

"He knows the mechanism of my being in this house and can drive me from it," he said. "But that is *all* he knows. Whatever else I am—my heart, my mind, my soul—he knows nothing of, cares nothing for. He's going to drive me from one hell to another, don't you see? Only you can help me. I can leave this house tonight if you'll help me. Please." His voice began to fade. "If you care for me at all, have pity. Please have pity. . . ."

"*Daniel*—"

For several moments she could hear his wretched sobbing; then the room was still. She stared at the spot where he'd been standing. "You know I can't," she said. "Daniel, please. You know I can't. *You know I can't.*"

10:23 P.M.

Barrett's eyes were slitted as he climbed the stairway slowly, his arm across Edith's shoulders. He tried not to put too much weight on her, tried not to make any sounds of pain. She'd had enough distress today; and it was only temporary, after all. Another pill, a good night's sleep, and he'd be fit enough by morning. He could endure the pain another day or so. The Reversor was almost ready for use. Another hour's work tomorrow, and he'd be prepared to prove his theory. After all these years, he thought, the final proof. What was a little pain compared to that?

They reached the top of the stairs, and Barrett tried to walk by himself, despite the throbbing in his leg and back. Hobbling weakly, he made a sound which he intended to be wry amusement but which, instead, emerged as one of pain. "After we're home," he said, "I'm going to take a month's vacation. Finish up the last few pages of the book. Relax. Enjoy your company."

"Good." She didn't sound convinced. Barrett patted her shoulder. "It's going to be all right," he said.

Edith opened the door and helped him to the bed. She watched in concern as he sank down heavily on the mattress. "Lie back," she told him. She propped pillows against the headboard, and Barrett hitched himself against them as she lifted his legs onto the bed. He slumped back. *"Oh."* He forced a smile. "Well, no one can say we aren't earning our money."

"You are." Edith flinched as she pulled off his shoes; they were on so tightly. Peeling off his socks, she began to massage his feet and ankles. Barrett saw that she was trying not to show distress at the swollen look of them.

"I'd better take another codeine," he said.

Edith stood and moved to his bag. Barrett tried to shift his weight on the mattress, hissing at the effort. He felt as heavy as a statue. He wouldn't mention it to Edith, of course, but it might not be amiss for him to undergo a short period of hospitalization after they got home.

He was winding his watch when Edith returned with the pill and a glass of water. Reaching out, he set the watch on the bedside table, then washed down the pill. Edith started to unbutton his sweater.

"That's all right," he said. "I'll sleep in my clothes tonight. It'll be simpler."

She nodded. "All right." She unbuckled his belt and loosened the top of his trousers. "I'll sleep in my clothes, too."

"You may as well."

Edith sat beside him on the bed and, leaning over, pressed herself against him. Her weight on his chest made it hard to breathe, but Barrett said nothing.

"If only today had never happened," she murmured.

"We can work it out." Barrett rubbed her back, wishing he cou'd think of some excuse to get her up that wouldn't hurt her feelings.

"Would you get my tie?" he asked after several moments.

Edith sat up, looking at him curiously.

"It's hanging in the closet."

She rose and got the tie, handing it to him.

"You want to wash up, brush your teeth before you go to bed?" he asked.

"All right."

Barrett lay, half-sitting, on the bed, listening to the sounds she made in the bathroom—the splashing of water as she washed, the brushing of her teeth, the rinsing of her mouth. Symphonie Domestique, he thought.

In hell.

He stared across the room. It was difficult to believe that they had been here only three days. He looked at the rocking chair. Two nights ago, it had moved by itself. For all the sense of time he felt, it might have been two weeks ago, two months.

His gaze moved lingeringly around the room. Grotesque, he thought. It could be a display room in some museum; the house was a treasure trove of art works. Thousands upon thousands of creations conceived and executed in the name of beauty—ending up in this house, which had to be the epitome of ugliness.

He blinked, refocusing his eyes as Edith came back into the room. "Can you stand to lie beside me in this tiny bed for one night?" he asked.

"I'd love to."

When she was lying beside him, both of them covered, Barrett started to fasten one end of the tie to her wrist. "I'm doing it so you won't sleepwalk." He tied the other end of the tie to one of the headboard posts. "That should give you enough freedom of movement."

Edith nodded, then, as Barrett put his arm around her, pressed against him, cradling her head in the hollow between his arm and chest. She sighed. "I feel safe now."

11:02 P.M.

If only I could sleep, she thought. Her smile was barren. The human mind, she thought. This afternoon she'd wanted to stay awake until their stay in Hell House was ended. Now she wanted nothing more than to drift into unconsciousness, eliminating eight or nine hours of their remaining time here.

She closed her eyes again. How many times had she closed and opened them now? Forty, fifty, a hundred? She drew in a long, slow breath. That smell; always that fetid smell.

Hell House should be burned to the ground.

She opened her eyes and looked at Lionel. He was deeply asleep. Moving her right hand, she felt the tug of the tie on her wrist. Had he really done it because she'd walked in her sleep last night? Or was it Fischer he was worried about? Did he really fear she'd go to Fischer again? She couldn't fathom what had driven her to him the first time. Had it truly been the house? Or was it something in herself? She'd never had such overt sex desires before—not even about Lionel, much less other men. Or women; she shuddered at the thought. She was frightened and appalled by the things she'd said and done.

She pressed her lips together. It was more than just herself; it had to be. Something had invaded her, some virus of corruption which, even as she lay here, might be spreading its disease throughout her mind and body. She would not believe it was herself alone, some unsuspected evil in her nature starting to emerge. It had to be the house. It had affected others. She could scarcely hope to be immune.

Her chin jerked up. She stared across the room.

The rocking chair had started moving.

"Lionel," she murmured. *No.* He needed sleep. It's force, she told herself; unguided, unintelligent; kinetics taking the path of least resistance—slamming doors, winds, footsteps, rocking chairs.

She wanted to close her eyes but knew that, even if she did, she'd hear the rhythmic squeaking of the chair. She stared at it. Dynamics. Force. Residuum. Her mind repeated the words again and again.

Yet all the time, she knew, she really knew, that it was someone sitting in the chair—someone whom she couldn't see. Someone cruel, implacable, waiting to destroy her, waiting to destroy them all. Was it Belasco? she thought in horror. What if he were suddenly to appear, gigantic, terrifying, smiling at her as he rocked? There's no one there! she forced herself to think. No one there at all!

The chair rocked slowly back and forth. Back and forth.

11:28 P.M.

The room felt hot. Groaning, Florence peeled aside the top blanket and dropped it to the floor. She turned on her side and closed her eyes again. Sleep, she told herself. Tomorrow we'll get back to it again.

A few minutes later she thrashed onto her back and looked at the ceiling again. No use, she thought. She wasn't going to sleep tonight.

Daniel's words had stunned her. She had always thought in terms of working with Dr. Barrett, but it had never occurred to her that such an alliance was an absolute necessity.

She'd almost gone to see him, tell him that they had to solve the problem of Daniel Belasco together. Then she'd realized that it would be a waste of time. As far as Dr. Barrett was concerned, there *was* no Daniel Belasco; he was a product of her own subconscious. What good would talking to him do? He hadn't accepted the body or the ring. Why should a Bible entry make any difference to him?

She drew aside the covers restlessly and sat up. *What was she to do?* She couldn't just stand by and let Dr. Barrett force Daniel from the house, without giving him peace. The thought appalled her. To plunge his desolate soul into limbo would be a crime against God.

Yet how could she prevent it? She mustn't even consider what Daniel had asked. She mustn't.

She stood with a mournful sigh and crossed the room. Entering the bathroom, she ran a glass of water. What other way *was* there, though? her mind probed. She'd been praying steadily since morning, pleading, importuning; all to no avail.

And, by tomorrow, Dr. Barrett would be ready with his machine.

For a moment she had the wild urge to run downstairs and damage the machine. She shook that off, angry at herself for even thinking it. She had no right to stand in Dr. Barrett's way. He was an honest, conscientious man who had devoted his life to his work. That he was so close to the truth was incredible. It was not his fault that the answer he'd found was only partial. He didn't even believe in the existence of Daniel Belasco. Obviously, he could not feel responsible for persecuting him.

Florence put down the glass and turned from the sink. There has to be an answer, she thought; there *has* to be. She started back into the bedroom.

She stopped with a gasp and looked toward the Spanish table.

The telephone was ringing.

It can't, she thought. It hasn't worked in more than thirty years.

She wouldn't answer it. She knew what it was.

It kept on ringing, the shrill sounds stabbing at her eardrums, at her brain.

She mustn't answer it. She wouldn't.

The telephone kept ringing.

"No," she said.

Ringing. Ringing. Ringing. Ringing.

With a sob, she lunged across the room and jerked up the receiver, dumping it on the table. She leaned against the edge of the table, suddenly weak, palms pressing on its surface. She could scarcely breathe. She wondered dazedly if she were going to faint.

She heard a thin voice coming from the earpiece. She couldn't hear what it said—a single word repeated—but she knew that it was Daniel's voice.

"No," she mumbled.

The voice kept speaking the same word, over and over. She jerked up the receiver, spoke into it desperately. "No!"

"Please," said Daniel.

Florence closed her eyes. "No," she whispered.

"Please." His voice was pitiful.

"No, Daniel."

"Please."

"No. No."

"*Please.*" She had never heard such anguish in a voice before. "*Please.*"

"*No.*" She could barely speak now. Tears were trickling down her cheeks. Her throat felt clogged.

"*Please,*" he begged.

"No," she whispered. "No, no."

"*Please.*" The voice of someone begging for his very existence. "*Please.*" She was his only hope. "*Please.*" Tomorrow he would be thrust into horror by Dr. Barrett. "*Please.*" There was only the one way. "*Please.*" He started crying. "*Please. Please.*" The world was gone. There were only the two of them. *"Please."* She had to help him. *"Please."* He was sobbing. *"Please!"* Dear God, her heart was breaking! *"Please! Please! Please!"*

She hung up suddenly, a violent shudder racking through her body. All right! she thought. It was the only way. Her spirit guides would help her and protect her; God would help her and protect her. It was the only way; the only way. She believed in Daniel, she believed in herself. There was only the one way; she could see that now with vivid clarity.

Moving to the bed on trembling legs, she sank to her knees beside it, bowed her head, and clasped her hands together tightly. Closing her eyes, she began to pray: "Dear God, reach down your hand and give me your protection. Help me, this night, to bring to your care the tortured soul of Daniel Belasco."

For five minutes she prayed without cease. Then, slowly, she rose and undid her robe. Removing it, she laid it across the other bed. She shivered as she drew the flannel nightgown over her head. She looked down at her body. Let this be the temple, then, she thought.

Drawing aside the bedclothes, she lay on her back. The room was almost dark, the bathroom door nearly shut. She closed her eyes and started breathing deeply. *Daniel,* she called in her mind. *I give you, now, the love you never knew. I do this freely so that you will gain the strength to leave this house. With God's love and with mine, you shall rest, this night, in Paradise.*

She opened her eyes. "Daniel," she said, "your bride is waiting."

There was a movement near the door. A figure drifted toward her.

"Daniel?"

"Yes, my love."

She held out her arms.

He crossed the room, and Florence felt the drawing from her body as he neared. She could just make out his features, gentle, frightened, filled with need for her. He lay beside her on the bed. She turned to face him. She could feel his breath, and pressing close, she gave her lips to him.

His kiss was long and tender. "I love you," he whispered. "And I love you."

She closed her eyes and turned onto her back again, feeling his weight shift onto her. "With love," she murmured. "Please, with love."

"Florence," he said.

She opened her eyes.

In an instant, she lay petrified, heartbeat staggering as she gasped at what was lying on her.

It was the figure of a corpse, its face in an advanced state of decomposition. Livid, scaly flesh was crumbling from its bones, its rotted lips wreathed in a leering smile that showed discolored jagged teeth, all of them decayed. Only the slanting yellow eyes were alive, regarding her with demoniacal glee. A leaden bluish light enveloped its entire body, gases of putrefaction bubbling around it.

A scream of horror flooded from her throat as the moldering figure plunged inside her.

11:43 P.M.

Fischer jerked up, gasping, at the sound of screaming in the next room.

For several moments he sat frozen, bound by dread. Then something drove him to his feet and carried him across the room. Flinging open his door, he lunged into the corridor and rushed to the door of Florence's room, twisted the knob, and pushed.

The door was locked.

"Oh, my God." He looked around in panic, the sound of Florence's mindless screams draining him. He glanced at the door to the Barretts' room as it opened suddenly and Edith peered out, her expression taut and stricken.

Lurching across the corridor, Fischer grabbed a heavy wooden chair and dragged it to the door. He started crashing it against the wood. The screaming broke off. He kept slamming the chair against the door. One of its legs snapped off. "Damn!" He battered at the door dementedly, seeing, on the edge of vision, Barrett and Edith hurrying toward him.

Suddenly the jamb was splintered and the door flew open. Hurling the broken chair aside, Fischer reached inside and switched the light on, then rushed into the room.

The sight of Florence made him gag. He heard the sound of Edith being sick. "Dear God," Barrett muttered.

She was naked, lying on her back, her legs spread far apart, her eyes wide open, staring upward with a look of total shock.

Her body was bruised and bitten, scratched, gouged, and running with blood.

Fischer looked at her face again, the face of a woman who had just been driven mad. Her lips stirred feebly. Compelled, he leaned over to hear. At first there were only rattling noises in her throat. Then she whispered, *"Filled."* She stared at him with wide, unblinking eyes. *"Filled."*

He was unable not to ask. "With what?"

With hideous abruptness, she began to smile.

DECEMBER 24, 1970

7:19 A.M.

Fischer sat slumped in an armchair, staring at Florence. He hadn't closed his eyes all night. When Barrett's pills had finally put her to sleep, he'd dragged the heavy armchair to her bedside; and Barrett and Edith had gone back to their room, Barrett with the promise that he'd return in several hours to take over watching. He'd never returned. Fischer had not expected it. He knew how badly Barrett had been physically and mentally abused the last two days in Hell House.

He shivered as a chill ran through him. Sitting up, he rubbed his eyes and yawned, wondering what time it was. He could use some coffee. Straining to his feet, he trudged into the bathroom, twisted the cold-water faucet, and cupped his right hand underneath the icy stream. Bending over, he splashed the water into his face, hissing at the sting of it. He straightened up and gazed at his reflection in the cabinet mirror. Water was dripping from his chin. He puffed out breath and misted drops of water on the mirror surface. Reaching out, he slid a bath towel from its rack and patted it against his face.

He went back into the bedroom and stood beside the bed,

looking at Florence. She looked at peace; a beautiful woman, asleep. It had not been that way during the night. Despite the sleeping pills, she had dozed erratically, limbs twitching, whimpering at times as though in pain, trembling periodically with paroxysmal seizures. He had been tempted to wake her from whatever terrors she had been experiencing. It had proven unnecessary. At unexpected intervals, she had jolted awake on her own, eyes staring, face disfigured by a look of dread. Each time, he'd held her hand, trying not to wince when her grip became painful, her clutching fingers as white as bone. She'd never spoken. After a while her eyes had fallen shut, and in seconds she had gone to sleep again.

Fischer blinked, refocusing his eyes. Florence was awake and looking at him. Her face had no expression. It was as though she'd never seen him before.

"How are you?" he asked.

She made no reply, gazing at him fixedly, her eyes those of a doll, glasslike, unmoving.

"Florence?"

There was a crackling sound in her throat as she swallowed. Fischer rose and walked into the bathroom, returning with a glass of water. "Here." He held it out.

Florence didn't stir. Fischer held the glass awhile, then set it on the bedside table. Florence's gaze shifted to the place where he had put it, then sprang back to his face.

"Can you speak?" he asked.

"Have you been here all night?"

Fischer nodded.

Her gaze shifted again, moving to the chair, then back again to probe at Fischer's eyes. "There?" she asked.

"Yes."

She made a noise of cynical amusement. "*Stupid.*" She ran an appraising gaze over his body. "You could have slept with me."

Fischer waited guardedly.

She pulled the covers down from her chest. "Who put on my nightgown?"

"I did."

Florence smiled with derision. "Fun?" she asked.

"After we cleaned you off."

Something flared in her eyes—a nova of awareness. Her body was convulsed by a wrenching shudder. "Oh, my God," she whispered. Tears welled in her eyes. "He's inside me." She reached out tremblingly for him.

Fischer took her hand and sat beside her on the bed. "We'll get rid of him."

She shook her head.

"We *will*." He squeezed her hand.

Florence pulled her hand away so fast he couldn't hold it. She began unbuttoning the front of her nightgown.

"What are you doing?"

Florence paid no attention. Breathing hard, she yanked aside the edges of her gown, exposing her breasts. Fischer winced at the sight of them. The teeth marks around her nipples looked purplish and infected. Florence clutched a hand around each breast, compressing and pulling them erect, their nipples hardening. "Look at them," she said.

Fischer grabbed her hands and forced them to her sides. In the instant that he did so, Florence lost rigidity and, with a faint groan, turned her head on the pillow. Fischer pulled the covers to her chin. "I'm taking you out of here this morning," he said.

"He lied to me." Her voice was strengthless. "He said it was the only way."

Fischer felt ill. "You still believe there's a Daniel—"

"Yes!" She turned back suddenly. "I know there is. I found the entry of his birth inside the chapel Bible." She saw his look of startlement. "He let me in to prove that he existed.

He's the one who always kept me out. He learned about my brother, picked it from my mind—just as you said. He knew I'd believe him, because the memory of my brother's death would make me believe." She clutched at Fischer's hand again. "Oh, God, he's *inside* me, Ben; I can't get rid of him. Even as I'm speaking to you, I can feel him in there, waiting to take over."

She began to shake so violently that Fischer drew her up and put his arms around her. "Shhh. It's going to be all right. I'll take you out of here this morning."

"He won't let me go."

"He can't stop you."

"Yes he can; he *can*."

"He can't stop me."

Florence jerked away from him and thrashed back, thumping hard against the headboard of the bed. "Who the fucking hell are you?" she snarled. "Maybe you were hot stuff when you were twelve, but now you're shit. You hear me? Shit!"

Fischer stared at her in silence.

A flickering in her eyes revealed the change, like the evanescent shimmer of sunlight across a cloud-darkened landscape. Instantly she was herself again; but not emerging from amnesia. It was, instead, a sudden, brutal surfacing to self, with total memory of every vileness she'd been forced to utter.

"Oh, God, please help me, Ben."

Fischer held her tightly, sensing the congested turmoil in her mind and body. If only he could dig inside her like some psychic surgeon, rip away the cancerous mass, and fling it from her. He couldn't, though; he didn't have the power or the will.

He was as much a victim of this house as she was.

Fischer drew back. "Get dressed. We'll leave."

Florence stared at him.

"Now."

She nodded; but it seemed the jerk of a marionette's head as the operator moved the string from overhead. Drawing aside the bedclothes, Florence rose and walked to the bureau. Fischer watched as she drew some clothes from its drawers and started for the bathroom.

"Florence—"

She turned to face him. Fischer braced himself. "You'd better dress in here."

The skin grew taut across her cheekbones. "I have to *piss*. Is that all right?"

"Stop it!" Fischer shouted.

Florence jerked so hard she dropped her clothes. She looked at him bewilderedly.

"Stop it," he repeated quietly.

Florence looked painfully embarrassed. "But I have to . . ." She couldn't finish.

Fischer stared at her sadly. What if she became possessed in there, did something harmful to herself?

He sighed. "Don't lock the door."

She nodded once and turned. Entering the bathroom, she closed the door. Fischer listened for the sound of the lock, relaxing gradually when it didn't come. Standing, he walked across the room and picked up the clothes she'd dropped.

He looked around with relief as Florence opened the bathroom door and came out. Without a word he handed her her clothes and turned away. He sat on the bed with his back to her. "Keep talking while you dress."

"All right." He heard the rustle of her nightgown as she took it off. He closed his eyes and yawned. "Did you sleep at all?" she asked.

"I'll sleep when you're out of here."

"You're going too, aren't you?"

"I'm not sure. I don't think I'm vulnerable as long as I'm

shut off from the house, not fighting it. I might stay. I have
no qualms about lifting a hundred thou from old man
Deutsch's bank account. He won't miss it." He paused. "I'll
give you half of it."

Florence didn't speak.

"Talk," he said.

"Why talk?"

The tone of her voice made him twist around. She was
standing by the bureau, naked, smiling at him. "Take off *your*
clothes now," she said.

Fischer stood up quickly. "Fight it."

"Fight what?" she asked. "My love of cock?"

"Florence—"

"Strip. I want to wallow. Like a pig." She started toward
him angrily. "Strip, you bastard. You've wanted to fuck my
ass all week; now *do* it!"

She seemed to think his sudden movement toward her
indicated interest, and she ran to him. Fischer grabbed her
wrists and jerked her to a halt. "Fight it, Florence."

"Fight what? My—?"

"Fight it."

"Let me go, goddamnit!"

"Fight it!" Fischer gouged his fingers into her wrists until
she gasped in pain and rage.

"I want to fuck!" she screamed.

"Fight it, Florence!"

"I want to *fuck*, I want to *fuck!"*

Releasing her left wrist, Fischer slapped her face as hard
as possible. Her head snapped to the right, her expression one
of shocked amazement.

When her head turned back, he saw that she'd been given
back her mind. For several moments she stood trembling, gaping at him. Then she glanced down at her body, shamed.
"Don't look," she begged.

Fischer released her other wrist and turned away. "Dress,"
he said. "Forget your bags; I'll bring them later. Let's get out
of here."

"All right."

God, I hope it *is* all right, he thought. He shuddered.
What if he was not allowed to take her from the house?

7:48 A.M.

More coffee?"

Lionel twitched, and Edith realized that he'd been half
asleep, despite his open eyes. "I'm sorry; did I startle you?"

"No, no." He shifted on the chair, grimacing; started
reaching for the cup with his right hand, then did it with his
left instead.

"You've got to have that thumb looked at, first thing."

"I will."

The great hall was without a sound again. Edith felt unreal. The words they'd spoken had seemed artificial. Eggs? No,
thank you. Bacon? No. Chilly? Yes. I'll be glad to leave this
place. Yes, so will I. Like dialogue from some inferior domes-
tic drama.

Or was it a carry-over from the tension between them last
night?

She stared at Lionel. He was drifting off again, his eyes
unseeing, almost blank. He'd been working on the Reversor
for more than an hour before they'd eaten, laboring without
cease while she dozed in a nearby easy chair. He'd said that
it was almost ready now. She turned and looked across the
hall at it. Despite its imposing size, it was impossible to believe that it could conquer Hell House.

She looked back at the table. Everything about this morning had conspired to make her feel unreal, a character manip-

ulated through some inexplicable role. Coming down the stairs, they'd seen the cat go running down the corridor to-ward the chapel—soundlessly, a fleeting, orange-mottled form. Then, while Lionel had been working on the Reversor, she'd heard a sound, and starting awake, had seen an old cou-ple crossing the hall, carrying a coffeepot and covered trays. Half asleep, she'd stared at them in silence, thinking them ghosts. Even when they'd set the trays on the table and begun collecting the supper dishes, she hadn't realized who they were. Then, in a rush, it had come to her, and smiling at her own deluding mind, she'd said, "Good morning."

The old man grunted, and the woman nodded, mumbling something indistinct. In moments they were gone. Still groggy from sleep, Edith had begun to wonder if she'd really seen them. She'd drifted back into a shallow sleep, jolting awake with a gasp when Lionel had touched her shoulder.

She cleared her throat, and Lionel twitched again. "What time will we be out of here?" she asked.

Barrett tugged at his fob and pulled the watch from its pocket. Opening the cover, he gazed at its face. "I'd say early afternoon," he answered.

"How do you feel?"

"Stiff." His smile was tired. "But I'll mend."

They looked around as Fischer and Florence entered the hall, dressed for outdoors. Barrett eyed them questioningly as they approached the table. Edith looked at Florence. She was pale, her gaze avoiding theirs.

"You have the car keys?" Fischer asked.

Barrett repressed a look of surprise. "Upstairs."

"Would you get them, please?"

Barrett winced. "Could *you*? I really can't face those stairs again."

"Where are they?"

"In my overcoat pocket."

Fischer glanced aside. "You'd better go with me," he said to Florence.

"I'll be all right."

"Why don't you join us, Miss Tanner; have some coffee?" Barrett invited.

She was about to speak, then changed her mind, and nodding once, sat down. Edith poured a cup of coffee and passed it across the table. Florence took it from her, murmuring, "Thank you."

Fischer looked uneasy. "Don't you think you'd better come along?"

"We'll keep an eye on her," said Barrett.

Fischer still hesitated.

"What Ben doesn't want to tell you," Florence said, "is that I was possessed by Daniel Belasco last night and could lose control of myself at any moment."

Barrett and Edith stared at her. Fischer could tell that Barrett didn't believe her, and the realization angered him. *"She's telling the truth,"* he said. "I'd rather not leave her alone with you."

Barrett regarded Fischer in silence. Finally he turned to Florence. "You'd best go with him, then," he said.

Florence looked up pleadingly. "Couldn't I have a cup of coffee first?"

Fischer's eyes narrowed with suspicion.

"If anything happens, just take me outside."

"I'll buy you coffee in town."

"It's such a long way, Ben."

"Florence—"

"Please." She closed her eyes. "I'll be all right. I promise you." She sounded as though she were about to cry.

He stared at her, not knowing what to do.

Barrett spoke to break the painful silence. "There's really no need to stay," he said to Florence. "The house will be cleared by afternoon."

She looked up quickly. "How?"

Barrett's smile was awkward. "I'd intended to explain it to you—but, under the circumstances . . ."

"Please. I have to know before I leave."

"There isn't time," said Fischer.

"Ben, I have to know." Her look was desperate. "I can't go until I do."

"Damn it—"

"If I start to lose control, just take me out," she said. She turned to Barrett pleadingly.

"Well . . ." His tone was dubious. "It's somewhat complicated."

"I have to know," was all she said. Fischer sat down gingerly near Florence. Why am I doing this? he wondered. He didn't believe that Barrett's machine would have the least effect on Hell House. Why wasn't he dragging her out of here? It was her only hope.

"To begin with fundamentals," Barrett said, "all phenomena occur as events in nature—a nature the order of which is larger than that presented by current science, but nature, nonetheless. This is true of so-called psychic events as well, parapsychology being, in fact, no more than an extension of biology."

Fischer kept his eyes on Florence. She had slipped in and out of possession so frequently before.

"Paranormal biology, then," Barrett said, "setting forth the premise that man overflows and is greater than the organism which he inhabits, as Doctor Carrel put it. In simplest terms, the human body emits a form of energy—a psychic fluid, if you will. This energy surrounds the body with an unseen sheath; what has been called the 'aura.' It can be extruded beyond the borders of this aura, where it can create mechanical, chemical, and physical effects: percussions, odors, movement of external objects, and the like—as we have seen repeatedly these past few days. I believe that when Belasco spoke of 'influences,' he may have been referring to this energy."

Fischer looked at Barrett, ambivalent emotion rising in him. The older man sounded so confident. Was it possible that all the beliefs of his life could be reduced to something one could probe at in a laboratory?

"All through the ages," Barrett continued, "evidence in proof of this premise has been forthcoming, each new level of human development bringing about its own particular proof. In the Middle Ages, for example, much superstitious thought was directed toward what were called demons and witches. Accordingly, these things were manifested, created by this psychic energy, this unseen fluid, these 'influences.'

"Mediums have always produced phenomena indigenous to their beliefs." Fischer glanced at Florence, seeing that she'd tightened at these words. "This is certainly the case with Spiritualism. Mediums adhering to this faith create its own particular phenomenon—so-called spirit communication."

"Not *so-called*, Doctor." Florence's voice was strained.

"Let me continue, Miss Tanner," he said. "You may refute me later if you wish. By record, the only time religious exorcisms have an effect on haunted houses or possessions is when the medium who causes the phenomena is highly religious, thus profoundly moved by the exorcism. In far more cases—including this house—gallons of holy water and hours of exorcism fail to alter anything, either because the medium involved is not religious or because more than one medium has contributed to the effect."

Fischer glanced at Florence. Her face was pale, lips pressed together.

"Another example of this biological mechanism," Barrett was saying, "was that of animal magnetism, which produced psychic phenomena equally as impressive as those of Spiritualism, but entirely devoid of any religious characteristics.

"How does this mechanism function, though? What is its genesis? Reichenbach, the Austrian chemist, in the years between 1845 and 1868 established the existence of such a physiological radiation. His experiments consisted, first, of having sensitives observe magnets. What they saw were gleams of light at the poles, like flames of unequal length, the shorter at the positive pole. Observation of electromagnets brought about the same results as did observation of crystals. Finally, the same phenomenon was observed on the human body.

"Colonel De Rochas continued Reichenbach's experiments, discovering that these emanations are blue at the positive pole, red at the negative. In 1912 Dr. Kilner, a member of the London Royal College of Physicians, published the results of four years of experimentation during which, by use of the 'dycyanine' screen, the so-called human aura was made visible to anyone. When the pole of a magnet was brought into proximity with this aura, a ray appeared, joining the pole to the nearest point of the body. Further, when the subject was exposed to an electrostatic charge, the aura gradually disappeared, returning when the charge was dissipated.

"I oversimplify the progression of discovered facts, of course," he said, "but the end result is irrefutable; *the psychic emanation which all living beings discharge is a field of electromagnetic radiation.*"

He looked around the table, disappointed at the flatness of their expressions. Didn't they realize what he was saying?

He had to smile then. There was no way they could realize the import of his words until he'd proved them.

"Electromagnetic radiation—EMR—is the answer, then,"
he said. "All living organisms emit this energy, its dynamo the
mind. The electromagnetic field around the human body be-
haves precisely as do all such fields—spiraling around its center of force, the electric and magnetic impulses acting at right
angles to each other, and so on. Such a field *must* impinge
itself on its surroundings. In extremes of emotion, the field
grows stronger, impressing itself on its environment with more
force—a force which, if contained, *persists* in that environment, undischarged, saturating it, disturbing organisms sensitive to it: psychics, dogs, cats—in brief, establishing a
'haunted' atmosphere.

"Is it any wonder, then, that Hell House is the way it is?
Consider the years of violently emotional, destructive—*evil*, if
you will—radiations which have impregnated its interior.
Consider the veritable *storehouse* of noxious power this house
became. Hell House is, in essence, a giant battery, the toxic
power of which must, inevitably, be tapped by those who
enter it, either intentionally or involuntarily. By you, Miss
Tanner. By you, Mr. Fischer. By my wife. By myself. All of
us have been victimized by these poisonous accumulations—
you most of all, Miss Tanner, because you actively sought
them out, unconsciously seeking to utilize them to prove your
personal interpretation of the haunting force."

"*That isn't true.*"

"It *is* true," Barrett countered. "It was true of those who
entered here in 1931 and 1940. It is true of you."

"What about *you?*" demanded Fischer. "How do you
know *your* interpretation isn't wrong?"

"Simply answered," Barrett said. "Shortly, my Reversor
will permeate the house with a massive countercharge of
electromagnetic radiation. This countercharge will oppose the
polarity of the atmosphere, reverse and dissipate it. Just

as the radiation of light negates mediumistic phenomena, so the radiation of my Reversor will negate the phenomena of Hell House."

Barrett leaned back in his chair; he had not been aware, until now, of leaning forward. Florence sat in stricken silence. Edith felt a rush of pity for her. After what Lionel had said, how could anyone doubt that he was right?

"One question," Fischer said.

Barrett looked at him.

"If the aura can restore itself after an electromagnetic charge is turned off, why can't the power in this house?"

"Because human radiation has a living source. The radiation in this house is only *residue*. Once it's been dissipated, it cannot return."

"Doctor," Florence said.

"Yes?"

She seemed to brace herself. "Nothing you've said contradicts what I believe."

Barrett looked astounded. "You can't be serious."

"I am. Of course there's radiation—and, of course, it persists. Because its possessor survives after death. *Your radiation is the body it survives with.*"

"Here we part company, Miss Tanner," Barrett said. "The residue I speak of has nothing whatever to do with the survival of personality. The spirit of Emeric Belasco does not prowl this house. Neither does that of his son or any of the so-called entities you have believed yourself in contact with. There is one thing in this house, and one thing only—*mindless, directionless power.*"

"Oh," she said. Her voice was calm. "There's nothing else to do, then, is there?"

Her movement caught them by surprise. With a fluid, twisting stand, she was on her feet and running toward the Reversor. The three sat frozen for a moment. Then, simultaneously, Barrett gasped and Fischer lurched up from his chair, knocking it over in his haste to rise. He charged from the table, dashing after Florence.

Before he'd gone halfway, she had the crowbar in her hands and was swinging it with all her might at the face of the Reversor. Barrett cried out, jarring to his feet, his face gone ashen. He jolted at the ringing sound of steel on steel, flinching as though the blow were striking him instead. "No!" he shouted.

Florence swung again, battering at the front of the machine. The glass face of a dial exploded underneath her blow. Barrett started from the table with a look of horror on his face. His right leg buckled under him, and with a startled gasp, he fell. Edith jumped up. "Lionel!"

Fischer had reached Florence by then. Clutching at her shoulder, he yanked her back from the Reversor. She whirled and swung the crowbar at his face, her expression one of manic rage. Fischer dodged, the crowbar missing his head by inches. Lunging in, he grabbed her right arm, wrestling for possession of the bar. Florence lurched back, snarling like a maddened animal. A bolt of shock numbed Fischer as she flung her arms up, breaking his grasp. *She was too strong!*

Blind to everything except the threat to his Reversor, Barrett didn't even glance at Edith as she helped him to his feet. Pulling free of her, he started hobbling rapidly across the floor without his cane. "Stop her!" he cried.

Fischer had grabbed at Florence's arms again. She heaved back, and the two of them crashed against the front of the Reversor. Fischer felt her hot breath on his cheek, bubbly spittle dribbling from her mouth. She jerked her right arm free and swung at him. Fischer ducked, the crowbar smashing against the metal face. He started reaching for her arm again, but she swung too fast for him. He threw his arms up, crying out as the crowbar struck him on the right wrist. Ragged, burning pain shot up his arm. He saw the next blow coming but could not avoid it. The crowbar smashed against his skull, and blinding pain exploded in his head. Eyes staring, he crumpled to his knees. Florence raised the bar to strike again.

Barrett was on her then, the strength of frenzy in his arms; with a single wrenching motion he had jerked the crowbar from her grasp. Florence spun around. Barrett's face had gone abruptly blank. Gasping, he was stumbling back from her, right hand clutching at his lower back. Edith screamed and started forward as the crowbar slipped from Barrett's grasp and thumped on the rug. He started falling.

Florence's sudden lunging movement made Edith freeze in her tracks. Florence snatched the crowbar up. Instead of turning back to the Reversor, though, she turned toward Edith and began advancing on her. "Now you," she said, "you lesbian bitch."

Edith gaped at her, as much unnerved by the words as by the sight of Florence stalking her, crowbar raised. "I'm going to smash your fucking skull in," Florence said. "I'm going to beat it into jelly."

Edith shook her head, retreating. She glanced at Lionel desperately. He was writhing on the floor in pain. She started toward him, then jumped back, looking at Florence again, as, with a savage howl, the medium broke into a run at her, brandishing the crowbar. Edith's breath cut off. She whirled and bolted toward the entry hall, her mind washed blank by panic. She heard the driving thud of shoes behind her, glanced across her shoulder. Florence was almost on her! She sprang forward with a gasp, darting across the entry hall and up the stairs.

She knew the moment she'd reached the landing that she couldn't make their room; side vision showed her Florence only several yards behind. Impulsively she raced across the corridor to Florence's room and plunged inside, whirling to slam the door and lock it. A groan of horror tore her lips back as she saw the broken lock. Too late. The door was surging in at her. She stumbled back and, losing balance, fell.

Florence stood across the room from her, panting, smiling. "What are you afraid of?" she asked. She tossed aside the crowbar carelessly. "I'm not going to hurt you."

Edith crouched on the floor, staring at her.

"I'm not going to hurt you, baby." Edith felt a spasm in her stomach muscles. The medium's voice was honeyed, almost purring.

Florence started to remove her coat. Edith tensed as she dropped it on the floor. Florence started to unbutton her sweater. Edith began to shake her head.

"Don't shake your head," said Florence. "You and I are going to have a lovely time."

"No." Edith started edging backward.

"*Yes.*" Florence removed the sweater, dropped it. Starting across the room, she reached back to unhook her bra.

Oh, God, please don't! Edith kept shaking her head as Florence moved in on her. The bra was off now. Florence began unzipping her skirt, the smile fixed to her lips. Edith bumped against a bed and caught her breath convulsively. She could retreat no farther. Cold and weak, she watched Florence drop her skirt, bend over to remove her panties. She stopped shaking her head. "Oh, no," she pleaded.

Florence dropped to her knees, straddling Edith's legs. Sliding both hands underneath her breasts, she held them up in front of Edith's face; Edith winced at the purplish teeth marks on them. "Aren't they nice?" said Florence. "Aren't they delicious-looking? Don't you want them?" Her words drove a spear of terror into Edith's heart. She stared up frozenly as Florence fondled her breasts in front of her. "Here, feel them," Florence said. She released her left breast, reached down, lifted Edith's hand.

The feel of the warm, yielding flesh against her fingers

broke a dam in Edith's chest. A sob of anguish shook her. *No, I'm not that way!* screamed her mind.

"Of course you are," said Florence, as though Edith had spoken. "We're both that way; we've always been that way. Men are ugly, men are cruel. Only women can be trusted. Only women can be loved. Your own father tried to rape you, didn't he?"

She couldn't know! thought Edith, horrified. She jerked both hands against her chest and pressed them tightly to her body, jammed her eyes shut.

With an animal-like sound, Florence fell across her. Edith tried to push her off, but Florence was too heavy. Edith felt the medium's hands clamping on the back of her head, forcing up her face. Abruptly Florence's lips were crushed on hers, mouth open, tongue trying to force its way inside her mouth. Edith tried to fight, but Florence was too strong. The room began to spin around her, burgeoning with heat. A heavy mantle fell across her body. She felt numb, detached. She couldn't keep her lips together, and Florence's tongue plunged deep inside her mouth, licking at the tender roof. Curls of sensation flickered through her body. She felt one of Florence's hands wrap her fingers around the breast again. She couldn't pull the hand away. There was a pounding in her ears. Heat poured across her.

The sound of Lionel's voice cut through the pounding. Edith jerked her head to one side, trying to see past Florence. The heated mantle vanished. Coldness rushed across her. She glanced up, saw the twisted face of Florence looming overhead. Lionel called her name again. "In here!" she cried. Florence pulled away from her, looking at herself with sickened realization; she lunged to her feet and ran into the bathroom. Edith struggled up and moved across the room unevenly. She fell against Lionel as he ran in, clinging to him, eyes shut, face against his chest. She started crying helplessly.

9:01 A.M.

You'll be all right." Barrett patted Fischer's shoulder. "Just stay in bed awhile; don't move."

"How is she?" Fischer mumbled.

"Asleep. I gave her pills."

Fischer tried to sit up, fell back, gasping.

"*Don't move*," Barrett told him. "That was quite a blow you took."

"Have to get her out of here."

"I'll get her out."

Fischer looked at him suspiciously.

"I promise," Barrett said. "Now rest."

Edith was standing by the door. Barrett took her arm and led her into the corridor. "How is he?" she asked.

"Unless he has a more serious concussion than I think, he should come around."

"What about you?"

"Just a few more hours," Lionel said. Edith saw that he was holding his right arm against his chest as though it were broken. There was a stain of fresh blood on the thumb bandage. When he'd wrenched the crowbar out of Florence's hands, he must have torn apart the edges of the cut. She was about to mention it, then gave it up, a sense of utter hopelessness oppressing her.

Lionel opened the door to Florence's room, and they crossed to her bed. She was lying motionless beneath the covers. After Lionel had spoken to her for a long time, she'd emerged from the bathroom, a towel wrapped around her. She hadn't spoken, hadn't met their gaze. Eyes downcast like those of a repentant child, she had accepted the three pills, slipped beneath the bedclothes, and in moments closed her eyes and gone to sleep.

Barrett raised her left eyelid and looked at her staring eye.

Edith averted her face. Then Lionel was taking her arm again; they crossed the room and went into the corridor. Moving to their room, they went inside.

"Would you get me some water?" he asked.

Edith went into the bathroom and ran cold water into the glass. When she returned, Lionel was on his bed, propped against the headboard. "Thank you," he murmured as she handed him the glass. He had two codeines in his palm. He washed them down his throat. "I'm going to telephone Deutsch's man for an ambulance," he said. Edith felt a momentary burst of hope. "Have Fischer and Miss Tanner taken to the nearest hospital."

The hope was gone. Edith looked at him without expression.

"I'd like you to go with them," Lionel said.

"Not until you go."

"It would make me feel much better."

Edith shook her head. "Not without you."

He sighed. "Very well. It'll all be over by this afternoon, at any rate."

"Will it?"

"Edith"—Barrett looked surprised—"have you lost your faith in me?"

"What about—?"

"—what happened just before?" He drew in a hitching breath. "Don't you see? It proves my point precisely."

"*How?*"

"Her attack on my Reversor was the ultimate tribute. She *knows* I'm right. There was nothing else to do—her very words, if you recall—except to destroy my beliefs before they could destroy hers."

Barrett reached out his left hand and drew her onto the bed. "She's not possessed by Daniel Belasco," he told her.

"She's not possessed by anyone—unless it's by her inner self, her true self, her *repressed* self."

Like I was yesterday, she thought. She stared at Lionel hopelessly. She wanted to believe him, but it wasn't in her anymore.

"The medium is a most unstable personality," he said. "Any psychic worthy of the name invariably turns out to be a hysteric and/or somnambulist, a victim of divided conscious-ness. The parallel between the mediumistic trance and the somnambulistic fit is absolute. Personalities come and go, methods of expression are identical, as are psychological struc-tures, the amnesia upon awakening, the artificial quality of the alternate personalities.

"What we've witnessed this morning is that part of Miss Tanner's personality she's always kept hidden, even from her-self—her patience turning into anger, her withdrawal into fu-rious expression." He paused. "Her chasteness into wanton sexuality."

Edith declined her head. She couldn't look at him. Like me, she thought.

"It's all right," Barrett said.

"No." She shook her head.

"If there are . . . things to be discussed, we'll discuss them at home."

At home, she thought. Never had a phrase implied such impossibility to her.

"All right," she said. But it was someone else's voice.

"Good," said Barrett. "In addition to my work, then, some extra value has come of this week, some personal en-lightenment." He smiled at her. "Have heart, my dear. Every-thing will work out."

9:42 A.M.

Barrett opened his eyes, to find himself looking at
Edith's sleeping face. He felt a twinge of worry. He hadn't
meant to sleep.

Taking hold of his cane, he slipped his legs across the edge
of the mattress and stood, wincing as he put his weight down.
He winced again as he slipped his feet into shoes. Sitting on
the other bed, he crossed his left leg over his right, and worked
the lace out of the shoe, using the fingers of his left hand.

He set the foot down. That was some improvement. He
did the same to his right shoe, then drew out his watch. It
was getting close to ten. His expression grew alarmed. That
couldn't be P.M., could it? In this damned, windowless hulk,
there was no way to be certain.

He hated to wake Edith. She'd had so little sleep this
week. Did he dare leave her, though? He stood irresolutely,
staring at her. Had anything happened to them in their sleep?
It was an aspect of the EMR he had not investigated, but it
did seem that one had to be conscious in order to be affected
by it. No, that wasn't true; she'd walked in her sleep.

He decided to leave the door open, go downstairs as rapidly as possible, make the call, and come right back. If anything happened, surely he'd be aware of it.

He limped across the room and into the corridor, setting
his teeth against the pain in his thumb. Despite his having
taken codeine, it still throbbed unrelentingly. God knew what
it looked like by now; he had no intention of checking. It
would undoubtedly require minor surgery when this was over;
he might even lose partial use of it. Never mind, he thought.
The price was acceptable.

He opened Fischer's door and looked inside the bedroom.
Fischer hadn't stirred. Barrett hoped he'd remain asleep when

they carried him out of here on a stretcher. He didn't belong here; never had. At least he was surviving once more.

Turning clumsily, he hobbled to Florence Tanner's room and looked inside. She was also immobile. Barrett gazed at her sympathetically. The poor woman had a lot to confront after she was out of here. What would it be like to face the lie of her past existence? Was she up to it? Most likely, she would slip back into pretension; it would be less difficult.

He turned from Florence's door and limped to the staircase. Well, it's been quite a week, all in all, he thought. He smiled involuntarily. That was, without a doubt, the understatement of his life. Still, all was well. Thank God Miss Tanner had been blinded by her rage. A few well-placed blows, and he would have been confronted by days, perhaps weeks, of work to put the Reversor into working condition. Everything would have been ruined. He shivered at the thought.

What would they all do after they had left the house? he wondered as he descended the staircase haltingly, his left hand on the banister rail. It was an interesting speculation. Would Miss Tanner return to her church? *Could* she return to it after this appalling insight into herself? What about Fischer? What would he do? With a hundred thousand dollars, he could do a great deal. As for Edith and himself, the future was relatively clear. He avoided thinking of their personal problems yet to solve. That was for later.

At least they would all be out of Hell House. As the unofficial leader of the group, he felt some pride in that, although it was, perhaps, absurd for him to feel it. Still, the 1931 and 1940 groups had been virtually decimated. This time, four of them had entered Hell House, four would be safely out by tonight.

He wondered what to do with the Reversor after today. Should he have it delivered to his laboratory at the college?

That seemed most likely. What a delivery that would be; tantamount, he thought, to displaying the capsule that had taken the first astronaut into space. Perhaps, someday, the Reversor would occupy a place of honor in the Smithsonian Institution. He smiled sardonically. And perhaps not. He was hardly deluding himself into thinking that the world of science would topple in submission before his accomplishment. No, there were still a good many years ahead before parapsychology was conceded its rightful place beside the other natural sciences.

He moved to the front doors and opened one. Daylight. He shut the door and hobbled to the telephone, picked up the receiver.

There was no answer. Barrett jiggled the cradle arm. A fine time for communication to be broken off. He waited, jiggled the cradle arm again. Come on, he thought. He couldn't possibly get Fischer and Miss Tanner out of here without help.

He was about to hang up when the receiver was lifted on the other end of the line. "Yes?" said Deutsch's man.

Barrett exhaled loudly with relief. "You had me worried there. This is Barrett. We need an ambulance."

Silence.

"Did you hear me?"

"Yes."

"Will you have it sent out right away, then? Mr. Fischer and Miss Tanner require immediate hospitalization."

There was no reply.

"Do you understand?"

"Yes."

The line was silent.

"Is something wrong?" Barrett asked.

The man drew in a sudden breath. "Oh, hell, this isn't fair to you," he said angrily.

"What isn't?"

The man hesitated.

"*What* isn't?"

Another hesitation. Then the man said quickly, "Old man Deutsch died this morning."

"*Died?*"

"He had terminal cancer. Took too many pills to dull the pain. Accidentally killed himself."

Barrett felt a numbing pressure on his skull. What difference does it make? he heard his mind inquiring; but he knew. "Why didn't you tell us?" he asked.

"I was ordered not to."

By the son, thought Barrett. "Well . . ." His voice was faint. "What about—?"

"I was ordered to just—leave you stranded out there."

"And the money?" Barrett had to ask, even though he knew the answer.

"I don't know about that, but under the circumstances—" The man sighed. "Is there anything in writing?"

Barrett closed his eyes. "No."

"I see." The man's tone was flat. "Then that bastard son of his will doubtless—" He broke off. "Look, I apologize for not having called you, but my hands are tied. I have to go back to New York City right away. You have the car there. I suggest you all leave. There's a hospital here in Caribou Falls you can go to. I'll do what I can to . . ." His voice faded, and he made a sound of disgust. "Hell," he said. "I'll probably be out of a job myself. I can't stand that man. The father was bad enough, but—"

Barrett hung up as a wave of dark despair broke over him. No money, no provision for Edith, no retirement, no chance to rest. He leaned his forehead against the wall. "Oh, no," he murmured.

The tarn.

Barrett whirled with a gasp and looked around the entry

hall. The words had leaped into his mind, unbidden. No, he thought. He clenched his teeth together tightly. No, he told the house. He shook his head deliberately.

He started toward the great hall. "You don't win," he said. "I may not get that money, but you're not going to beat me; not you. I know your secret, and I'm going to destroy you." He had never felt such hatred in his life. He reached the archway and pointed at the Reversor with a look of triumph. "There!" he shouted. "There it stands! Your conqueror!" He had to lean against the archway wall. He felt exhausted, racked by pain. It doesn't matter, he told himself. Whatever pain he felt was secondary now. He'd worry later about Fischer and Miss Tanner, worry afterward about Edith and himself. There was only one thing that mattered at this moment: his defeat of Hell House and the victory of his work.

10:33 A.M.

She felt herself begin to rise from darkness. Daniel's voice cajoled her. *You don't have to sleep*, he said. She seemed to feel her veins and arteries compressing, tissues drawing in, her body forcing out the darkness. There was burning pressure in her kidneys. She tried to hold it back but was unable to. The pressure kept building. *Go on*, Daniel told her; *let it go*. Florence groaned. She couldn't stop herself. She felt the gushing from her loins, and cried aloud in shame.

Suddenly she was awake. She pushed aside the bedclothes and stood, looking groggily at the patch of wetness on the sheet. He was so rooted in her, he controlled the very workings of her body now.

"Florence."

She jerked her head around and saw his face projected on the hanging silver lamp. "Please," he said.

She stared at him. He started smiling. "Please." His tone was mocking.

"Stop it."

"Please," he said.

"*Stop* it."

"Please." He bared his teeth in a derisive grin. "*Please.*"

"Stop it, Daniel!"

"Please, please, please, please, please, please, please!"

Florence spun around and lurched for the bathroom. A cold hand grasped her ankle, and she toppled to the floor. Daniel's icy presence flooded over her, his voice, demoniac, howling in her ears: "Please, please, please, please!" She couldn't make a sound; his presence seemed to suck away her breath. "Please, please, please!" He began to laugh with wild sadistic pleasure. Help me, God! she thought in agony. "Help me, God!" railed his voice. *Deliver me!* she pleaded. "Deliver me, deliver me!" his voice impersonated. Florence pressed both hands across her ears. "*Help me, God!*" she cried.

His presence vanished. Florence gasped in air convulsively. She struggled to her feet and started for the bathroom. "Leaving?" said his voice. She set her mind against its blandishment. Stumbling into the bathroom, she ran cold water and splashed it on her face.

She straightened up and stared at her reflection. Her face was pallid, marked by dark scabbed scratches and discolored bruises. What she could see of her neck and upper chest was scored by jagged lacerations. Leaning forward, she saw that her breasts looked inflamed, the teeth marks almost black now.

She stiffened as the door swung shut, then saw the full reflection of her body in the mirror fastened to the door. She started to resist, but something cold snaked up her spine. She gasped; eyes opening wide.

In a moment she began to smile. She leaned back, eyes

half-closing. Daniel was behind her. She could feel his hardened organ sliding deep into her rectum. His hands were clutched around her breasts, kneading them. Florence leaned back as Edith slipped into the bathroom, falling to her knees in front of Florence, darting her extended tongue to Florence's vagina. Florence's tongue lolled out. She bucked against Daniel eagerly. This was what she wanted, what she was.

She twitched as though electric current surged through her. Suddenly she saw herself, half-crouched before the mirror, face slack with vacuous abandonment, the fingers of her right hand thrust into her body. With a sickened noise she jerked the fingers free. A harsh laugh rasped behind her, and she whirled. The bathroom was empty. I was watching, his voice spoke in her mind.

She flung open the door and ran into the bedroom, Daniel's laughter following. She bent to pick her robe up. Something jerked it from her grasp and flung it away. She moved after it. The robe kept flapping from her. Florence stopped. No use, she thought, despairing. "No use," parodied his voice. The robe flew up and fell across her head. She jerked it off and pulled it on her body, buttoning it hastily. He's *playing* with me, she thought; making me do everything that's most abhorrent to me.

"—most abhorrent to me," his voice parroted, mockingly falsetto. He giggled like a girl. "Most abhorrent to me, most abhorrent to me."

Florence fell on her knees beside the bed and, resting both arms on the mattress edge, pressed her forehead to her tightly clasping hands. "Dear God, please help me; Red Cloud, help me; spirit doctors, help me; I have been possessed. Let the fire of the Holy Spirit burn this sickness from my mind and body. Let the strength of God rush through me, let his might instill me with the power to resist.

"Let his God cock sink into my mouth," she said. "Let me drink his holy, burning jism. Let me—"

A wail of torment jerked back her lips. She drove the knuckle of a fisted hand into her mouth and bit until the pain had filled her mind. Daniel vanished. After several moments she withdrew the still-clenched fist and looked at it. Her teeth had broken the skin; blood was trickling on the back of her hand.

She looked around uncertainly. It seemed as though the flare of pain had cleared her mind, driving him away. She pushed down on the mattress, standing. Now, she thought, the chapel. That was where the answer lay.

She ran across the room and jerked open the door. Hurrying into the hall, he turned toward the staircase. I'll reach it, she thought. He can't possess me every moment. If I keep on going, no matter what happens, I can get there.

She stopped, her heartbeat jolting. A figure blocked her way: a gaunt man dressed in ragged, filthy clothes; bones showing through his skin; long hair shaggy; face malformed by sickness; tiny, glowing eyes buried in dark-rimmed sockets; mouth distended, filled with thick, discolored teeth. Florence stared at him. It was one of Belasco's victims, she knew. He'd looked like this before he died.

The figure disappeared. Florence began descending the stairs. The acid coldness started up her spine again. She felt the gray defilement in her blood and fought it off, biting on her hand until the pain had driven it away. Pain was the answer! Whenever Daniel tried to take control, she'd drive him off with pain, because it filled her mind and left no room for him!

She stopped, hitched back. Two figures sprawled across the steps below, a man and woman. The man was plunging a knife into the woman's throat. He started sawing at the jagged wound, blood spouting, splashing on his twisted, gleeful face. He was cutting off the woman's head. Florence jammed her fist into her mouth and bit down, stiffening at the burst of pain. The man and woman vanished. She descended farther, wondering where the others were: Fischer, Edith, Barrett. It didn't matter; they couldn't help.

As she crossed the entry hall, she caught sight of Barrett in the great hall, working on his machine. Fool, she thought. It wasn't going to work. He was full of shit, the stupid—

No! She ground her teeth into her hand again, eyes wide and staring. Let her bite her fingers to the bone before succumbing to Daniel's sway again. She wished she had a knife. She'd thrust it far enough into her flesh to keep the pain there constantly. It was the answer: agony that blocked his contaminated soul from hers.

She started down the corridor. A wild-eyed man was hunched across a naked woman's back. She was dead, a sash cord pulled around her neck, her face purplish, eyes bulging from their sockets. Florence sank her teeth into her hand. Blood was running down her lips now, dripping onto her throat. The figures vanished as she reached the chapel door. A man was crouched in front of it. His face was white, his expression drugged. He held a severed human hand to his lips, sucking on one of the fingers. She bit into her hand. The figure vanished. Florence fell against the door and pushed it in.

She stood wavering at the head of the center aisle. A maelstrom of power filled the air. This was the nucleus, the core. She started down the aisle, then jerked back with a gasp as she saw the cat lying in the puddle of blood. It had been cut in two.

She shook her head. She mustn't stop now. She was almost to the answer. She had beaten Daniel; she would beat the house now. She stepped across the cat, advancing on the altar. Dear God, the power was incredible! It radiated through her, pulsing, driving. Darkness flickered in her mind. She thrust her aching hand into her mouth again and bit. The darkness cleared a little, and she moved against the power. It was like a living wall before her. She was almost to the altar now. Her eyes were staring, fixed. She'd win her battle yet. With God's help, she would—

Sudden weakness turned her limbs to stone. She fell against the altar heavily. The power was too strong! She looked up dumbly at the crucifix. It seemed to move. She stared at it in horror. It was moving toward her. No, she thought. She tried to back off, but she couldn't budge, rooted to the spot as though by some gigantic magnet. *No!* The crucifix was falling. It was going to hit her!

Florence cried out as it struck her head and chest and knocked her backward violently. She crashed to the floor, the massive cross and figure crushing down on her, knocking out her breath. The serpentine chill went lashing up her spine. She tried to scream but couldn't. Darkness flooded through her.

The possession ended instantly.

Florence's eyes bulged, her face distorted by a look of agony. She couldn't breathe, the pain was so intense. She tried to push the crucifix away, but it wouldn't move. The pain of trying made her gag. She lay immobile, groaning at the endless waves of agony that filled her. Once again she tried to push the crucifix. It moved a little, but the movement nearly made her faint. Her face was gray, dewed with cold sweat.

It took fifteen minutes to do. She almost fainted seven times before she'd finished, holding on to consciousness only with the most intense exertion of will. Finally she pushed aside the heavy crucifix and tried to sit up, gasping at the agony of the attempt. Slowly, ashen lips pressed together, she struggled to her knees. Blood started running down her thighs.

The sight of the phallus made her vomit. Hunching over, she expelled the contents of her stomach on the floor, eyes glazed with pain. *He'd tricked her.* There was no answer here. He'd only wanted to commit this final profanation on her mind and body. Florence rubbed a palsied hand across her lips. No more, she thought. She looked around and saw the huge nail sticking from the crucifix's back; it had been pulled out from the wall. She dragged herself across the floor until she'd reached the nail. Hovering above it, she began to saw the insides of her wrists across its point, hissing at the pain. She began to sob. "No more," she said. *"No more."*

She slumped back. Blood was flowing from her wrists like water. She closed her eyes. He can't do anything more to me, she thought. Even if my soul is held in bondage in this house forever, I won't be his living puppet anymore.

She felt life draining from her. She was escaping. Daniel couldn't hurt her now. Feeling had begun to leave; pain was fading. God would forgive her self-destruction. It was what she had to do. Her lips drew back in a surrendering smile.

He would understand.

Her eyes fluttered open. Were those footsteps? She tried to turn her head but couldn't. The floor seemed to tremble. She tried to see. Was that a figure standing by her, looking down? She couldn't focus her eyes.

Suddenly it struck her. Horrified, she tried to push up, but was too weak. She had to let them know! Florence struggled fitfully to rise. Clouds of darkness were enveloping her. Everything felt numb. She turned her head and saw her blood running on the floorboards. Help me, God! she pleaded. *She had to let them know!*

Slowly, agonizingly, she reached out to shape the moving scarlet ribbons.

11:08 A.M.

Fischer jarred up, heartbeat pounding, and looked around in dread. His head was throbbing violently. He wanted to fall back on the pillow, but something kept him from it.

He dropped his legs across the mattress edge and stood. He began to reel, and pressed both hands against his head, eyes closed, body rocking back and forth. He groaned, remembering that Barrett had given him pills. Damn fool! he thought. How long had he been unconscious?

He started for the door, moving like a drunken man, trying to maintain his balance. He moved unevenly into the corridor and started toward Florence's room. He entered and stopped. She wasn't in bed. His gaze jumped to the bathroom. Its door was open; there was no one there. He turned and stumbled back into the corridor. What the hell was wrong with Barrett, anyway? He tried to move faster, but the impact inside his head was too painful. He stopped and leaned against the wall, a billowing of nausea in his stomach. He blinked and shook his head. The pain grew worse. To hell with it! he thought. He staggered forward willfully. He had to find her, get her out of here.

He glanced into the Barretts' room in passing, jarred to a halt. He moved inside and looked around incredulously. Barrett wasn't there; he'd left his wife alone! Fischer clenched his teeth in fury. *What the hell was going on?* He moved across the room as quickly as he could and dropped his hand on Edith's shoulder.

She jerked back from his touch, eyes open suddenly, gaping at him.

"Where's your husband?" Fischer asked.

She looked around in shock. "He isn't here?"

He watched dazedly as she stood. From the look on her face, he saw that she was taken aback by his appearance.

"Never mind," he mumbled, heading for the corridor. Edith didn't speak. She brushed past him, calling, "Lionel!"

She was halfway down the stairs before he'd reached the landing. "Don't go alone!" he cried. She paid no attention. Fischer tried to hurry down the steps but had to stagger to a halt, clinging to the rail as pain drove spikes into his skull. He leaned against the banister, trembling. "Lionel!" he heard her calling as she ran across the entry hall. He heard an answering call below and opened his eyes. Where else? he thought bitterly. Barrett was so anxious to prove his point, he was leaving his wife alone now, ignoring Florence. Stupid bastard!

Fischer hobbled down the stairs and walked across the entry hall, teeth set against the jolting pain. Entering the great hall, he saw Barrett and Edith standing by the Reversor. "Where is she?" he demanded.

Barrett looked at him blankly.

"*Well?*"

"She's not in her room?"

"Would I ask if she was?" snarled Fischer.

Barrett started limping toward him, joined by Edith. From the look on her face, Fischer could tell she was upset with Barrett too. "But I listened," Barrett said; "I checked you awhile ago. And the pills I gave her—"

"To hell with your pills!" Fischer cut him off. "You think possession can be stopped with pills?"

"I don't believe—"

"Screw what you believe!" Fischer's head was pounding so hard now that he could barely see. "She's gone, that's all that matters!"

"We'll find her," Barrett said; but there was no assurance in his voice. He looked around uneasily. "We'll try the cellar first. She might—"

He stopped as Fischer clutched his head, his face distended by a look of agony. "You'd better sit," he said.

"Shut up!" Fischer shouted hoarsely. He hunched over, making retching noises.

"Fischer—" Barrett started forward.

Fischer stumbled to a chair and dropped down heavily. Barrett approached as fast as he could, followed by Edith. They stopped as Fischer jerked down his hands and looked at them in shock.

"What?" asked Barrett.

Fischer began to shiver.

"What is it?" Barrett's voice rose involuntarily. Fischer's look unnerved him.

"The chapel."

Edith's scream of horror pierced the air. She spun away and stumbled to the wall.

"*Oh, my dear God,*" Barrett murmured.

Fischer walked unsteadily to the body and stared at it. Her eyes were open, looking upward, her face the hue of pale wax. His gaze shifted to her genitals. They were caked with blood, the outer tissues shredded.

He twitched as Barrett stopped beside him. "What *happened* to her?" the older man whispered.

"She was killed," said Fischer venomously. "Murdered by this house." He tensed, expecting Barrett's contradiction, but there was none. "I don't see how she could have gotten up with all that sedative inside her," was all Barrett said, his tone one of guilt.

He saw that Fischer had turned to look at the crucifix lying nearby and did the same. Seeing the blood on its wooden phallus, he felt his stomach walls contract. "My God," he said.

"Not here," Fischer muttered. He shouted suddenly, as if he'd gone berserk: "*There's no God in this fucking house!*"

Across the chapel, Edith jerked around to look at Fischer

startledly. Barrett started to speak, then held it back. He drew in a trembling breath. The chapel smelled of gore. "We'd better get her out of here."

"I'll do it," Fischer said.

"You'll need some help."

"I'll do it."

Barrett shivered at the look on Fischer's face. "Very well."

Fischer crouched beside the body. Darkness pulsed before him, and he had to put down both hands to support himself; he felt them pressing into her blood. After a while his vision cleared, and he looked at her face. *She tried so hard,* he thought. Reaching out, he closed her eyes as gently as he could.

"What's that?" Barrett asked.

Fischer glanced up, wincing at the pain the movement caused. Barrett was staring at the floor near Florence. He looked down. It was too gloomy to see. He heard Barrett fumble in his pockets, then the scratching of a match end on a striking surface. The flare of light made his eyes contract painfully.

She'd drawn a symbol on the floor, using a finger dipped in her blood. It was a crude circle with something scrawled inside it. Fischer looked at it intently, trying to decipher it. Abruptly he saw what it was. Barrett spoke at the same moment.

"It looks like the letter 'B.' "

11:47 A.M.

They stood in the doorway, watching Fischer's slowly moving form until it vanished in the mist. Then Barrett turned.

"All right," he said.

She followed him into the great hall. Barrett hobbled quickly to the Reversor, and she stopped to watch him, trying not to think of Florence. Barrett made a final check on the Reversor, then turned to look at her.

"It's ready," he said.

She wished, for his sake, she could experience the emotion he obviously felt. "I know this moment is important to you," she said.

"Important to science." He turned to the Reversor, set its timer, turned several knobs, then, after hesitating for a moment, threw the switch.

For several seconds Edith thought that nothing was happening. Then she heard a resonant hum rise to audibility inside the giant structure and began to feel a throbbing in the floor.

She stared at the Reversor. The hum was rising in pitch and volume, the vibration in the floor increasing; she could feel it running up her legs, into her body. *Power*, she thought—the only thing that could oppose the house. She didn't understand it, but feeling its heavy throb in her body, its reverberation starting to hurt her ears, she almost believed.

She started as, behind the Reversor's grillwork, tubes began to glow with an intense phosphorescence. Barrett backed off slowly. His fingers trembled as he drew out his pocket watch. Exactly noon. Fittingly precise, he thought. He pushed the watch into his pocket and turned to Edith. "We have to go."

Their coats were on the table by the front door; Barrett had brought them down earlier. Hastily he helped her on with hers. As she assisted him, she glanced toward the great hall. The noise of the Reversor was painful even here now. She could feel its pulsing in the floor beneath her, hear the rattling of a vase nearby. "Quickly," Barrett said.

A moment later they had left the house and were hurrying

along the gravel path, around the tarn, the sound of the Reversor fading behind them. As they crossed the bridge, Edith saw the Cadillac standing in the mist, and tightened at the thought of Florence being in it.

Barrett pulled open the back door, flinching as he saw that Fischer had the blanket-covered body on the seat with him, cradling its head and upper torso in his arms. "Couldn't we—" he started, breaking off as Fischer glared at him. He hesitated, then reshut the door. No point in setting Fischer off. He was close enough to the edge as it was.

"She's in there *with* him?" Edith whispered.

"Yes."

Edith looked ill. "I can't sit in there with—" She couldn't finish.

"We'll sit in front."

"Can't we go back in the house?" she asked, fleetingly aware of the grotesqueness of her requesting to go back inside Hell House.

"Absolutely not. The radiation would kill us."

She stared at him. "All right," she finally said.

As they got into the front and closed the door, Barrett glanced into the rearview mirror. Fischer was bent over Florence's body, his chin resting on what must have been the top of her head. How badly had her death affected him? he wondered.

Remembering then, he turned to Edith. "Deutsch is dead," he told her.

Edith didn't respond. At last she nodded. "It doesn't matter."

Unexpectedly, Barrett felt a flare of anger. *Doesn't* it? he thought. He turned away. Why brood about it, then? He'd done his best to provide for her. If she didn't care . . .

He willed away the anger. What else could she say? He

straightened up, grimacing at the pain in his thumb. "Fischer?"

There was no reply. Barrett looked around. "Deutsch is dead," he said. "His son refuses to pay us."

"What's the difference?" Fischer mumbled. Barrett saw his fingers tightening on Florence Tanner's shoulder. He turned back to the front and, reaching into his overcoat pocket, withdrew the ring of keys. Fingering through them, he found the ignition key and pushed it into its slot. He turned the key enough to activate the dial needles without starting the engine. There wasn't enough fuel to run the engine for forty minutes so they could keep the interior warm. Damn, he thought. He should have remembered to bring more blankets from the house, some brandy.

He leaned his head back, closed his eyes. Well, they'd have to endure it, that was all. Personally, he didn't care— This moment was too engulfing for anything else in the world to overshadow it.

Behind those windowless walls some several hundred yards distant, Hell House was dying.

12:45 P.M.

Barrett snapped his watch cover shut. "It's done."

Edith's face was without expression. Barrett started feeling disappointment at her lack of response, then realized that she could not conceive of what had taken place inside the house. Reaching across the seat, he patted her hand, then turned. "Fischer?"

Fischer was still slumped over Florence, holding her body against himself. He looked up slowly.

"Will you go back in with us?"

Fischer didn't speak.

"The house is clear."

"Is it?"

Barrett wanted to smile. He couldn't blame the man, of course. His claim *did* sound preposterous after what had taken place this week. "I need you with me," he said.

"Why?"

"To verify that the house is clear."

"What if it isn't?"

"I guarantee it is." Barrett waited for Fischer's decision. When nothing happened, he said, "It will take only a few minutes."

Fischer stared at him in silence for a while before he edged away from Florence's body and, shifting carefully to a kneeling position on the floor, lowered her to the seat. He looked at her for several moments, then withdrew his arms and turned to the door.

They came together in front of the car. *Déjà vu*, thought Edith. It was as though time had been reversed and they were about to enter Hell House for the first time. Only the absence of Florence prevented the illusion from being complete. She shivered, drawing up the collar of her coat. She felt numb with cold. Lionel had run the engine and heater for brief periods of time during their wait, but minutes after he switched off the engine each time, the cold had returned.

The walk to the house was eerily reminiscent of Monday's arrival: their shoes ringing on the concrete bridge; her glancing back to see the limousine being swallowed by the mist; the circling trudge around the tarn, its hideous odor in her nostrils; the crunch of gravel underneath their shoes; the cold penetrating flesh; her feelings as the massive house loomed up in front of them. It was no use. She couldn't believe that Lionel was right. Which meant that they were walking back into a trap. They'd gotten out somehow; three of them, anyway.

Now, incredibly, they were returning. Even realizing that Lionel had to know the effect of his Reversor, it was impossible to comprehend the suicidal folly of their move.

The final yards along the gravel path. The approach up the wide porch steps; the click of shoes on concrete again. The double doors ahead of them. Edith shuddered. *No*, she thought, I won't go back inside.

Then Barrett had opened the door for her, and without a word she'd entered Hell House again.

They stopped, and Barrett shut the door. Edith saw that the vase had fallen to the floor and shattered.

Barrett looked at Fischer questioningly.

"I don't know," Fischer said.

Barrett tensed. "You have to open up." Was it possible that Fischer had no extrasensory perception left? The thought that he might have to bring another psychic all the way to Maine before finding out was appalling to him.

Fischer moved away from them. He looked around uneasily. It did feel different. That could be a trick, though. He'd been fooled before. He didn't dare expose himself like that again.

Barrett watched him restively. Edith glanced at her husband and saw how impatient he was. "Try, Mr. Fischer," he said abruptly. "I guarantee there'll be no trouble."

Fischer didn't look around. He walked across the entry hall. Amazingly, the atmosphere *had* changed. Even without opening up, he could sense that. Still, how *much* had it changed? How much faith could he really have in Barrett? His theory had sounded good. But Barrett wasn't just asking him to believe a theory. He was asking him to put his life at stake again.

He kept on walking. He was passing through the archway into the great hall now; he heard the Barretts' footsteps following. Entering the hall, he stopped and looked around. The floor was littered with broken objects. Across from him, a tapestry hung askew on its wall. What had the Reversor *done?* He wanted very much to know but was afraid to try to find out.

"*Well?*" asked Barrett. Fischer waved him off. I'll do it when I'm ready, he thought angrily.

He stood immobile, listening, waiting.

On impulse then, he dropped the barriers. Closing his eyes, he spread his arms, his hands, his fingers, drawing in whatever might be hovering in the atmosphere.

His eyes jerked open, and he looked around in bafflement. There was nothing.

Distrust returned. He whirled and darted past them. Edith looked alarmed, but Barrett grabbed her arm, preventing her from panic. "He's startled because there's nothing to pick up." he told her.

Fischer ran into the entry hall. Nothing. He raced down the corridor to the chapel, shoved the door in violently. Nothing. He turned and ran to the steps, descending them with avid leaps, ignoring the pain in his head. Straight-arming through the pool doors, he raced to the steam room, pulled open its door, braced himself.

Nothing.

He turned in awe. "I don't believe it."

He sprinted back along the pool and out into the corridor. He ran into the wine cellar. Nothing. He dashed back up the stairs, gasping for breath. The theater. Nothing. The ballroom. Nothing. The billiard room. Nothing. He raced along the corridor with frenzied strides. The kitchen. Nothing. The dining hall. Nothing. He charged across the great hall, back into the entry hall. Barrett and Edith were still there. Fischer rocked to a panting halt in front of them. He started to speak, then broke into a run for the stairs. Barrett felt a rush of exultation.

"Done," he said. "It's *done*, Edith. *Done!*" He threw his arms around her, pulled her close. Her heart was pounding. She still couldn't believe it. Yet Fischer was beside himself. She watched him leaping up the staircase, two steps at a time.

Fischer ran across the corridor to the Barretts' room. He plunged inside. Nothing! Spinning with a dazzled cry, he ran into the corridor again, to Florence's room. Nothing! Along the corridor to his room. Nothing! Over to Belasco's quarters. Nothing! God Almighty! *Nothing!* His head was pounding, but he didn't care. He raced along the corridor, flinging open doors to all the unused bedrooms. Nothing! Everywhere he went, nothing, absolutely nothing! Jubilation burst inside him. Barrett had done it!

Hell House was clear!

He had to sit. Staggering to the nearest chair, he dropped down limply. Hell House cleared. It was incredible. He thrust aside the knowledge that he'd have to alter everything he'd ever believed. It didn't matter. *Hell House had been cleared*, exorcised by that fantastic—*what?*—down there. His laugh broke hoarsely. And he had called it a pile of junk. Jesus God, a pile of *junk!* Why hadn't Barrett kicked him in the teeth?

He slumped against the chair, eyes closed, regaining breath.

Reaction came abruptly. If she'd lasted one more hour. Just another *hour!* He felt a sudden, anguished rage at Barrett for having left her alone.

It wouldn't last. It was overpowered by the awe he felt for the physicist. Patiently, doggedly, Barrett had done his work, knowing that they'd thought him wrong. Yet he'd been right all the time. Fischer shook his head in wonderment. It was a miracle. He inhaled deeply, had to smile. The air still stank.

But not with the reek of the dead.

2:01 P.M.

Fischer braked a little as the Cadillac moved into another pocket of impenetrable mist. He'd decided to keep the car and sell it if he could, splitting the take with Barrett. Failing that, he'd drive the damn thing into a lake; but Deutsch would never see it again. He hoped that Barrett had some way of getting the Reversor out of Hell House before Deutsch could get his hands on it. It had to be worth a small fortune.

Reaching forward, he turned on the windshield wipers, his eyes fixed on the road as he drove through the dark woods, trying to dovetail the pieces in his mind.

First of all, Barrett had been right. The power in the house had been a massive residue of electromagnetic radiation. Barrett had negated it, and it had vanished. Where did that leave Florence's beliefs? Were they totally invalidated now? Had she, as Barrett had claimed, created her own haunting, unconsciously manipulating the energy in the house to prove her points? It seemed to fit. It shook his own beliefs as well, but it fitted.

Still, why had her unconscious will chosen to effect a type of phenomena she'd never effected in her life? To convince Barrett, to whom physical phenomena were the only meaningful kind, the answer came immediately.

All right, there really had been a Daniel Belasco, he thought. He'd been bricked inside that wall alive by someone, probably his father. That much Florence had picked up psychically, reading the house's energy like the memory bank of a computer. That Daniel Belasco was, therefore, the haunting force had been her mistaken interpretation of those facts.

Why had she carried it to such suicidal extremes, though? The question baffled him. After a lifetime of intelligent mediumship, why had she literally killed herself to prove that she was right? Was that the kind of person she'd really been? Had her outward behavior been entirely a deception? It seemed impossible. She'd functioned as a psychic for many years without incurring harm; or inflicting it, as she apparently had on Barrett. Had the power of Hell House been so overwhelming that she simply hadn't been able to cope with it? Barrett would undoubtedly say yes; and it was true that, facing it that single time yesterday, he had almost been destroyed by its enormity. Still . . .

Fischer lit a cigarette and blew out smoke. He had to force himself back to the unassailable fact that the house was clear. Barrett had been right; there was no denying it. His theory made sense: shapeless power in the house requiring the focus of invading winds in order to function. What had the house been like between 1940 and last Monday? he wondered. Silent? Dormant? Waiting for some new intelligence to enter? Undoubtedly—since Barrett was correct.

Correct.

He tried to fight away encroaching doubts. Damn it, he'd been in the house! He'd run from room to room, completely opened. There'd been nothing. Hell House had been clear. Why were these stupid qualms assailing him, then?

Because it was all too simple, he realized abruptly.

What about the debacles of 1931 and 1940? He'd been in one of them and knew how incredibly complex the events had been. He thought about the list Barrett had. There must have been more than a hundred different phenomena itemized on it. This week's occurrences had been staggeringly varied. It simply didn't make sense that it had all been radiation to be turned off like a lamp. True, there was no logic to back up his misgiving, but he could not dispel it. There had been so many "final answers" in the past, people swearing that they knew the secret of Hell House. Florence had believed it of herself and had been lured, by that belief, to her destruction.

Now Barrett felt *he* had the final answer. Granted that he had what seemed to be complete verification of his certainty. What if he was wrong, though? If there'd been any recurrent method at all to the house, it had been that at the moment when a person thought the final answer had been found, the house's final attack was launched.

Fischer shook his head. He didn't want to believe that. Logically, he *couldn't* believe it. Barrett had been right. The house was clear.

Abruptly he recalled the bloody circle on the chapel floor, the "B" inside it. Belasco, obviously. Why had Florence done that? Had her thoughts been blinded by the imminence of death? Or crystallized?

No. It couldn't be Belasco. The house was clear. He'd felt it himself, for Christ's sake! Barrett had been absolutely right. Electromagnetic radiation was the answer.

Why, then, was his foot pressing down harder and harder on the accelerator? Why was his heart beginning to pound? Why was there an icy prickling on the back of his neck? *Why did he have this constantly increasing dread that he had to get back to the house before it was too late?*

2:17 P.M.

Barrett came out of the bathroom, wearing robe and slippers. He limped to Edith's bed and sat on the edge of it. She was lying down, the comforter pulled over her. "Feeling better?" she asked.

"Marvelous."

"How's the thumb?"

"I'll have it checked as soon as we get home." He wouldn't tell her that he'd tried to unwind the bandage in the shower but had been forced to stop because he'd almost fainted from the pain.

"Home." Edith's smile was bemused. "I guess I still can't believe we're really going to see it again."

"We'll be there by tomorrow." Barrett made a face. "We'd be there by tonight if Deutsch Junior wasn't such a—"

"—son of a bitch," she provided.

Barrett smiled. "To put it mildly." The smile disappeared. "I'm afraid our security is gone, my dear."

"You're my security," she said. "Leaving this house with you by my side will be worth a million dollars to me." She took hold of his left hand. "Is it really over, Lionel? All of it?"

He nodded. "All of it."

"It's so hard to believe."

"I know." He squeezed her hand. "You don't mind if I say I told you so, do you?"

"I don't mind anything as long as I know it's over."

"It is."

"What a pity she had to die when the answer was so close."

"It *is* a pity. I should have made her leave."

She put her other hand on his and pressed it reassuringly. "You did everything you could."

"I shouldn't have left her alone before."

"How could you have known she'd wake up?"

"I couldn't. It was incredible. Her subconscious was so intent on validating her delusion that her system actually rejected the sedation."

"The poor woman," Edith said.

"The poor, self-defrauded woman. Even to the final touch—scrawling, in her own blood, that circle with the 'B' inside it. She had to believe, even as she died, that she was right; that it was Belasco destroying her—the father or the son, I don't know which. She couldn't allow herself to believe it was her own mind doing it." He winced. "How pitiful an end it must have been; pain-racked, terrified—"

Seeing the look on Edith's face, he stopped. "I'm sorry."

"It's all right."

He forced a smile. "Well, Fischer should be back in an hour or so, and we can leave." He frowned. "Assuming he isn't detained when he brings in her body."

"Can't say I'll miss the old place," she said after a few moments.

Barrett laughed softly. "Nor can I. Although"—he thought about it for a moment—"it is my scene of—how shall I term it?—triumph?"

"Yes." She nodded. "It *is* a triumph. I can't really comprehend what you've done, but I sense how terribly important it is."

"Well, if I do say so myself, it's going to give parapsychology rather a leg up into polite society."

Edith smiled.

"Because it's science," he said. "No mumbo-jumbo. Nothing the critics can pick at—though I'm sure they'll try. Not that I argue with them when they cavil at the usual approach to psychic phenomena. Their resentment of the aura of trivial humbug which hovers over most of the phenomena and its advocates is justifiable. By and large, *psi* doesn't have an air of respectability. Therefore the critics ridicule it rather than risk being ridiculed themselves for examining it seriously. This is *a priori* evaluation, unfortunately—one hundred percent unscientific. They'll continue to overlook the import of parapsychology, I'm afraid, until they're able—as Huxley put it—'to sit down before fact as a little child—be prepared to give up every preconceived notion, follow humbly wherever and to whatsoever abysses nature leads.' "

He chuckled self-consciously. "End of discourse." Leaning

over, he kissed her gently on the cheek. "The speechifier loves you," he said.

"Oh, Lionel." She slipped her arms around his back. "I love you, too. And I'm so proud of you."

She was asleep now. Barrett carefully disengaged his fingers from hers and stood. He smiled down at her. She deserved this sleep. She hadn't had a decent night's rest since they'd entered Hell House.

His smile broadened as he turned from the bed. Hell House was a misnomer now. From this day forth, it would be merely the Belasco house.

As he dressed with slow, contented movements, he wondered what would happen to the house. It ought to be a shrine to science. Deutsch would doubtless sell it to the highest bidder, though. He grunted with amusement. Not that he could imagine anyone wanting to own it.

He combed his hair, looking at his reflection in the wall mirror. His eye was caught by the rocking chair across the room, and he smiled again. All of that was over now, the endless little outputs of meaningless kinetics. No more winds or odors, no percussions; nothing.

He crossed the room and went into the corridor, heading for the stairs. He was glad that Fischer had insisted on taking Florence Tanner's body into town immediately. He knew the other man would not have placed the body in the trunk, and it would have been terribly painful for Edith to ride all the way to Caribou Falls with the body in the back seat. He hoped that Fischer didn't take too long in returning. He was working up quite an appetite; his first of the week. A celebration meal, he thought. Poor old Deutsch, it suddenly occurred to him; he'd never know now. Perhaps it was kinder that way. Not that Deutsch had wanted—or deserved—kindness.

He descended the staircase slowly, eying the enormous entry hall. A museum, he thought. Really, something should be done with the house now that the terror had been exorcised.

He hobbled across the entry hall. He'd examined his body in the full-length bathroom mirror after taking his shower, imagining it was how a prizefighter's body looked after a particularly grueling bout—the purple-black contusions everywhere. The burned skin on his calf was still contracting, too; he could feel the tautness of the scalded area pulling at the skin around it. The abrasion on his shin still hurt as well; and, as for his leg and thumb—Barrett had to smile. The Olympics I'm not ready for, he thought.

He crossed the great hall, walking to the Reversor. Once again, he stared at the main dial in awe: 14,780. He'd never dreamed the reading could be so high. No wonder this place had been the Everest of haunted houses. He shook his head almost admiringly. The house had been aptly named.

He turned and limped to the table, frowning as he visualized the necessary packing. He looked at the array of equipment. Maybe he wouldn't have to pack it, after all. If they put blankets in the limousine trunk for padding, the equipment could probably be wrapped in towels or something. Maybe they should take a few *objets d'art* as well, he thought, repressing a smile. Deutsch would never miss them. He ran a finger over the top of the EMR recorder.

Its needle stirred.

Barrett twitched. He stared at the needle. It was motionless again. Odd, he thought. Touching the recorder must have activated the needle by static electricity. It wouldn't happen again.

The needle jumped across the dial, then fluttered back to zero.

Barrett felt a tic in his right cheek. What was happening?

The recorder couldn't function on its own. EMR was convertible to measurable energy only in the presence of a psychic. He forced a dry laugh. Grotesque if I discover I'm a medium after all these years, he thought. He made a scoffing noise. That was absurd. Besides, there was no radiation left in the house. He'd eliminated it.

The needle started moving. It did not jump or flutter. It inched across the dial as though recording a build-up of radiation. "No," Barrett said. His tone was irritated. This was ludicrous.

The needle continued moving. Barrett stared at it as it passed the 100 mark, the 150 mark. He shook his head. This was absurd. It couldn't record by itself. Moreover, there was nothing left in the house to record. "No," he said again. There was more anger than dismay in his voice. This simply could not be.

His head jerked up so suddenly that it hurt his neck. He watched the needle of the dynamometer begin to arc across its dial. This was *impossible*. His gaze leaped to the face of the thermometer. It was starting to record a drop in temperature. "*No,*" he said. His face was pale with malice. This was nonsense, totally illogical.

He caught his breath as the camera clicked. He gaped at it and heard the film inside it being wound, heard the lens click shut again, He gasped again, muscles spasmed as the rack of colored lights went on, turned off, went on again. "*No.*" He shook his head unyieldingly. This was not acceptable. It was a trick of some kind; it was fraudulent.

He started violently as one of the test tubes broke in half, falling from its rack to clatter on the tabletop. *This cannot be!* he heard a voice protesting in his mind. Abruptly he remembered Fischer's single question. "No!" he snapped. He backed off from the table. It was utterly impossible. Once dispelled, the radiation had no restorative power whatever.

He cried out as the rack of lights began to flicker rapidly. "No!" he raged. He would not believe it! The needles of his instruments were not all quivering across their dials. The thermometer was not recording a constant drop in temperature. The electric stove had not begun to glow. The galvanometers were not recording on their own. The camera wasn't taking photographs. The tubes and vessels weren't breaking one by one. The EMR recorder needle hadn't passed the 700 mark. It was all delusion. He was suffering some aberration of the senses. *This-could-not-be-happening.* "Wrong!" he shouted, face distorted by fury. "Wrong, wrong, *wrong!*"

His mouth fell open as the EMR recorder started to expand. He stared at it in horror as it swelled as though its sides and top were made of rubber. *No.* He shook his head in disavowal. He was going mad. This was impossible. He would not accept it He would not—

He screamed as the recorder suddenly exploded, screamed again as metal splinters drove into his face and eyes. He dropped his cane and threw his hands across his face. Something shot across the table, and he jolted backward as the camera struck him on the legs. He lost his balance, fell, heard equipment crashing to the floor as though someone were flinging it. He tried to see but couldn't, staggered blindly to his feet.

It struck him then, a crushing, arctic force that jerked him from his feet as though he were a toy. A cry of shocked bewilderment flooded from him as the glacial force propelled him through the air and flung him violently against the front of the Reversor. Barrett felt his left arm snap. He shrieked in pain, dropping to the floor.

Again the unseen force grabbed hold of him and started dragging him across the hall. He couldn't break away from it. Trying in vain to scream for help, he bumped and slithered along the floor. A massive table blocked his way. Sensing it, he flung his right arm up, crashed against its edge, his bandaged thumb driven back against its wrist. His mouth jerked open in a strangling cry of agony. Blood began to spout from the hand. Yanked across the tabletop and somersaulted down onto the floor again, he caught an obscure glimpse of the thumb dangling from his hand by shards of bone and skin.

He tried to fight against the power which hauled him brutally across the entry hall, but he was helpless in its grip, a plaything in the jaws of some invisible creature. Eyes staring sightlessly, face a blood-streaked mask of horror, he was dragged into the corridor feet first. His chest was filled with fiery pain as clutching hands crushed his heart. He couldn't breathe. His arms and legs were going numb. His face began to darken, turning red, then purple. Veins distended on his neck; his eyes began to bulge. His mouth hung open, sucking at the air in vain as the savage force bounced him down the stairs and drove his broken body through the swinging doors. The tile floor rushed beneath him. He was hurtled into space.

The water crashed around him icily. The clutching force dragged him toward the bottom. Water poured into his throat. He started choking, struggled fitfully. The force would not release him. Water gushed into his lungs. He doubled over, staring at the bottom as he strangled. Blood from his thumb was clouding everything. The power turned him slowly. He was staring upward, seeing through a reddish haze. There was someone standing on the pool edge, looking down at him.

The sound of his enfeebled thrashing faded. The figure blurred, began to disappear in shadows. Barrett settled to the bottom, eyes unseeing once again. Somewhere deep within the cavern of his mind a faint intelligence still flickered, crying out in anguish: *Edith!*

Then all was blackness, like a shroud enfolding him, as he descended into night.

2:46 P.M.

Edith's left hand jumped abruptly. Her wedding band had sheared in half and fallen to the bed. She snapped her eyelids back. The room was dark. "Lionel?"

The door was opened. The corridor was dark, too. Someone entered. "Lionel?" she said again.

"Yes."

She sat up groggily. "What happened?"

"Nothing to be concerned about. The generator just went out."

"Oh, no." She tried to see. It was too dark.

"It's not important," Lionel said. She heard his footsteps cross the room, felt his weight settle on the other side of the bed. She reached out nervously and felt his hand. "You're sure everything is all right?"

"Of course." The hand began to stroke her hair. "Don't be afraid. Let's take advantage of it."

"What?" She reached for him, but he was farther away than she'd thought.

"We haven't been together for a long time." Lionel's hand slid down her cheek. "And you're in need of it."

She made a questioning sound. His hand slid over to her left breast and began to squeeze it. "Lionel, don't," she said.

"Why not?" he asked. "Aren't I good enough for you?"

"What are you—?"

"Fischer's good enough," he interrupted. "Even Florence Tanner was good enough." His fingers tightened on her breast, hurting it. *"How about a little pussy for the old man now?"*

Edith tried to pull away his hand. She felt her heartbeat quicken. "No," she murmured.

"Yes," he said. The hand moved down abruptly, shoving up her skirt to clutch between her legs. *"Yes, you lesbian bitch."*

The lights went on.

Edith screamed. The hand released her, pulling back. It was bloodless, severed at the wrist, floating up above her chest now, gamboling in the air before her stricken face, vein ends dangling from it. Edith recoiled against the headboard. The hand dropped to her breast again, pinching her nipple between its thumb and index finger. She cried out shrilly, tried to knock it loose. The hand jumped forward like a leprous spider, clamping on her face, cold and smelling of the grave. A crazed shriek flooded from her, and the gray hand flew back. Edith jerked her legs up, kicking at it berserkly. The hand jumped up and started gesturing in the air, fingers wriggling wildly.

Suddenly it darted downward, vanishing into the bedclothes, and the comforter began to swell, ballooning quickly. Gasping, Edith flung herself across the mattress, springing to her feet. She lurched around the corner of the bed, fleeing for the door. The comforter flew upward. In an instant, she was covered by a cloud of moths. Flailing at the surge of insects, she stumbled blindly across the room. The moths enveloped her completely, gray wings beating at her face, bodies fluttering in her hair. She tried to scream, but moths flew in her mouth; she spit them out in horrified revulsion, pressed her lips together. Moths flew in her ears. Their dusty wings whipped frenziedly against her eyes. Both arms flung across her face, she crashed against the octagonal table and began to fall.

Before she hit the floor, the moths were gone. She landed hard and scrabbled to her knees. The table thudded down nearby, pages of Lionel's manuscript spilling across the rug in front of her. The pages leaped into the air. She swung at them in mindless panic as they tore in shreds before her eyes. The pieces shot into the air and fluttered downward like a rain of giant snowflakes. Edith backed away from them, pushing at the floor with hands and feet. A man began to laugh. She looked around in terror. "Lionel," she muttered. "Lionel." She heard her own voice played back like a tape recording. "No," she pleaded. "No," her voice repeated. Edith whined. She heard the whine again. She started crying, heard an echoed crying in the air. With a desperate lunge, she found her feet and dashed across the room. She jerked the door in, leaped back with a choking scream.

Florence stood in the doorway, naked, staring at her, dark blood running down her thighs and legs. Edith shrieked. Darkness swept across her. She began to fall.

She jerked erect as an electric current spasmed through her body. Darkness fled; she was acutely conscious, knowing even as she flung herself into the empty doorway that she hadn't been allowed to faint. She lunged into the corridor and headed for the stairs. The air was thick with mist. She smelled the odor of the tarn. A figure blocked her way. Edith jolted to a stop. The woman wore a white gown. She was soaking wet, her dark hair plastered down across her gray face. She was holding something in her arms. Edith stared at it in loathing; it was half-formed, monstrous. *Bastard Bog!* a voice screamed in her mind. She backed off, a demented moaning in her throat.

Something spun her, slammed against her back. To keep from falling, she was forced to run. She wasn't headed for the stairs! She tried to stop herself and turn but couldn't control her limbs. She screamed as Florence rushed at her. She felt the cold arms clamp around her, and her scream was cut off as the dead lips crushed on hers. She reached up, gagging, crazed with terror, tried to pull the head away.

Florence vanished. Edith's yanking motion made her fall. She landed on her knees. "Lionel!" she screamed. "Lionel!" roared a mocking voice. Cold wind rushed across her, whipping at her clothes and hair. She tried to stand. Something icy crashed against her neck. She screamed as teeth dug deep into her flesh. Her hands flew up, but there was nothing. Fetid spittle trickled down her skin. She felt the pitted indentations. "Lionel!" she screamed in anguish.

"Here!" he answered. Edith's head jerked up. He was running down the corridor toward her! She scrambled up and rushed toward him. She threw herself against him. Instantly she jerked back, staring at the man who held her. It was her father, with the slack expression of an imbecile on his face, his red-rimmed eyes regarding her with stupid glee, his mouth agape, his tongue protruding. He started pulling her against him, a sound of animal amusement rumbling in his chest. He was naked, bloated. Edith wrenched away from him. She tried to run, but something smashed against her side. She lost her balance and went floundering toward the banister that overlooked the entry hall. She crashed against it, crying out in pain. Her father advanced on her, holding his enormous penis with both hands. She started clambering across the rail, to die below, escape this horror.

Strong hands grabbed her. Edith whirled in horror. Lionel was holding her. She stared at him, refusing to believe. "Edith! It's me!" The sound of his familiar voice made her fall against him, sobbing. "Take me out of here," she begged.

"Right away," he answered. Left arm fixed around her back, he ran her to the stairs. She looked at him. He had no cane, he wasn't limping. "No," she moaned. "It's quite all right," he said. He rushed her down the staircase. Edith tried to pull away from him. "It's me," he said. She sobbed again. He wouldn't let her go. Hollow laughter rippled in the air. She looked around and saw the people grouped below, watching them elatedly. She turned to Lionel, but it wasn't Lionel anymore. It was a monstrous caricature of him, every feature gross, exaggerated, his voice a vicious mocking as he said, "It's me. It's me." "No!" she screamed. She wrestled with him helplessly. His grip was too strong. He wasn't even looking ahead. He was grinning at her as they ran. Edith closed her eyes. Let it be quick! she pleaded.

The entry hall, the corridor. She felt herself rushed along the floor. She couldn't make a sound. The theater door flew open; she was thrust inside. She opened her eyes and saw a crowd of naked people sitting in the velvet chairs, keening with amusement at her plight. She was half-dragged up the steps. The bloated parody of Lionel bound her to a post. She looked out at the audience. They howled with fierce anticipation. Edith cried out as her clothes were ripped away. The people cheered. It sounded muffled, from another world. Edith heard a coughing growl and turned her head. A crouching leopard stalked across the stage. She tried to scream, but nothing issued from her throat. The audience screamed. Edith closed her eyes. The leopard sprang. She felt its huge teeth sinking deep into her head, its heated, blood-sour breath flooding across her face. She felt its rear legs start to thrash berserkly, felt the talons ripping out her stomach. Black pain seared her, and she fell back, shrieking.

She was crumpled on the dusty stage. Heartbeat staggering, she sat up. The theater was empty. No. There was someone, sitting in the shadows of the last row, dressed in black. She seemed to hear a deep voice resonating in her mind. *Welcome to my house*, it said.

She tried to stand. Her legs began to buckle, and she fell against a wall. She pushed away and staggered to the steps. Lionel stood in front of her. "It's me," he said. She cried out, agonized. Laughter boomed inside the theater. Edith stumbled to the door and pushed it open. Lionel was standing in the corridor. "It's me," he said.

She tried to make the entry hall but couldn't; her body was turned to the side. Lionel was waiting on the landing of the cellar stairs. "It's me!" he cried. The stairwell yawned before her. Lionel was standing at the bottom, grinning up at her. "It's me!" he cried. Edith whimpered, clutching at the banister rail, half-pushed, half-descending on her own. Lionel was standing by the metal doors.

"It's me!" he cried. The swinging doors flew open, crashed against the wall inside. Lionel was standing by the pool. "It's me!" he cried. The force impelled her toward him. Edith staggered forward, stopped beside the pool. She stared into the bloody water.

Lionel was floating just below the surface, staring up at her.

Madness took her then. She backed off, screaming, stumbling out into the corridor. A figure came leaping down the stairs and grabbed her by the arms. She fought it with demented strength, shrieks of frenzy flooding from her throat. The figure shouted at her, but she heard only her own voice. Something struck her on the jaw, and suddenly she was falling, screaming endlessly, as she went plummeting into the depths.

3:31 P.M.

Edith stirred again. Her eyes fluttered open. For several moments she stared toward the front of the car. Then she turned in confusion, twitching as she saw him. She looked at him in questioning silence.

"I'm sorry I had to hit you," he said.

"That was you?"

He nodded.

Edith looked around abruptly. "Lionel."

"His body's in the trunk."

She started for the door, but Fischer restrained her. "You don't want to look at him." She continued struggling against his grip. "Don't," he said.

Edith fell back, averting her face. Fischer sat in silence, listening to her cry.

She turned to him abruptly. "Let's get out of here," she said.

He didn't move.

"What is it?"

"I'm not leaving."

Edith didn't understand.

"I'm going back inside."

"*Inside?*" She looked appalled. "You don't know what it's like in there."

"I have to—"

"You don't know what it's like!" she cut him off. "It killed my husband! It killed Florence Tanner! It would have killed me if you hadn't gotten back! No one has a chance in there!"

Fischer didn't argue.

"Aren't two deaths enough? Do you have to die too?"

"I don't plan to die."

She clutched his hand. "Don't leave me, please."

"I have to."

"*No.*"

"I have to."

"Please don't do it!"

"Edith, I *have* to."

"No! You don't! You *don't!* There isn't any reason to go back inside!"

"Edith." Fischer took her hand in both of his and waited for her crying to abate. "Listen now."

She shook her head, eyes closing.

"I have to. For Florence. For your husband."

"They wouldn't want you to—"

"*I* want it," Fischer interrupted. "I need it. If I leave Hell House now, I might as well crawl into my grave and die. I haven't done a thing all week. While Florence and your husband were doing everything they could to solve the haunting—"

"They couldn't solve it, though! There isn't any way of solving it!"

"Maybe not." He paused. "I'm going to try, though."

Edith glanced up quickly at him, then said nothing, silenced by his look. "I'm going to try," he said.

They were silent. Finally Fischer asked, "You drive, don't you?"

He saw a telltale flare of hope in her expression. "No," she said.

He smiled gently. "Yes, you do."

Edith's chin slumped forward on her chest. "You're going to die," she said. "Like Lionel. Like Florence."

Fischer drew in a slow breath.

"Then I will," he said.

Fischer crossed the bridge and trudged along the gravel path which ringed the tarn. He was alone now. For several moments the realization filled him with such dread that he almost turned and ran.

Edith had been crying when she left; she'd tried, in vain, to control it. Tears running down her cheeks, she'd turned the Cadillac and driven off into the mist. He had to go inside the house now anyway. He couldn't walk to Caribou Falls in this cold.

The bottoms of his tennis shoes made crunching noises on the gravel as he walked. What was he going to do? he wondered. He had no idea. Had Florence accomplished anything? Had Barrett? He had no way of knowing. He might be confronted with starting from the beginning all over again.

He began to shake, stiffening his back to fight it off. It didn't matter what he had to do. He was here; he'd do it.

Edith would bring back food and leave it on the porch for him. How long it lasted didn't matter either. Only one thing counted at the moment.

As he continued walking, he became conscious of the medallion Florence had given him pressed against his chest. He'd told Edith he was doing this for Barrett too, but really it was all for Florence. She was the one he could have helped, the one he should have helped.

The house again, a mist-obscured escarpment up ahead. Fischer stopped and looked at it. It might have stood there for a thousand years. Was there an answer to its haunting? He didn't know. But if he couldn't discover it, then no one could: of that much he was certain.

He padded silently across the porch steps to the door. It was still ajar, the way he'd left it when he'd carried Barrett's body to the car. He hesitated for a long time, sensing that to walk inside would decide, finally and irrevocably, his fate.

"Hell." What fate did he have, anyway? He went inside and shut the door. Moving to the telephone, he picked up the receiver. The line was dead. What did you expect? he asked himself. He dumped the receiver on the table. He was cut off absolutely now. He turned and looked around.

As he crossed the entry hall, he had the feeling that the house was swallowing him alive.

6:29 P.M.

Fischer sat at the huge round table in the great hall, eating a sandwich and drinking a cup of coffee; Edith had brought two sacks of food and left again without a word. It's insane, Fischer was thinking. He'd thought it endlessly for the past hour.

The atmosphere of Hell House was completely flat.

He hadn't even had to open up to realize it. The awareness had developed quickly as he'd toured the house, first upstairs, all the bedrooms, used and unused. If there'd been any presence in the air, he would have sensed it. There was nothing. It was grotesque. What had killed Barrett so violently, then? What had almost killed Edith? He'd felt that presence strongly as he'd rushed down the cellar steps to rescue her before. Now it was gone; the house felt as clear as it had after the Reversor had been used. It wasn't any kind of trick, either; he was sure of that. When he'd opened up the first time yesterday, he'd known that there was something lurking in the house. He'd miscalculated its power and its cunning, but he'd known it was there.

Now it wasn't.

Fischer stared at the floor. One of Barrett's galvanometers was lying near his feet, its side cracked open, springs and coils protruding from the gash like polished entrails. His gaze shifted to the other equipment lying broken on the rug, shifted to the Reversor, and held on the huge dent on its face. Something devastating had struck this room, struck this equipment, struck Barrett.

Where had it gone?

He sighed, and propping the soles of his tennis shoes against the table edge, leaned the chair back slightly. Now what? he thought. He'd come back imbued with fine dramatic resolution. For what? He was no further along than he'd ever been. There wasn't even anything to work with now.

He'd walked through every room on the first floor, stood for almost twenty minutes in the dining hall, looking at its wreckage: the massive table wedged against the fireplace screen, the giant sanctuary lamp battered on the floor, the overturned chairs, the debris of broken crockery and glassware, the coffeepot and serving dish, the scattering of silverware, the dried food, the coffee stain, the sallow blots of sugar and cream. Staring at it all, he'd tried to calculate what had happened. Which one of the two had been correct? Had Florence caused the attack, as Barrett had claimed? Or had it been Daniel Belasco, as Florence had insisted?

No way of knowing. Fischer had walked through the kitchen, out through the west doorway and down the corridor to the ballroom. What had made the chandelier move? Electromagnetic radiation, or the dead?

The chapel. Had Daniel Belasco possessed Florence?—or suicidal madness?

He'd gone into the garage, the theater, the cellar, walked along the pool, into the steam room. What had attacked Barrett there? Mindless power, or Belasco?

The wine cellar. He'd stood there for minutes, staring at the open section of wall. Nothing there; a void.

Where was the power?

Fischer picked up the tape recorder and set it back on the table. Finding the extension cord, he plugged it in, surprised to discover that it still worked. He reversed the spool, then pressed the PLAY button.

"Hold it!" Barrett's voice said loudly. There were shuffling noises. He heard heavy breathing; was it his? Then Barrett said, "Miss Tanner coming out of trance. Premature retraction, causing brief systemic shock." After several moments of silence, the recorder was turned off.

Fischer reversed the tape farther, played it back. "Teleplasmic veil beginning to condense," said Barrett's voice. Silence. Fischer remembered the mistlike fabric which had covered Florence's head and shoulders like a wet shroud. Why had she manifested physical phenomena? The question still disturbed him. "Separate filament extending downward," Barrett's voice said. Fischer reversed the spool and switched the recorder to PLAY again. "Medium's respiration now two hundred and ten," Barrett's voice was saying. "Dynamometer fourteen hundred and sixty. Temperature—" He stopped as someone gasped; Edith, Fischer recalled. Momentary silence. Then Barrett's voice said, "Ozone present in the air."

Fischer stopped the spool, reversed it, let it run. What could he possibly hope to learn from reliving those moments? They hadn't added up to anything, except to confirm to Florence what she believed, and to Barrett what he believed. He stopped the spool, began to play the tape. "Sitters: Doctor and Mrs. Lionel Barrett, Mr. Benjamin—" Fischer switched it off and ran the tape back farther still.

He stopped and played it, starting as the hysterical voice— Florence's, yet so unlike hers—cried out, "—don't want to hurt you, but I must! I *must!*" A momentary silence. The voice near choking with venom as it said: "I warn you. *Get out of this house before I kill you all.*"

Sudden banging sounds. Edith's frightened voice asking, *"What's that?"* Fischer stopped the spool, reversed the tape, and listened to the threatening voice again. Had it been the voice of Daniel Belasco? He listened to it five times, gleaning nothing from it. Barrett could have been right. It might have been Florence's subconscious creating the voice, the character, the threat.

With a muffled curse, he reversed the tape again and played it back. "Leave house," said the imperious voice of Red Cloud. Had there ever been such an entity, or had it, too, been a segment of Florence's personality? Fischer shook his head. There was a grunting noise. "No good," said the voice, deep-pitched, but conceivably Florence's, forced to a lower register. "No good. Here too long. Not listen. Not understand. Too much sick inside." Fischer had to smile, although it pained him. It was such a poor excuse for the voice of an Indian. "Limits," it was saying. "Nations. Terms. Not know

what that mean. Extremes and limits. Terminations and extremities." A pause. "Not know."

"Shit," said Fischer, jabbing in the button which stopped
the spool. He reversed it farther, switched it on. Silence.
"Now, if you'd—" Barrett began. "Red Cloud Tanner woman
guide," Florence interrupted in the deep voice. "Guide second
medium on this side."

He listened to the entire sitting: the rumbling voice of the
Indian; the description of the caveman entity; the "arrival" of
"the young man"; the hysterical voice, threatening them; the
fierce percussions; Barrett's voice describing the unexpected
onset of physical phenomena.

The second sitting: Florence's invocation and hymn; her
sinking into trance—the low-pitched, wavering moans, the
wheezing inhalations; Barrett's impersonal voice recording instrument readings; his description of the materialization; the
rolling laugh; Edith's scream.

The tape moved soundlessly. Fischer reached out and
switched off the recorder. *Zero*, he thought. Who had he been
kidding, to come charging back in here like Don Quixote?
What a laugh.

He stood. Well, he wasn't leaving. Not until something
happened. Not until he started to pick up the threads. There
had to be an answer somewhere. All right, he'd walk around
the house again. He'd keep on ferreting in corners until he
found that little mote of insight he was searching for. The
house felt flat, but somewhere there was something still alive,
something powerful enough to murder.

He was going to find it if it took a year.

As he moved across the great hall, he began to open up.
There seemed no danger to it now. There seemed no point to
it, either. Still, he had to do something.

He had scarcely let the last of his defenses down when
something pushed him. He was moving into the entry hall,

and the unexpected shove almost made him fall. Staggering to one side, he crossed his arms automatically, braced for resistance.

There was no more. Fischer scowled. He knew that he should open up again. Here was something tangible at last. Except that it had caught him by surprise. He didn't dare expose himself the way he had yesterday.

He stood hesitantly, sensing the presence hovering around him, wanting to confront it but afraid to.

Enraged at his weakness, he opened up.

Immediately something clutched his arm and flung him toward the south corridor. Fischer stumbled to a halt. He removed his crossed arms, which had, with instant self-protection, covered his solar plexus. He had to stop this opening and closing like a goddamned frightened clam!

He opened the door inside himself enough to feel the presence squeezing in. Again he was impelled toward the corridor. It was as though invisible hands were plucking at his clothes, holding his hand, clutching at his arm. He moved along with it, amazed by the blandness of the presence. This was no dark, destructive force. This was like some unseen maiden aunt hastening him to the kitchen for milk and cookies. Fischer almost felt inclined to smile at the feel of it— insistent, yes, demanding, but totally devoid of menace. He gasped at the sudden thought: Florence! She had sworn the answer lay in the chapel! A rush of joy burst through him. Florence helping him! He pushed in through the heavy door and went inside.

The chapel was oppressively still. Fischer looked around as though to see her. There was nothing.

The altar.

The words had flashed across his mind as clearly as though someone had spoken them aloud. He moved quickly down the aisle, wincing as he stepped across the cat, then the fallen crucifix. He reached the altar and looked at the open Bible. The page he saw was headed BIRTHS. "Daniel Myron Belasco was born at 2:00 A.M. on November 4, 1903." He felt a chilling disappointment. That wasn't it; it couldn't be.

He started as the pages of the Bible were flung over in a bunch. Now individual pages began to whirl by so fast he felt a breeze across his face. They stopped. He looked down, couldn't tell which paragraph he was meant to see. He felt his hand being lifted, let it move to the page. His index finger settled on a line. He bent across the book to read it.

"If thy right eye offend thee, pluck it out."

He stared at the words. It seemed as though Florence were standing beside him, anxious and impatient; but he didn't understand. The words made no sense to him.

"Florence—" he started.

He jerked his head up at the tearing sound behind the altar. A strip of wallpaper was hanging down, revealing the plaster wall behind it.

Fischer cried out as the medallion burned against his chest. Reaching frantically inside his shirt, he yanked it out and dropped it with a hiss of pain. It broke in pieces on the floor. Fischer stared at it in dazed confusion. A wedge like the head of an arrow had fallen from the other parts. It seemed to be pointing at—

It came with an appalling rush. Like some native paralyzed to mindless terror by the roar of an approaching tidal wave. Fischer looked up dumbly.

In the next moment, the power had smashed against him violently, driving him backward. He screamed in horror as it flung him to the floor and covered him with crushing blackness. There was no resisting it. Helplessly, he lay there as the cold force flooded through him, swelling every vein with dark contamination. *Now!* a voice howled in his mind, triumphantly. And suddenly he knew the answer, just as Florence

Tanner had, and Barrett had, and knew that he was being told because he was about to die.

He didn't move for a long time. His eyes did not blink. He looked like a dead man sprawled on the floor.

Then, very slowly, face without expression, he got up and drifted to the door. Pulling it open, he walked into the corridor and headed toward the entry hall. He walked to the front door, opened it, and went outside. Crossing the porch, he descended the broad steps, reached the gravel path, and started walking on it. He stared straight ahead as he walked to the edge of the tarn and stepped into the glutinous ooze. The water rose above his knees.

He seemed to hear a distant cry. He blinked, kept moving. Something crashed into the water with him, grabbed his sweater, jerked him back. There was an acid wrenching in his vitals and he gasped in pain. He tried to throw himself into the water. Someone tried to pull him back to shore. Fischer groaned and pulled away. The cold hands grabbed him by the neck. He snarled and tried to break away from them. His stomach muscles knotted, and he doubled over, falling to his knees. Icy water splashed across his face. He shook his head and tried to rise, to move into the tarn again. The hands kept pulling at him. Looking up, he saw, as through a veil of gelatin, a white, distorted face. Its lips were moving, but he couldn't hear a sound. He stared up dazedly. He had to die. He knew that clearly.

Belasco had told him so.

7:58 P.M.

For the past half-hour Fischer had been hunched in the corner of the seat, face as white as chalk, teeth chattering, arms crossed across his stomach, eyes unblinking for minutes at a time, staring sightlessly ahead. His shaking had kept dislodging the blanket from his shoulders; Edith had had to draw it around him repeatedly. Fischer had not responded to her attentions in any way. She might have been invisible to him.

It had taken her what seemed an endless amount of time to prevent him from walking into the tarn. Although his struggles had become progressively weaker, his obvious intention to drown himself had persisted. Like a somnambulist, he had tried stubbornly to wrest himself away from her. Nothing she'd said or done seemed to help. He hadn't spoken, was almost soundless in his single-minded attempt at suicide. Pulling at his clothes, clutching at his hands and arms and hair, slapping his face, Edith had thwarted his efforts again and again. By the time his struggles had finally ended, she'd been as soaked and shivering as he.

She looked around, trying to see the gasoline gauge. She'd been running the motor and heater since she'd gotten him into the car; the Cadillac was warm now. She saw that there was still more than half a tank, and turned back. The temperature did not appear to have the slightest effect on Fischer. His shivering continued unabated. Still, it was more than cold, she knew. She stared at his palsied features. Full circle; she could not avoid the thought.

The 1970 attempt on Hell House was one more item on the list of failures.

Fischer twitched convulsively and closed his eyes. His teeth stopped chattering; his body was immobile. As Edith watched in anxious silence, she saw faint streaks of color returning to his cheeks.

Several minutes later he opened his eyes and looked at her. She heard a dry, crackling sound in his throat as he swallowed. He reached out slowly toward her, and she took his hand. It was as cold as ice.

"Thank you," he murmured.

She couldn't speak.

"What time is it?"

Edith looked at her watch and saw that it had stopped. She twisted around to look at the dashboard. "Just past eight."

Fischer sank back with a feeble groan. "How did you get me here?"

He listened as she told him. When she was through, he asked, "Why did you come back again?"

"I didn't think you should be alone."

"In spite of what happened to you before?"

"I was going to try."

His fingers tightened on hers.

"What happened?" she asked.

"I was trapped."

"By what?"

"By *whom*."

She waited.

"Florence told us," Fischer said. "She *told* us, but I didn't have the brains to see."

"What?"

"The 'B' inside the circle," Fischer answered. "Belasco. Alone."

"*Alone?*" She couldn't comprehend it.

"He created everything."

"How do you know?"

"He told me so," he said. "He let me know, because I was about to die.

"No wonder the secret was never found. There's never been anything like it in the history of haunted houses: a single personality so powerful that he could create what seemed to be a complex multiple haunting; one entity appearing to be dozens, imposing endless physical and mental effects on those who entered his house—utilizing his power like some soloist performing on a giant, hellish console.''

The motor was off now; the car was getting cold. They should be getting into town, but sitting in the darkness, stunned, subdued, she couldn't stir herself as Fischer's voice droned on.

"I think he knew, from the second we entered, that Florence was the one to concentrate on. She was our weakest link; not because she had no strength, but because she was so willingly vulnerable to him.

"When she sat on Monday night, he must have fed her various impressions, looking for one that would create a response in her. It was the young man that 'took' in her mind—the one Florence came to identify as Daniel Belasco.

"At the same time, in order to use her against your husband, Belasco caused her to manifest physical phenomena. It served a multiple purpose. It verified your husband's beliefs. It was the first wedge in Florence's assurance; she knew she was a mental medium, and even though she tried to convince herself that it was God's will, it always distressed her. She knew it was wrong. We both did.

"And, as a third effect, it prevented your husband from bringing another psychic into the house after I refused to sit for him." His eyes flinted. "Belasco keeping the group to a workable number.

"Then," he continued, "he started to evolve a situation of hostility between Florence and your husband. He knew that they disagreed on their beliefs, knew that, subconsciously. Florence would resent your husband's insistence on the physical examination, the intimation—however politely phrased—that she was capable of fraud, even if it was involuntary. Belasco worked on that resentment, worked on their differences of belief, built them up, then caused the poltergeist attack in the dining hall, using some of Florence's strength but mostly his own. Again, a multiple purpose was served. First, it weakened Florence, made her doubt her motivations. Second, it increased the animosity between her and your husband. Third, it further verified your husband's convictions. Fourth, it injured him, frightened him a little."

"He wasn't frightened," Edith said; but there was no conviction in her voice.

"He kept on working on Florence," Fischer said, as though she hadn't spoken, "draining her physically and mentally: the bites, the cat's attack—undermining her strength on the one hand, elaborating her misconception about Daniel on the other. When her confidence was flagging most, because of what your husband said, Belasco let her find the body—even staging an apparent resistance to her finding it, to make it more convincing.

"So she became persuaded that Daniel Belasco haunted the house. To guarantee the conviction, Belasco led her to the tarn in her sleep, let 'Daniel' rescue her, even gave her a fleeting glimpse of himself rushing from the tarn. She was positive then. She came to me and told me what she thought—that Belasco controlled the haunting by manipulating every other entity in the house. She was so close. *My God!* Even fooled every step of the way, she almost had it. That was why she was so certain. Because, in everything she said, there was only the thinnest wall between her and the actual truth. If I'd helped her, she might have broken through, might have—"

Fischer stopped abruptly. For a long time he stared through the window. Finally he went on.

"It was a matter of timing," he said. "Belasco must have known that, sooner or later, Florence would come up with the right answer. So he concentrated on her even more, used her memory about her brother's death, and tied it in to her obsession about Daniel Belasco. Her brother's grief became Daniel's grief, her brother's need"—Fischer clenched his teeth—"became Daniel's."

His expression was one of hatred now. "He clinched it by finally letting her into the chapel. Admitting her to the very place she was positive possessed the secret of Hell House. It was his final stratagem, showing her the Bible entry made when his son was born. Belasco knew she'd believe it, because it was exactly what she was looking for—a final verification. There was no room left in her mind for doubt after that. There *had* been a Daniel Belasco, and his spirit needed her help. Combining the facts of his son's existence with her lasting sorrow for her brother's death, Belasco had convinced her."

Edith twitched as, unexpectedly, Fischer drove the edge of a fist against his palm. "And I sensed what that help was going to be. I knew it inside!" He turned his face away from her. "And I let it go. Let her do what she should never have done, let her destroy herself.

"From then on, she was lost," he went on bitterly. "There was no way I could have gotten her out of the house; I was a fool for thinking that I could. She was his . . . a puppet to be played with, tortured." Again, the sound of self-derision. "There I sat at the table while your husband explained his theory to us, knowing she was possessed, yet not even questioning why—suddenly, illogically—she was so quiet and attentive, on her best behavior. Because it wasn't her listening at all; it was Belasco.

"He wanted to hear the details."

"Was it him that tried to break the Reversor, then?"

"Why should he break it? He knew it wasn't any danger to him."

"But you said the house was clear after Lionel used it."

"Another of Belasco's tricks."

"I can't believe—"

"He's still in that house, Edith," Fischer interrupted, pointing. "He murdered your husband, murdered Florence, almost murdered you and me—"

His laugh was cold with defeat. "His final jest. Even though we actually know his secret now, there's not a damn thing we can do about it."

8:36 P.M.

Fischer held back as they reached the house. Edith turned to face him. He was staring at the doors. "What is it?" she asked.

"I don't know if I can go back in."

She hesitated, finally said, "I have to have his things, Ben."

Fischer didn't respond.

"You said if you were closed off, Belasco couldn't touch you."

"I said a lot of things this week. Most of them wrong."

"Shall I go in, then?"

He was silent.

"Shall I?"

Stepping to the doors, he pushed the right one open. He looked inside for several moments, then turned to her. "I'll be as fast as I can," he said.

Fischer stepped inside the house. For a few minutes he stood motionless, anticipating. When nothing happened, he started across the entry hall, heading for the stairs. Again the atmosphere was flat. It did not assuage his fears this time. As he ascended the steps quickly, he wondered if Belasco was still in the chapel or moving about the house. He hoped that being closed off was enough defense. He wasn't even sure of that now. Entering the Barretts' room, he threw their suitcases on the bed and opened them.

What had unnerved him as much as anything, he thought as he started packing, was the realization that Barrett had been wrong. The man had seemed so confident; everything he'd said had made so much sense. Still, what did that weigh against the fact that he'd failed?

Fischer moved quickly between bed, closet, and bureau, grabbing clothes and other personal belongings and tossing them into the two open suitcases. Belasco must have decided, from the start, never to show himself, he thought. If no one ever saw him, they could never think him that important a part of the haunting. If, instead, they observed a fantastic array of phenomena, all apparently disconnected, they would work on separate elements of those phenomena, never once realizing that he was the cause of all of them. Bastard, he thought. His features hardened, and with angry movements he began to cram things together in the suitcases so he could shut the lids.

The only thing he couldn't understand was why Belasco—so diabolically efficient when it came to plotting Florence's and Barrett's overthrow—had chosen such an inefficient way to finish him. Sending him away from the house could not have been fail-proof under any circumstances. If Belasco's power was unlimited, why had he chosen such an inept method?

Fischer stopped packing abruptly.

Unless that power was not unlimited any more.

Was it possible? He'd certainly been vulnerable to Belasco in the chapel. If there had ever been a time when Belasco should have been able to crush him, that had been the time. Yet, despite that, the most he'd been able to do was direct him to commit suicide in the tarn. *Why?* Had Florence been right about him, too? Was his own power really so vast? He shook his head. That didn't make sense. It was ego-flattering, but unconvincing. Maybe when he was a boy, but not now. More acceptable an idea was that Belasco hadn't been strong enough to destroy him after destroying Barrett and Florence.

Again, *why?* With such power at his disposal as he'd manifested all week, why should he be weakened now? It couldn't be that the Reversor had worked. If it had, Belasco would be gone.

What was it, then?

Edith stamped her feet on the porch, waiting for Fischer's return. The blanket she'd wrapped around herself was not keeping her warm; her clothes, still damp, were getting chilled again. She looked into the entry hall. Would it hurt to step a few feet inside and get out of the worst of the cold?

She had to do it finally. Entering the house, she closed the door and stood beside it, looking toward the staircase.

It seemed as if they'd come into this house in another life. Monday seemed as distant in her mind as the time of Christ. That had been one reason she'd come back. Now that Lionel was gone, nothing seemed important anymore.

She wondered how long it would take before the full impact of his death hit her. Maybe when she saw his body again.

She thrust aside the thought. Had it been only yesterday that she'd come down those stairs after Fischer? She shivered. She'd been such an easy prey for Belasco.

When she was examining Florence, it had been Belasco looking in at her, noting her embarrassment. Belasco had shown her the photos, made her drink the brandy, turned her fear of possessing lesbian tendencies into a thoughtless counterdesire for Fischer; she winced at the memory. How weak she was; how easily Belasco had manipulated her.

She thrust aside that thought as well. Every thought about

Belasco was an affront to Lionel's memory. She was almost sorry she'd come back, to discover that he'd been wrong in everything he'd said and done.

She grimaced with self-accusing guilt. How could his entire body of work have been for nothing? She felt herself tighten with anger against Fischer for destroying her faith in Lionel. What right had he to do that?

A rush of sudden anguish made her start across the entry hall. Ascending the stairs, she crossed the corridor. The two suitcases stood outside their room. She looked around, heard sounds in Fischer's room, and moved there rapidly.

He started as she came in. "I told you—"

"I know what you told me," she interrupted. She had to get it out before he spoke. "I want to know why you're so sure my husband was wrong."

"I'm not."

The impetus of her anger carried her past the point of reaction. She began to speak again, then had to catch herself and backtrack. "What?"

"I'm wondering if he might have been partially right."

"I don't—"

"You recall what Florence said?"

"What?"

"She said, 'Can't you see that *both* of us can be right?' "

"I don't understand."

"I'm wondering if Belasco's power is electromagnetic radiation, as she said," Fischer told her. "I'm wondering if he was weakened by the Reversor."

He scowled. "But why would he allow himself to be weakened? It doesn't make sense. Especially when he had a chance to wreck the Reversor."

Edith wouldn't listen to his objection. Eager to restore validity to Lionel's work, she said, "Maybe he *is* weakened, though. You said he trapped you in the chapel. If he was still powerful, why would he have to do that? Why not attack you anywhere you were?"

Fischer didn't look convinced. He started pacing. "It might explain why he lured me there," he said. "If, in coming out after the Reversor had weakened him, he used up most of his remaining energy to destroy your husband and attack you—" He broke off angrily. "No. It doesn't add up. If the Reversor worked at all, it would have dissipated all his power, not just part of it."

"Maybe it wasn't strong enough. Maybe his power was too great for even the Reversor to destroy it entirely."

"I doubt it," he said. "And that still wouldn't explain why he'd allow the Reversor to be used at all when he had a chance to destroy it *before* it could be used."

"But Lionel believed in the Reversor," she persisted. "If Belasco had destroyed it before it could be used, wouldn't that be as much as an admission, to Lionel, that he was right?"

Fischer studied her face. Something was needling up inside him, something that had the same exhilarating sense of rightness he'd felt when Florence had told him her theory about Belasco. Seeing his expression, Edith hurried on, desperate to convince him that Lionel had been right, even if only partially. "Wouldn't it be more satisfying to Belasco to let Lionel actually use the Reversor, *then* destroy him?" she asked. "Because Lionel must have believed that he was wrong when he died. Wouldn't that be what Belasco would want?"

The feeling was increasing steadily. Fischer's mind struggled to fit the pieces together. Could Belasco really have been so determined to destroy Barrett in just that way that he'd deliberately let himself be weakened? Only an egomaniac would—

It sounded like a groan that shuddered upward from his vitals.

"What?" she asked in alarm.

"Ego," he said.

He pointed at Edith without realizing it. "Ego," he repeated.

"What do you mean?"

"That's why he did it that way. You're right; it wouldn't have been satisfying to him any other way. But to let your husband actually use his Reversor, apparently dissipate the power—and when your husband was at the peak of his fulfillment, to get him then." He nodded. "Yes. Only that way could satisfy his ego.

"He had to let Florence know before she died that it was him alone. Ego. He must have told your husband, too. Ego. He let you know in the theater. Ego. He had to let me know. Ego. It wasn't enough to lure us to our destruction. He had to tell us, at the precise moment when he had us powerless, that it was him. Except that, by the time he got to me, most of his power was used up, and he couldn't destroy me. All he could do was direct me to destroy myself."

He looked suddenly excited. *"What if he can't leave the chapel now?"*

"But you said he made you go there."

"What if he didn't? What if it *was* her? What if she *knew* he was trapped in there?"

"But why would she lead you to destruction?"

Fischer looked distressed. "She wouldn't. Why *would* she lead me there, then? It had to be for a reason."

He caught his breath. "The Bible entry." There was a throbbing in his system he had not experienced since he was a boy, the pulsing of force inside him, crying for release. *"If thy right eye offend thee, pluck it out."* He paced restlessly, feeling himself near the edge of the precipice, the mist about to part in front of him, the truth about to appear. *"If thy right eye offend thee—"*

He couldn't get it; turned his mind away from it. What

else had happened in the chapel? The torn wallpaper. What had that meant? The medallion—broken, like a spearhead pointing at the altar. And, on the altar, the open Bible. "God." His voice was trembling, eager. He was so close—so close. *"If thy right eye offend thee, pluck it out."* Ego, the thought recurred. *"If thy right eye offend thee, pluck it out."* Ego. He stopped, his inner senses heightening with awareness. He was almost there. Something; *something.* *"If thy right eye—"*

"The tape!" he cried.

He whirled and rushed for the doorway. Edith ran after him as he plunged into the corridor and over to the staircase. He was halfway down before she'd reached the landing, springing down the steps with vaulting leaps. Edith descended as quickly as she could and ran across the entry hall.

He was at the great-hall table, listening to the tape recorder. She bit her lip involuntarily as she heard Lionel's voice. "—causing brief systemic shock." Fischer made a grumbling sound and shook his head as he pressed the REVERSE button and turned the spool back, pressed the PLAY button again. "Dynamometer fourteen hundred and sixty," Lionel's voice said. Fischer made an impatient sound and reversed the spool again, waited, pushed the button for PLAY position. Edith heard Florence's voice saying, *"Get out of this house before I kill you all."* Fischer snarled and punched the REVERSE button again. He switched to PLAY. "Here too long," Florence's voice said deeply, supposedly the voice of her Indian guide. "Not listen. Not understand. Too much sick inside." There was a pause. Fischer leaned across the table tensely, unaware that he was doing so. "Limits," said the voice. "Nations. Terms. Not know what that mean. Extremes and limits. Terminations and extremities."

Edith flinched as Fischer cried out with a savage glee. He reversed the tape and played it again. "Extremes and limits. Terminations and extremities." Fischer snatched up the tape recorder and held it high above his head in triumph. "She knew!" he shouted. "She knew! She knew!" He flung the tape recorder across the room. Before it had crashed to the floor, he was running for the entry hall. "Come on!" he shouted.

Fischer sprinted across the entry hall and down the corridor, followed by Edith. With a howl like that of an attacking Indian, he flung open the chapel door and leaped inside. "Belasco!" he roared. "I'm here again! Destroy me if you can!" Edith ran in beside him. "Come on!" he yelled. "Both of us are here now! Finish us! Don't leave the job half done!"

Massive silence fell, and Edith heard how strangely Fischer breathed. "Come on," he mumbled to himself.

He shouted suddenly, *"Come on, you lousy bastard!"*

Edith's gaze leaped toward the altar. For a moment she could not believe her hearing. Then the sounds grew louder, clearer, unmistakable.

Approaching footsteps.

She drew back automatically, eyes fixed on the altar. The footsteps were louder now. She was unconscious of Fischer's hand restraining her. She gaped at the altar. The sounds were getting louder every second. The floor began to shake. It was as though an unseen giant were approaching.

Edith whimpered, pulling constantly at Fischer's grip. The footsteps were almost deafening now. She tried to lift her hands to shield her ears but could lift only one. The chapel seemed to shudder with the thundering noises coming closer, closer. She jerked back hard, her cry of panic engulfed by the titanic, crashing footsteps. Closer; closer. We're going to die, she thought.

We're going to die!

She screamed as a violent explosion filled the chapel; closed her eyes involuntarily.

Deathly silence made her open them.

She lurched back, gasping. Fischer held her. "Don't be

afraid." His voice was taut with excitement. "This is a special moment, Edith. No one's ever seen his nibs before; not unless they were about to die, that is. Take a good look, Edith. Meet Emeric Belasco. *'The Roaring Giant.'* "

Edith gaped at the figure.

Belasco was enormous; dressed in black, his features broad and white, framed by a jet-black beard. His teeth, bared in a savage grin, were those of a carnivore. His green eyes glowed with inner light. Edith had never seen such a malignant face in her life. Deep within the frozen dread she felt, she wondered why they weren't being murdered at this very moment.

"Tell me something, Belasco," Fischer said. Edith didn't know whether to feel reassurance or terror at the brazen insult in his tone. "Why didn't you ever go outside? Why did you eschew the sunlight,' as you put it? Didn't care for it? *"Or was it better hiding in the shadows?"*

The figure started toward them. Released, Edith drew back quickly, horrified to see Fischer move forward.

"You walk with a labored tread, Belasco," Fischer said. "You dominate your movements at a cost, don't you?"

He shouted abruptly, fiercely, "Don't you, Belasco?"

Edith's mouth fell open.

Belasco had stopped moving. His features were ablaze with fury, but it seemed, somehow, a fury of frustration.

"Look at your lips, Belasco," Fischer said, still advancing. "Spastic pressure holds them together. Look at your hands. Spastic tension holds them fisted at your sides. Why is that, Belasco? Is it because you're a fraud?"

His mocking cackle rang out in the chapel. "Roaring Giant!" he shouted. "You? My ass! You bullshit artist! You sawed-off little freak!"

Edith caught her breath. Belasco was retreating! She rubbed a shaking hand across her eyes. And it was true.

He *did* look smaller.

"Evil?" Fischer said. He moved at Belasco steadily, a look of ruthless animosity on his face. "You, you funny little bastard?"

He stiffened as a cry of anguished rage burst from the lips of the dwindling figure in black. For a moment Fischer couldn't react. Then the grin returned. "Oh, no," he said. He started shaking his head. "Oh, no. You couldn't be *that* small."

He started forward again. "Bastard?" The figure drew back farther. *"Bastard? That* disturbed you? Oh, Belasco. What a funny little man you really were. What a funny little crawling bug of a ghost. You weren't a genius. You were a nut, a creep, a deviate, a slob, a loser. *And a sawed-off little bastard in the bargain!*

"BELASCO!" He howled. "Your mother was a whore, a slut, a bitch! You were a bastard, Emeric! A funny little dried-up bastard! Do you hear me, Evil Emeric? A bastard, *bastard,* BASTARD, *BASTARD!"*

Edith flung her hands across her ears to shut away the hideous wail that gorged the air. Fischer stumbled to a halt, his features washed of fury by the sound. He stared at the nebulous figure behind the altar—cowering, rat-faced, beaten—and it seemed as though he heard Florence's voice in his mind, whispering: *Perfect love casteth out fear.* And suddenly despite everything, he felt a sickened pity for the figure standing there before him.

"God help you, Belasco," he said.

The figure vanished. For a long time they could hear a screaming, as of someone falling down into a bottomless pit, the sound fading slowly, until the chapel was still.

Fischer moved behind the altar and looked at the section of wall revealed by the torn wallpaper.

He smiled. She'd shown him this too; if only he had known.

Leaning over, he pushed at the wall. It opened with a grating rumble.

A short staircase declined in front of him. He turned to Edith and extended his hand. She didn't speak. Moving across the chapel, she circled the altar and took his hand.

They descended the staircase. At the bottom was a heavy door. Fischer shouldered it open.

They stood in the doorway, looking at the mummified figure sitting upright on a large wooden armchair.

"They never found him because he was here," Fischer said.

They entered the small, dim-lit chamber and crossed to the chair. Despite the feeling Edith had that everything was over, she couldn't help cringing from the sight of Emeric Belasco's dark eyes glaring at them from death.

"Look." Fischer picked up a jug.

"What is it?"

"I'm not sure but—" Fischer ran his palms across the surface of the jug. The impressions came immediately. "Belasco set it down beside himself and made himself die of thirst," he told her. "It was his final achievement of will. In life, that is."

Edith averted her face from the eyes. She looked down, leaning forward suddenly. The chamber was so gloomy that she hadn't noticed before. "His legs," she said.

Fischer didn't speak. He set down the jug and knelt in front of Belasco's corpse. She saw his hands moving in the shadows; made a tiny sound of shock as he stood up with a leg in his hands.

" '*If thy right eye offend thee,*' " he said. " 'Extremities.' She was giving us the answer, you see." He ran a hand over the artificial leg. "*He so despised his shortness that he had his legs surgically removed and wore these instead, to give him height.*

That's why he chose to die in here—so no one would ever know. He had to be the Roaring Giant or nothing. There simply wasn't enough stature inside him to compensate for his shortness—*or* his bastardy."

He turned abruptly and looked around. Setting down the leg, he crossed the floor and put his hands against the wall. "My God," he said.

"What is it?"

"Maybe he was a genius, after all." He walked around the chamber, touching all the walls, examining the ceiling and the door. "The final mystery solved," he said. "It wasn't that his power was so great that he could resist the Reversor." His tone was almost awed. "He must have known, more than forty years ago, about the connection between electromagnetic radiation and survival after death.

"The walls, door, and ceiling are sheathed with lead."

9:12 P.M.

The two walked slowly down the steps, Edith carrying her suitcase, Fischer carrying Barrett's suitcase and his duffel bag.

"How does it feel?" she asked.

"What?"

"To be the one who conquered Hell House."

"I didn't conquer it," he said. "It took all of us."

Edith tried not to smile. She knew it was true, but wanted him to say it.

"Your husband's efforts weakened Belasco's power. Florence's efforts led us to the final answer. I just polished it off, that's all—and even that would have been impossible if you hadn't saved my life.

"It had to be that way, I guess," he said. "Your husband's

mentality helped, but wasn't enough by itself. Florence's spirituality helped, but wasn't enough by itself. It took one more element, which I provided—a willingness to face Belasco on his own terms, defeat him with his own weaknesses."

He made a scoffing noise. "Then again, Belasco may have beaten himself; I suspect that's part of it, too. After all, he'd been waiting thirty years for more guests. Maybe he was so eager to utilize his power again that he overextended himself, made the first mistakes of his existence in this house."

He stopped at the door, and both of them turned. For a long time they stood quietly. Edith thought about returning to Manhattan and to life without Lionel. She couldn't visualize it, but for now a kind of inexplicable peace had taken hold of her. She had the remnants of his manuscript with her. She'd see to its publication, see to it that people in his field learned what he'd accomplished. After that she'd worry about herself.

Fischer looked around, extending tendrils of unconscious thought. As he did, he wondered, consciously, what lay ahead for him. Not that it mattered. Whatever it was, he had a chance to face it now. It was bizarre that, in this house, where his horror had first begun, he should feel the returning stir of self-assurance.

He turned and smiled at Edith. "She isn't here," he said. "She just stayed long enough to help."

They took a final look around. Then, without another word, they went outside and moved into the mist. Fischer grunted, mumbled something.

"What?" she asked.

"Merry Christmas," he repeated softly.